# Hollow Stars
## A Paladin's Saga

### Matthew Martella

Copyright © [2022] by [Matthew Martella]

All rights reserved.

No portion of this book may be reproduced in any form without written permission from the publisher or author, except as permitted by U.S. copyright law.

To Murphy, for none of this would be possible without you. Late in the night while hunched over a laptop, it was your watchful eyes that kept me diligent, and I miss every single day without you.

# PROLOGUE

They did not belong here, four shadows against a world of red. The air was thick and humid and seemed to add weight to their shoulders as they descended deeper into the earth. There were rocks and boulders three times the size of a man all around them, boiling so hot that they could have burned skin and bone alike with a single touch. Each rock was a shade of deep crimson, like a dying flame burning at the end of a wick. The small crannies between the rocks were black as coal, enhancing their already formidable size.

It was an endless labyrinth of tunnels, each darker and tighter than the previous. The one assurance they were not going around in circles were the footprints left in the sand as they walked. Rallock turned around and traced the steps back with his eyes until they disappeared into the shadowy void. He let out a deep sigh as the four men pressed on, fully acknowledging that those footprints were his only way out of the tunnels.

"Something wrong, Rallock?" Xavier asked, his voice as mighty as it was condescending. "You're welcome to go back to the ship. We need someone to flush out the toilet before it backs up."

The darkened figure beside Xavier squeaked in approval. "The squid's too far away from the sea," he jeered. Little Ben was his name, but Rallock had grown accustomed to calling him more expletive things behind his back.

"Nothing is wrong," he lied, unwilling to reveal his trepidations among the men, let alone two humans. Rallock was a being of the sea trapped in a world of dust and fire, and the humans did not hesitate to point out his disadvantage. "I just don't think this is the safest way to travel."

Xavier grimaced. The human had fair skin and a neat red beard burning beneath the veil casted by his silver hood. His neck was covered in tattoos, the most prominent being a diamond-shaped eye at the center of his throat. He looked at Rallock with cold eyes that said everything in a single glare: there was no reasoning with Xavier. "You want safe travels?" he mocked. "How's that possible with Planters lurking about?"

"Maybe he wants us off our guard." Little Ben suggested. He had short black hair, a squished-in face, and three long hairs sprouting from the small lump that was his chin. The two humans bonded rather well during the journey. They had a mentor-apprentice relationship, and Xavier taught the boy as much in the art of mockery as he did sorcery and swordsmanship.

The fourth and final shadow chimed into the conversation. "Don't question Rallock's loyalty, boy. He's been serving under the Inquisition long before you were born. I've fought beside him, and he's done more for our kind than you ever will."

Geherris was his name, a Drakonid from some moon Rallock had never heard of. Geherris had auburn-colored scales lined in silver, a long, sinewy neck, and yellow eyes that glowed vibrantly in the night. He was their source of light in the maze of darkness, summoning it from his slithery fingertips. It was his gift, each of the shadows had their own.

Thankfully, Little Ben had quieted down as the four Inquisitors wandered on. The silence gave Rallock a chance to meditate on the mission at hand. He had never seen a Planter. In fact, he hardly believed in their existence, but this was not to say he was particularly motivated to test his notions of myth and legend. The boy was more excited than the rest of them combined. Little Ben was innocent, spending his young life learning to hate everything that was not mage-kind. Rallock had been the same way, until he realized the enemy had a face, a personality, fear, a family too, probably.

"Do you think we'll find any Paladins lurking around?" Ben asked, rather suddenly.

"Absolutely not. But if there were, they'd be Maelstrom," Xavier wagered, "They're the ones with the fortitude to keep this war going. If anyone else is hunting Immortech weaponry, it must be them."

"Why are we wasting time on this treasure hunt?" Rallock asked. "Maelstrom may have found your supposed cache."

"Because with that kind of arsenal, the Inquisition would have felt it by now." Xavier fired back. "Besides, if they're too braindead to accept the war is over, then they definitely won't be able to find this cache."

*And what makes you so sure we will?* Rallock asked himself. The word *Paladin* was almost an obscenity among their ranks. Hearing the word spoken aloud and with such casualness was alarming. Xavier was correct though, to a certain extent. The last militia of the Paladin Order, called Maelstrom, were always lurking around this sector of the galaxy. Elusive bastards too, as the Inquisition had spent nearly a decade and a half trying and failing to eradicate them. *We used to label them as desperate radicals, holding up in the ruins of Last Bastion and searching endlessly for Immortech that did not exist. Xavier is no better than the worst of them.*

"Well, if I see a Paladin," Ben began, hyping himself up. "I'm gonna take my blade and shove it right through his belly."

"And how many Paladins have you encountered before?" Rallock asked, knowing the answer.

Ben paused. "Uh, none, but-"

"Let's hope you're right, Xavier." Geherris interrupted, twisting his long neck so he could match eyes with the human. He could cast light from his hands without any concentration, a tribute to the mastery of his gift. "Mages of Maelstrom are more mercenaries than Paladins. Should be quick work, which is favorable considering our losses."

Xavier frowned. "Just light the way, lizard. You're not here for your inputs."

The Drakonid spoke brashly, but truly. Ten Inquisitors departed inconspicuously from the obsidian cities, but only four remained. They had stolen two spaceships with them fitting five Inquisitors each. When they crossed Hallyan space, a decision Rallock did not endorse despite making the journey quicker, they were inevitably surrounded by star-splitters. One of the ships was shot down immediately. Rallock shut his eyes, imagining at any second that their ship would fall next. Fortunately, the Gods let them live another day. Unfortunately, one of his crewmates was of the Hallyan race, and was subsequently executed by Xavier for treason she certainly did not commit.

He did not mourn the Hallyan girl, nor did he mourn the five Inquisitors lost in space, he only cared about getting back to his ship safely.

They entered an abandoned mining factory many miles ahead, a refreshing change of scenery from the endless tunnels, yet no less dreary. The metal floors and walls had bent and rusted from decades of abandonment, and the dripping water some distance away echoed often enough to drive anyone insane. There were massive carts attached to a conveyor belt at least a century out of use. Rallock examined one of the carts and found a thin pool of stagnant lava inside.

"Energy," he said aloud.

"What do you mean?" Little Ben inquired.

"Heat and lava were used as an energy source. This is what powered Last Bastion."

Little Ben made a quizzical face and said, "For a squid, you sure know lots about lava. What's the matter with you?"

Rallock shrugged. "I should be asking you the same thing. This is important history everyone should know." He offered to teach the young Inquisitor more, but Ben simply turned away, disinterested. *What is more disappointing than a stagnant mind?*

"This is nothing more than an antique shop," Geherris said, examining the remnants of a computer room. "Remind me why we are here again?"

"A cache of Immortech weapons and armor," Xavier said, investigating every closet, trap door, or hidden room he could find. Rallock searched passively, imagining a time when the factory was shiny, organized, and bustling with many people of many races all working as one, rather than the dank, broken, and barren home it had become for insects and other creatures skittering around in its wake.

"As I said, an antique shop."

"Fool." Xavier answered. "You should understand the value of Immortech by now. One sword by itself is worth tens of thousands of credits. If we find this cache and sell it all, each of us will be millionaires."

"Traders love'm on Prisilla, I hear." Little Ben added, clearly on a script from Xavier. "Merc companies too are always sniffing for'em."

"Underground bartering," Xavier pitched with the heightened charisma of a salesman. "We won't even have to pay taxes."

"Yes," Geherris agreed, although his low, lingering voice expressed the opposite. "But the tunnels of Last Bastion are a massive search for the four of us. I don't suppose you know exactly where they are."

"In the heart!" Xavier stated, proudly. "In the final standing place of the Immortals."

Geherris chortled. "And what are your sources for this information? Religious texts? Myth and rumor? Why are we risking Planter infection on this futile treasure hunt when we could be halfway to Laktannon?"

Rallock nodded absently in favor of his friend. Like crossing Hallyan space, this quest into Last Bastion was another of Xavier's brilliant ideas. He was thrilled someone finally challenged the headstrong human, but did it come too late?

"Treasure hunt, is it?" Xavier asked, grinding his jaw beneath his red beard. "You must not understand our situation. We can't go back to Dakahaan, unless you want to face *His* wrath. After the choice we made, there's not a single alcove in the galaxy safe for us anymore. So, if you want any hope of surviving, you're going to need an endless supply of credits to purchase that safety."

The Inquisitors fell dead silent, allowing the dripping water to take prominence in the cool air once again. It was true, they had all chosen freedom knowing the extreme vulnerability of abandoning home. Geherris did not ask another question after that, and all the Inquisitors were better off for it.

After hours of searching every corner of the three-story factory, Xavier declared it empty, and they moved on. They descended a few flights of rickety stairs until the tunnels were back in sight. There was something different though. The air felt cooler, the tunnel's appearance smoother, and the black rocks that closed in around them appeared to sweat in the bleak light Geherris casted. Sand no longer rested at their feet. In its place was hard, rigid rock that crunched with every step they took.

"We should turn back," Rallock suggested. "Without sand, there's no way we can retrace our steps."

"We don't turn around until we find the bloody Immortech," Xavier said.

"But how're we supposed to get back?"

"Afraid of Planters? You sound like His bloody priests, always whispering lies and superstitions. We're miles deep into the cavern, what more proof do you need to dispel these imaginations?"

"Don't talk down to me!" Rallock protested. "What terrifies me is getting lost and starving to death in these godforsaken tunnels!"

Xavier laughed as if he was dispelling the nightmares of a child. "Simple, as soon we've looted the cache, we walk in the opposite direction from which we came. Now come on, you're wasting time."

"No," Rallock stamped his foot down.

"No? I'm in charge here. It's my duty to keep us safe. Defying me is defying your commander, and that's treason." He gave a wink to Geherris. "We all know how I deal with treason."

"You've already murdered one of us today." The sudden nerve he acquired caused his whole body to shake. "Now you mean to get us all killed down here. I won't have it."

Xavier chortled at the threat. He swaggered over to Rallock and said, "What are you gonna do about it, fishy?" He pushed his long, silver cloak from his hip and put a hand on the hilt of his sword. Rallock did the same, as did Little Ben. Geherris could not, for his hands were preoccupied summoning the lone light they had for miles.

"Xavier, please!" Rallock objected, whatever courage he once possessed now a distant stranger. "You have Immortech attached to your belt. Let's sell the sword. Buy a better ship and more fuel than we'll ever need."

"He's right," Geherris added. "Be rational now." The Drakonid's scaly fingers itched.

Xavier looked at the hilt of his sword, then back to Rallock. Without a word, his answer was obvious. "Your magic's useless without any water, mine on the other hand..."

Rocks began to rumble and shake while dust and pebbles fell like hail as the world began to turn upside down. The tunnel choked up and Rallock could feel himself losing his balance. Xavier raised his hands up and large boulders came with them. His smile was menacing, ready to crush the entire group. Rallock went to draw his sword but he stumbled over, coming close to stabbing himself in the process. He made another attempt to stand, but it was all in vain for the ground rose and crashed like the crack of a whip. He slipped, and when gravity pulled him down, there was no ground to land on.

Falling for what felt like forever, Rallock believed he was flying until abruptly landing hard on his knees, nearly shattering his bones as they made graceless contact with the hidden rocky surface. He screamed out as lightning beams of pain shot up his legs and into his spine. He laid in the rubble, cradling his legs, rocking back and forth, eyes closed. *This is a nightmare! Soon, I'll wake up... and have a good laugh about it!*

With great reluctance, he opened his eyes. The nightmare, however, continued. It was entirely black around him, but the angry rumbling of boulders and stones as they rolled down into the cavern sounded like a war in full eruption.

"Geherris!" he called. "Light!" There was no answer. He switched his body weight to relieve his knees slightly.

When the rocks finally rested, Rallock was rendered both blind and deaf. He sat on his backside for a while. It was so dark, so utterly silent that he may as well have been drifting through space. He called out for hours, to the point where his throat turned raw and his voice gave out. His mind wandered in the suffocating night, collecting morbid thoughts.

Life on Dakahaan, although not perfect, was superior to his current situation in every way. *Why did I leave anyway?* Rallock wondered, his hands cracking as they dragged his useless body forward. *Out of pride? Because I didn't like His twisted cult? I was secure with the Inquisitors.* A new revelation made his stomach churn. *But things were better before the Inquisition. The Paladins are wiped out, and I'm partially to blame. One way or another, the Immortals will have their vengeance... And now it's time to pay my debts.*

He persisted for a while longer, his voice being the only thing separating him from the realm of the dead. But with constant, ripping pain in his knees and a quickly dying voice, Rallock inevitably gave up. Before he prepared to lie down for the last time, something grabbed him by the shoulder.

The hands were fast, with thin, nervous fingers. They patted him, felt around his shoulders, neck, and face. When the hands reached the tentacles on the back of his head, a voice whispered, "Rallock?"

"Yes Ben. It's me. Where are the others?"

"I don't know, I don't know!" Ben said, frantically. "Gods... Gods what happened?"

"Calm yourself," Rallock insisted. "Are you hurt? Please, tell me you can you walk?"

"Yes, I think so," Ben guessed. Rallock wished he could see the boy's face, or anything at all. "I've been c-crawling around for hours. I thought I was d-d-d-dead."

"You're not dead." Rallock reassured him. Their sudden attraction was almost brotherly. Admittedly, he felt a touch of sympathy for the frightened boy, despite his insults. "Let's find the others."

Little Ben had to help him to his feet, heaving at his shoulders while his knees continued to drag lifelessly along the ground. Eventually, he was up, and with an arm around Little Ben's shoulder, managed to proceed forward with a limp. In the darkness, he prayed to the Immortals of his home-world that he wouldn't fall into another pit.

"Xavier," Ben called, "XAVIER!" There was no answer, except for the distant echoing of his own voice. Rallock no longer cared about the cache of Immortech artifacts, or where his companions were, or even where he was; all he desired was light. Whether it was the unbearable aching in his legs or the mental toll of the situation he was caught in, Rallock's mind began to wander uncontrollably.

In the cold silence, his thoughts brought him to the memory of his old sword, expertly forged in the finest Immortech and so weightless that he could swing it without applying any force. They were one in the same, the blade a mere extension of his own arm. He felt safer with it on his hip, stronger with it in his hand, but it was a memory now, and memories could do nothing for him.

Despite his antipathy toward Xavier, he reluctantly understood his unwillingness to part from his own Immortech sword. Knowing such a celestial metal was designed specifically for you made it impossible to do without. Losing his own sword was like having a part of his soul ripped from his chest. The mere idea of willingly giving it away was blasphemous.

Ben yelled until his voice went raw. Rallock would not have considered pulling Ben's tongue out so many times if the constant screaming was not targeted directly into his left eardrum. The worst part was that no one ever responded. Ben's calls served no purpose. Everyone else must have died from the fall.

After the millionth call for Xavier, Ben finally got a response. "Ben?" Despite the blackness, they instinctually turned to each other for reassurance that the voice was, in fact, real. "Ben? Is that you?"

"Yes? Where are you?"

"Where's Geherris?" Rallock impatiently included.

"Come here and I'll show you."

With the support of Little Ben, Rallock limped to where he believed Xavier resonated. "Don't walk any closer or you'll step on me," he warned. "Look down here and try not to fall."

Rallock snarled. "What the Hell was your plan? I made a suggestion, and you tried to kill me for it."

Xavier shrugged off the guilt. "This is all a result of your insubordination, fish-face."

"So you thought the best course of action was to cause an earthquake. Are you mad?"

"Just look down the damn ledge!" Xavier commanded. If they ever survived this, the human deserved nothing more than a bullet in the back of his head. It would at least double the group's odds of survival. Even Ben, by this point, would probably not protest.

Rallock approached the ledge cautiously. There was a dim, yellow glow from within the lower plain of earth. He peered down the hole to find Geherris in the cavern below. Lying on the ground, he casted a light spell from his hands, yet it did nothing in the sea of darkness. Although the light was poor, he could see one of Geherris' legs bent improperly. "How can we get down there?"

"Doesn't seem very safe," Xavier mocked.

"Without Geherris' light, we won't get anywhere. Which means you won't find the cache and I won't get off this cursed rock."

Xavier's mouth twitched, but he consented to Rallock's logic. "Is there a way down?" he called to Geherris.

"No. Can't see anything," Geherris said. "Maybe we could-" His head snapped behind him, as if something bit the back of his long neck. He put one hand on the hilt of his Immortech mace while the other hand continued to cast an orb of yellow light. He bent is knees and arched his back into a defensive position and studied his surroundings furtively.

"What is it?" Xavier asked, eagerly. "Planters?" Rallock's own skin started to sweat. *Our nightmare is far from over. One way or another, punishment will find us.*

"Something's down here." Geherris called back. He bared his sharpened teeth as if about to strike. His growl was low, and it echoed like a motor against the spacious cavern.

The earth shifted again, but this time it was not by Xavier's doing. Rallock grabbed the hard ground for stability and was surprised to feel no vibrations. The noise only came from below. Eventually, he realized it was not the ground that was moving, but feet.

"Get out of there, Geherris!" Rallock called quite uselessly. The Drakonid twisted back and forth, surrounded by enemies no one else could see. The sounds of shuffled feet grew and grew to a number impossible to determine. Geherris did not speak, but his cowering body told them everything they needed to know.

"Get back!" Geherris commanded to an invisible enemy. He raised his mace to strike, but at what?

There was no scream, no effort to prepare a defense, and no attempt to comprehend what was happening. Geherris was absorbed into the darkness, and the light died with him.

"Where is he?" Little Ben asked, incredulous. The other two Inquisitors were equally clueless. Rallock considered an idea, but it was as stupid as it was impossible. The instant quietness was absurd considering the evil they had witnessed. No man thought to move, without light they were out of options.

The ominous shuffling of feet started up again, this time on their level. The three Inquisitors could see nothing. To fix this, Xavier unsheathed his Immortech sword, which illuminated at the touch of the mage's hand. Orange and yellow lights danced on the symbols and glyphs engraved on the smooth blade. It was lost in time, crafted from material beyond this galaxy. Rallock admired it, longing for his own once again.

The sword granted them some vision, but one must be careful of what he wishes for. Before them stood a swarm of apparitions, shuffling ever closer. A horde of husks inconceivable in size, they navigated the ruins in pure silence. The light was too dim to see the features of their faces, but no figure looked exactly the same. Little Ben pissed himself as they came close enough to take form. Rallock nearly did the same.

"Ben, draw your sword!" Xavier commanded. His tone was oddly inspiring. Ben obeyed, reluctantly, and unsheathed his weapon. It was an ugly blade, in truth, all jagged, pitted, and crafted from inferior Enfari crystal. It lacked the glyphs and weightlessness of the divine Immortech.

Being trapped at the edge of a cliff, the three men prepared for a fight, but instead the shrouded figures stopped in their tracks mere feet away from them. They stared with cold, lifeless eyes, and it was at this point that Rallock could distinguish the familiar species that made up their adversary. Xavier yelled and cursed, but they paid him no attention.

"Does anyone feel that?" Ben asked. Rallock turned and saw the crystal sheen of sweat that drenched his face. He grasped his stomach, then collapsed, dropping his sword in the process. Rallock was on top of him immediately. The boy screamed in agony, clutching his stomach. Rallock asked what the problem was, but Ben was delirious. Still, the figures stood sentry, surrounding the three mages.

Xavier joined him on the ground, although he was less empathetic. He cut Ben's shirt at the waist with a swipe of his sword, exposing his pale stomach. The scene before his eyes almost made him sick. Something was moving inside Ben's stomach, rising up and down as if trying break through the skin like a battering ram. "Help me, HELP me!"

"Oh, fuck it." Xavier cursed, cutting through Ben's stomach. The skin folded, revealing his insides. Rallock was not a professional of human anatomy, but what he saw was clearly unnatural. Millions of fleshy hairs arose from every organ, his intestines twisted like tapeworms trying to break his skeleton. It was a new biome of lurid, distorted spores wriggling and writhing from within the young mage. The body possessed a unique life to itself, thousands and thousands of demented souls in one, reaching out with a countless number of miniscule hands and breathing a horrifically alien existence. Ben got one look at himself before passing out.

Rallock retreated. He wanted answers from Xavier, but the other Inquisitor appeared equally confused. The tattoos on his neck shifted as well, bubbling on his skin. His eyes dripped in unnatural colors down his cheeks, although he did not notice.

"You bastards!" Xavier cursed. He took his pistol out from his belt and fired green, diamond-shaped lasers at the monsters. When the twisted beings merely absorbed the shots and continued their slow pace, Xavier returned to his sword and presented it to his enemy. The blade illuminated brilliantly, annihilating the darkness. Glyphs that flamed orange and red ornamented it beautifully.

The frontline of figures was more easily seen in the light. Each one, regardless of the race, was covered in a thick fungus possessing the same lurid glow as the insides of Little Ben. Skin cells seemed to move and vibrate on their own. Sacks of dead skin and fungus hung like beards from their faces; misshapen masses grew from their bodies in large, grotesque mounds and lumps. *And the dripping! The unholy dripping!*

Xavier gazed at his sword, his face oozing and sliding to the ground.

He slashed at one of the beings, and the blade cut through like paper. He cheered, but when he went to pull the sword away, he found it to be stuck. The monstrosity's spore-covered skin reformed where the cut was made, trapping the Inquisitor's sword within its stomach. Xavier went to kick the creature away, but his foot was absorbed too.

The figure collapsed, bringing him down with it. As if given a command, several more of the fungus-covered creatures surrounded the human Inquisitor and embraced him.

"Damn you," Xavier said, "Rallock, help me." Rallock wanted to, but he found himself frozen, shell-shocked at the horror.

Xavier swore to all the Gods he knew of as he struggled, but eventually he lost his shape to the embracing swarm. The pile of men all formed into one, their skins sticking and mixing together. What remained of Xavier was hidden somewhere in the mass of fleshy overgrowth.

Rallock bowed his head, knowing he was bested. The horde shuffled closer, encircling him even tighter. They gazed at him with thousands of haunting, dispassionate eyes. Rallock looked at his own hands and saw the same fleshy hairs stand up on his fingertips, swaying back and forth like blades of grass in the breeze.

*There were worse ways to die*, Rallock concluded as his body merged with the horde. *The true Gods have made their will known, the end is near.*

# KENT (1)

For a while, it was quiet. The refugees sat and drank and kept to themselves. The band eloped when the bartender passed out behind the sandstone counter, taking more than just their paychecks with them. But music did not exactly fit the Bar-With-No-Name. Dead and absolute silence proved to be much more suitable.

Kent tipped a small glass over, what number glass it was he could not say, and slammed it down on the table. The loud clang shocked the bartender awake and, like a trained dog, he went over with a refill. *It's a shame such strong alcohol must be served in a small glass*, he thought to himself as he watched the jowly bartender slither over on his pink, wormlike tail. He eyed the very drunk Kent until he pulled out his coin, then poured a raspberry red potion into the inadequate glass.

"Thanks," he muttered, not meaning it. The bartender may have been a portly slug, but dull-witted he was not. He knew well enough how desperate his clientele was, how much they wanted to forget, and like any good businessman found profit in their turmoil.

Most of his days were spent hiding in the Bar-With-No-Name on the deserted desert planet he called home. The planet was so empty, so dry, and so bland it might as well have been nameless too. But despite the many hungover mornings, followed by buzzed afternoons, and finished off with drunken nights, Kent still remembered everything, including the name of the planet he lived on, Narood.

He looked into his empty glass and saw his own sad reflection. Rough skin dark and green like a swamp. A crown of small, ivory horns around his head. Yellowish brown eyes with heavy lines around them. He was of the Druin species and had the rare honor of being a member of two dying breeds.

His cunning often betrayed him. He kept the reminder of his past, of his shame, beneath his bed, so his ghosts could not see his digression. Death was the only salvation from history, the penance for past sins, and it would be his to embrace soon enough.

Another drink washed down his throat, followed by the familiar sound of glass meeting the hard table of rusted metal scrap. But this time he did not call for another, something else caught his attention.

"You like this piece boys?" a scrappy voice bragged from a booth behind him. It was absurdly loud for the bar. "Don't touch it! It's an incendiary rifle. Can burn a bastard to ash with one shot. Look, it even has the Triumvirate brand."

*Triumvirate.* The word bit at his bones. "I've been workin' on my shot too," the scrappy voice continued, "Heard the Timanzees are on their way. When they see my skills, they'll be beggin' me to enlist."

Whoever the voice was, he was not wrong. The Timanzee accepted any species into their ranks, on the concealed condition that they would be sent to the frontlines before their own kind. Kent would know, he'd killed plenty of them.

He slowly stumbled from his seat to feast his eyes on the wannabe soldier. The slug of a bartender cackled at Kent's drunken stumper as he shuffled around to get a sense of his own feet. *Laugh behind your counter,* he encouraged the slug, *I've accomplished more in a day than you have your entire life. I once helped the depraved, you merely exploit them. But I suppose we'll all soon be equals as our bodies burn in the same ditch.* Balancing himself, Kent felt foolish, but it wasn't like he had to impress anyone of the refugees. His eyes were heavy, his movement delayed and feelingless. Not all of this sedation, in honesty, could be blamed on drunkenness. Eventually, though, he mastered the art of putting one foot in front of the other without teetering too uncontrollably.

The wannabe soldier was found with a posse of freaks, crowded around a circular table in the corner of the bar. The one with the incendiary rifle, a *Bakar* if Kent was not mistaken, sat between them as a true leader should. He had the typical features of the Bakar race: wrinkly blue skin, large oval eyes, and thick orange tusks protruding from the roof of his mouth that he did not hesitate to bare as Kent approached. "What do you want?"

"I couldn't help but overhear your discussion of weaponry from my... home away from home over there." He pointed to his sad table of rusted scrap. Being several feet away, a sense of longing overcame him. "I happen to have an ear for the subject, and I had to admire your piece. You said something about a Triumvirate branding? That means it's in good quality."

Kent asked a redundant question. The branding on the hand guard of the rifle was unmistakable: an emblem engraved with the entwined laurel wreath of the King of Humanity and the platinum ring worn by the Emperor of the Timanzee, and between the two was the silver and sapphire staff of the Denvari Consul. A cluttered emblem in truth, forged by three rulers unwilling to be showed up by the other two.

The wannabe soldier gave Kent a weary look. The Drakonid beside him extended his long, scaly neck to whisper in the Bakar's ear. "Test it out on him, Grogg," he hissed, "I wanna watch him burn." Kent could clearly hear the proposal, but he pretended not to. Drakonids were typically renowned warriors throughout the galaxy, but this one was thin and homely, a reject of his kind.

"Go back to your corner, drunk. Or I'll personally kick you out of *my* bar," the Bakar named Grogg said, confident with his Drakonid to the left and his human to the right. After them were two more of his cronies from mutt species Kent could not recognize.

"Your bar?" Kent asked. "I did not know it was yours. In fact, I've never seen any of you here before, which puzzles me because, how do I put it... I'm a bit of a celebrity here."

"It's because we're taking over," Grogg insisted. "We're the Sand Snakes, right boys?"

"Sand Snakes rule!" the four cronies shouted, in unison.

Grogg continued: "And you better get used to taking orders from us... at least until the Triumvirate gets here." Kent laughed to himself, *when the Triumvirate gets here, the only command you'll hear is 'Kill them all.'* The Sand Snakes were getting restless, and their conversation was starting to attract the other bar-dwellers.

He was alive inside the minds of the Sand Snakes, but he was dizzy, fading in and out of reality. He kept his face frozen, though he feared it was a matter of time before his mental struggle became obvious.

"How unfortunate," he said. "We'll be on opposite sides of the battlefield when the war comes to Narood. A pity, truly. I'm starting to like you."

Conflict was coming, but "battle" was a generous term for what was surely to be a slaughter. Kent and a ragtag group of refugees had formed a makeshift militia. When he wasn't at the bar, he was digging trenches around the outside perimeter of the small town. In fact, the militia spent so much time digging that they hardly trained with what few weapons they had. No one ever questioned it. Each soldier knew they had no chance of defeating the impending Timanzee Empire. It would be one last moment of glory, a payment for a death-debt owed many, many years ago.

"Doesn't surprise me. Scum like you wouldn't be welcomed into the Triumvirate." Grogg turned to his men who nodded in agreement. "It will be a glorious battle though, a great first victory in my military career."

"Do you know how many planets there are in the galaxy?" Kent asked, not realizing he had laughed his way through the question.

"I don't know," Grogg said, a finger furiously scratching the handle of his Triumvirate-issued rifle.

"Hhhmmm, 'I don't know.' I'm sure the phrase is quite familiar to you," Kent said, "But that's not the point I'm trying to make. There is an infinite number of planets in our galaxy alone, and we are living on perhaps the loneliest and most forgotten one. It is incalculable how insignificant this moment is."

"What's your point?" Grogg barked, his finger again itching at the trigger. His boys sensed it too. *Animals, waiting for their leashes to be unhooked.*

"You expect me to be afraid of you when neither you nor your motley band of misfits matter?"

Grogg shot up from his seat, banging his knees fiercely against the table, and pulled out his rifle. His thick orange tusks snarled through his mouth. "Liar! I'll incinerate you into less than nothing!" The sights targeted Kent. Grogg placed a pudgy blue finger on the trigger. The barrel began to ignite with scorching flames while the other Sand Snakes admired lustfully.

"Before you kill me," Kent said, calm and with arms folded across his flat chest, "Look at your friends." Grogg fancied his request and considered the Sand Snakes. At first, he thought nothing of it, but he eventually realized something was off. The Drakonid, the human, and the two mutt soldiers sat straight and tall, unblinking and thoughtless, utterly unresponsive to the world around them.

"Ed? Rek? Dizo? Knock it off!" Grogg commanded to the ears of his incoherent gang. Kent smiled mischievously. He smacked the Drakonid on the snout, but received no response.

"Have you heard of the Paladins before?" he asked the frantic Bakar.

"Yeah, why? They're dead. The Triumvirate killed them."

"If only that were true. Another question: are you afraid of the Paladins?"

"No!" Grogg laughed frantically. "As I said, they're all dead. Them and their magic. The only mages left are part of the Inquisition… and they're on *my* side."

"Really?" Kent asked, "Are you sure?" All four heads of the Sand Snakes came crashing down, meeting the cold metal table mercilessly with one large CLANG. Although still alive, their bodies fell lifelessly to the floor. Waterfalls of blood from four shattered noses dripped methodically down their chins.

"What the…WHAT?!" Grogg panted with fear. By the time the Bakar understood what had happened, his own arm, gun in hand, turned against him until he was looking down the barrel of the same weapon he prided himself on. He screamed, cursed, and spat as he tried to will the weapon away, but Kent was in his head now. He let the Bakar struggle for a time until even he became bored with it. Grogg cried in terror, begging for mercy. Kent felt nothing.

"A bit too dramatic, don't you think?" Kent cackled. "I merely hurt your friends, it's nothing to kill yourself over."

"I'm not doing this!" Grogg cried. He was shaking and sweating and whimpering away, attracting the attention of the other refugees. It must have been quite a sight, seeing one drunkard laugh while another attempted suicide above a pile of unconscious bodies.

Surely this news will spread, and the Timanzee would likely put an extra special bounty on Kent's head. *I hope they do.*

"Make it stop!" Grogg wailed, "Save me, please!"

"Very good," Kent sarcastically complimented. He considered the variety of other things he could make him do.

A stroke of exhaustion crashed over his body like a tidal wave. Reality faded to utter blackness, and his body trembled. If he stood for much longer, his legs risked crumbling from underneath him. "Although I've enjoyed our engaging conversation," he muttered breathlessly to the Bakar, relenting his mental grip. "I have to go home. If you'd like to talk again some other time, I live south of here in a sad, lonely shack. But please visit me soon, before the Triumvirate wipes us all from existence."

The drunk used his last morsel of strength to escape the Bar-With-No-Name and into the starry night outside. The cool, nearly freezing, air kept him awake long enough to find his sand-bike and set a course for home. Other refugees were lighting fires or hanging lamps around their huts to keep warm in the frigid night. A large man filled two larger barrels at a nearby well and lugged them away, likely needing one barrel for his own people, and the other for a neighbor's. Kent saw they depended on one another for survival. If there was one was positive thing a galaxy at war brought, it was a sense of unity among the losers. Even though Kent was as much a loser as anyone else on Narood, he preferred his own home, his own fire, and his own food surrounded by nothing else but endless skies and sand dunes.

Although it huffed and puffed, the sand-bike hovered swiftly over the mounds and mounds of dusky desert. The propellers that elevated the machine blew the grains of sand below them in a flurry. Wherever the bike went, a miniature sandstorm followed. He wore goggles and a thick, hooded cloak of brown wool to help keep the sand off, but they were mostly ineffective.

He hated the desert, yet when looking from afar, the bronze hills appeared like waves of an endless ocean met in equal harmony with the slate of black, starry sky above. He occasionally tricked himself into thinking there was some magic in the air, that some God had sculpted Narood and there was a divine beauty embedded within. He wanted to believe it, but he didn't. Although beautiful from afar, Kent knew the desert was nothing more than sand over sand.

It was a struggle to keep his eyes open. His body was so weak that he had to use all of his weight to steer the bike forward. Using his power, his *gift*, carelessly was a mistake, especially in front of so many people. Surely the whispers would spread like a forest fire, and the whole galaxy would know a Paladin still draws breath.

*But that problem will be taken care of shortly. The Timanzee are on their way.*

It had been years since he used mind control. It was his gift and, for a time, he had mastered it to a fault. He was slow, even though he had possessed all five Sand Snakes, they were easy targets and the process still nearly killed him. In his prime, he could have possessed fifty low life creatures such as them all at once and without breaking a sweat. He could have wiped the memories of everyone in the bar, and with that the Paladin could disappear without a trace. But the strength he had once earned only existed in the present through memories.

The wood-carved shack resting in the middle of a barren desert was more like four-walls-and-a-roof than a genuine home. Inside, lying on the swept, sandy floor was a cotton bed and a thick blanket not shy of bugs and other sorts of creatures. Underneath the bed lay the last remnant of the Paladin he once was, and he felt it every single night as he tossed in his sheets. A bucket of water sat unused in one corner, probably contaminated by this point. A small rug covered the center of the ground to prevent some of the sand from rising. His bathroom was the entirety of the desert.

*I need a pet*, Kent thought to himself, but it was a lie. Any poor creature trapped with Kent Kentoshi would be lonelier with him than by itself.

The drunk hardly made it to the door before passing out. He collapsed on his bed, face planted on a worn pillow. Granted, it had been the first natural sleep to fall upon him in a while. A generous sleep, as a result of exhaustion rather than intoxication. Unwanted dreams haunted him in his slumber, nonetheless. They were dreams he had before, but not for a while. They were strange at first, but as always, Kent remembered everything.

He saw a sword forged of Immortech beneath the crypts of the ancient Spyre. The white-gold steel beamed brilliantly in the light shining from the circular, crystalline window that made up the roof of the Elemental Hall. Its hilt and pointed cross guards were traced in silver and platinum. The man holding it was equally as magnificent. Like the blade, the man's hair was whitish gold, but somehow even more stunning, and he wore rich purple robes with streaks of white lightning bolts running down the creases. He was encircled by others of varying alien species, all wearing the same white armor and robes and armed with swords, axes, or maces made of Immortech. Their weapons combined could not match the brilliance of the one held by the man, the human, in the middle. The Lightning Lord. *The Stormcaster*. The Archmage.

As much as he preferred the reality of his dreams, sleep always ended. Kent woke hours later and started his morning by cursing out the Immortals. His body was hot and itchy, his head pounding after the severe effort he forced it through the previous night. *How many more days until the Timanzee come?* he asked himself, rolling from his bed.

The next couple of days followed a similar pattern, although with a bit less violence and a bit more intoxication. The villagers were wearier around him as he wobbled down the street. Not that the village was at all friendly to begin with, but Kent was growing suspicious that he couldn't seek refuge with refugees anymore. The bar owner still let him in, given he had the credits to pay.

Some of the militiamen were more enthusiastic, one soldier even going as far as to ask him if he was indeed a Paladin. They were alone at the time, making Kent's next move easy.

"No," he said, before wiping the young man's mind and ripping hope from his soul. *It would not be the first time… but hopefully it would be the last.*

The dreams continued to deliver at night; a mocking reminder of what used to be. He was told since childhood not to take his gifts for granted, but how could he possibly foresee the annihilation that occurred seemingly at an instant? *Perhaps I'm even taking my current situation for granted*, Kent thought one night at the Bar-With-No-Name, *but probably not.*

The numbers of the ragtag militia dwindled with the passing days. Even the inspiration of fighting alongside a Paladin couldn't triumph the fear of opposing the Triumvirate. Those who stayed were either moronically optimistic or desired their end. The latter of which were skeletons, fighting a war that had been lost over a decade and a half ago. They stayed not because they believed in opposing the evils of the Triumvirate, but because they wanted a noble and certain end before joining their loved ones in death.

Food was low across the whole village, and weaponry and ammo were nearly non-existent. At this point, it would take a single Timanzee slave-squadron to finish off his starved and depraved militia. After digging, he returned to the bar. After the bar, he drove back to his shack. And after that, he dreamed, despite his best efforts not to.

With mornings came a peculiar feeling. Each sunrise over the sandy dunes could be his last. Each day increased the likeliness of a Timanzee invasion, and each day he prayed they would come.

He awoke at the crack of dawn to a thunderous commotion outside. It was a ship, practically landing on top of his lonely shack. The sounds of its whining jets cut through the flimsy walls. He charged out, unarmed, to find a puny black ship with pointed wings and a glass cockpit. After some struggle, it descended on the flattest ground available. A ramp dropped from the rear and a cloaked figure walked down.

The figure was unrecognizable by sight, but he knew who approached by the indescribable aura that accompanied her. "Best turn your ship around, Tali. I have no reason to talk to you."

"Do you have other company?" the strange figure asked, shuffling over. "If not, I don't see why we can't talk as friends? If you are busy, say so. I can come back again some other time."

Tali made her way to Kent, who barely presented more than his head outside the shack. His walls shook anxiously as the vents on the ship berated them with waves of winds and sand. "Okay *friend*, what do you want?"

She looked at him with her heart-shaped face and large violet eyes. "What I want is some common hospitality. Aren't you going to invite me inside?" Kent sighed, but obeyed. At this rate, he would have been more hospitable to the Timanzee.

Perhaps using his powers attracted more attention than he expected.

"You look good, Kent." Tali smiled as she entered. The years had been kind to her. She belonged to a small race of people from an orbiting moon around the Denvari home-world. Her skin was as dark and brown as tree bark, but smooth as the bottom of a chestnut. Her hair was long and wild like hundreds of tiny twigs sprouting from her head and falling down her shoulders. Her mystical presence had not left her either; even his drunken cynicism could not abate that.

"Minimalist approach." she said, awkwardly, her mystique unable to conceal her disappointment. "Admirable, although a window or two couldn't hurt."

Kent would not fall for the old teacher's charms. He sensed more than Tali on the puny ship, and he hardly expected she came for a friendly visit. *I will refuse her. Whatever she asks of me, I will refuse. She is not my superior anymore; she's just a creature now.*

"I would offer you a drink, but I have none," he said, deeply embarrassed that she had to see the pathetic state of his living conditions. His own throat was dry, and he would have dipped his head into the water bucket if not for his company.

"Don't worry, Kent Kentoshi, I will not be staying long. And you will be coming with me."

"Don't be so sure," he warned. "I have nothing but respect for you, but my destiny has led me here, and here it's meant to end." They stood in an awkward silence in the cramped shack, listening to nothing else but the running ship outside. He begged internally for her to leave. She was part of his past, and that was where she needed to stay.

"It doesn't have to end like this." Tali said, her eyes wide and drowning in sympathy. "How did you come to this desert?"

"Don't act like you don't know. We show our faces anywhere there's a camera, and expect Triumvirate hitmen to be right on our ankles. This past decade, I've had more homes than I can count. I managed to stay out of harm's way too... until now."

Tali received the hint. "Even on a planet such as this, we cannot stay hidden. I heard news of a sorcerer who seized the minds of a few clients at a bar in Narood. Rumor has it, he pulled their brains out from their skulls. I took that last part with skepticism."

"So, what the Hell have you been doing?" Kent asked, his tone uncordial. "I can't imagine you've been drifting through space listening for rumors."

"It's not completely inaccurate," she admitted. "I've been listening to reports of spotted mages for years. All end in nothing, or worse. You're the first I've managed to catch alive." Something about her presence alarmed him. His old life was too distant to be real, and yet it was all coming back as if raised from the dead.

"Do you still have your sword?" Tali asked, much to the drunk's surprise. He pondered for a moment, and remembered the blade was under his mattress, sticking him in the back as he slept, serving more as a dust collector than a weapon.

"Of course, but I don't use it."

"Then it's a good thing I came along. Immortech is such a rarity these days, it would be a shame to see it go to waste." Tali smiled. She was friendly and amiable, making Kent feel absurdly uneasy. Ultimately, the drunk decided to say nothing. Silence was better than saying something he would inevitably regret. "To be blunt, I have a mission for you, which will require your blade and skills of the mind."

Kent scoffed, "You cannot send me on missions. Your power over me vanquished with the Order."

Tali lifted an eyebrow. "I was not aware our Order, the Paladin Order, had died? We are still here, aren't we?"

Kent scoffed again. There was no point in acting polite. He should be drinking, but instead he was talking to a memory. "Our Order died when the Inquisitors betrayed us. Our Order died when Spyre crumbled to dust. Our Order died with the Archmage." He turned away from Tali, head down to the earth. "Do us both a favor and leave."

"Not until you hear my quest. You idolized Archmage Zoltor, did you not? He would have done anything to keep the Order alive, and I know you would too."

"The Order is dead. Mages are despised and killed on sight. Either of us casts a spell in public, we're dead." He was insulted that she would use the Archmage's name for bargain. If this was what Tali had become, she was not worth another moment of his consideration.

"But there is a way to bring back the days of old. After some time, I've located the children of Archmage Zoltor. They are young, but they have potential. They do not know how powerful they are; they need guidance. I want you to find them and I want you to teach them."

"NO!" he barked, regretting it immediately. It was disrespectful to speak in such a tone to a professor. "The Archmage's children died with their mother."

"Not true," Tali corrected him. "They are very much alive. It's a cruel secret to hold, but I had no choice. I'll admit, I had no idea what do to with them until now, but since I've found you, I believe it's the perfect time to unite the Archmage's children and start a new Order."

*Impossible.* The Zoltor line died along with Spyre. No one could possibly keep them hidden. *What trick is she playing?*

"I'm shocked you didn't turn your ship around as soon as you laid eyes on me. Look at me, Tali." He raised his arms in mocking embrace. "Am I someone worth following?"

"Maybe, or maybe not," she shrugged. "I was overwhelmed when I heard of your presence. Although optimism may have set my expectations too high, if there is some semblance of the Paladin I once knew, I'd say you are the perfect teacher."

Their eyes met. He could not deny the seriousness, the sincerity, written on her face. "With these children, we could restore the Order. We could create the first truly safe beacon for mages in fifteen years. And by the looks of it, they can save you from whatever your life has become."

Kent clenched his fists. He considered entering her mind and forcing her out the door under his own volition. *First she lies, then she insults me. Living on the run has changed us all for the worse. Best to let the past die, before we've ruined the legend.*

"Mages have never seen darker days than the ones we live in now." Tali admitted, her tone turning serious. "You're the only Paladin I know to still be alive. But if not for me, then fight for the thousands who died so this one small spark may exist in the darkness. It's the least you can do."

Kent marched over to his mattress and recklessly turned it over. Hidden beneath it was a sword, his sword, made from the divine Immortech metal. He wiped the dust off with his sleeve and considered its majesty. It was a ghost in his hand. Even in the dark cabin, the sword with its swirling glyph carvings radiated brighter than the sun.

"Now you have two options," Tali said. "Turn the past into an ally and help make a better future for our people, or waste your life away trying to forget it."

The Paladin swiped the blade up and down. It felt natural in his hand, as if a part of him. For the first time in a long time, Kent Kentoshi smiled.

# ARIEL (1)

The flashing neon lights that blanketed the towering buildings were far too bright for her to see the stars. They were everywhere, to the point where actual colors around her became unknown. One moment the walls around her were lime green, and the next they were blood red, and then sunburst orange. Most onlookers were impressed or even hypnotized by the psychedelic displays that followed them wherever they went, but Ariel desired something more authentic.

For a world which appeared so bright and polychromatic, Ariel felt nothing but blackness on the inside. Behind those collages of lights and sounds were things less appealing. There were cracked walls and broken windows, dark alleyways with even darker people, and more crime and corruption than one could possibly imagine. But this was home for her, she was her city, or more accurately, a product of it. She wished she could see her home, Prisilla, with fresh, rather naïve eyes, but the grand spectacle of the proclaimed "Greatest Planet in the Galaxy" was a living, breathing joke to her.

But she had more urgent priorities than self-reflection. Her name was not Ariel anymore; it was Canary, her working name. She did not like it, but her master had given it to her, insisting that someone of her profession could not run about the districts shouting her real name to any "fuckwad" on the street. Ariel, or Canary, did not object to her master. He was smarter than her and, for the time being, she was dependent on him.

Hovering by her side was her Pup, a premium model "BOT," from of a heavily coveted brand of robotics typically used as servant and occasional bodyguard to its owner, depending on the situation. They were expensive, and the deftest tradesmen could get fatly rich selling them in the upper levels of New Horizon. *That, or you could steal one.*

Pup had been in her life since she could walk, and this night was no exception. Slightly bigger than Ariel's head, its metal was mostly white, decorated with blue and orange stripes she had painted horizontally and vertically around its circumference. She and her master had upgraded it with a variety of weapons... because you never knew what could happen on the job. Pup may have been a robotic sphere constructed to inflict pain upon her adversaries, but it still whistled with delight as she scratched under what she imagined to be its chin.

"Canary," the transmission came in through her earpiece, "Remember the mission. You are to follow Graznys and find out who his associate is, that's it. Kagen has a high bounty on this guy so don't screw it up!" The chatter was mostly static, but the voice was so gruff that it fought through the poor connection. It was the third warning her master had given her that evening, as if she was some dumb kid.

The bounty was high, impossibly lucrative, and Wulf was beyond lucky to have been given the contract in the first place. And when they succeeded, business would boom. Bounty hunters were paid their dues in many different hard currencies, as online transactions were too easily traceable by authorities. When Ariel did the conversions out into Prisilla's credits, they'd be rich enough to look for property on New Horizon.

She had followed her target for an hour, blending in with the masses which populated the streets of the Market District and dodging in and out of alleyways and stores to keep hidden. This Graznys, a Levian from the planet Morque, had a reputation for being paranoid to all those around him. He needed to be, with that line of work. Like most of his species, Graznys was absurdly quick and agile, making it impossible to match him in a foot race. Any suspicion that he was being tailed could jeopardize the mission irreparably. And she wondered why her heart pounded in her throat.

Ariel assured herself it would not come to that. She kept her face cloaked under her hood, and hid a pistol in the holster on her belt. Graznys would have to search her to find it, and if he got that close, she'd be sure to stun him first. She heard the voice inside her head say: "Kagen has a high bounty on this guy so don't screw it up!"

She shadowed Graznys on an empty street in the Market District. Typically, the Market District would be stuffed of full shoppers, vendors, and pan handlers alike, but not at this late of an hour. Prisilla was a planet of hundreds of levels, each one stacked upon the other. Each floor was a new bustling globe to itself. Effectively an overly ambitious space station, Prisilla was the hub of the galaxy. Ariel hailed from one of the bottom-most levels, closest to the core, known as the Underbelly, but she knew the Market District's layout better than anyone. It was a maze she had mastered through practice. Despite her bounty's quickness, she knew she could use the environment to her advantage.

"Stay back." Ariel whispered to Pup, who whistled sadly in response. "I can't risk having Graznys see you. You can follow, but not too close." Reluctantly, her BOT hovered away.

The Levian crossed a jammed street and entered a building of glass walls. She tailed him, being extra stealthy in the empty atrium. The ceiling above was covered by a black shroud, implying eternity. Her target continued; his steps soft against the polished floor but they echoed nonetheless in the quiet air. Ariel stood frozen as far away as she could while still maintaining eyesight, peeking over a potted plant placed in front of a large window. The lobby was sparse of furniture, meaning she had nothing to hide behind if Graznys caught whiff of her.

The impending doom of a failed mission pushed the oxygen from her lungs.

The common hall was dark save some neon lights from the streets outside that reflected a variety of colors against the glass walls. Ariel watched from far away as her target changed from one hue to another depending on what light pooled over him. Graznys was nearly out of sight before she could tell what he was doing.

"He's calling an elevator," she said into her comm, in a tone barely high enough to be a whisper.

"Don't pursue," her master barked. "There will be other chances to find him." That was a lie. This was the only lead the two bounty hunters had on their target, and it costed them everything to buy it from a secrets-broker.

Her master sounded forgiving enough through the headset, but Ariel would not be fooled into taking it as a promise of mercy. He would beat her bloody for this, though she did nothing wrong. It was his form of stress relief. When provoked, he was as indifferent to her well-being as another would be to a punching bag. The elevator was on its way down, spit out by the blackhole above.

"We know where he's meeting the associate; I can try to find him there." Ariel offered. She bit her lip, waiting for permission to pursue, but her master would have none of it.

"No, Graznys is too quick, and we can't risk any pearls finding you out in the open. Report back to me in the junkyard this instant, before you fuck this up further!"

The elevator stopped at the Levian's feet and its doors opened horizontally. Despite her master's command, Ariel felt herself moving forward, each step faster than the previous. Entering the lobby as softly as she could, she had to walk slowly, at least until the elevator closed, or Graznys would hear her. No one was around either; she had no means to disguise her intentions. When the doors did close, Ariel broke out into a sprint across the flat polished floor.

The elevator ascended at a quicker speed than she predicted. She ran as fast as she could, but the elevator was faster and any chance of her completing the mission vanished as it crept into the darkness above. Believing she was close enough, she leapt hoping to get a grip on the threshold.

Her hands wrapped around cold metal, but not the piece she wanted. Instead, she was clinging for her life to the end of an iron bar attached feebly to the bottom of the elevator. Her feet dangled as they tried to land on something solid, but the ground below her was rapidly disappearing.

"Kagen has a high bounty on this guy so don't screw it up!" she heard the voice reprimand her. Pain shot up her arms and lower back as her body tugged her down to the earth. Her fingers screamed but she refused to let go. Her nails clawed at the cold iron. She kicked her feet up to rest them on anything, but they embraced only airy darkness. The elevator was going up, and she would either hold on or be cleaned off the ground the following morning.

Despite the panic and pain pouring within her body, the outside was calm and cool. Only the elevator's fast vertical ascension and Ariel's muffled grunts for life could possibly be heard. She wanted desperately to cry out for help, but who would come to her rescue? Certainly not her master, and it would be unprofessional of her to ask a bounty for any assistance.

Her lower back joined in her body's protest. Her spine was ready to snap as gravity pulled at her with lustful hands. Her eyes watered. The grip of mortality squeezed her passionately.

Without knowing, her left hand gave way. She would have screamed, but it felt unreal. Being close to death made her numb, as if everything happening was part of a lucid dream and her life wasn't actually in danger. The nothingness had deflated her fear of dying. If her right hand gave way and she fell, there was no longer a ground to crash into and she would fall forever, trapped in a boundless void.

Her right hand would not betray her to the legitimate doom awaiting hundreds of feet below. The doors opened and Graznys stepped out into another level. Which level it was, she could not determine, for Prisilla consisted of hundreds, but judging by the sweeping ranges of circular and rectangular buildings etched in chrome and hundreds of narrow walkways flooded with disillusioned creatures from across the galaxy, she determined she was still in the Market District.

Ariel worked her way up one of the sides of the elevator and jumped for a hanging chain used to operate it. From there, she climbed the chain and opened a vent with the help of a red laser blast from her pistol. She used what little strength she had left to swing the chain toward the opened vent and dive into it. Fortunately, the vent wasn't blazing hot. Unfortunately, its exterior was slimy, dusty, and populated by an army of two-headed insects that scattered up her arms and legs. They wouldn't bite her, yet, but she sent them scurrying off with the flicker of her lighter before they could muster the courage.

The other exit was not far off. Ariel broke the hatch and emerged on the sidewalk of a new level of the Market District, a few yards from the elevator. A new city, above hundreds of others, but beneath hundreds more. It was quite an odd sight coming out of the ground like that, but those walking the sidewalks were too preoccupied with racing to the next shop to acknowledge her.

Graznys was sitting at a table on a balcony looking down upon the city. He appeared rather relaxed with a cocktail glass in hand and an empty chair across the table. Ariel continued to pursue, this time walking with more of a swagger and removing the hood from her head. It was risky, she knew. Floating barges, called whaleships, hovered in the sky above the cityscape, containing Prisilla's notorious police force known as the *Pearls*. They searched for her and her kind with their blazingly white spotlights drilled into the decks of their barges. Most of the people she knew were hunted by them. To be able to say she was on the pearls' wanted list was something to brag about in the Underbelly. It was a rite of passage into adulthood. Her master was on this list, and Graznys was certainly on it too.

The barges she did see were drifting away, allowing her the confidence to show her face. Her name was out but her master had done a good enough job concealing her identity, so she gambled that any pearls wouldn't recognize her.

Ariel removed the inhalator from her belt, put the piece to her lips, and took a deep breath. The effects were immediate. Her brain achieved euphoria, her senses vibrating exuberantly. A sudden whip of confidence boosted her forward. It took many uses, but once she learned how to operate under the enchantments of Blast-off, she became a better bounty hunter.

She removed her hood and let her hair tumble down her shoulders. That was her weapon, intertwined strands of silver and gold. Alluring to most men, regardless of species.

Ariel performed exactly how she had seen it done many times before. *Approach him from behind,* she told herself. *Not too slow, not too fast. Trace your forefinger gently on his shoulder. Don't say a word, just sit. Don't make eye contact unless he engages you.*

"Not even two weeks on this shit-stain planet and I'm beginning to smell like shit myself." Graznys said when Ariel took a seat. She could feel his lustful gaze on her hair.

She did not turn to him immediately, instead preferring the view from the balcony. The blaring lights from below and the pitch black space above turned the sky into a ghostly gray. Now and again a flicker of orange or red light from the hover cars speeding across the sky would flash from the gray. The walkways were like a neon collage from high up, swallowing pedestrians as they roamed about.

"You should be thankful that you can tell it's shit. Some of us are surrounded by it so much that we forget." Ariel said, making eye contact. Graznys was a Levian, and a fairly unattractive one. His scales were spiky and the color of rust. His lizard eyes were candlelight yellow with a sloppy film plastered over them. He had four long claws on each hand and his voice sounded as mistrusting as his appearance.

"We must be some of the lucky few who haven't forgotten," Graznys raised his cocktail glass. "Cheers to us." He stopped when the rim touched his mouth to consider her. "I see you don't have a drink, would you like some of mine?"

Ariel pretended to be flattered, "I don't drink on the job."

"What? That's half the fun for a girl of your profession." Graznys leaned back in his chair and licked his forked tongue across his lips. They were not alone on the balcony. Other races sat, drank, and mingled with one another. The more she blended in, the less attention she would draw from the barges.

"And what is my profession?" she asked with a malicious smile on her face. It was a risk, one wrong move and Graznys would be gone forever, but the coy smirk he returned showed it paid off. She had to get him comfortable enough to let his guard down so she could pull out her pistol and stun him, but it was easier said than done.

"You have a mouth on you." Graznys said, ordering another cocktail. "You're not the prettiest one I've seen, but your mouth makes up for it. I'd like to put it to better use."

A spotlight of an overhead barge cut through the open lounge area. Instinctively, yet foolishly, Ariel crouched down.

"You in some trouble?" Graznys asked. He tapped his cocktail glass somewhat tentatively.

"As much as any Underling." Ariel replied, coolly. "We're inclined to not trust pearls, it's in our DNA, I think."

Graznys took another sip of his drink. His movements were clumsy, his eyes occasionally wandering when they weren't conspicuously gawking at her. "They gave me some shit when I was trying to enter the planet, but I told them off."

She nonchalantly took out her inhalator and puffed it. "I'm a bit paranoid. It happens when all your friends are taken away and never seen again. That's the scariest thing: no one knows what happens when the pearls take you in, you just disappear forever."

Ariel was unsure why she was speaking honestly to her bounty, revealing secretive thoughts she would never dare to share with her master. Regardless, what she said was true. Pig-Faced Willy was arrested for shoplifting some convenience store, the mutt Javella was taken in for harassing a tourist up in the Market Districts where Underling scum did not belong, and Savelind was caught pickpocketing when he was eight years old, abducted and never seen again. Her old "friends" served as warnings to her now, and she was better off because of it.

Graznys, however, was too preoccupied with other intentions than to listen to her. "I'd like to take you back to my place. I've got a stash of fade-away for us."

Ariel swallowed bile back down her throat. "I'd like the same thing. Are we going back to your place? I'm sure a guy like you owns a condo on the Horizon levels."

"Not here," he said. "Not yet, at least. I have powerful friends that have promised me a large sum of wealth. It's practically mine, do you see it?" He raised his hand, palm stretching across the neon skyline. "Once I get it, I could buy a whole level on New Horizon if I wanted to. And maybe I could buy you as well, permanently."

"Oh, that does sound wonderful," she admitted, pointing her pistol at her target underneath the table. She had it set to stun, or she thought she did. Regardless, the Levian would not leave his chair without taking a laser shot to the groin.

"Let's go back to my place," Graznys ordered. "It's not a condo but remember we must think long term." He made a move to get up, but she wouldn't budge.

"I'm not leaving with filth like you," Ariel said with a sweet smile. Horns from the hover cars above protested wildly. The owner of the balcony made his last call for drinks before closing up for the night.

Graznys took offense to her words, but that offense soon turned to fury. "Filth like me? You should speak. You're the ugliest human girl I've see. Tits of a child, too. I shouldn't have wasted my time, not when there are other options."

There were still too many people on the balcony for her to shoot him and drag him away without anyone alerting Prisilla's police. The bar was closing soon, she just needed to keep him for a few minutes longer, give some of the clientele time to clear out.

"By other options, you must mean porn," Ariel inquired. "I looked through your search history, that's how I discovered your fondness for human girls. Funny, lots of them on your computer, but not so many wanting to cozy up to you in the low-rate bunk you can barely afford." She arched her weapon over the table, then gestured him to stay seated. Ariel took note of the paranoia that sparked in his eyes, but his pride was a live grenade in his pocket. He may have been afraid, but he was willing to stick around to put a whore in her place.

Others on the balcony showed no mind to them, being too focused on getting their last drinks before the balcony closed.

Prisilla was a noisy city. More hover cars raced from above, hordes of common folk muttered from below, and somewhere in the middle was the constant explosion of ads from every sound system seen and unseen.

"I know what you're thinking," she said. "It seems cliché for a woman best a man by manipulating his sexual cravings, but Kagen has a high price on you, and I was told not to screw it up."

"Kagen?" Graznys said, half a gasp. "Who are you?"

"I asked you to guess my profession before, but you refused. I'm a bounty hunter. Well, I'm an apprentice really. I work for my master, Silver Wulf. He works for Kagen, and Kagen works for the

Triumvirate. So, in a way, I work for the Triumvirate too. They don't like you selling weapons to terrorist groups, so I have to stop you."

"N-No!" Graznys stuttered. "You can't, my f-friends won't have it."

"What your friends want means nothing to me. Now, we can leave smoothly, or I can stun you under the table and drag your twitching body to Kagen. I prefer the first option but don't think the second is something unfamiliar to me."

The first option died as soon as she said it. Graznys desperately darted from his chair, throwing the table up with him as he made his escape. Ariel could see it telegraphed in his eyes and fired a stun laser, but the weight of the table threw her off balance, the resulting shot barely scraping his thigh. It wasn't much, but she managed some damage. Graznys screamed and swore as bolts of electricity fired up and down his leg. He was limping, but even the Levian's limp was speedy, and before she knew it, he had thrown himself over the balcony and into the crowd.

Ariel followed, praying the oncoming drop was not a deadly one. She fell on the tarp of an outside shop, landing on the display table, rolling to her feet, and continuing the chase, not taking a second to look back and thank the owner who cursed her existence for ruining his shop.

Graznys limped as fast as he could to safety, throwing unsuspecting bodies at his pursuer left and right. Ariel was agile, though, and could dodge whatever he threw at her, but there was an ever-growing distance between them. Finally, she stopped and pulled out her pistol. "EVERYONE! OUT OF THE WAY!" she demanded as she aimed down the sidewalk. Although he was fast, Graznys was running in a straight line, so all Ariel had to do was aim right down the middle and...

A fierce orb of electricity fired down the sidewalk between masses of people like a pinball launched through a shaft. The shot was perfect, Ariel could feel it, but it did not hit Graznys, not directly. The ball of electricity hit an unfortunate spectator as he ignorantly strolled into the pedestrian-made tunnel. The impact of the shot sent the poor man reeling backwards and into the Levian, knocking him down face-first onto the concrete surface. Some gasped, others ran for their lives, but most took out their phones to record the event as it happened. Ariel didn't care. She'd rather them take videos than call the pearls, but she needed everyone to scatter in order to get to her target, who was getting back to his feet, albeit in a slow, dazed sort of way.

By the time Graznys gained control of himself, Ariel was on top of him. She kicked him as hard as she could in the leg and stomped down until there came a sickening crack.

"Bitch!" Graznys hissed through his sharpened teeth. He did not make another attempt to flee, but Ariel gave him another shot of electricity to make sure. She let her target shake violently on the ground for a few moments before cuffing him and picking him up to his feet.

"This didn't have to be hard," she reminded him, utterly breathless from the chase but soaking in the pride that came with her accomplishment. But that pride was short-lived.

A blaring, white light loomed over her. Another struck down on the streets, then a third. "Pearls." Her heart fell to the floor. More white lights appeared from the heavens as everyone on the ground retreated to the darkness. More lights meant more barges, and more barges meant more pearls. Ropes were thrown from the docks above, but she was gone before the men sliding down felt the surface of the ground on their boots.

Ariel kept a cuffed Graznys in front of her as she navigated through a maze of dead and dark alleyways. "Now you got pearls tailing us," he wailed. "Why'd you have to bring me down too?"

"Shut up!" she commanded, hearing the impending march of soldiers. No matter how many dark corners they cut through, the march grew louder. Graznys' limp did not help either. If she were by herself, she could have climbed into a building or hid in a sewer. Despite temptation, she had worked too hard to abandon her target now. She considered calling her master, but what was he going to do? Yell at her, most likely, then beat her senseless. She tried to be as quiet as possible, but Graznys' manacles clanged and banged as he ran.

The impending radio chatter coming from the pearls echoed louder down the narrow aisle of the alleyway, and Ariel knew it would not be long before she became someone else's cautionary tale.

Despite her master's valuable words, there was one relationship she did keep, if one can consider a bond between a girl and her robot to be legitimate.

Her sphere of screws and bolts which she named Pup came zipping around the corner of a building to her rescue as the pearls closed in. "What the Hell is that?" Graznys asked, half delirious from the wound in his leg.

"THAT is going to save your life," Ariel said. She looked into the round, black lens and saw the eye of her best friend.

Pup pushed by her to confront the marching pearls. They stopped and stared at it in confusion. "A Bot?" one of them said through his helmet. "Should we shoot it?"

"No!" another objected, rather harshly. "We'll take it back to the station and dismantle it for parts. These things are worth a fortune. Come on, hit it with a shock ray."

Pup responded to their hostility by opening a compartment under its lens, from which a metal tube poked out. In an instant, a wave of fire sprouted from the tube and created an unrelenting storm of heat around the pearls. The shadows of the alleyway were vaporized by a myriad of yellow and red flames. The front line of pearls screamed as they cooked in their armor, and the survivors were forced to retreat.

Pup returned to Ariel, whistling with delight; he was quite jovial for a killing machine. "Good job," she said. "Now get us out of here." Pup nodded by moving its lens up and down. He allowed her to get a strong arm around him. The magnets in her white gloves seamlessly attached to her robot's body. "You might want to grab on too," she suggested to Graznys, who approached the BOT with heavy trepidation.

"This thing can't support both of us; it's too small!"

"You just have to hold on until we find a roof," Ariel assured him. Pup hovered wherever he went, and he could fly hundreds of feet in the sky if commanded to. "Would you rather come with me or get taken by the pearls?"

"No way I'm getting up in the air only to slip off that floating circle," Graznys said, stubbornly. "I'm not moving."

"Fine." Ariel grabbed his manacles with her free hand. Pup soared upward. Graznys dangled in the air, swearing and screaming his head off while she struggled to hold on to both him and Pup. She discovered rather quickly that the magnetic pull of her gloves lacked the strength to carry so much weight.

To increase to morbidity of their predicament, the pearls had regrouped at the bottom of the alleyway and were firing lethal lasers up at them. A random cry of pain cut through the night as a laser grazed by her head, but she did not think to look back. "Faster, Pup!" she ordered. Her BOT ascended with newfound fortitude. Ariel laughed, grateful for her friend.

The sky around the tops of buildings was an abyss of lifeless black. Most of the roofs were pointed or in half-domes decorated with lights, but Pup came across a flat-top soon enough. When her feet touched ground, a great sense of relief filled Ariel's back and shoulders, pleased for no longer being pulled in opposing directions. She gave the manacles a tug and was astonished by how light they were.

Ariel turned her head, her heart stopping. Locked within the manacles were wrists and hands, but that was all that remained of Graznys. She ran to the edge of the roof and gazed down, seeing no signs of her target, just the gloom of distant barges filled with pearls still on the hunt.

*Failure.*

It would not be long until they started checking the roofs too. She would have to find her master before things got out of hand, yet she found herself moving to the edge of the roof and sitting, allowing her feet to dangle over the neon city below. Pup hovered over her cautiously. It did not look like too far of a fall from here. Her heart was racing, her eyes red and hot, and yet she felt a sense of complete numbness throughout her body and mind. She inched further to the edge, for the thrill of it.

Then, she heard a voice.

"What did you do now, Canary?" her master said into her earpiece.

"I captured him, but pearls surrounded us." There was a long silence.

"Can you make it back to the safe house without a thousand pearls on your ass?" Silver Wulf asked.

"They haven't found me yet; I can be there by tomorrow night." Ariel said, her throat raw with defeat. Silver Wulf strategized on the other end, he always grunted when he was strategizing. A part of her wished for abandonment, after all she deserved it. Her life rested on this bounty, and she blew it.

"Don't do the safe house. I'll meet you at the subway station between the last level of the Market District and the first of the Underbelly. It's always crowded there so we can hide in plain sight, saying you can handle it. Pearls won't risk the bad publicity of opening fire in a populated area. Do you understand?"

"Yes," Ariel choked.

"Canary," he said, his voice lingering. "You fucked both of us."

"Wulf, I'm sorry, please, I really tried, I really, really tri-"

"I said, you *fucked* both of us. Is that clear?"

Ariel would not respond. The lump in her throat would have made her voice crack, and Silver Wulf could never hear that. She examined the manacles one last time. Graznys' hands were thin, scaly, and rust-colored. His sharp claws were not as menacing up close; they were thin as paper and dull at the ends. She examined where the arms had been cut off, presumably by a laser fired from a lucky pearl. She assumed Graznys had been left behind miles back. Reflecting, it would have been impossible to hold on to him and Pup at the same time without falling to her death, and Graznys was probably torn away mere seconds after leaving the ground.

His blood was a boiling, bright green. She examined her clothes only to find the ooze painted all over them. It would not be long before they began to reek. "Kagen has a high bounty on this guy, so don't screw it up!" She took another gulp of sadness and watched the green blood slowly ooze over the edge of the roof and drip to the illuminated streets far below.

# TROYTON (1)

Destiny had brought him here. Of all the planets in the galaxy and of all the people he could have been, he had the fortune of being a soldier, fighting for Rome and for King Gaius Julius Caesar. Troyton reminded himself of that every morning as he woke up, and each time he spoke those words, he hopped out of bed with an austere commitment to carry out his duties to the absolute best of his abilities, all in the glorious name of his king and kingdom.

Back home, he had been bombarded with stories of Caesar's great victories during the Civil War against the evil Republic and of the heroic accounts from soldiers who fought in the frontlines for truth, justice, and a long-lasting peace for the Kingdom of Humanity. They had inspired him to become a soldier, to perform his own courageous deeds in the name of the KOH. Troyton wanted to fight in the frontlines, to hold the golden eagle standard, commonly called *the Aquila*, into battle against enemy forces and assist in the expansion of the greatest empire to ever exist. Caesar devoted his life to the betterment of the KOH, and now it was his job to help the king maintain his life's work. It was a small task compared to the burden of his leader, but still not one to be underestimated.

Troyton was a soldier now, the best thing to ever happen to him, and yet not entirely what he expected.

The mission was to be six months long once they landed on their first assigned planet in Grayspace. The journey to the Edge, where galactic civilization met its end, was about four weeks long, even with a Roman engineered starship. The task was simple: search the planets of the Edge for any Synth activity. If any dangerous activity was to be found, eliminate it.

Scipio oversaw the daily records of their mission, but because none of the planets in Grayspace had names, his reports came off as lazy, vague, and rather dry of engaging content. Troyton opened a tablet and read some random report one night while the rest of his squad slept. "Day Three," the report began. "Quill Squad is still searching their first assigned planet for Synth activity. Although the planet does not seem to contain any sort of intelligent life forms either now or in the past, it has the ability to sustain life, including that of humans. We traveled by vehicle for twelve hours today, then by foot for an additional four. The starship sent out four probes in opposite directions, each probe with a tracking area of 200 kilometers. No life signs were reported in any of the data. The water in the rivers is clean and drinkable but we rely exclusively on the rations from the starship. We expect there will be at least another week of searching before we can be completely sure that there is no Synth activity on this planet and move to the next."

Troyton sighed when he finished the closing lines, it wasn't worthy of a story, unless the person reading it wanted to be bored into sleep. At this rate, the campaign into Grayspace would earn him and his squad no *auctoritas*, the prestige and respect of KOH society. Many a young soldier made a name for themselves through fighting bitter campaigns into the unknown, Caesar included. The king, before he donned the laurel wreath, fought for the Roman Republic, accumulating so much auctoritas through his successful campaigns that the government he supported feared his popularity and turned against him.

Troyton tried reading Scipio's report with a fresh mind, but he hardly got a few sentences in before putting it down.

The next day was no different, nor the day after that, nor the week, nor the month. The days began to blur into one long, monotonous cycle of walking along a never-ending road to nothing. They were on their third planet, and it was exactly the same as the other two: cold, dark, with jumbles of twigs and leaves that barely qualified as bushes, and long stretches of lakes and rivers with water so colorless they looked like thick clouds strapped to the earth. The weather was dreary, and rain poured down on the squad frequently.

By now, Troyton could write Scipio's reports for him: "Barren, wet wasteland. No Synth lifeforms found... or anything at all."

"I'm doing this for Caesar, I'm doing this to keep Rome safe," he muttered while marching the endless path. "If this is the job they want me to do, I will do it to my best ability." He received odd stares from his fellow squad mates, but Troyton chose to ignore them. He would not be frazzled by distasteful stares.

"Is this all you had hoped it would be?" Lucius asked in a friendly yet undeniably mocking tone. His sarcasm would have bothered Troyton if he had not known Lucius to be playful.

"As soon as we find some Synths, it will be," Troyton assured him with a smile. Lucius stood seven feet tall. He had milky white skin, crystal blue eyes, and shaggy brown hair to match his equally long and unkempt beard. Troyton stood seven feet and two inches tall, a fact he frequently reminded his friend of. His skin was caramel-colored, his hair short and black, and his face cleanshaven. They could not have looked more different from each other, yet they shared more similarities than with the rest of their squad.

Quill Squadron consisted of twenty Roman foot soldiers specializing in guerilla warfare, three tech officers from three different colonies, two armored tank drivers, two starship pilots who were back with the starship, a scribe, a medic named Alfred from Mercia, a diplomat, and Troyton and Lucius, lab-born humanoids from the Casca moon genetically altered to excel in warfare.

They were all afraid of Troyton and Lucius, but the Romans tried to mask their fears by mockingly referring to them as "Lab Rats." The name bothered Troyton at first, but he would not allow juvenile insults to take away from the fact that they all fought under the same banner. Lucius, on the other hand, was not so forgiving. He nearly came to blows with his comrades multiple times, but Troyton would be there to hold him back whenever these situations became too heated. The two of them could have killed the rest of the squad without breaking a sweat. They were designed to do so, but it would be treason and, above all, immoral to take the lives of fellow soldiers.

"Why don't we ditch this pack of fools, hijack the starship, and leave this cluster of nothing," Lucius suggested. "We were made for war, searching one empty planet after another is an insulting waste of our potential."

"If we come back home without the squad we'll be executed." Troyton said, half listening. He briefly admired a lone shrub crouched in an endless valley of short, gray grass.

"I never said anything about going home. We'll be free lancers. Make money on the infighting between crime bosses. Travel to Laktannon and fight for some disposed king in the Bloodlands. The entire galaxy will be our home!"

"Why would you want to be a mercenary? They're scum, recluses. No loyalty to anything other than themselves. It's not a good life."

"But it is for those who are good at it. We're designed to decimate organized military forces. In the underworld, we can be Gods of war."

"Yes, but we'll be working for other criminals. We would be fighting bad guys, but for the gain of other bad guys. And we'll be hunted down by the Triumvirate for the rest of our lives." Troyton chose to leave out that he liked fighting for humanity. Lucius returned his squad's hostility with greater hostility, and his enmity towards humans in general grew day by day. He was obsessed; they hardly spoke of anything else. "Be patient. We haven't been given a chance to prove ourselves yet. Wait until a real battle comes along. Then they'll be happy to know we're all on the same side."

Lucius scoffed, "Same side? We aren't humans, we're weapons. And once we stop working, we'll be discarded as quickly as a broken rifle. You may not have accepted it yet, but you'll have to at some point. I don't understand your loyalty to a species that we owe nothing to."

Troyton stared at his friend, who was grinding his teeth in frustration behind his brown and bushy beard. "Without humans, we would not exist. What debt could be greater than that?"

He thought of home the most. Casca was barely a small rock circling Orbis, but it was his rock, and it meant nearly everything to him. The base where he grew up was mostly white rooms and windows. When he was not engaged in military training in the battle-room, he was learning about human history, and when he was not being lectured on history, he was taking pills and running tests in the lab, and when he had what little free-time he was allowed, he would gaze out the ceiling window in his bedroom and admire Orbis. The hub of humanity consisted of three massive continents: Mercia, Tisoni, and Carcia. When he was a boy, he asked his doctor where the city of Rome was. He pointed to the southernmost tip of Carcia, "There, looking right back at you. That is the home you must protect."

Traveling to Rome was his top priority. The capital of the human race and the foundation of the Triumvirate seemed so close from his bed on the Casca moon, yet so far at the same time. Almost humorously, he felt closer to Rome at the edge of the galaxy than he ever did at home. *If I just get a chance to prove myself*, he thought as he went through the daily walking routine, *I can show my worth. I need something better than this, it's in my design.*

The setting sun was distant and could easily be mistaken for any other star. The latest planet they were scanning was the farthest from the sun any of them had ever been. Most of the soldiers wore jackets under their already thick, plated armor. Troyton did not take part. *The more layers a soldier wore, the stiffer he becomes and the easier a target he makes.* Regardless, he did not mind the cold. As a student, he had developed an indifference to it through combat drills in rooms set to below freezing temperatures.

On top of the cold and an overall lack of unity among the squad, a new problem emerged. Food was thinning faster than he had planned. The twenty Roman soldiers that made up the majority of the party had fancied themselves to more than the allowed rations of hot meals per day to keep themselves warm. The tech officers and pilots could not complain, for they were outnumbered, and Lucius would not speak a word about it because he too was doing the same thing. It was up to Troyton, Quill squad's supposed leader, to say something. *Perhaps another day.* They still had plenty of food left, and an increase in hostility between him and his squad was not favorable. The Romans hated Troyton for what he was, but they were content with making their distasteful comments behind his back. If he dared to take away their food, their disdain may become physical.

The mission was the priority, which required Quill squadron to remain subordinate to its commander. If a few extra meals a day meant keeping his squad in line, Troyton would allow it.

Across the system, no human squadron had discovered Synth activity. The idea of being the first to find the Synth army was a desire he kept close to himself. No organic life had dived this deep into Grayspace for thousands of years. In fact, no race across the galaxy truly knew what the Synths were, but each believed their own interpretation to be true. Troyton imagined the history he could make, being the first person to interact with this fantastical species. Perhaps that would get Caesar's attention.

"Commander Vorenus," one soldier called as they walked the eternal path. They were both on foot, while a majority of the soldiers rode in the armored tank, huddled together like penguins to keep warm. "Do you have a moment to talk?"

Troyton smiled at the soldier warmly. He recognized the man as Gnaeus Scrupio, a sergeant and Roman foot-soldier. Unlike the others, Gnaeus had not japed about the "lab rats," or if he did, he kept it well disguised.

"Of course, Sergeant."

"I've been meaning to ask you; how does somebody have the means of making someone…like you?" Gnaeus asked, the words 'lab rat' wanting to jump from his tongue.

"I don't know the exact logistics, but I was designed by scientists on a moon base. I went through the same stages of birth as any other human, only substitute the womb for an incubation tank."

"I see," said Gnaeus. "And I heard your training is the most intense across the worlds."

"I wouldn't know, I haven't completed every training the galaxy has to offer. It was difficult, but the same can be said for all soldiers in the KOH." Troyton kind of laughed. "I think we are all the best of the best."

"No need to be humble, Commander Vorenus. You already tower over the lot of us." He gestured toward his men riding the tank. They were looking with greedy eyes, as if they knew something was about to happen. Troyton turned around to see Lucius stalking behind them, hands firmly on his rifle. He was many things, but above all Lucius was loyal to his people.

"I'm curious, with that special training and those fancy modifications, how do they help you in battle?"

"Well," Troyton paused. He gave the sergeant a dubious look, realizing the intentions of this conversation were not friendly. "I haven't seen real battle yet, but I have passed every combat trial Casca put me through." He did not let the sergeant speak, believing it best to be blunt and honest with the man. "If you have any trepidations about my command, allow me to relieve you of them. I have been shaped my whole life to lead, I am completely competent in my position and the safety of you and the rest of the squad is my top priority."

"You are competent," Gnaeus agreed. "When the mission is to walk in a straight line, searching for an enemy that doesn't exist. How confident will you be when lasers start flying, when bombs explode, when ships fly above your head and rain down hell? I fought for Caesar during the Civil War, I've seen chaos in its most glorious form, day in and day out for years. It's drilled into my skull. But you know where that got me? Now I must take orders from some *lab rat* so green he shits grass in the morning."

The other soldiers began to laugh. They would never act this cruelly to a human officer, yet because Troyton was a lab rat, insubordination was acceptable. For a split second, he considered punching Sergeant Gnaeus Scrupio directly on his square, Roman jaw. That would infuriate the rest of the soldiers. Pride tested, they would rush him like starving dogs, giving Troyton a valid reason to tear every one of them apart. As tempting as it may seem, he would not lift a finger. They fought under the same banner, they were his brothers, and they needed his leadership.

"I am sorry you feel that way," he said, calmly. "You are within your rights to bring this matter up with the generals as soon as we return home."

Gnaeus winced. He pointed an accusing finger at Troyton and prodded his chest with it. "Listen here, you disgusting lab rat. I didn't fight for the KOH my whole life to be taking orders from a walking experiment. You speak of returning home, what's that for you? Certainly not Rome. You'll return to that lab of yours and be dissected for the next batch of genetic freaks-"

An explosion came from the ground, followed by a deafening noise. Dirt, ash, and fire flew into the air, lifting off like a rocket ship. Blood and limbs rose to the sky as well, spraying the ground with red liquid and burned flesh. The clean air turned thick with smoke and dirt, morphing into its own putrid substance.

He sat in a mound of dirt and sand. There was ash all over his white uniform, and blood too. *Not my blood*, was his first reaction. Lucius was there to lift him up, shouting and pointing out to the hills some distance away. Troyton could hear nothing, his ears flooded with a sharp ringing. He hit his head with the palm of a gloved hand, trying to grasp some sense of the world that had become a blur.

*Battle.* He had been desiring this moment for his entire life, and the Immortals granted it. This was his chance to impress Caesar, and he sat there in the dirt like an oversized bug. Finally realizing what exactly was on the line, he gained the ability to say, "Form up...Form up around the tank!"

"Form up around the tank!" Lucius mimicked, his voice possessing urgency. For once, the soldiers did as they were told, leaping from the tank to form a complete circle around it. They drew their weapons and waited for another order.

Troyton grabbed Lucius by the shoulder, "Sergeant Gnaeus-"

"Shot up into space!" Lucius finished, dragging his delirious friend to the circle.

"What do we do now, sir?" a soldier called.

*Sir*, Troyton thought, *don't you mean Lab Rat?*

"We wait," Troyton said. "Did anyone see a Synth?"

"What do Synths look like?" another soldier called out. *Excellent question...*

"Where's Gnaeus?" said a third soldier. "He disappeared!"

"Worry about the sergeant later," Troyton said. "Just look for the Synths!"

Lucius gestured to the range of hills again, like black mountains against the setting sun. "They'll attack from the hills, most likely. It's a good place to hide, they'll have the high ground and the sun at their backs if they charge our position." Troyton knew what that meant. If the sun was at the backs of the enemy, it would be in their eyes.

He hopped on top of the tank and opened the hatch. Inside were the two armored drivers, a woman named Williams and an old man named Henrik. Scipio also sat inside the tank, shaking violently as if there was an earthquake right below him. Troyton could not blame the boy. His job was to observe and record, not fire a weapon, but if another gunman was needed, he would not hesitate to order Scipio outside. "Williams! Henrik!" he yelled, forgetting only he had a landmine explode in his ear. "Target the hills. Use your scanners to locate the enemy, we're blind in the sunlight."

"Scanners, sir?" Henrik said. "They're Synths, will they show up?"

*Another excellent question.*

"Just do what I say." He slammed the hatch shut and regrouped with his squad.

Troyton, Lucius, the three tech-officers, and the now nineteen Roman soldiers stood in silence, waiting anxiously for the impending storm. This was his moment, he knew, his first taste of conflict and the start to an outstanding military career. He gripped his rifle, put his finger on the trigger, and aimed at the hills.

He waited, and he waited, and he waited. Still, Troyton kept his eyes peeled, his gun at the ready. His mind was in a rush, his lone instinct was to find the attacker. *They will come, their games will have no effect on me.* But night came before any enemy. It was his sole indication that time had passed.

"What do we do, Troyton?" Lucius asked, relaxing his firearm. They had stood in a circle for an hour at this point, and there was still no sign of Synth activity.

"We press on." Troyton declared, already starting his march. "There is something out here, we can be certain now."

"What about Gnaeus?" a soldier asked.

"He's dead. He gave his life for Rome, hopefully some day we can all do the same." Troyton pointed forward. "We continue on and bring Caesar's justice to the bastards that killed him." His soldiers followed with vigor in their steps.

Troyton walked on, never looking back to see if he was being tailed. He was certain Synths were going to attack; he wanted them to. The fact that they had been standing for an hour like a school of scared children pestered him. A real commander would have rallied his men and staged a counter offensive, not hide behind a tank and let the enemy come again at their own will. What if the enemy staged an ambush? Then, the entirety of Quill squad would have been slaughtered.

It was a mistake Troyton would not make again. He would find the Synths and make them pay for murdering a Roman soldier.

Night was on them. Cold winds blew from every direction, penetrating layers of coats and armor like a knife in the back. Stars were non-existent in the deep, black slate of sky, and the only natural light shining on the world were two distant moons the size of peanuts from where they orbited. Tall trees barren of all leaves became more prominent as Quill squad passed the endless span of valleys. Twisted branches and twigs like the fingers of an ancient monster reached out from the earth.

Troyton sent two scouts ahead of the party to search for any Synth traps. His human soldiers were more obedient. They realized the threat was real, something he had rightly taken seriously from the start, and that war with an unknown enemy was imminent. He reminded himself to keep a cool head because, at least according to General Marcus Pullo, "A leader who acts out of fear is no leader at all." Back in his day, Pullo was a stanch supporter of the Roman Republic, but considering his superb military career, Troyton took his words with the upmost value.

"Commander Vorenus!" a scout shouted as he charged towards the group. Troyton would have to punish the scout later for his failure to keep quiet. "There's a base, I think, over the hill to the west."

"How are you not certain of this?" Lucius asked. "Didn't you get a good look at it?"

The scout panted furiously as he tried to explain what he saw, "It's so black, it blends right in with the night. If I hadn't used my night-vision glasses, I wouldn't have spotted it. You have to see it for yourself, sir."

Troyton asked, "Did you spot any Synths? Was there ANYTHING guarding it?"

"No sir, and I checked a long while," the scout said. "Can I please get some water?"

Troyton gestured Lucius to the tank to grab the scout a canteen. The situation was peculiar. He still possessed nineteen Roman soldiers and a tank at his command, but whether or not those were poor or favorable odds against whatever resided in that base was the unanswerable question. There was an enemy out there that no one had seen since the earliest records of history, and their number ranged from zero to infinity. Troyton also had to consider what artillery, turrets, and traps the Synths might have. If there were mines like the one that had killed Gnaeus, a technician could easily scan the ground for more.

The whole squadron followed the scout to where he spotted the base. Troyton was handed night-vision goggles to locate it. The base was like nothing he had seen before. It was oval-shaped and as dark as a shadow, defying the gravity it stood on. It even appeared to be hovering and rotating in place. Disturbingly alien, the sight of such an abnormal construction gave Troyton an unfamiliar sense of pressure in his gut. He put the goggles down and sighed, having no idea what to make of it.

He turned to Lucius and was immediately brought back to his days on the Casca moon. His officers and professors had taught him how to kill Mages, Denvari, Enfari, Drakonids, and even the Khav. Troyton could survive for days in the harshest environments and still be in better condition than the freshest human soldier. What he never learned was how to fight a myth.

"What's the plan Commander Vorenus?" Lucius asked through his thick beard. The other soldiers had gathered around, equally as curious.

"You want revenge for Scrupio? Well, you'll get it beyond those hills. I don't know what's out there or how strong it is, but like everything else in this galaxy it can be killed." The soldiers nodded in approval. "We're as much a stranger to them as they are to us, only a Roman does not fear his enemy just because he is unfamiliar, am I right."

"Yes sir!" they declared.

"Good, I have a plan." Troyton lied, he opened his mouth and let whatever came to his mind spill-out. "As soon as we get a good look at the base, I'll place five men on the opposite side to set up a flank. The rest of us will hide to the right. Then, the five men will fire shots to get the Synths' attention. When they go to investigate, the rest of the squad will ambush. From there we should learn something from the bodies and plan the taking of the base accordingly."

"But what if the Synths don't come out?" a soldier asked.

Troyton smiled. *Confidence*, he thought, *confidence, confidence, confidence*. "Then they are afraid of us, and fear is the best weapon there is. This is the start of something historic, men. From this day on, Quill Squad will be remembered until the very end of days. Are you with me?!"

"YES!" they shouted.

"FOR CAESAR!"

"FOR HUMANITY!"

# Marion (1)

"FIGHT! FIGHT!" The voices thundered in their demand for bloodshed. They encircled him. Each body became a bar of the prison cell that entrapped him. They grew taller and stepped closer, tightening the space between him and the beast, forcing him to shrink before his opponent.

Marion stumbled to his feet, his knees as shaky and uncertain as his head. He wiped a streak of bloody spittle from his lip with the sleeve of his uniform and looked around with swollen eyes. They were shadows, more akin to the silhouettes of featureless statues than his classmates. "Fight!" they demanded. Marion wanted to fight them all, but the numbers were too overwhelming.

Vintrus was his real concern, however, and was standing before him like a mountain over a small forest. He puffed his chest out like the great Roman animal he was, but kept his arms by his sides as an open invitation for Marion to strike. He gladly obeyed, making a fist of broken fingers and swinging wildly at the older boy's rock-solid stomach. If he had hurt him even slightly, there was no sign of it. Instead, he laughed at Marion's efforts.

He recoiled to prepare for another swing, but was cut off by Vintrus' large, sinewy hands as they grabbed him by the face and shoved him heedlessly into a line of metal lockers.

Marion saw a flash of gold, which came and went faster than a crack of lightning, then it was dark. The crowd roared with approval as Vintrus loomed over him, considering if another assault was worth the effort.

"Stay down," he advised. "You started this, and I'm ending it."

But Vintrus started it years ago, along with all the other students who adored him. Fueled solely by fury, Marion rose to his feet, this time with more certainty than his previous effort. The shadowy statues that were his prison bars began to take form into familiar faces, faces Marion hated with all his being. Vintrus raised his arms and basked in the crowd's approval. The shadows turned flesh chose him as their champion against Marion, and he took the challenge of squashing the school's parasite with stellar enthusiasm.

Vintrus was held to a higher standard than most, the academy's golden-haired hero embracing his role as leader with an ostentatious sense of entitlement. He wore the same blue-on-gray cadet uniform that the entire class body was assigned, yet his godly physique, flaming blue eyes, square jaw, and perfectly white teeth made him a celebrity among the masses. He was their hero, but what was a hero without a villain to oppose him?

The promising future of the KOH versus its greatest shame. Picking a side was too easy.

"You're embarrassing yourself," Vintrus said. "Somehow you manage to keep lowering the bar."

"Are you going to keep stalling?" Marion asked, struggling to keep the world from spinning. He sensed his eyelids puffing up, fragmenting his vision. At most, he would have a few minutes before he was completely blind. *Let's make the most of it.* "For Romulus' star-student, you're kind of a pushover."

Vintrus laughed. "I have standards. Must be a strange word to you." He smiled arrogantly. "You did attack me first, so anything that happens next is in self-defense."

Marion responded with an equally arrogant smile. He spat a messy glob of blood at Vintrus' polished black boot, which ended with a plop as it splattered over his ankle. The crowd went silent. Vintrus winced. He spun around, too quickly for Marion to calculate, and put all his momentum in a fist landing squarely on his jaw. The boy went reeling backward, smashing his head hard into the lockers yet again. The clang of flesh and bone meeting metal echoed throughout the hall.

This time, he did not get up. The crowd exploded in vicious approval.

Marion wasn't even given the chance to properly digest the pain. He felt a violent tug on his collar and was yanked upward like a ragdoll. The hot-blooded breath of Vintrus hit him like dragon's breath. His swollen eyes rendered him blind, but he still flinched as he waited for another barrage of punches. They never came, but if he knew what was coming next, he would have preferred the fists.

"What is going on here?!" a voiced boomed from down the hall. The other students fled like caged animals finally set free, leaving Vintrus and Marion to deal with the headmaster.

Mister Antrius Polanis was a short, stocky man with arms and legs thick as kegs and a neck so wide it verged on swallowing his chin. His wiry brown hair receded past the tips of his ears, his mouth and jaw were locked in a permanent scowl, and his close-set, rage-filled eyes were targeted on Marion.

"Would someone care to explain?" the headmaster asked in a softer but equally intimidating tone. He stood like a brick in the center of the polished hallway, squatting in preparation to chase them down.

"Sorry sir," Vintrus spoke first. "Marion tripped and fell against the lockers, so I tried to help him up, but he fell again. I know this looks bad, but there's only so much one man can do for someone of his nature."

"And what nature is that?" Mister Polanis asked.

"Well, forgive me for being frank, but he's the bastard spawn of traitors. It doesn't seem fair to hold him to the same standards as a true Roman." The rage rushed through him again, but he could not garner the strength to move his body. He craved to rip Vintrus' throat out, so none of his insults could escape his vile mouth. He turned his head and gave Marion a coy smirk, a gratuitous acknowledgement of his own wit.

Headmaster Polanis was not amused.

"Do you take me for a dullard?" he asked, although it sounded more like a command. Vintrus' smile died on his lips, unable to answer. Polanis continued, "Has this school taught you nothing? Is lying to your headmaster some small thing to you? This should not come as a surprise, but publicly assaulting another student, another soldier, has its consequences. You're popular among the other boys and girls, but don't for a second think it grants you any immunity from the rules."

Vintrus put his hands up and stepped back, "If I could explain, sir. Marion challenged me. I was defending myself and the name of the prestigious Military Academy of Romulus. It's my duty as a student and obligation as a soldier."

He wasn't lying; Marion had marched right down the golden halls of Remo's Tower and challenged him to a fight. The older boy was caught off guard and hesitated a moment to consider the request, but with his fans watching with equal amounts of adoration and thirst for carnage, he was easily persuaded to accept. Sitting in a state of beaten disillusionment, Marion could not recall why he had challenged Vintrus to begin with. He was used to getting himself into stupid predicaments, and thus had stopped questioning his actions, as anything illogical also seemed inevitable.

Polanis' internal temperature appeared to spike higher with every word spoken from Romulus' star-student. "So you mercilessly beat another classmate in the name of our academy? And were you expecting a reward in return? In the real worlds, assaulting another soldier is considered an act of treason, and your only reward will be a noose around your neck. Would you like that, Vintrus?"

Marion chortled. Each breath sent a shock of pain into his lungs. He answered it by quite uselessly pounding his chest. As if alerted by his amusement, the headmaster fixed his glare on Marion. "And you, Mister Donatus. Can you go a day without causing trouble? I'm beginning to realize why no one likes you. Your discipline comes later, or maybe I should expel you now and be done with it."

"Fine by me," Marion wheezed and coughed, reliving each punch as if it were happening all over again. "Wasn't my decision to be here in the first place."

"Nor did I decided to have you, but life's unfair and some of us handle it better than others." Polanis turned back to Vintrus. "And you, star child, follow me back to my office so we can come up with a proper punishment."

"You can't," Vintrus objected. "I have a clean record!"

"You give yourself too much credit. If you're the best the Academy of Romulus has to offer, then I've failed as a headmaster. I pity the soldiers and officers who must fight beside a short-tempered juvenile such as yourself."

Vintrus was speechless. He bowed his head to hide away the tears and stomped on the ground. "Marion," Polanis said sternly, yet not without mercy. "Go to Everec, he'll make you look decent before reporting back to me. Normally I would let this slide considering Vintrus' involvement, but your frequent misbehavior has forced my hand."

Marion nodded, refusing to meet Polanis' eyes.

"Good, now I want you to limp to Everec. If I hear that you asked for a guard or another student for help, I'll beat you worse than you could ever imagine. There's a soldier in you, Marion Donatus, you're just fighting for yourself rather than Rome."

"I don't care about Rome. I don't want to be a soldier and humanity is the last thing I would ever fight for." Marion forced himself to his feet, feeling internal snaps and cracks as he struggled. He looked at his headmaster and grinded his teeth, half in contempt and half in agony.

Polanis sighed, "That's the worst thing you could have said to me."

The grandfather clock ticked and ticked and ticked in what would otherwise be a silent space. The office was a perfect cube, consisting of a flat ceiling and floor and flanked by four walls made of solid oak. There were no windows. A red carpet laid across the floor and towering bookshelves hugged the left and right walls, making for a rather deceptive prison.

Marion sat on a cushioned chair opposite a tall, black desk for two hours, listening to the endless toll of the grandfather clock. Placed promptly in the center of the desk and staring him directly in the face was a golden desk sign, which he read repeatedly to pass the time. "Mister Lyndon Everec, Academic Dean of the Military Academy on Romulus".

Marion suspected the wait for the Academic Dean was part of his punishment, until he heard the door behind him turn and open. The sound of something other than the obnoxious ticking of the clock was so gratifying that he nearly leaped from his seat in excitement.

Even the slightest movement sent shockwaves of pain up his body. Vintrus was many horrible things, but a weakling he was not. The man who approached the desk was not as intimidating physically as Vintrus, but Marion feared him more than anyone else on Romulus.

"Marion," Mister Everec said, taking his seat behind the desk. Every motion he made was soundless. "How are you today?"

Marion scoffed, "You already know the answer".

"Then you are doing quite well. You wanted to pick a fight with the most beloved student on Romulus and you got it. I'm surprised there isn't a smile on your face from ear to ear."

"I got demolished. The only positive thing to come of this is he'll go down with me."

Everec shook his head. "Vintrus is the son of an honored Roman officer, you're some boy abandoned by his deserter parents. I can promise you that your punishments won't be the same."

"Don't call them that!" Marion demanded.

Mister Everec was struck with confusion. "Am I wrong? Did you conjure parents out of your lunch today? If so, I would have to report you as a mage."

Marion shot up from his seat as a splash of anger swept across his face, sending his chair reeling behind him. He clenched his fists tight and in preparation to smash the desk in half. His jaw clenched and he bared his teeth like an ape. But after a second of hesitation, his attitude changed when his eyes met the Dean's.

He was an older man, nearing his sixties, with a lined and gentle face and shallow green eyes. He was significantly taller than Marion, as well as most of the other students, and maintained the stature of a soldier despite his years. His snowy white hair was long and flowing and fell past his thin shoulders. Marion checked himself, fixed his chair, and sat back down.

"What am I supposed to do now?" he asked, composed.

Mister Everec put his elbows on the desktop and folded his hands. He wore a similar gray suit to Marion, except for the décor that distinguished his honorable rank. On his heart was the golden pin of the Aquila. A purple sash of satin hung in proud showcase from shoulder to hip.

"Hope and pray that you will not be expelled," Everec said. Marion anticipated something more insightful.

"Is it likely? This isn't the first time Polanis has threatened me."

"Don't sound so reassured. If it was your first warning, I would not be too worried, but Mister Polanis did not get to where he is today through hollow threats and pandering. Are you forgetting who he is?"

"Polanis-"

"Mister Polanis."

Marion took a deep breath in through his nose, held it, and exhaled through his teeth. "Mister Polanis was a commanding officer of King Caesar's army during the Civil War. Caesar himself honored him after taking Rome from the consuls."

"Correct," Mister Everec said. "And what would have happened if Mister Polanis' enemies did not take him seriously or if his company thought he was a coward?"

"He wouldn't be headmaster of a Roman military academy." Marion said, well past seeing Everec's point, yet the old man proceeded anyways.

"Mister Polanis' students are his company now, and they are just as likely to rebel if they detect weakness in their commander. If Mister Polanis expels you, it will not be because he dislikes you, but because he has to if he wants to maintain his dominance over the student body that outnumbers him by the thousands."

"Great. I'll be a message for everyone to not stand up for themselves."

"You will be a reminder that brash actions lead to unwanted consequences. Do you even know the dangers you face with expulsion?"

Marion shrugged, "I'll get to leave this golden Hell. Honestly, it's about time."

*Golden Hell* was not a clever nickname for the academy, but he deemed it fitting as nearly everything on the inside was made of gold (or, more likely, cheaper materials similar enough in appearance). From the hallways to the lockers, from classrooms to dorms and even bathrooms, every speck of Romulus was pretty and shiny, and it aggravated him endlessly.

"And what happens when you leave?" Everec asked with a hint of annoyance. It was one of the few times in his life that Marion had seen the old man express impatience. Even on his worst days, Mister Everec found something to smile about. Expulsion must have been serious, indeed. "You have lived inside the academy for all of your life. You have no idea what the real worlds are like. You have never felt a rain drop, never met an alien, never worked a job. You are ignorant to everything that exists outside of Romulus and if you leave, I will not be there to guide you."

"Maybe it would be for the best," Marion snarled. "Did your 'guidance' help me make friends? It's a little more than coincidental that you're the only person in this damn school I can speak to. We should go our separate ways, for all I know you've been holding me back." He experienced an undeniable sense of power, lashing out on the one man who ever showed him any empathy, but he regretted his words as soon as they left his lips. The grandfather clock tolled in the quiet tension he had created in the cramped office. Mister Everec made no notion to speak, and that was what shook him the most.

"Mister Everec, I-I'm sorry. It's been a long day, I should leave."

"If you are angry about something, best let it out on me." Everec said. "Ever since you were a boy, I have failed at controlling your temper. Get all the frustration out now, I implore you, before you have to see the headmaster again."

"I'm fine, thank you." Marion was too embarrassed to look the older man in the eyes. Lyndon Everec was the closest thing to a father he had, and Marion demonstrated his gratitude by shoving all his problems onto him. "I should go back to my dorm. I don't know when Mister Polanis will want to speak with me."

"You do that. I will talk to him and try to sway his decision for a lesser punishment."

Marion went for the door. The bookshelves loomed over him like two massive waves on the brink of crashing. Mister Everec claimed to have read every single book in his office, which was something worthy to boast about considering each case contained shelves several feet long with books so tightly packed together that not even dust particles could squeeze between opposing leatherbound book covers. Everec's intelligence far exceeded his, and he would do well to remember that next time he spoke out.

"Marion," the older man said as he reached for the doorknob. "I do not want to be a heckler, but I give you these lessons for your own good. If you pull a stunt like you did with Vintrus in the real worlds, the consequences will be much more severe than a mere detention. This galaxy can be cruel. You are not like them, and they will do everything they can to drag you down because of it. All I am trying to do is to prepare you." Everec smiled in his kindly way. Marion responded with a crooked one before turning on his heel and limping back to his dorm.

The Academy of Romulus consisted of three main buildings: Myker, Lorneway, and Despir. Myker was primarily used for student housing. Lorneway was twice the size of the other two structures combined and was dedicated to classrooms, large lecture halls, and physical training rooms. Despir was built for faculty offices and housing, lounges, conference rooms, and had a docking bay for ships on the ground floor.

Marion was in Despir and had to make it all the way across Lorneway to reach his dorm room. Crossing Lorneway proved to be challenging, not because he was exhausted from the day, but because he found it nearly impossible not to fight every student that gave him a dirty look as he struggled down the golden corridors. "Pompous assholes," he muttered to himself, limping along the cold hallway. By now, the entire student body knew of the brawl, and likely knew of Marion's pending expulsion too.

He was instructed to see a nurse, but he felt the best way to treat his wounds was to lick them in the privacy of his own room, alone. It was nighttime when he finally got to Myker, or at least that was what the clocks declared. Romulus lacked a single window across the whole academy to tell what time of day it was. Windows were distractions from learning, so logically they were not allowed.

The walkways along tower were empty when he arrived. He passed busts of many a legendary Roman, living in sweet, nameless immortality. As he made his way to his dorm, an echoing shriek followed as he dragged his left foot along the smooth floor.

The Academy of Romulus hosted tens of thousands of students, each with their own dorm. Marion peered up to the rows and rows of iron vaults reaching such a height that he could not see the top. Each door was exactly the same, except for the room number engraved upon the top threshold. His number was 304.

Marion went up an elevator to his room and put his hand on the security lock to open it. It took a few attempts for the scanner to recognize his hand which had become crusty with dried blood, but the iron door eventually gave way and opened like a bank vault.

He let out a sigh of relief when he saw home, although home was not much. Inside his four golden walls was a bed, a bathroom, and a desk with a laptop that would automatically shut off after ten o'clock. A small rug covered the floor and hanging on the left wall was a portrait of his king, Gaius Julius Caesar. Over the years, Marion had become accustomed to Romulus' ostentatious display, but stark offerings.

304 had looked exactly the way it did when he moved in at the start of primary school twelve years ago. It would have looked exactly as he left it in the morning, if not for the redhead girl sitting patiently at the edge of his bed with a glass bottle in her hand.

"Octavia?" he said, not sure if he should have gone to the nurse for a brain scan.

The girl stood up and rushed to him, leaving the bottle by the bedpost. "What happened to you?" she asked, brushing a thumb against his swollen eye. The touch would have hurt if done by anyone else.

"Vintrus and I had a disagreement, but we settled it," Marion said. The girl examined the scratch marks on his neck, then his broken fingers.

"Settled?" she asked. "Seems to me like you lost. Don't you know any better?"

"I haven't learned in sixteen years, why start now?" He tried to laugh it off, but she only answered with genuine concern in her eyes. Like with Mister Everec, the unbearable guilt hit him harder than Vintrus' fists ever could. "Octavia, I'm sorry. I don't want these things to happen, but they do. You know how it is."

"I know you might get expelled; everyone is talking about it. You might think that expulsion means you're sticking it to the academy, but if you're gone, I'll never see you again."

Marion abruptly kissed her but received nothing in return.

"I'm serious," she said when he gave up. "Unless you really can't wait until graduation to get rid of me."

"I don't want to get rid of you. I love you." Marion said, honestly. She was the one student who took the time to understand, the one who treated him as something more than a bastard son of traitors.

"But your actions prove the opposite," Octavia declared with a taste of frustration. "I don't want you to give up who you are, but the next time you want to do something stupid, consider how it affects *us*."

"You're right," he admitted. "I'm selfish, but speaking of stupid decisions, why're you here? If you're caught in my room after dark, we'll get expelled together."

Her concern shifted into a mischievous smile. "I thought I'd take care of you, looks like you need it." She turned to the bed and showed him the bottle. "This will heal the wounds, I think. Actually, it really won't. At the very least it'll numb your head."

Marion did not join in her delight. "Is that wine?" The glass bottle was a shade of olive, concealing a dark purple liquid inside. "Where did you get it? How are you even here?"

She shrugged. "The security system on the vault was easy to hack. Tech like that gets archaic pretty quick when not updated. The safe inside the teacher's lounge was harder, I'll admit, because it's too old-fashioned." She popped the cork and took a swig from the bottle. "Try some, it's Denvari."

The Denvari were one third of the Triumvirate that conquered most of the known galaxy, with the help of the Kingdom of Humanity and the Timanzee Empire. Marion learned about the mystical Denvari race in his classes, but oddly nothing about their vintages.

"This isn't a good idea. You could get in trouble."

Octavia grimaced. "Why is it that you can break the rules all you want, but I can't? I'm completely capable of making my own decisions, I hope you realize."

"I don't want to see you get in trouble," was what he said, but what he meant was that he did not want her to follow his reckless path. "You have the potential for something great, and I don't want you to jeopardize that for me."

"Poor Marion," she mocked. "What a big martyr you are. Get the fuck over yourself. I chose to come here tonight. I want to get drunk and have fun, and I want to do it with you. Clearly you don't want the same thing, so I'll just leave."

She went for the door, bottle in hand, but Marion grabbed her by the arm. "No. Stay. But you should be aware of the consequences."

"I'm not stupid," Octavia said. "In an hour, the doors will be locked for the night. Even if we got drunk, it's not like we could run around the academy." She pursed her lips in thought. "Sounds kind of fun though, could be a grand graduation prank."

"Okay," was all Marion said. He pulled her close and wrapped his arms around her waist. He kissed her again, and this time she kissed him back, her soft hands tenderly caressing his neck.

Octavia handed him the bottle and he drank. The wine was thick and sweet, tasting like freshly picked grapes, but he preferred the taste of her tongue. They kissed again, this time longer and harder.

"I like to break rules too," she said in between breaths. "I'm just better at it than you."

# Kent (11)

The monstrous iron claw plucked the Seshora Araman from outer space like an apple from a tree, its long fingers forming the thick bars that engulfed the small ship. As they were pulled toward the docking bay, the hand closed so tightly that Kent believed they would be accidentally crushed beneath the weight of unconcerned steel.

*It would be an unexpected end to an unexpected quest,* Kent thought as the Seshora Araman was scanned all over by red, spotty lasers shot from distant watchtowers. It was a security scan meant to detect bombs or chemical weapons and was unlikely to trigger any alarm over a few handguns his newly formed crew had on the ship. He kept his blade on his hip in case a signal did sound off and he was surrounded by pearls. It was a rarity to have a Paladin die of old age, and Kent did not foresee himself to be the exception.

"Please remain calm, this is a simple security check," a robotic voice from an intercom boomed. "Traffic officers will direct you to the nearest landing zone momentarily. If you have any questions, please be sure to ask one of our travel agents located by every elevator and rest stop. We thank you for your cooperation, welcome to Prisilla."

The last word sent a shiver down Kent's spine. He had not been to Prisilla since he was a boy, barely a mage let alone a Paladin. He squired under Paladin Dallo Woh at the time, who was tasked with finding a dealer selling chemical weapons in the Underbelly. It was a fond memory upon reflection: Dallo had sent most of the dealer's clientele scurrying away at the sight of his Immortech battle-axe.

The dealer was less timid and even offered the Paladin all the credits he could ask for to forsake his vows and work for him as hired muscle. Dallo obviously refused, and had the dealer punished accordingly for his violations against galactic law. Kent had been terrified of failing his first mission, as he had heard stories of how brutal merc companies could be, but that day black-hearted criminality was bested soundly by the forces of Paladin justice.

But Dallo was dead. He died fighting bravely during the Battle over the Blood Moon. *No memory is truly pure.*

Feeling the Seshora Araman land was a relief. Kent had been traveling with strangers for weeks and it would be refreshing to see some new faces. He kept his distance from most of his new crew during the voyage and hardly learned anything about them except for their names, but if Tali trusted them, he would too.

The ship's captain was a female Kalmar named Matiyala. Her skin was as green as spring's grass and she had a mop of long tentacles for hair. There was a wit about her fitting of her youth, which was what made her Kent's favorite crewmate to talk to, not that there was much competition from the others. She had named her ship the *Seshora Araman*, which meant "Mermaid of the Stars" in her native tongue.

Sara was the second member of the crew and the biggest mystery to Kent. She was native to a moon in the territory surrounding the Kingdom of Humanity. She resembled a wolf in human form, with her black pelt and haunting yellow eyes, and yet she stood on two legs, thankfully wore clothing, and acted relatively like a civilized being. She was annoyingly quiet, but Kent did learn that her home had fallen victim to one of Caesar's many conquests before the Civil War. That alone was enough for him to trust her, at least momentarily.

The final member of the Seshora Araman was a human named Brutus Cirileo. He possessed the typical features of a battle-hardened, ex-Roman soldier: leathery skin, short brown hair, and angry, close-set eyes under bushy eyebrows. He was tough to the bone and had the scars to prove it. He was belligerent and hated all things KOH for some reason he would never disclose. Kent engaged in a few verbal sparring sessions with Brutus while voyaging, but of late they found it best to leave each other alone.

Kent determined that Tali formed her squad not based on content of character, clearly, but enmity for the Roman army. An intelligent move on her part, for shared hatred is unity in its superior form.

The hatch dropped, and Kent, Sara, and Brutus descended to the docking bay. Ships of all shapes and sizes buzzed around at insane speeds as they fought for empty spaces. The metal on the floor was a dull gray, but the directional lights scattered throughout the floor were bright greens, yellows, reds, and blues. *Blue lights lead to the nearest elevator, the only way to travel quickly through the levels of Prisilla.* He thought of the mission once again, given to him by a mentor he believed to be dead. The Archmage's daughter lived on one of these levels, the question that remained was which of the thousands was she on?

Three soldiers garbed head to toe in vivid, cream-colored armor swaggered over to them, sporting their rifles conceitedly across their torsos. The armor they wore was too thick to recognize their races and their visors were too black to see their eyes. "Bloody pearls," Brutus muttered. Kent prayed the human would not quarrel with others so quickly.

The soldier in the middle stepped forward and commanded them to halt. He separated himself from the others with his satin cloak of crimson fastened at his shoulders. "State your business on Prisilla," he said through the voice modifier in his helmet.

Kent broke in before his comrades could speak. "We're traders. We thought we'd try our luck with the best of the best."

"That's what everyone says," the pearl agreed. "But there are billions of traders here. You'll need something to distinguish yourself, or end up like a billion other losers."

The pearl was arrogant, which subsequently made Kent cautious, as if he was out of the loop on a conspiracy against him. In his prime, he could have taken over the guard's mind in seconds, and the whole conversation would never have happened. He was weaker now, his skill having dulled from lack of practice. As long as the pearl wore his helmet, his brain was impenetrable.

Other passengers exited their ships freely, which meant the pearls made Kent and his crew a special case. He had no doubt the scan from the watchtower detected his Paladin sword. There were other pearls lurking about in hidden places, waiting for an excuse to engage. Luckily for Kent, he had predicted this.

"We have something that'll catch a few eyes." He gestured to Sara, who unsheathed the Immortech sword from its scabbard fastened to her hip. In the hands of a mage, the sword's blade would have illuminated, allowing the glyphs and symbols engraved into the steel to catch fire with divine light. But in the hands of anyone else, the sword looked rather average, the only evidence proving it was indeed a Paladin sword were the glyphs on the blade and the crafted hilt. Kent gazed longingly at the sword, no longer whole without it.

"Impressive," the guard admitted. "How is it that the pack of you got your hands on a Paladin sword?"

"We're bloody traders, we bloody traded for it!" Brutus Cirileo butted in. The malice in his voice was surely going to get them killed. "Do you talk this much to everyone?"

"Not usually, but when our scanners identify a human, a Druin, and…" the pearl paused to consider the wolf-girl. "Whatever it is that you are, our curiosity got the better of us. And when the human has a temper, well, it makes us even more curious."

"You won't find any trouble from us," Kent assured him. Admittedly, he was slightly on edge due to the lack of alcohol on the Seshora Araman, but he did his best to patiently reason with the pearl in the crimson cloak. If he could keep a level head, they should at least get through customs unscathed.

"Oh, we look forward to trouble." The pearl gestured to his men with their heavy machine guns that matched their cream-colored armor. "And if there is a problem, my boys will be there to settle it. Understood? Good, you're free to go for now."

And with those words, Kent and his crew departed to the elevators, but before they were out of view, the pearl in the crimson cloak called back to him. "Hey Druin. Best be careful with that blade; my men have orders to kill any Paladin on sight."

"Yes," Kent agreed, "So does everyone else in the galaxy."

It was a noisy planet to say the least. Not including the constant barrage of jingles and voices of commercials bashing against his ears, Kent could also hear people of a variety of races bartering in a variety of tongues all around him. There were hover cars soaring above the narrow walkways, their engines roaring like wild beasts as they zoomed by. They were flanked by glass facades that stretched for miles above and beside them, and on those facades were balconies where pearls and other members of Prisilla's law enforcement eyed the crowds of travelers. Each shop was restricted to several feet in space, causing incredible confusion as to which signs represented their stores.

The difference between the docking bay and the first level of the Market District was jarring. There was hardly an inch of space between pedestrians, making the line of traffic move at a crawl. If the other hundreds of levels on Prisilla were crowded like this, finding the Archmage's daughter would take decades.

His companions were not faring well either. Brutus pushed and cursed his way through the crowds, his consistently truculent behavior making Kent feel nothing but utter disgust. Even the slightest hint of what they were doing would have gotten them killed, yet Brutus behaved like a bull in a glass shop. The wolf-girl kept herself somehow smaller and quieter than usual. Every blaring advertisement, honking horn, or hollering pedestrian startled her. She could not conceal her discomfort in her big yellow eyes. She was a creature of the natural world, but Prisilla was a world of metal, and it contradicted her instinct at every turn.

"We should split up here." Kent suggested at a rest stop around an open plaza. He leaned on a guardrail beside an over-stuffed food court. Some distance away, a holographic projection of some featureless purple being stood waiting to be of service. It was one of Prisilla's travel agents, a hub of information tasked with directing visitors to wherever they needed to go. Kent chuckled to himself over his brief consideration of merely asking the ghostly projection where the Archmage's daughter was. If the mission was that easy, Tali could have done it herself.

"I agree," Brutus said. "You go wherever you want; I'll check the New Horizon levels."

"Is that a good idea?" Kent respectfully asked. "Only the rich live there. You'll stick out dressed like a trader, and it's unlikely the girl would be up there anyways."

"It's unlikely the girl is alive at all. Your precious master's contract is keeping me here. The sooner I fine the dead body, the sooner I get paid." Brutus' voice was rank with anger.

"Tali wouldn't send us on such a hopeless quest. What would be the point in it?"

"You hold that bitch in such a high regard considering she abandoned your cult when the galaxy turned against it. This precious girl is either dead or someone's slave. I've seen it before, especially on this shithole of a planet."

Kent had to watch his words. One slip of the tongue and someone was bound to hear it. Even the mention of the word *Paladin* or *Archmage* could cause them trouble.

"Fine," Kent relented. "Go there and get arrested, just don't rat us out when the pearls start cutting you up. Sara and I will keep searching the Market District. Keep in touch if you find anything."

Brutus smiled wickedly. "You think I care if I'm wrong and you find her in perfect condition? I don't, as long as I get what's mine. And don't worry, any pearl who tries to arrest me will sorely bloody regret it."

"I'm not," Kent insisted. If anything, he'd prefer Brutus to be dead and silent. The Paladins and their Order had kept the galaxy stable for countless generations, and he treated them with as much respect as a discarded piece of trash. But what was Kent to expect from some freelancer? A mage devoted years of his life to mastering the arts of sorcery, diplomacy, and swordsmanship before possibly being considered for the Paladin Order. All a mercenary needed was enough funds to buy the newest killing machine. Freelancing was a lazy business for vile people, and Brutus fit the personality standard perfectly.

In the end, the merc went up while Kent and Sara went down. The elevator descended silently, as if it was not moving at all. Nevertheless, the doors opened horizontally to another level of the Market District, this one somehow more populated than the last.

They were moving faster now. People on this level walked with an incentive, to spend or make money, and soon enough Kent refamiliarized himself with how the traffic flowed. He did not share the same intention as those around him, but telling the pearls at the landing zone he was a trader was not a total lie. What he valued was information on where the girl could be, and Tali had given him a large sum of credits to buy secrets.

Although credit was the common currency used in most of the galaxy even after the fall of Last Bastion, Prisilla had its own twist on the system. Transactions were typically done through cards, but seasoned traders had created their own, more efficient way of the process. To prevent pickpockets from stealing said cards, traders put their credit information on chips designed to cover one's fingernail. When making a transaction, one would simply place their finger in a machine that all shop owners had, and the deal was finalized. Tali had specifically found a chip that matched Kent's pointed fingernails before finding him, and he was incredibly grateful for it.

Back on the ship, Matiyala questioned why credit was necessary in the first place. "You're a telepath and a Paladin," she had told him in a tone suggesting he was not aware of his own nature. This was one of the many aimless conversations they had while travelling to Prisilla. He had spent many of his nights lying in bed with her in the captain's cabin. "Can't you read their minds or something? We could spend it on something more practical, like ship upgrades."

Kent laughed. "When I was younger, I could force a large squadron of men to throw themselves off a cliff without a second thought... Not that I did. But when it comes to determining a truth from a lie, I have the same judgement as anyone else."

"Do any Paladins know how to read minds?" she asked, realizing her dreams of a better ship were fading.

"Can't say that I do. Even if I did, chances are they'd be dead now anyways."

"Oh," Matiyala said. "I'm sorry."

She was the most honest of the crew members on the Seshora Araman and he wished she had not decided to stay on the ship. Kent missed her company, especially when compared to what little companionship Sara offered. Her nose, which supposedly possessed a superior sense of smell, proved to be utterly useless as they went along. How could she pick up a scent when she was too preoccupied shuttering at every electric buzz or beep in a mile's radius?

Matiyala was not the only one left behind. Tali stayed on the ship as well. Having one Paladin in Prisilla was dangerous enough. "You'll have a better chance convincing her of who she is," Tali said one night on the ship. "Paladins of the Saighdiúir guild have always been the most inspirational of us all."

It was a severe underestimation of her own persuasive abilities. After all, she managed to get Kent off Narood, a task that should have been impossible. "If you say so," he had said, walking to the window and looking out to the stars. Being so deep into space again was unnerving. He had not realized how long he'd isolated himself on Narood until experiencing a rough reacquaintance with space travel.

"Don't pretend to be cynical, Kent." Tali had added. "There has to be some optimism in you, or else you never would've come along."

"It wasn't optimism," Kent stated. "I just had nothing else to do."

Tali laughed lightly. "Is that so? Well, whatever it was, channel it when you find her. I lost track of her years ago, so only the Immortals know what state she's in."

Kent's mind journeyed deeper into cynical conclusions. "When you landed on Narood, did you truly think I'd be on board with your plan?"

"Honestly? No, I thought you would tell me to screw off. But you surprised me, and I'm a little more hopeful because of it."

"Have you seen a human girl?" Kent asked for the thousandth time. "About sixteen years old with golden hair." By the end of the day, these phrases had come as naturally to him as breathing. He asked shop owners, construction workers, clerks, traders, thieves, and even a few of the homeless loiterers around street corners. All of them were equally useless, more concerned with how much he was offering for their secrets rather than if they had the answers he needed. Kent was not a mind reader, but it did not take a genius to tell when someone was lying to make a quick profit.

This agonizing process repeated for the next several days.

Kent had spent those days wandering the streets like a lost animal, desperately talking to useless strangers. Those nights he was out cold in the closest motel room. Sara typically slept on the bed while Kent settled for a couch if it was not infested with insects, mold, and rot. He tried hard not to think that if Matiyala went with him over Sara, he would have a nice bed to sleep in and someone warm to hold on to every night. But sleep would not improve his attitude. Consistent defeat put them both on edge, and they started going days without sharing a word. In addition to their hopelessness, Kent could not help but notice they were running out of credits.

He counted himself fortunate, regardless of how mind-numbing the adventure had turned. Out on the streets and sidewalks were the longest stretches of homeless communities the Paladin had ever seen. The poverty was hidden during the day, but at night the outside world became an entirely new entity, and it got worse as they descended deeper into Prisilla.

The dream of a restored and glorious Paladin Order kept Kent going. Finding the girl would be the biggest obstacle, Tali assured him. The Archmage's son was in the reach of one of her allies, but the girl was completely lost to her. Tali was deceptive on how close of an eye she kept on the daughter. After some questioning, it was revealed that she had not heard about the girl in years, but her whole life after the fall of Spyre had been lived on Prisilla. And if she was not on Prisilla, then she was lost to the void forever.

Had Kent known what kind of aimless search he would be sent on ahead of time, he doubted he would have left his shack on Narood. Of the crew on the Seshora Araman, only Kent was told of the son's whereabouts, and he planned on withholding that information for as long as possible in hope that finding the daughter would spark enough courage in them to willingly travel to a territory far more dangerous than Prisilla.

But these were worries for another time. If Kent started considering the suicide mission of rescuing the son, he'd have even more reason to give up on Prisilla. Finding the girl was his priority for now, although the cost of completing it would likely be his sanity.

Prisilla was lacking in many ways, but security was in an excessive abundance. Pearls ruled the rooftops in their heavy, flamboyant armor, looking down upon the masses as killer birds do over their prey. Police barges hovered over the streets like moons made of steel. *They're watching us. The war has been over for fifteen years and still the sight of Immortech makes them anxious.*

Kent tried to scout humans from the crowd while Sara used her nose to find a scent. There was a human male he ran into earlier in the day. He was a shop owner, specializing in the building, repairing, and selling of drones. When Kent asked about the girl, the human said he had not the slightest idea who she was. He suggested Kent buy a drone to aid him in his search, to which he respectfully declined. The drone was expensive, but it would have been better credits spent than all the bribes he generously gave out before. Had he run into the drone seller earlier, his offer may have convinced him.

Wandering the streets yet again, his thoughts turned to Brutus for the first time in days. In one way, Brutus finding the girl would have been splendid news, but the fears lingered in the back of his mind that the mercenary would betray them and sell her to a higher bidder. Brutus held no reverence for the Order, so why wouldn't he sellout?

*If Tali trusts him, then I trust him too.*

Before he knew it, the world had turned dark, and he was walking from pool to pool of streetlights. Natural light could only reach the top few levels of Prisilla, so day and night cycles had to be simulated in the other hundreds. It was like any other planet, except without a sun, a moon, or any refreshing air.

The coolness of the night was a welcoming embrace on Kent's skin. Another day of absolute failure had taken a major toll on him, but it was not half as bad as what it did to Sara, who may as well have been walking corpse.

Kent could not resist feeling pitiful for the wolf-girl. Although he did most of the mingling, Sara guided him through level after level under the impression she found a human scent, but every scent ended with the wrong human.

"How about a drink?" Kent offered. "Then we'll buy a room for tonight with whatever credits we have left."

For once, Sara agreed. She nodded wearily, her eyes large, empty black pools, considerably tamer than days before. Her mane had tousled and fringed from the day's affairs, making her look abandoned. Prisilla, whether purposefully or not, had domesticated the wolf-girl.

As the shops closed down, the clubs came alive with booming music and fluorescent lights to attract people inside. The streets had emptied out, finally allowing Kent and Sara the space to stand more than a foot apart. After cutting through some black alleys, Sara suggested they try their luck at the quietest bar they had come across.

"The Wasted Wallack" was its name, presumably owned by a Wallack who enjoyed the party lifestyle.

The club was shaped like a dome from the inside, with an upper level consisting of a bar and lounge and a lower level for dancing. Kent would not go to the lower level.

The lines separating the floor and ceiling from the curved walls were decorated with fiery red lights that gave the otherwise darkened bar a haunting gloom. It was difficult to make out faces in such a setting, for everyone's features were either half or entirely covered in flashing shadows. The music was nothing memorable, except for the bass, which was so heavy and low that it forced his heart to change vibrations and match the beat. After but a few minutes, a pain sprouted between his ears.

The dance floor was overrun with an army of silhouettes shaking and shifting in an exhibition of bloodred luminosity. Their stiff movements matched the beat of the music, as if the sounds were controlling them like the strings of a marionette show.

And when the bar was finally spotted, Kent concluded that a drink was necessary.

Much to his disappointment, the bartender was not a "Wasted Wallack", but a Hallyan of the Tri-World. Like most Hallyans, the bartender was bald with a thin head shaped similar to a downward-facing triangle but with subtly rounded edges. His circular eyes, with small black pupils in pools of hazel gel, were on opposite sides of his head, and his nostrils were two small holes punctured directly between them. His chin ended the bottom point of the triangle, where a thin pink mouth scowled as Kent approached.

"What do you want?" the Hallyan asked. Kent determined it to be a male.

"Strongest thing you have." he said, "Doesn't matter the price."

That was a lie.

"And for your woman?"

"She's not my woman."

The bartender snorted. "Okay pal, and for *the* woman?"

"Water." Sara said, shy as always.

"If you insist, but water here'll likely fuck you up more than the alcohol does."

Sara growled. "Then I don't want anything."

Within moments, the bartender came back with Kent's drink. He grasped the cylinder cup holding a neon green liquid inside. He noted how long and thin the Hallyan's arms and fingers were. His species was one of the most respected and feared in the galaxy, made evident by the Triumvirate who hesitated to declare war against them despite having hundreds of planets under their domain. Their strength wasn't in their physicality, but in their minds. Hallyan engineers could design weaponry that closely rivaled Immortech.

"My thanks." Kent said, paying his credits with his fingernail scan. "It's been a long day."

The Hallyan licked his thin, pink lips and said, "That's the motto here. I can't complain though. The more brutal everyone's day is, the more business I have at night."

Kent drank to that. "You've beaten the system. Admirable if you ask me."

"Surviving is more accurate," said the bartender. "The folk on New Horizon have beaten the system. Either that, or they are the system. I can't decide, but I'll leave that conundrum up to the philosophers."

"Someone who has the time to sit around and think about nothing?" Kent joked.

The bartender, surprisingly, laughed along. "Yeah, exactly the type."

"Surviving is just as impressive, considering all the homeless on this level alone. It's more than I've seen my entire life."

"You think that's bad? Go to the Underbelly levels, they're built on poverty and crime. That's what Prisilla does, it swallows people in from across the galaxy, sucks them dry of everything they have, and shits them out into the Underbelly."

Kent considered his drink for a moment. "Would you say you've met a lot of people in your life?"

The Hallyan gave him a dubious look. "Yes, it's part of my shitty profession."

"Ever meet a human girl? Mid-teens with pale gold hair."

"Can't say I have. I'd stick with that wolf if I was you. No man knows what he has until he loses it."

Kent smirked. "No wonder why Hallyans are renowned for their intelligence. Your life advice is impeccable."

The bartender snorted and went back to cleaning a glass with an old rag. Kent looked out into the crowd. Among the group of shadowed figures mingling amidst rays of multi-colored lights, Kent saw his reflection. It was only for a moment before being swallowed by the crowd, but what he saw was unmistakable. *Druin*, he thought, and pursued his evasive reflection.

Sara tailed him as if knowing what he was after. They cut their way through the bar in pursuit of what must have been another Druin. Kent had seen one of his kind before, and he too was a Paladin. *Long since dead... or so I thought.*

He went down a dark tunnel. Gray fog rested around the floor. At the end of the passageway pulsed red and green lights that would sporadically illuminate the tunnel in time with the musical tempo. Stark against these lights were several figures. Kent, hoping his eyes would not deceive him, followed his doppelganger.

He tracked the figure to the lounge, a small area with a sleek, jet-black floor and a series of thin, circular tables scattered about. Large lava lamps were erected like columns along the sides and down the center, changing colors like a bad psychedelic trip captured in a bottle. The Druin sat at one of those tables, an open chair planted firmly beside him.

The Paladin approached, cautiously accepting the invitation. They sat in silence for a moment, listening to the wall shaking bass boom from the speakers. Smoke swirled around the ceiling, like a tornado forming over their heads.

"Find her?" the man asked. He wore a black leather jacket with a high collar that hid part of his face. Even then Kent could still tell this Druin was not the one he had imagined.

"What girl?" Kent said unconvincingly. He must have known about the mission, but how? Could he be working with Tali too? Unlikely, as she had no reason to withhold this kind of information from him. Maybe Brutus was captured and forced to talk, adding more parties at play for the Archmage's daughter. Confused, Kent had to be solid as a statue, hoping the Druin pretended to know more than he did.

"The Archmage's daughter, of course!" the other Druin said aloud.

Kent looked around to see if he caught anyone else's attention. "I'm searching for a girl, true enough, but last I heard all mages were dead." The sentence came out awkwardly like a child attempting to lie for the first time.

"I heard the same thing," the Druin said. "And yet two traders carry an Immortech sword. May I see it?"

"Of course," Kent said, peering around. They were, at the very least, not attracting the attention of the other customers. "Sara?"

The wolf-girl went to draw the blade from her belt, but the Druin stopped her. "No, no. I want to see one of my own kind hold it. Never seen too many Druins before, let alone one holding a Paladin sword."

"You'll either see it in my partner's hand, or not at all."

"I know for a fact it would look better in your hands. Such a delicacy, Immortech is. Everyone in the club would love to see it. If only they knew…"

Kent considered grabbing the blade and cutting him down. It would be the last thing he would ever do before his own demise, but it may have been worth it. Ultimately, he chose a more passive route.

"We both know what will happen if I draw that sword," Kent said with blunt honesty. *It will illuminate, and your blood will glisten in its shine.*

The Druin smiled. He looked similar to Kent: small coals for pupils surrounded by brown irises, rough reptilian skin, and fingers that ended in yellow claws. The other Druin possessed a brownish-green complexion, while Kent's was a shade lighter like tree leaves under a twilight sky. Whereas Kent had a crown of small horns around his head, the other Druin had a forearm's length horn sprouting from each of his temples.

"Should we get to the point?" the Druin proposed.

"Let's," Kent said, prepared to do whatever he could to protect Tali's mission and the lives of the Archmage's children, no matter the cost.

"Okay then," he began. "I am Bato, Justiciar of Prisilla and champion of the defenseless. I have dedicated my life to right the wrongs committed by the fat pigs on New Horizon."

*He's not a humble soul.* "Your people? Do you mean Druins?"

"No, the people of Prisilla. The ones who work day and night, the ones who live under the constant boot of a corrupted elite."

"Good for you," Kent said sarcastically. "But what does this have to do with me and my mission?"

"Everything. This girl you are trying to find is special. The common man yearns for a symbol of hope to rally behind, so a new era of righteous stability can dethrone the crushing grip of those who thrive on New Horizon. Who better than the daughter of a legendary hero? A girl who is not only a Paladin, but a product of the Underbelly herself. With her leadership, she could rally billions against their overlords."

Kent considered correcting Bato. The girl was not a Paladin, not yet at least. A mage does not simply become a Paladin by virtue of being "magical."

"I did not know the Archmage was so beloved in Prisilla," Kent said instead. He found the theatricality of the other Druin to at least be slightly amusing.

"Him and his Paladins did what they could to help us. Corruption persisted, but not at the levels it does now. Unlike the Triumvirate that has no regard for us, the Archmage did what he could to aid us in our struggle."

Kent said, "Even if we find the girl, I have for her an even greater mission. The Paladin Order must be rebuilt before we can take any more responsibilities. Your revolution would have to wait."

Bato shrugged. "I play a long-term game. Freeing Prisilla has been my life's work, I can wait a while longer. Besides, I have known Paladins to be particularly consistent at keeping their word."

"You're very generous," Kent noted. "There must be some sort of short-term game you desire."

"Being justiciar is not cheap work," Bato admitted. "I will need some sort of payment for helping you find the girl. Being justiciar also means killing pearls, the vile instrument of New Horizon. I believe this mission will require killing many of them."

"I would rather grab the girl and leave without raising an alarm, but there is a great risk of violence."

"Then you've sold me."

"But how do I know this isn't a setup?" Kent asked. He looked to Sara, who appeared equally uncertain.

"You don't!" Bato declared. "That's the beauty of it. I've been following you for days. I can name every motel you've stayed at since landing on Prisilla. Watched you dip into alleyways where I could have mugged you freely if the desire existed. Basically, if I wanted to cheat you, we wouldn't be having this conversation."

Kent sighed. Sick of day after day of futile searching, desperation gave him no other choice. "When would be the earliest we can start searching?"

Bato laughed. "Searched! I found her through a pearl radio transmission. Not that she was ever lost. Nothing on my planet passes me by."

"You have access to police radios?"

"Obviously. Most of my people do. Pearls have their special codewords, but I've developed an ear for them."

Kent was skeptical, "How do you know it's her?" The idea that finding her could be this easy was utterly too good to be true.

"Does a young human girl with golden hair fit her description? Of course it does." He stood up and drew from his jacket the largest handgun Kent had ever seen. "We must go quickly; they are hunting her as we speak. There are pearls that need killing!"

Kent was utterly shocked that no one heard his revolutionary cries. Bato got up, headed for the exit, and never looked back. Kent turned to Sara, who only shrugged. A blond human girl meant nothing really, but at least they had direction. Following Bato, he did not let his guard down until they stepped outside the club and he knew for certain that Prisilla's police weren't waiting for them.

Kent followed his new friend down a barren street in the dead of night, chuckling to himself that he had put his fate in the hands of a psychopath.

# ARIEL (11)

Failure stung like a bitch.

Ariel sunk to her knees, tenderly caressing her cheek as if she could brush the pain off like dirt. Greeting her with gloved slap was her master, Silver Wulf, whose disdainful grimace expressed complete dissatisfaction with her punishment thus far. Her eyes watered, knowing it was far from over.

"Not only are the pearls on us, but now we'll have Kagen's men on us too. Probably every gang in the Eight soon enough. He's expecting a body for the advancement he gave me, not a pair of fucking bleeding hands. Remember when I commanded you to let him go? Immortals forbid you listen. Your incompetence has killed me!" Wulf was on fire, his long, furious rant rendering him breathless.

"Master," Ariel responded, feebly. She felt her face grow hot as the spectral fingermarks seeped their way into her skin. "I don't think we would've found him again. I didn't have any option but to follow-"

Wulf belted her again with another right hand, this one to the gut. He despised how Ariel absorbed the pain, but she could not bring herself to put on a show for him. Wulf got onto one knee and put his face directly into hers. His breath smelled faintly of warm whiskey. "I could give fuck-all to whatever you think. What I know is that two of Prisilla's most ruthless groups are after us, and it's all because of you. Information on what Graznys was doing would've been just as valuable to Kagen as the man himself, but now we have neither!"

Ariel caught the words in her mouth that would have explained Graznys was out looking for a prostitute, that she had not interrupted a potential deal, but such reasoning would only reward her with another steel-plated smack. Pup hesitantly hovered around her shoulder, wanting to intervene but unable to defy the master of his master.

After the botched job, the two bounty hunters regrouped in a metro on a lower level of the Market District on the border of the Underbelly. The metro was packed with travelers, allowing them to hide in relative plain sight. Even pearls were unwilling to fire on large groups of civilians, as someone would certainly catch it on camera. Wulf had dragged her to a cranny within the gray-tiled lobby to escape the bustling crowds, roaring subway trains, and exploding ads. He needed the silence to come up with a plan, he needed the isolation to avoid drawing the eyes of an empathetic traveler who would not tolerate how he vented his frustrations.

Even in the dimness, Wulf's disappointment was quite conspicuous. The bounty was issued from a source well above his paygrade, but they both suspected it was from Rome. A chemical weapons dealer in Prisilla was as much a valued adversary as he was an ally, and without knowing who he was selling to, the number of factions with stakes in Graznys' well-being was incalculable. The risk was evident from the start, but the reward had admittedly blinded them both. Wulf saw it as a golden ticket to the New Horizon levels, a reward well overdue for his years in the underground system of Prisilla.

Silver Wulf was a top-tier bounty hunter operating in the black market of Prisilla, at least that's what he himself claimed. His name stemmed from his armor. It was a remarkable set, which he kept supremely polished and glistening despite it being even older than Ariel. Wulf himself was a portly human, growing fatter by the day, and the years of struggle had not been kind to his pale, well-worn face or his crowning hairline. His armor was the one thing that remained from a better time. What caused Wulf's fall from grace was a question Ariel would never dare to ask.

"What's the plan, Master?" Ariel inquired, adding "master" in an attempt to mitigate his anger. Silver Wulf wore a mask of cruel certainty, but he was scared, nonetheless. Although not spoken, it was understood by the two Underlings of the Underbelly that they were trapped. If they went up, Prisilla's pearls would arrest them and lock them away forever. If they went down, Kagen's men would capture them, torture them, and make their execution a public display as a warning for those not to disappoint the King of the Underbelly. If they stayed still, then it was a race to see who would catch them first.

"We can't stay here," Wulf finally said. "Best chance we have is to head up, evade pearls, and hijack a ship on the docking bay."

Ariel could not hide her skepticism.

"What?!" he barked, grinding his teeth to hide the self-doubt. "We won't be walking around in the goddamn open. You know the vents and elevator shafts. We'll sneak by them that way. Can you try not fucking that up?"

Ariel thought for a moment. She knew the vent systems by heart in the Underbelly and in most levels of the Market District. She had never reached a level as high as the docking bay before, so the ventilation systems would be completely alien to her. She almost said no, but remembered this was all her fault anyway, and the least she could do was save her master's life after endangering it.

"I can do it," she stated.

Silver Wulf nodded.

"But… uhhh. What happens when we get a ship?"

"We leave Prisilla, permanently."

Ariel's heart nearly stopped. "Leave? And do what?!"

Silver Wulf did not like being challenged. He looked ready to smack her again. "Join a merc crew. They like acquiring kids into their ranks. I could sell you and make a good profit."

Ariel's heart nearly exploded. "You can't abandon me. I've never left Prisilla in my life. I'd have no idea what to do!"

"You should've weighed those consequences before putting me in danger." Wulf responded, dispassionately. "Maybe if you prove yourself here, I'll change my mind, but don't start thinking I owe you shit. Remember, I treat you a Hell of a lot better than any bounty hunter treats his apprentice."

Ariel sighed, but nodded. "I won't let you down, Master. We'll get on a ship, I promise." *Or die trying.*

They waited in a shadowy corridor on a far-off street until it was nightfall. The wait was agonizing, having to stand in the dark for hours and praying that each passerby walked away unaware of their presence. The wait was made even worse by Silver Wulf's cold, spiteful stares. He was furious; the only thing stopping him from unleashing said fury was the undeniable fact that she was his passage out of Prisilla.

The crowds began to thin inside the metro; signifying to Ariel that it was time to make her escape.

She peeked her head out from a stairwell connected to the metro. Shop owners were closing up, pulling down metal curtains over their doors and locking them tightly. The homeless population appeared with the night. Many different races made up this poor, wretched flock, but none were refused from the trash fire shrines lit along the sidewalks. From afar, each one of them garbed in layers of rags and tatters looked like a silhouette of shapeless mass against the rising flames.

It was difficult to comprehend that they were technically in the Market District. In the abandoned dark, this level was just as eerily quiet as most levels of the Underbelly. *We're spreading,* Ariel thought. *Day by day the Market District loses ground to us. Eventually, there will be nothing to separate us from the elite pigs of New Horizon.*

The cold air of the lower levels hit hard. She had gotten used to the warmth of the Market District and foolishly did not prepare for spending the night near the Underbelly, where proper heating was considered an unnecessary expense by the rulers of New Horizon. Proper lighting was also deemed more of a luxury than a necessity for the Underlings, but Ariel learned how to use the darkness to her advantage...

The lustrous armor of the pearls would make them easy to spot, even in the dimmest light of the Underbelly. The same could not be said for Ariel; she was a child of the darkness, a demon and a slayer of the blue-blooded gods and their warrior angels. The rulers of New Horizon had deprived her people of light, a fatal tactic meant to cripple the Underlings and keep them permanently locked away in the dungeon. But her people learned to embrace the blackness forced onto them. It served to unite them in their anger against their oppressors.

Pearls were out of their element down here, no matter what high-powered death machines they possessed. *They do not know my Hell.* Here, *they are at MY mercy.*

With Kagen's gang, she was less confident. They were Underlings like her, and they could navigate the Underbelly just as well, even better with their large numbers. With no dress code, they were untraceable too, meaning she may as well have been walking down streets covered in landmines.

An elevator would be their salvation. From there, she could break into a shaft and navigate the vents she knew so well. They could move throughout the planet undetected, all the way, she prayed, to the docking bay. She and Pup were masters of moving through tight spaces, but Wulf was the uncertain variable.

As she walked with a mind full of determination, the doubts crept in. Wulf was a large man made larger by his bulky armor. If he managed to squeeze into the vents, the darkness would certainly terrify him, or the thick, pungent smells would make him violently sick, or the hives of insects who built their nests within the cracks of metal would send him into an uncontrollable panic.

Despite these uncertainties, Ariel pressed on, guided by the apparition of absolute faith she could bring Wulf to a ship, even if it killed her.

They came across a large square in the center of the level. Ariel hugged the corner of an abandoned house, analyzing the open area from a safe place. The square itself was sparse, looking like a long valley of dull alloy in desperate need of a paintjob. The center contained the remnants of a humongous water fountain, now filled with garbage and unrecognizable filth. The black outlines of a hundred rectangular buildings were stark against the gray sky. Pearl barges floated in the distance, scanning the ground with blazing white lights.

"Why are we stopping?" Wulf asked, impatiently.

"The square," she stated, as if it answered his question.

Wulf rolled his eyes, "Yes, but what about it?"

"If we cut through it, that'd shave at least an hour off our time. But I can't tell if it's worth the risk. We'll be out in the open, and I don't see any cover to hide behind."

Wulf frowned as Ariel considered her odds. Finally, he made the decision for her. "Going around will give the pearls too much time to set up a perimeter and lock us down. We'll go through the square."

Ariel nodded; her master knew best.

They treaded hastily across the open expanse of metal. Yellow streetlights sparsely lit up the plaza, revealing signs of abandonment in a once lively level-center. Shrouded figures lurked all over the concrete area, each one with the undeniable possibility of being a hunter. Ariel became overwhelmed by the suspicion that they were being pursued. She kept one shaky hand on the holster of her pistol. If anyone made a move toward her, she would not hesitate.

Pup drifted loyally by her shoulder. She accepted its allegiance was based on programming, but she loved her Pup back, programming or not. Wulf stayed well behind them, calculating that he had a higher chance of survival if she went first, giving him more time to flee with the added protection of a human shield. Ariel did not object, taking it as part of her punishment.

On one of the gray facades facing the square was a massive canvas depicting something Ariel could not see until she was very close. As they walked on, she began to notice that on the canvas was the outline of a person, a human woman with large, square glasses, full red lips, and long neon-green hair with bangs that partially hung over her left eye. She was Selina Vortex: an activist, a rock star, and a martyr.

As the image came more into view, Ariel realized it was not just one canvas, but hundreds of smaller squares each portraying a minute feature of her icon. Selina Vortex was illustrated in fluorescent paint, her figure beaming against the gray void that loomed over a forsaken sky. She was not an Underling by birth, but she had united her people like no one else through her words, actions, and, most of all, her music. Now, her presence lingered in no man's land, a permanent reminder to the pearls that they could kill the woman, but not her revolution.

Ariel wished more than anything that she could have been alive at the time of her uprising, but she missed it by twenty years. At times, she imagined herself as the next Selina Vortex.

Her heart grew stronger. She persisted through the square with greater swagger, the spirit of the rock star guiding her along. Selina would never cower in fear, nor would she.

An exit appeared on the opposite side of the square between rows of abandoned houses and shops. Ariel hurdled herself over a derelict hovercraft before safely making it to the other side. After a few quick turns, she had successfully brought her master to their deeply coveted elevator. Before approaching, she squatted down beside the remnants of a broken wall from across the street. The black ash covering the crumbled pieces suggested a recent bomb was the culprit. A *battle, no doubt, but between who?*

Ariel peered furtively across the street, then cursed her luck.

"What's the problem now?" Silver Wulf asked, crawling to her position. The amount of walking had rendered the veteran bounty hunter breathless.

"Pearls," she said. "Six of them patrolling the elevator doors." Six made their presence known, at least. Four stood by the elevator doors, while two stood as sentries on the balcony above. Their stances expressed determination, as if expecting trouble at any moment.

Wulf peered out next and cursed as well. Sneaking by would be impossible, and they were too fortified to defeat in a firefight. Ariel was silent, bereft of a solution.

"You're going to distract them," Wulf said abruptly.

"I'm what?" Ariel asked, convinced she misheard him.

"You heard me fine. Get them away from the elevator. You'll be difficult to catch, giving me more time."

"But you need me to escape." Ariel reminded him in a desperate bargain for her life.

"I'm not going to leave you! If you take them down some alleyway, I can set up an ambush. We can only beat them with the element of surprise. Agree?"

"But what if they catch me?" She had flashbacks to her childhood friends abducted by pearls. She tried her whole life to eliminate her emotions, but the closeted anger, the helpless frustration still lingered.

Wulf rolled his eyes. "They won't if you run really, really fucking fast. Let's go, before we have even more to worry about."

She nodded with great reluctance.

Farther down the street was an abandoned citadel with a rounded structure and a cone-shaped roof. The building's front side was fifty yards long and four stories high. Ariel climbed the steps to verify the door was indeed open. The windowless citadel was fortified by thick walls of steel, meaning any noise that happened inside would not escape, for better or worse.

Wulf observed the architecture and astutely concluded that the citadel was once an embassy for the Galactic Council, which made its base of operations on a massive space station known as Last Bastion. Both the Council and the station had dissolved long before Ariel was born, but Wulf claimed to have visited Last Bastion in his youth. Ariel asked him what the platinum Halo symbol on the front of the building stood for, and Wulf pompously explained that it was the symbol of the Galactic Council before yelling at her to stay focused.

The trap was set.

Wulf crouched behind a fence bordering the citadel. At his command, Pup stayed with him, leaving Ariel on her own. She walked down the street to the elevator, this time doing nothing to hide herself. She strutted with confidence, but on the inside her stomach was a queasy mess. When she got close enough to the patrolling guards to be barely in sight, she pulled her pistol from her hip and set it to *lethal*. She raised the gun high above her head, breathed in and held it in her lungs for as long as she could, and fired, the shot echoing throughout the desolate, black street. As she planned, the pearls took notice.

One of the armed men by the door raised his head to his helmet and spoke into his comm. They spotted her instantly, and Ariel turned as soon as she saw two of the guards start their pursuit.

She sprinted back down the street, not taking the time to turn back and see who was following. Slowing down could be a mortal mistake, one she refused to make. She approached the doors of the citadel and made a quick glance to the fence. Wulf was not there. He must have been in cover. *Gods please be in cover.* She wanted to look again, but it simply was not an option. The impending sounds of clanking boots told her that she had not a second more to spare.

"Stay where you are!" one of the pearls commanded. Ariel responded by doing the opposite.

The inside of the citadel was lit with yellow, flickering ceiling lights on the verge of death, but she could see enough to know the circular room was fully equipped with a myriad of hallways to escape through. On opposite sides of the room were semicircular tables meeting between a podium under the same Halo symbol outside.

Chairs, papers, and archaic technology were left scattered throughout the floor. For a moment, Ariel thought she saw the remnants of skeleton lying face down on a desk, but the heart-stopping sound of laser fire flying by her ear sent her running for her life, again.

She vaulted over one of the long tables and chose a random hallway to retreat through. She was aimless and loud, stealth could not save her, only her master could. Her heart fluttered, images of all her lost friends cycling rapidly through her mind. She took a blind turn down a connecting passageway, completely unlit and hiding who knows what kind of obstacles begging to be tripped on.

The pearls used their words, for the most part. They ordered her to stop, to surrender, to give up the chase. Their mercy would only last so long. Soon, the lasers they fired would not be warning shots. Ariel double-checked that her pistol was set to lethal for when that happened.

In the end, the pearls did not need force to capture the Underling. They had her trapped at an unforeseen dead end caused by a collapsed ceiling. She searched frantically for an escape, but there was not a sliver of space to move through.

Ariel observed her pursuers. There were two of them, just two, each with a loaded rifle locked down on her. If she reached for her pistol, it would be suicide.

"Nowhere to go," one of the pearls said. "Take off your hood and put your hands behind your head."

She hesitated; Wulf's number one rule was to never reveal herself to a pearl. Once they had her face, she would never be safe on Prisilla. "Why should I?" she asked, purposefully being uncooperative to buy her master more time. *He's coming. He has to be...*

The pearl pointed his rifle at her again, with intent. "Do it now."

This time, she obeyed.

Although their helmets kept the pearls' faces concealed, their frozen bodies revealed their astonishment. One brought his hand to his mouthpiece to speak into his comm, but after an abrupt flash of red light, the hand was vaporized.

The pearl hollered at the cauterized stump, but his vocalized agony was promptly silenced by another laser shot to the throat. The other pearl turned quickly, only to get his helmet and face shattered by a third laser blast.

*Wulf came for me!* she realized, almost surprised.

But it was not Silver Wulf. Two figures stood at the end of the hallway, one holding in his hand an absurdly large (but incredibly powerful) pistol.

Both strangers were not human. Each had rough, green skin, but the one with the pistol had long, ebony horns at each temple while the other had a crown of smaller horns around his head. Ariel was sure they were of the same species, but she was completely clueless as to what that species was.

"Ariel Zoltor," the one with the crown of horns said. He reached into his jacket and proudly displayed something so mesmerizing it must've been a ray of sun. The hallway illuminated in half a second and Ariel had to squint as her eyes adapted to the sudden, brilliant light. "You are a hard girl to track down."

# KENT (III)

Bato was his guide in their decent through Purgatory.

The public elevators would only take them so deep into the heart of the planet, but Bato swore he knew the labyrinth that was Prisilla's abandoned subway system, so they pressed on into the eternal darkness with a radio to lead them toward the Archmage's daughter. Bato assured Kent that his radio was connected to the central police station's wavelengths. The voices talked in mundane riddles, but his new acquaintance insisted the pearls were after her and the best way to find her was to follow them.

"Why are visitors blocked off from the levels beneath the Market District?" Sara asked. She moved swiftly, far away from the abundant crowds and alarming noises of the upper levels. Her eyes were also better adapted for the darkness. For the first time since Kent met her, she almost looked happy.

"The elite of New Horizon are doing their best to cutoff what they see as an infection," Bato said as he dropped down into a hole that severed a pair of train tracks. "They think if they ignore the Underlings, we'll go away. But even an infection starting in the toe will find its way into the brain if left untreated."

Kent hardly trusted Bato, and he bluntly disliked him even more. His self-aggrandizing rants against the wealthy of Prisilla were irritating after the first, and Kent could not shake the suspicion that at any moment, he would be surrounded by thugs. Immortech was worth a fortune throughout the galaxy. If Bato was as righteous as he claimed to be, selling Kent's sword to the right bidder would give him more than enough credits to fund his war against New Horizon.

Sara did not share Kent's distaste. In fact, she urged him to trust Bato whenever he was out of earshot. As Kent dove deeper into the depths of the never-ending maze of passageways, he realized he had no other choice.

"And how did you find yourself back under the service of the Paladins?" Bato asked for the sake of creating a noise to mask the constant crunchy echo of boots meeting rocky ground.

"Tali found me," Kent said. Bato's question was wrong, he was not acting for the Paladin Order. The Order was dead, and his actions were a means to resuscitate it, vain as it may be. "I was on a refugee planet called Narood waiting to die. She saved my life."

"Is this Tali another Paladin?" Bato asked.

"Yes, well... sort of." Tali never wielded a weapon. She was a teacher of young mages. Her expertise was to find the gift within every young mage and help them control it. This was not to say she stayed exclusively in the classroom. When on the field, she was one of the best healers in the Order. "She was a well-respected member of the mage council and a trusted advisor of the Archmage. Maybe the most trusted, if my memory serves me right."

"Interesting," Bato remarked, his mind energized. "And she leads your rebellion against the Triumvirate? Does that make her the Archmage?"

"Of course not," Kent said. "One must be elected to the role by the council. It's a balance of power to prevent one family or faction from taking over the Order."

"What's the importance of the dead Archmage's children? It's not like they can inherit his position." Bato's bluntness irked Kent.

"I can't say I know for sure. Tali believes the Zoltor name still carries reverence throughout the galaxy, and with that reverence comes support. As it stands, the only way a mage can find protection in the worlds is to join the Inquisition, but that's a dark path for the worst of us to consider. The way I see it: if the Archmage couldn't save us, no one can."

Bato continued his prodding. "And what happens if the rebellion fails?"

"Then the Paladin Order is dead for good."

"I'm not receiving much optimism. Why bother with your friend's cause if it appears so futile?"

"Everyone has to die sometime," Kent said. "I might as well do it fighting against the Triumvirate."

"Aye," Bato agreed. "And these children will die with you."

Kent rehearsed meeting the girl a million times in his head, each attempt sounding dumber and more absurd than the last. Based on Tali's information, the girl had lived her whole life on Prisilla never knowing her real identity. Kent was a Paladin; he'd witnessed the magnificent breadth of the Order firsthand. And even with that knowledge, the notion of a new Order was pure fantasy. He imagined the girl laughing in his face when he told her that she was the daughter of perhaps the most powerful Paladin to ever take the mantle of Archmage. *Hell, if an old drunk told me the same thing, I'd do him the courtesy of ending his misery.*

"I present to you: The Underbelly." Bato announced as they emerged from the final abandoned tunnelway. The nearest street corner was thinly populated and mostly gray. The air was cooler too, almost chilling. The inherent darkness veiled the years of rust that marked the skyscrapers erected around them. Kent felt a chill run down his spine, but whether it was from the frigid, lifeless air or the hauntingly dead atmosphere of a wide expanse of abandoned, urban ground, he could not determine.

"Is this the right level?" Kent asked, looking over his shoulder after every step. The anxiousness was peculiar. Having not experienced real fear since the Blood Moon, he questioned why his body trembled down here.

"Police transmissions seem to indicate that this level has the highest number of police blockades in the area. It won't do them much good. Anyone who knows the ins and outs of the Underbelly could avoid a thousand pearls without raising a single suspicion," Bato declared as two police barges scaled over a horizon of broken roofs.

Kent looked up, naturally expecting to see the sky but instead finding thousands of blocky structures facing back at him, reaching out with massive, cold fingers. It was like gazing at another city sprouting from the heavens, or rather an impossibly long concrete labyrinth. No longer able to tell up from down, Kent felt sick.

There was an elevator further down the street guarded by a small group of pearls like a pack of wolves around a fresh carcass. They stopped anyone who came into their circumference, demanding to see their faces. When a long-necked Drakonid tried to avoid the pearls as he walked by, his face met the butt-end of a rifle.

"Pearls are aggressive down here," Kent noted.

Bato agreed. "No one's down here to keep an eye on them. Stories escape to the Market levels from time to time, but no one takes the word of an Underling seriously. They'd rather remain ignorant." He scoffed as the pearls continued the beat the helpless Drakonid as he sprawled across the pavement. "Don't forget about us while you're fighting a war with the Triumvirate."

There was a silence between the two Druins, broken by Sara's sniffing as she tried to pick up a human scent.

A shot fired into the air. A red beam of light skyrocketed into the gray night as its blast echoed throughout the entire level. A long wall obstructed Kent's vision of the culprit. The pearls by the elevator stopped their beating of the lone Drakonid to investigate. Within seconds, two of the guards broke rank to chase the fiery comet.

Without a word to his companions, Kent sprinted after them. It did not take long for Bato to catch up and take lead, guiding them into a roofless, derelict factory on the bordering sidewalk. The factory was long and spacious, meaning they could run as fast as they could without the risk of being spotted. Sara leaped from a lower balcony to a conveyor belt and ran the flat, unperturbed surface until its very end before jumping back down to the ground, using her hands and feet to navigate the rusted factory like it was a jungle. Bato was right behind her, forcing Kent to play catch-up.

The factory eventually ended, and they found themselves back outside. Kent was sweating, the cold air making his body shiver. However, his heart was hot, his mind more vibrant than it had ever been. An indescribable, untraceable sense screamed to him that a mage was nearby.

Bato spotted the pearls before anyone else. They entered a wide, dome-shaped building, one of them firing a shot as they kicked down the entrance door. Kent's first thought was of the Archmage's daughter, and how he did not come this far to have her die in some small skirmish.

Kent recognized the platinum Halo on top the threshold of the building as he sprinted up the steps. Past the atrium, the main room of the Galactic Council embassy was spacious, though dark and decrepit. Relying on his hearing, he took a sharp left down a hallway, kicking up blankets of dust and narrowly dodging a crumbling pillar in his pursuit.

"Why should I?" he caught the girl saying. Kent's heartbeat accelerated. *Gods, she even sounds like a Zoltor.* She stood under a dim white light, her hood casting a shadow over her face. Her back was to a pile of debris that collapsed the hallway, blocking her escape.

"Do it now," a pearl ordered, aiming down the sights of his rifle.

The girl hesitantly pulled her hood off, giving Kent not the slightest doubt as to who she was. Golden and silver strands of hair fell down together in perfect harmony, as if written in a poem. Her eyes were a deep orange, an unnatural color for most humans, but the Zoltors transcended their species.

"Caella," Kent whispered unconsciously. Something that could only be described as blissful nausea filled his stomach and head. What stood before him should not be real.

Tali's arrival, after all, was a blessing.

Soundwaves of two thunderous shots ricocheted off the narrow hallway walls. An invisible foot crushed his lungs. Kent believed for half a second that his brief bewilderment allowed the girl to get shot, but those fears subsided when the two pearls collapsed in fatal succession. Bato was beside him, arm extended holding his smoking, long-nosed pistol.

Kent shook his head to bring himself back down to reality. Any doubts he had about what to say to the girl had vanquished. He did not need a long-winded speech to win her over. Instead, he did the same thing that convinced him of the eminence of the Paladin Order so many years ago.

"Ariel Zoltor," he said in a commanding, confident voice. He released his Paladin sword from its scabbard to let the Immortech vaporize the darkness. "You're a hard girl to track down."

A laser zipped his way, but Kent had the reflexes to block it with his sword. The laser hissed as it was absorbed into Immortech metal. Before he could speak, another laser was fired, and he was forced to block again.

"Who the fuck are you?" she screamed, running at him with her pistol drawn. "What did you do with my master?!"

Kent was utterly stupefied. He saved her life, and this was how she showed gratitude? She continued to attack with unbridled rage, as if trying to obliterate Kent into a pile of ash. Before she could do just that, he managed to gather enough of a defense to enter her mind and calm her down. Even his worst imagined interaction with her still went better than the one currently.

"Answer me!" Ariel commanded, no less calm. At least she wasn't actively trying to kill him anymore.

Bato too prepared to fire at the girl, who was still, despite his placating spell, a slight finger squeeze away from removing Kent's head from his shoulders. She stopped dead in her tracks when Sara arrived, dragging with her a large and stubborn human male. Behind the two of them was a hovering, spherical BOT that rushed to her side.

"I found him hiding in the back courtyard." Sara said. "He says he's a bounty hunter, and that he knows the girl."

"Is this true?" Kent asked Ariel. Her BOT made a jovial whistle at the question.

Ariel gave the fat man a skeptical look. He was dressed in fierce, lurid armor that contradicted the quivering, petrified man who wore it.

"He's my master," she said. "What's it to you?"

"What do you mean by 'master?'" Kent asked cautiously. "Are you his... slave?"

"No!" she declared. "He's a bounty hunter, and I'm his apprentice."

"Most bounty hunters have one," Bato said. "Someone to take a bullet in their stead. Most apprentices don't live long enough to make their own business, or else there'd be millions of bounty hunters running around Prisilla."

"He means nothing to me," Kent said, wanting to change the conversation to more pressing matters. But first, he turned to Sara. "Did you see any more of these policemen coming?"

"No," Sara said. Kent continued to stare at her, waiting for her to get the hint. She never did.

"Serios save me!" he muttered. "Could you stand guard outside the citadel?" He felt it necessary to add: "And if you see any pearls coming, please inform us."

Sara departed. With her gone, Kent could finally tell the Archmage's daughter everything she needed to know. He paused to prepare for the potential embarrassment of his next words. "There's no simple way of saying this, so here it is. I'm a mage of the Paladin Order on an assignment to find you. I'm not sure what you know about your parents, but you are the daughter of the last Archmage, Marius Zoltor. Ariel, we need you more than you could possibly understand… to bring back the Paladin Order."

"Archmage?" she asked, expectedly unconvinced. "This is strange… and wrong. I don't know any magic."

"Not yet, and I can't blame you. Most mages can't access their gift for the first time unless under the guidance of a teacher. But there is magic inside of you, it runs thick in the veins of your family. I sensed it as soon as I met you."

"Bull. Shit." Ariel cursed. The flicker in her eyes warned that she might shoot again. "Who are you working for? Kagen? Emerald Suns?"

"If we were employed by any of those outfits, would we be speaking right now?" Bato interjected.

"This is too weird," Ariel said, rubbing her temples. She looked at the bounty hunter, then back to them. Even her movements were familiar. *Immortals, she is a Zoltor.* "You really expect me to believe any of this?"

Kent groaned lightly. Pearls could be coming at any moment, but what choice did he have but to cooperate? His safety was not worth the price of losing her. "How can I prove it to you? Keeping in mind the finite amount of time we have."

"Fine," Ariel said. "Show me your powers."

The Paladin smirked. He turned to the fat bounty hunter and took over his mind. He forced the human to pick his head up and look Ariel in the eyes.

"Is that it?" she asked.

"If you have any questions for your master, now is the time to ask."

Ariel arched an eyebrow. "I have one: were you planning on saving me from the pearls, or was I just a diversion for you to escape?"

Silver Wulf growled and cursed all of them with the foulest language imaginable. Kent made the man punch himself in the face, the steel gauntlet shattering his front teeth. Wulf howled in agony.

"You were a distraction," he admitted through a bloody mouth. "I expected more than two pearls to follow you, but you managed to fuck that up as well."

"I put my life on the line so we both could escape," she spat. "You selfish bastard!"

Wulf snarled, a vein popping from his neck. "I raised you, I kept you in my service no matter how many times you failed me. I'd be on New Horizon if not for you ruining my reputation."

Bato bashed the man on the back of the head with his sidearm, knocking him out instantaneously. "Make your decision, young one. More pearls will come to find their fallen friends, and I won't be here when they do."

"It's true, Ariel. I know you have a lot many questions, but we have to leave." Kent said, in a more endearing tone.

She glared at her unconscious master, then turned back to the Druins. "I'll go," she said with obvious reluctance. "I was leaving Prisilla anyway."

Kent smiled. "You've made the right decision. I know this is a lot to process, but everything will make sense once we leave this damned forsaken planet."

Ariel bit her lip. "It's not just the pearls who are after me. Kagen wants the both of us dead too. If you could find me, they'll find me too."

"Who's Kagen?" Kent asked, dreading the answer.

"Kagen is the deadliest crime boss in the Underbelly." Bato said as he casually looted the bodies of the fallen pearls. "His men are ruthless. Worst of all, they could be anywhere."

There was an odd sparkle in Bato's eye, something Kent felt obligated to address. "Why so optimistic about yet another obstacle?"

Bato said, "I've dealt with him before. He and his men hate the pearls as much as I do, and down here they have an empire of their own."

Ariel smiled wickedly. Kent became uneasy by her thin face and wide, devilish eyes. "That makes them confident, perhaps enough to go toe-to-toe with a pearl squadron… if given the proper motivation."

"I'm not following…" Kent started to say, but his ignorance was brief. The old Paladin realized what the two Underlings were concocting. He gripped the hilt of his Immortech sword realizing, solemnly, that soon it would be tasting blood once again.

# TROYTON (11)

Troyton could not remember the last time he had slept. Trapped on a ship for what felt like forever, the last few weeks were a hazy dream he had finally awoken from. Touching land again proved to revitalize his senses, for this was no ordinary land, this was Roman land. He required constant self-reminders to restrain his near irrepressible emotions. The last thing he would ever want was to make a fool of himself in front of the gracious and noble people of Rome.

He considered his attire. The outfit was not unfamiliar: a solid square of unrelenting metal on his head adorned with red rubies along the visor to match the heavier chest plate and shoulder armor on his person. Sharpened points stuck out from the ends of the shoulder pieces, while the chest armor was decorated with a carving of the Aquila, wings spread and talons sharp, at its center. Below his belt was a thigh-length skirt colored gold and red, finished off by thickly padded pants and cleated boots.

He felt at ease in armor, even if it was slightly more embellished than what he was used to. He did question whether he would make the noblemen and women uncomfortable wearing a soldier's garb, especially considering his towering height, but his newly appointed tailor insisted they would in awe at his near Godly appearance. Troyton laughed, having grown rather fond of the man who picked and designed his clothes. Unlike the guards who watched his every move during his stay outside the capital of Orbis, his tailor was warm and welcoming to the overwhelmed humanoid.

Givani was a small city no more than thirty miles outside Rome. The city was overflowing with visitors who sought passage into the capital of the KOH to participate in the upcoming New Year's festivities. All of the ports had been closed in Rome for the arrival of the Queen's family and the many other nobles from the continent of Mercia, leaving Givani as the closest landing zone. Not even Troyton was considered important enough for direct passage into the capital city, not that he minded. In fact, he was blessed purely to be near Rome, let alone be an honored guest.

After two days in Givani living in what was essentially house arrest, a private shuttle finally arrived. Troyton's experiences of Orbis were limited to the warm air of southern Carcia that flowed into his window and the squat, multicolored houses along the elevated road looking like they were etched from clay. He highly anticipated the opportunity to leave his room to explore the land and meet the people he was fighting for.

Troyton gazed outside the shuttle window to admire the rolling hills and short, light grass sprawling endlessly past the horizon. An abundance of vineyards thick with golden-leafed plants popped up everywhere on the open expanse. Southern Carcia was known for its exports of wine and fruit. He had tasted the fruit before and loved it, but wine was not allowed in a humanoid's diet. *Maybe just a sip while I'm here.*

The rich and warm colors of Carcia were a welcome change to the drab grays of Grayspace and the sterile, white metals in the lab on the Casca moon. Orbis must have been the most beautiful planet in the whole galaxy.

"Almost there," Lucius said, dressed in similar military apparel as Troyton.

"Still planning on speaking your mind to King Caesar? These thoughts have been brewing for twelve years, if I'm not mistaken. I expect you have a novel's worth of complaints."

"I've had a change of heart," Lucius smiled through his thick, although recently trimmed, beard. "I love the King of Humanity and all he's done for his people."

"And this has nothing to do with the honors he's bestowed upon you?"

Lucius leaned back in his chair, "Absolutely nothing."

They had been separated for the voyage home. Lucius landed on Givani around the same time, but on the opposite side of the city. This was the longest Troyton had gone without his friend, worsening the long and arduous voyage by its loneliness. He even missed the constant treasons flowing from his mouth. When the first thing Lucius said to him after arriving was that he'd kill the next Roman who tried to lock him up on a three-week flight, Troyton admittedly felt his soul warm.

The two humanoids never mentioned the Synths. All the way to Rome they filled the empty air with memories of the Casca moon or future ambitions now that they were in Caesar's favor, knowing full well what they were avoiding. Troyton had a difficult time recalling the events. The adrenaline rush at the time left him in a surreal state-of-mind, and the following weeks of confusing isolation further muddied his memory.

"Have you spoken to anyone else from Quill squad?" Lucius asked. Troyton was relieved that his memory of storming the Synth base was not a fabrication.

"I haven't seen anyone besides you since that starship picked us up. Have you?"

"No one."

"Whoever is responsible for us is going above and beyond to ensure our safety. Makes me curious," Troyton said.

Lucius furtively darted his eyes around in every direction. "Think it's Caesar?"

"I can hope, but he has a galaxy to run. What time can he spare for us?"

Lucius raised his finger. "He has one-third of a galaxy to run. It's not called a Triumvirate strictly for formality's sake."

"Whatever," Troyton Vorenus brushed the comment aside. "The amount of protection still doesn't make sense. It's not like we were the only two to make it off the base." He sighed for a moment, remembering the other three soldiers who had fallen in the process of taking the Synth stronghold. A simple mistake that could have been avoided.

"Things can go wrong," Lucius cynically noted. "Immortals only know what's out in Grayspace."

Troyton's weak laugh barely escaped his throat. He had left the base near hours after the arrival of Imperator Hirtius Tarquinius and his legion of about ten thousand elite Roman soldiers. Tarquinius was first out of the starship to greet him, sporting scintillating medals on his chest armor. They had all but exchanged formalities before Troyton was rushed onto the same starship bound for Orbis.

"Ten thousand Roman soldiers can handle anything," Troyton stated, unconvincingly.

Lucius slouched in his chair, "Whatever you say."

They came to the train station not long after. He was excited to hear the screech of the sliding doors marking the end of the uncomfortable silence that had grown between him and Lucius. A voice sounded off on the intercom overhead, but it was too muffled to make out against the chattering of thousands on the station concourse.

As soon as Troyton and Lucius were out, they were surrounded by guards. These soldiers were dressed in silver and black, their bodies covered head to toe in metallic armor, looking more machine than man. Each of the guards had a badge on their right breast of a snarling dog on a yellow field.

*The Black Dogs, Rome's police force.* Trained to master the brutal arts of stealth and close-range street combat, the Black Dogs struck fear into the hearts of any evildoer inside Rome. They knew the streets of their city better than anyone else, and Troyton only spotted them because they allowed it.

"Commander Vorenus, a pleasure to have you in Rome," a woman's voice as hard as iron said behind a black helmet, fittingly etched in the design of an exceptionally fierce dog. "We've been tasked with escorting you into the city. Unfortunately, I cannot say any more until we've reached a secure area."

"And by that, do you mean the Capitoline Hill?" Lucius chimed in.

"Again, I cannot say until we've reached a secure area."

They were taken through the security block swiftly, while thousands of others stood in lines longer than Troyton could see. They were all humans, as far as he could tell, but all exotic to him, nonetheless. Compared to others, Orbis was a medium-sized planet, but each of the three continents possessed several fully unique cultures. That wasn't including the hundreds of moon colonies which belonged under the KOH, many of whom Troyton did not know the names of.

Cars were waiting for them to the right of the station's entrance. Troyton and Lucius were forced to separate again, as neither car could fit them together. The driver cut through the heart of the city on their way to the Capitoline Hill. Hover cars were banned in Rome for fear of damaging the countless towering buildings in the city center. Canals ran deep into Rome, despite being miles out from the Elvezian ocean that surrounded the city on three sides. The Black Dog woman pointed out that roofs were intentionally slanted so rainwater could run into the deep canals and prevent severe flooding.

Rome felt like a preserved city from the past. Troyton was used to lab life on his moon, where he was surrounded by the detached, dull lifestyle of the modern age. On the Casca moon, weather was simulated, food was synthetic, conversations were mostly held through projections, and the environment never changed.

Rome, on the other hand, possessed a personal electricity. People were out and about, preparing for the New Year's festivities, walking along the streets and socializing with their neighbors. Each person dressed differently; every interaction was unique in its intention. Artists set up small shops along the sidewalks, proudly displaying their canvases and offering to immortalize bystanders as they passed by. The cityscape perfectly merged temples and monuments plucked from centuries of old with the modern skyscrapers befitting of a galactic hotspot. Every inch of Rome had a story.

The Capitoline Hill was separated from the rest of the city by a massive wall compounded by blackened steel. Troyton judged the height of the deific structure to be at least seventy-five meters tall, but it was probably higher. Its name was Pullo's Shield, in honor of the great Republican whose war ended the first dynasty of the KOH. There were hints of railway tracks sprouting from the ramparts. The Black Dog leader, who formally introduced herself as Legate Liscinia Drusilla, informed him that these unfinished railway tracks stuck high in the sky were the start of a transportation project led and funded by Caesar himself.

There was a roadblock ahead, but the patrolman let the group pass on as if they had been expected. They went through a tunnel beneath the massive steel wall, one car among a sea of hundreds slowly traversing into a giant maw. Troyton turned around to find the other car containing Lucius had disappeared. Butterflies started to flurry in his stomach, making the forward crawl excruciating. When it felt like they would be perpetually trapped in a blackhole, the driver mercifully turned on the upcoming exit and ascended the ramp back into the outside world.

The buildings on the other side of the mighty defensive wall were better spaced out, the whole area, in fact, was less claustrophobic and, unexpectedly, more verdant. Troyton guessed they were houses for the patrician and equestrian families living in the city. Some of the houses had front lawns and gardens far more vivid than anything in Grayspace. A pond on the opposite side of the houses glistened in the rays of a low hanging sun. Way off in the distance was another wall encircling an even smaller section of the Square, although it was more of a picket fence in comparison to the one they previously passed under.

"We'll take you to our barracks so you can get situated. You will spend the night with us where it's safe." Drusilla said, purely business.

"Do you know who I'm meeting with?" Troyton asked. He longed to explore the city on his own, but the chain of command needed to be upheld at all costs. *There will be time to experience the city, just not now.*

"With the king himself." Drusilla said, sounding confused under her helmet.

In an instant, Troyton's world turned upside down. He had fantasized about meeting his king countless times before, but that was where the interaction belonged, in his fantasy. "C-c-c-Caesar?" he slobbered.

"Affirmative," Drusilla replied. She took a long pause to let Troyton return to earth. "Our king's schedule is unpredictable to say the least. I would imagine you should have a private meeting with him in the next few days, and that's because your situation is of the upmost urgency to him. High ranking officers and patricians would be jealous of how much His Majesty has made you a priority."

"I should have prepared something to say." Troyton muttered to himself, his blood pressure rising.

Drusilla stared at him through her snarling dog helmet, "To that, I cannot say."

The barracks of the Black Dogs consisted of a series of tall, rectangular building cutting high into the air. The architecture was blunt, devoid of any of the subtle art design that decorated other facades in the city, and perfectly in line with the personalities of the Black Dogs he had encountered thus far. They turned into a garage and Troyton was allowed out of the vehicle. Lucius was not far behind.

"Better be a toilet here," Lucius roared as he stepped outside. "I've had to piss since we got to Rome, and I'd hate to desecrate your capital city."

The humanoids were escorted inside and brought to a small conference area. "Your rooms are being prepared," Drusilla said. "Commander Vorenus, Lord Poncius Tarquinius has requested your presence tomorrow night for dinner at his villa."

"Why doesn't he want to speak to me?" Lucius asked.

"He has requested Commander Vorenus alone. As to why, well, that's neither your business nor mine. He did tell me that he would like Commander Vorenus to update him on his brother."

Lucius shrugged and turned away to pursue the nearest bathroom. Troyton stayed in the windowless lounge area. "I hardly shared a sentence with the imperator before I was sent to Orbis." The atmosphere of the wide room was a controlled kind of hectic, with countless Black Dogs running around in varying directions, but every single one of them moving with a definitive purpose.

Drusilla, annoyed by the constant inquiring by the humanoids, said: "I'm carrying out the orders I was given. The meeting will be tomorrow evening, I shall escort you there personally."

"Thank you, Legate, I will be ready," Troyton said. "If you don't mind, I would like to retire to my room now. This day has left me quite exhausted."

Drusilla nodded. "Of course, Commander. Rest up. Caesar may call you at any moment."

The first thing Troyton did once the door of his private room shut behind him was strip off the suit of armor. Once his body could breathe, he flopped right onto the bed and closed his eyes, letting his long legs dangle over the bedposts. His head raced with memories and dreams as his mind dodged in and out of sleep. Just a month ago he was an average soldier, but now he was in Rome and about to meet his king, his hero. Troyton could thank the Synths for leading him to this moment, but it would be as much an act of treason as it was heresy.

Sleep was an impossibility at the moment, so he decided to workout instead. The exercise was light, consisting of sit-ups with his feet tucked beneath the bedframe, pullups on the threshold of the bathroom door (although even with his knees bent, he still touched the ground), and push-ups on the dull orange carpet. These were performed in rapid succession to maintain his cardio. The room wasn't conducive for a soldier over seven feet tall, but by the end he had worked up enough of a sweat to warrant a shower.

An hour later, Troyton found himself again sitting on the bed, resting his back against the gilded post, and reading a magazine previously left on the bureau.

Then, a knock on the door. He got up to answer it, expecting Drusilla or another Black Dog, but instead receiving an unexpected but familiar face.

"Commander!" the man exclaimed at first sight. Dressed in a plain tunic, he likely wasn't one of Drusilla's guards. Nervous, the man invited himself inside the room.

"Scipio?" Troyton asked, recognizing Quill squad's laconic scribe. "Where have you been? How'd you get here?"

"I was escorted here just like you," Scipio said. The scribe appeared healthier than he did on assignment in Grayspace. Troyton recalled the contrived daily reports he had typed up that were so disappointing to read.

"Have you seen anyone else from Quill?" Troyton asked. "I've been traveling with Lucius. We're supposed to meet with King Caesar any day now."

Scipio scratched the back of his head. He had a difficult time making eye contact with Troyton, although it had nothing to do with the near two-foot height difference. "Funny thing about that… I was the only one supposed to come to Rome, but it was mandated that you and Lucius come to."

"You seem disappointed." Troyton noted, a bit taken aback.

Scipio reached into his back pocket and pulled out a thin tablet. "This should do all the talking."

Troyton unlocked the screen and read the last entry date on Scipio's report. After a minute, he put the tablet down and glared at the scribe wrathfully.

"You lied!" he scolded. "Not just to our king but to the entire KOH. Do you understand the magnitude of this deception?"

"It means we have a reason to go to war with an enemy that wants the same thing. If anything, we're helping the KOH. This will allow us to take the Synths by surprise."

"You said we lost three men while assaulting the Synth fort. How could there be a battle when all the Synths inside were dead? I didn't see any mention of that in your report." Troyton remembered taking the fort and seeing the lifeless bodies scattered about the inside. The cadavers were like nothing he had seen before, looking like some twisted amalgamation of man and machine. He did not let his guard down until it was more than obvious that something got to the Synths before they did. As for the three dead Romans, they met their demise toying with Synth weaponry Troyton specifically commanded them not to screw around with.

"No one will know the difference," Scipio pleaded. "I have pictures to prove it. All I need you to do is tell Caesar the same story."

"I can't," Troyton said. "I won't lie to our king. Even if I did, the truth will come out eventually."

"How? The rest of Quill squad joined Imperator Tarquinius' legions. Hell, they've certainly found living Synths by now. What's the problem?"

"This is absolutely wrong," Troyton sighed. The mere thought of lying to Caesar's face made him ill.

"Please," Scipio pleaded. He constantly looked to the door to make sure no one was coming. "Imagine the glory! The auctoritas that comes with our achievement! You always talked of that. If you snitch, Caesar won't believe for a moment you weren't complicit, and you'll be locked up same as me."

"Immortals! You really are scum!"

"Think about it for a minute," Scipio begged, but Troyton had already given his proposition more time than it deserved.

"If you don't leave now, Caesar will have two reasons to throw me in prison."

"Fine." Scipio backed to the door. "But you're screwing yourself over. This war is inevitable. What about Gnaeus? Those bastards put the land mine there that blew him into ash. Because of you, his murder will never be revenged."

Troyton sighed heavily once he was gone. The day kept getting wilder, and he just wished for it to be over. In a way, he almost missed the simplicity of Grayspace. Minutes ago, he was thriving on his highest high, but how quickly does fortune change?

He was going to meet Caesar and knew, unquestionably, that he had to tell the truth, no matter the consequences.

# ARIEL (III)

Liberation.

Her whole life to this point had been confined to Prisilla, surviving by the skin of her teeth. There was a new life for her beyond the Underbelly and the hundreds of levels above it. Freedom was in sight; it was a finger's touch away. Ariel dreamt of adventure, of traversing uncharted territories. The galaxy was smaller, easier to grasp. Fantasies of exploring the great Colosseum of Rome, Halo and the cosmic tear into another dimension that it surrounded, and the remnants of Last Bastion were no longer fantasies, they were goals.

Ariel felt a peculiar sense of freedom. She walked with a chain around her ankle for as long as she could remember, forever restrained by Prisilla. Each person, contract, and stupid rule served as an iron link that held her back. But those links were shattered, including the fattest, most self-serving one.

Silver Wulf was left unconscious, face down on a cold tiled floor and hopefully inhaling decades worth of dust and filth. She was furious at him, not solely for his most recent betrayal, but because of the years of inhumane treatment. She embraced her long-concealed emotions like a painter with a blank canvas, free to be as brave and honest as she pleased. *Why did I restrain myself for so long? For Wulf?*

She won, she was superior to the man she once called "Master," and now he was useless and could be disposed of. She stole his pistol too, as payment for her years of servitude.

The Paladin, Kent, was a different matter. He would be the one to take her off the planet, to guide her into her new life, to teach her *magic*. In truth, she feigned most of her knowledge of the Paladins and of Marius Zoltor, her supposed father. The little she heard about the Order was through mercs, bounty hunters, and other criminals. Their opinions were universally negative, most claiming the mages to be "self-righteous pricks."

She came close to killing Kent Kentoshi, believing him to be one of Kagen's men with the intention to do the same to her. The glowing sword engraved with enchanting glyphs was her first clue that he wasn't some common thug, but hesitation in the Underbelly meant certain death. She nearly ripped up her own ticket out of Prisilla by blowing the mage's head off, thank fate she missed.

Kent gazed at her with his dark eyes as they waited in an abandoned shack for Bato to return. She learned they were both Druins, a species of people she'd never seen before. Based on the awkward hostility shared between them, she guessed they were more likely strangers than friends. Sara, the wolfwoman, was with her too, and Pup, but Pup was always there.

Bato was scouting the surrounding area, scanning for groups of natives who likely belonged under Kagen's payroll. She was told to be quiet, but questions nearly overflowed from her lips. She did not particularly like Kent, but he was useful in that he may have known more about her past than she did. *Remember to be skeptical. He could be deceiving you. Stick with him for now, but when he's no longer needed, ditch him.*

Kent returned from the lone window of the abandoned shack, his right leg anxiously shaking. "There's a painting of a woman on one of those buildings. She's a human with green hair. Do you know her?"

Bemusement crossed Ariel's face. "That's Selina Vortex? How don't you know her?"

"Is she a friend of yours?"

"She's my hero," Ariel stated, obligated to lecture the mage for his ignorance. "Selina was a pearl once, but on her first job in the Underbelly she saw how terribly the pearls treated our kind, so she rejected them and worked to make the rest of the planet aware of our suffering. The oppressors of New Horizon tried to silence her, but she was a rock star, and she used her music to spread her demands for justice. She united the Underlings like no one before, and she nearly overthrew New Horizon."

Kent seemed to not share her passion. "Sounds like an impressive girl. Have you met her?"

She froze. "Well, no. She died before I was born, betrayed by a pearl informant desperate to escape a life sentence."

The creak of an opening door was startling after the moment of pure silence that assumed as Ariel and Kent tried to figure each other out. He went for his sword, she for her pistols, and Sara revealed her razor-sharp claws.

"It's me," Bato said. He squatted beside them. "Pearls got a pretty good lockdown on the street. We won't be strutting out of Prisilla any time soon."

"Must've found their guys," Kent said.

"Won't be long till they've searched every building in the level," Bato figured. "Also saw a tank a few blocks over."

"What about this Kagen's gang?" Kent asked.

"There are a few members, five or six maybe, moving along an open square, far too regimented to be a coincidence. They're also wearing some unusually long jackets."

"I wonder what's in those jackets..." Kent asked flippantly.

Ariel assumed it was the same square she crossed a few hours back. She must've just beat the gangsters to the spot, or else she'd surely have been captured.

"Now we lead the pearls over to the square and let the two sides kill each other. That's the agreed upon distraction." Kent said, his disgust for the plan was palpable.

"It won't be that easy," Bato said. "Kagen's influence is strong here, but his outfit won't start a firefight with pearls just to flex it." He considered Ariel. "Perhaps if they had something worth fighting for..."

"No!" Kent barked. "She's the reason why we're here. I won't have her put in such explicit danger."

"It's okay," Ariel inserted, "I've made it this far, I don't need babying now."

"Of course, because you were perfectly fine when we found you." Kent retorted, dismissively. "You're too important to be thrown into the middle of a firefight."

Bato laughed. "In that case, we might as well hand ourselves over to one side or the other. It would save them hours of searching. There's no way off Prisilla without a distraction, and we won't have a distraction without her. You pick, Paladin."

"It'll work, Kentoshi." Ariel said. She remembered Graznys and how he was torn apart at the wrists, leaving nothing more than a pair of bloody hands locked between her shackles. "They're not just after me, they're after my bounty too. I don't know why, but he's a high value target to both Kagen and the pearls. If you show me to his outfit, you can convince them that you have my bounty too. That'll be worth fighting for, trust me."

Kent sat in silence for a long while, grinding his teeth. "Fine," he conceded. "But I'm by your side the whole time."

"You want to keep her safe?" Bato asked. He handed Kent the assault rifle of a freshly killed pearl. "You'll need this."

Ariel took out her inhalator and puffed some Blast-off. She'd need it for the fight ahead, so she could be braver, stronger, overall better. Her action caught Kent's eye. He wasn't sure what to make of it, but his anxiety stripped his attention away from her instantaneously.

Police barges covered the skies like a flock of giant metallic birds, the aggressive rumbling of their engines tearing a hole into the quiet night. Sporadic window lights popped up in mostly dead building, like earthly constellations. The air was cold and lifeless, as it always was, but nothing could kill the fire inside her soul.

Ariel's bound wrists bumped against her thighs as she walked across the formidable open square. Kent Kentoshi firmly grasped her forearm, guiding her as if she were infirm. He looked the part of a bounty hunter, hooded and dressed in a long coat, concealing his weapons and identity alike. He even smelled like a brewery. Nice touch, but Ariel guessed it was an unintentional detail.

Ariel dressed herself as much like Canary as possible. She wore her white, leather jacket and hood, nylon running pants, and high boots with spiked cleats. She was hardly a famous bounty hunter, but she guessed Kagen's men and the pearls were using security footage of her encounter with Graznys as the means of identifying her. Of course, the irrefutable evidence laid under the hood.

Kent touched his ear and whispered something into his comm, tucked inconspicuously into his sleeve. "Bato's in position," he told Ariel.

She nodded. Bato was several blocks away along with that wolfwoman who hardly spoke. Bato was setting up bombs along the pearls path to the main square to create an illusion of a hostile attack. The more bombs, the more pearls get sent. Kent's task was simpler, though vaguer: hold Kagen's men in the square for as long as possible and give them a reason to hold their ground.

They approached five figures loitering in a corner like rats in the shadows. Ariel spotted them as agents for Kagen, but she wasn't certain until they swarmed, as if on silent command, by her approach. A few meters away was the same derelict water fountain she had spotted hours ago. All around the square were other Underlings loitering about. Ariel suspected some, in one way or another, were also agents of Kagen in disguise.

"What's dis we have," the largest of the gangsters said. He stood seven feet tall, with blue skin and three eyes. His lips and mouth were bloated like that of a hippopotamus. He raised his hand and revealed four brick-sized fingers, signaling Kent to halt. *Jurishan*, she thought, *from Denvari space*. Ariel took pride in her wide knowledge of races across the galaxy, that was until she met Kent, Bato, and Sara.

"I need to speak to your employer," Kent said, stiff as a stone. "I have what he's looking for." Ariel's eyes rolled to the sky. The Paladin sounded nothing like a bounty hunter, let alone a bounty hunter on Prisilla.

"My employer?" The blue beast laughed, spitting red slime from his round mouth. "That's a fancy way 'o puttin' it."

"Make'm talk s'more," another one of the men said. It had green skin and a bald head, with a long, wriggly beard of tentacles. *Kalmar*. He wore a sleeveless, coal-black tank top, emphasizing his malnourished body and twiggy arms.

"Just kill'em. Hear pearls er workin' undercover dese days. Why risk it?" said another voice so raspy Ariel couldn't believe it came from a human woman. She was bald too and well-advanced in years. Her face was painted in tattoos, and she favored an excessive amount of violet eyeliner.

"You wouldn't want to do that," Kent promised. "Because I made your night easier."

"'ow so?" the Jurishan asked, his voice inconceivably deep. Some of the Underlings in the perimeter stopped moving to listen in. *Definitely part of Kagen's gang.* She hoped Kent caught on too.

"I know you belong to Kagen. I know you're searching for a bounty hunter named Silver Wulf and his apprentice." Kent said with increased confidence and flow. "But I can't quite remember why either of them is important to you."

The blue beast smiled through his underbite. "Thas Canary, ain't it? She took money from Kagen for a botched bounty, but never turned 'em in. Heard 'er master spent t'all on booze 'n bitches."

The Jurishan laughed thunderously at his own joke.

"Sounds like he's getting the pleasure of the crime, and she's getting the pain of the punishment," Kent observed.

The Jurishan shrugged. "Don't matter 'o me. You didn' see deh bounty, did you?"

"In fact, I did. He's in a separate spot, I just needed to know you were the right businessman before I showed up with all my assets."

The Jurishan's face turned lustful. He opened his massive hands before them. "Dis is great news. Da shoo'in star of my destiny righ' befo'e me. You gonna be makin us both celebrities in da Underbelly." He sneered at Ariel. "Da girl was worth it alone. Kagen's got his eyes on 'er. Coulda fooled me. She ain' nuthin special."

An explosion sounded off on the opposite side of the square. The noise was distant but profound.

"Hear that?!" the raspy woman squealed. The fourth member of the gang, a Wallack no taller than three feet, pulled an ill-fitting shotgun from behind his back that had to weigh as much as he did. "Yep," he said. "No need to yell 'bout it." The Wallack possessed a thin neck and a small, squished in face ending in a beak. His wiry white hair was shaggy and unkempt and completely covered his eyes.

A second explosion went off, this time much closer to the open square. Kent reacted quickly, pulling down Ariel's hood. "Remember your prize," he tempted the Jurishan.

The blue beast admired the top of Ariel's head before speaking. "I'll nevah let dat happen."

"Good," Kent said. "How do I get my credits?" He stuck out his finger with the credit-chip installation.

Ariel nearly kicked him. *Cash, moron. Bounty hunters deal in CASH.*

"Credits?" the blue beast groaned. A third explosion sounded, practically on top of the square. Ariel was shocked she didn't see it. The skinny Kalmar and human woman were growing anxious. The Wallack cocked his shotgun. The fifth member of the outfit trailed behind, waiting like the runt of the litter content with the scraps of what was left behind.

"Yes. My credits." Kent insisted in his same arrogant tone. Despite his growing confidence, his utter stupidity shattered any illusion of professionalism.

"Righ'... just 'ow much is she worth?" the Jurishan asked. He gestured to the Wallack and Kalmar to investigate the impending sounds

"Uuhhh..." Kent froze. Ariel tried to reach for her pistols, but came to the morbid reminder that her hands were bound and her weapons were on Kent's belt. She still had Pup, but he would only be in use once guns were drawn.

The Wallack climbed the old water fountain in the center of the square with impeccable speed and agility. He perched his stubby legs on the top of the fountain and looked out across the metallic expanse. The Kalmar drew is old fashioned, six-shot repeater and positioned himself at the base of the fountain by the pool.

"Jas." the Jurishan said.

"What?" said the bald woman.

"Point yah gun at deh 'bounty hunteh.'"

"Why me?" she objected.

"'cuz I'll kill you if you don't."

The barrel of her handgun centered right between the eyes of Kent Kentoshi. The woman looked reluctant, but not so reluctant that she would not pull the trigger if provoked. The fifth member of the outfit continued to stalk around in the back. Its body was thin and its movements robotic. Ariel wondered what in the Hell it could be.

"Whaddya see, Fince?" the blue beast called toward the Wallack. He, however, did not respond.

"Fince?"

The Wallack turned to face them, his eyes bulging out of their small sockets. He started to yell "PEARL-"

A sharp whistle pierced through air and eardrum alike, followed by an earthshattering explosion rendering the decrepit water fountain to dust. The Wallack and Kalmar were engulfed into the tornado of stone, metal, and fire. The rising tornado roared, spitting out hundreds of pieces of shrapnel as it encompassed the entire square. Ariel would have caught a piece of shrapnel herself, if she had not been knocked off her feet first by a mighty gust of wind.

The dust and smoke eventually settled and cleared, bringing into sight a bright, shiny, and impeccably lethal tank as it thunderously rolled into the square. Twenty pearls followed, showering everything in sight with fire-hot lasers. Those who ran away fell dead on their faces, while those who stood their ground fell dead on their backs.

The Jurishan pulled out his comm and made an order to stand and fight. Wherever the rest of Kagen's gang stood, Ariel could not tell, until more shots fired from behind her, resonating from the towering skyscrapers she previously believed were abandoned. A battle assumed instantaneously between the conspicuous pearls and the inconspicuous Underlings. Although the number shocked her, more of Kagen's gang likely patrolled nearby, and would soon be called by the sounds of warfare.

"Shoot 'im!" the Jurishan commanded to the human woman named Jas. She aimed to do so, until her chin was yanked back, and a red line was drawn across her throat by an ebony-colored claw.

Sara threw the dead woman to the side and howled. She focused her fury on the Jurishan, who responded with all the punching and kicking he could to keep her at bay.

Kent unlocked Ariel's cuffs and she immediately grabbed her pistols from his belt. She admired them for a moment, then turned to the distracted Jurishan. He was gaining control over Sara with the help of his overwhelming girth. Ariel shot him twice in both legs, forcing him to collapse to his knees.

He had enough time to see his killer before another laser blasted through his thick skull and sent his brain matter splattering in all directions.

Sara nodded, whispering: "Thanks."

The battle became lopsided in moments.

The pearls, led by the combat tank, had already taken half the square by the time Ariel could redirect her attention to them. Resistance dwindled, and she questioned whether her actions were for nothing.

A barge hovered around the buildings, deploying additional police forces onto the firefight. As their numbers grew on the ground, so did the perimeter they occupied. The support turned into a detriment when a rocket from one the surrounding buildings zipped through the sky and utterly destroyed the barge's engine. The flying hunk of metal nosedived on the spot, crashing and incinerating several pearls on the ground.

More shots fired off from the abandoned buildings, red, yellow, and blue blips of death alike. Both sides fought viciously, baring decades of contempt in one firefight alone. Suddenly, the pearls were the ones falling back, and they would have been in an all-out retreat if not for their tank.

"To the elevator!" Kent yelled, dodging debris and fire as he pulled Ariel out of no man's land. She had been so captivated by the spectacle of brutality that she was actually thankful for Kent's concern. She and her allies got down on their stomachs and crawled under the slaughter spiraling around them.

"What about Bato?" Sara asked as they retreated from the wide-open square and navigated through an old merchandise shop for cover. The foundation of the building had rusted, and the roof gave way to what had once been an office space above. One missile from the tank and the whole thing would collapse, Ariel determined.

"We'll meet him at the elevator," Kent said. "Best leave before the battle spreads. Bato knows the plan!"

They emerged on another block a good distance away from the square. The sounds of warfare were distant but foreboding. More pearls, aligned in rows of six, were marching ignorantly into their impending doom. Their futile efforts made her smile. Kagen's gangsters were likely using the subways and underground vents to flank them. It wouldn't be long until they had the pearls surrounded, all the while not raising a single suspicion.

Adrenaline pumped through her bloodstream. *Silver Wulf couldn't pull off a scheme like that. I was always better off without him.*

"We did it!" she belted, letting out a joyous laugh.

Kent nodded sullenly, "We did."

Bato was at the unguarded elevator when they arrived. "Isn't it glorious?" he asked. Even from far away, Ariel could still see explosions from the battle peek over the hundreds of roof tops. This would be her last look at the Underbelly, a world she was brought into as just another pawn, but a world she left in chaos by her own bidding.

Silver Wulf tried to control her, Kagen tried to kill her, and the pearls tried to lock her away, but she took control of life and made her antagonists suffer the consequences of restricting her. It had taken sixteen years to realize it, but now her world was expanding, and yet she held it more in her grasp than ever before. She skipped to the elevator door and never looked back.

While they ascended to the docking bay, Ariel posed the question: "What now?" to Kent Kentoshi.

"Now we find your twin brother," he said, flatly.

She broke out in laughter, hunching over and breathless. Kent tried to hold it in, but he too joined her in the absurd merriment.

She felt a sense of weightlessness as the elevator went up, rising to freedom, rising to opportunity, rising to the stars.

# Marion (11)

Marion peeked his head out of the iron-vaulted door and searched furtively to the left and right. It was 8:30 in the morning, meaning the dormitory should be completely empty, as classes began at 8. He was currently missing statistics class, an utter shame.

Octavia crossed the flap over her student uniform to her right shoulder and buttoned it down to her waist. She smoothed the creases with her hands and met Marion's eyes. "All clear?" she asked.

"All clear," Marion confirmed. "Won't it seem suspicious if we show up at the same time?"

Octavia went to the bathroom mirror to fix her shoulder-length, auburn hair. "Different classes on different floors. I doubt it."

"You should go," Marion suggested. "I'll take a lap around the gym, just in case."

Octavia snickered. "If there's anyone who needs to spend more time in class, it's you."

"Hey!" Marion said with theatrical sternness. "I'm only in danger of failing two courses this semester. I keep this up and I'll be top of the class."

She laughed at the absurdity of his proclamation. She grabbed her bag by the bedside and went for the door. "I'm sure Cornelius is shaking in his boots." Pausing, she sighed. "Anyway…"

Octavia hugged him and kissed him on the cheek before leaving. Marion held onto her for an extra moment longer. Her warmth was absent, her heart drumming to an unfamiliar beat.

"Promise me you'll stay out of trouble," she begged.

"I promise."

"If not for yourself, then for me."

"Do you want to know the worst part?"

"Tell me."

"I can't remember why I wanted to fight Vintrus. It just happened. I'm getting expelled and I don't know what stupid reason it was for."

She lingered by the threshold. Whether she was upset, concerned or both, Marion could not determine, but he felt overwhelmingly guilty, nonetheless.

"Whatever happens, I-"

"I'll see you later." Marion interrupted.

She forced herself to smile and left before tears could well up.

The weight of self-righteous stupidity berated his mind with barely a second of relief. Marion could not escape the path of what might have been. Had he obeyed the rules of Romulus, had he tried to assimilate with his classmates, had he listened to any of Mister Everec's wise words, how different would his life end up? If he had not pushed Headmaster Polanis beyond his breaking point, in a year he would graduate from Romulus and be on his way to a respectable career as an officer in the KOH. Best of all, he could have worked beside Octavia, but that reality was squashed by his own boot.

Polanis could call him down at any moment with the verdict of his fate. Marion wondered if he was making him wait on purpose, to make him suffer for as long as possible. It was gratuitous, and Marion did not think it was in the headmaster's character to do so, but it would send one Hell of a message to the rest of the student body who were undoubtedly anticipating his expulsion.

His first mental relief came from the daily combat session. He normally hated this period, which was always right before lunch, but today was different. He was a horrible marksman, an uncoordinated hand-to-hand wrestler, and naturally disobedient during exercise drills, but he possessed an inherent skill for whacking people with an electrically charged baton, and he exercised that skill mercilessly.

Matches were typically six-on-six and carried out like a game of capture the flag. The underground arena was narrow but long and consisted of three obvious routes to the enemy's base separated by a series of white, pyramid-shaped obstructions. They were scalable and could serve as a quick and stealthy way to make it to the enemy's fort where their flag was stationed, but anyone other than the most agile and silent of navigators would soon find themselves surrounded by the enemy team and destined for an electrical elimination.

Marion tended to take the middle route, undeterred by whoever confronted him. Although the other boys and girls feigned bravery whenever their batons sang with his in combat, their eyes always betrayed the fear of the inevitable pain awaiting them. Big or small, strong or fast, Marion conquered all who dared defy him. He had the footwork and instinct to predict his opponent's move before it could be made. He was always on the offensive, always planning the demise of the next opponent before his current one had fallen. The routes were narrow, allowing him to handedly defeat each player on the other team one at a time.

Regardless of his impeccable talent, he was always picked last. One of today's captains, Cassian, reluctantly accepted Marion onto his team when he had no other choice. His teammates knew victory was inevitable, but with the foul taint of having the match won by a non-Roman and seedling of deserters.

Their spitefulness irked Marion, as did too many other things, but it was more motivating than bothersome. This game was his opportunity to get revenge on his classmates without the risk of academic discipline. His task was to conquer the other team, whether it be by eliminating all the other players or by capturing their flag. For him, the answer was easy.

While Cassian and his teammates planned their attack, Marion paid them no attention. He had his own plan in mind, and it would be much more effective than what any of these pretend Roman officers could create.

From the boundaries, Officer Brody, a former Roman soldier turned drill instructor, sounded the bell through an intercom to announce the start of the game.

Marion sprinted to the arena. The pain Vintrus had inflicted on him a day prior vanished. His hand gripped the electrically charged baton better than ever and his legs felt strong enough to kick through the entire enemy team. Fate was out of his hands. If these were truly his final hours on the Academy of Romulus, he would make them unforgettable.

His liberated desires flatlined when he received a bolt of electricity straight into his spine.

He crashed to the ground, his body spasming like a fish out of water as both teams surrounded him. They held their batons like daggers, anxious for another excuse to shock him. Cassian was the one who stabbed him, grinning wickedly at his betrayal.

One of the other students could not resist the temptation of sending the orphan student into another uncontrollable spasm and whacked him on the leg with his charged baton. A jolt of lightning shook him all the way to his neck, forcing Marion to bite down on his tongue to prevent himself from screaming out.

"That's enough." The crowd parted for Officer Brody. He was a thin man with a protruding gut. Both of his hands were dull metal, a reward for his military career with the KOH. A pink burn scar covered the left side of his face, another medal of his service.

"That's treason on the battlefield." Marion managed to say as his whole body went numb. "Aren't you going to punish them?"

Brody smirked, his burn mark twisting like old gum. "You hold yourself in too high regard. You're not a part of this army. Besides, it's an order straight from Principal Tarius. He thinks Polanis' expulsion is too easy of a punishment. I'd have to agree."

"I haven't been expelled," Marion protested. A slight chortle mumbled from the crowd of students.

"Oh, you naïve boy. You aren't ready for the galaxy. Gods I'm curious as to what will come of you, but I'm certain it won't be good," Brody sneered. He turned his attention to the other students and said, "You've had your fun. Go back to your bases and we'll run the game again."

Marion went to get up, but Brody pinned his chest to the ground with a boot. "Not you, you're eliminated."

"But we need a sixth player." Cassian complained. "It won't be fair."

"Fair?" Brody chortled. He clenched his metallic hand and admired it with cold, black eyes. "Are you stupid enough to think war is fair?"

Cassian said nothing. Something about the Officer's bitter aura made them all turn away.

"I swore an oath to King Gaius Julius Caesar vowing to turn the lot of you into intrepid Roman soldiers, no matter how insolent you all may be." Brody leaned forward, the weight of his boot flattening Marion's lungs. "Perhaps it will be easier once this filth is gone, but I won't set my expectations high."

He frowned from the sideline while his team was trampled by the enemy. Cassian, still upset over the disadvantage, lacked the patience to keep his squad organized. He chose to go for the enemy flag alone and left his team as a distraction. The plan technically worked, but the diversion did not last nearly as long as Cassian anticipated.

Each of his teammates wandered through the maze like sheep without a shepherd, and they were subsequently hunted down and neutralized with remarkable speed and precision by the enemy. Cassian managed to grab their flag, but not without being surrounded and forced to surrender the match.

Marion laughed at their expense, and he made no objection to running laps with them as punishment for losing. The show was well worth the price of admission.

He still found the miserable failure quite humorous when he retold it to Octavia at lunch. The emotions were not reciprocated. Every word, every action, and every expression she made was delivered with such fragility that Marion became convinced she was going to reveal to him that he was dying.

Octavia was a portrait of division. Beneath the wall of feigned happiness was an interior precariously built on the expectation of doubt and loss. They talked like strangers on a first date; always nice but never genuine. Their life-long bond became a story from a closed book, their emotional history fading from their minds fast like an old memory.

*It's the uncertainty. We were fine yesterday. Fear is playing tricks on us.*

He dwelled on where she would be this time tomorrow. At lunch, surely, but with whom? She had friends and other tables to welcome her. He was the loner; he was the leash constantly tugging her away from everyone else.

"How'd it go with stats?" Octavia asked between bites of a sandwich. The dining hall was a sprawling valley of long, rectangular tables. It could fit hundreds of students at once, and yet lunch time needed to be split into several periods for every student to have a chance to eat. *We are just one military academy of hundreds, maybe thousands.* The scale of the military machine of the KOH was incalculable.

"I ended up skipping," Marion answered. "Decided to stay in the room and read one of Everec's books."

Octavia inclined her head, "Oh, what book now?"

"It's on the religious stories and traditions of the Khav, documented by some mage diplomats from the Paladin Order. It's a decent read, not one of Everec's best recommendations though. It's kind of hard to get engaged about such a… niche topic."

"Was it written before the…" she made an explosion sound with her lips and raised her hands and arms to symbolize the rising clouds of nuclear waste.

"No," Marion said. "It was back when the Khav were primitive. Well before the Hallyans got to experimenting on them."

"And did you learn anything interesting about their religion?" Octavia asked, milking the subject for all it was worth.

Marion pointed to the dome-shaped ceiling over the dining hall. The mighty Roman Gods, all muscular and deified, decorated the canvas above. In between them all was Rhomigius, the Immortal who, according to the KOH doctrines, saved humanity and all the other races from extinction during the Creation War. On the ceiling, he was the largest of the Gods, spear in hand and pointing it divinely forward in symbolism of humanity's eternal forward progress. Marion laughed under his breath. Artistic impression was, most likely, the extent of their righteousness. "All the same stuff Romulus teaches us, just switch out the names and places."

"You might want to watch your words," Octavia whispered. "Their Gods could be listening, and they won't be happy to hear you accuse them of plagiarism."

Marion smirked. "They aren't the only ones accused of it. If the Khav Gods wanted to interfere on the petty affairs of mortals, they could have saved their own worshippers from living in a wasteland."

"Maybe they tried. Maybe the Khav ignored their Gods and brought their own downfall."

Marion shook his head. "But they're Gods. If they are truly all-powerful and all-knowing, why put the Khav at risk in the first place? If their Gods existed, the Khav would be ruling the galaxy."

Octavia responded without hesitation. "You make the foolish assumption that all Gods are good. When in a competition, the greater likeliness of losing makes victory all the sweeter. The Immortals seek the pleasure of winning just as much as we do. We are made in their image, after all."

"Are you suggesting the Khav Gods made a game out of whether their species could survive?"

"Why not?" was Octavia's answer. A genuine smile crossed her face. "The game is hardly over. The Khav are still around, although not the powerhouse they once were. I did read that both Khav males and females have a remarkably high libido, so maybe a comeback is inevitable."

Marion shrugged. "I disagree. Why gamble a guaranteed victory? The most fun I have in a game is when I'm most certain I can win."

The lunch bell rang, causing hundreds of students to stand up in unison and waddle to the exit doors of the dining hall. Octavia sighed as she turned away from him. "Well Marion, you love to be the exception."

On this particular rotation of the course schedule, history class followed lunch. Marion had this course with Professor Quintus Lictinius, and the focus of the subject was on the contemporary history of the Kingdom of Humanity.

Marion was fond of the study of those who came before him. No matter what hideous sights marked his report card, his grade in history was always the best. For this accomplishment, he owed a tremendous amount of gratitude to his Dean of Students, Mister Everec.

As soon as he was of an age to develop the basic abilities of learning, Everec had him reading about the old and long since extinct Gasardi Kings, the hub of the dissolved Galactic Council known as Last Bastion, and, of course, the Creation War that set the groundworks for life as all people knew it. The latter subject was more based in myth than fact, but Marion enjoyed reading the stories with a detective's eye. As his knowledge increased, his passion intensified. If given the chance, he could have taught his classes better than the professors.

Everec warned him that history was written by the victors, and thus a victim to much subjectivity. The statement was never more apparent than in his school curriculum.

In the past week, Professor Lictinius lectured on the Bodewin rebellion and how it almost destroyed the KOH if not for a young Gaius Julius Caesar, who at the time was a no-name military officer. Lictinius was careful not to portray the Bodewins as villains, as Reynard Bodewin, Overseer of Mercia, Lord of Erron, and Admiral of the Crimson Fleet, was currently King Caesar's most powerful ally. However, Caesar's victory in the rebellion was nevertheless stated with the upmost solidarity. This lecture was all well and correct, but Marion could not help but notice his omissions of Ademar Vikander and Marius Zoltor, who also played crucial roles in the victory over Reynard Bodewin. Ademar at the time was one of Caesar's closest friends and Zoltor was the final Archmage of the Paladin Order. Both men fought bravely the day the rebellion was put down, but both men eventually ended up on the wrong side of history and were subsequently erased for their mistakes.

Marion considered bringing this issue up during the lecture. The last time he said anything related to the Paladin Order during class, he was forced to clean toilets for a week. For now, the actual truth, at least on Romulus, would remain between himself and Mister Lyndon Everec.

Despite how any other history class would draw him in to the point where minutes passed like seconds, Marion found himself fidgeting restlessly in his seat at the front of the class. No matter what, he could not distract himself from the danger that may or may not be awaiting him. His fate was being written by another man, leaving him at his most vulnerable and depraved. His classmates knew it too, enticed by the blood in the water and awaiting his devourment.

They would not strike; the show was satisfying enough for them. Headmaster Polanis had his teeth tight around Marion's neck, and he had given him little reason not to chomp down.

The intercom sounded, and the secretary called him to the headmaster's office. He stood and sensed the condemning eyes of the other students burn holes through his cadet uniform. *Will I at least get to keep the suit?* Marion wondered dejectedly as he shuffled down the endless golden halls.

# TROYTON (III)

The sun dipped below the thick steel walls around the Capitoline Hill when Troyton heard a knock on his door.

He was tired and sore, having spent the whole day turning his small quarters into a personal gym. No matter what exercise he did or in how rapid a succession, exhaustion could not mitigate the spite he held for Scipio. By the time he shamefully conceded that his mind would not escape his inevitable court-martialing, his entire body was glossy with sweat and his arms and legs pulsed thunderously in tandem with his raging heart. He still managed enough time to shower and don a simple, black and white tunic tied around the waist with a leather belt. Troyton was hesitantly clipping a red Roman eagle pin to his uniform when the knock finally came. Making a last second decision, he pierced the pin through the fabric.

Legate Liscinia Drusilla waited for him at the threshold. Her suit was more casual than the heavy, jet armor that covered every centimeter of her body the day prior. She wore a doublet of red silk with scintillating steel reinforcements around her neck, shoulders, chest, and legs. To Troyton's surprise, she was not wearing her snarling dog-shaped helmet.

"Are you ready to go, Commander Vorenus?" she asked, her voice lighter than it sounded beneath the mask, but no less commanding.

"Of course, Legate Drusilla. Will we be riding to Lord Tarquinius' residence?" Troyton asked.

"If you would like, but I assumed you'd rather walk and get to see more of the Capitoline."

Troyton considered the request. "That sounds wonderful," he said, recognizing his freedom to do such things was on borrowed time.

Legate Drusilla escorted him out of the military barracks and onto the street. The air was cool and peaceful, and the crescent moon was beginning to appear over the oceanic horizon. His nerves eased as he walked down the concrete sidewalk, side by side with the legate.

"I read in a file that you're from the Casca moon," Liscinia said as they passed rows of connected three-story houses, each with a staircase leading up to the entrance, large windows with colorful shutters, a small balcony on the third floor, and topped by a triangular roof. The white-painted facades soaked in the ominous glow of the crescent moon. This was just one residential neighborhood of hundreds in Rome.

"I lived my whole life on Casca up until recently. My first chance of freedom came when I passed my final tests and was given a legion and shipped off to Grayspace." Troyton saw moving figures prowling in the distance. *Black Dogs, no doubt.* If he was a normal human, they would have been impossible to detect.

"Must've been scary for you? Grayspace is still a mystery to most of the galaxy, and yet it was your first time away from home."

Troyton chuckled and shrugged it off. "If I had been anyone else, maybe. It was such an incredible honor to finally serve the KOH that I didn't care. If I was going to die, at least I knew I was dying for the greatest cause in the worlds. You must have similar feelings."

"I have the same loyalties as you," Drusilla assured him. "But, honest to the Immortals, I've never left Carcia in my whole life."

"Seriously?" Troyton did not mean to sound as shocked as he did. Considering her rank of legate, he assumed she earned years of military service outside the boundaries of the KOH. That's how most young soldiers gained auctoritas, by proving themselves out in the worlds and claiming new territories in the name of the Triumvirate.

"I was born in a small village ten miles north of Pullo's Shield. I came to Rome when I was twenty, joined a provincial police force soon after, then the Black Dogs. And now I'm a legate."

"Impressive," Troyton congratulated. Liscinia Drusilla was not the woman he expected her to be. Under the helmet and suit of the Black Dogs, he imagined her as a stern veteran of the Roman army, with a lined face proudly displaying her years of military prowess. What he saw now was a woman, probably in her mid-twenties, with a long face, olive skin, and deep brown eyes. She was strong, unquestionably, but the silk clothing revealed her true, slimmer form disguised by the bulky armor of her professional attire. Her hair was long and raven black, with a thin braid running down the center.

"Are your plans to eventually leave Orbis?" Troyton asked as they took a scenic route down a snaking stone path. The houses were spread farther apart, each accompanied with a lawn, trees in the backyard, and sprawling gardens planted with olive trees, grape vines, and exotic flowers he had never seen before. The houses were bigger and grander in this area too, and they were allowed copious amounts of privacy with the help of corpulent trees and bushes planted along the narrow pathways.

"I have no intention of leaving Carcia, let alone Orbis," Liscinia said before pausing. "My dream, or rather, my goal is to become a knight of the Praetorian Guard."

"You want to be a member of Caesar's private army?" Troyton asked, finally finding someone whose aspirations were even more daunting than his. Only the most venerable warriors were allowed into the ranks of the Praetorian Guard. They were the last line of defense between King Caesar and his enemies. The guard was originally founded by the first Gasardi King when he unified the KOH thousands of years ago, and the tradition was recently resurrected by Caesar when he took his crown. Legend boasted they could defeat an army twice or three times its size in close quarters. Troyton had no doubt this was true.

"I want it more than anything," Liscinia stated with absolute determination.

"Well..." Troyton began. His mind drifted toward Grayspace and the dead Synths. He thought of Scipio and imagined King Caesar's rightful fury when Troyton told him the truth. "When I talk to the king, I will be sure to put in a good word for you."

The manse of Lord Poncius Tarquinius came upon them unexpectedly, well hidden in the brush wrapped around the short wall surrounding the property. Troyton noted they had walked away from the Capitoline Hill and headed for the western bank of the city. Rome was surrounded on three sides by water, which was why the air was fresh and breezy.

Tarquinius was already waiting, standing on the steps leading up to the entrance of his manse and flanked on either side by an armed guard. Compared to his estate, Lord Tarquinius looked no larger than an ant.

"Commander Vorenus," he welcomed. "I'm privileged you could make it."

"The privilege is all mine, sir." Troyton replied, unsure of how to properly greet his host. When in doubt, he went to the proven method of saluting.

"A soldier to the bone, but those honors are for my brother." Tarquinius said, gesturing him inside. "Thank you, Legate, but I can take it from here."

Drusilla spoke up, "If it would not be too much of a bother, sir, I'd rather stay. Commander Vorenus is my responsibility, and I would prefer to be nearby."

"My house is well-fortified," Tarquinius said. "Besides, from the stories I hear of humanoids, Commander Vorenus won't need any protection."

Drusilla restated her intentions firmly, but respectfully. "Again, if it's not a bother, I would rather be present, as I am under orders to keep Commander Vorenus safe."

"It is not a bother at all," Tarquinius assured her. "You have your orders, and I certainly know where they come from."

The inside of the manse was spacious, especially when considering the heavy rugs over the maple hardwood flooring, the multitude of rich couches and chairs made of fabrics from all across Orbis, and the paintings that decorated the jade-colored walls. The proudest of the paintings hung over the living room fireplace depicting the coat-of-arms of the Tarquinius family, a fierce brown boar stampeding across a brilliant yellow background. *The sigil of an ancient warrior family,* Troyton recalled, *the sigil of a patrician house as old as Rome itself.*

He was invited into the dining hall and sat at a long marble table under a looming crystalline chandelier. The wide windows on one side of the room were slightly shrouded by magenta draperies that almost touched the floor. The manse was undoubtedly the most sumptuous home Troyton had ever seen, and it served as a testament to what the KOH had to offer for anyone with the determination to pursue it.

He imagined himself living in such a place after a long and successful career fighting under the Roman standard. He could have kids of his own to tell his war stories to and inspire the next generation of soldiers who would continue to preserve and expand the KOH. *You have to be a competent soldier to earn such a luxury,* he reminded himself, *you must maintain control of your squad and not let them commit vile treasons like Scipio.*

But it was not the time for contempt. He was a privileged guest, and he needed to start acting like one. "This is a magnificent home," Troyton complimented as he took his seat.

Tarquinius chuckled. He was a middle-aged man with receding brown hair and a clean-shaven face. His features were not as sharp as his brother's, Imperator Hirtius, but the similarities were quite obvious. "Don't compliment me, for the property is not mine. I'm renting it for the New Year's celebrations, then I'm back to Vispania and its mind-numbing bureaucracies."

Troyton cursed his idiocy. Poncius Tarquinius was the Lord of Vispania, the largest city in the continent of Carcia with the sole exception of Rome.

"Hirtius was given firearm and shock baton, and I was handed paperwork. He commands soldiers across the galaxy, and I sit in a chair and listen to complainers and preachers who lecture me on how I can do my job better. And why did this happen? Because I was born first. Vispania was mine by laws of inheritance. My brother was fortunate enough to be born without a destiny, so he created his own."

"The KOH is a massive machine, and each of its parts is just as vital as the others to keep it operating." Troyton said, sincerely.

"Don't take me as a bitter man," Tarquinius said. "All people from time-to-time dwell on what might have been."

Troyton nodded, feigning empathy with the Lord of Vispania.

"Speaking of my brother, I arranged this meeting to ask you about his well-being."

"I spoke to him briefly before I boarded the ship to Orbis, but he seemed to be in good health." He tried to recall a small interaction that at this point occurred weeks ago but felt like a different lifetime. "Last I heard, he had taken the rest of my squadron deeper into Grayspace. If it is any assurance to you, my men boast and practice absolute loyalty to their human commanders."

"My brother always looked the part of a fierce leader; someone a soldier could put his faith in when a battle turned to its most desperate. That's the hardest part, looking like you know what you're doing. Once you achieve that, your subordinates will do anything you say like it's the word of Rhomigius."

"I have no doubt, sir."

"But of course, you know that," Tarquinius continued. "You must be over seven feet tall! You might be able to convince me to fight weaponless against a Khav war-party."

His servants came into the dining room with glasses of wine and small silver platters covered with an array of finger foods. Troyton's hand lingered over it as he chose between slices of salami and other salted meats, dry cheese, and brown and green olives. A sudden hunger caused his mouth to salivate. While in the barracks of the Black Dogs, obsession over Scipio's lies caused him to forget to eat anything all day. With the rich aroma of food trapped in the dining room, the craze flooded his attention.

"My men learned to trust me." Troyton said, tempted to take a sip of wine to dull his hunger. His hands glistened with sweat as he struggled to keep the glass from slipping.

"Please, sample it." Tarquinius proposed, detecting his hesitation. "You won't find better wine anywhere else in the galaxy, or food for that matter."

Troyton puckered his lips and planted them on the rim of the glass. Slowly, he tipped it upward, so a small sample of wine could touch his tongue. The taste, disappointingly, was horribly bitter. *Immortals! Is this what alcohol tastes like? Who would ever drink more than one drop?* he asked himself, but to the lord, he smiled forcefully and complimented the vintage.

"Don't drink it if you don't like it," Tarquinius advised, not appearing to be insulted. "It is, at least, fascinating to find someone who does not enjoy Carcian wine."

"Please don't take any offense, my lord." Troyton replied, deeply embarrassed. The aftertaste was poisonous. "We were never allowed to drink wine, beer, or any alcoholic drinks on the Casca moon. It's a strict part of our training. You're actually the first person to offer it to me."

The Lord of Vispania studied Troyton like an experiment. He was clearly the first advanced humanoid Tarquinius had ever seen, but the air between them was not stinking with rancor, but curious admiration.

"Why don't we cut to the chase," Tarquinius suggested. "Tell me about the Synths."

Troyton choked. He did his best to snuff out the erupting coughs into his sleeve, but the sounds of his suffering bounced off the compacted walls of the dining hall, nonetheless. He excused himself to his host, who did not seem to mind.

"They've left you speechless!" Tarquinius jested. "I can only imagine. Until now they were fairy tales, but you've brought fantasy back into the worlds. Your story will be passed down until the end of civilization, and it's just beginning."

"Thank you, sir," Troyton croaked. *My story will be remembered all right, but not for the reasons you think.*

"No need to be humble. You've accomplished something children have fantasized about for generations, and at such a young age too. Commander Vorenus, Finder of Synths, could be Imperator Vorenus, Conqueror of Synths, by the end of your career."

"I can only hope to live up to the great humans who lived before me." The name "Imperator Vorenus" danced in his head for a moment, until he swatted it away.

Tarquinius leaned back in his chair and said, "You are on the right path towards glory, but this discovery did not benefit you alone."

Troyton took the bait. "What do you mean?"

"The Triumvirate needs this war." Tarquinius stated, impaling a slim piece of meat with his fork. "With the Fyrossians nearly beaten, the mighty alliance between the KOH, Timanzee Empire, and Denvari Union has written the final chapter in the largest war our galaxy has ever witnessed. What scares me most is what will be written in the next chapter, and who will be the ones to write it.

"The downfall of every great superpower is complacency. When the Gasardi Kings and Queens finished their foreign wars, all of humanity realized how incompetent their rulers were and had them overthrown. When the Paladins stopped sticking their noses into the affairs of the rest of the galaxy, they warred against themselves. The second time, of which, destroyed their little cult beyond repair."

Troyton was incredulous. "Are you questioning Caesar's ability to rule over the KOH? Or the Triumvirate's governing of the galaxy?"

"Certainly not," Tarquinius assured him. "But war brings the opportunity for glory and auctoritas! Names are made through battle, and humanity as a whole is united. Our leaders, when tested, perform at their best, as I'm sure Caesar can attest to. Plus, with war comes profit. Employment opportunities abound, and not just on the frontlines. From a business perspective, the KOH is the largest weapons selling company in the galaxy, so with war comes a stimulated economy."

Troyton leaned in close, never breaking eye contact with the Lord of Vispania. His collar tightened, as if a serpent was constricting around his neck. "But what if, hypothetically, the war wasn't justified. What if we went to war on an innocent race?"

Tarquinius chortled. "If there is one thing I've learned through all my years in politics: there is no such thing as innocence."

Tarquinius walked with Troyton to the front lawn of the rented manse, accompanied by his guards and Drusilla. Troyton expressed his gratitude for the lord's hospitality, and Tarquinius expressed his gratitude for Troyton's company. Leaving, he regretted the night and hated himself for lying to a patrician lord even more. *When Caesar hears the truth, it must come from my lips alone.*

That moment would come sooner than he anticipated, as Drusilla reported his meeting with the king of all humanity would be on the morrow. Troyton's face creased into a smile when he was told the news, but any appearance of happiness was purely superficial. Drusilla attempted to make conversation with him as they walked back to the barracks, but his attention was stuck somewhere else. His consciousness was placed in a small black box deep inside his mind, compacted together by unbreakable layers of guilt and anxiety. *Hmph, not much unlike a prison cell.*

Marble pillars held up the outside entrance to the Temple of Rhomigius in an ostentatious display of divine affluence. The front of the temple was approximately one hundred yards long, with giant iron doors at its center. The marble exterior was so burnished that it looked chrome as it sizzled in the midafternoon sun.

*Even the Gods will witness my judgement,* Troyton muttered to himself, marching up a small mountain of steps and through the portico. King Caesar was waiting for him, and the Black Dogs took him through the underground passageways of the city to ensure his punctuality.

He was hurried up the nave and past the altar. At his feet were multicolored mosaics depicting the epic stories of Rhomigius and the Immortals. They were beautiful and detailed, nearly as divine as the legends themselves, but utterly irrelevant. His mind was racing, his vision such a blur that he could not admire the inside of the temple. He had yearned for this moment his whole life, and yet he had never anticipated something with such extreme dread before. He would do the right thing, no matter the consequences, even if it would ruin the rest of his career and the careers of many others.

He thought of Lucius, and how his confession would be exposing his friend's complacency in treason too. It was wrong for him to agree to Scipio's scheming, but Lucius held no loyalty to a race that labeled him a 'Lab Rat.' After today, not only would his king hate him, but the one person to ever have his back would likely despise him more than he did the humans.

Friendship and imminent betrayal dispersed like flames dowsed in water when Troyton's eyes met those of King Gaius Julius Caesar.

"K-King Caesar," he barely whispered. The king was immaculate. Square-jawed, olive-skinned, and with searing brown eyes that stared into his very soul, Troyton was convinced he was in the presence of an Immortal. He had seen countless videos and pictures of Caesar before, but nothing could have prepared him for the real thing. The laurel wreath upon his brow glimmered like a halo. The man radiated an ethereal confidence and royalty. He was a patrician hero from the annals of legend turned flesh.

*This is him. Only a man like this could govern the whole galaxy.*

Thankfully, Troyton's instinctual reaction was to salute, or else he would have stood in a slack-jawed, bumbling state for an eternity. He held the position until his king told him otherwise.

Caesar approached him in the tight, windowless room deep within the bowels of the Temple of Rhomigius. Troyton coiled in the presence of such a daunting figure. He held his breath, not feeling worthy to breathe unless his king allowed him to.

"So, you're the humanoid I've heard so much about." King Gaius Caesar spoke, his voice unrelenting. "Commander Troyton Vorenus of the Casca moon, if I'm not mistaken."

"That's-that's-that's correct, my king." Troyton replied, his eyes wandering frantically. Would looking down to his king be rude? Would looking beyond him be an insult? These questions rendered Troyton Vorenus terrified.

"I have already spoken with the scribe and the other humanoid, but war stories are best told by the captain, don't you agree?" Caesar asked. He was thin and fit, with sturdy shoulders and a tight stomach. His hair was short and dark brown to match his eyes that continued to burn holes into Vorenus.

*Did Lucius turn on Scipio?* he asked himself. Caesar may have already declared Troyton a traitor, and the purpose of this conversation was to determine the severity of his punishment.

"I agree, sire." he choked. *Imbecile, tell him the truth.*

"You'll have more stories to come. With the Fyrossians subdued, the KOH will be able to focus its efforts solely on the Synths. Of course, the biggest threat Rome faces at the moment is making sure the New Year's celebration ends with the kingdom still intact."

"Under your authority, sire, it will go as smoothly as it possibly can."

Caesar smirked, the sharpness of his smile making Troyton shake. "I wish others were so convinced of my competence." He turned to his desk on the other side of the room and picked up a tablet set on a stack of files and documents. "I've seen the pictures your scribe took. It's difficult for me to believe I'm in the company of a man who has not only encountered Synths, but killed them too."

"I was following your orders," he replied, the words slipping from his mouth. Trapped simultaneously in both a dream and nightmare, Troyton's body and brain operated on spectral threads.

"Don't belittle yourself, Commander, or else you'll never make it far," Caesar warned. "You defeated an enemy thought to be extinct for thousands of years. You were put in an impossible situation, and you proved your valor."

"Your Majesty, I-"

"If I may continue," Caesar interrupted. *Stupid! Don't interrupt the king.* "This display of military proficiency will not go unrewarded, which is why I have a proposition for you."

"Anything Your Majesty orders, I am his to command," Troyton said. His conscience screamed to confess, implored that the longer he maintained the facade, the worse his punishment would be. But these righteous declarations of morality were met with deaf ears. The drab room sparkled as he shrugged off his nerves and floated to the ceiling.

"Your knowledge of the Synths is invaluable. Grayspace is the alcove where myth and superstition reign supreme, and your presence among my soldiers would help to dampen the powers of the unknown. Of course, you would be in command of a much larger legion than you've taken on before, which also means a promotion is imperative."

"Promotion?" Troyton gasped. The nightmare dissipated; the dream enveloped all things in a fantasy-like haze. The greatest man the galaxy would ever know viewed him as an asset. All the years of training were finally rewarded, but in a much grander way than he could ever have anticipated.

"As is fitting, Centurion Vorenus." Caesar declared vigorously. Troyton held himself as still as a statue, resisting every urge to get on his knees and kiss the king's feet.

Caesar continued, "As you already know, I have legions combing Grayspace as we speak. Although you should return to your duties as soon as possible, I have but one order beforehand."

"Anything," Troyton begged.

"You will be detached to the Fyrossian home-world to participate in the final invasion. I have three frigates invested in the operation already. I don't want you leading the frontlines, but this would be a good opportunity for you to get accustomed to military leadership on a larger level. I will have you serve with one of my best officers."

"Thank you, sire." Troyton said, fully accepting the training wheels Caesar had put on his bicycle, but nonetheless eager to prove why he did not need them. *Baby steps*, Troyton reminded himself. He demonstrated his value to his king once, and he was confident that he could do it again.

"You are dismissed, Centurion. I wish you best fortune in the wars ahead."

Troyton saluted and drifted out of the temple like a deity himself. He would need to make travel arrangements soon. He was no longer acting under the nebulous commands of "Rome," but by the spoken word of Gaius Julius Caesar. The Fyrossians would not stop him, nor would the dreaded Synths, as he already proved.

"Centurion Vorenus," Troyton spoke aloud.

*Legate Vorenus.*

*Imperator!*

# ELYSANDE (1)

Her hands reeked of sweat and metal; her body gleamed in the mirror beneath radiating ceiling lights. Elysande took a moment to admire herself. Wearing nothing but a sports bra and a pair of tight-fitting shorts, she had an impeccable view of the mountain range running across her shoulders, the valley of abs stretching down her abdomen, and the steel thighs she had dedicated years to expertly crafting. She was beautiful, her body comparable to the statues erected in the Forum or outside the Senate. Approaching thirty-five years of age, Elysande knew she was in the best shape of her life, if only she could show it off.

"Towel, my queen?" her personal guardsman, Ser Richard Dance, offered. In the private gym set beneath the basement of her manor, Richard was the one man allowed to see her in a state of near nakedness. And yet, he lacked the equipment to act upon his desires. *Takes all the fun out of it, really.*

The Queen of the Kingdom of Humanity grabbed the towel and wiped away the perspiration from her forehead and neck. She felt the tingling sensation inside her chest and shoulders as the old, weak flesh tore away and new, harder flesh took its place. Receiving the immediate feedback for her hard work was rewarding all to itself. She had tried to get her son to train with her, but he refused. Lance was the stubborn one. Julia was more than eager to join, but she was still too young.

"You should expect heavy activity in the streets today, my queen." Richard Dance reported, watching her towel off and feeling nothing. "Should I order a heavier retinue of security guards for your escort into Rome?"

"Are you as capable of a fighter today as you were yesterday, Ser?" she asked.

"Yes, my queen."

"Then you alone should satisfy."

Elysande had concerns far greater than her own protection. Dance had served her deftly and dutifully for a decade now. And if someone was to defeat her royal guardsman, she was always looking for a fight herself. For humans, a simple palm-pinch takedown, as made famous by the Denvari, would be enough to render a man's arm useless for the rest of his life. The defense tactic was basic, but highly effective and impossible to counter if the fighter was quick enough. Elysande trained in a variety combat techniques from across the galaxy. All it required was ambition, study, and practice.

She showered, dressed in a black tunic with crimson fringe around the collar and cuffs, and threw on her favorite pair of red boots that clapped thunderously with every step. Despite the many liberties she possessed as queen, the freedom to choose whatever she wanted to wear was not one of them, but that did not mean she was completely powerless in her options.

Unlike most other ladies who walked the Forum, Elysande felt it to be completely unnecessary to wear a suffocating dress whenever she presented herself to the public. Instead, she dressed to intimidate. Besides, the useless sacks of flesh she would be in the company of today were not worthy to see her looking her best.

She combed her stunning auburn hair so the long mane on top flowed down the right side of her head and gingerly touched her pale shoulder. It was a hairstyle in honor of her mother's people in the northern districts of Mercia. Most Romans labeled them savages, but Elysande simply thought of them as unabashedly cultured.

She left the manor with great haste, hopped into the car parked outside, and took off to the Palazzo Reale. Normally, flying cars were strictly prohibited in all sectors of Rome, but rules only applied to those without the title of "Queen." She was already risking tardiness for her meeting, therefor her means of transportation could be considered a service to the KOH.

She looked out her window to the city below. Although unmatched by the beauty of Erron, Rome was well-kept for a place of such mass. The Forum was bustling as usual, but even with thousands of pedestrians walking about, the vast open space was not obscured in the slightest. The temples were as magnificent as they were divine, and the ancient canals that snaked between city blocks and through parks were always a pleasant sight. Rome was as modernized as any other city on the planet, and yet, it cherished its history and honored it in both boastful and secretive ways. Perhaps the singular eyesore was Pullo's Shield, a putrid and impudent piece of defensive architecture constructed by an animal. Although Elysande had to admit, the massive wall did serve the practical purpose of separating expendable Romans from the nonexpendable ones. To that, she was eternally grateful.

The car took a sudden dip and, in a matter of seconds, she was at the doorstep of the Palazzo Reale. A sprawling building made of marble, concrete, and crystalline steel, the palace was especially luminescent today in the late morning sun. Along with Ser Dance, Elysande ascended the long set of steps, flanked on each side by a series of massive columns. She made her way through the atrium, where she received half-a-hundred impassioned salutes and had to return the favor with half-a-hundred laconic ones before entering the private council chamber of her king.

Gaius Julius Caesar dressed modestly. He wore no crown on his brow, nor flaunted any jewels to distinguish his wealth. He did, however, sport the familial ring of Caesar on his finger, ruby red with gold plating, the perfect symbol of his prestige and how he acquired it. His ebony-colored hair was short and his sharp face clean-shaven. He could have passed as an ordinary citizen if not for those fierce, calculating eyes and posture that commanded respect and obedience.

"My queen," he said, the emotion behind his voice was inconspicuous. "We were about to start our meeting without you."

Elysande saluted indifferently. "My apologies, husband, tardiness should be expected from time to time when one does not live in the Palazzo. Unless someone wants to waste more time, I will take my seat."

Caesar let it go. He would never obsess over a trivial matter. He was a fastidious man, but somehow managed to delegate it to the most necessary of conflicts.

Joining the King and Queen of the KOH were the chief advisors who made up the private council. First among equals was Caesar's younger brother, Tullius, Supreme Commandant of the entire KOH military and an accomplished war hero nearly on par with his brother. Although he lacked King Caesar's natural charm and dashing looks, Tullius' brutish appearance disguised a wily and calculating brain.

Beside Tullius was Sutorian, the Prefect of the king's Praetorian Guard. An aging man just shy of sixty, Sutorian possessed the confidence and strength of a man half his age, while also benefitting from the wisdom of his storied career. Wearing his golden armor with the eagle sigil of the Caesar family engraved on his breastplate, the old warrior was nothing short of a living legend.

"If I may begin today's session, I would like to compliment Sutorian publicly for his watchful eye over Rome. Even in hectic times such as these, you have kept the city under control." Elysande spoke, genuinely.

Sutorian nodded, "The acknowledgement is appreciated, my queen, but undeserved. The most challenging weeks are still to come. The New Year's celebration tends to unleash a madness within people, but this madness will be subdued as it always has been."

Elysande appreciated the old prefect's bluntness. It was a refreshing form of diction unfamiliar to most Carcians who spoke so lavishly while expressing so little.

"Oh, the Year's End," Tullius remarked. "Everyone wants to take one last dip into their vices before the new year magically changes them. And yet, each year no one changes."

"We are all perfectly understanding of how chaotic this time of the year can be," King Caesar said, shooting a glance at his brother. "Rest assured, Sutorian, you have all the resources you need to maintain the peace within Rome."

The prefect saluted. "Thank you, King Caesar."

"On the topic of the New Year's celebration," Admiral Kassa Savon spoke up. "Ships from all over the planet have been docking at Paranthon's Cross, as Your Majesty has requested. The method has worked smoothly, although security is flimsier than I would prefer. The sheer number of ships entering through the Cross will increase over the upcoming weeks, so I request adding more security checkpoints for travelers on their way into Rome."

"Granted," Caesar spoke. He respected Admiral Savon for her forethought and honesty. Having no connections with anyone from the royal family, her prestigious position was owed to her own work alone. "Any updates on Omir?"

"I have heard nothing from my friends and family in Tisoni, other than Haisam Omir's apparent intention to attend the celebration." Kassa reported.

"I hope he does not mind sharing a city with Timothy Mauvern." Tullius remarked, half in jest and half in grave seriousness.

"Allow me to speak more on that matter," Shota Nakamura, First Censor of Rome, replied. Shota was a young man with honey-colored skin and long, smooth black hair. Every word from the censor's mouth rang smoothly like a song. "Timothy Mauvern's transition as Overseer of Tisoni has been tremulous but nonviolent, so far. Lord Haisam Omir has been hosting a variety of cultural parades in his city of Malike, seemingly in protest of the new overseer's arrival."

Caesar asked, "Has Omir spoken out on Mauvern's rule? Tisonians have worshipped his family like royalty for generations. If he obeys, the rest of the country will follow."

"Omir has not made a public condemnation of Mauvern's appointment." Nakamura responded. "Behind closed doors, who knows."

Overseer was one of the most prestigious positions in the KOH. There were three active at a time, one for each continent of Orbis. Elysande's father was Overseer of Mercia, and Timothy Mauvern the newly appointed Overseer of Tisoni. Rubio Brunetti was the Overseer of Carcia, but the title was somewhat hollow when the continent Rubio had jurisdiction over was the same continent of his king. Poor Brunetti did not even have an office in Rome.

"A true politician," Elysande spoke up. "Omir is more worried about losing control of the spice trade than anything else. And he should be. Mauvern took on the responsibility of an entire foreign continent to get his hands on those spices. He best pray the riches he receives can pay off all the bounties the Tisonian nobles will surely put on his head."

Elysande had little love for Timothy Mauvern. The Mauvern family were nobles of Mercia, the continent that the Bodewins held supremacy over since the beginning of time. The two families clashed on countless occasion during the thousands of years of recorded history alone. Perhaps Timothy was the smartest of his brood, as he was the first to realize that Mercia would never be his as long as a Bodewin was there to stop him.

"Timothy Mauvern is ambitious, but he is not so shortsighted," Caesar warned. "For now, we will observe how he behaves in the role. Regarding more immediate concerns, Shota, make sure the Mauverns and Omirs are housed in opposite sides of Rome."

Shota bowed. "It will be as you command, my king."

"Admiral, your family has close ties with Omir. If you hear anything about his departure to Rome, you must tell me directly." Caesar said.

Savon nodded. She and Haisam were from the same region of Tisoni, where the sun burned the hottest and the land was an endless desert of scorched sand and death. The Tisoni people were survivalists, a merciless culture where the weakest of their kind were still leagues tougher than Mauvern and his spineless retinue.

Tullius Caesar spoke next. "A new election season in the Senate is a few months away. Expect much pandering from the wonderfully duplicitous representatives of the KOH."

"Are you considering running for election?" Elysande snuck in.

Tullius sneered. "And demote myself? My point is: most of these stick-thin patricians will enter themselves in the lists for the Gladiator Games. It's a publicity stunt, I understand, but I fear that any of the real soldiers they face-off against will choose to yield instead of fight. Millions anticipate the event every year, and it would be a colossal disappointment if half the matches showed young knights surrendering their weapons to kiss the asses of old men."

Elysande rolled her eyes, but Caesar considered the matter more assiduously. "Unfortunately, brother, it is well within their rights as noble citizens of the KOH to enter the tournament. I can see, however, that the registration lists take the long road to the Senate's hands."

"As long as Magnus is on the list, I can at least guarantee he won't yield to some entitled senator," Tullius said.

Caesar opened the floor again. After a prolonged silence, the final member of his advisors, Cira Dei Tra, made her presence known.

"The Grand Inquisitor thanks you for inviting him into Rome for the celebrations. Regretfully, he will not be able to attend, but hopes to make his way to Orbis on a later date." A frail thing covered in bulks of silver robes belted together with purple velvet bands, Cira was the oldest woman Elysande had ever laid eyes on. Despite her appearance, Cira's voice was as strong as titanium, and her gray eyes cloudy like an ominous stormfront. She represented the Inquisition on the council and, despite being surrounded by non-mages, she was never the least bit intimidated.

"Unfortunate news," Caesar stated, skeptically. "It has been years since I've seen the Grand Inquisitor, I do pray he is in good health."

"His service to the Faiths is far from complete. Until then, he is protected." Cira returned.

A *pity*, Elysande nearly said aloud. Life in Rome was stressful enough without any wretched mages running around. Cira was human, and yet she devoted herself to some ghastly Inquisitor lurking in the obsidian palaces of the Enfari home-world. Elysande had pleaded with Caesar to no end to remove the Inquisitor from their council for she served little purpose but to be an informant for her own people, but he was hellbent on fulfilling his pact with the Inquisition.

"I, on the other hand, cannot say the same," Cira continued. "Zealots roam the streets. They curse me, spit at me, and even throw rocks and garbage my way. I am bound to the Inquisition. These robes are not a choice, they are my life. I do nothing to draw attention to myself, and yet I feel targeted."

Elysande could not stifle her anger any longer. "Zealots, you say? Those are the good worshippers of Rhomigius. Perhaps their passion for our Gods is alien to you, true faith has a power to it you could not possibly understand."

"Power?" Cira scoffed. "Magic flows through my veins. It is as real as the ocean waves that lick the docks outside Rome, as the winds that berate the Senate walls and ricochet throughout every street corner. I am of nature, and nature is entwined within me. What do your zealots have? Their imagination? Their ignorance? Illusions of lesser beings."

"Mighty accusations coming from a dying breed," Elysande laughed. "I'm not a biologist, but I do know that the superior species tend to survive longer than the weaker ones. It would appear you are on the wrong side of evolution."

"Enough of this nonsense," Caesar interrupted. "We're all humans, can we agree on that?"

"I'm not so convinced," the queen retorted.

"Quiet Elysande," Caesar commanded, stern but never raising the volume of his voice. He addressed Cira directly. "My apologies for the way you have been treated in Rome. If it will make you feel any better, I can spare a few of my guards to watch over you throughout all hours of the day."

Cira was hardly content. "It will suffice, my king. Please make sure these guardsmen do not hold similar prejudices."

"Good," Caesar said as he took a survey of the room. "Before the council is dismissed, I have one more issue to bring up. This may sound absurd, but I have received evidence of hostile Synth activity in Grayspace."

Tullius titled his head. "Synths? What kind of evidence?" The room was silent, no one was really sure if their king was playing a prank.

"We have been searching Grayspace for months, and there is finally a sign of life. A humanoid and his squadron encountered what they believe to be Synths while on a scouting run, and they defeated the enemy after they were fired upon. I have spoken to the humanoid and his scribe, and they both tell the same story. Imperator Tarquinius is still out there, but news takes so long to get back to Rome that there could have been another Synth encounter and we just don't know it yet."

"This is a tremendous discovery." Sutorian said, scratching his head. "What do you need from us?"

Caesar looked around the room. Elysande questioned whether or not she was dreaming. *Synths are a myth, but now my foolish husband expects me to believe they've risen from their storybooks?*

"I can see everyone's skepticism. I assure you that I too am not fully convinced. The scribe showed me the photos, and the humanoid commander is eager to return to Grayspace and fight the Synths once again. All I am sure of is that Roman soldiers were fired upon, and that is an act of war. Synths or not, whatever is out there in Grayspace is hostile."

"You have my support, King Caesar." Sutorian said.

"And mine too," echoed Tullis and Admiral Savon.

"For the time being, I will not make any public statements on the matter, but it won't be long until rumors start to spread. When I bring this issue up to the Senate, my hope is that people will already begin to believe the Synths are real. As for now, we wait until there is more news from Imperator Tarquinius and act accordingly from there."

Caesar dismissed the council soon after. Elysande watched as each member took their leave. The feeble Cira shuffled her way down the marble floor, each step sending chills down the queen's body. *I could kill her, regardless of her powers. Whatever spells she has, they're certainly as decrepit as she is.*

Sutorian was the last to exit, closing the door on his way out and standing guard.

"Would you care to explain yourself?" Caesar asked. He removed himself from the circular table to gaze outside a small window in the back. Elysande rested her elbows on the table and watched him.

"She's a menace. She serves no beneficial role to our council. Best send her back to-"

"You came close to starting a war just then," Caesar interrupted. "And for what? I won't trivialize your history with mages, but it's no reason to act the way you did. The Grand Inquisitor is an enigma, who knows what can tip him over the edge. Why give him a reason to hate us?"

Elysande groaned. "We could obliterate the Inquisition if we so choose. Their numbers are small, they're licking their wounds as we speak. Strike at them before they can recover."

"Have you learned nothing from your own life?" He directed his eyes back to hers. "Look where I am now, look where you are. If our enemies had not underestimated us, we'd not be standing here."

A *shame*. "Your enemies were as incompetent as they were stupid. I would not make the same mistakes."

Caesar drew in a deep breath. He loosened the collar around his neck and unbuttoned the cuffs at his sleeves. He pulled out a chair and took his seat across from the queen. After all the years, all the battles, and all the strife, not a crack of it showed on Caesar's olive-skinned face. True, he did look his age of forty-five, but the man had lived several lives in one. An ordinary man would be content on his deathbed having experienced a quarter of the king's adventures thus far.

"How big of a fool did I look when discussing the Synths?" he asked, earnestly.

Elysande shrugged. "You appeared as sane as you possibly could be. I don't believe it myself, but everyone in the council sees you as a rational man. They may be unconvinced, but they have the faith you will make the right judgement in time."

"That's the best I can ask for now. If they are real, Tarquinius will find them." Caesar said, his brow furrowed as one idea in his head was replaced by another. "I've been meaning to talk to you about your father. He is just days away from Rome, traveling with a couple guests and a handful of guards. Will he be staying at the estate, or did you arrange other accommodations?"

The Queen of the KOH pursed her lips. She had not spoken to her father; she had no idea he was heading to Rome. "Other arrangements."

# KENT (IV)

"Fuck. No." Matiyala stated with unwavering certainty. Kent was prepared for her reluctance, but not to this extreme.

"Will you at least listen to me?" Kent asked, politely. Both he and Tali had planned to break the news to her when she was in the best mood possible. With the Seshora Araman back in space, this moment was as good as they were going to get. But Matiyala's high spirits made her no less willing to embark on another mission that, at first glance, maybe could have been considered a "suicide mission."

"It IS a suicide mission!" Matiyala screamed as if Kent was delirious. She stood while the rest of the crew sat at a round table likely carved from a hunk of scrap metal. The room effectively served as the ship's canteen, which was so small that Kent nearly hung himself a number of times on loose wires dangling from the ceiling. The entire ship was dank and cramped, made worse by the additional crew members picked up on Prisilla.

"It's not a suicide mission," Tali insisted. "I have a contact who has eyes on the boy. We'll be in and out before the Romans even know what happened."

Matiyala stared at them, incredulous. "We aren't just heading into Triumvirate space, we'll be grounded on Roman-occupied territory. My ship has no missiles, no defensive shields. If even one Roman star-splitter picks us up, we're dead."

"Without missiles, we won't draw any suspicion. The KOH is preparing for the New Year celebration, meaning there will be hundreds of thousands of ships in KOH space. We'll blend right in," Kent said.

"Also consider the space between us," Tali proposed. "Romulus is one of the furthest colonies from Orbis. It's practically in Fyrossian territory. My contact picked it for a reason. Trust me, we won't be anywhere near any serious KOH stations."

Even in the dull lighting of the canteen, Matiyala's green Kalmar skin was vibrant. She considered Kent with her lilac eyes, eyes that exposed her willingness to concede. "Who's the contact?"

"He's an old friend of mine." Tali said, delighted. "He's been watching the Archmage's son ever since they escaped Spyre. He works at the academy; it won't be another blind chase like it was with Ariel."

"It was a blind chase until you met me." Bato corrected, leaning back and placing his boots on the table. The other Druin had assimilated seamlessly into the crew by proving himself to be quite handy with maintenance on the ship. Bato made his bed in the boiler room, preferring a noisy room that was isolated over the tight sleeping conditions of everyone else.

Kent looked for Brutus, who preoccupied himself by watching Sara sharpen her claws from across the table. "You're oddly quiet, Cirileo. Are you having cold feet about heading back home?"

"Some colony for rich kids on a planet millions of miles away from Orbis isn't my home. As for the mission, you're right for once. Seems like the difficult child was found."

Brutus Cirileo's affairs on New Horizon were still a mystery to him, but they were on amicable terms and Kent wanted to keep it that way. "There you have it, let's set course for Romulus."

Matiyala wasn't finished yet. "I was only paid to transport one galactic hero; I'll need double for the other one."

Tali shook her head. "We both know I don't have that kind of money."

Matiyala crossed her arms. "Then it appears we are at an impasse."

"There're bound to be some Roman antiques on Romulus. I'll be sure to steal any if they cross my path. Whatever I find is yours to sell," Kent proposed. He was proud with how quickly the idea occurred to him. "Deal?"

Matiyala shoved her hands in her pockets and leaned against the wall. "Yeah, deal. But you're not getting back on my ship without bags filled of goddamn priceless KOH shit."

Ariel Zoltor was found lying on her bed, appearing as if she was independently drifting through space as she rested beside a long stretch of windowpane. On her lap was Archmage Tye Crossford's book: "Intergalactic Encounters with Unknown Entities." Tali had given her the book, as it was required reading for all aspiring Paladins. It taught the intricacies of parleying with foreign parties, particularly if those parties were potentially hostile races. Tye's recorded adventures were beloved among training mages. Kent hoped that Ariel would find it even more inspiring because Tye was a human like her.

"You're enjoying Crossford's book," Kent said as he entered the room. Within a few days, she had reduced the two-thousand-page book to under a couple hundred. "I read it decades ago, but I still remember every story."

Ariel closed the book and sat up, letting her feet dangle over the bed. Her spherical BOT hovered around her, extending its lens to better scrutinize Kent. "I am. He's so descriptive; I just get lost in all the places he's visited. I can't imagine doing half the things Tye has done."

Kent smiled. "You may have more adventures. Before the Civil War, Paladins were revered in every corner of the galaxy and were honored guests no matter where they visited. And not with undo cause, we dedicate our lives for the betterment of every world."

"And what about my father?"

"What about him?"

"Was the galaxy a safer place with him as Archmage?"

"Safer than it had been in over a hundred years. Archmage Zoltor was responsible for putting down the Bodewin Rebellion against the Roman Republic. He modernized Paladin bastions all over the worlds and recruited more young mages than any previous Archmage. My words can't do him justice, I just wish you could have seen how great of a man he was."

Ariel paused to fully consider his words. "Then why did the Order collapse under his rule?"

Kent could not answer the question at first. There was so much she did not know, and to an extent, much he did not know either. He was a common diplomat and soldier during the Civil War, but Tali surely knew more than he did. Unfortunately, she wanted little to do with Ariel since they first met. Despite his ignorance, Kent decided to tell his perspective.

"Nothing about Archmage Marius' leadership caused the downfall of the Order. The blame lies solely on the shoulders of his friend and apprentice, you may know him as Lord Zakareth, Grand Inquisitor."

Ariel's ember eyes widened at the recognition of the name. "What did he do?" she asked, eagerly.

Kent scowled. "Zakareth raped the Archmage's sister, your aunt, and tried to steal her away to the obsidian palaces beneath the Enfari home-world. He failed at his plot, and your father had him and his pack of traitors beat until they aligned themselves with Caesar and his belligerent forces."

"The Triumvirate?"

"No, the war between Caesar and the Roman Republic had not enveloped the galaxy yet. The Order was aiding the Republic in ending Caesar's rebellion, and he capitalized on our division. Thanks to him and Lord Zakareth, trillions more died than what was ever necessary."

Ariel scratched her head. "I don't get it. If my father was as loved as you say, why would anyone want to follow Zakareth?"

Kent drummed his index and middle fingers on his thumb. "It's a complicated matter. The galaxy as a whole was increasingly divided. With Last Bastion in ruins, the Paladin Order was the last of the glue that kept the worlds together. You see, our Order operated as the arm of the Galactic Council. While the Council still operated, Paladins had diplomatic immunity across the worlds. When it dissolved, so did our protection… but that was even before I was born."

"Let me guess," Ariel started. "My father wanted to continue the role of Paladins as they were, immunity or not. But without protection, their missions were more dangerous, and his mages became resentful."

"More or less, yes," Kent admitted. "There was always a small party of mages on Spyre who believed our kind should sequester themselves from the rest of the worlds, create our own faction and live selfishly. They were vocal but contained. Zakareth's mutiny was the excuse they were looking for. Traitorous bastards, all of them!"

There was a silence between them, only broken by living walls that constantly dripped and creaked. Kent gazed out the window and saw a huge planet, coated in multiple shades of green and surrounded by three red rings. As he breathed, his body temperature cooled.

"I'd like to change the subject," Ariel said. He could sense her conflict. She devoured his story like an epic tale, but for Kent, he was retelling a nightmare.

"What did you do to my– to Silver Wulf?" she asked. "It looked like you were controlling him."

"I was," Kent said. "It's my gift, it's what makes me a mage. You have your own gift too."

"Will it be the same as yours?"

"Maybe. The range of magical abilities that have been a part of the Paladin Order knows no boundaries. You could be a telepath, a pyromancer, a shadowbinder, or something completely different. No two mages are exactly the same, but I suppose we could share similar gifts."

"What if I don't have a... gift?"

"I wouldn't worry yet," Kent assured her. "Do you know about Serios?"

Ariel shook her head.

"Not surprising," he sighed. "He was an Immortal, one of the handful of Gods who crossed dimensions to help our realm defeat the Planters. Our history tells that he was the leader of the Immortals, and the most powerful too. His sacrifice in the first Planter war caused a disruption in the atomic fabric of our realm. As his blood spread across the galaxy, beings from every world began showing signs of his divine powers. Hence, the birth of mages.

"You're lucky in that you're the descendant of one of the most prevalent mage families the Order has ever known. Serios' mutagen has been active in the Zoltor line since its inception. You do have a gift, Ariel, and in time it will come."

She nodded, although her starstruck eyes expressed an overload of confusion. "So, this mutagen is hereditary?"

"It could be," Kent considered. "It is stronger in some family lines than others. For example, I'm the only one of my family to have a gift, but that doesn't mean I'm the first to have the mutagen. In all honesty, some scholars of Spyre theorized that every being in the galaxy possesses Serios' mutagen… it's just a matter of awakening it."

Ariel went along with Kent's explanation as if it was a work of fiction. He, however, could not blame her. The Creation War took place thousands of years ago, and the tales were passed around today more like fables than facts. Every race had their own theological interpretation of the epic conflict that consumed men, Gods, and the still mysterious microscopic race known as the Planters, but only the doctrines of the Paladin Order acknowledged the role of Serios in preserving the galaxy as they knew it.

"Could you have killed Wulf if you wanted to?" Ariel asked, finished with story time. Kent's thoughts brought him back to the Underbelly, where she had killed the Jurishan creature without a moment of hesitation.

"I could have," he admitted, "But that's something else we need to discuss. As a unit, the Paladin Order was nearly unstoppable, so we have a code to prevent ourselves from becoming the same tyrants we swear to fight against."

"Is it presumptuous of me to guess that this code prevents killing?" Ariel said, an unnerving glint sparkling in her eyes.

"Killing is permitted when absolutely necessary. Diplomacy always precedes violence for a Paladin," Kent insisted. Ariel rolled her eyes.

"You wanna know where hesitation and diplomacy get you on Prisilla?" she growled. She made a gun with her hand, put it to her temple and pulled the trigger. "You almost got us both killed back there, remember that next time you want to give me advice."

"I don't know what it's like to grow up on Prisilla," he admitted, trying to keep tempers cool. "All I ask of you is to consider my words and try to live by them."

"Okay," Ariel said, flatly. She stretched out on her bed once more and picked up Tye Crossford's book. Despite Kent's presence, she continued to read.

He found Tali alone in the canteen. He had planned on retiring to Matiyala's chamber early but seeing the forlorn face of the other Paladin made him pause.

"Where are you off to, Kent Kentoshi?" Tali asked, the sluggish tone of her voice very familiar to him.

"Off to sleep for the night. Maybe you should too."

"Oh Kent, you cannot be covert on a ship this size."

*Neither can you.* "Okay, I'm going to go fuck Matiyala if she'll have me. I am deep in her debt now."

Tali laughed. "Thanks to me, right?"

"Thanks to you." He waited in silence for the inevitable question.

"How'd it go with her?"

Kent shrugged. "Could've been better. I let her know about the Order's code on killing, suffice to say she did not take it well." Again, the image of Ariel killing the blue beast flashed through his head. The way she gazed spectacularly at the gruesome battle between pearls and Kagen's gang unnerved him. *If I hadn't pulled her away, how long would she have watched?*

"She's not the girl I imagined her to be." Tali admitted, her face in her hands. "Prisilla's a rough environment, but I thought she'd be different. I don't know what I expected, but it's not what I got."

"Perhaps you expected a flicker of warmth in her?" Kent suggested.

Tali let out a faint laugh. She muttered something in a language Kent did not recognize, then switched back. "Maybe that, maybe more. I tried to talk to her directly. I walked into her room while she was inhaling Gods know what into her lungs."

"Blast-off, I believe it's called."

"Whatever it was, I didn't know how to react. I freaked out, and she got defensive... It was a mess." She rested her head in her hands, drowning in morbid speculation. "I'm used to teaching students when they're young. She's nearly a woman, Prisilla has molded her and I fear the clay has already settled."

Kent sensed her mood would worsen the longer the conversation stayed on Ariel. "Any news on the Archmage's son?"

"Not recently. My contact says he needs a two-day notice for our arrival. Was Matiyala right? Is this really a suicide mission?"

"You said Romulus is near the border of KOH and Fyrossian space. Regretfully, what remains of the war is on the doorstep of Fyrossia."

"That essentially puts us in no man's land?" she asked.

"Not quite, but very, very close." Watching her, he felt obligated to include: "It won't be easy, but we will make the most of it."

Tali laughed again, "And I thought I had to restore hope in you. We've found the Archmage's daughter, a girl I've worried over for sixteen years. Now she's in my grasp and I'm as miserable as ever."

The stress ate at her. She was holding back even more grief, but he decided not to probe any further. "If you broke my drunken cycle, you can get through to Ariel too. She's young, and perhaps as warm as a blizzard, but if there is someone who can guide her through our path, it's you. You had the spirit to track her for a decade and a half, that same spirit can overcome a few awkward interactions. She's read Tye Crossford's book faster than anyone I've seen. The Archmage's soul is inside her somewhere, she just needs to trust us."

"Pray that's the case. But there are two of us for a reason. When my spirit is drained, it's yours that must continue the fight."

Kent's words came more from pity than honesty. He wanted to make Tali feel better, much good it did, but he too had his doubts. No matter what actions Ariel made to contradict her family, her appearance was still the damning evidence that she was indeed a Zoltor. The pale golden hair and the fiery orange eyes all screamed her heritage. She looked like Marius' sister, albeit with an entirely different energy.

And yet, he found something unfathomably alluring about Marius' daughter. She would not abandon him when the battle in the square became chaotic, and she made him laugh along with her at the absurdity of their situation as they ascended the floors of Prisilla. Kent felt privileged to witness her first time traveling through space, and he could not help but smile at her awestruck expression as she admired stars and planets for the first time. The galaxy was an arcane void to her, and yet she wanted to delve into it head-on, like Caella would.

These thoughts lingered with Kent deep into the night, as he laid in bed under the embrace of his Kalmar confidant. He stroked the many tentacles on her head as she rested her chin on his chest. Matiyala's face was youthful and pretty, but something in her eyes bragged experience and character.

"You seem out of it," she said. The room was pitch black, except for the luminous glow of a burly purple planet entering ominously through the sky roof. They drifted slowly in empty space.

"I have the daughter of the Archmage under my protection now. Forgive me if the pressure gets to me now and again."

Matiyala shook her head. "No, don't lie to me. You welcome the responsibility. I've known you for a short time, but the drunken bum who entered my ship on Narood is not here anymore. You need the pressure, or else you wouldn't have joined us. There is something else bothering you."

"It's the boy," Kent admitted. "I'm afraid of what he'll be like."

"I see," Matiyala noted. "The girl, Ariel, was not everything you dreamed of and more?"

"Are you mocking me?" Kent asked.

She sat up, sheets raised to her neck. "Your Archmage was born into royalty, destined for greatness. She, I assume, started working odd jobs the moment she could walk and talk. Probably held a pistol before she held a boy's hand."

"That can't change the fact that a whole galaxy won't rally behind a delinquent."

"I never said she couldn't change, but you would be a fool to assume she would give up everything she is to fit your bill of perfection. The wise move would be to use her skills to your advantage. You and Tali could help her incorporate the Paladin code into her own, therefor giving her the best of both worlds."

"And when did you become so learned, Captain?" Kent teased. His years of self-imposed exile allowed him to forget the warmth of companionship. He was thankful to have Matiyala in his life now.

"I wasn't much unlike her when I was that age," Matiyala reflected.

"And how long ago was that?" Kent teased again.

She smiled. "Funny, but you insult yourself more."

They laughed for a moment. When it was silent, Kent rubbed his head and sighed. He recalled his Immortech sword hidden beneath the bed. "This still doesn't ease my trepidations about the boy. Tali says he's been living on a Roman military academy his whole life. He could be brainwashed beyond repair."

Matiyala shrugged. She got up and sat herself on top of Kent. She put a hand on his chest, leaned in, and kissed him on the mouth. "The time will come to worry about these things that we cannot control. Let's enjoy the now."

And they did.

When Kent awoke, he was alone. He stumbled to the canteen to find the entire crew already active. Brutus was polishing one of his rifles (as he normally did), while Sara was setting the table for breakfast. Matiyala was opening canned food to be thrown into a pot already heating under the stove. Any hunger Kent might have had rapidly retreated.

"For captain of the ship, I don't think I've seen you in the cockpit." Bato jested at Matiyala's expense.

"It's on autopilot," she fired back, "Have you not flown a ship in the past 300 years?"

"No," Bato conceded. "Have you?"

Ariel was beside Brutus, inquiring about his weapons and bragging about her own. The human merc was not thrilled about the conversation, but he was eager to show off his assault rifle to someone who could appreciate it. Ariel too pulled out her pistols. She placed them on the table and slid them to the other side. Then, she stretched her gloved hands, causing sensors on her fingertips to glow and the pistols to fly through the air and land back into her palms. Brutus scowled, knowing he had been beat.

"Ariel," Tali said, hesitantly. "Has Kent showed you his Immortech sword?" Being a master of healing magic, she was not normally the one to talk about weapons. *She must be truly desperate.*

"Briefly. I've seen Immortech before, but not in that good of a condition."

"Really? How'd you come across it on Prisilla?"

"Wulf and I used to steal parts and sell them to Kagen. He liked to redistribute it as armor for his guys, that's what makes his army strong."

"I used to make a fortune on selling old Immortech parts," Brutus Cirileo added. "Better money in that market than the killing market. Problem is, Immortech gets harder and harder to find, whereas bounties are in an abundance."

"Now I don't even know if what I was selling was the real thing," Ariel said. "Wulf said it was, and it was good enough for me at the time. After seeing Kent's sword, I have my doubts."

"As long as the client believes it, why give a shit?" Cirileo asked. Ariel laughed in agreement. Kent was unable to contribute anything to the conversation.

Ariel leaned back in her seat, taking out her inhalator and sucking into it. Cirileo and Bato made nothing of it, the same could not be said for Tali.

"Do you have to do that right now?" she asked, annoyed.

"I don't have to," she said, her eyes already starting to dilate. "But I want to. It helps keep me calm. You want some?"

Tali shook her head. "No, not in a million years."

Ariel shrugged. "Are you sure? Might help you lighten up."

"No. I do not need drugs to feel better about myself." Tali stated. Brutus revealed a sinister smile.

"And are you saying I do?" Ariel asked in a tone daring her to continue.

Thankfully, Matiyala came just in time with the freshly heated cans of slop. Kent felt a tension in his spine release its tight grip. Everyone ceased talking to eat, except for Tali who excused herself from the room, insisting that she did not feel well.

# MARION (III)

The iron cuffs and chain were unrelenting.

Marion strained and yanked, grunted and gritted, but to no avail. He acted as much in belligerence as he did in hilarious terror. This was how he awoke, pinned to the ground like a rabid beast, arms intwined around an immovable desk and backside firmly planted to a carpeted floor.

His mind fell into an unhinged state upon realization of his imprisonment. The delusions that flooded his thoughts were elevated by a throbbing headache, a parched throat, and an overflowing bladder. Confusion was an oiled whip, keeping him frantic, making his reasoning delirious, forcing his body into a feral dance.

Breakout possessed him. He struggled against the chains that pinned him to the desk. *I need to get out, I need to get out, I need to get out!* Pull and yank as he may, Marion was trapped. Neither the desk nor the manacles showed the slightest hint of relent. Eventually, his body tired, and his mind stepped into the forefront of his thinking.

Memories returned in sporadic mental images, as if he were dreaming during a restless sleep. Something about an office, not unlike the one he was in now, a man slumped over, something rolling around, and the stains, *oh Gods the stains*.

The small bronze clock on top of a coffee table moved along, the tick hypnotic in its endlessness. His cadet uniform was completely disheveled, the sleeves especially torn and tattered. A red stain covered the front of his uniform, its smell putrid and unbearable.

When he tried to look around the room, his eyes strained and watered. The right eye was especially sluggish as it began to swell and puff-out.

Starved for questions, Marion instinctually called for help. First at a normal pitch, then shouting, then screaming, then, finally, crying. "Let me out," found no return, nor did "help me," or "what the Hell is going on?" Even the incoherent hollers he had no idea his throat could make after hours of forlorn calling sought no sympathy from whoever had locked him inside.

Octavia was the first to appear to him. She came out of nowhere, standing over him with a distraught, no, disappointed look on her face. Lonely beyond belief, her presence alone was enough to elevate his spirits.

He tried to stand up himself, but his fettered wrists thwarted his efforts mercilessly. He begged her for help, but she responded with nothing but a cold stare. Asking again and again did nothing to change her mind or the horrible glare on her face. He pleaded with her to answer, to explain what was going on, but she gave him nothing in return.

It was like talking to a mannequin. Any sort of relief her presence had brought him before evaporated. He must have appeared so vulnerable, so pathetic in his current state, and he hated she could see him like this.

"You're disgusted, right?" he asked, spittle flying from his lips. "Why don't you leave? Get the Hell out of my sight if you're just gonna be useless."

Before Marion could stop her, Octavia dissipated into thin air.

The anguish was too much to handle, and the bestial impulses returned fiercer than before. He fought the cuffs, tried to break the leg off the desk that was implanted into the floor, and, in his final and most ineffective attempt of escape, stomped at the carpet until it folded away from his reach.

The more Marion struggled, the more feral his actions became. By the end, he was performing nothing more than unrelenting spasms and thrashes. He was a creature reduced to one goal: escape. He was free of the pain, exhaustion, and confusion that he had woken up with, but this invincibility ended abruptly when his final act of defiance involved smacking his head against the bottom of the desk and putting himself to sleep.

When he awoke again, a new person appeared. This time, Marion did not know what to think.

"Marion?" the old man said, their noses nearly touching. The age marks sketched on his face had always been there, but they were deeper now than ever before. "Can you see me? Those bastards beat you well, didn't they? Please say something."

"Mister Everec," Marion said, his voice groggy like he had slept for an entire day. The headache returned, along with bruising on the back of his head where he had collided with the desk. "What time is it? What day is it?!"

Everec sighed. "It's been six hours since…." The old man looked unnerved. His wise mentor could not mask the obvious concern on his face. "This is an ordeal, Marion, but not an unsolvable one. I need time to think. Of all people, it had to be Polanis."

"Polanis!" Marion yelled, the memories hitting him like a car crash. He was called into the headmaster's office, presumably to hear the verdict on his tenure at the Academy of Romulus. He passed a guard chatting, or more accurately flirting, with a teacher several doors down. The receptionist's desk was empty, so Marion took the liberty of entering on his own.

And that was where he found the body.

The cut was clean. Even with a neck as thick as Polanis', he was seemingly decapitated with a single swing, but a swing with what? Certainly not a knife, for even the sharpest of knives would have a difficult time cutting through the headmaster's sinewy throat.

By the time Marion saw Polanis in his most mortal state, only drops of blood secreted between shoulders from which a Roman head once proudly stood, but the red mess on his jacket, dress shirt, and carpet beneath suggested there had once been a waterfall.

Marion had never seen a dead body, let alone a freshly cut one, and the sight of it rendered him frozen. He nearly cried and vomited all at once. He also considered running away, but any action would have been better than the befuddled stance he was caught in when the hallway guard returned to his post.

Vision blurred, he stared back at Mister Everec and only saw fractions of a face. He went to touch the skin around his eye, which had been busted open anew after a night of healing from Vintrus' knuckles, but the manacles that bounded his wrists halted the motion. To stay calm, Marion reminded himself that he was no longer in Polanis' office, and that the body was far away.

"Immortals!" he exclaimed, swallowing hard and feeling bile boil up in the back of his throat. He turned desperately at Mister Everec, "Get me out of here! Please?"

"Right." Everec ordered the guard to step inside. "Uncuff the boy. He'll be taken back to his room."

The guard was hesitant. "Principal Tarius said-"

"I don't care what Tarius said. He's had a student chained to a desk for hours. Whatever his intentions were behind this display, they've been made and surpassed."

"Well, I-"

"How about you do as I say, or I'll put you on trial myself for abusing a student." Everec declared. There was an urgency in his voice Marion had never detected before. The guard obeyed and released him. "Good, escort him back to his chamber. Marion, do tell me if this man harms you in any way. I'll make sure he's kicked out of Romulus with nothing but the clothes on his back."

"Yes, Mister Everec."

The walk back to the dormitory was brutal. His legs, which had grown stiff after hours of being locked in an awkward position, were the opposite of obedient. He limped along the golden halls of Romulus. The guard, observing his pathetic state, made him promise not to lie about his limp and say he caused it.

Despite the struggle, he did eventually make it to room 304, and shut the vaulted door on his escort before the man could help him inside. From there, Marion stumbled to his bed and collapsed. Before he knew it, sleep encircled him, and he woke up with the dried blood all over his student uniform smelling even more putrid than before. He stood, his body regaining some of its strength, and stripped off his clothes, lazily leaving them in clumps by his bedside.

*I'll pick them up later*, he thought as he limped to the shower.

The steaming hot water rushed down his skin, easing his bones and regenerating his mind. He stood in the shower for a long time, pondering, letting the heavy steam fill the entire bathroom. *Polanis is dead, and I was the first one to find him. Was he going to expel me? Who cares? They tied me up like I'm the one who did it. Fuck Romulus.* The physically healing shower did nothing to improve him emotionally. Marion shut the shower off and dried himself. From there, he collapsed on the bed, just as frustrated and confused as he had ever been.

The sight of the headless body seeped inside his brain like poison. The stench of Polanis' blood still lingered in his clothes, but he was too exhausted to do anything about it. The whole day had been a nightmare, but at least nightmares had the luxury of being woken up from. He remembered his morning with Octavia, the dread that haunted him then was incomparable to what it was now. Any senses of safety and security were rendered absurd concepts, while the scope of future horrors was limitless in its possibilities. With that knowledge, he tried his best to not think of what awaited tomorrow.

Marion checked his clock; it was close to midnight. Naturally, he drifted off into sleep once again, perhaps the pitiful hope that his problems would disappear by the next morning lingered somewhere in the back of his consciousness.

The vault turned open from the other side, the noise of it disturbing him enough the pull him from a deep sleep. He raised his head languidly, half expecting Polanis' killer to come for him next.

"You look better," Mister Everec said as he entered. The Dean, typically exuding a natural confidence, seemed unnervingly unsure of himself. "How are you feeling?"

"Good," Marion lied. He checked the bedside clock and realized he had slept the whole night. However, he hardly felt rested. "Any news on the headmaster?"

Everec sighed. "Unfortunately, there's something we need to talk about."

"I didn't kill him." Marion declared. It was more of a plea than a statement.

"I know you didn't." Everec was pacing around the room, as if his legs were transmitting the energy to his brain that allowed him to think. "I saw the body, there is no way anyone could expect a boy like you to do it."

"What do you mean?" Marion asked, his voice cracking. "Am I a suspect?"

Lyndon Everec rubbed his temples. "You're *the* suspect. Tarius has already sent an envoy to the nearest relay station. He is requesting a judicial representative from Rome to come to Romulus and conduct the trial. He has already convinced the guard who found you to testify."

Marion came close to fainting again. He had been betrayed by his capture the flag team earlier in the day by the will of Principal Tarius, but this was a cruelty he did not believe Tarius capable of.

Everec detected his unease and sought to placate it. "I advise you to not get too worked up. It will require at least a week's travel for the representative to get here, depending on the speed of the vessel and how quickly they detect the signal from our relay station."

This deep into space, directly speaking to Rome was impossible. Relay stations constructed all throughout the galaxy facilitated communication between space vessels and bases. They were originally designed by the Galactic Council, but with the council dissolved for over half a century, many of these stations were failing due to improper maintenance. If he was not mistaken, it would require a multiday travel to find the closest one to Romulus.

"He can't have me convicted!" Marion protested. Everec wanted to comfort him, but something kept him away. He was Marion's lone hope, but even now the Dean of Students seemed incredibly powerless.

"With Polanis deceased, Tarius can do as he pleases. He's had the entire school under lockdown since the body was found. It's a miracle I was able to get to you at all."

"So, what do we do?" Marion asked, desperately. The smell of blood scratched the insides of his nostrils, the stench was so pungent that it made him nauseous. His eyes moistened too, but he wiped them on his sleeve before any tears could form.

Mister Everec swiped his fingers through his long, white hair. "All you need to do is wait. Tarius will play his tricks, but I won't, under any circumstance, allow the Roman representative to see you chained down like a psychopath. As for the trial, I will be your defense. Tarius might have the influence of the entire academy, but I'll be far more convincing."

"Do you have a background in law?" Marion asked, legitimately curious. Everec was an encyclopedia of history, but never had the two discussed law before. Marion, frankly, was completely uninterested in the subject.

"Not exactly," Everec admitted. "But I can be persuasive if the situation calls for it. Besides, a shoe would have an easy time outwitting Principal Tarius." A sudden thought hit the Dean of Students, his eyes dancing around the room as he let the idea ruminate. "If the murder weapon is uncovered, it could have fingerprints on it. That's our best chance of getting you off the trial."

"And if you don't find it?"

"Then we'll find you innocent the judiciary way. The process may be more tedious, but as long as the ending is the same, that's all that matters."

Marion bit his lip. He started a word, stopped, realized he had to continue, and asked: "What if I'm judged guilty?"

Everec smiled, almost genuinely. "No need to dwell on 'what ifs' just yet. If you will excuse me, I'm going to get you out of this mess."

Marion appreciated his attempt at optimism, as vain as it was. Although he could not read Mister Everec as well as Mister Everec could read him, Marion could at least tell the mask of confidence that the Dean of Students wore was hiding a black shroud of doubt.

When he left, Marion drifted toward Octavia yet again. What did she know? Had she been manipulated into thinking he was a murderer? Was she a defiant supporter of his among a hive of eager condemners? Neither sounded particularly favorable, but he secretly wished that she held on to what little faith he instilled in her.

Mercifully, his speculations were disturbed once again.

He popped his head up like an excited dog at the sound of the dormitory vault turning open. He needed Mister Everec, he longed for Octavia, but he received neither.

Principal Tarius was a rotund man, rounded like an overly inflated ball and possessing a waddle appropriate for such a figure. His stare was unrelentingly spiteful, his close-set eyes like two onyx gems in a sea of milky flesh.

"Stand by me, men. I don't want the murderer to be provoked again." Tarius ordered to the guards who flanked his right and left sides. If he planned such an ostentatious display of defense in the audience of Marion alone, he shuddered to imagine the spectacle he would put on for the judge from Rome.

"Here to help me out?" Marion asked, knowing the answer.

"Of course not. I've come to interrogate the criminal. How could you kill the headmaster like that? After all he did for this academy." He shook his head in great sorrow.

"I'm unaware the verdict was decided," Marion answered bitterly. Indifference, and an amount of mental exhaustion, had emboldened him. "Can't say I'm disappointed. Romulus has always been quick to judge me guilty."

"Not guilty yet, but it's inevitable," Tarius promised. "Immortals, why didn't I see it earlier. The bad pup has turned into a monster. We all should have expected it. You even managed to surpass your traitorous parents; they must be proud."

"I didn't do anything!"

Tarius smirked. "He's not just a murderer, he's a chronic liar too. Thankfully, Marion, you'll be shipped off to Rome once Caesar's man sorts out this tragic situation. The Academy of Romulus will be cured of your one-man insurgency soon enough, but I'll make sure you receive the guilty verdict first."

"Fine!" Marion spat. "You won't be the only one relieved. This fucking academy has wasted my life."

He cursed his own temper. Tarius was trying to incite him. *That's why he's brought the guards, for further witnesses to my insanity.* Thus far, he proved he could play Marion like an instrument. Belligerence would do him no favors now, as if it ever did.

Tarius chortled at the cadet's pathetic acts of defiance. "Your arrival to Rome won't be met with adoring crowds and celebrations. You will enter as a prisoner." He gazed around the room in mock astonishment. "Whether or not you ever see the light of day from your cell is not for me to say, but the murder of a veteran Roman officer is historically met with the harshest, yet most appropriate punishments."

Marion almost screamed out in defiance again, but he promptly halted the words as they threatened to escape him mouth. He would not perform for his principal any longer.

Tarius grunted. He gave Marion a sideways look, continuing to taunt him. "Of course, any punishment can be eased with a confession. Caesar is a merciful king; a confession could mean an escape from life imprisonment, or worse."

The bait was too obvious. Marion refused to belittle himself with a response. Instead, he focused his eyes on a wall and turned into a statue.

A flash of rage crossed Principal Tarius' fleshy face. "I'm clearly getting nowhere with the murderer." He signaled his guards out of the room, but the principal himself stopped at the threshold. "Sleep long and well, killer. I'll make sure you don't have any special visitors tonight."

# ELYSANDE (11)

The sight of the Crimson Armada still gave her chills.

Tens of thousands of ships roared passed the Forum in the center of Rome, the eruption of patriotic admirers rendered unheard by an army of roaring engines. The wind picked up, swirled, and nearly blew the watchers off their feet. Elysande remained unbroken, she had learned to keep her feet planted firmly to the ground.

Several minutes had passed before the entirety of the Armada finished its parade above the Roman skyline. The tailing star-splitters shot fireworks from their holsters, changing the sky from blue, to green, to gold, and finally red. The crowd adored it, clapping and laughing and making merriment of the most destructive naval force the galaxy had ever known. Caesar clapped too, like the proud owner of the best-dog-in-show.

One ship, a carrier, broke off from the pack with a masterful turn up into the sun and a spin that would make a planet jealous of its circular form. It descended, slowly and deliberately, onto the Forum square, landing near meters from Elysande and her king. The latch of the carrier dropped, and out came Reynard Bodewin, Lord of Erron, Overseer of Mercia, Commander of the Crimson Armada, and Father, the last title reserved for Elysande and her brother alone.

"Hail, King Caesar!" Reynard said, saluting. He was accompanied by a score of guards, each donning the crimson-on-black armor of their commander's noble family. Reynard dressed himself in a red velvet doublet laced with golden silk, a tribute to the families of Bodewin and Caesar alike.

Gaius extended his hand, and Reynard shook it. "A pleasure as always, Lord Bodewin."

Reynard eyed Caesar up and down. "I must say, my king, it doesn't seem like you've aged a day. Many a ruler has crumbled under the pressure of leadership, and yet the immense responsibility has had no impact on you."

"It's friends like you that make my job all the easier." Caesar complimented. "You too must have found the cure for aging."

*A blatant lie*, Elysande thought. *Father, you've put on some weight since the last time we met.*

Reynard addressed her, as if sensing her concealed disdain. "And it is my greatest joy to see you again, Elysande, no matter how peculiar your hairstyle becomes with each passing year."

She smiled. "It is to honor Mother and her people. If not me to carry on her memory, then whom?" An awkward silence ensued, until Reynard broke it off.

"Of course, we only joke with each other." Reynard lied, kissing his daughter on the cheek.

Caesar admired the smoke-filled sky over their heads. The strength of Reynard Bodewin's air force lingered in black clouds. "The sight of the Crimson Armada still thrills me. You've truly built a formidable force."

"It is quite impressive. The Roman Republic was terrified of the Crimson Armada, back when it was but half the size it is now," Elysande said. "I only hope I'm a worthy successor, Father, when I inherit it."

Bodewin shook his head. Being the eldest of her father's children, she was technically the heir to his fleet. *I always longed for the Admiral's cap, but he forced a laurel wreath upon my brow in its stead.*

"It is not my armada. I am merely a vessel for you to command it, my king." Bodewin answered, rejecting the point of contention entirely.

*And am I a vessel for you to fuck Caesar?* Elysande asked herself.

"I see you've added to it," Caesar said. "From what I've observed, you carry a few more frigates in your arsenal."

"We have the most excellent engineers in Erron, always eager for a new project. And I can't help but provide it to them. Perhaps it is the paranoia of the past that haunts me, but I'm anticipating another war on our doorstep." Reynard admitted.

"I've found it helpful to hope for the best, but prepare for the worst," Caesar agreed. "But this is no place to catch up. Why don't you come to our home? Lance and Julia can't wait to see you."

Reynard bowed his head humbly. "As you command, my king."

The three retired to the king's estate in the outskirts of the city by the western waterfront. King Caesar was a stranger to his own four-story mansion, as he typically elected to sleep in the city center in case of an emergency. He and Lord Bodewin shared in their amazement of the ground floor living room Elysande had personally designed. Marble flooring, an iron fireplace with a holographic fire, and opulent red curtains draping over a large-framed window allowing an unparalleled view of the setting sun over Rome.

Standing in the center of the living room surrounded by barriers of couches and chairs were the prince and princess of Rome.

"Good evening, Grandfather," they said in unison.

Reynard studied his grandchildren, Lawrence first, then Julia.

"You're a thin boy, Lawrence. How old are you?"

"Fourteen," he answered, shyly. Lawrence was the spitting image of a Bodewin: red hair, blue eyes, and skin as fair as a summer's cloud.

"No matter, you're still young." Reynard assured him, although he followed it with a condescending glare at Elysande. In a flash, his interest turned to his younger grandchild.

"This one's beautiful. She's a Caesar to the bone."

Julia smiled, as if relieved by his approval. "Thank you, Grandfather." She responded with a curtsy, quite well for a twelve-year-old.

"Where have the years gone, Gaius?" Reynard asked, solemnly. "My grandchildren are on the cusp of adulthood, and I've missed out on the joy of being a grandfather."

"There is still plenty for them to accomplish," Caesar assured. "This is just the beginning."

"Ah yes, I do await eagerly for... for... whatever comes next." Reynard caught himself a little too late. Elysande's internal thermometer spiraled upward. Caesar pretended not to notice the stutter. He could stay cool under an erupting volcano. *Bastard.*

The two children between King Gaius Julius Caesar and Queen Elysande Bodewin were, unfortunately, not the king's only offspring. Gaius had been married before his Civil War, and with that marriage came a daughter, Natalia. She was away from Rome at the time, studying at a university, but her presence was felt everywhere.

*If he would pick his heir, I'd know how much of an enemy Natalia is to me and my children.* Reynard had the power to force Caesar's hand, but he would not. He would rather his grandson be passed up as ruler of the KOH if it meant not causing any friction between him and his son-in-law.

"Lance, Julia, you may run along. Your mother and I need to speak with Grandfather in private." Caesar advised, calmly.

Sensing the intensity within the room, the two children darted for the door and escaped upstairs. The king called to one of his servants for drinks, and a few empty glasses later the three managed to forget any bitterness as best they could. Natalia's name was never spoken aloud, and yet she loomed over the room like a spirit.

"Elysande," her father said between sips of wine from the mystical Denvari orchards. "I'm shocked you haven't inquired about your brother yet."

Elysande put her cup down. Denvari wine was beloved in Rome, but she preferred the heavier, darker beers of northern Mercia. "If something exceptionally favorable or, conversely, exceptionally unfavorable has occurred to my brave brother, I imagine I would have heard by now."

Reynard grimaced. "How rational, how cold. A great victory awaits Drake. He's headed for the Fyrossian home-world as we speak. He will be commanding the attack on their capital city, the Fyrossians' final defense before this horrible war is put to an end."

"I'm aware, Father. Although 'great victory' is slightly hyperbolic. The three KOH frigates are conquering the planet quickly. They are months ahead of schedule, and the operation is developing better than any of our generals could have expected. The Fyrossians have lost their enthusiasm to resist. By the time Drake begins his siege, he'll be fighting ghosts."

"There's no value in underestimating the enemy. The three of us should know better than anyone else."

"True," Elysande agreed. "I'm happy for Drake, honestly. However, I must admit that I will miss his participation in the Gladiator Games, something about watching him humble those Mercian nobles and Roman patricians is endlessly entertaining."

Caesar drank to that. "Yes, but this New Year's lists will be increasingly unpredictable without him."

Reynard's bushy eyebrows twitched as an idea entered his brain. "Speaking of the lists, Timothy Mauvern hasn't been subtle about his intention to enter the tournament. If he should face-off against any of Omir's supporters, or any Tisonian really, I fear the violence will not be contained to the Colosseum."

"My censor, Shota Nakamura, is handling the brackets as best as he can. Mauvern is old, and he was never an athlete to begin with. He should not make it past the first round, if we have the favor of Rhomigius."

"Tournament or not," Elysande began, "Tensions will be feverish. Tisonians and Mercians will cross paths, regardless of our efforts. We'd best pray for another war, the only way to stop us from killing one another is to find another species to kill instead."

Caesar laughed, although the truth to the statement was unnervingly genuine. Reynard remained serious. "Rumor has it that a Roman squadron was attacked by Synths out in Grayspace. This may belittle my intelligence, but I have to ask..."

"We are still investigating the matter, but the evidence is there." Caesar said. "I spoke to the survivors and I've even seen pictures. My plan of attack is to have the three frigates finishing off the Fyrossian home-world lead the first wave of the invasion out into Grayspace. Hopefully by then Imperator Tarquinius can report on more Synth sightings, if not I may look like a fool when I bring this news to the Senate."

"Just when the worlds can't get more exciting, you manage to uncover a myth." Reynard raised his glass to Caesar. Elysande followed. The talk of Synths had become so frequent of late that she was beginning to think they were real.

Just as Reynard was about to inquire further about the existence of Synths, the sounds of a hover car landing outside filled the room. It parked on the street directly outside the estate. Caesar's Praetorian guardsmen sprung from nowhere and were on top of the vehicle.

"Are you expecting more company?" Reynard inquired.

Caesar watched the car with controlled curiosity. One man exited the vehicle. The soldiers saluted the figure. The house steward walked into the living room and reported, "The Praetorian Prefect has urgent news for His Majesty. He requests permission to enter the estate."

"Why would he not call me?" Caesar asked.

"He would not say," the steward confessed.

"Then let him in. Let's see what this is about."

Seconds later, Sutorian, flanked on both sides by knights of the Praetorian Guard, entered the room. The aging prefect dressed in his garnished, yet lumbering armor set, his subordinates looking anorexic by comparison. He saluted upon entering, and Elysande caught his silver eyes darting around the room and surveying for threats.

"Apologies, my king," he said. "But I have news that seems as risky as it does inappropriate to report over the phone."

"What's the problem?" Caesar asked, his stare as solid as steel. Elysande leaned in. The prefect was a capable leader and hardly one to dramatize, so the urgency of this meeting was ominously intriguing.

"A member of the Praetorian Elite has died, my king." Sutorian reported. Caesar leaned back, allowing the statement a chance to breathe. The king and his family had hundreds of protectors in their service, but the Praetorian Elite were a special class of knights who served as the king's very last line of defense. It was mandatory that at least several Elite Guardsmen be with Caesar at all times.

"Who is it?" Caesar demanded.

"Fulvius Galla," Sutorian obeyed.

"Damn," he cursed. "What was the nature of his death?"

Sutorian spoke apprehensively, but honestly. "Although a full autopsy report has not been completed, the likely cause of death is a drug overdose. The body was found in an alleyway several miles outside Pullo's Shield, hiding carelessly under a pile of garbage bags. He had not been wearing his Praetorian armor, so there is a chance that the body was not recognized by any civilians."

"Galla has been a member of the Elite guard since I took my crown. How am I supposed to believe he was a drug addict?" Caesar paused, fists clenched. "And if he was an addict, he would never have deemed himself fit for his position."

Elysande could not object; Galla was about as exciting as a beige wall, but to say he was not a humble and duty-bound soldier would be an abject lie. Then again, she never found a reason to scrutinize him more carefully. *Perhaps his demons hid in the shadows of my indifference.*

"I should have seen this coming," Sutorian confessed. "He's under my command, so he is my responsibility alone. I've left you compromised for Gods know how long. I propose my immediate resignation as Praetorian Prefect."

"You're tired, Sutorian. Galla's death is equally as alarming to me." Caesar reassured him. "Until all the information is collected, there is no point in jumping to conclusions. Send your people to his family, let them know of his death but not of the circumstances."

Sutorian saluted. "It will be done, my king."

"Blast-off has become a hot commodity in the poorer districts of Rome. There's always the chance Galla discovered this addiction recently," Elysande theorized.

Caesar still was unsure. "I can't help but find this unlikely. We would've noticed. Besides, Blast-off provides a quick high. How could a dose of it kill a Roman soldier on his feet?"

"Bad batches exist for every type of drug. I've seen it all during my years with the Black Dogs," Sutorian said. "The wrong concoction of chemicals can do irreparable damage to the human body. You'd be surprised by how quickly this filth can kill a man."

"It could be a coordinated hit from a dealer," Elysande proposed. "Maybe he was recognized and was purposefully given a lethal dose. The crime syndicates outside Pullo's Shield aren't fond of Praetorians."

"They're fond of no one but their own factions." Reynard added. "And yet, to defy the KOH so publicly is uncharacteristically brave for their kind. It may be a declaration of war."

"But a war on what?" Caesar inquired.

"A war on the spread of Blast-off throughout your city." Reynard responded, coldly.

Sutorian clenched his fists. "Say the word, my king, and I will lead a whole legion out into the streets tonight to find answers."

"We can't rule out any possibility," Caesar stated. "But this is no time to crack heads without appropriate cause. Have the Black Dogs investigate. They know the underworld of Rome better than anyone else."

"This is an undeniable and unwarranted tragedy," Reynard spoke up. "But we also must consider the consequences of Galla's body being identified before it was taken in."

Sutorian reminded the Overseer of Mercia that Galla was dressed in civilian clothes, but Bodewin was hardly relieved.

"Unless he miraculously found a way to change his face, he is still at risk of being identified. Wherever our king goes, the Praetorian Elite follow. Although he wasn't a celebrity, Galla has been seen publicly with King Caesar for over a decade, meaning only the blind don't know who he is. If word was to get out that a member of the Praetorian Elite was found dead in an alleyway while loaded on drugs, well, it would call into question the intelligence of those who lead the KOH."

"And what do you suggest, Father?" Elysande asked.

Reynard's face turned grave, purely for theatrics. "We come up with our story before someone else does. For all we know, Galla died while fighting bravely against the criminal scum that plagues the great capital of the KOH."

Elysande cocked an eyebrow. "Are you suggesting we lie to the good people of the KOH? If we get exposed, the consequences will be even more dire."

"You overexaggerate the risks," Reynard warned. Everyone turned to the king for his input. Caesar, however, was focused on his hand, watching his forefinger rub against his thumb.

"My first instinct will never be to deceive my people," Caesar said. "But if Galla was a drug addict, it could be an insult on the entire royal guard."

"My sentiments exactly," Reynard agreed. "We can make Galla's death mean something. Make him a martyr against the rise of Blast-off. After all, it is the highest honor for a Praetorian guardsman to die in service of the king."

# TROYTON (IV)

When the sun rose over Drusk-El, the four pyramids that made up the capital city of Fyrossia remained defiantly liberated from the Triumvirate. By the time the sun set, the whole planet was conquered in the name of Caesar. The four pyramids, surrounded by miles of scorched earth, rested in a slate of cool shadow, and would not see the light again without the golden Aquila mounted atop each pyramid's apex. *Well, at least three would.* One pyramid crumbled during the battle, a result of being caught in a crossfire between a KOH frigate and its own antiaircraft weaponry.

Troyton stood atop a windswept ridge cresting around the scene of the battle. Smoke and hot air filled his lungs, glory and triumph caressed his face. Today was the proudest day in which he could call himself a centurion.

Breaking up the peaceful silence of a dying battle, he heard footsteps crunch in the dirt behind him. He turned around to discover those footsteps belonged to Lucius. The other humanoid was drenched in ash and soot, his ragged beard looking as if it was caked in flour. Despite all this, nothing could hide the elation on his face

"Nothing beats your first, right?" Lucius asked.

"I can't tell yet." Troyton lied. Never had his body felt so alive than during the battle. Never had his mind felt so stimulated than in the middle of a firefight. The rush of storming a Fyrossian stronghold was euphoric; the thrill of conquering the enemy unparalleled. The Fyrossians were tough, intelligent warriors, and Troyton embraced the competition and found himself hungry for more in its wake. "We had it easy by Caesar's design. We were fighting outside the city because he didn't want us risking our lives in the frontline."

"The real challenge comes later," Lucius agreed. He pulled out a pack of cigarettes from his pocket and offered it to Troyton. When he refused, Lucius elected to smoke by himself.

"When did you pick up that habit?" Troyton asked.

"Some soldier gave it to me. He says it helps calm your nerves after a firefight. I don't understand why anyone would want that."

"So, you smoke it anyway?"

"When you're a foot taller than the next tallest human, you do what you can to assimilate. Of all people, you should know."

The two humanoids stared over the city of Drusk-El as it burned. *Hundreds of generations of humans will read about what I'm seeing with my own eyes.*

"Do you ever think about what will happen if we find nothing in Grayspace?" Troyton asked, raising the unspoken demons.

Lucius shrugged. "It's been a while. Over a month, has it? Another sorry squadron has run into Synths by now. Don't worry about it, you know how damn long it takes to get news in and out of Grayspace."

"I know," Troyton said.

Lucius laughed and slapped his friend on the back. "Let's talk about what's really bothering you. You're feeling guilty about lying to the king. Well don't be. He's putting our lives on the line to do his bidding. There's no shame in finding a way to profit from a bad situation."

Troyton sighed. Guilt had crippled him in the subsequent weeks of his first lie. Selfishness seduced him. Caesar spoke the word "Centurion," and Troyton's better judgement went awry. But as time passed, his sins healed like a middling wound. It still hurt on the occasion, but its presence faded as the dreamlike gloss of his new life took over. Though with Lucius' words, the wound was torn open anew.

"We exist for the betterment of the KOH, but now we've concocted a war over a landmine. I looked my king in the eyes and I lied to him. If three frigates invade Grayspace and find nothing, what will we do next?"

"I don't think that far in advance." Lucius said. "Quite frankly I'm surprised you even played along with Scipio's plan."

Troyton arched an eyebrow. "Then why'd you go along with it if you thought I'd snitch?"

Lucius raised the cigarette to his lips and took in another breath. "The prize was worth the gamble I guess."

"And what if I told the truth?"

"You're a good man. I wouldn't have been mad at you. Hell, by now I would've been court-martialed for one reason or another if not for your concern. You showed me the benefits of siding with the KOH, but I like to think I've taught you a couple life lessons too."

"You did, despite my best efforts." Troyton laughed, faintly. Lucius joined in, but their merriment was drowned out by a soaring aircraft that flew over their heads and into the city. The humanoids watched as it dropped three bombs into the heart of Drusk-El, the subsequent fiery mushroom clouds towered over the crumbling skyscrapers.

"We've done pretty well together thus far, my friend." Lucius said, the smell of burning skin and ash swirling through the air.

Troyton stood and brushed the dust and dirt from his uniform. Centurion armor was bulkier than he was used to. It was awkward to maneuver in at first, but he was beginning to understand its purpose. Black seared marks dressed its white plates, warnings of enemy laser fire that would have killed him had his armor not been so substantial.

"Where are you off to?" Lucius asked, watching Troyton board a one-man hoverbike.

"To find General Marko. I'd guess he's in the city by now. Centurion Decius wanted me to report to him after the city was taken." Decius was the officer Troyton studied under during the siege of Drusk-El. Unfortunately, the good centurion had perished during the battle, a result of a cowardly Fyrossian sniper lurking behind their lines. Decius was ordered to bring him to General Marko, had his head not exploded from his shoulders.

"And Marko did not want to see me as well?" Lucius asked, offended.

"Not sure." Troyton said, revving up the engine of his hoverbike. "I'll ask him when I see him." As he sped off, he glimpsed Lucius in the rearview mirror standing alone in the scorched field, middle finger raised in the air.

He took his hoverbike to a path on the right where the ridge swooped down to the level of the pyramids of Drusk-El. The bike picked up ample amounts of ash and soot in its wake, and Troyton was thankful that he wore a loose-fitting robe over his armor to prevent it from getting dirty. From afar, the setting sun over Drusk-El was an enormous, fiery mouth about to swallow the city whole.

Three mighty dragons of black steel loomed over the dying city. Human Fury, Immortal's Awe, and Spear of Rhomigius were their names. They were the frigates of the KOH, perhaps the largest and deadliest vessels known in the galaxy. Virtually impenetrable, one frigate alone could carry five-hundred-thousand men. It was, undoubtedly, the perfect war machine.

The Roman outposts were finally letting people in and out of Drusk-El as Troyton approached the city's entrance. As he continued, the alien appearance of the cityscape stunned him. The dome-shaped buildings with sunburst roofs, some massive and others puny, the tight and narrow streets of red asphalt and the archways over them, the skinny autumn trees with contorted trunks protruding from the alleys between buildings, and the broken monuments of Fyrossian heroes made of what appeared to be pure diamond all made Troyton eager to explore the old capital. Human soldiers roamed the naked streets, stepping on the blood and bodies of Fyrossian soldiers which were carelessly strewn about in their death poses. The only enemies he could see were dead ones, the rest were likely locked up in their domes or thrown into KOH prison transports heading out of the city.

He could not keep his eyes focused as he navigated the urban environment. Lawlessness covered the streets at every turn. A small band of soldiers had committed themselves to fill one of the larger domes with explosives, and the resulting explosion turned half the block into fireworks. Troyton assumed the perimeter was already cleared of civilians.

A few miles further into the city, he finally laid eyes on a pair of living Fyrossians who were fighting over a cart of food until one pulled out a sidearm and shot the other in the chest. As the surviving Fyrossian made his escape, a sniper on an archway over the street turned his brains into pudding and let the body skid across the asphalt.

Deeper into the capital was where Troyton found a Roman legate. The man was ordering soldiers to track down and arrest some Fyrossian refugees who were spotted sneaking around a nearby boulevard. The legate was an older man, no stranger to war judging by his indifference to the chaos.

"Sir!" Troyton saluted.

"Gods, you're a big one," the legate said. "Are you one of those Lab Rats?"

Troyton cringed. "My name is Troyton Vorenus, centurion of the KOH. I was told by my commanding officer to report to General Marko once the city was successfully taken. He died during the battle, and I have no clue where to go."

"And what makes you so special that you need to see the head boss?" the legate asked, eyes narrowing.

Troyton thought of Grayspace and Scipio, the Synths, and the small pit in his stomach that gradually sunk deeper. "I commanded a squad that found Synths out in Grayspace. Although, I may have just revealed classified information."

The legate laughed heartily. "Not as classified as you think. Your story has spread throughout my ranks, it's inspired many of them to continue the fight toward the real enemy." A bomb exploded a few blocks away, followed by gunfire and screams. Neither soldier paid it any attention.

"Meaning no disrespect, sir," he continued, standing on his toes. "I do have urgent business with the general."

The legate nodded. "I'll bring you to Marko. Grab your hoverbike and follow me." The two soldiers boarded their respective hoverbikes and headed southwest to one of the pyramids.

"I didn't get your name, Legate." Troyton said as they zipped through the streets. The Fyrossian capital was nearly the scale of Rome, but without any of the people walking along the sidewalks or cars in the streets. It possessed none of the electricity that a capital city should have. He imagined Rome would as a warzone and shuddered.

"Mirius, from Tisillio, a few miles outside Rome. You from one of those moon bases?"

"Casca…" Troyton said, struggling to talk while maintaining the same breakneck speed of his guide.

"Never heard of it," Mirius said

"It's not much to see." Troyton told him, remembering what the legate had said earlier. "So, everyone knows our frigates fly to Grayspace next?"

"Most of the officers know. There is no official order from Rome yet, but we are anticipating a long campaign ahead."

Troyton took a long time to absorb that information. Mirius misrepresented his contorted face as a struggle to keep the conversation going, so he continued. "This has to be one of the most deftly performed invasions I have ever had the privilege to participate in."

"It must be a favorable sign from the Immortals." Troyton replied absentmindedly, his focus dedicated to dodging scrap metal strewn about the broken city by shifting his bodyweight on the glider.

They passed a small factory building with a rounded roof sticking out from an otherwise crumbled block. KOH soldiers gathered around it. As soon as they were in order, they lobbed grenades through the broken windows of the upper floor. A few muffled screams rang from the factory's interior, but all sound was overshadowed by the harsh snap of the grenades detonating at once. Troyton slowed his bike to get a better view.

Smoke spilled from the shattered windows. The soldiers stood stealthily by the walls, watching each exit. A handful of Fyrossians rushed from the building, most covered in ash but some too were on fire. As soon as they saw sunlight, they were met with a hail of lasers and bullets. Troyton wondered what crimes the Fyrossians committed to deserve such hostility.

The legate continued casually: "The Immortals may have played a role in this victory, but the day is owed to Drake Bodewin."

Troyton's attention shifted back to Mirius. "How so?"

"Lord Bodewin aligned himself with a terrorist faction of Fyrossians. They gave him access to the city's sewer system, including a route leading to each pyramid's shield generators. Before the battle started, Lord Bodewin and a small battalion destroyed the generators before a single shot was fired. The result is the sound victory we're witnessing now."

"An excellent strategy," Troyton complimented. Drake Bodewin was a legend coming from the Civil War. The brother of the Queen of the KOH, putting such a vital leader behind enemy lines seemed like a major risk. But that was the beauty of the KOH, no sacrifice was too great for the betterment of humanity.

The buildings became more spacious and sumptuous as they neared the pyramid. The facades of each building had windows placed in patterns that formed squares, triangles, or rhombuses. The windows radiated a range of luminescent colors coming from strange, glowing orbs hanging from inside.

The stink of fire and death swelled as they went on. Troyton guessed this stench stemmed from the dead bodies baking in the sun, some of which had likely been there throughout the day. Many of the KOH soldiers kept their helmets on even after the battle was over, and now he understood why.

The massive obstruction that was one of the great Fyrossian pyramid looked to be made of pure, black hematite. The thin golden scrawl sketched over the pyramid shimmered in the sun and pulsed like the heartbeat of an enormous beast. At first, it looked like the unhinged scribblings of a child. Only upon further study did he find himself feeling the reverence of the golden-laced sketches, despite being completely oblivious to their significance. An unworldly weight elicited from these symbols and onto Troyton, overwhelming him with the guilt that he could be desecrating something sacred, something beyond his ability to comprehend.

Knowing there was no turning back, he thanked Mirius for his help and climbed the steps to the atrium.

The first floor of the pyramid was spacious with windowless walls that ascended at a nearly unnoticeable upward angle. Human soldiers buzzed about the place, sharing stories with one another of the battle, other adventures, or home. Troyton walked aimlessly across the tiled floor, searching for General Antonius Marko.

The general was a familiar name to him, but it did not carry the same esteem as many of the legendary military leaders he had studied. Marko was a child during Caesar's Civil War but distinguished himself as a student in one of the off-world military academies and further surpassed his potential when granted governorship of a KOH colony after his graduation. Marko's triumphs in colonization earned him the title of 'general' at a young age and made him a necessary mind behind the invasion of the Fyrossian home-world.

If rumors were to be believed, General Marko would be chosen to spearhead the attacks on the Synths. At least, this is what Troyton was told by some soldiers milling about the pyramid. As much as he enjoyed gossiping among the other soldiers, he had to remain focused on his mission. Perhaps he would ask Marko when he found him.

The ancient throne room of the Fyrossian Emperor was simplistic in design, moderate in its luxuries, and a time capsule of culture from a classic era. Globes of light were scattered about the pointed ceiling, heavy rounded pillars were erected on the sides of the room leading to the dais, and the same pulsing gold writing on the outside of the pyramid was sketched into the interior walls. Troyton's cleated boots echoed thunderously as he approached the throne, making him feel reckless like an animal inside a glass shop.

Eight figures stood in a semicircle by the dais, every eye on Troyton as he made his raucous entrance.

"Who in the Hell are you?" a man asked. He wore a fine gray tunic with a plethora of silver and gold badges adorned on his right breast. He was a young man, in his late twenties by his appearance, with wide eyes and an oddly nervous demeanor. Troyton guessed him to be General Antonius Marko.

"Centurion Vorenus, sir. I was told to report to you once the battle was over."

The general's laugh was weak and snobbish. "If you were anyone else, I would have told you to find a Fyrossian whorehouse and fuck off. But you're the Synth conqueror, I'm not sure which one of us has the greater pleasure of this meeting."

Beside the general was a Roman soldier who, judging by his abnormally heavy armor set, was likely a personal bodyguard. Three other figures stood behind them in the shadows of the dais. Troyton absentmindedly assumed they were more of Marko's soldiers.

Across from them were two Fyrossians; orange-skinned with long, bony foreheads, almond eyes, and lines on their cheeks that may have been gills. The male Fyrossian was bald, while the female had long, black hair wrapped in dreadlocks. They both wore lavish silk robes and sported elegant diamond bands on their arms gleaming in the dimly lit throne room.

It dawned on Troyton that he was in the presence of royalty.

"If we could return to our negotiations, general," the Fyrossian emperor stated. "My wife and I are eager to go over the terms of this surrender." There was child in the arms of the empress.

Marko nodded. "You are dismissed for the day. We'll continue our conversation once the heat of battle has cooled. I will call for my guards to escort you back to your room." The "And keep a watchful eye on you" was heavily implied.

"Your generosity meets no ends," the emperor said, all cordial. As he and his family turned, the three specters closest to the dais finally spoke up.

"The child stays," one of the shadows demanded. They had been so quiet, so covert, that Troyton had hardly noticed their presence. He saw the billowing silver robes of all three shrouded figures and scowled. *Inquisitors, the rebellious brood of the Paladin Order. Witches and warlocks, manipulators of the dark arts, and allies of the KOH and Triumvirate.*

The emperor did his best to conceal his uncertainty. "Excuse me, Lord Inquisitor?"

The Inquisitor stepped forward, his bone pale face touching the light. Small, bloodred eyes considered Troyton for a moment, then returned to the Fyrossians. This mage was of the Enfari race, the rejected brothers and sisters of the Denvari Union. "Put the boy down."

The empress turned to her husband, who reluctantly encouraged her to obey.

"He's not any harm to you," she pleaded. "We promised to publicly renounce our titles as soon as we can. None of our children will have any claims to the throne. He'll just be another Fyrossian boy."

Marko hummed. "We are well aware of your three children, empress. Two are accounted for, the middle one you've been trying to hide from us."

The emperor chose his words carefully. "My son is a priest, off-planet studying and spreading the word of the Immortals. He renounced any of his allegiances to me years ago. He is of no one's concern but the Immortals themselves."

"Then pray tell me which temple he serves," Marko insisted. "KOH databases are quite dense. We'll certainly find it, and swing by and say 'hello' to the priest."

"I don't remember the name of it..."

"It is against the rules of his brotherhood to tell us," the empress added. "It is an especially strict religious order. Those who join must separate themselves from their past lives entirely if they are to spread the graces of the Immortals."

"Your children hold as much value to me as the Fyrossian blood on my boots," the lead Inquisitor declared. He struggled to make his raspy voice sound deep and menacing, but it only came across as an unconventionally loud whisper. Troyton spotted a metal casing over the right side of his face, like a chrome jawbone.

The Inquisitor continued. "That thing in your arms is an unregistered mage, and it looks to be well over the age of appropriate registration. As you know, the Triumvirate has only one punishment suitable for this heinous crime."

Marko jumped in, his voice shaking. "It's a law loosely enforced. Surely Caesar will overlook this matter –"

"The child needs to die, by order of the Triumvirate," the Inquisitor demanded. His companions, two faceless demons dressed in similar silver cloaks, stepped forward. Each wore a white mask with black holes around the eyes and a slight crest in the center for the nose. Enfari masks, Troyton knew. One of the masked Inquisitors was tiny, maybe five feet tall at the most, and swaddled in silver cloth. The other Inquisitor was giant, perhaps taller than Troyton, with mountainous shoulders and a barreling chest. Considering the Inquisitor's massive breastplate and long warhammer at his back, only a creature of incredible strength could support that additional weight.

    The Fyrossians cowered as the Inquisitors advanced. Marko meekly commanded the mages to stand down, but his orders were met with deaf ears. Troyton's stomach fluttered, having never before witnessed the implausible, yet all too real Inquisitors in action.

    The small Fyrossian boy trembled, clutching at his mother's skirts, unable to comprehend the situation entirely but realizing all too well that the cloaked apparitions were coming for him. *Such innocent eyes.* He imagined what the Inquisitors would do to him: set him afire with the snap of a finger, eviscerate him with a crooked glare, or turn him into water and watch his remains wash down the steps. These images accelerated his thoughts into a rapid pace, his mind slipping away and his body becoming a puppet to impulse.

    Marko stood stupefied, the Fyrossians stuck in aghast horror. *No one will intervene.*

    Troyton palmed his belt and found a flash grenade in a holster. The flash would render everyone in the room blind for several moments, except for Troyton whose genetics could resist the effects. How the flash grenade would affect the mages, especially the big one, was a mystery, but this was not the time to ponder such questions. Without hesitation, the flash grenade spiraled across the floor.

    A sharp, piercing bang followed by a scintillating flash of light turned the whole world into white nothingness. Troyton's eyes burned, his brain pounded inside his skull, but the advanced humanoid powered through. He searched with blind hands until they wrapped around the Fyrossian boy's wrist.

    He ran aimlessly, armed solely with the instinct to protect the child, a child who had meant nothing to him moments ago.

    Concerns for Scipio and the Synths vanished, the dreams of glory and prestige in the KOH military nonexistent. Caesar would not stand for the execution of a child, no matter the race.

Troyton pulled the child along, unaware of the boy's resistance. He heard a shriek from behind but did not take the time to look back.

With his vision returning, black shapes took form against a white void, noiseless apart from an incessant ringing. Freedom was in reach, but prohibited by a set of hidden stairs that abruptly turned Troyton's heroic stride into a perilous tumble.

He shot back to his feet as soon as his bearings were with him again. His first concern was for the boy. He snapped his head back and forth in frantic search, but the child was nowhere in sight. However, the Inquisitor was.

The flash grenade had no effect on the Enfari Inquisitor. His red eyes were cold and emotionless, but his teeth grinded relentlessly in pained animosity. Troyton became paralyzed by an untraceable fear, and when the metal-jawed Inquisitor revealed a long, pointed fingernail, he was unable resist. The cut left on his cheek was shallow, but the poison soon filled his veins, and the sickly sensation that overwhelmed his body was the last of his memories.

# MARION (IV)

Frequent blackouts delayed the trial several days after the arrival of the judicial representative from Rome.

Marion found this odd, as Romulus rarely suffered a single power outage, let alone a series of them in a short period of time. He could imagine Tarius' panic. With Headmaster Polanis short of a head, he was effectively in charge of all the academy's operations and was certainly behaving as the most obedient of pets for the representative to ensure this position became permanent. These blackouts could not have favored Tarius; if anything, they benefited Marion's case against his incompetent principal.

The thought of Tarius as headmaster was horrifying. In a way, Polanis respected his rebellious attitude, which he took for granted until he finally pushed the headmaster's patience over the edge. "Tolerance" was not a word in Tarius' vocabulary, so even if Marion could escape expulsion and imprisonment, he would have a target on his back until his very last day on Romulus.

And that day may be imminent.

A Roman soldier dressed in full military attire entered his chamber unannounced and ordered Marion to the auditorium. He obeyed without objection and followed the soldier.

Located on the ground floor of Lorneway, the auditorium was by far the largest and most spacious room of the academy. The floor and walls were painted black, making the room appear dimensionless, while the metal seats were cream-colored and the stage an unmissable white spectacle.

Three thousand faces turned to Marion as he entered through a pair of wide doors and descended the long range of steps to the stage. He refused to acknowledge the crowd, knowing he could easily be overwhelmed by stage fright. Everec advised him to maintain a confident exterior in front of the judge, and for once Marion was going to follow every word of the Dean's advice wholeheartedly.

He had been coached endlessly by Mister Everec in the weeks spent anticipating the arrival of the judge. The Dean of Students drilled him on every possible question Tarius could ask, any method the principal could use to push him toward self-immolation. At first, Marion was ungodly nervous. Everec morphed every statement he made into an indictment. But as they practiced, he grasped the rhetoric of a man on trial for his life.

Two paper-thin tables were propped up on either side of the stage. At one table sat Principal Tarius and three other members of the academy's teaching staff, who unsurprisingly were also members of the Law department. At the other table, Mister Everec sat by himself. Between the two tables was a podium of darkened wood with the crest of the golden eagle of Rome proudly displayed at its center. At the podium stood the man who held Marion's life in his hands.

He crossed Mister Everec first as he walked up the stage. They shook hands and Everec pulled him close in embrace. "Keep your eyes on the judge as you approach him," he whispered. "Shake his hand and address him as 'sir.' Please don't forget to salute."

Marion turned to the judge and marched to the podium like a true Roman soldier. "Hail Caesar!" He saluted more passionately than ever before.

"Hail Caesar," the judge returned. He was much thinner than Marion expected, with thick, salt-and-pepper curls and a goatee consisting of little more than a couple wisps of hair. His handshake, too, was shockingly pathetic and bony.

"It is an honor to have you oversee my trial, sir," was all he could come up with before retreating to Mister Everec. He prayed that the statement was not as dumb as it sounded. He scrutinized the crowd, searching for his flower among the piles mud, but she was not there as far as he could tell.

The judge raised his hand, signaling to everyone in attendance to sit and be attentive. Marion soothed the creases of his uniform, though he had already ironed it to perfection. His anxious hands grasped and clawed for something to do. Across the stage sat Principal Tarius, whose disdain was palpable enough to build a wall between them. *Tarius will have to earn his ambitions,* Marion thought, anticipating the principal's defeat as much as his own victory.

While interned to his room for the weeks before the trial, servants came to his vaulted door to drop off meals. Consistently, these were heavy meats cooked bloody red. This may have been by Tarius' design, to remind him of Polanis' head every time he had to eat. If this was his tactic, it worked. He had lost several pounds during his internment, due to his newfound disgust for red meat.

The judge made an echoing thump as he tapped the microphone on the podium with his forefinger. Every single audience member heard him raucously clear his throat before delivering a prepared speech. "To King Caesar, every loss of human life before its time is viewed as a terrible tragedy, but few tragedies can be so horrific as the murder of a Roman veteran. To the students, faculty, and staff of the revered Academy of Romulus, my promise to you is that I, Pompilius Metarsus, on my honor as a consul, a Roman, and above all, as a human, swear to each and every one of you that Headmaster Polanis' death will not be in vain. His murderer will meet justice and his legacy will carry on through every student here today and every graduating class from Romulus in the future."

The crowd roared with vehement applause. They were not cheering for Polanis' storied career, but for Marion's indictment. Because most of the students who filled the auditorium were part of the graduating class, Marion did not recognize those who vocally craved his guilty verdict. Notoriety alone was enough to warrant such gleeful hatred. *They're using the same tactic as Tarius, they want me to lose my temper, to commit self-sabotage right before the judge.*

When the crowd settled down, Pompilius continued his speech. "Because I have been granted sole agency over this trial, I have taken it upon myself to plan out the proceedings. Today, the plaintiff will produce his evidence against the defendant as well as call upon any witnesses. Tomorrow, the defendant will be given the same privileges. On the third day, I will have my verdict to declare publicly."

Tarius smiled and thanked Pompilius in a way only the most egregious sycophant could. He walked to the edge of the stage, allowing for an intimate moment between himself and his audience.

His diction when addressing Marion was more flowery and less abrasive than it was when the two spoke in private. He attempted to draw sympathy from the crowd for Marion, but not in a way that suggested his innocence. The bastard son of traitors may as well have been declared a wild animal in front of Consul Pompilius and over a thousand of his peers. He was a creature that could not be held accountable for his actions, for they were done out of primal instinct, an instinct that Romans were too evolved from feeling. However, such a beast could not reside in the great halls of Romulus and must be thrown out of the academy and into a cage immediately.

A drip of sweat sunk down his forehead. What could a beast do when his master was so cruel? Tarius chained him to a desk, unfairly. If not for Everec coming to the rescue, he may have stayed chained until the day of his trial. It sounded absurd in his head, but he should not be naïve enough to underestimate the cruelties of his principal.

When Tarius concluded his opening diatribe, the crowd received him with applause. Pompilius was forced to thump on the microphone once again to have the auditorium quiet. The students had little love for their principal, as he was an unreasonable dictator to them as much as he was to Marion, but at least for today they had all united under the cause of removing the traitorous stain from their academy.

*The enemy of my enemy.*

Tarius called several of his teachers to testify, all of whom stating in a variety of forms that he was a troublemaker, a derelict to the bone who showed a psychopathic urge to resist proper social etiquette. These statements were mostly discarded by Pompilius, and Mister Everec's choice to not cross-examine sought to further emphasize their irrelevance. "A rogue student is not an anarchist,"

Pompilius said. "Many of the great military leaders of the KOH were deemed 'unteachable' during their youths."

Tarius' eyes twitched, and his fingers turned purple from being intwined together. He struggled to speak civilly to Marion and Everec, wanting rather to strangle them in their seats. *If one of us will boils over, it will not be me.*

Officer Brody was called up next, his metallic hands absorbing the white lights projecting from above the stage. "The bastard Marion has a gift for hitting other students with an electrified baton," Brody stated, his voice low and cruel. "He's strong and agile, I'd bet money he could beat any of our senior cadets." Marion appreciated the comments although they were meant to do him harm.

Pompilius observed Brody with more interest than any of the previous witnesses. "Forensic reports state that Polanis' head was taken off by a single swing of an unidentified object. Would you say he has the skills to do this?"

Brody's eyes shifted to Tarius. "It depends on the weapon, sir. If it can be retrieved, I would be more than willing to provide my insight. But if there is a student who could do the job, it would be the defendant."

This tickled the imagination of the Consul, and also deflated some of Marion's repressed optimism. Tarius, on the other hand, was revitalized by the newfound smell of blood in the water.

Vintrus delivered his testimony with the rehearsed charisma and enthusiasm that only the star-student of Romulus could possess. His testimony, or more accurately, his self-adulating victory speech, recounted several instances where Marion "cruelly" and "unreasonably" attacked him from behind, leaving Vintrus with "no choice" but to defend himself.

"He is the son of traitors," the star-student said, reiterating a point that was made to no end. "And with that taint comes the genetic inability to tell right from wrong."

Mister Everec approached the podium with the grace of a silent hunter. "That may be so," the Dean considered. "Just a day before Polanis' death, you were attacked by Marion, weren't you?"

Vintrus smiled smugly. "Yes, sir. The traitor walked right up and challenged me for no rightful reason. I had no choice but to defend myself." The star-student could not resist but to add: "And I did defend myself properly."

Everec paced across the stage, deftly spun on his heel, and returned to Vintrus. "Let me ask you this: are the bruises on Marion's face a result of you 'defending' yourself?"

"Uh, yes, sir."

The Dean of Students stroked his pointed chin. "And after this act of self-preservation, did you then try to beat the correct moral principles into the defendant?"

"What do you mean?" Vintrus asked, sounding innocent.

"The bruises on Marion's face indicate you acted well beyond the means of defending yourself. Boys will be boys, of course, but I find it shocking that one cadet would go to such excessive lengths to harm another student, a future brother on the battlefield. To say I'm curious of your explanation would be an understatement."

"I-I-I uhhhh..." His face was shiny beneath the hot, white overhead lights.

"As a matter of fact, I'd go as far as to say it looks like you enjoyed brutalizing the defendant. An unnecessarily violent act such as this forces me to wonder if we have the wrong student in the defendant's seat. Wouldn't you say?"

"Well-uh-well- I-can't-uhhh..."

"That will be all, cadet." Everec said, acting with a civil hostility that Marion never had the pleasure to witness before.

Vintrus sprinted from the stage as if he had discovered a bomb beneath his seat.

Then, it was Marion's turn to take the stand.

Every step he made awkwardly clapped throughout the auditorium as he walked along the stage. He gazed out into the seats, searching for Octavia once again. And once again, she was invisible. Tarius pointed his arms in the direction of the hot seat, as if he could not find it himself. He took the chair and slid it closer to the table, the metal supports grinding and screeching against the wooden stage.

"Mister Marion Donatus..." Tarius began.

"Principal Tarius," Marion returned, trying his best to seem cool.

The principal chuckled lowly. "We're no strangers to each other, are we?"

A *lead*, Marion knew, Everec's coaching ringing in his ear. A *student familiar with the principal is a troublemaker.* "We are. It's your job to be close to every student."

Tarius grimaced slightly, betraying his truth for just a second. "But you I'm extra familiar with. As was the late headmaster. In fact, he had ordered you to his office moments before his murder."

"He did. That's when I found him."

"No, no, no. You're jumping ahead." Tarius said, wagging his finger. Marion cursed under his breath. "Why were you called to Headmaster Polanis' office in the first place?"

"He caught Vintrus and I fighting the day before. This meeting was to decide on my punishment." *He has no way of knowing the threat of expulsion, does he?*

"To warrant a private meeting, the punishment he decided on must have been extreme," Tarius led again.

Marion shrugged. "I have to idea, sir."

"But I think you do. As a repeat offender against the code of our great academy, I would imagine this punishment to be more severe than any of the rest."

*He doesn't know,* Marion tried to convince himself. He took a deep breath and considered Mister Everec's teachings. "At this point, it would be blind speculation."

The principal's jaw clenched. For the first time, Marion was the one causing the anger. It made him feel quite smart. "As the bastard product of traitors, I suspect nothing but deception from you!" Tarius declared vehemently. A deafening silence assumed the auditorium. The principal searched for support, but found none of it. Defeated, he retreated back to his table.

Marion, coolly, turned to Consul Pompilius and said, "What my parentage has to do with this trial is beyond me. I have no memories of my mother and father, and thus no influence from their traitorous ways. I was raised by the academy, and so I am Roman."

"I would have to agree with the defendant." Pompilius said, directing his scorn at Tarius. "I will not have my court descend into a barrage of irrelevant name-calling."

Tarius' expression returned to a fiery unease. He had expected Vintrus to do his job, but Romulus' favorite cadet proved to be ineffectual in everything outside fist fights. Other than Brody's testimony, the plaintiff's case was unveiled to be ungrounded and hollow. Unless Tarius could uncover the murder weapon, Brody's speculations were all but worthless too.

Marion let out a sigh of relief, being pleasantly surprised that the judge was not as eager to condemn him as his peers.

"Is there anything else that the plaintiff would like to present before the trial is closed for the day?" Pompilius offered.

Tarius shuffled a handful of papers on his desk and pushed the chair backwards with a screech as his sausage legs extended. "One last piece of evidence, sir. These documents were found in Headmaster Polanis' desk drawer."

He handed the papers to Pompilius. The judge scrutinized them for a long moment. The auditorium was silent, with the occasional rustling of papers to break the stillness. Marion's own heartbeat thumped in his stomach, causing instant nausea.

"Is this Headmaster Polanis' signature?" Pompilius asked. The judge's face contorted. He looked at Marion as if he had two heads. Marion, in turn, swallowed a brick.

Tarius nodded. "And there are many more documents in our storage room to verify it." The judge returned to observing the papers. No one made a notion to speak. Everec anxiously scratched the side of his head.

Finally convinced that what he had been handed was legitimate, Pompilius said: "It appears I have been presented with documents signed by Headmaster Polanis finalizing the expulsion of the defendant from the Academy of Romulus."

The audience responded with a universal gasp. Marion swore by accident and Tarius revealed the most self-satisfactory grin a man could ever make. Eruption ensued in the auditorium and, within the mix of screams and hollers, rancorous accusations of "murderer" shot his way.

Pompilius demanded order, but seeing that effort futile with a crazed and confused crowd, he quietly dismissed the plaintiff and defendant until tomorrow.

Lyndon Everec took Marion by the arm and snuck him behind the stage to an emergency exit, dodging thrown shoes as they made their escape.

"I had no idea about the papers." Marion said, half in a daze. Everec moved swiftly, at such a speed that he had to jog to keep up. They were crossing over to the dormitory, where his room had become his prison cell.

"Did you hear me?" Marion asked, with a spice of attitude.

"We'll talk when we get somewhere private."

They arrived at room 304 in complete silence. When Everec sealed the vault door shut, Marion blurted: "Is it okay to talk now, SIR?"

"You might want to sit."

"I don't want to sit! I'm screwed. Even if, by some miracle, Pompilius finds me innocent, the whole academy will still see me as a murderer." *Octavia will hate me. I'll have nothing. Expulsion would be a mercy.*

Everec bit his lip to fight back the words in his throat.

Marion continued his tirade. "After all my time here, I get kicked out a year before graduation. Say something, Everec! Are you going to visit my jail cell in Rome? Because there is no point in defending me tomorrow."

"You're right, there will be no need to defend you tomorrow." Everec said, still apprehensive.

Marion groaned, "What?" The Dean of Students was speaking nonsensically now. Truly, there was no hope.

"I've hidden this from you for a long time, perhaps unjustifiably so, but you must remember that I only have the best intentions in mind."

Marion felt as if he had a terminal illness. "Is there something wrong with me?" he asked, desperately.

"No, no." Everec shook his head. "It's the opposite, actually. You're special, Marion, it's just difficult for me to explain."

He sat on the edge of his bed and crossed his arms. "So, start at the beginning."

Everec processed his advice, then said: "You will not be here tomorrow to be defended. By the time the trial resumes, we will both be far away from Romulus."

Marion smiled, unconcerned about the who, what, where, when, why, and how of it. Everec did not form a defense for his trial, he had crafted an escape plan. "Explain."

# ELYSANDE (III)

"When can I go to academy?" Julia asked one morning on the backyard veranda outside their home. Elysande had finished eating breakfast with her daughter and was enjoying a moment of tranquility before a day full of mundane conversations with Rome's honored guests of the New Year's celebration.

"You're already in school." she replied, playing dumb. A cool breeze graced the veranda, carrying with it the sweet fragrance of the flowered bushes in the front yard.

Julia shook her head. "No, no, no. I mean military school."

"Soon, you're almost old enough. Are you in such a hurry to leave me?" Julia was twelve years old, so in truth, she was plenty old enough to enlist into a military school. Some of those off-world academies even take them before they can walk. But she was a princess, enlisting into an academy would be… complicated. The other students would love her, and she would excel above the rest, but she was royalty. She would never fully immerse. Supreme nobility was her privilege and her curse.

"Lance does his schooling from home, but I won't." Julia's face turned guilty. "I would come back and visit as often as I can."

"Sweet girl," Elysande smiled. Looking at Julia was like gazing into the past. Not so much in appearance, but in demeanor and mind, all the important qualities.

"I think it's a waste if Lance goes to military school in my place. He doesn't care about learning; he just mopes around."

"Mind your tongue, Julia." Elysande warned. She wasn't wrong, however. Lance had not taken to his studies well at all. *He should* have been shipped off-world to attend school, but I was weak and let him stay home. The vulnerability would be good for him, as he takes too many of his luxuries for granted.

The queen sipped juice from her glass and gazed at the light green hills, olive trees, and rows of lucrative grape vines. Rome was located on the southernmost peninsula of Carcia, the closest city to the equator besides Paranthon's Cross. Cool days were a rarity, something Elysande grew to appreciate during the cold season around the New Year. If she ate breakfast outside in her motherland this time of the year, her food would have frozen before the plate hit the table.

"You're the princess of the KOH. Orbis could be yours to command one day. Why would you give that up for a life in the army?"

Julia stared out into the yard, the sun beaming down on her curly, reddish-brown hair. She was exceptionally reflective for a twelve-year-old girl. "Let Natalia be the princess. I want to go on adventures."

Elysande sneered. *Silly girl, Natalia is your enemy. She is Caesar's firstborn, and your safety will not be assured as long as she lingers about.*

"Can I tell you a secret?" Elysande asked; Julia nodded eagerly. "You're the only one in Rome I like to talk to. Everyone else is a bumbling, pea-brained fool. You want an adventure? Once the New Year festival passes, how about we visit your grandmother's home in northern Mercia?"

Julia giggled. "I would love it!"

"Then it's a deal." They each raised their respective glass of juice and clinked them together to solidify this newly formed pact.

The Senate was filled to the brim with senators from around Orbis and the surrounding colonies on foreign worlds. The massive stadium was alive with incoherent chatter, but all noise died when Caesar entered the stage and approached the podium. Elysande was by his side, along with Reynard and the king's brother, Tullius. The Praetorian Elite stood sentry in the background, conspicuously missing one member.

"Noble Senators of the KOH!" Sutorian announced, his voice louder than a microphone. "I present to you, King Gaius Julius Caesar!"

"HAIL CAESAR!" the faceless mob called out in return.

"Thank you, Sutorian," Caesar said. "Everyone must be noticing an absent member of my Elite guard. To dispel any rumors before they can spread: Fulvius Galla, one of my most-trusted Roman knights, died while off-duty far away from the city center. Although not every fact is known at this time, I can confirm to everyone here that he perished in combat against enemies of the state."

*Good for Galla*, Elysande thought to herself, *his reward for being a junkie is a hero's death in the history books… I hope I can be just as lucky.*

A senator at the front of the stage raised his hand in a request to address the king and fellow senators.

"Felix, you may speak freely," Caesar allowed.

The senator stood from his seat. He wore the same white toga as every other member of his profession, save the colored sash that divided each senator by their district. Felix's sash was colored magenta. "Thank you, King Caesar. I believe I speak for every senator here when I offer my condolences to Ser Galla and his family. It is truly a tragic end, but a brave death most of the Praetorian Guard strive for."

Caesar agreed. "I am fortunate to have the most loyal protectors on the planet. However, I did not call everyone here to mourn the loss of a Roman knight; I stand before you all today to humbly request your support. Although the Fyrossians are nearly defeated, a new threat looms at our doorstep, a threat unlike anything we have encountered for thousands of years. Reports of Synth sightings in Grayspace are growing by the day. My legions sent to contact the Synths have been met with violence in return. And now, I need the help of every senator in a war that is becoming more likely by the day."

Another senator stood to speak. "You will always have our backing, King Caesar. However, I don't believe I am the only one who finds this request unusual. We've all heard the rumors, surely, but rumors do not make bedtime stories any more real. This is not doubt or suspicion, my king, just curiosity."

Elysande laughed to herself. It would take more than some brittle-boned senator to shake the king.

"No offense taken, Senator Lucio. I bring to you strange and unexpected news, but it is true, nonetheless. I've spoken to three soldiers who were attacked by Synths, I've seen videos and photos of creatures far beyond the scope of imagination, and soon enough all will be revealed to my kingdom. Imperator Tarquinius combs the Grayspace cluster as we speak, and he needs our support."

"And what will be required of us?" Senator Lucio asked. *Gods, he's so old and decrepit. Is this the best Carcia has to offer for politicians?*

"My first wave of the invasion is set to begin after the turn of the New Year." Caesar said, speaking fearlessly in front of thousands of noble senators. "I propose a formal declaration of war against the Synths. While you are all in the city, I suggest this be voted on within the fortnight. If my proposal is passed, I will need each of you to rally support in your home districts. This enemy is an enigma, but it will require full participation from the entirety of the KOH if we are to ensure victory."

The next half an hour involved a handful of senators taking the floor one at a time to proudly proclaim their support to King Caesar. This was not so much a testament to the dedication they had for the KOH, but rather a display of how desperate each man and woman was to win their senatorial seat back in the next election. Caesar welcomed the overwhelming support wholeheartedly, but even he must have recognized the duplicitous nature of his senators.

Elysande entered a trance to pass the time, a skill she had mastered throughout her years of laborious talks and meetings. When she was disturbed, she expected it to be from a guard telling her that the session was over, but much to her surprise it was a senator.

"My word means very little in Carcia. If you want to do some meaningful bootlicking, get into my husband's line."

Senator Felix smiled. "My seat is not on the market this season. How about we go for a walk? Get away from the stuffiness of the Senate."

Elysande gave him a quizzical look. Felix was a senator from Rezza, a city in the northernmost district of Carcia. He was the picturesque northern Carcian: tan skin, but not quite as dark as his southern counterparts, black hair cut short but with long bangs, and a slightly protruding gut befitting of the lackadaisical lifestyle of the region.

"I'm flattered, but I can't at the moment," the queen said, she barely knew the man apart from his growing reputation, but she liked his forwardness. Felix had become a rock star of sorts in the Senate, obtaining a large amount of popularity in a short period of time. She vaguely remembered at a council meeting Caesar complimenting his sudden rise to fame. To say the least, she was curious about him. "I have a lunch appointment with my sweet stepdaughter. But perhaps tonight?"

Felix bowed. "I am at my queen's command. Tonight, outside your estate?"

Elysande looked to Caesar, who was surrounded by a legion of adoring senators, much to the displeasure of Sutorian and his guards. "You'd best be there, or it might cost your head."

Natalia Caesar was the spitting image of her father. Tall, with curly brown hair, a long nose, olive skin, and a perpetual aura of clear determination. Natalia was a Caesar through and through. She welcomed Elysande and her father warmly, and the queen pretended to be happy in return. They met at *Il Cacciatore*, a restaurant near the Senate building and bordering the Forum. Although the establishment did not discriminate, the prices were uniquely reasonable for those of the patrician class. Anyone else would simply turn away in disgust or shame.

Elysande grabbed her seat by the window. Peering outside, she saw the wide-open Forum bustling with people. It was a unique time in Rome, with humans from across Orbis converging into one city. The New Year season may be stressful, but it was an unparalleled time to people-watch.

"How did your Senate meeting go?" Natalia asked. She wore a light, black, button-down blouse with white trousers. She was a simple dresser, but her Roman beauty could make even the most mundane attire stunning.

"As well as they all go," Caesar responded. "But I'm more interested in you."

Natalia shrugged. "I finished up my semester and spent some time with friends on the Kappelli Isles. I thought I'd come to Rome for the New Year... and ask you about the Synths."

Caesar sighed. "The rumors have spread that far, haven't they? These damnable creatures have swarmed my life of late. I would like one conversation where I don't have to explain myself like a madman."

"Very well then," Natalia said. "I do have some exciting news for you: Proconsul Indro Bebti has accepted me as his censor. I'm set to start in two months' time, so I won't be able to stay in Rome for long."

"I had no idea!" Caesar said, elated. "Bebti is one of the best proconsuls in the kingdom, learning from him could be the best thing for you."

"I would have to agree." Elysande said, feigning equal enthusiasm. "The legislative work will likely be daunting, but no task is insurmountable for a Caesar." *The girl is already trying to make friends in high places.* Bebti was the proconsul of Paranthon's Cross, the last and most fortified base on the road to Rome. If enemy forces could accomplish the impossible and break through the mighty fortress, then nothing could stop them on their path to Rome. To be proconsul of such a strategic position was no easy feat, and Bebti was more than capable for the job. Yes, *Natalia does choose her friends wisely.*

"How did this come to be?" Caesar asked. "Did you reach out to him?"

Natalia smiled. "Of course, I did. Opportunities don't make themselves. This is the kind of job I've been studying for. I just hope I can live up to the family name."

"I have no doubt," Caesar said, confidently. "But, as a father, I must warn you of the environment of Paranthon's Cross. It's cut-throat, as I trust you know."

He was right in his cautions. The Cross was a military district. It possessed a civilian population, but it mostly housed hosts of legions and war machines serving as Rome's reserves in case of a crisis. Unlike cities and towns, military districts were not overseen by lords and ladies, but instead proconsuls who were elected to the role, rather than inheriting it. With that said, Proconsul Bebti had a target on his head. His mistakes increase another ambitious general's chances of snatching the consulship away from him. As censor, Natalia in many ways helped decide the tenure of her proconsul.

Natalia stared at her father and winked, "I anticipate the challenge."

A waiter came by and poured each one of them a glass of white wine. Gaius and Natalia drank it fervently. Elysande would have preferred something else, something less Carcian. "There is something I would like to propose to you." Caesar said, strategically waiting until the wine was out before raising the issue. "Timothy Mauvern will be arriving in Rome within the next few days, I was hoping you would join me in the greeting party to welcome our esteemed guests."

"And will Jacob Mauvern be present?" Natalia asked, raising her eyebrows.

"Of course."

"And would you like me to display my feminine charms for him upon arrival? Or should I wait until the banquet where I am sure you've already assigned our seats together?"

"Are you seeing anyone?" Caesar asked.

Natalia crossed her arms. "Well, no…" She was fast, but not fast enough.

"Are you opposed to the idea of seeing anyone?" Elysande added. She liked watching Natalia get defensive.

"No, but this seems… archaic."

"Look Natty," Caesar said. "You are your own woman, and I won't force you into anything, but there is an opportunity here to strengthen the bond between our families, and I only ask for you to consider it."

Elysande added: "Plus, I hear Jacob is quite the gentleman. You could have an easy life ahead of you profiting from the spice trade without needing to raise a finger."

A marriage between Natalia and the Mauvern runt would mean she would be sent off to Tisoni, permanently. Caesar would never make her the heir if it meant bringing the Mauverns into the royal line. They could undo his decades of hard work in an afternoon. A *Mauvern in Rome gives him nothing, but a Caesar in Tisoni grants him countless benefits. If Lance could marry a Roman girl, the throne would be as good as his.*

"Why Jacob Mauvern? Wouldn't a nice patrician be a better fit for me?" Natalia asked.

"It could be," Caesar said. "But the Mauverns are unequivocally on the rise. If Timothy can successfully transition into his role as Overseer of Tisoni, his family could become one of the richest on Orbis."

"But why take the position away from Omir? His family was hardly a problem to us before. Why risk putting an outsider in charge of Tisoni?" Natalia asked, trying to learn from her father.

Caesar steepled his hands on the table. "The Omirs for centuries have cared more about controlling the spice trade than unifying their country. A legitimately unified Tisoni will be a powerful ally for us, and it is something that will never be accomplished with an Omir in charge. Centuries of bad blood exist between the noble families of Tisoni, so much so that they will never allow one family to rise above the rest. They would more likely pay homage to an outsider who proves his worth than they ever would to one of their own."

"It seems like a bold decision," Natalia said.

"It's the curse of ruling: no decision is ever made without consequence."

Natalia pondered her father's request. She finished her wine as if the right answer was written at the bottom of the glass. "Fine. I will talk to Jacob Mauvern, I'll dine with him too if he makes a good impression. However, I will be serving my time as censor regardless of how this goes."

"I wouldn't have it any other way," Caesar said. They communicated with more than words. Nothing was more dangerous than two of the shrewdest minds in the world working in cohesion, especially when they opposed her.

Queen Elysande retired to her estate as soon as she could without appearing impolite. Ser Richard Dance was the one to take her home, and she ordered him to drive by hover car despite

Rome's insistence that she did not. Dance would not object, nor would any officer of the law attempt to stop her.

Senator Felix would be arriving in two hours, so Elysande made best use of the available free time. She returned to her personal gymnasium in the basement of the estate. Treadmill, stationary bike, rowing machine, all in rapid succession. During a festival that necessitated plenty of eating, drinking, and sitting, these would be the exercises that would help her maintain the figure she worked so hard to achieve. Elysande pushed herself until she was breathless, rehydrated, showered, then felt good as new. By the time Richard Dance announced Felix's arrival, she had accomplished everything she desired given the short timeframe.

"My queen," Senator Felix said as she opened the door. He took a moment to fawn over her tight, crimson red blouse, the gold necklace embedded with green emeralds around her neck that was once her mother's, and her long black boots decorated with glittering rhinestones. She barely put in a moment's effort to dress up for the senator, but she appreciated the compliment, nonetheless. "I hardly feel worthy to look upon you. Say the word and I will gouge my eyes out for committing such a sin."

"Save the seductive talk for Carcian girls, for Mercian women are made of stronger material." Elysande advised. "Few men possess the gall to invite me on a night out on our first meeting, I'd hate to have my expectations disappointed by such trite tactics."

Felix bowed. "I will be more alert then, knowing I have quite far to fall. Anyway, where is your husband? It would be rude of me to not pay my respects before we leave."

"If you want Caesar, go into the city center, that's where he spends all of his time." Elysande said.

Felix's face expressed no disappointment. "Never mind, shall we go?"

"We shall." She looked for Ser Dance and ordered him to stay at the house, which was code to follow her but remain out of sight. Dance nodded, a statue in fleshy form.

Walking in the night air, she wished she had done this more often. The western outskirts of the city were quiet come nightfall, and the gentle ocean breeze that rolled in from the not-too-distant shore was cool and refreshing. The winds here were nowhere near as strong as the ones in Mercia, but the chill was welcomed when most days in Rome ranged from hot to unbearably hot. All around her rang the echoes of bugs and birds living in the ample bushes and trees that decorated the outsides of every estate she and Felix strolled passed. Rome had never felt so beautiful.

"I have a question that's been bothering me," Elysande started.

"Please, by all means, ask it." Felix insisted.

"This may be blunt, but how old are you?"

"Thirty. I'm one of the youngest in the Senate. For that, it's hard not to be grateful."

"Don't sell yourself short, Senator. Plenty of Carcians twice your age only achieve half the success. We are a warrior people, regardless of all the social formalities. We are addicts of war and auctoritas. You, however, have achieved popularity without bloodshed. What's your secret?"

Felix pondered the question for a moment, then said: "Love of country, maybe. My people sense it, and that's how I earned both their trust and admiration."

"What do you miss about Rezza when you're gone?" Elysande asked the senator.

"I can't say I've been gone long enough to truly miss anything," Felix answered. He touched his pointer finger to his chin. "The people, maybe. In Rezza we keep things relaxed. Rome is the hub of Orbis, so it's busy by necessity. That makes people less trustworthy and more ambitious. Personally, I'm happy with my birthplace."

The queen laughed. "You contradict yourself, sir. You've been playing our game for a short time, and yet you're one of the most recognizable names in the Senate. A Rock Star from Rezza; you might be the only name I know from the whole region, let alone the city."

"Out of the living, maybe, but Rezza is rich with human history. Elvezio Gasardi was rumored to be born in Rezza, and he was the best of us all," Felix said. Elvezio was the first King of Humanity from roughly one thousand years ago, reigning in the longest and most successful dynasty humankind had ever known. *The Roman*

*Republic saw that the dynasty end, and then my husband repaid the debt.*

"True, you could be a descendant of the venerable Gasardi Kings." she said, half sarcastically.

Felix was not so flippant. "Then I'd be the luckiest man in the world."

They walked in silence for a moment. Elysande found the man's bluntness to be oddly alluring. *Are all northern Carcians like this?* "I noticed you dodged my accusation; I want to know what your game is. You're not as complacent as you want to appear to be."

"True, I am ambitious, but not for a selfish cause. I have dedicated myself to one purpose, a purpose no sacrifice is too worthy of. This allows me to take chances when other politicians, no matter how aspiring, will not. I owe a great deal of who I am today to outside influences, and I have every intention to return those favors."

Elysande inclined her head. "And what is this purpose?"

Felix stopped in his tracks. He turned to her with a face completely void of any false niceties. "Tell me this, my queen: who is the heir to Caesar's kingdom."

Elysande scowled. "Why do you deserve to know?" she asked. *Is he one of Natalia's spies? Did she fill his head with the promises of auctoritas if he helps her seize the throne? Well, the Rock Star of Rezza will need to be put in his place.*

Felix nodded, as if reassured about a secret hypothesis. "So you don't know. I would predict Natalia as the heir, as would many of the senators in our private discussions. She's the true Caesar, you and your children are outcasts, the black sheep, and you will be led to the slaughter when the time comes."

Elysande sneered. "Oh, so we're threatening each other now? I can have my personal security here in seconds and have you gutted in the street for speaking such words. I'm fully aware of my expendable position in Rome, and I'm prepared to defend myself for when that day comes."

"This is not a threat, but a proposition." Felix made sure to speak low. "I can offer you an escape from this life of uncertainty. If King Caesar truly valued you or the children you have together, his successor would be known. How would you like to never have to worry about this again? How would you like to remove Caesar from power?"

"You're mad," Elysande said. "Why would I trust you? Why would I think you care at all about me or my family?" She was still convinced that Felix was secretly Natalia's dog. *He could be leading me into a trap. Have my name disgraced to make her ascension all the easier. No, I won't have it.*

"Oh, you're right to not trust me. My duty is to the people of Orbis, and the best way to ensure humanity survives for the next thousand years is not to replace one king with another, but to overthrow the KOH and resurrect the Republic." Felix's convictions nearly masked his delusions. The Republic had been dead for two decades thanks to Caesar, and she was unaware anyone desired it to come back.

"You're asking me to willingly abdicate my position as queen to support some conspiracy?"

"I am granting you and your children the chance to carve out your own lives in the Republic, not to live each day in terror. True, you will be relinquishing significant authority, but you will win your own destiny in return."

Elysande shook her head. "Oh, I'm not in control? I could wrap my hands around your throat, squeeze the life out of you, and I won't suffer so much as a slap on the wrist. You may be the Rock Star of Rezza, but you're a bug in Rome."

"Killing me won't solve your problems," Felix assured her. "But listening to me will."

Elysande considered him for a long time. She kept her stare firm, giving him the impression that she could strike at any moment. "Say my ears are open. Say for a moment I'll take these delusions with an ounce of legitimacy. What then?"

"Plenty of us have been longing for the days of the Republic, and now is finally time to strike."

"Stop speaking vaguely!" she commanded. "Who craves the Republic?"

Felix laughed, shaking his head. "I won't go into specific yet, not until your allegiance is proven. But think of this practically. More territories of the KOH are ruled by elected officials than ever before. Governors and proconsuls, staples of any republic, are on the rise. Lords and ladies may still possess most of the power, but they are a deceptively dying breed. Another war between humans is coming, one fought between future and past. It's up to you to choose a side."

"And what if I give this news to Caesar?" Elysande challenged.

Felix was unfazed. "I knew the consequences of coming to you, and the role you could play in our glorious overthrow is more than worth the risk. But I won't be the only one who suffers the consequences. Fulvius Galla challenged us. A similar, tragic fate may await you and your loved ones too."

# MARION (V)

Kent Kentoshi was the first alien Marion had ever laid eyes on, and the words he spoke nearly caused him to lose his mind.

The girl in Everec's office, with pale golden hair and a look in her eyes that could only be politely described as off-kilter, was his sister. *Twin sister*, he thought, needing to sit down to support the burden of knowledge unloaded on his shoulders, *fathered by Marius Zoltor, the Archmage who waged war with King Caesar and the Triumvirate*. Marion said nothing, firmly expecting to be the victim of a bad dream or a cruel joke. *Perhaps Polanis is alive too, and this is all some ridiculously elaborate lesson in Roman morality.*

"It's true, Marion." Mister Everec said, delivering the deathblow to any semblance of sanity. "It was my responsibility to protect you until the Paladin Order was ready. Now they've called, and you must answer."

They had this conversation before. Right after the first day of the disastrous trial, Mister Everec told him the truth. At least, it was a fraction of the truth. Consul Pompilius had delayed the second day of the trial indefinitely, and Marion lived every subsequent day trying to come to terms with the apparent fact that he was, indeed, a mage. House arrest allowed him plenty of time to come to terms with this revelation, but any mental recovery he had made was promptly shattered with the further revelation of his parentage.

The Druin shot a glare at the Dean of Students, obviously having expected this conversation would not be necessary.

"Mister Everec," Marion began, addressing the Dean of Students politely but incredulously, "Were you going to tell me of my... family history if not for the arrival of... Kent?"

"You were destined to learn someday." Everec said, regret written on his face. "But not until we were both far away from Romulus. I made the judgement that you were safer living in the confines of a Roman academy thinking yourself the son of traitors than the son of the Archmage."

"You should have told me everything at once. I could have handled it," Marion lied.

"I know, but it took all my strength to tell you the truth. I pray you can forgive me."

"I am an advocate and experienced practitioner in the process of making amends, but this can be settled on the Seshora Araman, leagues away from this dreaded place," Kent interrupted. The Druin's paranoia was obvious, as not another soul on the academy had green skin and a crown of horns sprouting from the head. Just a glimpse of him would be enough to warrant a lockdown.

Marion wondered how the alien could have possibly made it to Everec's office undetected. *Maybe the hood? And an absurd amount of luck.* He peered up at the ceiling lights and noticed a flicker. *I guess those blackouts weren't a coincidence after all.*

"Agreed," Ariel said. She tugged at the collar of a cadet uniform she had buttoned the wrong way. *My twin sister.* "I won't allow myself to get caught by a hall monitor."

In addition to Kent and Ariel, another human, who stood at least six feet tall and possessed a hostile demeanor that could make walls jump out of his way, was in their company. His name was Brutus Cirileo, and he brooded and growled by the door of the Dean's office while the wine-smelling Paladin negotiated with Everec. Marion met eyes with his sister, but all four pupils darted away upon contact.

Everec continued: "I have control of Romulus' electrical system. I can stage blackouts, but for a short period of time. There's an exit in the basement we can use to slip away."

"And what about my ship?" Kent asked. "Our pilot only knows the entrance by the docking bay."

Everec shrugged. "Then let's hope we can contact your pilot once we get outside, I'll bring flares just in case. I would go to the docking bay again, but it is an awful long walk to go undetected with Marion."

"Yes, he found trouble at the most inopportune of times," Kent sighed. "Let's get out of here, this place makes me want to vomit."

Marion had one apprehension: "What about Octavia?"

Kent and Ariel rolled their eyes in unison, not knowing who Octavia was but strongly suspecting what she meant to Marion. Lyndon Everec smiled reassuringly. "I'll find your friend. If there is a blackout while I'm gone, get to the basement and wait for me there." The aging Dean reached into his pocket and handed Marion a laminated card, his faculty ID. "This will get you outside. It's more valuable to you than me."

"I'll wait for you, no matter what happens," he promised. Everec half-smiled and left the office.

Marion and the three strangers stood in the room for what felt like hours as they waited for him to return with Octavia. Kent grew restless, questioning the old man's loyalty. Marion knew better than that and found the Paladin's distrust to be repugnant. All the while, Everec's grandfather clock ticked, accentuating the tension in the silent office.

"So, how long have you been looking for me?" Marion asked, trying to deflate some of the tension.

"I didn't know you were alive until a month ago." Kent answered, frankly. "Another Paladin on the ship has been watching you for over a decade. Her name's Tali. She's the one who contacted Everec." He gestured over to Ariel. "She was the migraine to find. That's why we went for her first."

Marion turned to his alleged sister and said, "I guess you're as lost as I am."

"Hardly," she sneered. Her accent was blunt and slightly disjointed. She sounded nothing like any of his classmates or faculty. He wanted to ask her where she was from, but her radiating displeasure abated his curiosity.

"Why come looking for me now?" Marion asked, redirecting his questions to the Druin.

"That's for Tali to know and us the piece together." Kent said, averting his eyes. "Although, I have my suspicions."

As time passed like nails down a chalkboard, Kent grew increasingly disinterested in Marion's questions. His restlessness returned, becoming rather obsessed with the location of Mister Everec. Even his feet, little by little, stepped closer to the door.

Reading the room, Ariel suggested they leave for the basement. Marion snuffed out the idea, firmly stating he would not abandon Everec and Octavia. Ariel declared his allegiances stupid, but he remained unyielding.

Kent's comms sounded before the impasse could be resolved. "Fuck me," he cursed aloud. Marion's stomach tightened as the Paladin's face filled with dread.

"That was Matiyala," he said to the room. "There's a Roman frigate outside the academy. They know we're here."

Cirileo cackled. "Those ships contain enough soldiers to cover every bloody centimeter of this damned place. It's a bloody miracle we haven't been found yet!"

"We likely just beat them." Kent guessed, his gaze long and hard.

Ariel continued, "Maybe they wanted us in the academy. Once we're discovered, the trap is sprung." She shifted her wild eyes to Marion. "And my brother is the bait."

"I'm not going anywhere until my people are back." Marion stated, hating the weird girl in Everec's office.

"Fine, then stay." She turned to Kent. "He's a lost cause. Let's leave while we still can. I am not getting taken by the KOH."

"We're not leaving without Marion." Kent said, his legs fidgeting as they paced the room.

"Why?" she begged. "He'll get us captured!"

"No," Kent firmly put his fist down. "I can't fail the Order. He's coming with us, whether you agree or not."

Ariel refused to give up. "He's a fucking Roman! They're all on the same side."

This made Marion's blood boil. He'd been rebelling against the academy for as long as he could remember. She knew nothing about him, despite the authority with which she spoke. Before he could defend himself, the intercom sounded off with a screech, followed by an unfamiliar voice. "Ahhh, here we go. Such mundane technologies have never been my specialty. Please state your name, sir, for formality's sake."

Everyone in the office went silent, all eyes staring at the overhead intercom. With both Octavia and Everec out of sight, Marion assumed the worst. Throughout all this, the grandfather clock continued its toll. Tick... tick... tick.

There was a pause, a staticky grunt, followed by obedience. "Lyndon Everec." Marion swallowed razors.

Tick... tick... tick.

"And where are we, Mister Everec?" the unfamiliar voice asked. Marion could not decipher whose it was. *Not Tarius, not officer Brody, definitely not Pompilius. Who could it be?*

".... Conference rooms in Lorneway." Everec grunted. Marion could sense his pain and it made him crumble. *This time, he needs me.*

Tick... tick... tick.

"Excellent. For everyone listening, Mister Everec and I are about to have a nice, long conversation. Once the conversation is over, I'm slitting the old man's throat and letting him bleed over his very rich suit. If you want to save him, Marion, come to me in the conference room before your dean expires."

Tick... tick.

Marion studied Kent, Ariel, and Brutus Cirileo, understanding they were prepared to leave Mister Everec in a heartbeat. It was his turn now to save his mentor. "The conference room is on the ground floor. We can rescue Mister Everec and still make it to the basement."

Kent shook his head. "He would want you to leave if it meant your safety, and we're already past that assurance."

"It's not out of the way at all!" Marion lied.

Kent gestured him abrasively to the door. "If only you understood the vulnerability of being a mage. You will, soon enough, but let's not make that day today."

He stomped his foot. "No! Mister Everec knows the academy better than anyone else, we could get lost without him."

Kent growled. "Marion, you're coming with us, whether it's by your will or my own."

"Mister Everec is more of a father to me than the Archmage, if you are unsure of where my loyalties lie," Marion said. "He must have told you about the death of Headmaster Polanis, and how the murderer is still unknown."

He eyed the hilt of the Immortech sword pointing out of the Paladin's belted robe. "His head was cut clean off, I saw it myself. Sure, the logistics of your arrival don't quite coincide, but a miniscule detail like that can be set aside for the perfect scapegoat."

Kent licked his lips, plotting. The intercom sounded again. They all waited eagerly for the mysterious man behind the microphone to speak. "Do you know who I am, Mister Everec?"

"Drake Bodewin, heir to Erron."

"Correct!" said the other man. *Drake Bodewin?* Marion considered the name like a math equation. *The brother of Queen Elysande. Why is he on Romulus?*

He heard Kent's grip tighten around the hilt of his sword. "Do you know exactly where this conference room is?"

"Absolutely." Marion replied, trying to conceal his excitement.

"Cirileo," called Kent.

"What?"

"Will you be able to find the basement?"

"I can bloody figure it out," Cirileo assured.

"Good, take Ariel and the key with you now. If Romans meet you before we do, leave."

Marion smiled to himself, impressed by his own powers of persuasion. Kent headed for the door, but his motions stopped when the staticky rumblings of the intercom came on again. The mysterious voice who identified himself as Drake Bodewin continued: "I do appreciate your use of formalities. I hope I addressed you correctly, for fear of revealing myself as a layman."

Mister Everec's voice followed on the intercom. "You are the furthest thing from a layman, my lord. Your father made sure of that."

Bodewin continued: "A man can be granted many titles, hold countless lands in this endless space, and win all the glory a lifetime allows, but every title I possess will never turn me into an intellectual."

Marion and Kent sprinted across the hall and down several flights of steps to the conference room. Kent kept a hood over his head, but it did nothing to disguise his identity. Whenever they came across a school guard, he would turn them away with a few words and a flick of the wrist. He was using magic, Marion knew, adding some credibility to the implausible tale he had heard thus far.

All the while, staticky voices echoed throughout the building like haunting spirits.

Drake Bodewin's tone was low, prideful even. He spoke with the certainty that Marion was coming. "In truth, Mister Everec, I am a savage. My firearm is my pen and paper, my means of self-expression. And I am hopelessly limited in all things that don't involve filling someone's body with beams of concentrated light. This is where you come in."

Mister Everec said nothing. *Is he stalling for me?* Marion asked himself as he searched for the conference room, likely doing the opposite of what the Dean wished.

Drake continued nonetheless: "I need you to clarify for me the difference between death and sacrifice. From what I gather, sacrifice is honorable, charitable, and elicits a greater meaning to one's own downfall. Death on the other hand is, well, death."

"Sacrifice is selfless," Everec said. "It can inspire others to think and act for something greater than themselves. There is nobility in sacrifice, a purpose."

Drake interrupted, "And yet, for the individual, both death and sacrifice have the same morbid destination. So, in my humble, layman opinion, there is no distinction between the two when the conclusion is the same."

Marion continued his stride, struggling as if he was running against the taunting words of Drake Bodewin. The Paladin followed, his magic deterring the actions of any guards who crossed their path. They descended the last flight of steps to the ground floor, sprinting across a carpeted hallway. They were flanked on each side by portraits and marble busts of legendary Roman figures. He felt their cold scowls as he passed them. *Stare all you want; I won't bow to any of you!*

"Did you force me in here to discuss philosophies?" Everec asked. Marion was disturbed as he imagined the current state of the Dean.

"Not quite, I wanted to know your stance on death before I continue with my questions. Given the circumstance of our conversation, you should be in no rush to finish." Bodewin assured him. Marion pushed forward as if each word Mister Everec spoke would be his last. The conference room was close, he just needed a few more minutes.

"What could you possibly mean?" Everec asked with tremendous disdain.

"We both know who Marion is, the son of the Archmage I killed fifteen years ago. What would you say his death was? A sacrifice? Of course not. Paladin loyalists will try to portray it that way, try to deify the man. But I was there, I did the deed. There was nothing noble about it."

Marion turned a corner into the conference area. He stopped himself just before the glass room where Everec was trapped with Bodewin. He would have charged into the room if not for the squadron of soldiers on patrol outside. Kent, in hot pursuit, stopped in his tracks as well. Marion peered around the wall and saw Drake Bodewin sitting across from the Dean of Students. The Mercian Lord was young and handsome, with shoulder-length auburn hair, cutting sky-blue eyes, and a self-assured smile that could make the dullest of creature dubious.

"I killed him the night Spyre fell, right in front of the few surviving mages who were still brainwashed enough to follow their God into one last, pointless battle against the Triumvirate. Their home was in ruin, their leader insane, and yet they still wanted to fight, they still wanted to die for something so futile." Bodewin moved his arm under the table, loosed a strap on his holster, and unveiled a pistol with a ten-inch barrel. A beautiful piece, in truth, if it had not been pointed at the forehead of his mentor. "It was only when I aimed this pistol at Marius' throat and pulled the trigger did that small flicker of light finally get snuffed out. Something about watching your leader choke on his own blood can really dampen morale."

"Is this a history lesson?" Everec asked, perturbed. "Or a lecture in mockery?"

Drake stood from the table and pointed the barrel of his gun at the head of Mister Everec. "By all accounts of everyone here, you are the boy's new father. It seems history will be repeating itself."

"STOP!" Marion pleaded, standing carelessly in the center of the corridor.

Tick... Tick... Tick.

"Oh good." Drake whispered through the microphone, his voice snaking throughout the halls. Their eyes met despite the distance.

Everec's head erupted in half of a second. His kind face, his lined skin, his magnificent flow of white hair turned into a collage of blood, brains, and bits of bone splattered on the glass wall behind him, all for Marion to see.

Before he would scream, cry, attack, or regret his actions, his wrist was seized by the Paladin. He was pulled along like a doll, his eyes blinded by tears and his throat closed by a sour lump. His body went limp; his legs stumbled forward, but not by his own will.

Deliriousness set in, but he was aware of the moment when they stopped moving. Kent spoke, but it was muddled by a ghostly ringing. Then, a girl's voice.

"I'm his girlfriend!" she stated defiantly. "Mister Everec told me everything."

"Octavia?" Marion whispered. He felt imprisoned in his own body, paralyzed by an influx of indescribable emotion.

"Is this true, Marion?" Kent asked, slapping him lightly on the face.

"Octavia?" he said again, this time with more emphasis.

The two voices sparred with each other, until one finally conceded. *I failed again, after everything Mister Everec sacrificed for me. Worthless! Worthless waste!*

"Fine, take him to the basement, I'll hold the soldiers off."

Marion was hoisted up. His hands touched someone with soft, familiar skin. He licked his lips and tasted Denvari wine, he sniffed the air fresh with the scent of strawberries. Weightless, his mind was off somewhere else, hypnotized by a ticking grandfather clock.

. . .

He returned to reality with the help of an ear-splitting clap of thunder. Louder than anything he had heard in his entire life, the sheer force of sound was enough to send him off his feet. He landed in the soaking, wet earth, his hands gripped tightly around overgrown and sodden blades of grass. Noises surrounded him: harsh winds whipping trees, a grumbling dark sky, rain lashing against his muddied uniform. These new elements, thrust upon him relentlessly, scrambled his cognitive abilities into near irreversible disarray.

Marion curled into a ball, the gravity of the outside world bending him into submission.

"Marion!" a voice called upon realization that he was awake.

"Octavia? Where are we?"

She caressed his face; she smiled warmly when he recognized her. "We're outside! You're free from Romulus."

Marion grabbed her and pulled her close. He buried his face in her neck and kissed it, her short hair sticking to his fingers when he held her head. Convinced that their lives together had come to an end, he was thankful for the second chance. He had been careless to her, and granted with a new life, he swore that she would come before anything else. Octavia was a head rush unmatched in its euphoria, and absence only enhanced his addiction, so much so that he could never live without it again. Unfortunately, it was not the only thing he remembered.

"Mister Everec..." Marion began, "He's..."

Octavia nodded, tears sprouting in her emerald green eyes and mixing with the rain on her face.

"Isn't this fucking amazing!" another woman abruptly screamed from up ahead.

Marion sat up and saw it was his sister. Ariel embraced the weather joyfully. She opened her mouth to the sky to taste the rainwater, she climbed the largest rock she could find to feel the greater strength of the stormy winds, and, as she raised her arms above her head, lightning struck the nearby ground as if by her command. She could have easily passed as part of the storm, the way she so naturally and lovingly danced with it.

Marion feared for his and Octavia's safety, and deeply wished the Paladin Kent was present to watch his wicked sister.

"We should try to find shelter." Octavia suggested. "Start a fire and wait for help."

Marion agreed. Ariel supported the decision too, although she made no effort to conceal her dissatisfaction. They walked guideless through the dark, wooded world. While wandering, he nearly drowned in several underestimated puddles, and the constant chill he felt tickle down his spine was becoming tedious. The outside world of Romulus was a dangerous and foreign beast, lacking the warmth and cleanliness he took for granted on the inside.

Ariel and Octavia walked unabated by their surroundings, forcing Marion to do his best to suppress his discomfort.

"What the Hell is going on with you?" Octavia asked as they walked along.

"I assume you know she's my sister," he said, gesturing to Ariel who was leading the pack. In return, she waved sarcastically.

"We caught up while you were out cold," Octavia said. "Met the Druin and the big scary human soldier too. They stayed behind to distract the guards."

"We have a ship on the planet," Ariel said. "My pistol has a flare attachment, but if there's a frigate around, I don't want to take any chances."

"Best not," Octavia said. "What do you want with Marion anyway?"

He interrupted before she could answer. "I'm a mage. At least according to Mister Everec. It's... it's one of many things that will take a while to process." The image of Everec's head exploding clawed at his brain.

"I'm sorry, Marion." Octavia said, turning back to him. "I'm so sorry for all of this."

"Thanks," he returned, sullenly. "But it helps that you're here."

The three travelers stumbled upon shelter concealed by a tangle of thick green bushes. When Marion went to move the stringy vines, a horde of small black birds flew from the brush and into the abyss above, giving him a near heart attack. Ariel and Octavia got a good show and hardy laugh from it, which was amplified by his attempt to appear calm and collected afterward.

Their shelter was a half-roof structure molded in reddish clay and made by some primitive culture by the look of it. The inside was dry enough to seek some warmth from the storm, but unfortunately there was no wood in sight.

"I'll go find some dry wood," Octavia suggested.

"No," Marion objected. Her breath was calm and steady, while his was loud and laborious. "I'll go."

She put a hand on his shoulder and said, "If you're half as tired as your face suggests, then it's better if I go for now. You can get the next run."

He conceded. "Okay, but please don't go out too far. I won't get any rest worrying about you."

Octavia arched an eyebrow. "Are you guilting me into coming back? Fair enough, it's an effective tactic." Marion watched as she disappeared into the verdant brush.

Inevitably, curiosity crept into the minds of the twins. This outside world was entirely new to him, tickling his interest at every sight. When Ariel vocalized her desire to explore, Marion hastily agreed, desperate to escape the trite small talk he felt obligated to exchange with her. Ariel responded to his attempts at conversation with disinterest, making him feel terribly boring about himself.

On top of it all, every moment that passed with Octavia out of his sight was agony-inducing. With enemies all around them, his imagination naturally assumed the worst.

"A walk would be good," he said. "Octavia's been gone for a while; we should go make sure she's all right."

"Yeah," was all Ariel contributed.

As they explored, Marion's head started to float, his breathing more strained outside than it was in the academy. This clouded mindset prevented him from accurately judging the distance and size of the countless rocks, tree stumps, and overgrown roots that threatened his path, so he committed himself to following the exact footsteps of his sister.

They came across a cavern dug into a topless cliffside of smoothed white stone. The exterior gleamed under the sheen of rainwater. Ariel pulled her pistol from her belt and went to fire it down the mouth of the cave.

"What are you doing?" Marion asked.

She displayed her weapon like it was a piece of classical art. "It has three modes: stun, lethal, and flare. Guess which one will help us see down the cave."

"At least shoot a flare up so Octavia knows where we are." Marion said, wondering why stupidity could conquer him so quickly. Octavia could have been back at the shelter, worried to death over him.

"Can't do that. Not with a Roman frigate in orbit. Come on, don't you want to see what's down there?"

Marion sighed. "Fine, then we go back to the shelter."

The cave took on an ominous, red glow as the flare dived into the unknown. A path of descension became clear, but it was ambushed on all sides by jagged rocks and deep crevices that would punish harshly for even the slightest slip or misstep. Ariel and Marion ventured on, and a few yards deep into their descent, the cave drawings appeared.

The figures were circular in shape, with antennae and small black dots for eyes. Each possessed several pairs of mandibles and rounded claws and had small stilts for legs. These two-dimensional creatures appeared in every section of the spacious cavern, gazing at Marion, daring him to continue his downward plunge into their home.

Epic scenes of history played out before his eyes. He saw these creatures engaged in various acts of love and war; kings selfishly sending their soldiers out to battle in the name of forgotten glory, young lovers fleeing from their homes to fulfill a forbidden romance that would inevitably end in tragedy, Gods engaging in the affairs of mortals and tormenting those who defied them. These stick figures magnanimously displayed the entirety of their history and culture for Marion to absorb, and he loved them for it.

Not much further down, the real creatures were found, a storied civilization reduced to bones and dust in the bowels of the cave.

Genocide. The heaping pile of remains left neglected and alone, forcibly erased from galactic legacy. They were so small too. Marion judged that two of the alien skeletons on top of one another would only be as tall as his shoulders. Spears and axes of bronze were strewn about the cavern floor, assumedly their futile weapons of choice.

Unable to indulge in the cataclysmic showcase any longer, he hastily retreated to the surface, leaving Ariel behind. On the verge of crying, he could not help but feel disgusted for the extinction of a species he had only just discovered. *But why?*

He stumbled into the open air. Cold rainwater drenched his shoulders. He lifted his face to the sky and embraced nature. The shelter was nearby. He readied himself to head back, to ease Octavia's worries, but he was hit with the disturbing sense that he was not alone.

"Are you Marion Zoltor?" someone asked. He looked up and saw a figure dressed in silvery robes with long sleeves and a dark cloak pinned to his shoulders. Beneath the cloak was a thin breastplate black enough to make his body invisible in the stormy night.

"It depends. Are you one of Kent's people?" Marion asked in return. Judging by his red eyes, the figure was of the Enfari species, and the Enfari were no friends to the Paladin Order. He heard Ariel emerge from the cave.

"And you, are you Ariel Zoltor?" The Enfari kept his voice cold, but his eyes failed to conceal his inner lust.

Ariel raised her pistol. "Who the Hell are you?"

The Enfari smirked. His cloak caught the wind and, instantaneously, he vanished. Ariel rapidly turned in place. She fired a lethal shot into the dense grove, swallowed whole by the brush without effect. Marion clenched his fists, useless without a weapon.

The twins gravitated toward each other, half out of strategy, half out of fear. Before they could formulate any sort of defense against the Enfari, an apparition formed behind Ariel. It grabbed her by the head and, emerging from the silvery robe, came a sharpened fingernail of a grotesquely yellow shade that plunged into her neck.

Ariel's eyes bulged in a plea for help as the shock of pain ripped through her. She gasped for air as the veins in her neck turned into wriggling black worms. She too wriggled in a desperate act to escape the clutches of the Enfari, but his embrace was unbreakable. Seconds later, she was unconscious, landing lifelessly into the mud.

Another chill crept up Marion's spine, followed by a poke and the feeling of complete paralysis.

# KENT (V)

There was never a more beautiful day than the one when Kent Kentoshi was declared a Paladin of the Order.

It was midmorning, when the sun shone directly and fully into the Elemental Hall of Spyre, reflecting off the massive, multicolored glass murals that adorned the back walls and filling the room with polychromatic radiance. These murals did not depict Gods or other deities, but the legendary Paladins of old, forever looking down upon their successors and giving them something to aspire toward.

In the center of the Elemental Hall was the mighty statue of Serios, the legendary Immortal whose sacrifice brought forth the existence of mages. The crystalline tribute reminded all Paladins of the Immortal who crossed dimensions with a band of his own kind to help the races of their realm defeat the Planters. Thousands of years later, Serios still watched over his creation, still stood guard to aid the Paladins in whatever trials were placed before them.

Archmage Marius Zoltor, whose formidable career was already worthy of a mural, stood at the dais of the sprawling hall. In his hand was Starfire, the ancestral Immortech sword of the Zoltor family. He could have been a God himself, with a shock of pale blonde hair, clean-shaven face, broad shoulders, and arms as wide as tree trunks. He dressed in rich, vibrant fabrics of emerald green and gold with a purple velvet sash going across his shoulder. The Immortech armor worn over it all shimmered like platinum. He was a sight not easily forgotten; an image that could inspire even the most morbid of souls.

Kent knelt in a semicircle around the dais along with a dozen other mages, eagerly awaiting his call. Behind them stood row after row of other Paladins and mages, so numerous that they filled the entire hall.

Finally, Kent was called upon. His unbridled excitement at the time made the memory hazy, but he would never forget kneeling before the Archmage, stating his vows, and feeling Starfire tap his shoulders.

When Marius Zoltor commanded him to rise, Kent did so on wobbly legs. With a booming voice, the Archmage declared, "I hereby name you, Kent Kentoshi, Paladin of the Order and Justiciar of the Galaxy!"

An eruption of applause followed. Kent bowed humbly to his Archmage and then to his peers. The moment was incredible, heavenly even, but fleeting. The claps and cheers were drowned out by a strident alarm that shook him back to the present.

He was trapped in the narrow corridor again, Immortech blade in hand and awaiting an incoming legion of KOH soldiers. Lacking possession of both Zoltor twins, Kent was reminded of how unqualified he was to carry out Tali's mission. *I can give them time to escape*, he thought, *it's the best I can do.*

The first enemy approached him from around the corner. He admired Kent in dubious and vague recognition. Kent, however, knew exactly who stood before him.

"Ah, it's coming back to me." Drake Bodewin said with a devious smirk. "You're Kent Kentoshi, the mage with the mind tricks. I thought you died on the Bloodmoon."

*I should have.* The soldiers behind Lord Bodewin formed in rows of two in the narrow corridor. They considered Kent like a rabid animal. He raised his sword in response, to encourage their skepticism, to resurrect the mystique of the once revered Paladin Order. Drake Bodewin, in all his arrogance, was not entranced by the spectacle.

Bodewin licked his lips. "Last I saw you, you and thousands of other mages were being led to the slaughter. And to think the Archmage cared for his underlings."

"It wasn't Marius' fault!" Kent fired back. Bodewin knew of his mind control, but not of how much it had dulled over the years. He was trying to scramble Kent's thoughts, incite him to act irrationally. It was tempting to assume Drake's body and force the vile traitor to give himself the same fate he did to the Archmage, but he had an awareness to magic few other non-mages possessed, and he would sense Kent's mind control before it could overcome him.

"That is true," Bodewin agreed. "He, instead, handed you off to Imperator Ademar Vikander, and what a great shepherd he was. Guided all his legions and Zoltor's mages into the worst defeat the galaxy had ever witnessed, and all thanks to the shrewdness of King Caesar and my beloved father.

"I did hear, however, of how valiantly the mages fought to their deaths, not including you of course. Isn't it ironic, believing you're dying for something grander than yourself, only to see it end in embarrassment?"

Kent could smell the alcohol on the breath of Drake Bodewin. The tolling alarm pounded at his senses. "You don't know what it's like to serve for a truly righteous cause. You spent half your life by the side of the Archmage but absorbed none of his wisdom."

Bodewin chortled: "You speak of Zoltor as if he was a God among men. I can assure you, he died like everyone else, with the same amount of indecency. Would you like to know what he sounded like when I shot him in the throat? Or describe the terror on his face as he gasped for air? I remember it like it's happening right before me."

Abruptly, a soldier in Bodewin's retinue charged his rifle and opened fire. The man was such a dullard that, even with a helmet on, Kent assumed his mind like a marionette. He felled two soldiers around him, aimed his sights at Bodewin, but even having the drop on the young lord was not enough to seize the advantage.

Drake turned, agile as a wildcat, and in one smooth motion aimed the barrel of his pistol at the witless soldier and blew his head into nonexistence, helmet and all.

The opportunity presented itself. Bodewin was distracted, long enough for Kent to impale him with his Immortech sword, relishing the victory before succumbing to a hail of gunfire.

Instead, he opted to retreat, sprinting down the corridor and praying to any Immortal listening to help him escape the wretched academy.

Kent ran in an aimless dash. Whenever he attempted to pause and consider his surroundings, the ominous trot of soldiers in between intervals of a blaring alarm encouraged him to keep running. Every office, locker, and lobby looked exactly the same: marble flooring, square walls glinting like gold in the lurid overhead lights, and the busts of "great" Romans erected along the sides of every hallway. Their stone faces glared at Kent, mocked him, taunted him, waited eagerly for him to bleed. *The basement! Where is this Goddamn BASEMENT!*

"Kentoshi!" Cirileo yelled from afar. Kent was, to say the least, incredulous to find him casually loitering without the Zoltors.

"This isn't as bad as it seems," Cirileo began. He was perspiring profusely beneath his leather and steel.

"So you have the twins?"

Cirileo shook his head: "No."

Before Kent could berate him, the merc explained himself.

"Roman soldiers were on us. Some redhead girl dragged Marion to me loonier than a moon man. I had to lead the soldiers away if they were to escape, you caught me doubling back."

Kent would not object, not that there was any time to argue. He bottled up his frustrations, his own gnawing inadequacy. Brutus led him to the basement, which was thankfully nearby and concealed only by his hysterical state. When they got to the exit, the vault door was wide open. On the floor beside the threshold was the laminated card of one Lyndon Everec. Whipping rain lashed at them even before they could step outside.

Kent charged out into the elements, searching wildly for any clue of where the Zoltors had gone. The muddy river running through his boots would have covered any footprints, and the dark, cloudy sky made it impossible to see more than several yards away. He considered shouting, but the ferocious thunder above would drown him out.

"Is tracking something they teach you in mercenary school?" Kent asked Brutus.

The merc nodded, shutting the vaulted door. "Hunting, more like it, but we're in the wrong party." Brutus pointed up ahead. Kent spotted hundreds of scintillating white lights from afar, their march mightier than the storm. "If you want to live, now's the time to act like prey."

Hours passed before the Seshora Araman spotted them. Forced to hide in trees while KOH soldiers searched the muddy forest, Kent felt beyond exhausted and soaked to the bone when he was finally in the safety of his own ship. When Matiyala met them in the cargo area, he immediately asked for the Zoltors.

"They should be with you," she said, defiantly. "Did you want me to land and have my ship blasted into oblivion by that frigate?"

Kent was beyond reasonable. Human interference was the last thing he needed, especially when he just had the Archmage's children in the same room. Everec seemed self-assured, and yet this rescue had become more disastrous than the one on Prisilla.

Tali was next in line for obvious questions, cornering Kent as if it would make him answer faster. "You lost the children? Where's Everec?"

"If you want Everec, you can find his brain matter on the ground floor of the academy. The kids are gone because the plan went to Hell." Kent stated bluntly.

"I'm bloody fine too." Cirileo swore, taking off his boot, tipping it over, and letting a lake spill out.

"That frigate came from nowhere," Tali insisted, her eyes large.

"Did it now?" Kent asked. "You know who else we met? Drake fucking Bodewin."

Tali sighed; she was turning pale with grief. "I don't know how any of this happened. Those kids can't survive out in the storm for long."

"Then we search Romulus until we find them!" Kent barked.

Matiyala saluted with mock dramatization, "Aye, aye!"

Searching was futile.

If hundreds, or possibly thousands, of foot soldiers could not find two kids while combing the deep brush of the forest, a small merchant ship with cheap flood lights would not either.

Kent, Matiyala, Cirileo, Tali, and Ariel's metallic oddity she called Pup scrutinized the wetland through the circular front window of the cockpit. Kent needed sleep and a hot meal, but he craved beer or wine or something to dull his senses. He clung to the fleeting hope that Ariel and Marion would show in the floodlights, with the justification that he had worked too hard for it all to end so anticlimactically.

"How did a frigate know we were here?" Kent muttered, but purposefully loud enough for everyone to hear.

"I warned you all," Matiyala reminded. "What were you expecting to happen in KOH space?"

"No, no." Kent said, frustrated beyond belief. A migraine was kicking in, encouraging his rage like a stimulant. "Someone knew we would be here. This was a fucking trap."

"You're tired Kent, let's think this through." Tali said, holding on to diplomacy.

"I've been thinking this through for quite a while," he replied, addressing Tali alone. "I don't know if you had anything to do with that frigate, but you're hiding something from me. ALL of you are hiding something from me."

"I don't know what you're talking about," she insisted, a clear lie.

Kent continued, "It was awfully coincidental that the one Druin I find in the rest of the galaxy just happened to be able to guide me to Ariel. Bato is quite convincing as the hero of the people, but someone is paying for his benevolence. On top of that, it's a miracle you were able to hire a crew of freelancers who are somehow loyal enough not turn over a handful of mages for millions of more credits than what you're paying them." He laughed hysterically. "There's something strange going on here, and I want answers."

Tali's eyes grew wide with remorse, making Kent feel guilty. "I'm sorry, but now's not the time. Not while we're missing the Zoltors."

Kent stepped back, his heart flinching. "Why keep secrets from me? Out of anyone here, you should trust me the most."

Tali grimaced. She went to speak but was interrupted by a sudden screech of radio chatter.

"Everyone!" Matiyala shouted. She directed the crew's attention to the radio, which was fizzling with static. She went to turn the microphone on, but hesitated.

"Is this the Seshora Araman?" the radio asked after about a minute of silence. "Is Kent there. Kent uuuhhhh Kentoshi?"

He recognized the voice but could not recall why.

"Kent Kentoshi? I know where Marion and Ariel are.... I won't say anything else until I get a response. Can you hear me? Kent? I'm with them now, sort of. Please pick up."

"Everyone, leave." Kent ordered with pure authority.

"This is my ship," Matiyala objected. "You don't even know who's on that line."

"I know who it is." Kent said, technically not lying. "And this is my mission, so when I say get out of the cockpit, that's what you do."

Matiyala stood up from her armchair, ready to strangle the life out of her bedmate. Instead, she stepped away, making sure to elbow him in the ribs before exiting.

Kent turned to his crew, "I don't trust any of you. A Roman frigate was waiting for me at the academy, and I need to figure out which one of you tipped them off. I don't mean to be blunt, but I have the suspicion that I'm being played in more ways than one."

# ARIEL (IV)

She broke the number one rule of the Underlings: never, under any circumstance, let yourself be captured.

*Authority* was a vague and menacing concept, one that did not just apply to the rulers of Prisilla up on the levels of New Horizon who tortured her kind by proxy of their doggish pearls. Silver Wulf taught her well in one regard: any force that has her outnumbered is an authority. This creed made Wulf cowardly and indecisive, a leech when he could have been a lion, but Ariel used it to her advantage. In her eyes, every authority, whether it be Kagen's gang or the Triumvirate, needed to be respected as equals so, if their paths crossed, she would never fall victim to underestimation. This was how she survived longer than any of her peers.

Now, she was in the clutches of THE authority of the galaxy, a threat that was impossible to underestimate.

General Antonius Marko analyzed her with considerable disdain. She guessed he was young for the all the medals he sported on the breast of his officer's tunic. He stood in the prison cell with her, his hands behind his back in fists while hers behind her back in cuffs. She was placed in the corner of the cell, surrounded on three sides by clear plexiglass and one of ashen metal. Above her were blazing ceiling lights, giving the whole cell a white glare abrasive to the eyes. This was in stark contrast to the neighboring cell, which was drowned in so much darkness that she could not tell who or what was inside.

Ariel stayed in the corner of the cell, stooped over in pain after taking the butt-end of a rifle to her stomach. This was her punishment for fighting back while being escorted around the corridors of the frigate. Pride convinced her that she could disarm one of the soldiers if she caught them by surprise, but it failed, and miserably so.

Marion was not so bold and received more dignity because of it.

"You two have caused quite a problem for me." Marko said through gritted teeth, primarily addressing the complaint to Ariel. "I should be on my way to Grayspace, off to fight the Synths in the frontline. Instead, I must turn the whole frigate around to deliver you before the king."

"Synths?" Marion laughed. "They haven't been seen since the Creation War, and those sources are dubious to say the least."

The general stared at them sternly. "Synths have been seen for the first time in thousands of years, and I find myself in a room with the brood of the last Archmage. Now seems the perfect time for the absurdly peculiar to become reality."

"How did you find us?" Ariel asked, not fully convinced of Marion's innocence.

Marko shrugged. "A rat, but not my own. Wrong place, wrong time situation. I was closest to the informant when he called for home, making it my responsibility to decide what to do with you."

"I'll kill whoever it was from our crew that betrayed us." Ariel swore, feigning rage. She had no idea if the rat was on the Seshora Araman. Marko would never willingly reveal his source, but she hoped her wording would accidentally spill some of his knowledge.

Instead, the general answered with a sneer. "Clever, but not clever enough. I never said the rat was in your company, nor will I tell you. But as it seems we'll be stuck in space for a long while, you'll have plenty of time to ponder."

"Scoundrel…" Ariel muttered.

"You're really going to take us to Orbis?" Marion asked, inserting himself back into the conversation. Orbis was the home-world of humanity. It was a destination Ariel often imagined herself exploring if she ever left Prisilla. *Although never, ever like this.*

Marko considered his surroundings, his teeth continuing to grind in deep contemplation. "Perhaps if there's a working relay station in this damnable sector, I can contact Rome and have them do most of the traveling, but of course you had to be on the academy furthest away from Orbis. You deprived me of my auctoritas for mop up duty of an old war... I should have you both shot and done away with."

And with those words, Marko marched out of the cell.

Ariel and her brother were given an extraneous amount of time to get to know each other. He tried to speak with her when they were stuck on Romulus, but something about his gaze and tone had shut her off entirely to his prying. She was some sort of spectacle to him, a rare animal in a zoo admired as much for its grace and mystery as it was for perceived primal stupidity. Whether it be a tool or a toy, Ariel would not let herself be treated as a "thing" any longer; Marion would have to indulge in oddities elsewhere.

Regardless of how he may have viewed her when they first met, day after day of sharing each other's company dissipated any shroud of novelty either of their characters may have possessed.

"So," he said at one point during their eternal internment, "You know where I'm from, how about you?"

"Prisilla," Ariel answered. Marion's silent implication told her to continue. "I lived in the Underbelly. Worked as a bounty hunter." *An apprentice to a bounty hunter... but he doesn't need to know the details.*

She could feel his fascination perk up again. "How interesting! Prisilla is the hub of the galaxy, with the most diverse population of any planet since Last Bastion. It's funny that both just happen to be artificially made, more like giant space stations than planets."

Ariel said nothing; she wondered if he knew that half of Prisilla's people lived in the garbage of the other half, or if he was aware of how many Underlings inconspicuously disappeared every night never to be seen again? *No, that sort of news is smothered by New Horizon.*

Marion continued as if he was a talking book himself. "Well, there are many differences between the two. For one, Last Bastion served as the sovereign hub of all life, while Prisilla is more of a trade center-"

"I know the difference!" she snapped.

Her brother turned away shyly. "Sorry. Everec... used to love to talk about this kind of stuff with me. I can't tell when I'm getting carried away because there was never a limit with him." He struggled to stifle his emotions: the wrath, the fear, the pain. Ariel felt an unfamiliar sense of pity; she almost wanted to comfort him. Marion covered his face, on the verge of sobbing. A barrier stood between them, one that followed her wherever she roamed.

And then an idea popped into her head. "You want to talk? Fine. Tell me about our mother."

She was met with a look of confusion, until he remembered they had the same mother. "Oh, yes. Sorry, I'm still adjusting to the Archmage revelation. Who could have guessed that having a long-lost mother would ever be the mundane news?"

Ariel giggled slightly. It snuck up on her, but she stifled it immediately. Marion saw it and he laughed with her, albeit more openly.

"It sounds funnier when you say it," she confessed. "Those Paladins speak so earnestly that I stopped seeing the absurdity of… whatever the Hell our situation is." She leaned her neck back and briefly stared at the lurid ceiling lights. "It's sad though, I have a mother… and I don't even know her name."

"Well, Marius' wife was Rosalind Gardener. She was from a noble family on the continent of Mercia. The Gardeners were loyalists to the Roman Republic, and their alliance with the Vikanders to remove Reynard Bodewin as Overseer of Mercia was what led to the Bodewin rebellion. You are aware of the rebellion?"

"Yes," she said, pretending to know.

Her brother continued: "Mister Everec made sure I was well-read on the noble families of the KOH, but I can't say I know too much about Rosalind specifically, other than the marriage to Marius being a political move. It worked for a while. The Gardeners had successfully pushed the Bodewins out of Mercia and became leaders of the Republic during the Civil War. And then, well, they all died."

"Dead? Every single one of them?"

"I think so. Rosalind's father, brother, and sister died in the war. She died when Spyre collapsed…" Marion shivered as if a phantom chill went up his spine. "So the family is extinct and their efforts in vain."

"Not extinct yet," Ariel corrected him.

"I grew up believing my parents were Roman. They were defectors, sentenced to permanent exile for their crimes of cowardice. I thought they sent me to Romulus as an infant to escape their fate. It's odd to think I'm part Mercian too... and a mage."

"I'm an Underling, and that mark will never fade. My blood is written by circumstance," Ariel said. "Who cares about these arbitrary differences between humans?" *Roman, Mercian, it's all the same. Is this what rich academy boys dwell on?*

He shook his head. "I honestly hate the Romans. I'd rather be anything else."

She considered continuing the debate further. Why humans of the KOH cared about imaginary lines in the ground, she could not decipher. Her supposed brother was adamant on his hatred for Romans, and so explaining her logic would be pointless.

"You want to know the really messed up thing?" Marion asked.

"Sure."

"Reports say when our mother was killed, we were killed with her... What do you make of that?"

The brother-sister duo eventually ceased all communication. Ariel developed an irrational hatred toward her cellmate, perturbed by the way he breathed and how he darted his eyes away whenever she caught him staring and the rhythm to which he slapped his knees at his most unbearable moments of boredom. He would sigh sometimes and gaze longingly past the plexiglass barrier and the stark steel corridor beyond that. He was dreaming about his redhead girlfriend, no doubt, and she legitimately considered strangling him whenever he fell into such trances.

Blast-off was missed severely during this perpetual internment in purgatory. The merciless Romans had stripped her of her inhalator right before throwing her into prison. Without it, life moved even slower than usual, her head sparked with pain, her fingertips twitched, and her mouth was dryer than a desert. Her thoughts were in a hurricane, haunting her, making it impossible to drift away and let time to fly by. Her emotions were tender like infected skin, and they continued to screech in the absence of her narcotic. She was desperate for another fix, her body and mind trapped in a war neither wanted to fight.

Despite this, the greatest enemy she was against was the tedium of being trapped in a cell of nothingness.

A brief surge of excitement occurred when Ariel spotted a foot sticking out from the shrouded cell across the hall. Considering her cell was perpetually burning with garish white lights, she absently assumed the darker cell was empty. The conspicuous foot flummoxed her and quickly became the center of all her attention and effort. Marion, too, was comparably enamored by this mysterious foot.

When asking politely for her neighbor to emerge from the darkness proved to be fruitless, Ariel turned to more petulant tactics. She and Marion rapped, tapped, and pounded upon the plexiglass wall. They yelled, sang, and hooted to contact their new and mysterious acquaintance. It was fun in an airy sort of way, and she even, in a moment of unconscious weakness, shared a smile with her privileged, obnoxious brother. Eventually, their combined raucousness forced their neighbor to reveal himself.

His eyes squinted when they touched the light, his face bending into an ugly and disoriented scowl. Ariel refused to believe what she saw in front of her was human. His features were normal: caramel-colored skin, short black hair that grew ragged from neglect, and a wild beard that covered a face not much older than her own, but his body was what made him inhuman.

Ariel felt her heart flutter. Standing two feet taller than herself, her cellmate manifested the appearance of a living God with his wide shoulders, mountainous arms and legs, and a lean, sinewy torso. Never had she seen a figure so muscular, so crisp, so… masculine.

Ariel shook her head of the arising fantasies. She would have deemed this immaculate specimen as the perfect candidate for her escape, if not for the iron shackles brimming with electrical sensors that bound him from head to toe.

"What?" he said, defeat distinctly in his tone.

"You're a humanoid!" Marion blurted out.

The man sighed, consciously moving as little as possible to prevent a hearty dose of electricity from surging through his veins. "Not a humanoid, a traitor."

"Hardly," Ariel said, cutting off her brother before he could speak again. "What did you do to end up here?"

The humanoid sighed deeply. "I was a Roman officer. I was given... given orders from C-Caesar himself. But I betrayed his trust, defied his command, and now I'm where I belong."

"We're prisoners, unfairly detained by the oppressive KOH." Ariel spoke with vigorous theatricality to incite some enthusiasm in the seven-foot embodiment of misery. "They took our freedom, leaving us with only one option."

"Yes," he said, slipping back into the shadows. "Die."

Ariel lost her sense of normalcy while imprisoned on the frigate. The jailers stopped coming at regular intervals for meals, and she became convinced they would allow days to expire without letting her eat. Not that she ever felt hungry, just the process of eating allowed her to flex senses and muscles she would never use otherwise. Time divulged into a nonsensical concept, to the point where even days lost their meaning and could've passed as quickly as minutes or as slowly as years. Had she been detained for a week, two weeks, or a month? It made no difference. The sole things that barely existed were the four walls of her prison.

She thought of Kent and Tali and Brutus Cirileo. Had they been captured too? Were they killed? Or, were they coming to save her? These mental gymnastics were the only forms of exercise she had. But overtime, bleak indifference erased them from her mind. Eventually, her thoughts abandoned in her too.

The metallic room with the lurid lights and the occasional grunt of the frigate moving through space were her only evidence that her senses still worked. The repetitiveness of her blank cycle turned into one image: inescapable, unavoidable, unknowing, and perpetual. She stared at Marion and could not see a person, only an illusion of the mind that never moved, never spoke, just existed.

When the creature in the featureless mask and silvery robes entered her cube of exile, she almost forgot how to react.

The creature was a giant like the humanoid, with heavy armor wrought into the shape of dragon scales. On his back was an equally formidable warhammer beautifully crafted in what must have been Immortech. Without saying a word, he raised his hand and pointed a steel studded finger at Ariel.

She was taken from the cell, blindfolded, and escorted through the frigate. Although she could not see, simply hearing the marching of soldiers or chattering of officers and technicians was enough the rekindle the flame inside her. She was led through a labyrinth, being turned constantly by her escort. When the blindfold was removed, she was in a room with the Inquisitor.

He was sitting casually on a desk, his back to a window viewing the vast void of space. "You may take a seat," the Inquisitor said, while politely indicating to her escort that he desired privacy. The other Inquisitor left in silence, pausing only to brush a mailed glove through her hair. She shivered at his touch, unsure if it was done on purpose or accident.

"I know your birthname," he began, "But I want to know your real name." His words were hoarse and painful, his face struggled to move by the crippling metallic case over his jaw.

"It's Ariel," she said. She recognized him as the Inquisitor who had captured her in the forest outside Romulus. His stare and smile were oddly welcoming, but she would not be deceived. "What's the point of this?"

"Blunt, are we?" he asked. "I thought you would be better at this game. Say the word and you'll be sent back to your cell." Her immediate silence was the only answer he required. "Please, take a seat."

Ariel pulled a chair from the desk stacked with handwritten documents. The words were completely foreign to her.

"Don't mind those, they're my poems. When I'm stuck in space I get to philosophizing, and I'm just conceited enough to consider my musings worthy of record. Are you well-read?"

"Somewhat." she said, never considering the topic before. "Reading is a job to me. I had to speak and understand so many languages growing up, and the best way for me to learn was by reading."

The Inquisitor nodded in understanding. He was of the Enfari race. His long, wavy bangs as black as a crow's feathers bounced lightly with the movement of his head. His skin was as pale and flawless as moonlight. Youthful, but lacking innocence. "Have you ever tried reading just for the sake of indulging in the prose? Depending on what you're looking for, it can be exciting, magnetic, tragic… fun even."

Ariel rolled her eyes. "What's the use of fun?"

"I don't believe you," the Inquisitor declared, boldly.

She shrugged, "Believe what you want."

The pale Enfari deliberately stroked the sword on his belt made from a hunk of the ugliest metal she had ever seen, rough and jagged like green stone at the bottom of an ocean. His eyes, like pools of blood, gleamed when he caught her distaste. "You don't like it? It's not as pretty as the Immortech that Paladins used to craft their own weapons. Those mines dried out or are lost forever, leaving new Inquisitors with the steel from my world."

"I see better material in my cell." Ariel said, intentionally mocking him.

"Yes, but only Enfari steel can conduct magic like Immortech." The Inquisitor smiled wickedly. He opened his silver cloak to reveal a belt. Well, it was not his belt, it was hers, and in its holsters were her two pistols. Ariel, not wanting to satisfy him, refused to acknowledge it. "You're well familiar with my gifts, aren't you?"

She nearly vomited upon recounting the Enfari's fingernail stabbing her in the neck and injecting some thick slime into her veins that rendered her paralyzed. It was the sickest she had ever been, and its damage still resonated somewhere deep inside of her. "Did you bring me here just to taunt me?" she asked, defiantly.

"Not at all. I've requested your company to make a peace offering." He paused to fully consider his next words. "But it cannot take place until you know my name."

Ariel indulged him: "So, what is it?"

"Slorne. Bastard by birth and left for dead in the ancient tunnels of Nezrath, now the heir apparent to the Inquisition."

She was silent. The Inquisitor would speak as he liked regardless of her input.

"Marko wants to take you to Rome as his prisoner, delaying the frigate's arrival to Grayspace significantly. He believes it's worth the sacrifice. Shame, I was looking forward to having a Synth's head mounted on my wall."

Ariel smirked. "I'm deeply sorry for being a burden."

"You're not a burden, Ariel." Slorne insisted. "You're a blessing. Unfortunately for Marko, his plans won't be fulfilled. We'll be far away before the King in Rome gets a hold of you."

He stood from the desk and turned to the window. His reflection in the glass was ghostly translucent. "I will take you and your brother to Dakahaan, my home-world and the citadel of the Inquisition. You will meet Lord Zakareth. Then, you will die by my hand."

The comment was not meant to shock her, nor was Ariel shocked to hear it. "I want to apologize in advance for what I will do, if there were any other way, I would take it. I've learned a lot about you in the past few days; an Underling from Prisilla, a bounty hunter, fugitive of the law. I can relate."

"Is that so?"

"It is," Slorne promised. "The Underlings of Prisilla have my sympathy. I've lived much the same life on my world."

"Hardly," Ariel declared. "If that were the case, you never would have made me a prisoner of the KOH." She picked up one of Slorne's journals and studied the symbols. The written word of the Enfari people was utterly strange to her, and yet she found the symbols alluring. She wanted to learn his language solely to read the prose. "Captivity is no place for someone like me. If you had any sympathy, you would have killed me."

Slorne's hands constricted so tightly his nails threatened to pierce his palms. "I come from nothing, deprived of even knowing who my parents were or why they left me in such a deprived state. A story most Underlings can relate to, is it not?"

"I guess so..." she admitted, reluctantly.

Slorne continued: "I joined the Inquisition as a child because I needed a place to sleep and was accepted into their ranks because of my blossoming skills in magic. Those without a gift died with their stomachs caved in and eyes bulging from their sockets. I knew I was fortunate, but fortune only helps you for so long. I honed my craft, spending night and day testing my abilities past the point of pain, all to create a better life for myself.

"Zakareth noticed my exceptionalism and took me in as his protégé. From there on, I was more motivated to improve, to evolve, to conquer. I bested all the young mages under his watch and some of his captains too, but it was never enough. No matter what trial I passed, or which of his pawns I defeated, he never showed me the appreciation I worked tirelessly to attain. One day, I spoke out; I asked him why, after everything I accomplished, could he not give me a sliver of his admiration? Zakareth, without even considering me, said it was because I did not deserve it.

"I lashed out, tried to strike him, tried to kill him honestly. I was one swing of the sword away from becoming Grand Inquisitor. He disarmed me before I knew what was happening, stroked my cheek with his dead fingers, and turned my jaw to ice!"

Slorne snapped toward her in bestial fury, charged headfirst, so his face was obtrusively in hers. "Do you like the reminder of my disobedience? He flicked the ice and my jaw shattered into tiny crystals." His breathing grew rapid, his eyes delirious. The more anger consumed him, the more it strained in his raspy voice. The metallic piece was directly in Ariel's line of vision, a capsule of all the Inquisitor's pain.

"Do you want to know what he told me after that?" His voice was low and breathless and nearly undeterminable. "When I stooped to my knees, clutching the melting shards of my own skin and bone, he said the son and daughter of Marius Zoltor are alive, and they are the heirs to the Inquisition. I'm nothing more than an obstacle for you to conquer, that is my fate!"

Slorne stepped back to regain his composure. Ariel was breathless herself, although she did such little speaking.

He continued. "I'm going to kill you not because I hate you. You and I both know what it's like to fight for our next meal, to fall asleep in an alley not sure if we'll ever wake up, to be fated by our lower birth. I'm doing this to defy the destiny another has cruelly written for me. I want Lord Zakareth to see his legacy crumble before his very eyes. He needs to be punished for trying to deny me of my agency. For all this, Ariel, I am sorry."

Marion was waiting for her when she returned. He was patient until the silver-cloaked mage left, then showered her with questions.

"It's nothing!" she screamed, turning to a corner and pretending to fall asleep.

# ELYSANDE (IV)

Timothy Mauvern was a slug of man. Fat, oafish, and with no awareness of the magnitude of his own voice, the new Overseer of Tisoni was the center of attention during the feast in the tall and sprawling halls of the Palazzo Reale. Located on the apex of the Capitoline Hill and bordering the Forum, Caesar fancied using the Palazzo for many political functions, including diplomacy conferences, council sessions, and, of course, business meetings disguised as long, lavish, and laborious dinner parties.

Above guests and hosts alike hung the red and gold banners of Caesar and the blue and yellow banners of Mauvern. The Mauverns fancied themselves as elk, but Elysande believed that animal to be far too majestic for their coat-of-arms. *A beaver would be more appropriate, or a pig.*

She sat at her king's left hand, while Timothy Mauvern sat at his right. To her left were her children, Lance and Julia, while to Mauvern's right was his equally oafish eldest son, Griffith, and his petite wife, Catherine. Timothy was a good deal older than Caesar, so their children did not share similar ages, leaving Julia and Lawrence to play with their food while the adults talked politics.

"I forget how beautiful Rome is this time of the year," Timothy commented between brief moments when his mouth was not full of food. "I've wasted my winters suffering in Lynwood when I could have taken a holiday here where it's warm." He grabbed a napkin to wipe his heavy, brown beard which was caked in grease.

"You will not have to worry about cold weather once you've fully settled into Hazelvale. I traversed those deserts years ago and received a sunburn I can still feel to this day." Caesar recalled. "If I may inquire, how is that process going?"

Mauvern shrugged casually, as if he was not making his home in a nest of vipers. "My soldiers and staff have started the process of integrating into Hazelvale. My son Edwin is there as well learning the intricacies of the spice trade. I will be leaving with Jacob once the New Year's festival is complete, while Griffith will be returning to Lynwood, as the stronghold has been governed by our family since its inception and I won't break that tradition now."

Griffith's bushy eyebrows perked up upon hearing his name, but his attention soon returned to his food when he found the conversation had drifted away from him. Elysande smiled coldly when hearing the name Hazelvale. Being the center of the spice trade on Tisoni, it was perhaps the most lucrative city in the KOH, but it was also the most dangerous. The cutthroat city devoured whoever dare try to tame her. Such potential profits tended to turn even the most civilized humans into savages. *The Omirs have gotten close, and they by no means are ready to surrender the progress they've made thus far.*

Further down the table, Natalia Caesar and Mauvern's third son, Jacob, were chatting with greater ease than Elysande had anticipated. Much to her surprise, Jacob was a handsome young man too, with a clean-shaven face, short nutbrown hair, and a lean body fitting of a warrior. Looks may be deceiving, but Elysande suspected that he possessed at least half a brain too.

"What's your strategy in appealing to the nobles of Tisoni?" she asked, boldly. "With such hostility in the continent, I'm curious as to how you plan to placate it."

Timothy looked stumped. "Well, I'm acting under the word of the king, and that is why they will obey me… Although, it could not hurt to do some research into the continent's history."

"One might think so," Elysande said, sipping her wine. *Caesar needs a leader who will unite Tisoni once and for all under the Aquila. And yet, our Lord Mauvern is apparently content with getting fatter than he already is off the spice trade. Be careful, sir, as you are more expendable than you may think.* Her husband's face was unreadable, as always. *You may have your unified Tisoni, but perhaps for the wrong reasons.*

Sitting on the opposite side of the table was Caesar's censor, Shota Nakamura, and he was eager to provide help to the overseer. "Tisoni is my home. If you need it, I will be happy to print out documentation on the region and the relationships between noble families. Suffice to say, most are volatile." The young man's honey-colored skin gleamed in the low candlelight as he smiled in an attempt to appear inviting to the overseer.

Timothy, realizing a great deal of work had been passed to someone else, sighed with relief. "Appreciated. You are Rome's censor, correct?"

"Yes, my lord." Shota replied.

"You are the one in charge of creating the tournament bracket for the Gladiator Games?"

Shota nodded. Mauvern kept his intentions secret, but Elysande sensed no hostility. "Then I have a gripe with you. You placed me against Robert Album, the old Lord of Buckleburn, in the first round of the tournament. Do you think I deserve to be on the old man side of the bracket?"

Shota answered without hesitation, as if prepared for the confrontation. "No, sir, I made the lists at random to keep the Games fair. I do apologize if I have harbored any ill will from you." This was a lie, but he spoke in such an innocent way that even the queen briefly perceived it as truth. Caesar ordered him to keep Mauvern safe and away from the Tisonians, and so elderly Lord Album of Buckleburn, a forgotten city in the southernmost region of Mercia, was considered the ideal first opponent. "The lists are not finalized yet. I could switch your opponent if you desire."

Timothy laughed hardily, slamming a fist on the table and nearly causing his glass of wine to spill over. The sharp squeal of delicate plates as they bounced in unison caused the whole hall to quiet. "I'm joking with you, son! The faster I get to the finals, the better." The Overseer of Tisoni slapped his gut and said: "I may not look it, but I have plenty left in the tank. Don't tell anyone though, it's my secret weapon."

Elysande saw the king's brother, Tullius, smile deviously. His head was perhaps filled with the fantasies of watching his prodigal son, Magnus, triumph over the fat Mercian aristocrat beneath the spotlights of the grandest stage in all of Orbis.

Mauvern continued, "Speaking of which, I'm disappointed to not see my king's name in the brackets. You're a cunning man, Your Majesty, surely you could still put the younger generation in its place."

Caesar shrugged. "I leave the glory of the Games to the youth. Tournaments were never my specialty, even twenty years ago. I've always preferred the game of wits."

"But that's how you could defeat them. Brains beat brawn every time. It's how we've both risen to prominence."

Elysande bit her tongue to stifle a laugh; Caesar, however, considered his wisdom with greater scrutiny. "That could be the case, but as king, I'd be concerned my opponent would let me win out of fear of angering me in defeat."

Mauvern brushed off the comment, "It's no concern of mine."

Caesar took a long drink of wine, then leaned in. "And what if we were on opposing sides during the Games? Would you strike at me with full force? Would you dare hurt the leader of the KOH?"

Timothy Mauvern stuttered: "I-I uh. No, Your Majesty, I would never dare to cause you harm. Never in any situation."

"I know you wouldn't, Lord Mauvern." Caesar subtly indicated with a slight nod down the table, where Jacob and Natalia were smiling and laughing with one another, as they had been doing the whole night. "I anticipate a long and prosperous relationship between our families."

Elysande eventually excused herself from the dinner for a breath of air outside. She walked to the balcony on the top floor of the Palazzo Reale and leaned over the edge to rest her elbows on the white balustrade. She looked out onto the storied city of Rome and saw an endless sea of pointed and circular rooftops erected from long, rectangular buildings. From their windows shown a million different lights in battle against the surrounding darkness. Close by was the massive expanse that was the Forum, which at the current hour served as the hub for young and restless socialites preparing for a night of unexpected escapades.

Sticking out like the fingers of a massive giant were the unfinished tracks of the sky-rails. Caesar began construction of the rails to facilitate travel in and out of the city center. The notion was pure, but the cost of it was already exceeding budget. He ordered that the construction be delayed until after the New Year. Elysande hoped they saw completion, as traffic within the heart of Rome was becoming more congested by the day, New Year or not.

To the north was the great Colosseum. From afar, the structure appeared to be a gigantic bowl gracelessly jutting out of the otherwise harmonious city, but soon the Colosseum would be decorated lavishly in lights and banners and would be the center of much commotion as the nobles of the KOH battered one another for their king's approval. She loved the event, in truth, but her mind was too distracted on other things.

Elysande allowed a warm ocean's breeze to brush over her back as she tried to enjoy the quiet night. Felix, the Senator of Rezza, threatened her, threatened her children, straight to the queen's face, and how did she respond? She allowed his boldness to go unchecked, establishing himself as the dominant in their relationship. Who was he? Some politician from an unremarkable city in northern Carcia. He may have had some mystique with how quickly he became a formidable name in the Senate, but he had no real sway in Rome. The Senate would crucify him as soon as she gave the word, so why didn't she?

Felix was vulnerable, but his behavior never gave it away. He had earnestly gifted her a demotion in status for playing along with his games. That, and a promise that she and her children would not become casualties in whatever was to come. Perhaps he was delusional, or maybe his conspiracy to resurrect the Republic was as grand as he implied. If they truly had a hand in Galla's death, the conspirators were to be taken seriously.

Informing Caesar would not eliminate the problem, saying there was a problem to be had. If she was to learn the true scope of the conspiracy, she would need to assimilate herself into it.

Footsteps marched ominously from behind her. She turned around and, unexpectedly, found Tullius Caesar in her company. The brutish man's eyes were overflowing with wine. *This should be interesting.*

"To what do I owe this pleasure, Commandant?" she asked.

"It must really get your temper flaring, seeing the Mauvern boy make a move on Natalia?" he said, swaying in place. "I can already see it: Natalia ascending the throne with her new husband, the Lord of the Spice Trade. A real power couple, wouldn't you say?"

"It's one night," Elysande retorted. "We both know the fickle nature of love, don't we?"

Tullius scowled. "I remember a time when Rome was ruled by Romans, now I walk about the city and I sit at council meetings and I can't help but notice the Roman influence is fading. You know, I tried to talk Caesar out of marrying you. I said having a Mercian girl as queen would muddy who truly ruled Orbis. Carcia has been the center of the KOH since the Gasardi dynasty, and having so many Mercians and Tisonians grasping for power truly irks me. It makes me question the years of hard work my brother and I dedicated to forming this dynasty."

Elysande raised her hand, having listened to her brother-in-law's ramblings for long enough. "You come out to mock me over those wretched Mauverns, when you're the one more perturbed by their presence."

Tullius shook his head. "No! I want Natalia, a true Roman, as the heir to my brother's dynasty, not your half-breeds. If a marriage with Mauvern allows that, I won't complain. They're a more docile breed than your lot. I like them that way."

"I've hardly lost yet. Caesar will be sending you off to fight the Synths soon enough." She put a finger to her chin and pretended to think aloud. "I just wonder what I can get done with you and my royal husband gone."

"Magnus will stay in Rome to keep you in line," Tullius objected. *The Commandant's eldest son, and an unfortunate identical picture of his father.* The boy knew the scope of his auctoritas and was unafraid to wield it.

"I'm shaking," Elysande said, clutching her forearms. "And how is your other son? Octavius, is it? I heard he's governing some colony with a formidable rubber fist. Will he also contribute to putting me in my place?"

Tullius growled. He looked ready to toss her over the balcony, which she invited him to try. It would be the easiest way to exterminate him, and she was confident she could get away with it. Instead, the Commandant turned on his heel and departed back into the dining hall. The Queen of the KOH did not follow.

She approached the decorated glass that looked down upon the dining hall. She spotted Caesar, who was laughing with the Mauverns, his brother, and his chief advisors. In Elysande's chair was someone else, a different Mercian girl likely part of Mauvern's retinue. She was elated as Caesar put his arms around her. No one questioned it, it was a scene as common as the sunrise. Elysande hoped she got everything she wanted out of her one night with the king.

Further down the hall at a different table and dressed in a bulk of silver robes was Cira Dei Tra, the wretched informant for the Grand Inquisitor disguised as one of Caesar's "advisors." She sat with other lesser Carcian and Mercian nobles. Some knights, some lords, ladies, consuls, or governors, all born into the servitude of greater families like her own. All were equally interchangeable.

Even at that table, Cira was an unworthy participant. *Timothy Mauvern does not have a court mage, so why do we?*

She had warned Caesar not to trust the mage, and he returned this wise counsel by inviting her to every important meeting he had. *She has no need to preserve the KOH and was likely contributing to its downfall, and yet he cares more of her advice than he does mine.*

Senator Felix valued her more than her husband, and for good reason. She was the queen, true enough, but the position meant nothing so long as it could be stripped away at any moment. Felix may be offering her and her children a demotion in status, but that status could have better stability than the one positioned high on the cliffside she currently occupied.

On her perch of the balcony, she searched for Lawrence and Julia and found them away from the table running around with some young nieces and nephews of Mauvern. *And yet, Felix threatened their lives*, she thought, her eyes becoming hot and red. It was an unforgivable sin, and she found herself swaying back to Caesar.

She returned to the balustrade facing the northern cityscape of Rome. On both sides, she faced uncertainty, so why pick a side at all? She could play the loyal Queen of the KOH for the public while also scheming with the conspirators behind closed doors. *And when the opportunity presents itself, take them both out.*

She turned to the city another time and discovered how differently it looked. Every part of Rome was on an incline heading toward the Capitoline Hill, as if bowing down in servitude to Elysande as she gazed out from the apex.

"My queen," Richard Dance said, appearing out of nowhere. It was a practiced skill of his. "Should we return to the dinner?"

Elysande shook her head. "No, let's head for home instead. I have much more urgent affairs to attend to."

# ARIEL (V)

She dreamt of Silver Wulf.

The bounty hunter, her master, her former master, dressed in his chrome armor, sending her that contemptuous glare she would only receive after an exceptionally bad blunder. She was on the ground, defenseless and frozen. His steel gauntlet closed in a hard fist. *He doesn't understand that I try my best.*

They were transported into the neon-melted world of the Market District of Prisilla. All around her were towering skyscrapers, lurid lights of every color in proud commercialized display, and people bustling along in endless waves through narrow streets. At every square-inch, the level was alive, zestful, but indifferent.

Ariel called for help as Wulf stalked her way, but no one paid any attention. She was on her knees and could not find the strength to move. Rain erupted from the sky, battering her face and blurring her vision, but she still saw the steel shimmer of Wulf's armor as he came forward. Giving up on the mercy of those around her, she was reduced to begging. *Begging? But for what?*

She turned away from Wulf in a frantic search for an escape. Her surroundings were not as they appeared. She was on the edge of a rooftop, an ocean of vibrant cityscape miles below her. Feeling damp, she peered down and saw her clothes were soaked in blood. Graznys' remains. The oozing stain of her inadequacy. Wulf was out of sight, but his presence was everywhere. Her feet shuffled closer to the skyline.

*Failure. Worthless fucking Underling.* The cold winds of empty sky embraced her. Her feet were fearless of the void. Ariel closed her eyes, uncaring, or accepting, or eager.

Her eyes opened to reality as the drop took her. The impact somehow crossed dimensions, abruptly and painfully shaking her awake. Marion, who was sitting on his side of the cell, was spooked by how violently she jolted to life.

"What happened to you?" he asked.

Ariel rubbed her eyes. The glaring ceiling lights still gave her migraines. Internally, her chest pounded like a drum. "Not sure. How long have I been sleeping?" Her racing heartbeat slowed to normalcy. *Pathetic*, a silent adversary declared, *pathetic, pathetic, pathetic.*

Marion considered her as if she were delusional. "How in the Hell am I supposed to know? A couple hours, a day maybe, I have no idea. How about you ask the Inquisitor for a clock next time you see him."

The comment went ignored. She still refused to tell her stupid brother about Slorne. Her reasoning? Not even she could decipher.

Marion continued, "Anyway, look at my friend. He's much nicer when you're asleep." He pointed to the humanoid who had returned to the light of his cell. With such a rundown appearance, she wondered what dreams haunted his sleep. "His name is Troyton. He was telling me about the battle for Fyrossia. If you were curious, the Fyrossians are defeated, and the Galactic War is over... not that it helps us."

She turned to the humanoid. "Troyton, is it? I'm Ariel."

The humanoid sighed. "I know that now. You're the children of the Archmage. Between you two and the Inquisitors, mage-kind has done nothing but torment me."

"Fortunately for you, we can't cast a spell between us," she said, trying to make light of his dour mood. "Can you tell us where we are going? Or how the frigate knew we were on Romulus?"

Troyton shook his head. He was apprehensive to speak, viewing her as an enemy, but he gave in, nonetheless. "I was arrested on Fyrossia and haven't spoken to an officer since. The frigate was heading for Grayspace, so the change in plans must have been made after I was locked up. Even if I knew who told Marko of your whereabouts, I wouldn't say anything."

Ariel assumed the humanoid was telling the truth. "Marko said something about finding a relay station, do you know where we could be?"

Troyton's eyes widened with contempt. "The nearest working relay station is hundreds of thousands of miles away from Romulus, and still we'll be traveling away from Orbis. All I want is to go back to Rome and face my punishment, why do the Gods keep me waiting?"

"You could be wrong?" Ariel suggested. "There are thousands of relay stations in space."

"Humanoids must demonstrate the ability to navigate each sector of the galaxy blind if they are to pass basic training. I know where the closest relay station is to Romulus." Troyton froze, as if startled by something in the room that only he could see. "I can't tell if we're moving... Marko must've sent a star-splitter to the station to cut time. Unless he's contacting Rome to pick us up, on a vessel like this we're over a month away from home."

"He's right," Marion confirmed. "We take mandatory cartography classes on Romulus too. I was awful at it, but I still know it's a Hell of a journey from the academy to Rome. What I can't understand, Troyton, is why be so hard on yourself?" He turned to Ariel to explain. "He tried to stop the Inquisitors from killing a child, that's why they imprisoned him."

"Was this on Fyrossia?" she asked, not really caring but so starved for conversation that she inquired anyway. Slorne may have been hospitable to her, but she had no doubt of the cruelty he was capable of.

"Yes!" Marion interrupted. "The child was the emperor's son. Marko sat back and did nothing. Only Troyton objected to it, right?"

"The child was an unregistered mage." Troyton fired back. "I interfered on the proper execution of justice, and I deserve whatever fate the king deems suitable."

"So what?" Marion asked. "The whole KOH system is shit. They forced me into a military academy before I could walk. They created you for the sole reason of being army fodder. King Caesar put us into roles we had no choice in playing, and when we resist, we're punished. The KOH wants tools, not people."

Troyton laughed bitterly. "It's relieving to meet someone else who wasted a good life granted to them by the KOH. Then again, at least I recognize my own crimes."

"A good life!" Marion laughed. "But at what cost? Apparently the lives of children, based on your own accounts."

"The emperor had an unregistered mage in his family!" the humanoid restated as if raising the volume of his voice added legitimacy to his words. "It's a simple rule to follow. If given the chance again, I never would have interfered."

"Why are you happy with being pawn? Every goddamn student on Romulus was so accepting of their role. No one cared about the oppression, everyone just wanted to satisfy the oppressor. Every day of my life I've been yelling at walls!" Marion was letting his emotions get the better of him. In a way, Ariel respected his lack of civility.

"The KOH represents the unity that can someday be achieved throughout the galaxy." Troyton answered. "One individual cannot achieve such a task on his own, only the collective can, and that collective is the Triumvirate. It is not that I'm content with being a 'pawn,' but I recognize their role for me in a much grander mission will mean far more than anything I can accomplish on my own."

"Unity?" Marion spat. "Everyone on Romulus hated me. Do you know why? The other students are from patrician families, while I was the abandoned son of defectors. They saw that difference and used my shame to feel better about themselves. The KOH may proclaim honorable ideals, but at its core, it's run by Romans. And I've hardly met a Roman who wasn't self-serving and egotistical. Can you say any different?"

Troyton went to correct him, but the objection lodged in his throat.

"It's easy to see the KOH, and not the people. I've made that mistake too many times," Marion said. Ariel was taken aback, wondering if her privileged brother was not so dull after all. "My hatred of the KOH blinded me from the people who actually cared about me. I believe we have two separate problems, but they are at such extremes that, somehow, we can relate. If we're ever given another chance at freedom, would you choose to be any different?"

The monstrous mage returned to the prison cell several days later. Ariel knew why he had come even before he gestured to her to step forward.

"Is the Inquisitor looking for me this time?" Marion asked, bitterly. The giant mage said nothing; he pointed at her to come, and she obeyed. In a way, she found the favoritism to be immensely satisfying, especially in how it neglected her brother. Marion switched his sly remarks to her. "Let him know I have all the time in the world for a chat."

What would her brother say if she told him the truth? If he knew Slorne was going to bring them to the Grand Inquisitor to be executed, would he be eager to speak with him then?

When she arrived to Slorne's room, the Enfari mage was hunched over his desk and scribbling something on a piece of paper. The giant Inquisitor exited without a word. Ariel expected him to touch her hair again, but he did not. Even with the door shut, his thunderous footsteps echoed all the way down the corridor.

"How do you feel?" Slorne asked. He put the papers away and invited her to sit.

"I'd like a bigger cell... and a better cellmate."

"That's not what I meant; how does it feel to be alone with me?"

She shrugged. "Are you asking if I'm scared? Well, I'm not sure how I feel, but it's unique and I want to enjoy it while it lasts."

Slorne gave her a quizzical look. "What do you mean?"

"I'm staring my killer in the face and you think I should shudder, but it's not the case. I get the chance to indulge in my own death, an opportunity not many people are given."

Slorne smiled. "So, I am death incarnate? I suppose I never considered death as a character. Very well, what would you like to know?"

Ariel nodded toward his desk. "What're you writing?"

"Why so curious?" Slorne asked, "You've made it clear you're not interested in the literary world."

"I lied," she confessed. "I'm not a lover of literature, but I am obsessed with adventure stories. I mean, real journeys written by people much braver than me. It's been a fantasy of mine for a long time, to wander into the unknown. The promise of an ever-expanding universe is so… alluring. No, I don't care about prose, but I love melding minds with an explorer."

"It sounds to me like you have a deep connection with prose, whether you know it or not. This is the point of reading, to briefly mingle with the thoughts and emotions of others. To experience something you would not normally have the chance to," Slorne said. A sudden and violent cough erupted from his lungs, stooping him over and nearly knocking him out of his chair. When he recovered, he tried to act as if nothing happened. "For a moment, the poor become rich, the boring become captivating… and the bereft become beloved."

"And which applies to you?"

"Any and all. But it's necessary not to become too obsessed. Living vicariously through others, whether they be fictional or not, becomes a crutch for some. They get their excitement from the page, and that's good enough. But for me, a brief change in perspectives strengthens the hunger for something more, something greater."

"It's sad, but inspiration leads to complacency. So many Underlings talk of leaving the Underbelly, but it's always something they'll do 'tomorrow,'" she said, her mind and heart blooming.

No one had ever challenged her to think critically. The things she said hardly felt like her own words, but sharing them was oddly liberating, as if they had been ruminating somewhere in the back of her mind for years. It was awkward to speak with this kind of candor. And yet, she sensed a subconscious encouragement from the Inquisitor to keep thinking, so she may match his philosophical ponderings word for word.

"The hope of change lets them continue to live their unfulfilled lives with the illusion that things will get better. And once the spell of inspiration fades, they find their fix somewhere else… and nothing ever changes."

Slorne rubbed his chin. "It's awful, isn't it?"

"My old master called me 'Canary,' a delicate bird unable to handle the limits of which her wings can take her. I left him for dead on Prisilla. I made it into space, and I handled the change on my own. I will always cherish my adventure books, but they can't capture the freedom of the first-hand experience."

An immense sadness overcame Slorne. "I can see the story now: the abandoned Underling of Prisilla defies the odds, escapes her Hell, and lives a life of travel and adventure as she dreamt of since childhood. Am I too cruel to cut that story short?"

"You've concerned yourself with battling destiny for much longer than I have," she admitted. "As long as your story is one worth telling, I will not object."

The Inquisitor considered his papers again. "We write what we know, and mine is great sadness. I'm a poet, of sorts, but only the most bereft souls would find any meaning in my words. I hope to someday create something different, something not so woeful." He gripped the papers in his pale hands, studied them, and sneered. "Tell me, how did it feel to defeat your master?"

Ariel smirked. Silver Wulf reappeared, face down in the dust and dirt. He was dead, certainly, by Kagen's gang or the pearls or even another Underling. "I won't spoil the experience for you."

Slorne went to speak, but another onslaught of coughing struck him. The attack was lighter than the previous but still reached the same chilling mortal pitch. "You've made me lose sleep of late. I keep pondering in my head the possibility of letting you live, of allowing us to create our own destinies separately, but it cannot be done. As long as you live, Zakareth's prophecy could come true. Even if I kill him, he will die with the hope that the spawn of Marius Zoltor could still succeed him. After what he's done to me, I cannot let that happen."

Ariel brushed her cheek. The sting from when Wulf slapped her for allowing Graznys to die had not faded. "My life doesn't deserve to be begged for," she said. "But I also won't follow your path willingly. If the opportunity of escape presents itself, I won't think twice."

"I expect nothing less. We are survivors, Ariel, and I won't deny you of your basic instinct."

When she returned to the cell, Marion did not bother to interrogate her. Nor did she have any interest in speaking with him. One question from Slorne still lingered with her: *how did it feel to defeat Wulf?*

She had not considered this before. She supposed this tremendous question went unanswered due to her world becoming so chaotic since leaving Prisilla that she never had the time to dwell on how she changed after ridding herself of the dead weight. Had she changed? Was she any different now without Wulf?

Ariel understood Slorne's internal conflict was slowly destroying him. Even with Zakareth dead and his prophecy broken, would he find vindication? When she had gazed into the red pools on his ghostly thin face, she saw nothing but anguish and despair. When one's identity was intrinsically tied to another, can that person ever achieve independence?

He would not find relief in killing Zakareth. He had made the Grand Inquisitor too large a portion of his own self, his actions to eliminate the man responsible for all his rancor were fundamentally a final act to receive his validation. And that deep hate, stemming from a loss of identity, would be as easy to remove as a vital organ.

She rested her head and fell into a smaller prison of self-reflection. Her egotistical pity quickly reflexed. Who was she without Silver Wulf? And could separation honestly change her from what Wulf had shaped her into being? These nebulous questions added up, but none reached a satisfying answer.

# MARION (VI)

After endless needling on his part, Ariel finally let her secrets spill.

Marko and the Inquisitor had summoned her to extrapolate more information on the Paladin, Kent Kentoshi, and his crew. They somehow found out she had been in their company for much longer than Marion and wanted to use her knowledge to their advantage. She swore that she remained vigilant, and that their threats were mainly idle.

"What did he say?" he asked. The first time he witnessed magic, it was used against him. The sickening substance of whatever the Enfari Inquisitor injected into his veins lingered inside him like an old virus. He read stories of mages who wielded fire and ice from their fingertips, summoned hailstorms out of clear skies, and created groundbreaking earthquakes powerful enough to split moons in half, but a magic as foul as the Inquisitor's was something he could never have anticipated.

"Marko did all the talking, the Inquisitor just stood around," Ariel said.

Marion cursed. He hated the Inquisitors, but his fascination outweighed his antipathy. Knowledge of the Paladins, Inquisitors, and mage-kind in general was mostly forbidden on Romulus. Even Everec was hesitant to teach of the people who simultaneously incorporated and sequestered every other race in the galaxy. These unspoken rules fueled Marion's interest, so the chance to speak to the Inquisitor unashamedly enchanted him.

While trapped in a prison of plexiglass, he strategized conceivable ways to prove his innocence. When presented to a

Roman court as an unregistered mage, he would hold nothing back when confessing his unconscious crimes. He would present himself as the fool he was, and maybe the court would show pity for his genuine ignorance. Then, he could reunite with Octavia and live a quiet life together somewhere on Orbis.

Or, they could sentence him to death. He would be executed, done away with in secret, disposed of, and erased from history before ever leaving a mark. The simplicity of it was almost attractive.

Octavia would manage to move on. He abandoned her again by the temptation of his reckless sister, despite the promise he swore under the heavy rain and black grove outside Romulus. The reminder of his stupidity came in waves of crippling regret. Octavia risked leaving Romulus to help him, and the academy may not welcome her back. In a way it seemed like a fitting final consequence. Despite all the warnings, Octavia stayed loyal to him, and the final punishment for her resilience would be the worst.

When a soldier entered the cell, Marion hardly gave her a second thought. Typically, visitors were the most enthralling part of his day, even though they would never interact. Today, his enthusiasm was absent. He assumed the visitor was the usual orderly making the rounds and delivering the prisoners their meals. Not one suspicion stirred when she walked straight to the plexiglass shield.

"I found that firewood for you."

Marion, incredulous, sprinted to the wall and placed his hands on the glass. "Oh Gods, please don't tell me you're a hallucination."

Octavia smiled under her heavy Roman helmet. Even at sixteen, she could pass for a soldier. "I'm one hundred percent real," she promised, putting her hands opposite his between the glass. For a moment, Marion could feel her warmth. "I can't stay for long," she said in a hushed voice. Her face was constricted to suffocate the emotions that wanted scream. "Help is on the way, that's all I can tell you."

She went to turn away, but Marion begged her to stop. "Wait, wait! How'd you get here? Who's coming to help us?" Ariel came to her feet and paced ominously behind his back.

Octavia made a quick head turn to check for any immediate threats. "I saw you get taken by an Inquisitor. I snuck on his ship and I've been searching for you ever since..." she let her words float. "We can talk later, I promise."

Like tearing off a bandage, Octavia charged out of the cellblock, leaving Marion with his jaw gaped. A sudden flash of madness overwhelmed him at the sight of the prison doors closing behind her, and he punched the plexiglass barrier with unrestrained force. The pain surged up his arm, but his body was uncaring. This sudden state of perceived invincibility allowed him to hit the wall again, and again, and again. Finally, he collapsed to the ground, exhausted, and resting his boiling face in his hands.

Again, she had risked everything for him. And for what? Gods only know how long she had been sneaking around the frigate, putting her life in danger. She should had given up on him, for her sake.

"She's quite the fascinating girl." Ariel said, not allowing him a moment to regain his composure.

"So, she is real..." Marion said, giving her a fragment of his attention.

"You've known her your whole life, right?" she asked.

"Yes."

"And how much do you trust her?"

"Completely." Marion replied, feeling tested.

Ariel arched an eyebrow. "It seems to me like this trust only works one-way. Now listen to me, let's say everything she told us is true. She had to sneak onto an imperial frigate undetected, assume an identity on this ship, and maintain that identity perfectly for as long as we've been trapped. I may be mistaken, but I doubt these kinds of lessons are taught on Roman academies."

Marion shot to his feet, "Who are you to question her loyalty?"

Ariel raised her hands in a mocking display of peace. "I'm not questioning anyone's loyalty, yet. But don't you find how good she is at this to be odd?"

"You don't know our history," he debated. "I would do the same for her if I had to. Maybe you're unfamiliar with it, but this is what we do for the people we *love*." An untimely smile crossed his face.

Handling extreme elation and tedium at the same time left his emotions conflicted.

She rolled her eyes to the ceiling. "You're missing my point. She's skilled, too skilled. Maybe this 'love' causes you to do stupid things, but it doesn't make you good at doing them."

"I think I understand," he said in a diplomatic turn. "You're saying that Octavia is lying to me, that she could not possibly have snuck onto the frigate herself. Maybe, somehow, she's deceiving me?"

"More or less," she answered.

"Okay." Marion swung at her, his knuckles meeting the outline of her jaw with accidental precision. The relentless crack upon contact bounced off the walls of their cell, and never truly left their presence. Ariel fell on her backside, her wild blonde hair covering her face in tangles. Marion rushed to her aid.

He pulled the bangs from her forehead, revealing a full, sinister smile, bloody teeth and all. She spat at him, the projectile crashing on his nose and splattering over his face.

Marion pounced on her, pinning her to the floor with his knees and shaking her by the collar of her shirt. He went to strike again, this time with more purpose, but she was ready. Her head moved a second too fast, causing his fist to embrace nothing but metal flooring.

The pain was intolerable, zipping through his body like bolts of lightning. His fingers began to swell, taking the form of puffy sausages. In this period of agony, he lost track of Ariel.

On his knees, he looked up and found his sister standing over him. Before he could react, she launched her right knee straight into his lips. The impact sent him tumbling backward but, instinctually recalling his training, used the momentum to roll back to his feet.

The siblings spat simultaneously, unconsciously comparing whose spittle was more entrenched in blood. They stood at a standstill, occupying separate halves of the cell. Marion breathed heavily, not from exhaustion, but as a reaction to the sudden transition from intensity to calmness. Romulus taught him to fight selfishly, to overpower his enemy by his own will. Ariel did not abide by these rules, electing to use her opponent's offense as her own. If he'd considered this strategy sooner, his brawls with Vintrus may have ended differently.

He could not read Ariel at this time, nor could she read him, he suspected. Marion did not want to keep fighting, but he also refused to be the first to yield. Her ember eyes burned brighter than normal, a disguised passion of anger or elation. He felt guilty for striking her, but she had questioned his love for Octavia, so she at least had some of it coming. Ariel was jealous, surely, and was trying to split them apart for her own selfish desires. He wanted to punch the wicked smile from her face, but he never got the chance.

The frigate halted abruptly, making a horrible screeching sound as the objects inside reacted to the sudden shift in momentum. Marion nearly lost his balance as the floor slipped from his feet. Then the lights shut off, and he was left in complete darkness with a lunatic.

A second passed before the emergency lights turned on, drinking in the darkness with a hazy, red glow. Ariel resided on her side of the cell, a demon in the new light.

The door out to the main hallway slid open and three Roman soldiers came barreling in, guns and flashlights aimed directly at their cell. Marion threw his hands in the air, but the soldiers were yelling incoherently at him, at each other, and into their comms.

An explosion fired in the near distance, and everyone went quiet. The sounds of cutting metal screeched down the desolate and dark corridor. The soldiers turned their sights to the entryway. They were hardly visible in the red gloom. Marching could be heard from all around, like the scattered pattering of rodents in the walls.

One of the soldiers spoke up. "You two, check the hallway. I'll stand back with the prisoners." The others obeyed, inching forward. Marion knew her voice.

The two soldiers were dropped with one shot to each head. Octavia turned to the cell door, typed in a code on the control panel, and set him free. She threw her arms around him, and he kissed her hard in return, nearly biting her in the passion of the moment. They embraced for a long time, until Octavia politely pushed him away.

"Not now. We're on a time limit," she said. Even in the darkness, her stunning green eyes mesmerized him.

"Are you a one-woman army?" Ariel asked, still in the cell. Marion despised the tone of her voice.

"Of course not, I'm working with your people," Octavia said. "Now, let's go."

"Wait." Marion stopped in his tracks. "Unlock this cell too."

Octavia looked skeptical. "You know who's in there?"

"He's my friend, please open it." Octavia shrugged and punched in a code. The door slid open, and out came the towering humanoid, Troyton Vorenus. His face was hidden in the weak red glow. Octavia was startled by the sight of him.

"Come with us if you want. Just remember, you don't owe the KOH anything," Marion said. He would not turn to see if Troyton followed, for it made no difference.

A Druin was waiting for them outside the cellblock, but it was not Kent. His green skin was darker than the Paladin's, and he had a long horn on each of his temples. He also smelled less of alcohol.

"You're Bato, I'm assuming." Octavia said. "I was told you have a way out."

"It's him." Ariel assured, nodding to the Druin. "But I trust this man as far as I can throw him."

"It'll have to do." Octavia insisted, the surrounding sirens almost drowning out her voice. Used to being out of the loop, Marion contributed nothing.

"Follow me, young humans!" Bato declared. "Our escape is in sight."

And so they did, but escape was most certainly not in sight. Bato took them down the main hallway and up a flight of stairs. Gunfire racketed in the surrounding rooms, but the path Bato took them on was thankfully clear.

Two men came from connecting corridors and fell in with them as they raced down the slick, grated hallway. One wore an ivory-colored mask adorned with glyphs and swirls while the other had a black bandana wrapped around his mouth. Their races were hidden, but they wore similar light leather suits reinforced by bronze-colored armor around the shoulders and chest. If Marion was to be shot at, he'd rather be wearing Roman armor.

More of these masked soldiers regrouped with the herd, until he counted ten of them in total.

"There's our ship!" Bato called out. Their pace doubled as they rushed through a shrouded hall connected to a plethora of other passageways separated by large, rectangular doors that started to close as they approached. Marion held onto Octavia's hand firmly, ensuring he would not lose her.

Roman soldiers sprung from secret passageways obscured in the poor lighting. The numbers were small at first but grew bountiful as they neared the ship. Naturally, a shootout ensued. Marion's protectors did everything they could to keep the small pack moving, stopping occasionally to shoot for the purpose of disorienting the oncoming enemy and preventing a barricade.

Two of the leather-clad soldiers elected to stand their ground, to no objection from the others.

Finally, freedom was in sight. There was a sizeable hole in the frigate wall and filling it from the vacuum of space was the entryway of a much smaller ship. Figures waited for them inside, but they possessed shapeless forms from afar. Meanwhile, sounds of spiraling bullets and lasers hailed from all around. Disorienting as it may be, Marion trudged on, his mind racing but his hand firmly in Octavia's and his eyes glued to their escape.

Ariel ran ahead, burdenless, but not to the exit. She stopped at the fallen body of a Roman soldier and relieved him of his sidearm.

He and Octavia were a few feet away from their ship, his heart rate rising with every step taken.

"Inquisitors!" a soldier hollered.

Three figures in haunting, silver cloaks emerged from the shadows. Two of them wore the traditional facemasks of the Enfari warriors, and the one with the horrible red eyes stood between them. In his hand was some grotesque, jagged sword that seemed to relish in the darkness.

Every one of Bato's crew focused on the Inquisitors. Friendly laser fire rained on the mages, but nothing hit. Marion, unconscious of the dire situation, watched in awe as they glided through potential death. Then, something tugged him by the collar. "RUN, BOY!" Bato demanded. Even with one arm, the Druin managed to push him helplessly in the desired direction.

With attention elsewhere, no one noticed a Roman soldier lob a grenade in their direction. One brave ally went to bat it away, and was successful to some degree, but not without the cost of his own life. The outburst of fire and shrapnel shook the hallway. Marion too suffered its effects as he and Octavia smashed into a wall and crumbled to the floor. The ear-piercing snap of the explosion stripped him of his hearing.

"We're surrounded!" someone called faintly against the intolerable ringing in his ear. The masked soldiers who remained fired aimlessly into the toxic mist. From ahead, Marion saw the darkened outline of Ariel, who stood stupefied like a frozen shadow.

"Get to the ship! Take the girl and go!" someone else yelled.

Marion helped Octavia to her feet. His back was to their escape when he finally got her up. The ceiling creaked violently from above, and the sounds of lasers, fire, and mortal screams encircled them. Smoke and ash swirled about, like a shield from the surrounding chaos. In that moment, Marion wondered blissfully if their unity could endure death.

He gingerly placed his hand on her cheek. She welcomed his touch at first as a sort of comfort against the bedlam, but her face turned to utter horror as she let out a tiny but screeching yelp from her throat.

"Are you hurt?" Marion asked, not understanding her behavior.

"What was it all for?" she asked, breathless.

Then the ceiling collapsed.

# ELYSANDE (V)

Richard Dance pulled up to the senator's estate in the dead of night. He got out of the car, opened Elysande's door, and assisted her out. They both dressed in basic, dark clothes, the queen going as far as to wear a hat. With the city center being most vibrant at night around the New Year, she suspected the west-end residences to be quiet and empty.

They approached the threshold of the estate and Ser Dance knocked. The door swung open, revealing a man as tall as her protector, with straw colored hair, striking teal eyes, and fair skin. He was dressed in heavy steel armor, with the crest of a mighty brown bear with its large paws raised above its head adorned on the center of his breastplate. The symbol looked familiar, but Elysande could not place it.

"My queen," the young soldier said with a hint of forced politeness. He gestured them to enter.

Inside, the estate was wide but sparse of furniture and decoration. It was practical in one way, because many of the nobles residing on the west-end would be returning to their homes as soon as the New Year's festival was through, but this degree of bareness was hostile.

Senator Felix Mareto of Rezza was waiting for her in the dining hall, along with Senator Lucio Privetera, who she recalled spoke at the last meeting Gaius had with the Senate. Along with them was a woman wearing the same senatorial robes as they did, but she was a stranger to Elysande.

Felix perked up at the presence of his queen. "Ahh, Elysande. How are you on this pleasant night?"

She waved her hand in dismissal. "Don't pretend like we're friends. We're two people working for one goal, that is the extent of our relationship. In fact, I'm not entirely convinced of your side as of yet."

"To flip back and forth would prove unfortunate for the both of us," Felix said, casually. "But I must have been somewhat persuasive to have you here, wasn't I?"

"For one night, maybe," Elysande conceded. "But I'm at Caesar's side every single day. Think about it: at any possible moment I could be revealing the conspiracy to him."

"How could you bring her here if you were not certain of her loyalty?" Lucio objected. He had dark Carcian skin like his fellow conspirators, but his was lined and spotted. "She will be the downfall of our cause!"

"Caesar forgave you once, Senator Privetera, when you sided with the Republic during the Civil War." Elysande reminded him. "Do you think he will be merciful again?"

Lucio scoffed. "I've done nothing wrong! Caesar is a tyrant. True, he allowed me to keep my seat in the Senate, but what is the Senate now? Lap dogs to the crown, that's all. The title may be the same, but the Senate has been stripped of its auctoritas!"

Felix shook his head. "Calm yourself, Lucio. What does she know? The worst she can say is she uncovered a few bad eggs."

The old senator was incredulous. "She could have the whole royal army outside! You've put our lives in danger."

"What are our lives worth in the grand scale of the cause?" Felix asked. "If you're concerned with your own well-being, I'm more worried about your damage to the Heirs than hers."

"I'm here, so whatever you're planning can be linked to me." Elysande objected. "I knew the risks of walking into this room long before I made my decision. I've come to help. The only question now is: what do you want of me?"

"See Lucio," Felix gestured. "She's already eager to serve. Rachele, if you will?"

The woman addressed Elysande. Judging by her features, she must have been Carcian too. "We need your name most of all. You are familiar with the brackets for the Gladiator Games, correct?"

"And who are you?" the queen asked.

"Senator Rachele Giordin of Venallia, but it's no matter at this moment. Again: are you familiar with the brackets?" Her voice was obscenely condescending. It took all of the queen's restraint to not put her in her place.

Rachele continued: "Then you will know that only a few spots remain open for the tournament. What we need from you is to sponsor a special knight so he may compete in the Games. The rest of the work can be left to us."

"You need me as an advocate?" Elysande asked, slightly disappointed. "You have the Rock Star of Rezza in your ranks. Surely, he will suffice."

"The compliment is appreciated," Felix said, smirking. "As you must know, getting onto the lists is no easy task. Most competitors need a significant amount of auctoritas just to be considered for the Games. Our champion is skilled, and we have the upmost faith in his abilities, but he has yet to earn the fame to make the lists on his name alone."

Elysande leaned in. "And who is this special someone?"

The tall soldier who welcomed her inside emerged from the shadows. The queen remembered that the roaring bear engraved on his breastplate was the coat-of-arms of a Mercian family, *but which one?*

Senator Rachele raised her arms as if presenting the soldier as a grand prize. "This is Ser Bryson Byrne, you may know his father, Edward, as the Lord of Riverford. He will be our champion in the Gladiator Games, and he will be victorious."

Elysande was not convinced. "I'm familiar with the Byrnes. They're sycophants to my father, if I recall. But what makes me the ideal advocate for this boy? You realize his family sided with Caesar during the Civil War? Lord Edward helped retake Mercia from the Vikanders, and now you think they'll help you?"

"If I may speak, my queen." Ser Bryson Byrne began. He was tall and built like the bear on his coat-of-arms, but that said nothing of his skill in the field. "I am acting under my will alone."

"Is that supposed to be reassuring?" she sneered. "You want me to vouch for a knight I've never heard of, and then what? What happens when he enters the tournament? And why is he worthy of my advocacy?"

Felix spoke calmly as if to reassure her. "As you said: the Byrnes are loyalists to your father, so it would not be implausible for you to sponsor him. Bryson may look young, but he's earned a remarkable amount of auctoritas for his bravery in the colonizing campaigns with General Tarquinius. King Caesar likely knows his name too. He's a valiant and seasoned solider, an unassuming but formidable threat to anyone in the Gladiator Games."

"Let's put that bravery to the test," Elysande proposed. "Ser Dance, cripple him."

In a flash, her guardsman pulled a baton from his belt, raised it in the air, and prepared to cast it down on Bryson Byrne. The young man grabbed the larger knight's arm and forced him backward. Dance's shoulders slammed into the wall, sending a quake throughout the house. Her protector was soon to regain a position of dominance as his wits returned, but Byrne would not submit. The two men wrestled in place, jockeying for position, neither allowing their feet to move an inch. The young knight was calm and his technique sound despite the sudden and powerful pressure Dance had forced on him. If the queen was not mistaken, it appeared that Byrne was taking advantage of her royal protector as the brawl transpired.

Before the two men could puncture any more holes into the drywall, Elysande called it off.

"Enough!" she commanded, slightly more convinced that Byrne was indeed a real soldier. With countless young men and women earning the title of knight without laying a foot in the warzone, she had to be sure.

"What in the Hell was that?" Lucio blurted. The old senator worked up more of a sweat than the two knights.

"A demonstration," Elysande said, rubbing her chin. The knight held himself like a hardened soldier, and she suspected their familial ties would make him a believable candidate for her sponsorship. "My apologies, Ser Byrne."

"It's nothing." Bryson responded, refusing to remove his eyes from Ser Dance.

Elysande continued: "I'd be risking a lot sticking my name out for him. How do I know you're not trying to screw me over?"

Felix shook his head. "The winner of the Gladiator Games is awarded one request before the king. When Bryson is victorious, he will ask to join Caesar's Praetorian Elite. As you can see, we gain nothing from you or our knight unless he wins the whole tournament."

"And if Caesar approves of the request, what happens next?"

"We have an Heir close to him. He will be around to hear Caesar's secrets, to master his schedule, to plot our overthrow."

"It will also give Bryson an impeccable position to… take a shot at the king." Elysande answered. She was not intimidated by the possibility, but she needed to prove to the conspirators that she could not be played for a fool.

"We will not have the foundation of the new Republic be built by bloody hands!" Lucio objected. "Caesar killed millions to take his crown, but we will not follow suit."

"Then I envy your naivety," Elysande said. The senators and Ser Bryson waited desperately for her answer. She supposed she had no choice but to go with it. If they needed Bryson to win the Gladiator Games, that would allow her plenty of time to earn the trust of the conspirators and discover their true scale in numbers. "I will advocate for Ser Bryson, but not publicly. I hope this act of faith will be returned in the future."

Senator Felix smiled. "The mutual benefits have already been set in motion, my queen. I admire your willingness to trust us, and I promise it will all be repaid."

She turned to Bryson Byrne, who was brimming with excitement. "Don't disappoint me. Many a knight and noble would kill for the position I'm granting you."

Bryson bowed. "Never. There's too much on the line. For the sake of the Republic, the tournament is as good as mine."

Elysande departed from the hive of conspirators soon after.

Lucio and Bryson Byrne were apes. Senator Felix's confidence indicated he was either a master manipulator or a brainwashed goon. Senator Rachele seemed to be a loyal servant to whatever the Heirs of the Republic was, and the practical nature with which she laid out her plan led Elysande to believe there may have been a few braincells swimming among the sea of idiocy.

Dance pulled out into the street and started to turn for home, until Elysande stopped him.

"Make a call to Shota," she said. Dance obeyed, and Shota picked up immediately.

"Hello, my queen?" he said, his voice coming through the car speaker.

"Shota, are you home? I know it's late, but I need to speak with you." Dance was already driving to the censor's house.

"Yes, madam. Anything for you. I will be waiting."

They drove for several minutes down the road toward the edge of the west-end neighborhoods, the pale moon stalking them from the rearview mirror. When Dance parked, Elysande peered out her window and saw the silhouette of Nakamura's house, stark and black against the explosion of lights resonating from the distant but buzzing city center.

Once inside, Shota welcomed her into the dining room, where the dense, maroon walls blocked any activity from the outside world. Surrounding her were the stark, vivid, and abstract paintings native to the Kygorro region of Tisoni. One picture depicted an ice blue river snaking through a snowy park. Using only three colors, blue, white, and black, Elysande enjoyed the simplicity of it, relying more on the viewer's imagination and less on hyperrealism. Another picture was of a massive black tree with long, winding branches covered in pink flowers reaching out into a sulfuric yellow sky. The tree and field were black against the brighter background, making it hard to distinguish the two. Despite the more sinister tone, she liked the painting equally to the first.

"These are such beautiful paintings," Elysande complimented. "Who's the artist?"

"My great-grandfather," Shota said, with some pride. "They've survived multiple generations. And now the onerous is on me to keep them protected."

"Impressive. Are you an artist yourself?"

"Depends on your definition," he said, somewhat passively. "I've never picked up a paintbrush in my life. Sitting back and admiring from afar is my preferred taste."

Elysande analyzed the paintings with greater scrutiny. The painting of the snowy park reminded her of her mother's homeland. Peace and longing overcame her, like the mixing and melding of paints themselves. "I wish I had time for either…"

"It's the beauty of looking at art, it helps us live in the moment, allows us to experience the present while taking us somewhere else completely." Shota said. As she continued to gaze, she glimpsed the outline of a woman by the icy blue lake.

"Could I bother you for a drink?"

Shota disappeared into the kitchen, reemerging with a large, clear pitcher containing a velvety purple liquid mixed with ice and lemons. He placed it on the long table between them, along with two small cups decorated with black and white painted shapes.

"This is angel's blood, from Hirosuma, my home city. It is one of our most treasured drinks." Shota Nakamura said. "I pray you like it."

He humbly poured the liquid into each of their cups. They raised their glasses in mutual respect and drank. The taste was smooth and sweet, but deceptively strong in alcoholic content.

"This is very good, Shota," Elysande complimented. "I'm grateful that you would offer such fine hospitality to a bad guest."

"How could you say such a thing? The Queen of the Kingdom of Humanity could never be a bad guest."

"I've come to your house in the middle of the night, uninvited, and still you treat me well." She eyed the censor up and down. He was dressed eloquently in a high-collared doublet of green satin with silver buttons going down a flap folding on the left side his slim body. She was relieved every day when she could strip off the constricting dresses that elitist society deemed she wear, but Shota's posture suggested indifference, or maybe pride in dressing sharply. "I hope you did not dress up just for my company."

Shota shook his head. "No, madam. Although I will always make myself presentable for royalty, this is simply what I like to wear. I find that I'm at my most productive when dressed for work."

"And when does work end and your personal life begin?"

"As the First Censor of Rome, work never ends." Shota replied. He was young, she guessed, somewhere between his mid to late twenties. To rise to such a prestigious position so early in his career, Shota must not have indulged in a "personal life" since his first day of primary school.

"That is the curse of working in political prestige," Elysande said. "We have our paperwork, councils, and public assemblies, but even when all that is over, I'm still Queen. At dinners I strategize with and against those I dine with. When I'm out in the public I smile and wave to the masses to let them think I care. I only wear my crown out in the open, but it follows me wherever I go, whenever I go… even now."

"It is my philosophy that we can only rise to such positions because our personalities suit them." He refilled her glass with angel's blood. "If I understand correctly, you are unsure if your position as queen has obscured who you really are. If your personality did not fit the role, you would never have survived in it, just as I would have been swallowed alive as Censor of Rome if I was not born to fulfill it."

"I haven't thought of it that way," Elysande said, drinking.

"You must have," Shota assured her. "As you alluded to, you're not here to discuss the human psyche. How may I be of assistance?"

The censor's directness was refreshing. "I wanted to ask about the lists for the Gladiator Games. More specifically… have they been completed?"

"They are nearly finalized. I've made sure Timothy Mauvern cannot encounter a Tisonian until the semifinals, if he can make it that far."

"Unlikely," she said. "But that's not what I'm here for. Are you familiar with Edward Byrne, Lord of the Riverford?"

"I'm familiar with every noble family."

"His son, Bryson Byrne, has asked me personally to help him enter the tournament. Normally, I would politely refuse, but he's fought bravely with General Tarquinius, and I think this would be an excellent way to show our appreciation to the Byrnes for their service."

"I see, but the same can be said about a million other soldiers. Placing Ser Byrne on the lists over more distinguished knights would be… controversial."

"I know, my lord, but I must admit: my actions are not entirely selfless. Although Timothy Mauvern swears one of his own will always rule Lynwood, part of me wonders if it will be forsaken once he settles into his role as overseer. Lynwood is too valuable of a city to be left ungoverned, so I have been tossing around the idea of granting it to the Byrnes. They may not have the prestige of other Mercian families, but they have been loyal friends to the Bodewins since the days we ruled Mercia as kings and queens."

"And one way to increase their prestige is to give Bryson a position in the Games, is it not?" Shota inquired.

"Precisely, my lord."

"Then I will try my best to place him in the brackets." The censor bowed before her. His posture expressed humility, but his tone suggested certainty that his queen's request would be fulfilled.

As she was about to leave, a creaking noise resonated from somewhere upstairs. The noise took the form of footsteps as they descended to the ground floor. Shota's eyes darted to the dark entryway where the steps were coming closer, his body language tensing. He went to speak but choked on his own words.

"Shota? What's that noise?" a woman's voice called. She cautiously entered the light of the dining room, and her face morphed into fear when she realized she was in the presence of royalty. "Oh Gods! Queen Elysande, please forgive me." The girl pulled her thin night robe close to her body in shame.

Shota shot up from his seat. "My queen, this is Mariko… my-my…"

Elysande stood up calmly and extended her hand. "Charmed." The girl meekly shook her hand, keeping her eyes to the floor. When she finally became comfortable enough to meet Elysande's face, the dim ceiling lights caught her flawless, honey-colored skin, much like Shota's. Her black hair was tied up in a bun, but with long bangs across her forehead. "You're very beautiful, my lady. No need to hide your face."

Mariko blushed. "Oh, thank you, my queen. I did not mean to be so rude."

"Nonsense," Elysande said. "Where are you from?"

"Near Hirosuma, in the region of Kygorro." Mariko said, confidence returning to her voice.

"A lovely area… I've been told," Elysande said. She assumed this Mariko was not a prostitute. "Forgive me, as I was unaware Lord Shota had other company."

"I owe you an explanation," he said, regretfully.

"No, my lord, you do not." She indicated to Ser Dance that it was time to leave. "Let some of your personal life stay that way, at least for now."

# KENT (VI)

Heroism was easy enough to fake.

Kent was the furthest thing from a hero... the battle over the Bloodmoon proved that, but as long as he could trick himself for a moment into believing he possessed an ounce of courage, the rest was easy. When he peered out from the rescue ship, watching as Ariel and Marion were surrounded by Romans, the false hero came to save the day.

Sitting in a private sector now, hands shaking and brow sweating profusely, Kent knew the false hero was gone. Not that he was ever really there. He sat still as the ship moved through space at an inconceivable speed, Ariel by his side, sprawled out on a bench and resting her eyes.

She was closest to the rescue ship when the false hero emerged. She was weaponless, reduced to running for her life as the ceiling above began to collapse. Kent, defying his better judgement, jumped into the fray inside the frigate and drew his Immortech sword. The sight of the blade alone was enough of a distraction to get her onto the ship, but when the sword was thrusted into action, he became the center of everyone's attention.

Kent blocked enemy fire excellently. Ballistic rounds ricocheted off the blade, while lasers were absorbed into the metal. One Roman soldier confronted him with an electric shock baton, and Kent cut through him like butter. His feet instinctually ran toward the large horde of humans, blood pumping furiously through his veins, but his mind worked to stop himself when he reached Marion's body. Through the putrid, rising smoke and chaos of a battle with no clear lines, it was a miracle that Kent spotted him. The poor kid was under a pile of ceiling boards, appearing dead in every aspect if not for the shallow rising and falling of his chest.

"Grab the boy," Bato said while shooting aimlessly into the smokey haze. The sound of his familiar voice, usually so cool, was startling. "I'll cover you!"

Without saying a word, Kent pulled the rubble away as fast as he could. He grabbed Marion by the shoulders and pulled, but a bastard Roman also beneath the rubble was holding onto him by the waist. In a hurry, Kent kicked her lifeless arms away, noticing she had been impaled at the chest by a sword... of Enfari metal.

The dreaded silver cloaks of the Inquisition billowed in the distance, fading in and out of the smoke as if part of it. A hunger shivered through Kent's body. An injection of adrenaline caused time to slow. He put Marion down and placed sword in hand. The Inquisitors walked forward, weapons drawn and matching Kent's focus. The tall one, the massive one, held his warhammer in two hands.

*Penance, finally. For me? Or you? Or for us all?*

The Battle over the Blood Moon flashed through his mind in one aggressive, assaulting frame. Throat dried, Kent could not stray his eyes from the Inquisitors, *the Betrayers*! He gripped the hilt of his Immortech sword tightly, its hardness inciting him to move forward.

Bato grabbed him by the collar and shook. "Come on, Kentoshi! To the ship."

Kent shuttered, sheathing his weapon and hoisting Marion's unconscious body over his shoulders. Taking one last look at the impaled soldier, he prayed a hunk of Enfari metal would not cut through his back as well. Once at the rescue ship, he handed the boy over to a medic but stopped before stepping into safety himself. The Inquisitors were behind him, creeping forward. *Someday*, Kent thought while boarding the vessel, *but not today. My second chance will be your downfall.*

Ariel sat up from the bench. How she could be so calm in the wake of such a disaster, Kent could not understand. Then, something patted his forearm.

"Thanks for saving me," she said, awkwardly.

"I owed you that much." Kent answered, his hands shaking. He still could not get used to her presence; it was like having a conversation with a memory.

"You didn't, not really."

The bruise on her lip made him wince. "Sorry it took so long. What happened on the frigate?"

"Nothing," she said, pausing to consider her next words. "Me and Marion were thrown in a prison cell. I thought I was going to lose my mind trapped in there, but now it kind of feels like a dream. This whole thing feels like a dream."

"Trust me, I believe you," he laughed.

Ariel maintained her seriousness. "We talked to some guy named General Antonius Marko; he's in charge of the frigate. He didn't say anything outright, but someone tipped him off that we were going to Romulus. It was a trap, Kent. And I think someone in the crew is to blame."

Kent sighed deeply. He remembered accusing the whole crew of the Seshora Araman of betrayal in his crazed state, when the wound of losing both Zoltors was at its freshest. The further he dwelled on it, the more he found each one to be equally untrustworthy. "I suspect that too. Can't say I have any idea as to who though. Gods know I've spent enough time dwelling on it."

Ariel's eyes darted around. "Where's Marion?"

"He's in the ship's medical bay. He's stable, but he has yet to wake up."

"Do you trust these people?"

"No," Kent laughed again. "Not at all. Everyone on the Seshora left me in the dark for months."

"Locking us in this chamber wasn't the best way to make amends," Ariel said. She was right, ever since Tali confessed her ulterior intentions, she had kept Kent isolated. When they ditched the Seshora Araman for the rescue vessel, the masked soldiers restricted him again to a separate space, only unleashing him when his sword was needed. Confiding with Ariel, the one person he knew wasn't in on the lie, was oddly endearing. "What's her plan anyway?" she asked.

"Tali's? She won't speak to me. I can't tell if she hired a private army... or if she's part of someone else's. I've never seen soldiers like them before. I can't recognize their coat-of-arms."

"She didn't tell you anything?"

"All I know is we're heading for Laktannon, the planet at the edge of the galaxy."

Ariel looked confused. "What's that?"

"It's a safe haven for refugees. Anyone of any race is welcomed as long as they have nowhere else to go. Many a usurped ruler has fled to Laktannon to make a new kingdom for themselves, and all end up failing."

"So Tali allied with some disposed aristocrat." Ariel concluded, her disdain palpable.

"Seems likely, but which one remains the important question. Laktannon is the biggest planet in the galaxy. It's a bloodbath of false rulers and faithless armies." Kent paused in reflection. "I nearly fled to Laktannon myself after Spyre fell. I was convinced I could make a good living selling my sword and sorcery until the day the Immortals called my name. Never got the credits for a ship, but fate has found a way to get me there anyway."

"Funny how that works out," she said. "What about Matiyala, she could tell you something."

"I don't understand your meaning?" *Gods! Does everyone know about us?*

Ariel smiled. "Come on..."

"She didn't tell me anything, never even alluded to it, so I don't expect her to say anything now." Kent conceded. He had grown more attached to Matiyala than he cared to admit. While exiled on Narood, he managed to eliminate his desire for intimacy, but after allowing the slightest embrace of warmth back into his life made having to sleep alone again colder than ever before. "Besides, she's on the Seshora Araman, but I'm dreading the conversation that's to come... if she cares to have one."

"She likes you," Ariel encouraged him. "There must be a reason why she didn't tell you. Give her the chance to explain herself."

"I didn't take you for the romantic type," Kent said.

Ariel's face turned quizzical in a moment of self-reflection. "I'm not... that should be a good sign for you."

"Maybe so." The Paladin stood from the bench. His eyes were frustrated from staring endlessly at gray spaceships. "Okay then, we aren't under arrest here, not aloud at least. I'm going to check on Marion. Will you do me a favor and stay here?"

She shrugged, "Sure."

"Good." He left the cramped room and headed upstairs on grated metal steps. All around him were patrolling soldiers in their concealing ivory masks. They gave him dubious glances as he passed, but Kent continued undeterred. One soldier specifically seemed out of sorts by his presence. He was tall, too tall, with mask and clothes that were ridiculously small for his body. The features behind his ill-fitting attire suggested he was a human… but Kent had never met a human so gigantic in size. Thinking not much of it and wanting to avoid any conflict, he chose to carry on.

A doctor stopped him as he walked through the bustling halls of the medical station.

"Where are you going?" he asked.

"To see the unconscious human. Do we have a problem?"

"He should not be disturbed. What's he to you?"

Kent tried to read the doctor. *Does he know who Marion is? Or who I am? Why else would he be concerned?* He watched others come and go unperturbed through the lobby. *Maybe I really am under arrest.* "I'm the guy who almost got his head blown off several times trying to save his life. Again, is there a problem?"

The doctor eyed him up and down, his attention taking an exceptionally long glare at the hilt of Kent's Immortech sword. "Go ahead."

The Paladin proceeded. The small medical bay filled substantially after the rescue mission. Soldiers were bandaged up like wrapped presents and hooked onto monitors and IVs. Some were crying out for their friends, their Gods, and even their mothers. A spectral coldness caused him to shiver. The bay had become so packed that many of the patients were left laying on gurneys strapped down precariously to the deck.

*Serios save them, how big was the operation?* Frigates were massive ships that could hold hundreds of thousands of people. In order to rescue the Zoltors, they must have launched several attacks on the ship to keep the humans inside disoriented. A smart tactic, but not without its consequences.

Kent opened the white curtain at the end of the medical bay and found Marion Zoltor still unconscious and with breathing tubes up his nose. He looked to be in a peaceful sleep, if one could ignore the raw, pink scar on the side of his head. The mop of blondish-brown hair on the right side of his head had been shaved off for the stitches, of which Kent counted five wrapped around the gash. *At least the scar will be hidden when his hair grows back.*

By his bedside, much to his surprise, was Tali. Sitting in a chair by Marion's head, she held his hand and was muttering rapidly in a language Kent could not understand. At the sound of his footsteps, she looked up with tired eyes and smiled solemnly. "Hey Kent."

"What's that language?" he asked.

"Godspeak. The tongue of the Immortals. I used to translate ancient texts for the Archmage, and the language never really left me. Now I use it to pray."

"Ah yes," Kent said. Godspeak was offered to young mages growing up on Spyre, but Kent and most of the other students never bothered to learn it. He used to be able to recite prayers and quotes in Godspeak, but the skill had faded so much that he might as well never have learned it. "Does praying in the Immortals' language let them answer faster?"

"Not from my experience... but I have to try." The seriousness in her tone served to condemn his attempt at flippancy.

"When was the last time you slept?"

"I'm not sure," Tali said, her mind clearly not concerned with her own health. "I didn't imagine this being my first interaction with him."

"He'll be awake soon enough," Kent promised. "In the meantime, you should get some rest."

"I've tried." She brushed her hand through Marion's hair. "What's he like? Was he happy on Romulus? I can't help but think he was better off without my interference."

"I talked to him once. To be honest, he seemed to hate Romulus and everyone on it. They were about frame him for the murder of their headmaster. If anything, we came at the perfect time."

"That's not what I was expecting to hear," Tali said, interpreting Kent's comment as another attempt at flippancy. "It doesn't make me feel any better though. What about Lyndon Everec?"

Kent scratched his head. He considered refusing her questions, given that she made no effort to enlighten him on whatever in the Hell she dragged him into. "Everec died. Drake Bodewin of all people was on Romulus, and he executed Everec to lure us out. Marion liked the guy too; his death will hit him hard."

"Damn," Tali cursed. "Everec was a good man. He'd been safeguarding Marion since the Archmage handed him over. That was a decade and a half ago. He dedicated his life to preserving the Order, but he won't get to see his hard work pay off."

"We may not either." Kent said. "But of course, you haven't been honest with me about the endgame for this revival. I didn't think we would be bedfellows with an army from Laktannon. If I'd known, I could have lowered my expectations earlier."

Tali sighed. Still, after all the demonstrations of his loyalty, she was reluctant to confess her true intentions. "We are not the pawns of some common warlord. I've formed an alliance with the Vikanders."

"The Vikanders? I didn't know any were alive." The Vikander family had sided with the Roman Republic and the Paladin Order when Caesar's war had yet to envelope most of the galaxy. Ademar Vikander was the leading general of the Republic at the time, and he would have bested Caesar if not for the interference of Reynard Bodewin and his Crimson Armada. Ademar was dead, so Kent was not sure how any Vikander could be helpful.

"Aethelwulf, Ademar's brother, has conquered Laktannon with the help of his niece," Tali reported. "I've seen their army and the government they've established, and it is undeniably formidable."

"Appearance can be deceiving," Kent warned. "Laktannon has known many displaced rulers. By the time we arrive, Vikander could be usurped by another exile."

"You don't understand, Aethelwulf has unified the entirety of Laktannon. As far as I'm aware, he's the first to do so in over a century. It's not some petty empire, Kent. I've lived there for years. It's the safest I've felt since Spyre. It can be the perfect foundation for the Order to rebuild."

"And by 'unify,' I suppose you mean 'conquer.' If that's the case, one does not easily conquer Laktannon and keep it stable." Kent said, doubtfully.

"But he's not what you think," Tali swore. "Yes, war on Laktannon is inevitable, but the Vikanders use diplomacy just as well in defeating their enemies. I've watched with my own eyes what Aethelwulf Vikander has made, and Laktannon and its people are safer because of it. I would never bring Ariel and Marion there if I wasn't certain of its security."

"I don't know." He vaguely recalled Aethelwulf being a solemn, levelheaded, and competent military commander. Ademar was the star though, while his brother tended to fade away in the background. "How did you manage to find him in the first place?"

"Like every other mage, I was desperate for a home. I kept my eyes and ears open for anyone promising safety. I came to Aethelwulf when he and his niece, Rachel, had yet to carve a territory for themselves in the Bloodlands. I had nothing to offer, but they still accepted me into their company." Tali rubbed her eyes, taking a moment to recharge her memory. "I was beyond lucky for their hospitality. They worked with me to watch over the Zoltors as best we could. They also helped me find you... Aethelwulf, at least, still knows the value of the Paladin Order."

"What do the Vikanders get out of a relationship with a few mages?"

"They get more followers. I do believe that countless mages are in hiding. If we can build a home for them, then Laktannon becomes all the stronger."

"And Aethelwulf gets a faction of mages for his army."

Tali shook her head. "I've known him for decades. He's done fighting the KOH. He accepts Laktannon is his home, and he's working to make it stable."

"If you're so confident in his ideals, why not tell me earlier?"

"They are a secretive bunch. The Vikanders have quietly built their own government, and they want to stay out of the crosshairs of the KOH. If their progress was to be discovered..."

"You thought I would snitch?" Kent growled.

Tali frowned, exhaustion combatting her wit. "No, not really. I mean, a lot can change in a decade, Kent. I had no idea who you were. Even if I had complete faith in you, if you were to get captured by the KOH and tortured…"

"I get it now. I wanted to trust you, truly. You made me lie to Ariel and Marion, you've dragged them into something none of us entirely understand. And for that, I can't forgive you."

"I'm sorry." Tali said, drifting backward in her chair. For a moment, Kent thought she had fallen asleep. "We've got a long trip ahead of us, so there's plenty of time to make amends."

# ELYSANDE (VI)

Twenty years.

Twenty years since she was forced into the bunker beneath Erron, listening to the high-pitched whistles of falling bombs and rushing footsteps of hundreds of thousands of invaders as they flooded her city. In the war room, below the red and white rose banners of Bodewin, stood her father and brothers, consulting with their generals as to how the city could be saved. They were Mercian Gods in their burnished, crimson armor and silver capes. Their stone faces expressed no doubt that the battle could still be won.

A scout rushed through the concrete halls of the bunker straight to the Lord of Erron. "Lord Reynard, Vikander forces are pouring into the city, led by General Ademar. They have passed two of our blockades already. Some reports say the Archmage fights alongside them."

"Leave it to the Consuls of Rome to enlist the help of mages," Reynard said. "What of Caesar?"

"Lord Caesar and his legions reside on the outskirts of Erron." the scout continued, breathless. He was covered completely in ash.

"At least the Republic possesses one decent man," Bodewin said, passively.

"The Gardeners have launched an assault on the northern district. It's been contained thus far, but it is dividing our forces."

"I can put down the Gardeners myself." Reynard said, his coolness keeping the bunker from melting. He turned to his sons, saying: "You two can take the bulk of the army to deal with Vikander."

The two young men saluted. "It would be our honor, Father."

Elysande, who was fifteen at the time, marched her way into the war room, rifle in hand. This was her city as much as it was anyone else's, after all, and she would do her absolute best to protect it. She had not considered the possibility of being left behind when the counterattack was launched, so when an officer blocked her from entering the war room, she responded with hostility.

"Get your bloody hands off of me!" she commanded to the nameless soldier who dared get in her way. She shoved him with all her might, and the force was more than enough to send him off his feet. Silence took over the room.

"What do you think you're doing?" Reynard demanded, perturbed. Elysande believed her father's wrath was directed toward the disobedient soldier. Rest assured, it was not.

"If I'm going to help in the counterattack, I should at least know the plans." Elysande objected.

"I don't have time for this nonsense," her father cursed; his crystalline blue eyes filled with disdain. "Go back into the bunkers with Drake, now."

"I won't!" She stomped her foot. The war room shook as bombs diving from heaven dropped closer to the center of Erron. Inside, her heart was filled with frantic doves.

"Fine, Ser Edwin, take her away. You may use whatever force is necessary." Reynard returned to his generals without hesitation. A large knight came for Elysande, but she refused to backdown. Ser Edwin was taken aback, expecting his presence alone to frighten her into submission. Before the situation could turn violent, cooler heads intervened.

"That won't be necessary, ser." Fredrick, her brother, said as he stood between them. The knight backed down, relieved he did not have to restrain the lady of Erron. "Elysande, walk with me." Fredrick put his strong arm around her compassionately and encouraged her to walk away.

"Are you scared?" he asked, earnestly.

"Hardly," she responded.

"Then you're braver than me." His auburn hair was long and slick, his skin pale like the moon, and his blue eyes flashing. He looked like the kind of young king that should have led Erron into battle, not her father.

"I'll follow you out into the field. We can give each other courage, for your sake."

Fredrick laughed. "I appreciate that. However, I can't let you go out there. You're much too valuable to be put at risk."

Elysande stopped. "You mean I'm too young! Or is it because of my tits?"

"No." Fredrick said, her language making him frown. "Any man with half a brain can command an army to charge forward. You have a mind for greater things. If I can't save Erron, our people will be put in a dire situation. They need someone like you take control and protect them."

"I want to be a general of the army, not a charity worker," Elysande stated. Her brother's willing ignorance irritated her from head to toe. "Father won't give me a chance, and I suppose I can't expect any more from you."

They arrived at the shelter where the pathetic people hid from the armies of the Republic. Her youngest brother, Drake, sat in a corner crying, cradled by one of the servants of their estate. "This is where I leave you, Ely. Remember, you will get your moment to shine, just not now."

The future queen crossed her arms. She tried to turn her gaze anywhere but his face. "You're very cruel with your false promises. I think I hate you."

Fredrick smiled, calling her bluff. "Is that my goodbye?"

Elysande, with tears welling in her eyes, threw her arms around her brother's strong shoulders. "Please be safe."

"Don't worry, Ely. We'll change the world someday," he promised, hugging her back.

"We're Bodewins," her other brother, Boltof, said as he walked into the conversation. "We'll change the whole fuckin' galaxy!" Boltof was an even bigger version of their brother; he was the brawn to Fredrick's brain.

"I can't handle two emotional goodbyes." Elysande said, drying her eyes.

"You won't have to," Boltof assured her. "We'll be back soon, little rose. I'll be sure to bring you a souvenir from the battlefield."

"Ademar Vikander's head will suffice."

Boltof winked. "So it shall be." An officer ran up to them, panic overflowing in his eyes.

"The Archmage is in the city," he reported. "Lord Bodewin says it's time to go!"

"We'll head out now," Fredrick replied. He turned back to Elysande. "See you in a bit. In the meantime, stay in the bunker." He sprinted back to the war room, Boltof in tow. Before they were out of sight, Boltof called back to her. "I'll bring you the Archmage's Immortech sword too!"

"I need a decoration above my fireplace!" Elysande yelled, although she was unsure if Boltof heard her. These would be the last words she would ever speak to them.

Boltof failed, Fredrick lied. Both of her brothers fought to the very last man in the center of Erron, so she had been told. They kept their army together until the Archmage Marius Zoltor appeared on the frontline, wielding lightning bolts from his fingertips and slashing Mercians to bits with his electrified Immortech sword. The sky turned black with the darkest clouds any soldier had ever seen, and ferocious rain falling like needles blinded the Bodewin army. Despite the ungodly powers of the Archmage, Boltof and Fredrick would not yield. They chose to meet the Archmage in combat, and their stupidity costed them their lives.

Her father mingled with her husband in the atrium on the upper decks of the Colosseum, amid a sea of Roman patricians and hundreds of other elites of the KOH. Caesar was dressed up in his best black and gold doublet, a laurel wreath resting upon his brow to distinguish himself as king. His Praetorian Guard watched over the crowd like battle-ready angels, as if the human aristocracy combined possessed the stones to cause him harm. Elysande chose to drift away from her king, in favor of scouting for the inevitable fight between Tisonians and Mercians. Nakamura did an excellent job keeping the two continents of people separate in the Games, but from the fan section there was little he could do.

The Colosseum maintained a steady rumble of excitement as the first round of the Gladiator Games was about to begin. Julia, by her mother's side, could not have been more energetic. Lawrence, staring at his feet, could not have been more apathetic.

"Can I go home?" Lawrence moaned. The collar on his doublet was stretched from his constant tugging.

"And do what?" Elysande asked.

"Anything but this."

"The good people of the KOH must see their prince in person every once in a while," she advised. "It's an easy way to earn their favor. They like seeing royalty share the same interests as they do."

"Fine." Lawrence whined, to the amusement of Julia. Natalia was in the crowd with Jacob Mauvern still by her side. Jacob's hand was on the small of her back as they spoke with the other young sons and daughters of nobility. Natalia's once straight hair now fell to her shoulders in ringlets. The newly declared Overseer of Tisoni, Timothy Mauvern, was near too, fawning over the young couple as if they were characters at the start of an adult film. The corpulent lord wore his battle armor in a bombastic statement of his participation in the Gladiator Games. Elysande prayed he lost in the first round.

The Omirs were running late for the New Year's festivities. A complete accident, surely. Considering no one in their family was entered into the Games, she supposed they had no reason to attend. On the other hand, some of their Tisonian loyalists were participating. If a tragedy were to take place, it would be easy for the Omirs to claim ignorance. She wondered if Timothy Mauvern was relieved by their absence, as he did not strike her as one who craves confrontation.

Poncius Tarquinius, the lord of the great Carcian city Vispania, approached her and saluted. "Hail, Queen Elysande. I see we are both bereft of someone to talk to."

*And I'd prefer it stay that way*, she thought in return. "It would seem so. Do you think it's due to intimidation?"

Tarquinius laughed. With olive skin and short brown hair, the man was Carcian to the core. On his breast was the brown boar coat-of-arms of his noble family. "For you, most definitely. Me? Not so much."

"Why is that? You're from a patrician family; your ancestors helped build Rome to what we see today. In fact, you may have more sway than me."

"I doubt it," Tarquinius said. "Patricians hardly exercise the control we used to. Today Rome is filled with people from across Orbis."

"And is it a bad thing?" Elysande asked, dubious.

"Not in the slightest. The patricians proved themselves unworthy rulers when their Republic crashed and burned in a most ungraceful display. Caesar came in, incorporated advisors from around the world, and we're all better off for it."

"I wish many of the other patricians shared your open-mindedness." Elysande remarked, having flashbacks to her interaction with Tullius atop the Palazzo Reale.

"They will in due time," Tarquinius said. His face was thin and long, possessing that indeterminable self-assuredness found in Carcian nobility. "Do you have a favorite in winning the Games?"

"No. I enjoy watching my peers bash each other in the name of myself and Caesar. As long as violence and humiliation are plentiful, I will consider myself a winner."

"I see." Tarquinius said, not the least bit intimidated. "I assumed you would favor Ser Bryson Byrne."

"Why would you say that?"

"He's your father's loyal servant. I assumed he'd play a role in getting young Bryson on the lists."

Elysande would not take the bait. "Bryson fought under your brother during a colonizing campaign. I've been told he is a valiant soldier and possesses much military potential. Many a knight and soldier pulled strings to get into this tournament, but I doubt Ser Bryson was one of them."

Poncius conceded. "Ah yes, anyone who fights alongside the great General Tarquinius is certain to gain substantial auctoritas. When compared to him, sometimes I can't help but consider myself as a failure."

"Hardly, my lord."

"Indeed, it's true. I was born with the destiny to govern one of the greatest cities in Carcia, while my brother polished the boots of some old Roman officer occupying a post on the Kappelli Isles.

He worked his way up to general, while I've been stuck in the same position since I've inherited it. Now he's leading the first campaign against the Synths, and I'm still here."

The sounds of the orchestra from inside the Colosseum sounded from the speakers above the atrium, signifying the start of the Gladiator Games. As the nobles of the KOH headed for their seats, Elysande had one more comment for Lord Tarquinius. "I've learned to stop abiding by the restrictions of my title, and you should too."

The Colosseum was a grand expanse of spectacle. Seating an audience of three hundred thousand, the Colosseum was the largest stadium on Orbis. From the top seats, the arena was nearly impossible to see. Thankfully, large monitors coming from the rafters projected everything that happened in the arena, so no occupant could miss the action. Ecstatic white spotlights hung from the catwalk above, moving over the endless sea of fans as they waited for the Games to begin. The Colosseum was designed in a perfect circle, allowing Elysande to witness the amazing scope of spectators.

As she entered with her king, the crowd erupted in a thunderous display of love for the royal family. Caesar smiled and waved briefly, recognizing their adulation without seeming desperate for it. Elysande did the same; it was one of the few philosophies they agreed on. Natalia was far more welcoming, smiling fully and laughing as Jacob Mauvern discovered his stage fright. Julia was equally as embracing of her subjects as her stepsister, while Lawrence kept his head down, not from fear but indifference.

The arena below was the combat zone. Barriers were set up around the floor to add an extra element to the fights themselves, but these were not the best gimmick to the Gladiator Games. A massive orb structure made of hexagonal plexiglass panes encompassed the arena. The panes shimmered in a bronze tint and pulsed whenever the spotlights shown directly on them. This orb was not for show. It acted as the prism for the gladiators to battle in once the arena forsook its gravitational pull.

Kassa Savon, Grand Admiral of the KOH and one of Caesar's chief advisors, was the first contestant in the Games. Her opponent was Centurion Publius Cato, dressed in heavy-plated bronze armor with a black skirt studded in silver pieces and the crest of an eagle on his helm. *I wonder if he's of the patrician class*, Elysande cynically thought.

Publius dressed opulently, but foolishly. Kassa Savon, who was no stranger to real combat, dressed in light Tisonian armor. Not only was it practical in the sweltering desert region from which she hailed, it would also allow her to use the zero-gravity zone to her advantage.

The crowd roared at the first bell commencing the Gladiator Games. Both competitors approached with measured steps, but their batons did not clash. Savon, right as she came into striking distance, cancelled the gravitational pull in her armored boots and pushed off the ground. Publius' baton hit nothing but air, leaving him stupefied as she soared to the apex of the orb.

The top hexagonal pane pulsed as she flipped and expertly kicked off it without losing any momentum. Publius Cato, not wanting to be outdone, followed her, disabling the gravity of his suit and aiming to cut her off as she descended back to the arena's floor. However, Savon did not shoot for the ground, instead electing for another pane on the left side of the orb. Publius, who had lazily left the arena floor and was now drifting lethargically through open space, lost sight of her.

With another deftly timed flip and kick against a side pane, Savon's direction changed horizontally and, as she predicted, collided directly with Publius as he was halfway between the arena's floor and the apex of the orb. She charged her shock baton and struck the patrician lord right in the back, sending electric shockwaves throughout his body and rendering him unable to fight. The siren sang once again.

Savon activated her gravity boots and she descended to the floor. Publius' body drifted aimlessly, so medics had to enter the arena and retrieve him. As Publius limped off the stage with the help of his subordinates, Kassa Savon reveled in the applause of half a million fans.

"For ISTOFAR!" she called, throwing her fists in the air. If the Omirs were present, they would have approved of her tribute to their homeland.

She exited the stage and out came the next set of opponents. In one corner stood Servius Venator, a young man of the venerable Venator patrician family. Servius was tall like a mountain and strong like steel, but his easy smile made the crowd chant with approval when his face appeared on the monitors. His long black hair glimmered in the stadium lights. Upon taking his position on one end of the arena, he bowed humbly in the direction of the royal family.

"This is Placus' son?" King Gaius Julius Caesar asked his brother.

"It is," Tullius answered. "He'd served as a legate for General Laberius Afer in his colonizing campaigns. He swears up and down that the boy has a promising career in the service of the KOH."

Caesar grinned. "I'll make a mental note of it. He's one of Octavius' friends from school, if I'm not mistaken."

Tullius' mood turned dour instantly. "He is. He went out of his way yesterday to find me and ask of my son's health. If only a portion of his maturity rubbed off on Octavius."

Gaius decided it best to end the conversation there. Elysande, however, chuckled loudly so the Commandant of the KOH could know her amusement.

Servius' opponent was Federico Paganelli, a short, bronze-skinned man who served as Lord of Ventrello, a breezy city in central Carcia just north of Paranthon's Cross. Federico, dressed in ostentatious red and green armor with a row of long multicolored feathers decorated down the center of his helmet, tried to appeal to the crowd like his younger opponent, but he received little more than a low rumble for his efforts.

The two men approached each other, raised their right arms in the air as tribute to their country and king, and the bell sounded to start the match. Federico waited for Servius to take the first strike, likely believing he could use the bigger man's strength against him. A reasonable strategy for a seasoned warrior, but for a man accustomed to the mundane art of bureaucratic combat, the implementation was ineffective and embarrassing.

Servius sent Federico reeling backward with a single swipe of his baton. The Lord of Ventrello managed to block the blow enough to prevent a hit, but his subsequent situation, laid out on his back and staring at the lights, was not much of an improvement. Servius Venator, ever the true Roman, allowed him to stand.

Federico rose, drew his baton, raised it over his head, and swung with all his weight behind him, praying that the momentum alone would break Servius' guard and win the match. It did not. Servius parried, spun, and kicked him away.

Sensing the end was near, Federico fell into a frenzy. With his focus on survival, the Carcian lord disabled the gravity suspenders on his boots and kicked off to the barriers of the plexiglass dome. He got off the ground but not out of harm's way. Servius, as powerful as an ox but as quick as a lion, grabbed him by the ankle and yanked him down. Believing the young patrician to be distracted, Federico tried to stab downward with his shock baton. The attacks missed, and Servius threw him to the ground and planted the offensive end of his baton into the Carcian's green and red colored chest.

Federico Paganelli whimpered as electric shock fried his body, but Servius was merciful enough not to hold him down for longer than what was needed. When the bell rang to mark the end of the match, Servius humbly bowed before his king and queen and departed from the arena. Paganelli, however, was dragged off.

Several more battles occurred before the A block of the first round was completed. Ending the block was no other than Magnus Caesar, first son of General Tullius. The father did little to hide is enthusiasm as his son took the stage, screaming and chanting their family name as Magnus waved condescendingly to the masses that filled the Colosseum. Both father and son possessed the same bear-like physique, but Magnus' sharp facial features, cutting brown eyes, and wavy onyx hair made him much easier on the eyes. He was so handsome, in fact, that many a lady of the KOH were too entranced to see the near psychopathic narcissism radiating from his posture and face. To the cameras, he flashed a grin, and the whole Colosseum erupted with high-pitched squeals.

Lord Yabu Taji, hailing from Kygorro, stood across from the nephew of the king. Yabu's black studded armor was especially heavy at the shoulders and arms, and his wide-rimmed helmet was as sharp as a razor. He dressed for real battle, heavy to reduce the threat of real bombs and lasers. As he appeared now, the zero-gravity environment would not suit him.

Taji was a young warrior, but not on the level of Magnus, who seized advantage of his opponent's weight and took to circling him to drain all his energy. Elysande, not in the least bit impressed by Magnus' actions, used the match as an opportunity to daydream. How would she perform in the Gladiator Games? She may have been one of the older competitors, but few people cared for their health like she did. She was strong, her body cut and sinewy. The weight of a knight or centurion alone could probably overpower her, but she had the endurance and agility to tire the bastards out. Then she could use her deceptive power to break their defenses and take victory.

Magnus' mountainous muscles flexed in his sleeveless armor as he continued to berate the Lord of Kygorro with his baton. The young Caesar hardly broke a sweat, while his opponent struggled to even shift his feet. *His muscle mass weighs him down, but he's trained his heart to endure it. Perhaps I've underestimated you, Magnus.* Before she could imagine how a battle between herself and her nephew could play out, the battle was over, with Magnus Caesar standing victorious over Yabu Taji, a foot on his chest to emphasize the domination.

Tullius stood and vehemently slapped his hands together until Gaius made him stop. "Tullius, enough."

The king's brutish brother bowed his head. "Apologies, my king." Although Caesar barely raised his voice, the whole section went silent as if they all were being punished by their father. Perhaps it was the glare that unnerved everyone. It was the same determined, unrelenting face that made enemies across the galaxy surrender and cower in fear.

The end of the A Block allowed for a reprieve for many of the royal retinue to retreat into the hall. Elysande followed her husband out, but they soon broke off once given the chance to speak to others. Caesar went to his daughter who was, of course, with her Mauvern boyfriend. Elysande spotted the First Censor of Rome and grabbed his attention.

"Lord Nakamura," she greeted. "I wanted to thank you for getting Ser Byrne on the lists."

Shota brushed it off. "It is my duty to serve." Remorse crossed his face. "I've been meaning to speak with you… could we talk in private?"

She already knew where this was going, "Let's walk."

The queen and censor departed from the large bulk of elites and aristocrats for a quiet, cooler space away from the lobby bar. "I need to explain myself for the other night…" he began.

Elysande raised her hand. "I'm not interrogating you."

Shota shook his head. "Please, I don't want to keep secrets from you or King Caesar. The girl you met, Mariko, she's not just some woman."

"Most girls aren't," she laughed, *especially in the eyes of men.*

"She's Mariko Reika, daughter of Nomura Reika, the former lord of Hirosuma."

"I see," Elysande said. "He was displaced by Omir during his reign as Overseer of Tisoni."

"Not displaced, madam. Executed. Lord Reika was overly ambitious. He'd expressed interest in taking Hazelvale for himself and was amounting a formidable army in Kygorro to challenge the Omir family for domination over the continent. He was found out, rightfully so, and punished justly for his crime. Lord Nomura's son and two brothers were sentenced to death too. Mariko was spared; I believe it was by Caesar's command."

"And how did she end up in your company?" Elysande inquired. In truth, she did not want to get involved in another affair, but that was the price of living on top of the world.

"We grew up together. My family were vassals to Lord Reika," Shota reflected. "She reached out to me, saying she had fallen on hard times. I let her into my home, but I should have asked permission from King Caesar first."

"If Caesar ordered she be spared, why the apprehension? She's not an enemy of the KOH."

"No, but she's an enemy of the Omirs and a majority of Tisoni. I want her to be as safe as possible, and if I was to bring this up in court, well, her whereabouts would not be a secret for long."

"A logical conclusion," she admitted. "What is your plan going forth? Sooner or later, Caesar will find out."

"I am waiting for the New Year celebration to end before introducing her to court. That way, the Omirs will be out of the city."

"That's saying they arrive."

"They will show," Shota seemed certain. "I have no quarrel with them. As a Tisonian myself, I understand how the Hazelvale spice trade seduces people. My hope is that Timothy Mauvern can bring stability to the country before it eats itself alive."

The Queen of the KOH rolled her eyes. "I wish I shared your optimism, Lord Nakamura."

Orchestra music sounded from the speakers once again, signifying the start of the B block side of the lists. Elysande found her king, and he in return took her arm and escorted her back to their seats. "You and Shota seemed to be having a pleasant conversation," he said among a wall of Praetorian guardsmen.

"We did," she agreed.

"May I ask what the content of the discussion was?"

"You could ask…" Elysande said. "But as king, you could command me to confess."

Caesar chortled, "Cute."

"Lord Nakamura is having troubles with women. Nothing more."

The Praetorian Elite, headed by Sutorian, cleared the stairs as the king and queen descended the concrete steps to their seats. "Odd to think Nakamura has a life outside his duties. Is it something that should concern me?"

Elysande shook her head. "You've remained ignorant to your own problems with women thus far. I can't say you'd be much help to him."

"If they aren't bothering me, are they really problems?" Gaius Julius Caesar asked. "My advice to Shota would be to stop deflecting his own shortcomings onto others. A little self-reflection can go a long way."

As she suspected, Ser Bryson Byrne was more than a capable gladiator. The young knight deftly and swiftly destroyed a Carcian legate in the opening match of the B Block lists. The legate was the second son of some noble family that she could not be bothered to remember and, at least for now, the name would continue to hold no auctoritas in the minds of the KOH aristocracy.

Two boxes of seats to the right of her sat a white sea of billowing togas that were the senators of the KOH. Elysande searched for Senator Felix of Rezza. Before she could realize it, they were making eye contact. Felix smiled his pompous smile and clapped as Ser Bryson received his victor's ovation.

*Smile, Felix. Your end will come soon enough. Imposters throw idle threats around to make themselves appear intimidating. Myself, I don't need harsh declarations to know I'll have no trouble putting you down.*

After several more matches, Timothy Mauvern was tasked with ending the first round of the Gladiator Games, and Elysande imagined he would do so in the most mediocre way possible. Not that he had a high bar to live up to, as many of the matches following Ser Bryson Byrne's were competent in execution, but unremarkable in their violence. *Maybe it will be a farce!* she predicted, in need of a laugh.

Mauvern's appearance was certainly a promising start. Dawned in his immaculate sky-blue armor with a helmet carved in the shape of an elk, even such an opulent costume could not disguise his portly figure or inept waddle. Elysande's ears caught some boos ringing out from the Colosseum as the new Overseer of Tisoni made his grand entrance.

Robert Album, the veteran soldier and Lord of Buckleburn, made his somber entrance after and paid respects to his fellow Mercian noble. Mauvern was greedy in his acceptance. Even from afar, Elysande could sense his lust to win.

The match bell rang, and the contest went along as embarrassingly slow as one should expect a fight between a crippled soldier and a corpulent nobleman would go. Mauvern was winded right at the start, while Robert Album, perhaps out of fear of showing disrespect, was unwilling to break the overseer's guard. This went along for a while, neither man using the zero-gravity arena to their advantage. It was just a barebones volley of batons.

The crowd turned on the match, jeering at the competitors and joking among themselves. "This is a mockery," King Caesar muttered. Elysande could not agree more.

Mercifully, Robert Album's guard broke, allowing Mauvern to check him with his meaty shoulder. Album fell flat on his back, dropping his baton in the process. All that was left was for Lord Timothy Mauvern to finish the job.

He approached, baton in the air, strutting his victory strut. The crowd cheered out of mercy as the match seemed to come to a close. Elysande, however, could have watched them "fight" for the rest of the day.

Timothy Mauvern stopped in his tracks right at the feet of his opponent. He pounded his chest, paused, pounded again, paused, then dropped his baton. He reached for his helmet and tried to loosen it at the neck.

"What's he doing?" Tullius asked aloud.

"He must want to look his opponent in the eyes before he slays him," Gaius figured.

Tullius snorted. "That's only on the field, for real battle."

"For Timothy, this is as real as it gets."

Timothy continued to struggle to remove his helmet, his fingers becoming more frantic as time passed. Suddenly, he fell to one knee… then collapsed to the floor. The audience gasped. Despite this, Elysande heard the crack of her king's knuckles as he clenched his fists. Lord Album was regaining his wits by this time, took to his feet, and skeptically stood over the body of his opponent. After a moment of hesitation, he approached Lord Mauvern, who still struggled on the ground with his fumbling hands around the helmet.

Album knelt by his elk-shaped head and, for the whole Colosseum to hear over the intercoms, shouted: "HE'S CHOKING!" Album joined his fellow Mercian in the struggle, heaving the helmet from Mauvern's neck but finding no success. Staff circling the arena took to the stage, but they were useless. Elysande knew they would not get the helmet off in time. In fact, it was already over.

Both Caesars leaped from their seats to the arena, their Praetorian Elite stumbling to catch up. The queen stayed where she was, searching through the box of senators. This time, she could not find Felix of Rezza.

# ARIEL (VI)

She waited in a private chamber for hours, looking out beyond the open balcony at the great expanse of sun-kissed ocean. The waves were tall and mighty, but they barely licked the feet of the cliff from which the Republic Manor was built on. Dark, sandy beaches occupied most of the land between sea and city, with the occasional stock of wiry yellow grass sprouting in patches throughout the plain. The site was a spectacle to behold, and Ariel especially admired the coastal breezes that danced into the chamber and filled the room with heavy smells of salt and sea.

How air could be so pure and vigorous, she could not comprehend.

Kent and Brutus Cirileo were far less appreciative of the world at the edge of the galaxy, showing less enthusiasm than Pup, who had clung to her side since their reunion. Kent's attitude suggested they were in a dubious predicament, but she felt secure with her hovering sphere of destruction at her shoulder.

"Look at this view!" Ariel said, pointing outside as if Kent and Brutus did not notice.

The Paladin shrugged. "It's fine. Nothing special."

"Nothing special?" she asked, taking a deep breath and letting the clean air fill her lungs. "It's incredible! So incredible!"

"Only someone who's never left a shithole like the Underbelly thinks this is incredible," Brutus said. "Kent's seen the galaxy, I've seen the galaxy, you haven't seen the galaxy. So, when we say it's a mediocre view, it's a bloody mediocre view."

"You go to Hell!" she declared. Out of everyone on the Seshora Araman, she had liked the merc above them all, mostly for his brashness. That changed once the lie was revealed. Now she could solely trust Kent, the only one who had been completely honest with her.

"It would be a mercy," Cirileo muttered under his breath.

Ariel shook her head. "What's this city called again?"

"Old Ulthrawn," Kent answered. "This week's capital city of the planet Laktannon."

"Well, I like the beauty of Old Ulthrawn." Ariel said, defiantly.

"Then that shows how bloody stupid you are." Cirileo answered.

"I'm not stupid, you're just cynical. A cynical, old merc."

"Cool it," Kent said. "Ariel, is this the first time you've seen the ocean?" She nodded, shyly. "That explains it. If you like the view, then enjoy it. You're right, Brutus and I are old and cynical, so our appreciation for beautiful sights may have burned out."

Ariel was content with the explanation.

The doors behind them swung open. Two masked soldiers entered first, armed with what looked to be spears, but were actually thin rifles with bayonet attachments. Both soldiers dressed in orange tunics reinforced by thick, black plating over their shoulders and chests.

Following them were a human man and woman, who took their seats across from Ariel and her crew.

"Please sit," the man offered. He was old, either in or near is fifties, and had a close-cropped brown beard and a crowning bald head flecked with gray. The lines on his face expressed experience as well as exhaustion, the small stones in his eyes revealed nothing of his character. He dressed practically for the hot day, wearing a plain silk doublet with baggy sleeves and an orange thread trim around the shoulders and cuffs.

The man turned to Brutus and said, "Would you care to introduce our guests?"

The merc rubbed the back of his head. "Ah, yes. I, uh, present to the Lord Aethelwulf and Lady Rachel Vikander of the Republic Manor: Paladin Kent Kentoshi and Ariel Zoltor, daughter of the dead Archmage."

"Late Archmage," Lord Vikander corrected.

"Yeah, late Archmage." Brutus returned to his seat as quickly as he could. Ariel smirked at his discomfort.

"Lady Ariel, it is an honor to meet you." Aethelwulf Vikander said. "I fought alongside your father for many years. He was as gifted a diplomat as he was a mage and warrior. Although I did not have the honor to know him personally, I already see much of him in you. I understand you were unaware of your bloodline until recently, I do hope you are adjusting to these revelations."

Ariel shrugged, "Thanks... Lord? I'm getting used to it."

Lord Vikander approached the next question with greater caution. "Have you practiced any magic yet?"

"No," she said. "I'm not sure how I could."

"Mages discover their gifts at different ages," Kent interrupted. "Now that she will be training with me and Tali, the process should be accelerated."

"I would believe so," Aethelwulf spoke with a skeptical undertone.

"And I must add," Kent continued. "We appreciate your hospitality. Both now, and for the home you've given Tali for years. Not a single crevice of the galaxy has been this safe for mages in over a decade. I don't exaggerate when I say that this kindness is exceptional."

"Consider it honor among refugees." Aethelwulf replied coolly.

"We were promised two Zoltors, not one." Rachel Vikander said. She was younger than Lord Aethelwulf by at least two decades. She was tall, with a thin face and high cheekbones. Her eyes were equally unreadable, and she possessed long, ebony hair slicked back behind her ears and ending in points. Her skin may have been naturally fair, but long hours in the sun had baked it into a deep bronze.

"The son of Zoltor is on one of your ships," Kent said. "He hit his head during the escape and hasn't woken up since."

"Superb," Lady Vikander groaned.

"Please forgive my niece. This new information is overwhelming."

"Yes, forgive me. Rescuing these mages has merely revealed our whereabouts to a KOH frigate and used up our best EMP bomb in the process."

"She raises an excellent point," Aethelwulf said. "How long will it be until that frigate arrives on our doorstep? And how long until the Triumvirate gets word of our existence?"

It was Kent's opportunity to speak. "If I may be blunt, I'm working for Paladin Tali. Your role in this was unbeknownst to me until long after our encounter with the frigate. I found these kids for Tali, and no one more."

"Unfortunately, we have not risen to such positions by boasting our names to a galaxy which exiled us." Rachel Vikander leaned back in her seat. "Tali held her tongue because we commanded it. Much can happen in years of hardship, so we were skeptical of how loyal you would be to the Order… especially if you were to be captured. Now, however, we know."

"How reassuring," Kent said.

"We have all the time we need to recover from hurt feelings," Aethelwulf interrupted. "There is more urgent business to attend to."

Through the discourse that ensued, Ariel began to grasp what was going on. She sat before exiled Mercians formerly belonging to the KOH. They were enemies of the Triumvirate, particularly of King Gaius Julius Caesar based on the disdain with which they muttered his name. They were raising an army to do… something, and whatever that something was, it involved her.

Lord Vikander made his intentions for the Paladin Order clear. Old Ulthrawn was to be the new safe haven for mages, designed much in the image of Spyre. Kent Kentoshi was to help build it, taking the role of teacher for any young mages seeking refuge. The Paladin winced in response, but he accepted with extreme apprehension. As for Ariel's role, nothing was made clear. The dialects of the Lord and Lady Vikander sounded like they belonged in a highbrow play or movie, making her not want to say anything at all for fear of sounding stupid.

By the end of the conversation, Aethelwulf said: "Our scouting ships have not returned, but I can assure you the frigate is coming our way. Suffice to say, we will take a peaceful resolution if possible, as I don't think any of us will survive the alternative."

Rachel shrugged off the warning. "Conquering Laktannon was considered impossible, and yet the entire planet is under our rule,

Uncle. This Roman frigate will simply be another battle, no harder than any of the previous we have overcome."

Aethelwulf wagged his finger. "Conquered subjects are not loyal ones. This is a lesson you should have learned by now. When the real war comes and loyalties are tested, you may find yourself more alone than you'd like to think."

"You would have our army disband out of boredom before we can test our strength." Rachel contested.

"Maybe so," her uncle considered. "But I've fought Caesar before, I delivered him his only defeat during the war for the Republic. You've proven yourself on the battlefields of Laktannon, but the KOH is an entirely different threat. Rachel, I'm sorry to say that you're out of your element here."

Without a retort, Rachel stormed from the room. "I'm sorry for that. She has the temper of her father," Aethelwulf said. "Is there anything else I can answer for you?"

"Yes," responded Kent. "This may be blunt, but I'm confused by what kind rule you have over Laktannon."

"We are not running a monarchy, I assure you. Myself and my advisors are in the process of setting up a republic here in the exact model of what once ran Orbis. Unfortunately, uprisings and rebellions persist, and they tend to get prioritized over bureaucratic matters."

Ariel laughed to herself. Prisilla's government was indeed a democracy, but a democracy run by the tyrants of New Horizon. They were dictators in every regard save one: their titles. Never had an Underling won a position in government, despite her kind making up well over two-thirds of Prisilla's native population. If her people wanted change, it had to be earned by force and bloodshed; the pigs of New Horizon would never hand them anything.

*Planet to planet, the rich and powerful are equally self-serving.*

"Tali has a lot of faith in you," Kent said to Lord Vikander. "If she thinks you are true to your word, so do I."

"Ah, yes, Tali. She's at the library with another Paladin you're familiar with," Aethelwulf said. The older man raised his eyebrows, purposefully playing with the imagination of the Druin.

"And who's that?"

"Atticus Zoltor."

Kent's face froze into such a stunned expression that, after a while, Ariel believed he was dead.

"Atticus Zoltor is alive?" he asked, incredulous.

"Who?" Ariel suspected another relative. At this point, anything was possible.

"Your grand uncle," Kent informed her. "I thought he died when Spyre fell. Tali told me nothing of this."

"He's very much alive," Vikander assured him. "You may go see him."

Acting as if a fire had taken over the room, Kent took Ariel by the hand and headed for the library.

They descended to the great foyer of the Republic Manor and went onward to the right wing of the estate. The interior décor was utterly magnificent with polished gray stone walkways, vaulted ceilings, pointed entryways, and rectangular columns for support. On the walls hung massive tapestries depicting various natural, verdant landscapes. Ariel guessed they belonged to Mercia. Guards were stationed along the hallways, each one wearing the same ivory mask and accompanied with the same spear-shaped rifle. Manor attendants in simple suits lurked about, eyeing the foreign mages as they hurried along.

Whoever designed the Manor sagaciously reveled in the scenic waterfront view, choosing to have an abundance of long, vertical windows built into the seaside wall. When the setting sun seeped into these windows, the walkways must have looked divine.

But Kent was not as concerned with stylish architectural tastes as he was finding the other Paladins. He frequently confronted bystanders to ensure he was heading in the right direction to the library. While they walked with a feverish pace, Ariel's mind conjured images of what her grand uncle could look like. Probably like her father, just older and grayer. Ultimately, her imagination was not particularly inspired.

Further along the wing, they might as well have passed through a portal into another time. The freshness of the Manor's center was absent, replaced by older walls cracked with neglect, and bland columns and thresholds absent of any artistic momentum. The windows were smaller and unwashed. The ceiling was gray and flat. Age reeked in this part of the Manor, reminding her of the countless buildings abandoned in the Underbelly.

When they arrived, she saw that the library was not a glorious harbinger of knowledge, nor was it even a pleasant location to read in. Rows and rows of books stacked on shelves as high as the ceiling were lined up so tightly that not a single person could fit between them. Lost papers and torn books were strewn across the hexagonal shaped lobby, and a patch of the ceiling was boarded up with planks of wood. Calling the library insipid would be a compliment, but calling it derelict would be honest.

Deep inside the library, Tali was sitting at a desk and reading a book with a faded cover. She smiled as Ariel approached, but a part of her was trepidatious. With her was an older man, a human like herself, with puffy blonde hair and dark blue eyes.

Tali put the book down and welcomed them in. "Ariel, let me introduce to you Atticus Zoltor, First Scholar of Spyre and your Grand Uncle."

"A pleasure," Atticus said, hardly granting her eye contact. His skin was pale in the low lights and his face fleshy from age. His studious brow furrowed as he scrutinized her up and down. "The Archmage's legacy lives on after all, for whatever it's worth."

Kent fell to one knee. He pulled his Immortech sword from its scabbard and planted it into the ground. "Master Atticus, my sword is yours to command. If I had known you were alive, I would have pledged it to you many years ago."

"Thank you, Ser Kent. Judging by your near-impossible achievement of finding my niece and nephew, I would say you've already proven your worth." Atticus said. "I'm sorry you had to be left in the dark until now. The Vikanders love their secrets, and whatever they say, we must obey."

"It's just good to see familiar faces again," said Kent.

Atticus patted his gut. "You've cared for your Immortech sword as well."

"It's the only valuable thing I own. The least I could do was polish it from time to time. To be honest though, I barely looked at the blade during my exile. I wasn't... worthy."

"Whatever sins you believe you've committed, absolve yourself. Those few Paladins that have survived as long as us are going out of their way to sully the name of the Order. You've accomplished more for mage-kind than anyone else since the fall of Spyre; I wish I had more Paladins like you in my service."

Kent said nothing. He bowed his head to prevent anyone from seeing whatever emotion had blossomed on his face. Sensing this, Atticus Zoltor continued: "Where is Marion?"

"He's still in the medical bay." Kent answered, recovering himself. "He got knocked out during our escape. Doctors say he will be fine, it's just a matter of waiting."

"He lived on Romulus. Did you have any trouble winning him over?"

"No. He was eager to leave."

"Lyndon Everec taught him well," Tali interjected. "Serios save him."

Atticus proceeded to analyze Ariel like she was a science project. "So, this is Ariel, right? You look like your father, that's for sure, but is that where the similarities end?"

"What if it is?" she asked, his tight and snobbish voice putting her on edge.

"It makes no difference to me," he returned. "I'm not the one who invested all this time and energy into finding you. What I see before me is an Underling from Prisilla. Unfortunately for you, the Vikanders don't care about Ariel the Underling, they want the daughter of Marius Zoltor. You are the rallying cry for the oppressed mages hiding in every crevice of the worlds, you are their beacon of hope. You are not who you are, you are who they want you to be."

"I don't owe the Vikanders shit," Ariel said, politely. "Nor do I feel any obligation to you." She pointed an accusing finger at Tali. "She did not tell me about any of this. If I'm such a disappointment, I can take a ship and make my own way."

"We are not the puppets of the Vikanders as Atticus may have you believe," Tali said.

"Is that so?" Atticus asked, stroking his wispy moustache. "The Vikanders have final say in everything we do. Our Order is nothing more than a component of someone else's army."

"Maybe you're right," Tali said. "But aligning with the Vikanders is a step away from annihilation." She turned back to Ariel, saying:

"I apologize for the First Scholar. We have endured a lot since Spyre fell, and it has caused the both of us to suffer from phases of unrelenting cynicism."

Atticus laughed. "I consider myself practical, but it seems the two ideologies run hand in hand. Do not think ill of me for what I have to say, my dearest niece. I only want you to know what you're involved in before we all find ourselves over our heads in the bloodshed still to come."

# TROYTON (V)

Old Ulthrawn smelled of dust, smoke, and death.

An ancient city on the outskirts of galactic civilization, Old Ulthrawn was stuck in a constant state of rebuilding. The streets were a collage of compounded sand and dried earth, with the occasional stretch of concrete or asphalt road along the more populous areas. The tallest buildings were half the height of those in Rome, most torn at their apexes and left with small fingers of scaffolding reaching out to the sky.

This was Troyton's home now; how far he had fallen.

The long, laborious travel to Laktannon had allowed him too much time to think, which had subsequently tied his mind into knots. He still loved Rome, loved Caesar, and loved the KOH. However, he tried to save the Fyrossian child, and he fled from his judgement by the persuasion of Marion Zoltor. He had digressed into a weakling, a failure to the highest degree. Not only was he a traitor, but he lacked the decency to confront his crimes against the kingdom which had given him everything. Now he lived on a planet of failures, traitors, and exiles. Perhaps this was the punishment he deserved, enacted by the Gods themselves.

A long way in the distance, the silhouetted outline of the Republic Manor loomed over the rest of the city. Troyton, disguised as a soldier, managed to escape the towering walls of the inner-city without a single objection. The sensation of earth rustling against his feet made him sigh with relief. Finally, he was out of space, no longer a prisoner and no longer pretending to be something he was not.

The triumph of his escape was overshadowed by the inability to come up with what to do next. He watched the massive antiartillery guns atop the ramparts of the walls, which seemingly followed him no matter how far he traveled away.

*Find a ship*, Troyton thought. *Buy passageway out of Laktannon. Get back to KOH space. Destiny waits for you on Orbis.* The idea of boarding a ship after months of space travel made him nauseous, but what was there for him to do on Old Ulthrawn?

The language barrier was the first of many unexpected and mind-numbing obstacles to delay his path. Whether the population of Old Ulthrawn spoke one language or one hundred, it was impossible to determine. The variety of races passing through the city blocks was jarring as well. He saw scaly Drakonids, corpulent Timanzee in cheap hover chairs, small and stocky Wallacks, and orange-skinned Fyrossians to name a few. The occasional Hallyan with their triangular faces and long, slim bodies were mostly found in tech shops set up in market corners, bartering with such passion that one might think they were preaching of the apocalypse. The humans Troyton sought after could not speak his language, instead retreating as they perceived his advances as an act of intimidation. Even on a planet brimming with all different types of species, the humanoid managed to be the most outwardly imposing presence.

*If only they knew how pathetic I was on the inside.*

Hunger overcame him. Even in his weakened state, he still had double the stomach of a normal human. Street vendors prepared what could generously be described as blackened meat on a stick, but Troyton had no means of purchasing it. Instead, the crispy smells followed him, made his mouth water, sent needles of starvation through his stomach. The bestial desire made his skin sweat. Despite an approaching deliriousness, his hunger never subsided, nor did the baking heat of a sun that refused to set.

Lost, Troyton stood in one place like a fool. He scratched at a patch of black hair on his chin. He hated beards, and yet his face was full of one. It would be ideal to find a room for the night, get some sleep before another full day of aimless wandering. But where would he stay? Where was it safe to stay? How would he get money to pay for a room? None of these questions would be answered if he moped around, so Troyton took a step forward.

Then another. Then a third. It was liberating to be in control. *I'm a humanoid, raised by the greatest nation the galaxy has ever known. It will take more than an empty stomach and tired eyes to stop me. So. Much. More.*

Not long after, he knew he was being followed.

The sun, which was so far away that it could have passed as any other star, was placed firmly in the drab, greenish sky. With no darkness to rely on, how else was a seven-foot-tall humanoid supposed to hide?

With every turn, a masked figure met him on the other side. They looked exactly like the soldiers who raided the frigate that freed him. Casually, Troyton took every turn he could, but they knew his route before he did and were likely herding him throughout the city. He tried cutting through the market square, thinking that the ragged tarps and hanging canopies would shield him from his pursuers. But while he struggled to squeeze through the large crowds and hundreds of small shops, his pursuers may as well have floated over them.

As he hurried along, his pursuers closed in. He was clumsy and utterly unfamiliar with the rules of walking through the bustling markets, causing locals to scream and curse at him at every direction. He stepped on feet, tipped over stands with his unconscious strength, and pulled down tarps with his large head. With this kind of attention, blending in was futile.

Desperately, Troyton pushed his way out of the market square and sought shelter inside a derelict building, believing it to be empty. Unfortunately, it was not.

At least a hundred figures, bundled in unkept clothing and rags, made their homes inside the open-roofed remnants. Some leaned against rusted metal beams, while others attempted to ignite a fire in a trash can. When they shouted at him, their speech sounded like the croaking of toads to his ears.

He crouched next to a wall half broken by the collapsed floor it once supported. He buried his face into his long knees, praying his pursuers would pass him by. Pungent smells of burning garbage and dead animals filled his nostrils. In silence, he wondered in vain what kind of land could be this horrible?

In the matter of a few months, Troyton had journeyed to two major landmarks in uncharted space, once as a soldier of the KOH, the other as a fugitive. Grayspace was on the opposite side of the galaxy to Laktannon. Most people, no matter which race or planet they belonged to, never considered venturing to anywhere passed the barriers of civilization, but for him it was becoming a regular occurrence. Grayspace was a mythical territory for brave, young warriors to venture into in the name of their country and king, while Laktannon best fitted the rejects of the galaxy to live the rest of their days in morbid contemplation of all their mistakes and misfortunes.

Lucius was likely cursing his name. He had left the other humanoid on Fyrossia, smoking a cigarette as the capital city burned. Troyton had always expected his truculent friend to be the downfall of them both, but instead it was he who ruined Lucius' grand plans of battling against the Synths together, as soldiers and brothers alike. He wondered how Lucius would survive on his own, if the humans would be more antagonistic knowing that another of his kind fell to insubordination.

His ears twitched as they caught the scratchy sound of boots grinding on sand and shards of metal. The low drum of marching echoed throughout the broken, concrete halls. Inevitably, the impending feet stopped at him. It was the Druin he encountered on the frigate, wearing the same maroon jacket with silver zippers.

"When I was told to hunt a man down on Prisilla, it often entailed many and much research," the Druin said, rubbing one of his long horns. "Where did he live? Who were his friends? His enemies? I made a trail of where he was spending money and what he was spending it on and used that information to predict his next move. For you, my friend, I just had to find the tallest head."

Troyton launched at him; he could take the Druin hostage and force his men to desist. But he was impossibly quick, drawing his pistol and sending a surge of electric shock energy throughout the humanoid's massive body. The blast left him paralyzed, face down on the ground and sucking filth up his nostrils.

"When you chose to board my ship, you chose servitude as well. Get him in the car boys." Troyton's body, so stiff it may as well have been dead, was lifted by several men and hauled away.

When he regained consciousness, he was in the company of a stranger.

She was a young woman with tan skin and long brown hair aggressively slicked back. She smirked when he finally became aware of his surroundings. The sandstone chair she sat on was absurdly tall and had carvings of prowling tigers at each end of its backrest. When she placed her hands on the long dining table, Troyton tried to do the same but realized his hands were shackled behind his back.

"You're the humanoid that Bato keeps talking about," the woman said. "He says you were a prisoner on a KOH frigate. I wanted to meet you earlier... but you disappeared."

Troyton said nothing. The room looked similar to Lord Tarquinius' dining area in the villa back at Rome. Black and orange tiger banners hung over the cream-colored walls, which had darkened in the aura of an impending evening. The hanging ceiling orbs barely elicited a glow, giving the entirety of the dining room a heavy, shadowy feeling.

"You must know who I am," the woman said with utter candor. "Or, at least, you have an idea."

Troyton spat. The woman responded with a condescending grin. "I pity those poor souls unfortunate enough to be born under the suffocating grip of the KOH. They're fed propaganda before they can let out their first cry. They're surrounded by so much of it that they forget it's even there. But the effects still remain the same, whether they know they're eating the shit or not." She slanted her eyebrows and stuck out her lower lip. "I can't imagine the types of brainwashing you've been subjected to."

"I don't call it that," Troyton muttered through gritted teeth.

"I'll challenge you," the woman said. "Tell me what you know of me and my family, and I will confirm its validity. Then we'll know who's the one being fed lies."

Troyton did not like this game she proposed, but he played regardless. "You are a Vikander."

The woman pulled at her light doublet and stared at the embroidered emblem of an orange and black tiger over her heart. "How perceptive of you. Can you guess which one I am?"

"Ademar's daughter, or Aethelwulf's."

"My name is Rachel, proud daughter of Ademar, former imperator of the Republic."

"Your father betrayed King Caesar by aligning with the Roman Republic after they tried stripping him of his legions. A fateful decision, as Caesar eventually defeated Ademar decisively over the Bloodmoon."

"Wrong," Rachel stated. "Caesar was too ambitious. He had gained such singular power that it went against everything the Republic stood for. My father acted on the behest of the Senate; it was your king who did the betraying. Continue."

Troyton gave her a long glare before he spoke again. Who was she to question the actions of his king? "After the loss, Ademar switched his campaign to the Timanzee Empire, a futile action made by a desperate man. He would later die in a hopeless battle against the Triumvirate."

Rachel wagged her finger. "Wrong again. My father turned to the Timanzee Empire for help, as this was before the formation of the Triumvirate, but he was misled. The Timanzee Emperor had him executed without a trial. All in an effort to appeal to Caesar."

"Liar!" Troyton declared, voraciously.

"I was very young, but I still remember the last time I saw him," she said. She took a long moment's pause to let the silence stew. As the game continued, the dining room became more obscured in shadows, to the point where the suspenders holding the dim lights vanished and the yellow orbs appeared to be floating magically over the table.

Rachel continued, "For someone so loyal to the KOH, how is it that you ended up in a prison cell? Surely not due to a lack of cots."

"I wasn't in a prison cell." Troyton lied.

"No? That's not what the Zoltor girl tells me. She said the Romans had you strapped down like a wild animal."

"That wasn't me."

"Ha, sure." Rachel said, raising her eyebrows. Her skin was smooth and healthy, but something in her voice and posture possessed the essence of grit.

"Why don't you believe me?" he asked, awkwardly. This war of words was exhausting. The beginnings of a migraine scratched behind his eyes.

"You left quite an impression on Bato when he first spotted you on the escape ship. He was so awestruck that he called me to ask when I recruited a humanoid to my army. I said that I had no such humanoid but was curious to meet one. The truth is, you don't blend in, not at all. So stop trying to outwit me, because you just look uncomfortable."

Troyton would not speak. Lady Vikander clicked her tongue to the roof of her mouth. "You've learned so much about me, it seems fair that you return the favor."

"I was on Fyrossia, stuck in the throne room with the emperor and his family, a Roman general… and three damnable Inquisitors. One of them demanded the emperor hand over his son."

"What would an Inquisitor want with a child?" Rachel asked.

"The boy was an unregistered mage…" No matter how many times he recalled his betrayal, the sting hurt more, the battering waves of his shame drowned him deeper. "The Inquisitor was going to have him executed."

"Fyrossia was not under Triumvirate rule. The emperor had no reason to abide to a government he was not dictated by."

Troyton shook his head. "It's his fault for resisting the Triumvirate in the first place. They are the ones working to unite the galaxy. The Fyrossians should not be excused for fighting progress."

Rachel interrupted his apprehensive speech with another question. "And what did you do when he pursued the child?"

"I grabbed the boy and tried to protect him. He was a criminal, and I interfered with justice… but I needed to do something to get him away from the Inquisitors. My general stood there stupefied. Since when does a Roman sit idly by while a mage murders a child?" Troyton's heart sank. "I woke up in a cell, chained like some psycho. I don't even know what happened to the kid."

Rachel expressed legitimate sympathy. "Now you see the hypocrisy in the principles of the KOH. They'll shove aside morals as soon as they conflict with their own agenda, and then tell you and billions of others that they fight for unity and peace. You cling more fervently to this creed than your leaders ever will, and that's how you ended up here."

"Because I'm a traitor?" he asked. Her eyes were too much to handle, so he kept his gaze to the table.

"Because you care for the betterment of people, no matter the race." Rachel gestured to two of her guards to approach the table, commanding them to remove Troyton's shackles. Even behind their masks, he could sense their mutual apprehension.

She shrugged. "He could've broken out of them at any moment. Are they not superfluous at this point?"

The guards obeyed. Before they departed, Rachel asked them to remove their masks. Despite the low lights, the vague features of a Drakonid and a Fyrossian were clear. Troyton's jaw dropped, as he naturally assumed a human noblewoman, exile or not, would surround herself with other humans.

Rachel continued, "My army is made up of races from across the galaxy. They are all my brothers and sisters, betrayed by their rulers and seeking retribution. Unlike the KOH, we don't allow for the murder of innocent children. To us, all life is sacred."

She stood from her seat and walked over to Troyton's side. "If you want to live the rest of your life on Laktannon as a recluse, I welcome you. But if you truly love humanity, you will join me to eliminate the filth that has misguided our people for close to two decades. The KOH will be overthrown with or without you."

The Lady Vikander turned on her heel and marched out, her soldiers in tow.

Getting out of bed the next morning was easier than any other prior to leaving Fyrossia in chains.

He rushed to the basin of his small room in a lodge Bato had directed him to for a free night of rest. He shaved the rodent fur from his face. When it was over, he rubbed his smooth cheeks and grinned. From there, he changed into the new clothes left for him in the dresser and went outside.

He headed for the courtyard of the Republic Manor, the headquarters of the Vikanders, at the break of a red sunrise. Still, he was not the only sign of life roaming around the outside area. If anything, the whole city seemed to have arisen before him. Massive orange and black banners billowed from the bannisters on the highest level of the Manor, depicting mighty tigers eyeing their cubs below.

Squadrons of soldiers, broken up into columns of at least one hundred a piece, were running drills on the expanse of the old, dried-up earth. From the view of the ramparts above, the marching soldiers must have looked like a kaleidoscope design. Consistency was a war tactic. Troyton was taught early on in his training that an enforced dress code was vital for an army's intimidation factor. This "army" may as well have been a dominion of unruly gangs playing pretend warfare.

But if the humanoid could ignore the crucial value of proper military attire, the soldiers acted equally as disciplined as any human army he had seen. One group of soldiers went through their physical exercises deftly and without leaving a single man behind. Another group by the shooting range hit all their marks with weaponry that appeared to be on par with the best of the KOH. Their air force, however, stood out among the rest.

Their frigates and troop carriers, although not the size of the models made by the KOH, were sleek and expertly designed, brimming with all sorts of weaponry. Their one-man combat ships, known throughout the galaxy as star-splitters, danced through the open sky, spinning and twirling with birdlike grace, but doing so at such a high velocity that Troyton's eyes strained to keep up with them. He had aspired to be a pilot when he was younger, but those dreams were quickly squashed upon trying and failing fit into a cockpit.

Bato spotted Troyton standing starstruck in the open field. When the humanoid saw him coming, he immediately put his guard up.

"Relax, friend." Bato said. "My job was to get you to the Manor, not to keep you there."

"What's with the show?" Troyton asked.

"Our Lady Vikander has called for her retainers across Laktannon. She wants the first thing they see when they arrive to be her military in full force."

The roaring of jets and whipping of propellers ripped through the greenish skyline. The savage chanting of soldiers rang hauntingly off the sounds of their war machines. It was beautiful music to the humanoid's ears.

"What's the occasion?"

"War," Bato said with a hint of anticipation. "And it's coming."

Troyton already knew what "it" was.

"Vikander scouts reported that the Roman frigate followed us and will soon be knocking on our door."

"Is it just the one frigate?" Troyton asked, making sure his tone did not undermine the Godly military might one Roman warship.

"As of now, yes. But more will be on their way."

"And Old Ulthrawn will be ready. When the frigate arrives, I will be there with you." The words spilled uncontrollably from his mouth.

Bato chuckled. "How long did you rehearse those lines? Looks to me like it was all night. I want to believe you, Troyton Vorenus, but neither of us know where your true loyalties lie until the legions of the KOH stand outside the city." He whipped out his pistol and admired it in the glow of the rising sun. "You can guarantee I'll be by your side when that time comes, and I won't hesitate to pass judgement."

# MARION (VII)

"What was it all for?"

The question, asked innocuously, bounced off the void of his mind. The realm was nebulous, trapped in nonexistence and forsaken by time. He felt asleep, yet he was perceiving the faded memories of reality that lingered in some alcove he could not quite trace. Only the question was truly concrete; the prism holding his thoughts restricted any other mental exploration.

Marion was left in solitude to roam the boundless yet isolating fields of his own consciousness. He assumed a formless entity and sort of hovered within himself, never entirely certain he was moving through his environment or if his environment was moving through him. Regardless, his awareness was deeply sedated, and any thought or emotion was quickly subdued.

And then the garish red lights flashed.

The alarms screamed murder.

The untraceable voices shouted muffled cries for mercy.

Chaos reigned around him, but Marion saw none of it. A shattering thud exploded above his head. The creaking of something large threatening to give way beneath its own weight scraped at the insides of his eardrums. As if the sky became a physical object, Marion could feel the world around him begin to collapse internally.

He searched around frantically until a girl came into view. Her skin was fair and her hair as red as an autumn leaf. Her eyes were like two blue diamonds mined from the darkest depths of a cave. A sense of tranquility washed over him, soothed him against the surrounding bedlam. He tried to speak to her but was ignored, her attention taken by something else. She was clutching something to her chest secretively. Marion approached her and lightly grabbed her forearm. When he went to move her hand, the sword took form.

A ghastly hunk of sharpened metal had pierced through her back, its point digging all the way through her body and proudly sticking out from her chest. She appeared frozen, like a living, bleeding statue. Her fair skin turned deathly gray. The warmth once on Marion's fingertips became ice-cold. Her eyes met his; the shameful acceptance of defeat shook him.

"What was it all for?" she asked through stone lips.

She dropped.

A figure loomed behind her, smiling. Cloaked and ominous, a silvery jawline flashed from under its dark hood in a taunting spectacle.

Marion screamed. He screamed at the girl's hopeless expression. He screamed at the silver-jawed man who mocked his agony. He screamed as his current state of being warped away, transporting him through the dark void and into another scene. His hands clung fiercely to the paper-thin bedsheets at his waist, his voice finally producing sound and startling him from its magnitude. He appeared to be back at the academy, back in the comfort of room 304 and far away from the nightmare too absurd to possibly be real. It was not so, as the alien woman at his bedside indicated.

She was gingerly toughing the side of his head with her fingers. Once his screaming fit ceased, she pulled her hand away. His clothes were damp with sweat, his breathing quick and shallow like he had spent the whole day running drills for Officer Brody. He attempted to roll out of bed to create a more comfortable distance between him and the alien, but his legs were about as cooperative as two beams of solid iron.

"Even with today's miracles of medicine, we mages still have a few tricks scientists have yet to figure out." the alien woman said, her huge, magenta eyes smiling at him. Her long hair, sprouting from her head like twigs, fell to her shoulders. She was odd to Marion's eyes, yet curiously enchanting.

He was not in the audience of just one. Kent Kentoshi and Ariel joined him inside the cramped room packed with boxes and other storage equipment. His bed had been thrown atop the most even assortment of packages and still he caught himself slipping off to the left. It was a makeshift hospital room, clearly, but what had led him here? Marion tried to channel his memories, but his pounding head served as an impassable barrier.

Kent Kentoshi appeared calmer than he was when trapped inside Mister Everec's office. In fact, he looked happy. Ariel was leaning by the threshold of a sliding door, her lower lip purple with the bruises he had given her back in the cell. She stared at Marion indifferently, and he pretended to forget about their brawl.

"Who the Hell are you?" Marion asked the alien by his bedside.

Disturbance crossed Kent's face. "This is Tali. She is the head instructor of the Healers guild on Spyre, and one of my teachers when I was your age."

"Apologies," he said, straightening himself upon this realization. Everec had taught him about the four guilds of the Paladin Order and that the leaders of each guild were some of the most revered mages in the galaxy. Marion was surprised to hear Tali was Kent's teacher, as the Druin looked to be quite a bit older.

"I've been waiting for this day for a long time," Tali said, excitedly. "Your father tasked me with keeping you and Ariel safe as he prepared to defend Spyre for the last time. I thought his orders would be impossible, but thanks to Lyndon Everec's watchful eye, he saw your father's requests through. It's a shame he could not be here with us." Her eyes started to glisten. Marion swallowed hard as he suppressed his own bubbling sadness.

"You knew Mister Everec?" he asked.

"I did. We were two of the Archmage's closest advisors. Lyndon could be wild during his youth, but he was dedicated to the Order more than any mage I had ever known. He was the perfect candidate to protect you. From the few conversations we had after Spyre, I can tell he thought the world of you."

Marion chuckled at the image of a young Lyndon Everec. "Wild, you say? Do you have any stories?"

"Yes," Tali assured him. "But for another time. You've been in a coma for over three weeks, and because of that you've missed out on so much."

"Three weeks?" he asked, incredulous. "Why not wake me up sooner?"

"Although rare, healing magic can have unforeseen consequences when working against the processes of one's own body. I would have preferred for you to wake up on your own, but with events unfolding as they are, we could not wait any longer."

"What do you mean? What's happening?" Marion asked, flustered.

Tali rubbed her hands on her thighs. "Well, to start, we're on Laktannon. You know where that is?"

"The planet of exiles. The bloodlands for displaced rulers across the worlds. I'm well aware." Marion assured her. Just when his current predicament seemed to have reached its limit of absurdity, Tali went on to explain that they were guests of the Vikanders, a forsaken family of Mercia. They helped in retrieving both him and Ariel and were willing to make Laktannon the new home for the Paladin Order.

*What would Principal Tarius think of me now? He always deemed me a rebel, and here I am in the company of some of the most notorious enemies of the KOH.*

"Did you know about this?" Marion asked, directing the question toward Kent and Ariel. By this point, he regained some control of his legs and was shaking them beneath the covers.

"Not until after I lost you on Romulus," Kent said. "Tali... had to keep it a secret by order of the Vikanders." A long silence filled the room, brimming with secretive animosity.

"It's a nice way of saying she lied to us all," Ariel corrected.

"Well, despite a few obstacles in the journey, I've managed to bring you all here." Tali assured them with a hint of aggression. There was an air of disgruntled familiarity between the three, making Marion simultaneously awkward and thankful that he was left out of the loop.

Tali continued: "Anyway, Marion, we'll give you some time to get yourself together. Your grand uncle is waiting for us inside the Republic Manor. I'll wait outside until you're ready."

"He's another 'secret.'" Ariel said as she turned on her heel. "Don't get your hopes up though, he's somewhat of an ass."

They departed after that, granting Marion the privacy to work the rest of his limbs back to his body. He could hear them bicker between themselves as they walked down the hall. *Damn it all*, he sighed, *can this life get any crazier?*

The mental process was much more taxing than the physical one. Connecting his brain to each limb was strenuous. His right arm was the first to gain full movement, then his left. His legs, which felt like the heaviest parts of his body, took the most concentration. After the laborious process was complete, Marion was flushed with exhaustion and soon drifted back into sleep.

He awoke more peacefully than before and promptly hopped out of his bed as his bones itched with restlessness. He was clumsy with his first steps, as if walking on stilts for the first time, having to maneuver over and around boxes of cargo. His room transformed into an obstacle course, with a clearly seen but difficult to reach exit. After massive, disjointed bounds over the cargo, a profound sense of accomplishment thrilled him as he stumbled out of the room. He passed a larger room filled with similar hospital beds and stretchers, some of which were stained with blood. Disgusted, Marion tried to keep his attention forward. Thankfully, his path out of the ship was just a hallway away.

He was met in the courtyard of the Republic Manor by Tali, who smiled warmly as he came into the overbearing sun. "That took longer than I wanted," he admitted.

"Don't worry, follow me." She led him through the open courtyard where soldiers were marching about at the command of their officers. Large concrete walls with high parapets surrounded the courtyard, blocking the view from the rest of the city. The air was hot and humid. After being outside for a few minutes, he was already perspiring horribly. Tali was less bothered.

His eyes could not help but study her. Her branch-like hair seemed to move on its own. Her smooth skin was a darkish brown like that of a tree, with a scent akin to the lush forests outside Romulus. Her elegant and earthly presence defied the arid terrain around her, but her gaze showed no hint of intimidation.

"I don't want to offend," Marion began hesitantly, "But I can't tell what species you are."

Tali grinned and chuckled slightly. "It's not surprising. My people are both incredibly insular and, well, incredibly few. I am of the Insharai, a sister race to the Denvari. We come from a moon circling their home-world, and it is, for the most part, where we stay."

"But you are the exception."

"Indeed I am. The Insharai are naturally gifted with powers others could conceive as magic. We've been on the losing end of many massacres in our history, which has made us cold to the rest of the worlds." She paused in a moment of recollection. "I left my home for Spyre not only because of my gifts, but because I wanted to rebuild a bridge between my people and everyone else on the outside. I've worked hard, but that bridge is nowhere near complete."

"Do you ever want to return home?" he asked, thinking of 304 and Romulus and all the classes he was missing.

"I've considered it, but there isn't much for me back there. The Insharai were not happy with my decision to leave the home-world, and I don't think I would be welcomed if I returned."

This caused Marion to dwell on his own legacy. Had he shaken the Academy at all with his departure? Did students and faculty alike speculate on his escape? Was his absence even noticed? Had Romulus moved on, continuing its normal business as if he never existed?

As they continued to trek through the courtyard, Marion's eyes couldn't stay in one place as they analyzed all those who roamed in and out of the many watchtowers and camps that spotted the area. *So many people of so many races, every one of them ostracized from their home-worlds.*

Years ago, he had come across the name Laktannon in one of his history books, a planet entirely ignored by the Triumvirate and the preceding Galactic Council. That encapsulated thousands of years in which a planet was sequestered from the rest of the galaxy, and Marion desperately wanted to learn why. Mister Everec regretfully informed him that no such records existed. Warlords came and went like passing seasons in the Bloodlands, none of whom ever possessing power long enough to record their victories before they too were disposed of.

"If you want the history, I'll sum it up," Mister Everec had said. "Pointless wars led by bloodthirsty commanders. Each battle and leader as nameless as the last. 'Peace' is a foreign term on Laktannon so long as it's the playground for tyrants."

Marion kicked the earth as hard as he could and watched the shiny dust particles drift through the air. *Thousands of years of history, and this is the only record that remains.*

"Can I ask you a question?" he proposed. Tali nodded. "Why did Everec take me to Romulus? It must have been the last place the Archmage would have wanted me to go."

"Everec was the understudy of the First Scholar of Spyre, your Uncle Atticus. He was one of the brightest mages in the Order, and so he believed he could forge an academic career with the KOH. He determined the best place to hide you was in their own backyard, play their pride against them. Soon after the fall of Spyre, rumors circulated that you and Ariel had perished during the siege."

Marion was hardly satisfied. "Did Marius know about Everec's plan?"

"He knew of Everec's intentions and trusted his intellect," Tali said. "Your father was Roman, after all. He may have been an enemy of Caesar's, but he admired Roman culture enough and respected their education."

"I still don't understand how Everec could have gotten us both into Romulus. Many professors dedicate their careers to working on an off-world academy."

Tali hesitated. "I have many fond memories of Lyndon… but there was always something wily about him. Never against the Order, but he had an unconventional way of taking care of assignments. Perhaps that's why the Archmage trusted him with you. Lyndon was crafty, he would do things other mages would never consider. We were in a dark time…"

Marion thought of the clean-cut Academic Dean and would never label that image as "wily." Technically, Mister Everec had been misinforming him all along, but somehow his actions seemed more protective than deceitful. *What other choice did he have?*

They ascended a large set of stairs outside the center of the Republic Manor. Its chalk white walls, long and open windows, and curved roof wowed him. Having never seen a building from the outside, the circular design of the Manor was a wondrous and epic sight. From the center atrium, it separated into two blocky wings with traditional triangular roofing. The right wing looked much like the center with its clear windows, long balconies barricaded by elaborate balustrades, and a magnetic white coating with a hint of windswept wear from the distant ocean.

The left wing was far less of a spectacle. Scaffolding and wood planks had shamelessly covered up the furthest end of the wing, and gaps in the walls were still conspicuous to the naked eye despite the distance. The top of the wing was flat, and the exterior walls were spotted with cracks and holes left unfilled by neglect. Some of the style from the other parts of the Manor was present in the left wing, but it was largely overshadowed by the glaring flaws.

To Marion's approval, Tali led him through the right wing.

The library did not match the quality of the wing it was built into. Hundreds of bookshelves on every floor stood barren and forlorn, documents and torn pages were scattered across the floors forgotten, a hole in the ceiling was patched up with boards in the most effortless way imaginable, and, maybe worst of all, not a single person walked its empty halls to care.

He found Kent waiting for him on the bottom level of the narrow and winding library. Ariel joined him, sprawled out across a derelict desk and kicking her feet up into the air. In her hands was a book with a cover so worn that it barely held the pages together. Also, there was an older human male with a sour face. This man, Tali told him, was his grand uncle, Atticus Zoltor.

Above them was a simple chandelier that lit the depths of the library in sporadic pools of ruddy light. Basking in one of those pools were two long and narrow cases of dark purple leather, decorated with golden trim woven into spirals and swirls. Marion became strangely and suddenly allured to the exotic nature of the cases and ever curious as to what they hid inside.

"How long were you waiting for me?" he asked, embarrassed.

"For almost sixteen years," Atticus responded. He gestured for Kent to come forward. Upon approaching, Kent placed a hand on one of the cases. "It is tradition for the Archmage to present a Paladin warrior with his first Immortech weapon, but no mage holds the title at this time, so the honor belongs to me."

The older mage seized the other case. He breathed deeply and sighed on the exhale. At this point, Ariel was shoulder to shoulder with Marion, both of them gripping their hands in unaware anticipation.

"You may open the cases," Tali commanded.

The two men released the silver clasps. The covers were lifted. Resting on top of a white, velvety fabric were two longswords, forged in Immortech from the mythical mines beneath Spyre.

Marion turned to Tali with unbelieving eyes. "How did you get these? Everec told me the mines collapsed when the Inquisition destroyed Spyre."

"And they did," Tali assured him. "And the last smiths with the knowledge to craft such weapons no longer live either. These swords have been waiting for you for a very long time. The Archmage had them prepared on the day he learned he would be a father. Do take good care of them."

"Can I hold it?" Ariel asked.

"Not yet. The swords are not quite finished," Tali said. "Atticus, if you will?"

Atticus Zoltor reached into his jacket pocket and pulled out a pen. It was gray and curved, more like a fossil than a writing utensil. "All the smiths may be gone, but one rune writer still lives." He took a sword from its case, laid it down on the desk, and started drawing with his pen on the Immortech blade. His movements seemed random and disjointed, yet as he continued, Marion began to detect some sort of art to it.

Atticus made several small rotations with his right hand, then flung the pen from tip of the blade to hilt with one exaggerated motion of the arm. Sparks flew from the metal where the line was drawn, causing both Marion and Ariel to jump back. The First Scholar of Spyre, however, was undeterred. He continued to scribble, now more furiously, beads of sweat stemming from his brow. The tip of the pen screeched against the metal blade as Atticus' efforts grew more aggressive. Another volley of sparks flew, then another, once blue like diamond, once emerald green, then ruby red.

Finally, Atticus put the pen down, wiping the sweat from his brow. "Marion, this one's yours."

The son of the last Archmage grasped the hilt of his Immortech sword and gingerly lifted it from the desk. Considering its formidable length, the sword was remarkably thin and nearly weightless in his hand as he swiped it through the air. Golden and ember glyphs whirled and danced on the smoothed blade that soaked and enhanced the ruddy light of the hanging chandelier. There was something ancient and fabled and mysterious seeded into the craftwork, and yet the fluid and sleek design along with its alluring sheen suggested something inspiringly futuristic.

While deep in admiration, Marion allowed time to slip away. A childhood dream long believed to be dead had finally come true. The sword felt incredibly natural in his grip, *like swinging a shock baton, but so much more... amazing.* He looked for Ariel to share his elation with, but her jarring reaction grounded him.

She held her sword by her waist, one hand on the hilt and the other under the flat surface of the blade. She stared down at it, scowling. Her feet were still.

"It's supposed to glow," she muttered under her breath. Her neck snapped up as she searched for Kent. "Those books you made me read, they said Immortech metal glows when in the hands of a mage." She then gestured to their swords.

"It means nothing," Kent reassured her, although his voice lacked certainty. "Immortech won't react to your touch until your powers have awakened. That is all."

"Then how do we 'awake' them?" Marion asked, implicitly forming an alliance with his sister on the grounds of their mutual ignorance.

"With time," Tali said. "Atticus was born on Spyre, Kent Kentoshi was taken in when he was a boy. They have lived their whole lives around mages, whereas you have just been welcomed into our world. Take this frustration and turn it into determination, then you will be on your way to becoming Paladins."

Her words were vague, but Marion found some comfort in them. Perhaps he just wanted to believe so badly that he could easily ignore the logical side of his brain. He was a fugitive of the Triumvirate, mixed with a crowd of even more notorious fugitives. If we had to be stuck with a rogue faction, he was glad it was the Paladin Order. But what if he wasn't magical? Would these mages disregard him?

Beneath the excitement of his newfound purpose and the prospect of becoming something only conceivable in the realm of fantasy, a sadness lingered. A silent stalker behind every corner, Marion sensed the eyes of a demon from afar. The sense haunted him throughout the day, his mind exhausted from trying to unveil the source of this depression. Whatever was causing this distress, it did not want to be uncovered.

He hid it from the other mages. When he was in the presence of the Vikanders, he suppressed his anxiety enough to be courteous. Hazy, he could not confess something that was indescribable.

Finally, the memories returned when he was alone, when night fell, as he laid in bed staring at the pale ceiling of his room in the Republic Manor. The rusted metal jaw beneath a darkened hood and eyes like two red moons. These were the features of his enemy, the man he would kill.

# ELYSANDE (VII)

"Explain to me the circumstances of Timothy Mauvern's death one more time," Caesar commanded. "I can't wrap my head around it."

Harry Holt, a young officer of Mauvern's retinue and the man tasked with applying his lord's armor to his fleshy figure, recounted the events, his voice cracking with every third word. "Well, my king, you see, it's very, it was a very unlikely occurrence of... events. My lord Mauvern's armor is top of the line, but the oxygen filter in his helmet turned off... blocking the, well, oxygen from coming through. It was working fine when I applied the armor, but a malfunction must have occurred." The whole table of advisors stared accusingly at little Harry Holt. He was in the Palazzo Reale, trapped and with no friends coming to help him.

"Sutorian!" the king declared without breaking eye contact from the Mercian officer.

"Hail, Caesar!" the Prefect of the Praetorian Elite answered.

"As the most accomplished warrior in my servitude, have you ever heard of a soldier's oxygen filter malfunctioning?"

"Not that I can recall," Sutorian stated. "And if it were to happen, the soldier should have had no trouble removing their helmet."

"Interesting. Would you say that the events Officer Holt is describing are... peculiar?"

"Suspicious would be a more appropriate word, my king."

"So, Officer Holt. First, I'm expected to believe Timothy Mauvern's armor, which you say is top of the line, malfunctioned and shut down for no reason at all. Then, I'm expected to believe two grown men could not remove a properly applied helmet before one of those men perished from suffocation. Tell me: what kind of fool do you think I am?" Caesar asked, his tone cool and venomous.

Harry Holt fell to his knees in an instant. The motion was so fast that the Praetorian Elite raised their rifles. "Oh please, King Caesar! I'm telling the truth. I don't know why it happened! Lord Mauvern rarely used his armor, but I know at least how to dress him properly! You must see my innocence, merciful king… I am nothing but loyal to my lord and to you!" Tears trickled down his puffy face.

"The king mustn't do anything you say!" Reynard Bodewin, the Overseer of Mercia, declared. He sat beside the right arm of Caesar, dressed in a rich doublet with the crest of the red and white roses of Bodewin embroidered over his left breast. Elysande tasted bile in the back of her throat. *If only Fredrick and Boltof could see you now, Father.*

"Guards, take Officer Holt to a cell. He will remain there until I've decided what to do with him," Caesar ordered. Two of the royal protectors promptly hoisted the sobbing Mercian by his upper arms and dragged him from the council room. The wails of his tearful pleas could be heard on the street outside the Palazzo.

"What are you thinking, Tullius?" the king asked when the room was finally free of Harry Holt's ghost.

"I'm thinking he's too stupid to pull off such a plot. Still, what happened to Mauvern was not an accident," the Commandant of the KOH stated. Elysande noted the red veins bulging in her brother-in-law's eyes. His voice, too, sounded exceptionally rugged.

"I would have to agree, but what do we know of Harry Holt and his family?" the king asked. What he meant was: do the Holts have any ties to Tisoni?

"The Holts have lived near Lynwood for many generations. They are as much a Mercian household as Bodewin and Mauvern." Shota Nakamura informed the council. "I know little of his past, but his family has never caused a problem in Mercia before."

"The Holts have served as the lapdogs of Mauvern for as long as I can remember," Elysande added. "With their master about to achieve more prestige than ever before, now would be the worst time to take him out."

"I understand," King Caesar, her royal husband, responded. "The Holts weren't proponents of my ascendency until a crown was practically placed on my head… but that can be said about many people."

"With Mauvern potentially leaving Lynwood behind, perhaps the Holts were not satisfied with how he planned to distribute his lands to his vassals," Reynard included.

"Unlikely," Caesar said. "My impression from Lord Timothy was that he intended to leave Lynwood to one of his sons. But still, that sort of information is something to look out for."

Elysande shrugged. "This is indeed an unnatural turn of events," she delivered an accusing glare to Cira Dei Tra, the wicked witch woman of the Inquisition. "My inclination tells me magic was involved."

Before Cira could curse her name, Caesar interrupted. "I'm still waiting for an autopsy report. Shota, make sure you find the best engineers in Rome to examine the armor. Tell them to study every screw of it, no matter how long it takes."

Shota bowed. Something was different in his posture. Now that Elysande knew his secret, uncovered his weakness, maybe she was just seeing a human behind the job.

"Sutorian, have your men question everyone stationed in the pit of the Colosseum. I don't need them breaking heads, but urgency is advised." Caesar commanded, his brow straight like a line. *He's thriving*, Elysande thought.

"As you command, Your Majesty." Sutorian obeyed.

"We can't make any decisions until all the information is out. In the meantime, are there any other travesties worth bringing up while we are convened?"

Kassa Savon, Grand Admiral of the KOH, spoke up. "Not a travesty, my king, but an offer. Given the current situation, I will relieve myself from the Gladiator Games in order to be better available to you."

Caesar waved his hand. "That won't be necessary. Stay in the Games; no need to incite any more panic. We don't know the scale of this problem yet, if there is a problem to be had." Savon nodded, happy she could still participate.

After a moment of pause, Caesar dismissed the council. Savon, Sutorian, Nakamura, and Reynard Bodewin exited without another word. Cira scowled as she left, her old, weathered face filled with disdain. The queen smiled in return. *If I can frame Cira for this, I can knock off every single one of my enemies with a single scheme.*

Tullius Caesar remained, his eyes locked on his steepled fingers placed on the table. Only when Sutorian shut the door did he speak. "Gaius, I have to tell you something, something that could not be said among the council members." He turned to Elysande with a look suggesting he wanted complete privacy with his brother, but she answered with a blank expression.

"What's the matter, Tullius?"

"It's Octavius. His governorship of the Italus colony is failing. No food is being produced, his generals disobey him openly, the colonists are frustrated… and the natives are in open rebellion." Tullius shook his head. "You generously granted him the position upon his own request, and now he has to suffer the consequences for his boldness." The Commandant shot up from his seat, his forehead steaming. "Say the word and I will renounce him as my own son! He's already brought too much shame upon our family. Italus shall be his fate."

"Did Octavius reach out to you?" Caesar asked, coolly.

"He did. Crying. Begging for help. Acting like a child. He's twenty now. Remember what we'd accomplished by that age?"

"Octavius was put into a difficult situation. Governing a colony is no easy task, hence why many of them fail." Caesar said diplomatically.

"But he keeps failing! That's the problem."

"I can have him recalled to Rome before his life is put in more danger."

Tullius chortled. "And have the shame of our family waltz around the capital? Gods know what more damage he can cause."

Elysande rested her chin on her hands. She did not like the idea of another Caesar roaming around court. "Our enemies could turn him into a political weapon," she said. "If one Caesar can't control a single colony, perhaps poor leadership can be twisted into a genetic disorder. Having Octavius hurry home with his tail tucked between his legs is not a good look, no matter how you spin it."

Caesar spoke after considerable thought: "I will offer him an administrative position in my court. Make him a procurator, present it as a promotion. Then, his recall is seen as an ambitious young Roman accepting a more prestigious role in his government."

"Tax collector? My son messes up and you punish him with a comfy desk job in Rome?" Tullius asked. "I swear, Gaius, I'm prepared to renounce him, it is no idle proclamation."

"I understand, but I see something in Octavius. Failure can better a man like nothing else. Look at us, we were hardly escaping battles with our lives when we first entered the military."

"Yes, but by twenty you were putting down rebellions in the name of the Republic," Tullius said. Elysande winced, the faces of her brothers flashing before her.

"Warfare may not be his specialty, nor governing, but he may find his passion in administrative work, but we'll never know if he rots on Italus," King Caesar debated.

"And who will take over the colony?" Elysande asked.

"I have plenty of retired governors eager for a chance to serve the crown once again. One of them can go to Italus and settle things," Caesar advised. "The colonists will not be forgotten about."

"You have final say," Tullius conceded. "If only he could've turned out like Magnus, or Natalia. Then I'd have no worries for the next generation."

"Our family needs to stay united. It's far more dangerous to set the precedent that we leave our own blood to the wolves upon their first failure over giving them a second chance."

Tullius, having nothing left to say, dismissed himself promptly. Elysande knew he would purposefully neglect to mention her children, but the pettiness still perturbed her more than she cared to admit. She wondered briefly what Octavius would think when he returned to Orbis and found it in an entirely new state devoid of his father and king. As she went to exit herself from the council room, her husband stopped her.

"Wait, there is still one more matter to attend to." Elysande waited in silence for the reveal. "Natalia will be arriving shortly with Jacob. I'm prepared to offer him the position as Overseer of Tisoni in the wake of his father's passing."

"And how does that involve me?" she asked. Her king proved to be a formidable obstacle in her plans for the day.

"You are the Queen of the KOH. Isn't it necessary to attend meetings of such magnitude?" Caesar asked, coldly.

"The decision was made without any of my input. How does it regard me now?"

"The Mauverns are in a precarious state. With their father dead, the sons may believe I intend to take advantage of them. If you're present during the negotiation, Jacob may find comfort knowing his Mercian Queen is involved." Elysande found no reason to object, as the king had already made up his mind.

Natalia arrived moments later, breaking the silence in the room with her solemn greetings. Jacob Mauvern followed in tow, dressed entirely in black. Without the energy of newfound love vibrating between them, the two looked like an estranged couple several decades into their marriage. *Nothing evaporates the thrill of blooming companionship like the dreadful reminder of death.*

"Jacob, thank you for coming today. Again, I offer my condolences to you and your family. The KOH lost a truly great man. If there is anything you need, please let us know." Caesar said, sincerely.

"Thank you, my king." Tears started to leak from his pretty eyes.

Natalia patted his back in support. "Jacob's brother Edwin is still settling in Hazelvale. He wants to return home for his father's burial, but he won't leave without your express permission..."

"Well, let him know he has my approval." The king turned back to Jacob. "That being said, I want to make it clear that the Mauvern-Caesar alliance will endure this hardship. The position as overseer will not be put on the market after your father's passing."

Jacob lifted his head. "What do you mean, Your Majesty?" He spoke cautiously, and rightfully so.

"I mean that I'm offering you the same position." Caesar said, eyes flashing. "Once you've taken the time to mourn, Hazelvale is yours to govern in my name."

The young Mauvern's eyes raised in pure elation. He looked to Natalia as if she would pull him from this fantasy, but her warm smile proved Caesar's words to be real. "Oh, you are too generous, King Caesar. I- I don't know what to say other than I'm completely honored by this appointment." Natalia wrapped her arms around her lord's imposing shoulders. *She'll hold on as tight as she can now.*

"No need to feel honored, Lord Mauvern. I am simply acting out of the best interest of the KOH. Queen Elysande and I agree, you are the ideal choice to rule."

"We do," she muttered.

Jacob's expression transitioned back to its original grave state once the heat of the moment passed. "And my father? Any news on the cause of his death?"

"The air filters in his helmet malfunctioned," Caesar said. "I have my best people investigating the matter, but no conclusion will be drawn until all the facts are in. You and your family are under my protection until then."

"I hope they have no reason to be worried." Natalia stated, nervously.

Caesar shook his head, "None at all, it's merely a precaution."

"What of his... body? My mother demands it be returned to Lynwood immediately," Jacob said. There was hesitation in his voice, desperate to make sure his mother's words did not sound like a command to the king.

"It will be done, once the autopsy report is complete," Caesar assured him.

"Very well," Elysande interrupted, capitalizing on the brief break in conversation. "Let's not keep the young couple trapped here. Jacob must want to be back with his family." *And I want to be done with all of you.*

"Ah yes, we should be returning," Natalia answered. "Lady Catherine is in shambles. She begged Jacob to not leave the villa."

"Yes, best not to keep Mother worrying," Jacob agreed. The young couple rose from their seats, said their goodbyes, and exited. Down the hall, the sounds of Natalia's sweet voice echoed as she soothed her lord. Elysande departed too, leaving the council room without a word and descending the marble staircases of the Palazzo Reale with Ser Richard Dance at her heels.

They exited the Palazzo and entered the warm, Carcian air of Rome. The city was quieter than usual for the New Year's celebration, due to the mourning of the lordly oaf who never got his ham-sized hands on the spice trade in Hazelvale. A stretch limousine was waiting on Via Vittoria. Richard Dance opened the door for her and followed her into the back seats. Elysande ordered the driver to the barracks of the Black Dogs.

The limousine embarked northwest, descending the mighty Capitoline Hill into the heart of Rome. Even from miles and miles away, Elysande could see the impeccable defensive wall that was Pullo's Shield, named after the Roman republican who dealt the death blow to the Gasardi dynasty. A variety of structures flanked them as they drifted lethargically like lily pads down the congested river that was Via Vittoria. Among the expected skyscrapers were smaller, older buildings with arched, tiled roofs and vibrantly colored facades.

Along the red-brick sidewalks were outdoor markets brimming with shoppers and vendors alike, bartering beneath vivid canopies along the canals that provided clean water to the city. Onlookers marveled at artists who sold their exquisite canvases through their traveling studios. Most of these artworks, of course, captured the stunning countryside of central Carcia through the fashion of acrylic paint. Some bold painters even offered to draw murals of anyone who had the credits to pay.

Elysande was perpetually impressed at how Rome mingled old and new architecture and culture so seamlessly. Any other city with such unmitigated bureaucracy would have forsaken its past for the practical gray alloy of the present.

Further down the Capitoline Hill was the First Bank of Rome. A massive edifice designed with the structural inspiration of a concrete croissant, the First Bank of Rome was essentially the galactic bank of the KOH. Much of the Crown's own resources resided in its vaults buried deep within the earth. Although the ground around it was flat with tiled flooring and decorated with fountains projecting epic pictures of Immortals and legendary humans in their purest form, somewhere hidden in the open was the most fortified military base in all of Carcia. If the bank were to collapse, then the dynasty would have no legs to stand on.

As they crawled through the city, Elysande took the moment of silence to think. Lord Mauvern's death had distracted her more than she predicted. She considered the likeliness that Senator Felix and his conspirators, the self-proclaimed Heirs of the Republic, had ordered a hit on the soon-to-be ruler of Hazelvale. Mauvern was about to be a major pillar in the KOH system, so taking him down could cause chaos if they desired it, but what would they have to gain? Felix and Lucio seemed content with executing their treachery in the shadows. The less damage they caused, the more likely they could get away with Ser Bryson's ascendency to the Praetorian Elite. Caesar was more cautious because of it, increasingly likely to be skeptical of Bryson's request... if he were to win the Gladiator Games.

On the other hand, Felix was reckless. He outwardly recruited her, the bloody Queen of the KOH, and threatened the lives of her children. He was putting everything on the line to win his Republic back, so killing off one of his major enemies was not out of the realm of possibility, as shocking as it may be. Lucio himself, along with thousands of others who had sided with the Republic during the Civil War, had been publicly pardoned by Caesar, so Felix may expect similar mercy if he was to get caught. True enough, Caesar was always willing to offer criminals the opportunity for life-servitude at Halo over execution, and maybe Felix was willing to risk it.

And perhaps Felix did not fear death at all. And perhaps Timothy Mauvern's demise was simply the result of a malfunction in his suit. With countless possibilities, Elysande felt her head spinning. Although she needed a break from such a mental workout, she persevered, nonetheless.

The commonality between the conspiratorial senators was obvious: they were all from northern Carcia. Felix was from Rezza, Lucio from Impesaro, and Rachele from Venallia. Elysande assumed if there were other conspirators, they were likely Carcian. It made sense in a way. Because Carcia was once the center of the Republic, the ones most attached to it were bound to be Carcians. She could safely suspect the lords and ladies of these cities as part of the conspiracy too, although she had no proof to confidently pass judgement.

What continued to needle her was Ser Bryson's involvement. He was Mercian to his very core, and he was too young to have lived during the brief years of the Republic. *How could he have gotten involved with the conspiracy?* Elysande wanted to narrow down the potential conspirators to one region, but the Mercian knight increased the magnitude of possible players by an unfathomable degree.

The limousine turned, heading more west than north. They drove further away from the city center and closer to the villas toward the waterfront. There, among an area of smaller buildings on the outskirts of the city, stood the formidable barracks of the Black Dogs. Although not their official title at first, the Black Dogs served as a division of the police force that specialized in eliminating organized crime, drug trafficking, and prostitution in the underground of Rome. Although their forces were more common in the districts beyond Pullo's Shield, a few barracks were required inside the city center to ensure people acted on their best behavior.

The driver pulled up to the curb right outside the main barracks. Imposing in its stark design, Elysande peered upward and discovered that she could not see the top of the building. Two soldiers, dressed in black and donning their snarling dog-shaped helmets, were in her way as soon as she stepped on the sidewalk. "Hail, Queen Elysande. My name is Quintus Longinus, commander of these barracks," the soldier said in a muffled voice. He removed his helmet to speak to her on a personal level. "This is one of my tribunes, Petina Docille."

"Hail, Queen Elysande," Tribune Docille shouted, followed by a salute.

Elysande grew tired of such inclinations toward formality. "A pleasure. You know why I'm here, correct?"

"Yes, my queen. The legate who discovered Ser Galla's body is waiting for you inside. I will take you to her personally. May I ask what the matter is about?" Commander Longinus asked. His long onyx hair was sleeked back from his forehead, as if boasting the signs of balding. His eyebrows were thick and grizzly. The shadow around his mouth suggested a forgotten morning shave.

"You may not, sir." Elysande answered.

The commander wisely would not push the matter any further than he had to. They walked through crystalline glass doors and into a wide, dome-shaped atrium flooded with patrolmen and officers. A bronze statue of her venerable King was erected in the center of the room, one arm by his side while the other raised before him as if in the middle of a bombastic proclamation. *Even when we are on opposite sides of the city, I can't escape him.*

The queen, her bodyguard, and the two Black Dogs crowded into an elevator. Commander Longinus punched a button to one of the top floors. During the awkward transition between spaces, Elysande's roaming eyes caught the right ear of Quintus Longinus, or rather, the mangled bits of skin that were left of it.

As if sensing her gaze, Longinus turned and caught her before she could dart her eyes away. "Got this during my first day on the job. Caught my first criminal after trapping him between an alleyway and a barbed wire fence. I had his ass on the ground, but I made the stupid assumption that he'd given up on freedom."

"And so he bit off your ear?" she asked.

Longinus' laugh was smokey. "He had a knife tucked into his sock. I take my eyes off him for a second, and the next thing I know I got half my face covered in blood and my ear laying in a dirty puddle."

"Sounds like something from a cop movie." Elysande added, unsure of whether to make light of the situation. "This must've taught you a valuable lesson, something to pass down to all the new trainees so they may hold on to their ears for many years to come."

"Yeah," he laughed again as the overhead light flickered. "The lesson's simple: no one gives up on freedom easily, especially those who don't deserve it."

When the elevator doors opened, Elysande stepped into the dormitory, a sprawling space equipped with an endless line of bunkbeds going down a long hallway. "The legate is here," Longinus said as he compelled her forward. Their feet echoed throughout the empty rooms. The sheer number of beds on just one level of the barracks reminded her of the scale of the KOH; impressive, daunting, too big to fail.

After passing through several rooms, the dormitory finally showed a singular sign of life. A woman, dressed in the coal black armor of the Black Dogs, leaned over her cot. She raised her head at the sound of their approaching and stood promptly in respect. Before she could exclaim her fealty, Elysande interrupted her: "At ease, Legate."

Commander Longinus pulled up a chair for his queen, a plain metal thing he was clearly embarrassed by as soon as he presented it. Elysande chose not to be slighted. Her escorts made no attempt to leave, so she took it upon herself to clarify. "I need to speak to the legate alone."

"Oh yeah, I'll give you some space," Longinus answered. The two Black Dogs exited, and Ser Richard Dance followed them outside as extra motivation.

Elysande sighed. For once, she could focus all her attention on one problem. She rubbed her temples to combat a wave of mental exhaustion. "Great. You're Liscinia Drusilla, the legate who discovered Galla's body."

"Yes, ma'am."

"You look quite young for your rank," she noted. "Plus, it's especially odd for a legate to serve with the Black Dogs."

Liscinia was unsure of how to interpret her words. "Thank you, my queen. I love Rome more than anything else. If an enemy army was to ever approach upon the city, Gods forbid, I'm the only one I trust to protect it."

The queen could not help but smile. She admired Liscinia for a moment: dark olive skin, deep brown eyes, long hair as black as a raven. *Quite young, and quite beautiful too.* "Nothing's more dangerous to our enemies than a headstrong woman," she said.

"You would know more than anyone else," Liscinia followed. Now it was the queen who was unsure of how to receive a compliment.

"It's nice to know that it is not just the king who inspires our subjects. Anyway, I need you to tell me everything you know of Ser Galla's death. Spare me no detail, I promise I can handle it."

Confusion struck Liscinia's face. "I was on patrol in the Cisterci district, several blocks north of Pullo's shield. There was a mob of people crowded around an alley next to a pub. Naturally, I had to investigate. Prepared for anything, I dispersed the crowd and found the body strewn about, his mouth still foaming postmortem. He was in civilian clothes at the time, but the body was later identified as Galla by a forensics worker on-scene."

"Did anything change when the body was identified? Did other officers show up? Or were you told to leave?"

Liscinia shook her head. "Nothing changed. I questioned what witnesses I could, then left when the body was taken away."

Elysande nodded. The chance that she could be working with the conspirators too had crossed her mind. "These witnesses you questioned, did any of them see if Galla was with someone before he died?" The legate expressed another sudden flash of uncertainty. "Why do you keep looking at me as if I have two heads?" the queen finally asked.

"I questioned a witness outside the pub who said she spotted Ser Galla walking down with a man described remarkably similar to a drug dealer in our database. His street name is Mercurio Shade, and he's a general in the war to bring Blast-off into Rome. Naturally, even before the body was identified, I was curious. Apologies for the confusion; I told this to a guardsman already, I just assumed you knew."

*Be careful*, Elysande warned herself, *cluelessness will ruin your aura*. "You said you were curious by Mercurio's involvement. Are you still investigating the case?"

"No, ma'am. The guard I spoke to said Galla was undercover, and that the case was a matter of the Crown."

"And you believed him?"

"Why wouldn't I? He had signed documentation from King Caesar," Liscinia stated, feeling her competence tested. Elysande was sure to pacify any tension. Caesar had publicly declared to the Senate that Galla was working undercover at the time of his death, and he likely signed some sort of documentation to verify it too. Making a copy would not be difficult, especially after it was out in the open.

"Did you get the name of the guardsman who spoke to you?"

"I did not," she confessed.

"What about his features?"

"He was dressed in his armor. His voice was distinct though, as it did not sound Roman, or even Carcian. But I must admit, I'm not especially well-versed in accents." Her eyes sparkled as a solution conjured in her head. "Commander Longinus was the one who brought him to me. You could ask him for the name."

*I would not be so hopeful.* Longinus' insistence to be part of the meeting became clearer. He likely knew more about Galla's death, but if she questioned him now, she risked raising the alarms of the Heirs. "This Mercurio, could you find him and bring him in for questioning?"

"I know where he hangs out. I could rally some Black Dogs to take him into custody."

"No need for that," Elysande insisted. She gestured to Ser Dance. "Get one or two of your closest soldiers, ones who can keep a secret. He'll be the only other manpower needed. And don't bring Mercurio into the barracks, I have another place in mind."

The legate shifted as she prepared to rid more guilt from her chest. "I would have searched for Mercurio on my own had this been a normal case. Once I was told the Crown was taking over, I let my guard down… I hope my negligence hasn't put anyone at risk."

"You answer to me now," the queen assured her. "I trust that you're fine with working off the record."

Legate Liscinia nodded. "If it serves my queen, I will do anything."

Elysande arched an eyebrow and smirked. *Smart girl, that kind of thinking will take you a long way once Rome becomes mine.*

# KENT (VII)

He had forgiven Matiyala twice that night, then once more in the morning as the bluish dawn emerged above the balcony outside his bedroom. Kent had sparsely thought of her since settling into Old Ulthrawn, had not even taken a moment to mourn the guiltless being he imagined for the deceiver she truly was. So, her arrival at his doorstep inside the upper court of the Republic Manor was the last thing he expected to happen on a night he planned on spending alone. Upon first sight, a sense of betrayal shook him, but he had come to learn that hard liquor heals all wounds, albeit temporarily.

The Druin was pleasantly surprised to wake up with a dull hangover, instead of the brain clawing one he probably deserved. Perhaps the exultance of victory combatted this, the pride of finding the Archmage's children and guiding them to safety allowed him newfound mental invincibility. In fact, he felt twenty years younger, and he wondered if Matiyala noticed his revived youthful vigor.

"How are you adjusting to Old Ulthrawn?" she asked in the morning, whilst they lied in bed. She rubbed her head and hissed as the rising sun enveloped the room. Kent laughed lightly. He had already been up for a few hours.

"Can't say yet. I've barely left the perimeter of the Manor. Although, anything is roomier than your ship."

"Don't slander my girl," Matiyala warned him. "What about the kids? Must be a lot for them to handle."

"Ariel is skeptical of the whole situation, Marion not so much." Kent said. "Tali can't reassure her. Even if she shoots moons from her eyes, she won't be convinced of her powers."

"You're confident they have powers?"

He sighed and fell back onto his pillow. Its softness granted him no comfort. "They must. I'm trying to be blissfully optimistic, can't you tell?"

"You both worry too much about the future. We've done the impossible once. Give it time and let these concerns of yours solve themselves."

"I don't remember how I first used my powers," he reflected. "I simply listened to my instructor and one day it happened. I had the naivety then not to doubt myself. They're different, more worldly; especially her."

Matiyala sat up, resting her back on the bedpost. "Caesar's war left us all more aware of the evils in our worlds, whether we were dragged through or born into it."

"I can't imagine someone as precious as you suffered any hardships," Kent joked.

She acknowledged the tease with a half-smile, but spoke seriously, nonetheless. "The Triumvirate sacked my home-world, overthrew its leaders, and claimed everything as their own. I didn't care much about any of the 'grander' implications at the time, only that my whole life had been turned upside down in a matter of days, and none of it was my fault."

She turned her gaze to the window, her eyes soaking in the calm, dawning ocean in the distance. "There was this vibrant coral reef near my village that me and my friends would venture off to after school. It was like living in our own little paradise away from parents and teachers. When we were young, we'd play all sorts of games in the reef, and as we got older, well, the games changed. Then the Triumvirate came. They slaughtered my friends and family and destroyed my village, but the image of that coral reef, and how they blasted it into bits of black soot floating in the ocean, still infuriates me.

"At the time, I thought if I could get off my home-world, those bad memories would just stay there. I fell into the company of bad people, you know desperate times call for desperate measures, but no matter what I did, my life remained inert. I knew I was destined for the execution line, it was only a matter of when. Before bitterness could consume me like it did the other survivors, fate offered me something new to believe in."

Matiyala looked to her nylon pilot's uniform hanging over a chair by the bedside table, the orange and black tiger of the Vikander family emblazoned on a patch stitched into the right sleeve.

"I fought with the Vikanders during the Galactic War," Kent said. "Ademar owned a certain aura of courage and faith about him; at the time I understood why humans would eagerly follow his commands."

"Rachel has inherited all the qualities that made her father a legend. It was her passion and determination that gave me faith again. If anyone can challenge the Triumvirate, it's her. And I would crash my ship into a Roman frigate if she needed me to." Matiyala's austere tone intimidated Kent at first, if only because it caught him off guard.

Even before Romulus, he had labeled her a mercenary, someone whose loyalty belonged to the highest bidder. Not to say it was meant to be a slight, as her stoic yet relaxed demeanor suggested a worldliness that contradicted the ignorance needed for a pure allegiance to a cause, let alone a human one. Then again, he too would have given his life for the Archmage if told to do so.

This realization of her loyalty allowed him to feel less insulted by her treachery. Matiyala's business with the Vikanders could not be weighed monetarily. She owed everything to them, so the deception was not performed out of indifference toward Kent, but devotion for her people. She may have even loved Rachel Vikander.

Kent picked himself up out of bed soon after. His schedule was slammed with activities, none of which would be accomplished inside his suite with Matiyala and all the booze a drunk could ask for. The implication in their goodbyes suggested that she would return again tonight. Kent licked his lips, suppressing a thoughtless and brimming smile with an iron lock. *Today will feel all the longer now.*

Before he could leave, the Paladin had to confess something: "Aethelwulf has asked me to become an instructor for the new

Paladin Order. I'm honored by the request but... teaching isn't something I'd want to do."

Matiyala sighed. "Lord Aethelwulf believes Laktannon is his salvation, as if the rest of the galaxy will just leave us alone. Whether he knows it or not, he challenged the Triumvirate as soon as he committed himself to unifying the Bloodlands. Although I hope that one day you will have your Order again, I would not plan on peaceful living anytime soon."

"Is it sad I'm relieved by that?" Kent asked.

"No. Were you an instructor before?"

His throat became dry like sandpaper. *No, it's too early to drink.* "I'm familiar with it. Maybe I'm intimidated by the thought of settling down."

Matiyala shook her head. "You recognize the threat of the KOH, that they won't allow more than one big fish in their ocean. Rachel Vikander knows this too. None of us will settle until they are rightfully removed from their tyranny. By then, I think, we will find our peace."

Kent met Atticus Zoltor outside the Tiger's Den, the grand embassy building neighboring the right wing of the Republic Manor. The First Scholar was taking his last bite into an apple when he spotted Kent, and subsequently tossed it to the earth. Although far from cheery, Zoltor was noticeably more pleasant on this day than any other since their reunion. Like Kent, he had donned Immortech armor and robes provided by Tali, who was unable to attend the conference personally as she was dedicating any and all of her free time to teaching Marion and Ariel.

To the unassuming eye, Paladin dress appeared like the blades of their weapons: polished, glinting, nimble, and decorated with glyphs and swirls that pulsed in different hues like erupting fireworks. Although light, Paladin armor was much more durable than the bulkiest steel plating of a Roman centurion. Paladins typically complemented their armor sets with robes, to hide the Immortech and surprise their enemies. Kent and Atticus would indubitably stand out among the other delegates; a firm statement that mages have returned to political relevancy.

After exchanging greetings, the First Scholar patted Kent on the shoulder and said, "We're about to enter a chamber filled with creatures who share next to nothing in common save their flaring tempers and haughty personalities. They barely speak the same language but can always detect when they're on the receiving end of an insult. The entirety of Laktannon will be on high alert for another world war until each delegate reports otherwise to their respective regions." Zoltor chuckled for a moment. "I feel young again!"

The aged diplomat held his belongings close to his chest and entered Tiger's Den with unexpected zest. The First Scholar of Spyre was required to be a role model of an ambassador for all mages, and Zoltor fit into the role perfectly in his prime. Thankfully, he seemed eager to prove he had not missed a beat. Kent was not so enthusiastic, walking into the embassy with the game plan of speaking when spoken to.

The Den was built like a saucer. Its center, where Aethelwulf and Rachel Vikander stood, was on the ground level. Curved rows of seats spiraled upward, every subsequent row stacking upon the former for support. Kent and Atticus took their seats in the second row closest to the ground. Peering out, many of the rows across the pit were barren.

Regardless of the unfilled seats, the embassy was alive with chatter from the delegates who circled the Vikanders like congregates to a shrine. Kent had never seen so much diversity in a council since the days of the Order. Aliens of almost every species represented the population of the "Hundred Provinces" of Laktannon, each possessing a face that looked down condemningly at the Vikanders, as if they were judges for a rigged trial.

Lord Vikander dressed in a plain, navy-blue uniform, bearing the badges of his former honors on his right breast. They were the medals of the Roman Republic, likely awarded to him by a consul long since scratched from the history of books of the KOH. Rachel, however, wore a fiery orange doublet and black leather pants. She stood at attention in the center of the pit, utterly unfazed and perhaps welcoming of the fact that she was about to be the center of attention.

A private set of doors opened at the top of the saucer and, descending the steps in rows of two, came a legion of ivory-masked soldiers with spear-guns in hand. Like robots, every soldier marched to their respective post inside the confines of the Tiger's Den.

One soldier arrived at his station behind and between the Vikanders. A giant brute of a creature, his attire was more elaborate than the rest of his guard. Lady Rachel Vikander nodded upon his entrance and addressed him as "Captain." When the man turned to face the crowd, his large mouth and snout and sky-blue skin marked him as a Jurishan. Kent Kentoshi shuttered. It was back on Prisilla where he watched Ariel execute a Jurishan during the firefight with the pearls. Granted, he was one of Kagen's gangsters and was prepared to kill them if given the chance, but something in the way she so unflinchingly ended him still made Kent uneasy.

The captain slammed the butt of his spear-gun on the floor to call for silence in the room. He spoke: "The council called by Lord Aethelwulf Vikander, Grand Admiral and Protector of Old Ulthrawn, is now in session. We wish that all delegates of their respective regions remain silent while the acting protector of Laktannon addresses the council. As always, every delegate will be given a chance to speak." The captain turned to Aethelwulf and saluted.

The Lord Vikander surveyed his audience coldly, with the fingers on his left hand scratching his palm unknowingly. "Before we begin, is there anyone unaware of the nature of this council?"

No one muttered a word. Atticus pulled out a pen and journal from his stack of belongings. Prepared for Kent's questionable glance, he muttered: "An archaic technique, I realize, but far more personal when documenting such events."

"A Roman frigate approaches us as we speak, and with it comes the possibility of war. As you may imagine, we will need all the manpower each and every one of you can acquire to fend them off." Aethelwulf spoke like a soldier out of time: strong, regimented, but completely uninspired.

One delegate took the pause in Vikander's speech to stand. Rounded of shoulder and waist, the blue-skinned balloon of a delegate could hardly reach his three-fingered hand to his mouth as he covered his cough. He was dressed richly in heavy velour robes that shimmered in the overhead lights. From his appearance, Kent guessed he was of the Jurishan species as well. A deliberate silence was thrusted on the Den. When he finally did speak, the delegate's saggy cheeks quivered with every word.

"I've heard rumors that a Roman frigate can hold half a planet's population and the firepower of an entire brigade of star-splitters." He gazed around the room in a theatrical jest and shrugged his shoulders. "By my generous eyes, I see no more than a third of the regions of Laktannon represented at this embassy."

With a hushed voice, the First Scholar kept Kent informed. The unruly delegate's name was Thalla Frorn, a magistrate of Old Ulthrawn from a long line of exiles despised by their own race. Atticus clearly had a poor opinion of the man, but he could not disagree with his point.

"And the absence of these regions has been noted." Aethelwulf said through gritted teeth.

Thalla went to make another remark, but he was cut off by Rachel. "I think it necessary to remind Magister Frorn that Laktannon has the largest population of any planet in the whole galaxy. A fraction of our army may double or triple whatever force resides on that frigate. Our soldiers are the best the worlds have to offer. So, even if we are outnumbered, each of our fallen should take three Romans to the grave with him."

A handful of delegates pounded their benches in excitement, the pure sense of patriotism overcoming them. Frorn did not share this enthusiasm as he stood, hands folded and drawing another breath. "I cannot and will not disagree with your claims, Lady Rachel, as your conquest and subjugation of our planet has made war and violence a familiar friend to all Laktonnians. I do ask, however, is why now?"

Rachel indulged him, enticing him to play his trump card. "Why what, Magister?"

"Why do you choose to unveil yourselves to the galaxy? It seems a risk for the greatest outlaws of the KOH to challenge Rome in such a public display."

The magister set a trap, and Rachel Vikander willingly walked right into it. Somehow, Frorn had learned of the botched mission to save the Zoltors and planned to use it against her. Exile or not, no one was willing to risk their lives for mages.

Another delegate stood. An old Hallyan woman with dry, gray skin and long hair dyed a vibrant green. Her reptilian eyes on either end of her triangular face looked condescendingly down at the Vikanders. Around her neck were a series of bronze rings that covered her from shoulder to chin. "They wish to wrap Laktannon in the petty affairs of humanity. And for what? You've risked the wrath of the Triumvirate for a handful of mages. If I'm not mistaken, I would say this was done on purpose."

"This is not the time to jump to conclusions," Aethelwulf warned. "When the frigate comes to Old Ulthrawn, I will make it my top priority to parley with whoever commands the vessel. The last thing I want is war with the KOH, but we need an army at the ready as a last resort."

"How can we believe anything you say, Lord?" Thalla Frorn asked, haughtily. "You conducted a secret operation to rescue a bunch of blasphemous mages without any of our consent."

"Caesar can be reasoned with!" Aethelwulf insisted.

"And do you think the KOH will let us live peacefully?" the Hallyan woman interjected. "Once King Caesar catches word that his rival family has taken over Laktannon, he will rain Roman hellfire upon us all!"

The delegates were in an uproar, making enough noise for double their actual number. Kent became uncomfortable, feeling more like a detriment than an ally. The raucous protests continued despite Aethelwulf's insistence. It was not until Rachel approached the stand again that the delegates quieted down.

"We are not the only outcasts to retreat here," Lady Vikander started. "And I can guarantee that each one of you has been wronged by whichever home-world you were forced away from." She walked with long, confident steps to the waist-high barrier separating her from the audience.

"True, one could consider this as a squabble between humans, one none of you should consider spilling an ounce of blood for. I would not blame you, but I choose to see it through a different lens, a lens much grander in scale than all the galaxies yet to be explored, a lens more magnificent than the very creation of our worlds by the Immortals. When Rome invades our home and we turn their frigate into scrap, it won't be just another affair in the long, tireless history of humanity, it will be the beginning of a Revolution that will defy the trajectory of this galaxy!"

Again, the delegates pounded their benches, except now the physical chant was joined in unison. They sat on edge, awaiting the words of the Tigress. Atticus no longer scribbled into his notebook, but was clenching his pencil tight enough to crush it in his grip. Kent caught his own foot tapping along, but promptly stopped it.

Another delegate called for attention. This one was a Drakonid with auburn scales flecked with blue as deep as the ocean outside the Republic Manor. One of his eyes sparkled with silver, the other was a sunken pit beneath his brow. When he spoke, his words were soft, but the hissing through his forked tongue and sharpened teeth cut through the crowd.

"Lady Rachel ssspeakss boldly, but wordss are worthlessss when action is not followed." The Drakonid turned his long scaly neck and, if Kent was not mistaken, was whom the next words were addressed to. "If the dogsss of the masster are left out in the cold and are fed promissesss instead of meat, their obedience will lead to hossstility quite fasssst."

Lady Vikander smiled, her onyx eyes flashing. "General Gressna, I will choose to take your words as counsel and not threats, as I completely agree. Do not interpret what I say next as a hollow promise, but as a proclamation, one I would not dare to announce unless I had absolute certainty in our ability to carry it out."

Aethelwulf ruffled his brow in disapproval, but she continued: "Our struggle exceeds that of a belligerent Roman frigate. It exceeds the KOH and even the Triumvirate. We've all lost so much from the people who have turned against us. I say we break the cycle of our ancestors, who lived and died abandoned and bitter, and take back a galaxy that is rightfully ours!"

Aethelwulf shot to his feet, sending his chair tumbling away. Atticus snapped his pencil in half, his puffy face boiling over. Lord Vikander demanded silence, but his voice was swept away in the tidal wave of roars raining from the benches. Kent kept himself stoic, but he too was on the verge of joining the erupting riot that inflated Tiger's Den.

It was not until the Jurishan captain-of-the-guard stomped the butt of his rifle to the floor that Lord Vikander received the silence to speak uncontested. "My niece speaks intrepid words, but they are utterly foolish nonetheless." Rachel went to cut him off, but she choked up at the battle-hardened glare of her uncle. "This assembly was called to discuss the immediate threat of the Roman frigate, not some fantasy war that will never end the way any of us imagine it will."

The energy within the Den fainted, but Kent could still sense the slightest of heartbeats. Finally, Aethelwulf seemed content with his ability to snuff the life from the crowd. "If we can get back to the topic at hand, I require every delegate to provide the exact amount of manpower and machinery they can send to Old Ulthrawn in three days' time."

. . .

Atticus stormed out of the embassy as soon as the session ended, muttering to the wind as he marched along. "The petulant bitch thinks the world revolves around her. War with the Triumvirate? She'd have better odds being crowned Queen of the Synths."

Kent Kentoshi was at his heels, unsure of how to comfort the First Scholar. Rachel Vikander was justified in her proclamation and determined in her speech; she would win the First Scholar over eventually. Having nothing to agree on, the two mages paced along in silence. Although Atticus did not say where he was going, Kent already knew.

They crossed the wide plaza at the foot of the Republic Manor, where the tiled flooring represented a history of war and reconstruction in its aimless diversity. The center of the Manor ominously stood like a tombstone ready for the massive burial to come. Kent turned his head away and on quick feet escaped the mortal shadow. As they walked by the right wing of the Manor, both flying and grounded cars alike passed them in rapidly increasing numbers, carrying with them the roar for war called by the Tigress of Old Ulthrawn.

A few blocks down from the Manor was Unity College, a small university consisting of several rectangular buildings all erected close to one another as if they were about to embrace. Kent trekked through the stone courtyard connecting the intellectually rich edifices together, the complete emptiness of the small community somewhat foreboding. In the back of the college was a grand, flourishing stretch of lawn that contradicted the hot and dry climate of the surrounding city.

The luscious green grass was split in half horizontally by a sand and stone pathway. The half that bordered the college ended with rows of dark green trees cut in rounded shapes like verdant moons. Chairs and small tables were placed in the shade, providing an excellent retreat from the overbearing sun. On the other half of the lawn, the impressive banks of vivid flower gardens and a six-foot-tall cobblestone wall provided an aromatic barrier from the outside congestion of the city. Kent considered bringing Matiyala to this place one night while the rest of the world slept. How one area could be so detached from its imposing surroundings, he could not understand.

Atticus could see Tali instructing Ariel and Marion, each with their Immortech sword in hand and listening attentively to her advice. As the swordsman, Kent should have been the one to train them. Besides a quick lesson here and there, his scattered life made it impossible to lay down a consistent schedule for their classes. He determined himself to make it up to Tali… eventually.

The First Scholar aimed to march right in on their lesson, but Kent politely grabbed his shoulder and advised him against it.

"You're right, Ser Kent." Atticus said, regaining his composure. "Best not to interfere with the morsels of training time the kids have. Come sit on the patio with me; we will watch and be amazed by the prodigal children of my late nephew."

They took their seats on a bench under a tilted canopy hanging over the college facade. Between them stood a small table holding emptied glasses not yet retrieved by a servant. It was not long until said servant hurried to their side to collect the cups and, before he could escape, was ordered by Atticus Zoltor to fetch more wine.

"Will it be one glass, or two glasses?" the First Scholar asked.

"One glass." Kent insisted, risking slight disrespect. Thankfully, Atticus appeared unperturbed. Kent wanted to limit his day drinking. Although he could typically function while under the haze of alcohol, every once in a while the deceptive poison bested him.

They surveyed the Archmage's children in silence for a time.

Marion was sturdy, possessed a strong form, and struck with precision. He fought like a Roman; pure confidence, absolute logic, choosing to win a fight on his own merit rather than his opponent's mistakes. Even in this environment, battling nothing but the breeze, Marion was a sponge, taking every word spoken by Tali to heart.

"Perhaps the Romans did us a favor." Atticus suggested, taking a sip of wine. Kent envied his ability to drink conservatively.

"He learned their discipline, that's for sure," Kent said. "He utterly despises his own people, but they made him one Hell of a fighter. I'll have to teach him some advanced techniques, but his fundamentals are sound." The Paladin leaned back in his chair, embracing the fragrant breeze that brushed by the patio. After everything he had accomplished thus far, there was still a mountain ahead of him to climb if the Order was to be rebuilt properly.

"An anti-Roman with Roman training? The Order stands a chance after all." Atticus cackled bitterly.

Ariel was reckless, not having the proper training of a KOH academy, but her quickness showed promise. Sure, Tali had to incessantly reteach her how to grip the sword, how to move her feet with her opponent, and how to stand when parrying an attack, but the elation she had through failure surpassed that of anyone else's on the field. For a moment, the Underling, the bounty hunter, the killer, was just a girl having the time of her life.

Kent also noted Tali's posture: relaxed shoulders, leaned back, and with a brimming smile on her face. This was the most comfortable he had seen her since being picked up on Narood. Instructing was her passion on Spyre, and the skill had not rusted over the years.

When the twins sparred with wooden practice swords, Marion won nearly every time. He was bigger, more reserved, and could provoke Ariel easily into an unstable string of attacks. She did not leave the session without a few victories of her own, although they were never earned by the most chivalric of ways. Her victory that got the greatest laugh from Tali, and the longest sigh from Atticus, occurred when Marion's boldness overcame him, and he hip checked her to the ground. She fell flat on her back and closed her arms around her head. Rightfully assuming she was in pain, Marion approached her with concern. In turn for his empathy, Ariel stealthily kicked her brother's shins from beneath him, forcing him to the ground as well. Before he could gain his bearings, the dull end of a wooden sword was at his throat.

"She's just like Caella," Kent whispered unconsciously. He hoped Atticus did not hear him.

"That's a name I haven't heard spoken aloud for a long time," he said. "Not that I've forgotten about her: the Wildflower of Spyre."

"She was one of the best of us," Kent said.

"One of? She was the best," Atticus declared. He put the glass of wine to his lips. "If she had been born first, we would've called her Archmage. Not that she cared. Marius relied on her as his best diplomat, and she embraced the role with an open heart."

"I only had the honor of working with her once," Kent reflected. "A Fyrossian trade ship got picked off by a Hallyan military station. The ship did not have permission to cross Hallyan space, so they had every right to lock them away and be done with it. However, the situation wasn't that simple."

"They never are." Atticus agreed, smirking.

"One of the passengers on board was the son of a Fyrossian chancellor. And the ship itself, well, wasn't in the business of legal goods. Turns out the kid was mixing in with drug smugglers. Whether the chancellor was linked to the drug trade was something we never bothered to find out. Regardless, the Hallyans wanted to punish them like any other criminals, but the chancellor threatened war if his son wasn't returned unharmed.

"An impasse with that kind of tension calls for the best diplomats to settle it, enter Caella Zoltor. The Archmage sent several of us to aid her, but we knew she was in command. Fresh off my knighting ceremony, I was shaking out of my boots as we entered the space station where the summit was to be held. Caella saw me on the verge of pissing myself and assured me everything would be fine. Representatives on both sides cursed at her as she tried to make peace. They called her horrible names, but her smile and civility endured it all. After hearing the wretched things they said, I would've let them kill each other. She talked to them for hours, searching for common ground."

Kent blushed as the memory came back to him. With her platinum blonde hair, elegant robes, luminescent skin, she was a Goddess dealing with the affairs of mortals. "Eventually, she won them over. The Hallyans surrendered the chancellor's son on the agreement that he never enters their space again. They kept the other smugglers to face their courts, and Caella prevented a galactic war.

"I was beyond relieved when we got back to our ship, and I knew the other Paladins were too. Our interrogation, best described as hours of stepping on needles and praying we didn't break skin, had worn us down. Not Caella though. She was as lively as ever, and she personally thanked me for my help. Her sincerity made me think I was the best diplomat in the worlds, but now I can't remember a single damn thing I did to help her."

"You probably didn't help, but her compliment was no less genuine." Atticus laughed, although not in an insulting fashion. "She understood the importance of maintaining unity among mages."

"Quite fortuitous. Look at us now."

Atticus nodded. "Thank you for the story. It's been a while since I've heard a fond memory. You say Ariel reminds you of Caella, but I disagree. It's in her face. Gaunt cheeks, darting eyes; she's hardened. She has Caella's fierceness, but not her beauty and grace, and I can't blame her for it."

"These things can change over time," Kent proposed. "She's been trapped on Prisilla her whole life. We need to give them both time to get used to their new surroundings."

"That's the problem with experience, it never truly leaves you. She's seen the worst of people; I don't know what it is, but it burns in those ember eyes. She knows the galaxy isn't worth fighting for." Atticus rose and parted Kent with a few closing words. "Caella believed in the best of us, or at least she did up until the end. She dedicated her life to keeping peace in the galaxy, but she herself was the motivation for its most destructive divide. And she knew it too… then she cut her own roots and the Wildflower of the Spyre wilted and died."

# ELYSANDE (VIII)

The second round of the Gladiator Games commenced with a match that impressed the whole stadium, including the queen who, despite her prior intentions to hate it, could not deny the zealousness for victory both competitors showcased for the people of the KOH.

The Commandant's son, Magnus Caesar, challenged Servius Venator, the heir to another prestigious patrician family of Rome. They represented the future of the KOH, and they battled as if the prize of standard-bearer for said future was at stake.

Magnus, dressed in his opulent golden armor with the winged Aquila sprawled in silver across his chest, engaged first. He swiped at Servius' arms and legs with his electric-shock baton, toying with him, attempting to intimidate him, but the young patrician was too seasoned to play such games. One petty slash too many made Magnus overconfident, and when he seized a moment of perceived rest to flex to the crowd, Servius punished him with a shoulder check that sent him flying off his feet.

The crowd roared with laughter, except for Tullius himself, who reprimanded his son from his seat as if anyone in the arena below could hear. Magnus returned to his feet, the cameras perfectly projecting his bottled contempt on the giant monitors hanging from the ceiling. Wiping his long brown bangs from his face, Caesar regained his composure and squared up against Servius once again.

Both men moved methodically, respecting the skill of the other while swinging their batons with the confidence that their own victory was imminent. The crowd was silent, reading each move in a grander story of two determined warriors fighting for the auctoritas that youth, thus far, had left them unfulfilled. The staticky sounds of clashing batons echoed throughout the stadium, creating a pulse to the battle like a melody gradually increasing in its tempo in anticipation of an epic climax.

Eventually, Servius began to overpower Magnus. He was the larger of the two, and the benefits of his natural strength were showing. Magnus' right arm quivered more and more with every blocked blow. The young Caesar, whose prior self-assuredness had led Elysande to think he would rather break in defeat than bend in recognition of his own weakness, expressed strategic humility and turned off the gravitational pull of his boots.

The silver eagle took flight, ascending rapidly to the top of the plexiglass dome. When his feet touched the apex of the barrier, the whole dome shivered in a bronze tint. Servius was on his tale, although he wisely elected to land several feet from his opponent to allow himself time to adjust to the change in perspective. The forethought paid off, briefly, as Magnus' sprint gave Servius just a sliver of time to regain his bearings.

The batons crossed yet again, this time Magnus with the clear advantage over a disoriented opponent. Elysande quietly rooted against Caesar. Her king was quiet on the matter, watching scrupulously as if determining the better of two products. These past few days, he spent nearly all his hours in the Palazzo Reale, so she sensed the Gladiator Games served as a merciful relief from his work.

*I've been busy too, Your Majesty, but the less you know of that, the better.*

Magnus continued his brutal assault, berating Servius with overhead strikes that pushed him further and further to the floor. The crowd watched in awe as the two men fought upside down. Finally, Servius managed a successful parry, granting him enough relief to force distance between them and jump away. Magnus predicted this move and latched on to his foot as he kicked off.

They struggled in the center of the arena, spinning like ballet dancers but clearing the distance of space at a scarily fast speed. Gasps emerged from the arena, mostly from girls worrying for the safety of both handsome boys. Elysande leaned over in her chair. Neither wore a helmet, so if their heads were to hit first, brain damage would be the least of their worries.

"Move him forward, Magnus!" Tullius declared, spittle flying from his brown beard. As if he heard his father's command through the flood of a hundred-thousand other screams, Magnus, whose arms were wrapped around the waist of Servius, shifted his opponent at the very last moment, causing his back to absorb the brunt of the impact. A large thud quieted the Colosseum, followed by the sight of Magnus skidding across the arena. Servius, on the other hand, did not move, sticking to the floor like a magnet.

"Finish it now!" Tullius ordered.

"He can't bloody hear you," Elysande shot back at him. A small spark of laughter came from the Praetorian Guard occupying the walkways. Tullius crossed his arms and grumbled.

Magnus stumbled to his feet and limped to Servius. Both shock batons were on the sight of the collision, so he claimed one and promptly stuck it into the abdomen of his opponent. The sirens blared in declaration of victory for Caesar. The Colosseum attendants roared with approval. They paid no concern to the man lying motionless in the center of the arena. Elysande assumed Servius was dead, until Magnus grabbed him by the forearm and pulled him up.

The two men embraced in competitive respect, inciting a tidal wave of applause from attendants who admired such a display of sportsmanship. Magnus' smile cut through the cameras and into the hearts of every girl watching, making Elysande groan in contempt. The young Caesar raised the arm of his defeated enemy, which was met with even more adoration from the audience. In return, Servius saluted his better and both men walked off the stage.

"A fine fight," Caesar noted, absent-mindedly. "Sutorian, would you agree?"

Sutorian, dressed in immaculate gold and crimson armor, studied the scene. "They showed great respect for each other. If the next generation of patrician leaders possess that kind of chivalry, Rome will see many more glorious years to come. As to the fighting itself, it's tough to say. The fight for one's life will hit them differently, but this is a promising start."

Tullius' ears perked up. "Rest assured, Captain, Magnus has served in a number of colonizing campaigns. He is no stranger to proper warfare."

"If you can call killing an animal with a spear in its hand 'proper warfare.' Perhaps the term is more generous than I remember," Elysande interjected. Tullius went to object but discovered he had nothing to object to.

Kassa Savon took the stage next. The Grand Admiral of the KOH was a fan favorite in the Colosseum, and she accepted their praise with open arms as she entered the arena. Sticking to her strategy in the first round, Kassa dressed in simple light armor that would allow her to navigate the arena and the surrounding dome with immense quickness.

Her opponent was Bernt Krudell, from the northern provinces of Mercia, Elysande's motherland. Like most men of that region, Bernt possessed a brutish body, standing about a foot taller and two shoulders wider than Kassa. His bluish armor was as bulky as he was, with the ornamented symbol of a snarling wolf displayed across his breastplate. Also like those from her motherland, Bernt's hair was magnetically blonde and his eyes crystalline blue. Despite his beastly disposition, the man was naturally attractive.

Bernt roared as he entered the arena. A small portion of the crowd hollered with him, as it was the traditional greeting for natives of northern Mercia. Bernt's strength allowed him the benefit of holding a baton in each hand. The crowd cheered wildly at the sight of him, unaware of how impractical the strategy was. Elysande at least understood his intentions to appear more intimidating, but a seasoned warrior like Savon would surely be aware of the clumsiness that comes with dual wielding.

The two competitors positioned themselves across from one another, waiting for the siren to holler to start the match. Before Elysande could test her predictions, she was interrupted by a short man who approached her with a retinue of guards at his back. His posture was absurdly confident, as if approaching the royal family unannounced was some casual thing for him. He wore a maroon doublet with violet fringes and white leather trousers. Pinned to his right breast were a myriad of dazzling badges. His skin was as dark as a coffee bean and his gaze was hard and soldierly.

Even Sutorian expressed humility as the man strutted by with scintillating determination. Speaking with a rich Tisonian accent, the lavishly dressed man said: "King Caesar and Queen Elysande, if I may have a word with you."

Caesar grinned slightly as he recognized the man. "Yes, Proconsul Bebti, have a seat if you will."

Indro Bebti, Proconsul of Paranthon's Cross, took a seat to the right of his king. As he walked closer, Elysande could smell a fruity fragrance emanating from his doublet. The two men sat beside each other with the relaxed disposition that only brothers in arms could have. Bebti's loyalty to Caesar and ability on the battlefield had earned him Paranthon's Cross, widely recognized as the last and most formidable defensive base in Carcia to keep invaders out of Rome.

"How are you, my friend?" Caesar asked. "It's been years, hasn't it? Immortals, I have no idea. Time just flies away."

"I've been busy keeping you protected, which is no easy task I must say," Bebti laughed. "And yes, I must agree. I barely recognize the man I see in the mirror every morning. Typically I look much older, but I made an effort to appear ageless for you today."

"The gesture has been documented," King Caesar said, tapping the right side of his head.

Bebti peered over to address Elysande. "Speaking of agelessness, my queen must tell me her secret. Which Immortal did you win the favor of to maintain such beauty?"

*Flatterer*, she thought. "The proconsul is too kind. I've made no effort to win the favor of the Gods, I assure you, but I am a fervent follower in the virtue of discipline."

"As clever as she is beautiful. You're a lucky man, Gaius."

The king did not say a word. Elysande felt the invisible strings of fate tighten them together. Wanting to relieve some of the tension, she averted her eyes back to the arena. Kassa was running circles around Bernt Krudell. The Mercian was learning the consequences of holding two batons at once, as they slowed him down significantly. *And yet, Bernt just needs Kassa to slip once, then she would be unable to resist his sheer power.*

Sensing the lack of air, Bebti continued: "I had to speak to you in person, Gaius, to let you know how honored I am to have Natalia work for me as censor. Both myself and my husband are excited to see what energy she brings to the Cross. We've met a few times already, and I have to say she is nearly the mirror image of you."

"She's equally as excited, and I must admit I'm relieved by her ambition," Caesar said. "It is the curse of the sons and daughters of successful parents to become lazy and complacent. They take their riches for granted and grow to believe success is deserved, not achieved."

"I would agree," Indro Bebti replied, leaning back in his chair. "Nothing changes a person like the uncertainty of tomorrow. We lived for years like that, under constant attacks from the Republic, forever unsure if our own allies would betray us for a larger profit. It puts things into perspective, helps one realize nothing truly worthwhile is handed over."

Caesar folded his arms. "I can't blame the next generation for their complacency, as they've grown up during a time relatively free of strife. My children show ambition, and I'm thankful for it, but the last thing our people need is an untested ruling class. These worries may be for nothing, as they could end up better than any of us having not suffered the long years of hardship."

"It's hard to say, my king. We dedicate our lives to making the best world possible for our children, but eventually it's up to them to reap the benefits."

Elysande could not help but agree. While Kassa wore down her opponent by dashing from barrier to barrier in the dome, the queen reflected on her own upbringing. Ambition may have been partially hereditary, but she doubted she would be as driven as she was without enduring a childhood and young adult life drifting through space on the Crimson Armada, endlessly searching for a new home while longing for the one she could not go back to.

When the Republic was defeated and it was safe to return to Orbis, home was not the beacon of security it had once been. The ghosts of her brothers, Boltof and Fredrick, haunted every street of Erron and every hall of her old estate. The Archmage was dead and the Order eradicated, but the stain they left would never be cleaned. She accepted that Erron no longer possessed the purity she once dreamed of, and no place for the rest of her life may ever fulfill the concept of what a "home" should be.

But Lance and Julia had a home in Rome, and she would do anything and everything in her power to keep it that way.

Simultaneous with that concluding thought, Kassa Savon swept beneath Bernt's wild, two-arm attack. The brutish man slowed with every progressive move, but this attack was insultingly lackadaisical. With his stomach completely exposed, Savon slashed her baton into his gut. The power of electricity made the larger man fall to his knees. The siren of victory wailed. Savon, too, was on the ground, breathing heavily as the adrenaline of competition relented to the exhaustion of mental and physical strife. And yet, she managed to recover quickly enough to embrace the fans who celebrated her victory.

The B Block competitors followed. Her man, Bryson Byrne, took to the arena. This round, he opposed Paola Mazzeo, a young woman and heir to the Mazzeo estate in the Kappelli Isles. Her patrician bloodline dated back to the founding of Rome. She had an impressive showing against a Carcian knight in the first round, but the Bear of Byrne was a whole different animal.

Lady Mazzeo displayed talent in the art of combat, achieving several hits on her opponent's arms and legs, but Byrne was in another class entirely. As Elysande analyzed his fighting style, which consisted of a constant state of attack that effectively prevented Paola from kicking off the ground and implementing the zero-gravity arena many smaller fighters used to their advantage, she was reminded of Byrne's legitimate military career. It was no easy task fighting alongside a war hero like General Tarquinius, and anyone who could come out of one of his campaigns alive was a better soldier for it.

Despite his naïve appearance, Byrne knew how to fight as if his life was at stake.

Paola Mazzeo was defeated abruptly and without objection. Her arms simply gave out from the never-ending pressure forced onto her by Byrne. To Elysande's surprise, his winning blow was merciful. The patrician lady was stunned, but not enough to make her collapse from the electrical shock. Understanding this act of kindness, a sigh of relief crossed the girl's face.

*Perhaps she'll have a better showing next year, once she's gained some legitimate combat experience.*

Bryson Byrne was heading to the semifinals of the Gladiator Games, something that did not sit right with the queen. This would make Senator Felix of Rezza and Lucio Privetera happy, and with that satisfaction would come a diminished paranoia to question or consider what she was doing on the side. As the Games transpired, Ser Richard Dance and Legate Liscinia Drusilla searched the outer regions of Rome for a Blast-off dealer named Mercurio Shade. By the end of the day, they would hopefully have him captured... as she spent the whole previous night anticipating a long conversation with this criminal scum.

Despite her scheming, it perturbed her to play the role of obedient pawn in Felix's game. The smug senator thought she had no cards to play, that threatening her children would make her crumble. Instead, it did nothing but ensure his downfall.

*Mercurio best be a treasure chest of information, or else it will cost him his life.*

Galla, the Praetorian guardsman murdered in the streets of Rome, may have been bested by these Heirs of the Republic, but she was more cunning. Felix could not be defeated through physicality, which was likely the game Galla tried to play, but he could be bested mentally. All she had to do was uncover the scale of the conspiracy, then exploit it.

The sirens in the rafters of the Colosseum sounded once again to start the next match, which would be the final bout of the round. Old Robert Album came to the arena, facing off against Shinjiro Ishii, of the Kygorro region in Tisoni.

Ishii looked to be a stone rhinoceros in his bulky gear and horned helmet. His presence and posture were magnetically eye-catching. Elysande found the combination of his stalky build and exaggerated pace to be quite eccentric, especially compared to the more self-conscious approach of his opponent. Ishii was a renowned warrior in his region, credited for his bravery during the storming of Hirosuma, where the delusional Lord Reika made his last stand in his failed secession from the KOH. Ishii had won the Gladiator Games once before and was a favorite to win again this year despite his veteran age.

There was an unnerving aura of death about the Lord of Buckleburn. Even from far away, it was easy to sense Album's difficulty with being back in the arena. Timothy Mauvern's mortality suddenly stunk the air of the Colosseum. It was an unwanted reminder to all attendants of the uncertainty of life and death. *It may be hard to fathom, but even the rich, famous, and powerful can die too.*

"It's a shame, what happened to Lord Mauvern," Bebti said as the two veterans in the arena squared up. Caesar was quiet as he rightly suspected that his friend had more to say. "If there is anything I can do to help in the matter…"

"No need of it," Caesar assured him. "As far as we know, Lord Mauvern's death was caused by a ventilation issue in his helmet."

"A one in a million accident," Elysande added. She analyzed the proconsul some more. "You seem distraught, Lord Bebti. What's the matter?"

"Nothing, just rumblings."

"And what are these rumblings saying?" Caesar asked.

Bebti scratched his thin, graying beard. "There are blind speculations that Lord Haisam Omir may have been involved, given the rivalry the two men have over Hazelvale. His absence from the Gladiator Games isn't relieving anyone of their suspicions."

"Lord Omir informed us that he could not come to Rome the day after Mauvern's death. He was not shy of stating his decision not to attend was for that very reason." Elysande said, returning her attention to the fight. Album had revived his confidence, but Ishii still held the upper hand with his longer reach and faster feet. "Seems valid to me. As a Mercian myself, I know my people are quick to jump to conclusions."

The two veteran warriors continued their spar, but as they went along, Elysande noticed a choppiness in their moves. They were swinging their batons sturdy enough, but the pushes and slaps between the swings were taking over. At one point, Album smacked Ishii on the crest of his helmet. Returning the favor, Ishii parried a strike and unabashedly delivered the hilt of his baton to the nose of Lord Album.

"Do you have any reason to listen to these rumors?" Caesar asked the proconsul, his inner speculations hidden behind a heavy veil of kingly aura.

"Not much," Bebti said. "I only bring this up to relieve any worries you may have. As you know, I grew up with Lord Haisam's father in Hazelvale. We both had our dealings in the spice trade too. The old Lord Omir was a cunning man, but he did not raise his children to resort to violence and deception to get their way."

A slugfest broke out between Album and Ishii. No longer caring about points, the two men set their batons aside in favor of colliding their shoulders into one another. Neither man broke. Ishii stepped back, charged for momentum, and shoulder-checked Lord Album, the clang of metal meeting metal cutting throughout the Colosseum. The old lord staggered, but his legs held true, sticking to the ground like tree trunks.

In return, Album paced backward, then sprinted at Ishii with all his might. Shoulder-plate met breastplate with an equally tremendous thud, but the rhinoceros of Kygorro did not yield. In fact, the stalky man was about as compact as a concrete wall. Album stepped back, incredulous as to how little he had shaken his opponent, but accepting the unwritten laws of the fight, stood his ground and anticipated Ishii's next demonstration in their test of strength.

"I trust your judgement," Caesar said, his eyes glued to the fight before him. "Regardless of what happened to Timothy Mauvern, I anticipated pushback from Tisonian nobles. The Mauverns will meet hostility no matter what, but I have a difficult time believing they would resist in such a public display."

"The Omirs I knew would never do such a thing," Bebti said. "But I haven't lived in Tisoni for decades. Things can change their as suddenly as a sandstorm. An Omir may still be in charge, but only the Immortals know which of the desert nobles are whispering in his ear."

"But you have family in Tisoni," Elysande added. "So you are not completely in the dark. If you had to give your impressions on the current Lord Omir, what would you say?"

Indro Bebti sighed deeply, folding his arms across his barreling chest. "Like myself, every man, woman, and child who lives in the deserts of Tisoni is a snake. The Omirs have reigned there for generations, meaning snake blood is strong in their veins. It must be, in order to hold Hazelvale for as long as they have."

Another profound thud of metal on metal sounded vehemently from the stage below, followed by the unanimous gasp of hundreds of thousands of spectators. Robert Album, having absorbed another blow from the rhinoceros, wavered on his feet before, ultimately, collapsing to the ground. Ishii, clutching his stomach, limped over to his downed opponent, picked up his baton, and claimed victory with a downward strike.

Bebti continued: "All snakes have fangs, so all snakes are dangerous, my king. You must learn which snakes are poisonous, and take your chances with the other lot."

The Gladiator Games were over for the day, which meant Elysande's time with her king and husband were through as well. She left the Colosseum first, flanked on her sides by two Praetorian guardsmen. A faint glimmer of red sunlight stretched across the western horizon of Rome while cool, nightly breezes drifted through the air. Exiting the stadium and walking out into the street, her car was waiting on the sidewalk underneath a white streetlight. Ser Richard Dance stepped out of the backseat and held the door open for her.

"Package is waiting for you, ma'am," he whispered.

"Excellent, Ser Dance. I do hope it was no trouble retrieving." Before entering the car, she ordered the guards rather directly to piss off somewhere else. Once both she and her royal protector were securely in the backseat, the driver took off. They had to stop at the villa by the western waterfront first. *Ditch the driver, then we leave.*

It was a slight detour in her plan, but overall the extra precaution was harmless. The driver dropped them off and departed from there. In her bedroom, Elysande put on a black leather jacket over a gray tank top. She made Richard Dance change into civilian clothes too, as a large man in pristine royal armor would stand out like a spotlight in the night sky for where they would be heading.

The villa felt empty besides the occasional servant snooping around. Lance was in his room reading, and Julia was at a friend's house. *Is she at a friend's house?* Elysande had been so mind-numbingly busy of late that it was hard to keep track of them. She wondered if they noticed her absence, and if they resented her for it.

*Love's a bitch, but they won't be safe until these revolutionaries are shot into space.*

"Ready to go?"

"Whenever you are," Dance answered. Elysande bit her lip to suppress the boiling laughter in her stomach. His mountainous arms were constricting in the tight sleeves, ready to burst at any second. His naked face was tense and desperate for a helmet to hide under.

"Good," she said, marching out the villa. "You drive. Take a cheap car from the garage. No loose ends with this, understand me?"

"Yes, ma'am."

North of the Capitoline Hill, well past Pullo's Shield, the streets of Rome were less spacious, the architecture grayer and blockier, and the people less diverse and warm. The air was heavier, almost metallic. Although not unpleasant, it was not the Rome that people from across the galaxy wanted to see when they traveled. Elysande kept her head low sitting in the backseat of the car, letting the night sky disguise her from those wandering the streets.

Scintillating signs from the long stretches of storefronts reflected neon red, purple, and yellow lights against the backseat window, mixing hypnotically with the few raindrops that pattered and stuck to the glass frame. Graffiti-covered walls were more abundant in this area of Rome. With the combination of honking cars and louder people babbling on the sidewalks, something about the districts outside Pullo's Shield felt abrasive. Elysande looked up and saw the dark, broken fingers of the skyward train system that Caesar was funding. It would be years before the project was complete, but as of now she hated the sight of these towering hangnails.

Dance drove on until they were away from the bustling biome and into a quieter, if not slightly more dubious, factory area. Numerous streetlights covered the barren urban land in lurid, yellowing pools of light. They pulled over to a tiny shack with a slanted roof that was one component of a factory building.

Elysande stepped out and breathed in the smoky air. Her chest was itchy and her mind a mess.

She turned to her protector and gestured him forward. "No time like the present, right?"

Ser Richard Dance took the lead, walking up to the stark, black house and knocking on the door. After a moment, they were greeted by Legate Liscinia Drusilla. Her immediate reaction was to salute her queen, but Elysande halted her.

"No need to draw any more attention than needed," she advised. "Now let's get inside."

They waited in a dreary gray room with a floor coated in dust. The walls, too, wore their chipped paint and cracked exteriors daringly. Whatever factory it was a part of, the shack had lost its use a long time ago. The only helpful accessory in the room was a thin, metal table which had a black gym bag on top of it.

"Where's Shade?" Elysande asked.

"He's in the other room, unconscious." Drusilla reported. There was a black bruise beneath the legate's lower lip. Despite this, she was still a sight to behold.

"Looks like you had trouble arresting him," she observed. Liscinia, however, brushed it aside.

"Nothing worth mentioning,"

"Did you need backup from your people?" the queen asked, skeptically. Quintus Longinus, the Black Dog with the mangled ear, rubbed her the wrong way from the start. Keeping him out of the loop was desirable, but someone of his rank must have had informants on every street in Rome.

"Not a single one," Liscinia said, eyeing Ser Dance up and down. "We found him in a club nearby with a few cronies, but we made short work of the lot. Your man is a tank. I've never seen anyone fight like him."

Elysande smirked. "Is he worth keeping around?"

"He's worth a raise, and so much more." Drusilla insisted. She looked at the bag on the metal table. "I bought the supplies you asked for. Should we get to business?"

*And I thought I detested pointless conversation.* "Let's," Elysande said, reaching into the bag and pulling out a black ski mask. She put it over her head, aided by the legate who helped her tuck any resisting strands of auburn hair beneath the wool. Ser Dance opened the door. Before entering, she greedily grabbed one last deep breath.

The queen followed the stains of dried blood across the cold, concrete floor. Mercurio Shade was tied to a wooden chair that creaked incessantly as he rocked back and forth. With his neck craned, greasy black bangs covered most of his face, save a pink scar on the tip of his chin. His shirt was ripped open, pointed ribs jutting from his body. *Gods, does this man eat?*

The sounds of her footsteps stirred the criminal awake. He was slow to process what was going on, but the sight of a mysterious masked woman filled his eyes with dread. Like his body, Shade's face was ghastly thin. He was younger than Elysande expected, perhaps in his mid-twenties, but the aroma about him expressed grit.

"You don't have fucking shit on me!" Mercurio swore. "Black Dogs got no right abducting me like this. I'm fucking clean."

"This is an off-the-books kind of justice," Elysande said.

Mercurio spat. "Yeah, well, I've seen the faces of your two bitches. Next time they roam my streets, I'll bury'em there."

"You're in no position to make threats." Liscinia promised, her voice strong and certain.

"She's right," Elysande agreed. "Think of it like bargaining. I'm going to ask you questions, and your responses will dictate how badly I have my people hurt you. You could walk out tonight without suffering another scratch, but that's entirely up to you."

Shade was silent, but his glare spoke volumes to the queen. She had no doubt he was planning his revenge. "First question: Did you know the Praetorian guardsman named Galla?"

"Name sounds familiar."

"It should, he was a protector of the royal family. I say 'was' because he was found dead in an alleyway outside Pullo's Shield, his mouth overflowing with a bad batch of Blast-off. Firsthand accounts say you were with Galla moments before his death. Have anything to say to that?"

Shade shrugged. "Unlucky fucking coincidence. I'm a frequent attendee of those."

Elysande looked to Legate Liscinia. She approached Shade and laid a right fist across his face. The sound was sickening, but he managed to stifle any cries. "How about a different answer?" Elysande suggested.

"How about you suck my cock?" Shade suggested, promptly followed by another punch to the face courtesy of the legate. This time, he did let out a whimper. The queen remained quiet.

"Okay, yeah, I dealt the knight some Blast-off," he confessed, the caverns of a red fist swelling on his thin cheek. "What of it?"

"That Blast-off killed him almost immediately. I'm not an experienced user myself, but from what I understand cases like Galla's are exceptionally rare." Elysande said. "Besides, you're a smart man. Why risk dealing out in the open when you can have a subordinate do it?"

"He's a high-value customer; had to make sure he got his order."

"Legate! If you were to spot Mister Shade dealing Blast-off on the street, what action would you have taken next?"

"I would have arrested the criminal personally," Liscinia reported. "From there, he would face a minimum of fifteen years prison time, not taking into account any previous offenses on his record."

Elysande turned her attention back to Shade. "That seems like a lot to risk just to prove you're an upstanding businessman, wouldn't you say?"

Shade bowed his head, allowing her to continue. "I think you wanted to ensure Galla got his Blast-off, not because you cared about your customers, but because you knew that specific batch was lethal. You were confident. Someone must've told you they'd look the other way, but who was it? Local police? Black Dogs? And who paid you to kill Ser Galla?"

"You fucking cunt!" Shade swore, launching a fat glob of spittle that landed right in the eye slit of her mask. His saliva was warm and smelled faintly of tobacco. She wiped it from her eyes and rubbed it off on her jacket.

Dance was on top of him, firing unrelenting punches into Shade's gut. The power behind his fists were more than enough to shatter bones. Now, Shade truly cried out. He kicked his bound legs frantically, but it did nothing to save him. Never having faced such blatant disrespect before, the Queen of the KOH had half a mind to let the assault continue.

"Enough!" she ordered. Dance stopped, turning to his queen in humility. She absorbed a deep breath into her lungs, calming herself before she did anything too bold. "Be a good lad and take off my jacket." Her protector did as he was told.

Liscinia rubbed a hand through her braided brown hair as she admired her queen's toned arms that were now out in the open. They were not brawny like a soldier's, but they were not the svelte things common for noble ladies either. Elysande cracked her knuckles, feeling liberated in a tank top. Shade, too, was shocked by her figure, although not the same kind of shock as Liscinia's.

"Congratulations, Shade." Elysande began, stretching her arms. "You've made the worst mistake of your life. On a positive note, no decision you make for what remains of your pathetic existence will ever be quite so dire."

# MARION (VIII)

"Elvezio Gasardi, born in the city of Crownhold located in the northernmost province of Carcia, was the fifth king of his line on his native country, and the first king of the entirety of Orbis. The third child of King Ludovico Gasardi, Elvezio was unlikely to inherit the throne, and yet fate possessed a different plan for him. It was through tremendous tragedy that Elvezio became ruler of Carcia, but his coronation would lead to decades of prosperity for the human race. With dark red hair and eyes carved of jade, Elvezio was a hero pulled from the pages of legend and brought to reality-"

Marion drifted away from his book. Octavia's hair was nearly the same color as the once great king of Carcia. *She could be a distant descendent of the Gasardi line.* She could have continued the bloodline if she hadn't... if he had not dragged her through his own misfortunes. No, the thought was absurd, delusional even. He shook his head and forced his attention back to the page.

"A majority of Gasardi's years were spent in warfare. By the time he had united the lesser kingdoms of Orbis, he was an old man. Despite being weak of mind and body, Elvezio was still graced with the foresight to form the first KOH, uniting the entirety of humanity under a single line of rulers, a line that would last many generations at-"

*Where was she born?* Marion wondered. Octavia's name was one hundred percent Roman, and she was from the same country as the Gasardi kings and queens. The once magnificent dynasty endured many generations, making it entirely possible that a lesser prince or princess found a lover in Rome...

*Stop!* he cursed, gripping the leatherbound book tightly in his fingers and digging his shoulders into the table from which he sat, as if the added stress would help him concentrate. The book was the first volume of the history the Gasardi family, documented intricately by the famed Roman scholar, Spurius. It was as old as Elvezio himself, a coveted possession for any historian. Marion discovered it crammed in the back of a shelf, matted in dust and lint and likely untouched for decades. The cover had frayed a bit from neglect, but the hundreds of pages inside were crisp, although slightly yellowed. He scrolled over the text with his eyes and realized he had not absorbed anything he had just read.

"Elvezio Gasardi, born in the city of Crownhold located in the northernmost province of Carcia, was the fifth king of his line on his native country, and the first king of the entirety of Orbis. The third child of King Ludovico Gasardi, Elvezio was…"

Mister Everec would have loved this book. Spurius' histories were absent in Romulus' libraries. In fact, Marion's history lecturers spoke as little of the Gasardi dynasty as reasonably possible, given their undeniable influence in all things "humanity." No, if he desired to learn anything about the galaxy outside Rome and its patrician heroes, he would need to turn to Everec. But the Dean was dead, his head splattered like a watermelon over an office wall. Marion shuddered; the image stapled to his eyes.

He forced his attention back to the text in his hand: "Elvezio Gasardi, born in the city of Crownhold located in the northernmost province of Carcia, was the fifth king of his line on-"

"Fuck it!" he swore, throwing the book across the table. The sounds of leather and paper hitting the floor echoed across the halls of the abandoned library. He stared at the book for a long time, unblinking, until he was interrupted by an old man. Marion winced, the presence of this new company reminding him why he came to the library in the first place.

"I'm not much a fan of Spurius' work either." Atticus Zoltor remarked, his voice as cool as it was indifferent. "You can't trust a history told by a man morally and politically opposed to the characters he writes about."

Marion stood from his seat. Frustration had blurred his intentions. Reading was supposed to be a distraction while waiting for his grand uncle, but instead his failure to engage with the text only disoriented him. "Apologies. My temper gets the better of me from time to time."

He saw little resemblance of himself in the face, body, and posture of his grand uncle. Atticus' hair was pale blond and puffy while his was brown and short. Atticus' cheeks were round while Marion's were thin and angular. There was a sense of self-assuredness in his grand uncle's straight shoulders, yet Marion felt his own body slouching drastically of late, the weight of living gravity becoming heavier with every passing day.

The derelict library at the end of the Republic Manor was the headquarters, of sorts, for the First Scholar. Motivation had carried Marion here, but the reason for wanting to speak to his uncle was lost along the way. His memory had been a scramble of late. Sleep never came easy, emotions were syringes, regret an undying cell.

"Is there something I can help you with?" Atticus asked, not unkindly, but not truly welcoming either. Marion stood and they nonverbally agreed to walk together through the eternal shelves.

"Uh, yes," he said, buying time. "Why are you called First Scholar?"

Atticus chuckled slightly. "My title was one of the most coveted positions in the Order at one time. This is a pleasant dose of humility."

"I meant no disrespect," Marion corrected, scratching the back of his head. His hair was greasy and unwashed.

"And none was taken. As First Scholar, I am the head historian of Spyre. I was in charge of maintaining all records of the Paladin Order and making sure the history that unfolded under my watch was properly recorded. I still do it to this day, although there is little point in it anymore. If anything can survive the apocalypse, it's our reliance on old habits."

"I think it's admirable. History must be celebrated, no matter whose it is. This passion must be hereditary."

"Your father was not concerned with records. Had he not appointed me as First Scholar, the great library of Spyre may have done little more than collect dust." Atticus quickly checked himself. "I mean no ill will to him. Marius was brilliant in his own right, and a worthy Archmage, but he was never one to sit still and reflect. No, our loves and passions can't be explained through genealogy, but through the strings of fate."

Marion was struck with confusion. A learned man could not be so beguiled by celestial predestination and, worst of all, religion. Obviously, this required a respectful approach.

"Do you think the Immortals decide who we are before birth? I find it hard to believe that Serios dictated my love for history. It makes life so... mechanical."

"First, Serios is dead. It was his sacrifice that created mages and Spyre to begin with," Atticus corrected. "And yes, to a certain degree I'd bet we all have our fates crafted for us. I've noticed a common theme that those who are joyful conclude said joy comes from divine influence, while those who are bitter believe their misfortune proves we're all falling endlessly through a blackhole of futility. Whether or not you agree with the prospects that life has given you, it has nothing to do with proving or disproving fate. Take me, for example."

Atticus stopped in his tracks. He raised his right hand and flicked his middle finger and thumb together. From that friction came a heavenly spark that lingered above his shoulder. Marion stepped back, impulsively anticipating the conjured light to attack him. The spark, however, remained passive. "This is my gift. Your father could summon lightning storms powerful enough to destroy cities. Your Aunt Caella was a healer who could grow blossoming gardens just by sticking her hands in the dirt. Me, I can summon a light over my shoulder to help me read at night."

"That's a strange power," Marion said, trying his best not to sound disappointed.

"It's underwhelming, I'm well aware." Atticus sighed. "But it begs the question: Did my passion for reading stem from my power, or were the passion and gift part of a larger thread woven into my destiny?"

"Why leave out blind chance?" Marion asked. That's what the galaxy was: an incalculable number of dice thrown by no one that determines the fate of everyone and everything. It was cosmic indifference that brought him out of Romulus, and it was the same implausible manipulator that permanently stripped away the love of his life.

"That makes the universe seem incredibly boring, doesn't it?" Atticus said. "When you've lived as long as I have, you start to see order in the chaos. You may not like it or understand it, but the strings are there, binding us together."

Marion's first instinct was to object, but found himself unable to. "I did not come here just to share philosophies," he began, finally remembering why he wanted to speak to his grand uncle in the first place. "My mentor, Mister Everec, was killed by a man named Drake Bodewin. Is the name familiar to you?"

A deep shadow loomed under the First Scholar's brow. "The name is a curse. And to this day the betrayer still torments our kind. I'm sorry for your loss."

"Drake said he was the man who killed my father during the fall of Spyre. I want to know what happened."

"It's a tragic story," Atticus warned. "I had evacuated Spyre by the time the betrayer had dealt the death blow to the Archmage, but I will tell you what I know… if you insist."

"I insist," Marion stated soundly.

"Very well. Drake is the son of Reynard Bodewin, Lord of Erron. When Lord Bodewin's rebellion against the Roman Republic failed and the man himself fled into outer space, Drake was the last Bodewin in Erron still alive to take hostage. Marius elected himself to take young Drake as his ward, so Reynard and what was left of his Crimson Armada would think twice before attacking again. The strategy worked, for a while.

"Marius treated Drake like family. Although he was not a mage, he was as much a part of the Paladin Order as anyone else. Even I was fond of the boy as he grew up, but it made me blind to his duplicity. He was a teenager at the time of the Triumvirate's takeover of the galaxy. When their army finally came to Spyre, Drake Bodewin shot Marius in the back as he rallied one last defense to save his home. All hope was lost after that, and the Archmage may as well have been murdered by his own son."

Atticus' jowls boiled red and hot. Marion, too, sensed an anger brew in his stomach. Drake Bodewin was another man who would need to meet justice. *This galaxy is terrible, but maybe I can clean some of the filth*. Not wanting to add more grudges than he already carried, Marion changed the subject. "What of my grandfather?"

"Ah yes," Atticus recollected, as if being pulled from a nightmare. "My brother, Caspius, was much like the Archmage. Headstrong, confident, ample charisma gleaming about him. He never achieved the title of his son, but Caspius kept our name in the ranks of the most revered mage families so his children could achieve the status they did. I hardly noticed when he died, as working in Marius' shadow was much the same as my brother's."

"And how did he die?" Marion asked, infinitely curious.

"Same as any mage of the Saighdiúir, or the Knights guild as they are called in our language. They serve as both diplomats and warriors. Although most conflicts reach a peaceful resolution, the job is no less deadly. To put it simply: Paladins of the Saighdiúir should not expect to die of old age."

"I'd like to be in the Saighdiúir," he said, head wandering. "I was trapped in Romulus for far too long. I won't return to confinement now that I've tasted freedom." This explanation, although true to a certain extent, did not express the entirety of his feelings. Settling down was no longer an option, as the one person he would ever dream of spending the rest of his life with was gone forever.

"What guild you belong to is not for you to say," Atticus declared. "The Paladin Order has four: the Saighdiúir, or Knights guild, the Tarrthálaí, or Healers guild, the Cosantóir, or Builders guild, and the Cruthaitheoir, or Conjurors guild. Your powers will determine which best fits you. Paladins of the Saighdiúir are historically the most inspiring to those outside the Order, so for all our sakes let's pray you make it."

Marion's heart warmed. No one had been this welcoming to his endless inquiries since Mister Everec. The First Scholar was an intelligent man and a wise professor willing feed his knowledge to Marion's hungry ears.

Afternoon light crept in from a row of long windows on the wall, illuminating the endless aisles of bookshelves. He had spent most of his sixteen years thus far reading a great wealth of books. And yet, he was nowhere close to reading even a fraction of all the great literature that the galaxy had to offer. *It's a pointless task to read it all, but the attempt alone is rewarding enough.*

Marion talked to his grand uncle for over an hour. Time finally passed quicker than it seemed, and he made a mental note to visit the library if he needed someone to talk to. Discussing history with someone else was always more engaging than reading it alone, especially when one person in the conversation had witnessed the events firsthand. Atticus' mind was a cave brimming with rich diamonds of knowledge. Mining it of all its wealth would require a lifetime of conversation.

Marion could have spent the rest of the day inquiring Uncle Atticus about their family history, but he had other matters to deal with.

The Immortech sword bestowed to him by Kent Kentoshi was waiting inside his room. Every free moment was spent with its platinum hilt in his hand. Training with electric-shock batons on Romulus had made the fundamentals of swordsmanship easy to grasp, but he needed more practice to ensure Octavia was properly avenged. He cut through the air, practiced spin moves, and rehearsed his footwork. Each day, he noticed improvements. His strikes were stronger, his movements more fluid, as if the sword was becoming one with his body.

At night, visions crept into what little sleep he received. They whispered that the Inquisitor was coming. No matter how impossible the odds, they would meet again. It would be Marion's last chance to prove his worth to Octavia, after all the endless disappointments. In his most secretive of thoughts, he prayed that his powers would come, that he would possess the same gifts as his father. But that was a fantasy, only his sword and the motivation for revenge were real. Until the moment of his inevitable showdown with the Inquisitor, he would use every opportunity available to enhance his ability to dispense vengeance.

Despite these brave proclamations, his last moments with Octavia almost felt like a trick. It was not a memory, but a hazy vision. The scar on his head was foreign as well, as if placed there via illusion. Octavia was gone, she must have been, but he could not shake the doubt from his mind. He needed another witness, someone else on the frigate who could confirm the images inside his head were real. Without that, his grief, no matter how it melted into every moment of his life, was oddly unearned.

He walked to the center atrium of the Republic Manor and climbed the steps to the top floor. An idea popped into his head as he walked to his suite. By chance, he crossed Ariel's door and saw it open...

"I need you to teach me how to shoot?" he asked, standing rather obtrusively at the threshold.

Ariel, from the desk, closed her book and turned casually his way. He perceived her opened door as a welcoming sign for any and all company. Besides, his thoughts were in too much of a storm to handle isolation, and the worst she could do was turn him away.

"They don't teach you how to use a gun in your little academy?" She pushed her book aside, allowing Marion to observe the cover. It was a volume three of Archmage Tye Crossford's "Intergalactic Encounters with Unknown Entities." When he was younger, Mister Everec encouraged him to read all of Crossford's numerous works... inconspicuously, of course. Little by little, Marion was piecing together the complex puzzle of logic that was his upbringing.

"I'm familiar with the fundamentals," he insisted. "Allow me to be blunt: I need you to teach me how to kill."

Ariel's brow twisted in skepticism. "So, I strike you as a killer?" Her spherical BOT, which she named Pup, hovered by her side, analyzing him with its lens.

"You strike me as someone who doesn't care about what others think of her. I could be wrong. Maybe you're more insecure than I thought."

Ariel stood from her seat in a dramatic display. She reached under her bed and revealed a rifle. KOH made. A sudden unease overcame him, knowing exactly where she found it. *What was it all for?* a ghost asked.

"Come on then, I'll show you."

Ariel took him to Unity College. She demanded that Pup come along too, and the irritable BOT whistled and beeped throughout the walk. Marion was growing sick of Old Ulthrawn, more specifically at the handful of locations they could access.

The oceanic view of the Republic Manor was grand for a while, but repetition had extinguished its mystique. The square outside the Manor was typically filled with training legions or ships transporting Laktonnian representatives in and out of the city. Unity College was quieter, and Ariel at least seemed to enjoy its design, but Romulus had tainted any fondness Marion could have for schooling facilities.

Ariel walked causally with the strap of her rifle wrapped around her shoulder. Her head was always looking up, watching the sky or analyzing the old edifices with their square parapets and protruding stone statues. She had killed before, unquestionably. Marion feared what would become of him after his first kill, but seeing her find happiness in their surroundings where he could not gave him confidence that his life would not be dramatically different after the deed was done.

They crossed the entrance into the dining common: a long, narrow hall with a vaulted roof flanked by dark, wooden walls covered in portraits of what Marion could best guess were the venerable professors at the College. Small angelic lights held in wrought, iron holsters added to the classical mystique of the hall. Three tables of long length and narrow width were placed on the floor. At the end of the common sat the dais, elevated above the rest and with fine candelabras atop its bright blue tablecloth.

"What are we doing here?" he asked.

"Teaching you how to kill," Ariel insisted. Pup whistled in agreement. She cut into a side door where the kitchen was. Clueless, Marion followed along. After some searching through cabinets, she found a box filled with wine glasses. She put it on the kitchen counter and presented it to Marion as if he had any idea what her plan was.

"We're gonna shoot these!" she exclaimed, somewhat agitated by his bemused expression. "Let the professor do her job."

"The kitchen staff won't appreciate us destroying their glasses," Marion warned. Why was he so turned off by trouble when it was anyone other than him causing it?

"Everyone living here has abandoned ship with the coming battle," Ariel insisted. "It's a ghost town, why not take advantage of it?"

He gave a conceding shrug. They headed back for the dining common and to the dais. He watched Ariel struggle with carrying the crate, but whenever he offered to help, she cursed him away. Mercifully, she placed the crate atop the dais, then instructed him to set the curvy wine glasses in a row along the edge of the table.

When it was done, they both took several steps away from the dais. Ariel handed him the rifle. "Now, shoot a glass."

He charged the rifle, peered down its sights, and aimed at a glass right in the center of the table. After a pause, he pulled the trigger and, in a flash, an eruption of crystalline shards exploded from the table. Marion laughed, impressed by his shot.

"Wrong," Ariel stated, arms folded. Pup beeped in agreement.

"I hit the thing!" he objected.

She rubbed her temples. "But you took too long. If you were in a firefight, that moment of pause would give you too much time to think about what's on the other end of that rifle. You'll realize that thing has a pulse, thoughts, feelings, maybe a family or a sweetheart at home. You'll think about yourself and the consequences of taking a life. You'll realize there's no going back, there's no forgiveness after that first kill. Most importantly, it gives your enemy the chance to do what you can't."

"I just needed time to line up my shot."

"You asked me to teach you how to kill, not shoot. Now kill a wine glass this time." Ariel instructed.

Marion grunted. He already regretted asking her for help. He put the butt-end of the rifle to his shoulder, raised the barrel, and, without a second thought, fired a shot at another wine glass. The shot missed, but only slightly.

"Better," she said. "You shot without hesitation, without remorse." She reached her hand out to take the rifle. When it was in her embrace, she took aim at the dais. "Here's a vitally important lesson: inhale as you set up your shot, exhale as you pull the trigger. Keep doing it until you can't exhale again without squeezing your pointer finger. That way, when you're in the heat of battle and your conscience betrays you, your exhale won't."

They practiced for about an hour. Every time the row of wine glasses was demolished into sparkling dust on the floor, they would go to the box and align a new row of translucent victims.

Marion followed his sister's instructions perfectly. *Aim. Breath in. Breath out. Squeeze trigger. Bang!* Eventually, the sequence of events came so naturally that he could shootdown several glasses without much concentration.

In a trance, he peered down the scope of his rifle at the last glass on the edge of the dais. As he continued to stare, the object in his view morphed in a horrific defiance of nature. The room grew dark and smoky, trapping him in a dimensionless prison. A siren blared from somewhere along the wall, deafening him. It was unnervingly familiar, like the return of a dormant disease. Beads of sweat sprouted on his neck. He shivered.

*What was it all for?* she whispered.

A head had taken the place of the glass at the far end of the dais. A silver hood over its face left most of its features in shadows, but the red, glowing eyes bled through the darkness. *Haunting me. Taunting me.* Marion pulled the trigger, but the laser that rocketed from the barrel missed his enemy by a hair. He shot again, this time the bolt of red light missing wildly. Watching his impotence, the head smiled sickly, revealing its metallic jaw.

He rushed to the dais, shooting his rifle wildly. The head laughed in return. "I'll kill you!" Marion declared. He continued to shoot until he was practically on top of the table. He held the trigger until the rifle overheated and the barrel hissed as it fried from the inside. Taking a breath, the illusion dissipated. There, he saw the shiny dust of what once was the wine glass, along with the charred remains of the right end of the dais. Smoke arose from the rubble. The surviving splinters were beyond fixing.

"You really got that one," Ariel said. She stared at him cautiously, "Everything okay?"

"It's fine, but I'm done with target practice." He dropped the rifle to the ground somewhat crudely. "Let's do something else."

Ariel's large eyes brightened. "I know exactly what to do." She approached the box of glasses and pulled out two. "Here, take these," she said, handing them to Marion and retreating to the kitchen. From the other room, he heard muffled sounds of clanging and banging. When she returned, she had a wine bottle in hand. "I don't know anything about vintages or whatever, but I like the designs on this bottle so…"

They walked to the entryway of the dining hall and sat on the cobblestone steps right outside. The rich aroma from the nearby garden left faint teases in the air as a warm breeze gently strolled by. The sky had a greenish hue that Marion still could not get over. It must have had something to do with Laktannon's location near the edge of the known galaxy. The yellow ball of sun, too, looked small like a midafternoon star.

He poured the wine into Ariel's glass first. It did not have the velvety purple texture of the Denvari wine he had shared with Octavia on their last night in his dorm, but drinking it still brought back memories of her.

"It's a beautiful day," Ariel said, taking in the scenery. "I don't think I'll ever get sick of it."

"My thoughts exactly," Marion lied. Fresh air had lost its novelty days ago. He had his mind on one thing alone. Until then, he did not deserve peace.

Ariel sipped from her glass. Although the healing process had started, her lower lip was still swollen and purple from the time he struck her. "I'm sorry for hitting you... back in the cell. I was beyond furious at the time, but it doesn't forgive my actions."

She brushed her fingers over her lip. "No harm done. I probably had it coming." They chuckled at the truth of her statement. "I'm not the person I was in the cell, and neither are you, I think. Whatever happened there is in the past."

"Can we get along now?" Marion asked flippantly. He drank another gulp of wine. The taste was bitter, faintly reminding him of lemon and thyme. It could never be mistaken for a Denvari vintage.

"Maybe," Ariel considered. She grabbed the bottle of wine and poured more into Marion's cup. He had not realized how quickly he drank the first and was caught off guard by her kind action.

"So, you've done something for me, what can I do in return?" he asked.

Ariel fell into deep contemplation, swirling the liquid in her glass around with her hand as if the answer was hidden at the bottom. Her face brightened when she found the answer, but something caused her to stifle whatever came to mind.

Marion raised his eyebrows to let her know she had been found out. "What is it?"

Ariel twisted her lips, accepting there was no evading it. "I'll say it, but you can't laugh."

"I won't make a promise I can't keep," he said, extending his tease. A flash of genuine anger on the face of the Underling led him to believe he had pushed her too far.

"Fine," she pouted. "I have a slight, and by 'slight' I mean miniscule, interest in… dancing."

Marion was incredulous. Ariel realized it immediately, causing her cheeks to flush and her eyes to fill with wrath. "Go to Hell! Just because I'm not some elitist academy kid doesn't mean I can't learn. I don't care that much anyway, so forget it!"

"Relax," he said, putting his hands up. "There's nothing to be embarrassed about, I was only caught by surprise. You mean formal dancing, right?"

"Obviously! Why is it surprising?" Ariel asked, still perturbed but not quite as hostile.

"I assumed you were better than all that."

"Well, I am, but I never thought I'd get the chance to learn on Prisilla. It wasn't practical then. Now that we're both in politics, sort of, the curiosity has returned."

"You wouldn't care that we're brother and sister?"

Ariel groaned. "I'm not looking to be felt up," she insisted. "Enough with these questions: will you help me or not?"

"I'll help," Marion confirmed. "I'm a pretty decent dancer. All the students on Romulus had to take classes for it. Faculty loved conditioning us for the stuffy rituals of patrician society."

She took a celebratory sip of wine. "Good. I'm glad I found a trainer."

Marion smiled, not from what she said, but from a memory that flashed before him. "Octavia loved school dances. She and her friends would make these elaborate dresses, and she'd be so excited to show them to me… Romulus always had these stupid, pretentious events for students to dress up and act nice to alumni, and naturally I despised most of them, but seeing her happy at those dances made me kind of like them too."

Ariel became quiet, her eyes looking everywhere but his direction. *She knows Octavia is dead. She must've seen the Enfari steel cut through her chest. Why isn't she saying anything? Does she think I don't know what happened? Does she think I can't handle it?*

The space between them was unbearably tense, the silence screeching, seconds in time passing like a millennium. Marion clenched his fists. His internal temperature rose to a scorching degree. *Don't keep me in the dark. Just tell me you know!*

He replayed the memory in his mind to check himself. Maybe she was clueless, and passing judgement on her would be as impetuous as it was spiteful. He saw Octavia, wrapped in his arms, a hunk of metal pierced between her breasts and sheer terror painted over her face. "What was it all for?" she asked, void of hope.

In the distance were the Inquisitors, the one with the metallic jaw smiling his malicious, no, his mocking smile. *He's the one who killed Octavia*, Marion guessed, but he needed to be certain. Ash and fire and death encircled them. The deafening alarms bellowing in an effort to scramble his thinking. He searched, internally, for Ariel. He saw Laktonnian soldiers fight desperately for survival against the overwhelming Roman legions, but she was untraceable.

The memory was utterly distorted, more like a nightmare than a real event. Marion could not trust his own judgement, as pain and grief muddied nearly all of it. He searched further, like digging in the dirt with tender hands. Ariel could tell him the truth, could direct him on the path of achieving justice, but her silence abandoned him. *Why? How much do you know? Regardless of how you feel about me, Octavia does not deserve this.*

She stood up and said, "I'll go clean up what I can inside. You can go do whatever." With great haste, she removed herself from his company. Marion was left on the outside stairs, a lone leaf in a hurricane of torment.

He sat on the stairs for an inconceivable period of time, pounding puzzle pieces into place. *She lied to me about her interrogation on the frigate. She was going off to see the Inquisitor. Her silence isn't to protect me, it's to protect him.* But what had they discussed during these engagements? And what had blossomed between them to cause betrayal of her own kin?

Marion heard a crack and saw the wine glass had shattered in his hand. Drops of blood sprouted from his palm. Atticus may have been right after all. Their showdown was written in the strings of fate, whether Ariel could accept it or not. The Inquisitor would come to Old Ulthrawn and face retribution by Marion's will.

*For Octavia. I owe her that, and much more.*

# TROYTON (VI)

The bronze statue of Jradex, the Foundation, stood proudly in the center of Old Ulthrawn, determination in his cold eyes, each hand gripping on the hilt of a mighty battle axe almost as tall as he was, and one monstrous leg stepping off his podium, as if prepared to walk among his people once again. Jradex was of the Kalmar species, as his beard of writhing tentacles would prove, and he was dressed in a suit with long coattails and tight pants tucked into boots large enough to crush a skull. Troyton stared in awe at the sun-bathed monument, his head spinning with ideas of what this legendary figure had accomplished in his lifetime.

Rachel Vikander was by his side, staring at the same statue not with awe, but aspiration. With them was her Captain-of-the-Guard, a burly, blue-skinned Jurishan who was not shy of his mistrust, or perhaps animosity, toward the humanoid. His name was Throd, or at least that was what Rachel called him, but Troyton only referred to him as "sir."

"He was the last person to unify Laktannon?" Troyton asked. "I've never heard of him."

"Doesn't surprise me," Rachel said. "How many historical figures can you name that are not human?"

He thought for a moment, then laughed. "Not too many, come to think of it."

She smiled too at the darkness of it all. "Jradex was not the last man to do so, he was the only one... until now. He was an outcast much like you and me, rejected by the galaxy through no fault of his own. He retreated to Laktannon as a broken man but emerged from it a conqueror."

Troyton gazed around at the architecture surrounding the statue of Old Ulthrawn's hero. Unlike whatever horrid area Bato had found him in, the buildings in the square a few miles from the Republic Manor were mostly intact, showing a few structural scars of war that cut deeper into the rest of the city. Old Ulthrawn did not amaze him like Rome did, but this culture that persevered through battle after battle was beginning to endear to him. It was a fisherman's village dragged through industrialization, but beneath the dry edifices, gray slates of walls, and conspicuous military weaponry existed a humble lifestyle that Troyton admired.

"So, about Jradex," he continued. "What happened to him once he united the Bloodlands?"

"He sought revenge on the rest of the galaxy, not just for himself, but for his people too. Jradex had formed the largest army ever known at the time, and he used it to stampede over his enemies by the millions! The years of brutal fighting in the Bloodlands had turned him into a masterful commander, and there was not a single general on any other world who could match his wits."

Troyton scratched his head. He sensed life did not end well for Jradex. "But… he did eventually fail?"

Rachel nodded. "Only when the rest of the worlds aligned against him. It was an act of pure cowardice if you ask me. Even with the combined forces of the old KOH, the Timanzee Empire, all three Hallyan Tri-archs, the Denvari, Kalmar, Fyrossians, and the damn Paladin Order, it was a traitor within Jradex's own ranks that dealt him the deathblow. Without that, who knows how he could have changed history."

"And this is what you want as well?"

"I want to follow in his footsteps. Jradex's war was waged over two hundred years ago, and Laktannon's population has increased since. I have a larger army at my disposal and the legacy of Jradex to guide me."

"As someone who was once part of the Triumvirate, I must admit that they will not be easy to challenge out in the open. You have an impressive army, unquestionably, but do they have the willpower to contend with a force like that? You could be facing years of warfare before the Triumvirate even shows a dent in its war machine." Troyton warned, trying hard not to sound like a loyalist.

"Our resolve is stronger than you can imagine. Those who live in the Bloodlands possess a fighting spirit like no other, it's in our DNA. Now that my people see the chance to retake their old homes for themselves and their children, only death will stop them from seizing the opportunity," Rachel said without a hint of uncertainty. "When Jradex challenged the galaxy, he did not achieve just a handful of fluke victories. His enemies struggled to match him for years. I will never underestimate the might of the Triumvirate, but the worlds are not as unified as they once were without Last Bastion."

Troyton had to agree. Last Bastion was once the galactic hub of the galaxy, holding assemblies in which representatives from across the worlds could attend. No such citadel existed anymore, making a centralized Laktannon even more threatening.

Rome, however, was a sacred city. Regardless of what side he was on, Troyton still loved the capital of the KOH, especially since experiencing it firsthand. Stunning architecture aside, Rome was the walking grounds of thousands of years of venerable humans, giving the city a certain untouchable mysticism. The image of a swarm of warships unleashing their firepower onto sacred grounds admittedly made him queasy.

"And how would you plan on taking Rome from Caesar if given the chance?" he asked, cautiously.

"When the opportunity presents itself," Rachel began, "I will obviously give the tyrants a chance to surrender. Rome may represent the worst of ambitious men, but it was once the citadel for the Republic, the thing my father gave his life for. When I've purged the corruption from the KOH, democracy will return to Orbis once again."

Rachel checked her watch and promptly turned on a dime back to the empty street. Old Ulthrawn was oddly noiseless. Troyton briefly wondered if the whole planet of Fyrossia was like this as its people braced for invasion. Quiet, still, anticipating inevitable destruction. "Come with me. My uncle has called a meeting with our generals. You will be needed to inform them on exactly what kind of threat approaches us."

"Me?" Troyton asked, as if she could possibly be referring to someone else.

"Of course, you. Tell my generals what you know, and they might start to like you." Rachel informed him.

"Who doesn't like me?" the humanoid asked aloud. He supposed he should have expected some animosity, but the fresh start had made him naively hopeful that others would treat him with greater warmth.

"Me, for one," the captain declared as he opened the car door for Rachel. "Now do as Lady Vikander commands, or I'll drag you in myself."

Troyton obeyed, although he would have done so anyway with or without the Jurishan's threat. He knew he could tear Captain Throd in half if provoked, but why incite any more ill feelings? Once inside, he was taken back to the Republic Manor, passing by the familiar, dumpy streets and alleyways.

As they drove along, Rachel said, "I have something to ask you." Her tone, surprisingly, was nervous. Troyton welcomed her to continue. "Humanoids have a different aging process than humans... and by that, I mean, your aging is accelerated to get you ready for battle sooner. May I ask how old you are?"

"Ten, I think, but that would be in traditional human years. I guess I'm as developed as someone in their early twenties, if it helps."

Rachel sighed. She peered out the window briefly to stare at the fields of cracked asphalt. "It helps in one way, but makes me feel guilty in another. Do you care that some scientist rushed you through childhood to put a rifle in your hands?"

"It doesn't make me feel anything." Troyton said. "As I see it, it's the price of living."

"Aaahhh, to be born with a clear purpose. I don't know to envy or pity you," she said. Troyton did not know how to respond, so he didn't. He never wanted to curse the scientists on the Casca moon for creating him. They made him for warfare, and he was grateful they succeeded in their design.

The car passed through the towering walls which surrounded the Manor and pulled up to the curb right outside the entrance. On the steps, surprisingly, was a mage. The Immortech sword on his belt made it obvious, but there was a scent about mages that Troyton was becoming overly familiar with. Immediately, he assumed the worst.

"You called for me?" the mage asked, standing up as Rachel approached the steps.

"I did, Ser Kent. You should be sitting in as we strategize. You will be taking part in the battle, after all."

"Won't I be protecting the Zoltor children?"

"How will you serve them better: fighting the KOH in the frontlines, or sitting in a bunker and waiting for the enemy to take our city? Now stop talking nonsense and let's go." Rachel charged up the steps. Kent relented and followed from behind. Troyton made sure to give the mage a glare as he passed him by. Why Rachel Vikander was associating herself with mages was something he could not understand.

They walked into the wide, vaulted-roofed atrium of the Republic Manor, then descended downstairs into the war room. They passed through a thick iron vault and into a small room heavy with cool air. In the center of the room was a table featuring an illuminated map of Old Ulthrawn. The model of the city itself was holographic and three-dimensional, and the outdated technology caused the map to glitch and shimmer. Surrounding the table were the generals who would be opposing the Roman frigate.

The lights resonating from the table highlighted Lord Aethelwulf Vikander's grim face as his niece entered the room. By his side was Sergeant Samuel Parkton, an equally sour-faced man with short hair brown like dirt, a sharp nose, and a pink scar embracing the left side of his face. His disdain was entirely directed toward Troyton.

Also joining them was a Drakonid named Gressna, with auburn scales and a cavernous hole on his face where an eye once was. Out of respect, he probably should have worn an eyepatch over it. Gressna hissed as he and Rachel approached the table, although her indifference allowed Troyton to assume the Drakonid meant no hostility. The final member of their company was a Denvari male with light blue skin, long silvery hair, and violet eyes like gems under his brow. The Denvari people were known for their near deific beauty, and this man was no exception. The enchanting aura he exuded did not come entirely from his pure features, but rather in some suppressed duality in his looks and actions that Troyton could not quite place. His benign smile flashed, daring a search for sinister intentions.

"Saryn Malor," the Denvari said, extending his arm. "And you?"

"Troyton Vorenus." He grabbed Saryn's right hand and realized it was made of metal.

Saryn unshyly analyzed him up and down. "I've never met a humanoid before, but I've heard of the legends. May I say, you do not disappoint."

Before Troyton could thank him, Rachel interrupted. "What's Lord Saryn doing here? Last I checked he does not possess an officer's rank."

"No but I do possess the Eclipse Syndicate, which is the largest army in Laktannon last time I checked," Saryn replied.

"You mean you bought the largest army." Rachel corrected him, boldly.

"If you want to argue over semantics, do it on your own time," Aethelwulf commanded. "For now, we have more vital matters to address."

"Should we discuss battle strategies in the presence of a humanoid?" Sergeant Parkton asked in a furtive tone as if Troyton did not hear. His pink scar twisted as he continued to glare. *You would fit quite well with Quill squad.*

"Commander Vorenus is on our side, I assure you." Rachel said. "He's been wronged by the KOH just as much as you have."

Parkton sneered. "Aye? Did he? All my comrades from the days of the Republic are dead or rotting in a KOH prison. Can this humanoid say the same?"

"This humanoid has ridden in the same exact frigate which opposes us. Is there anyone else who can provide more valuable information on what we're up against?" Rachel paused dramatically to allow time for a retort. "No? I did not think so."

"Don't assume the worst yet," Aethelwulf announced. "This assembly is purely for safety precautions."

"And how have the Romans responded to your attempts to parley?" Rachel asked.

Aethelwulf's eyes turned to his sergeant, then back to his niece. "The frigate has shot down two of our ships."

"Oh, so they've committed war crimes against us. What would you say are our chances for peace now, Uncle?"

"I would say the odds are shit, and getting worse by the day," Aethelwulf confessed. "And with that, Commander Vorenus, what can you tell us about this frigate?"

Troyton froze at the vagueness of the question. *What would he like to know? That one frigate alone has enough manpower to seize Old Ulthrawn? That if the city goes unshielded for even a moment, we could all be turned into dust. Should I tell them there are half a million humans on that ship, all of whom likely know their role in dismantling your defenses piece by piece?*

"The ship's called Spear of Rhomigius. The first piece of advice I should give you, Lord Vikander, is to make sure the city's shields are in their best condition. The firepower on the frigate alone can eviscerate Old Ulthrawn. I've seen your air force, and it's quite impressive. Use it to keep their star-splitters from gunning down your anti-artillery weapons and shield generators."

"The humanoid isss an exsssellent teacher of the fundamentalsss of warfare," General Gressna interrupted. His slithering voice was low enough for Troyton not to detect his sarcasm.

"He's right," Aethelwulf agreed. "Troyton, what kind of ground deploys do the Romans have?"

"Hundreds of thousands of trained soldiers," he said, feeling slimy as he spoke. If his teachers on Casca knew what he would become, they would have let him starve in his incubation tube. "Tanks and helicopters as well. Your walls are strong, but not strong enough. If they get close, they'll obliterate every line of defense."

Lucius may have been in their company too, the humanoid who was as formidable as a tank if he were to reach the frontline.

Aethelwulf looked for General Gressna and said: "I'll need your snipers and rocketeers to keep their machines at bay. Is your team good enough to hit a pilot in his cockpit?"

"The besssst," Gressna responded, casually. "Don't worry, lordly lord, we know how to buy the livesssss of an entire sssquadron for the price of one bullet."

"Kent, you could use mind control on them too. Cause some dissension in the ranks." Rachel proposed.

The Paladin rubbed his chin. "I could try. My gift works better when I can see who I'm using it on. Also, can't say I'm as good as I used to be... I have a difficult enough time breaking through someone's helmet."

*So what use are you?* Troyton wondered. A Paladin who could not control his powers spelled bad news for all. Judging by the atmosphere around the table, everyone else was similarly skeptical.

"Well, let's hope the rush of battle will motivate you." Aethelwulf said. "Troyton, is there anything else we should know?"

"One more thing, sir. The general in charge of the frigate is a Roman named Antonius Marko. He's a competent leader, but he's young and I would wager he has never conducted an operation on his own."

"That could make him bold," Saryn Malor said. "An experienced military leader like the one before me could take advantage of that." The Denvari's opulent eyes stared lovingly at Lord Aethelwulf Vikander.

"I'll take it into consideration, but youth does not necessarily mean ignorance." Aethelwulf replied. "I possessed youthful pride once too, and I used it to defeat Caesar."

Soon after, Vikander ended the meeting under the pretense that they could regroup at any moment for further strategizing. Not knowing where else to go, Troyton followed Rachel. Suffice to say, Throd was not pleased. He left the meeting believing his contributions had won the generals over. At the very least, he looked much better than the mage, whose lack of commitment rightfully caused concern. Just as he and Rachel were leaving the Manor, the voice of the mage called for them to stop.

"I didn't exactly win anyone over back there." Kent Kentoshi said, apologetic. "They may hate me even more now."

*As they should.*

"My uncle doesn't," Rachel assured him. "The others will take time to warm up to you... but honestly, Kent, you could have been a little more inspiring back there."

The mage sighed sorrowfully. "I know. The magic is coming back to me, but I was afraid of making false promises."

As they continued to speak, Saryn Malor entered their circle. His long, rich cape brushed against the floor as he walked. The symbol of a dark purple moon eclipsing over an orange sun was embroidered on his right sleeve. "Apologies for the interruption, but I will be brief. Ser Kent, I want to invite you and your Paladins to my estate tomorrow night for dinner. When I heard the news that the Zoltors were not only alive but on my planet, well, now I'm dying for their company."

Kent Kentoshi shot the Denvari a dubious look. "Can't this wait until after the battle?"

"I'm afraid not," Saryn answered solemnly. There was something subtly dramatic in his tone of voice. "With life being so uncertain, it's best to take advantage of the opportunity while we can. Lady Rachel, you are invited as well."

"Did it occur to you that Kent may have more pressing issues than to fancy your interests?" Rachel objected.

"It's fine, Lady Vikander," the mage said. "I'll talk to Tali, although we aren't on the most amicable of terms right now. Tomorrow night, you say? Where is your estate?"

Saryn Malor smirked. "It's just outside the city. Well, it's not an estate, but rather a large ship, so be on the lookout for it. I am eagerly awaiting your company."

The sun set below the opulent flower garden separating the verdant field of Unity College from the rest of Old Ulthrawn. A scorching red line rising over the land made its last stand against the dark green sky that overwhelmed the rest of the city. The swaying trees to his back were like the massive outlines of titans, while the flowers in the garden were so vibrant that their colors still blossomed against the embracing dusk. On the field stood three figures, two with practice swords in hand and stepping with and against one another as if engaged in some unconventional dance. The other, a feminine figure with what looked to be twigs growing from the back of her head, watched along.

Troyton clenched his fists, licked his lips, and marched forward. Unable to hide his over seven-foot-tall body in an open field, he was spotted rather quickly. Marion was confused by his arrival, although his slouched shoulders suggested no intimidation. The girl, however, kept her distance, prowling in the background and, if Troyton was not mistaken, prepared to strike.

"Sorry to interrupt," he apologized before turning his attention directly to Marion. "Is it okay if we talk for a moment."

The human shrugged. His brownish-blonde hair was longer than it had been on the frigate, except for one side of his head which looked somewhat recently shaven. Upon further inspection, he noticed a long scar hidden in the forest of hairs.

"It's all right with me," Marion said. He placed his practice sword on the lawn and told the alien woman he would be back soon. The woman glared at Troyton before they left, a not-so-subtle statement of her distrust. Marion walked with him to a small patio a few yards away from the other mages. They took chairs and faced them in the direction of the flower beds.

"That woman, is she your teacher?" Troyton asked, completely unaware of the practices of mages.

"She is, somewhat. Tali is helping us find our powers, but I haven't felt anything yet. She says it's her specialty, so I'm hopeful it will happen any day now." He leaned back and sighed. "It involves a lot of meditating and thinking, things that aren't very kind to me."

"She's also training you in combat." Troyton noted, carefully not including that Tali did not appear physically suited for the task. Of course, mages were a deceptive bunch, as unpredictable physically as they were mentally.

"She tries," Marion said. "Kent is supposed to be teaching us how to use Immortech, but he's never around. Tali has the spirit to teach, but I'll rely on my Roman training when the situation calls for it."

Troyton considered mentioning that Kent was with him and Lady Rachel earlier in the day, but he wisely chose not to. "You said you've been having trouble meditating, so what've you been thinking about?"

Marion met his eyes. The space between them hardened. Something about the boy's face was vacant. "What I've lost."

"Whatever you're feeling, I came here to say I'm grateful that you saved me. I was content with wasting away, but now Lady Rachel trusts me as her advisor. Finding a new path was easier than I wanted to believe, all it required was a step forward."

Marion smiled. "I'm glad Old Ulthrawn has treated you well. Freedom can be sweet, it's something I craved for my whole life on Romulus." He raised his hands to the sky and let a gentle breeze course through his fingers, which were covered in fresh scarring. "And now I have it. Tell me, was it worth the price?"

"Well... maybe. As you said, what the KOH presents itself as is not what it is. I'm no longer fighting for a lie, at least." The humanoid dwelled on this fact and found the resulting emotion to be quite liberating. "And you?"

"I despised how Romulus had tried to direct my life, but now that I can only see the path from a distance... it doesn't seem so bad. It was physical, safe, something I could follow and feel confident on." The human stomped his right foot on the brick patio. "Without it, I'm walking on air, guideless."

"You will find a new path soon," Troyton said. "If I could do it, you can as well."

Marion continued as if alone. "Fate is a tricky thing. You want to control your own destiny, but through that desire for agency you strip away someone else's. My need to play with life has cut another's short through no fault of her own, and for what? What was it all for?" His face turned pale; his stare so strained that blood vessels pulsed in the whites of his eyes. He begged Troyton for an answer, but he was utterly clueless as to what to say.

"Listen, I'm sorry I came here. I wanted to express my gratitude for your help. I did not mean to strike any sensitive chords."

Marion's intensity cooled. His posture relaxed once again, and he seemed at peace. "Don't worry, my friend. You've done the nicest thing anyone has done for me since arriving to this shit-pile of a planet. To that, I say thank you."

# ELYSANDE (IX)

The queen gazed at her bloodied hands. Her fingers were raw and starting to show signs of bruising. Her arms were warm and sore and jittery as if fresh from a workout. She leaned against the thin metal table, breathless. Fatigue, of every kind, weighted on her.

"Did I kill him?" she asked, lightly touching her knuckles to see which hurt and which did not. In the end, they were all in varying degrees of pain.

"He's breathing, at least." Liscinia Drusilla remarked. She considered her queen with the eyes of a psychologist. "Are you okay after all that?"

Elysande laughed faintly, "Do I look perturbed?"

"No, ma'am. You handled yourself expertly. If we were strangers, I'd say you were a veteran of the Black Dogs."

They were in a circle of disillusion. The boundaries surpassed to pry a confession from Shade were finally sinking in. They were already acting against the principles of KOH law, but whether or not they had defied the more ethereal rules of basic human morality too was the question whose answer was not so easily clear or willingly sought for.

"Excellent, I'd say we wake Mister Shade in an hour and get his confession on tape."

"Do you want to risk holding that kind of physical evidence?" Ser Dance asked.

"I have no choice now." Elysande remarked, gazing down at her battered hands some more. She would periodically clench them to prevent the oncoming stiffness. "I acted gratuitously out there, didn't I? I don't know how I'll explain these to my husband."

"You did what needed to be done, my queen." Liscinia said, her somber brown eyes dancing in every direction but hers. The guilt of what had occurred was seeping into her conscience, but the queen had a suspicion she would not crack.

"What's the matter?" Elysande asked, already knowing the answer.

"It's what Shade said about my commander. If Quintus Longinus was involved in the cover up of Galla's murder, he's a conspirator against the king. I've worked with him every day since joining the Dogs, and I truly can't believe I was blind to his duplicity." Liscinia admitted.

"Then learn from this mistake and grow from it," she advised. "Your king is not immune to them, nor myself. What we need to focus on is uncovering the breadth of this conspiracy before it's too late."

The legate's eyebrows narrowed. "But there's still another problem: the Praetorian guardsman I spoke to. He must be a part of the cover up, but Shade didn't have a name."

"Right…" By the end of the interrogation, Shade was an open book. Elysande nearly believed him when he proclaimed in merciful cries to have no idea who the mysterious guard was. She had to beat him to unconsciousness to prove his honesty, but at least the effort increased her trust. A cold shiver scurried down her spine. "Let's wake our friend up and get his confession on tape."

"And what is to be done after that?" Liscinia inquired. The urgency in her voice took her by surprise.

"It's no concern of yours, *bella*. We'll be in touch. I let you play your part in finding Shade, now let me play mine," the queen said. "Oh, and cease the formalities. Call me Elysande."

The Queen of the KOH watched the semifinals of the Gladiator Games as if she had bet her life savings on the outcome. In a way, the hyperbole was more accurate than she cared to admit.

Much to her disdain, Magnus Caesar defeated Admiral Kassa Savon in the A Block final. The duel was fierce, as both competitors traded the upper hand back and forth throughout, but ultimately a fluke slip on behalf of the admiral gave Caesar the window he needed. She tripped as she ran, and instead of chivalrously letting her regain her bearings, Caesar struck her when she was down and stole his victory. Magnus was skilled, a master of combat even, but he could not defeat Savon on his own merits, and the self-conscious grin plastered over his face as he celebrated expressed his awareness of this very fact.

Tullius would overlook the asterisk above his son's victory his inevitable boasting at the next council meeting. *If Magnus wins the whole bloody Games, his brute of a father will never let us hear the end of it.* Just as the sickening thought popped into her head, she noticed a slight awkwardness in Magnus' step. His right foot dragged, favoring the ankle. His assistants caught on and supported him off the stage with his arms around their shoulders.

Elysande replayed the match in her head and could not find the moment where he may have damaged his ankle. She recalled the fall he and Servius Venator took the previous day and concluded the injury may have started there. The subsequent bout with Savon served to make it worse. Most importantly, the whole Colosseum saw it, and whoever his opponent was in the Finals would surely make a mental note of it too.

Her husband was tucked away in some niche of the Palazzo Reale. Preparations for war against the Synths had become too overwhelming for him to afford a break like attending the Gladiator Games. On top of that, he had to arrange for Timothy Mauvern's body to be delivered back to Lynwood, as the rest of the Mauvern brood likely lacked the intelligence combined to put the right stamps on the packaging.

And yet, Elysande wondered how many ladies were shacked up in his office, diligently keeping his mind and body at ease during this abnormally stressful time. She tried to block Gaius' extramarital affairs from her head, as it was an unspoken leniency between them as long as their separate love lives remained out of the public eye, but with the king at her mercy it was difficult not to stew on all the ways he wronged her.

With that and the sight of his daughter Natalia and her lover Jacob Mauvern a few rows down fully returned to their infatuated ways, Elysande fell into a suppressed fury. She caught herself unconsciously digging her nails into the armrests of her chair and scoffed.

The finale of the B Block matches held her interest for a different reason. Bryson Byrne, the knight she advocated for to Shota Nakamura, took on Shinjiro Ishii, the rhinoceros of a man who had beaten Lord Robert Album to dust. Elysande watched with a finger on her lips. She needed Byrne to win to keep the conspirators satisfied and stupid as to what she was doing behind the scenes. On the other hand, if Byrne lost, she could be free of their commitments. Perhaps her advocacy was the scope of the plans Felix and the senators had for her. Was Ishii unknowingly fighting for her freedom, or her doom?

The answer to this riddle would never be solved. Bryson Byrne went up against his toughest opponent yet, but even the rhinoceros of Kygorro wasn't enough to fell the unstoppable Mercian knight. The Bear of Byrne refused to fall for Ishii's attempts to provoke him into a test of strength like he did against Album, and this restraint was rewarded with victory. Again, Byrne expressed respect for his defeated opponent and humbly walked off stage without taking the time to boast his success in the center of the Colosseum. The queen's ears perked up to the crowd, who cheered for Byrne louder now than any of his previous bouts.

*His auctoritas grows by the day. If only he was not so blindly loyal to the Heirs, he could have a remarkable career serving the KOH.*

The finals of the Gladiator Games were set: Magnus Caesar versus Bryson Byrne. The royal bloodline against the relative unknown. Judging from the crowd's reaction, Elysande had created an underdog. Ser Bryson was building his family's name before the hundreds of thousands of eyes inside the Colosseum. "Bry-son Byrne!" they exploded together, "Bry-Son Byrne!"

*If my knight wins the whole tournament, he will ask Caesar to join the ranks of his Praetorian Elite... according to Felix of Rezza.* Elysande rendered the idea absurd. She had not given Byrne the faith to make it past the first round. The Praetorian Elite consisted only of the most accomplished knights and soldiers of the KOH, the ones who spent years in the frontlines, gaining auctoritas through bloody battles and undying allegiance. Byrne, who for all purposes was a "nobody" a few weeks ago, surely would have insulted the king and his honored guard by making such an outrageous demand.

*How stupid am I? He's an underdog, and the masses love him for it. If Ser Bryson wishes to become part of the Praetorian Elite, the adoring crowd will give their king no choice but to accept.*

. . .

Felix of Rezza took a bite of his apple, pulled it away from his mouth, and admired the cavern. The senator had brought her to the back of his rented villa after the Games, the afternoon sun casting golden rays on the stiff grass and small, winding olive trees in his backyard. They sat around a circular glass table topped off with a wine bottle and two glasses. Felix was well into his second cup, while Elysande had not touched her first.

By the sliding door stood Bryson Byrne and Richard Dance, the two knights picking up their stare down where it last left off.

"I haven't seen you wear gloves before," Felix observed, his contrived grin not fooling anyone.

Elysande showed him her gloved hands. They were white leather with red trim, a tribute to her family's colors. On the inside, her hands were a collage of soars and bruises. "You haven't known me for very long. And if you did, is the queen not allowed to switch up her style from time to time?"

"It was merely an observation." Felix said, taking another bite of his apple. Seeing how the rest of the senatorial body had crowded around him as he exited the Colosseum, she became increasingly careful as to what kind of influence he wielded. Every senator, no matter where they came from, must have missed the days of the Republic. It was a time where they were at the height of their power, controlling consuls and generals and collecting lucrative favors from those who wished to cut their teeth in human politics, as foolish as they may be. But despite this immense influence, the Senate was prone to clash within itself. The Roman Republic became static, the position of consul was reserved for "yes men" to the most revered senators, and even then, little meaningful legislation was ever passed.

The Republic was a disaster, and the Senate was its greatest contributor. Caesar never would have gained the support he did otherwise. That being said, senators were hardly self-reflective, as expressing even a morsel of humility would mean absolute political deflation. They likely craved their old power back, no matter how Caesar governed them. If Felix could launch a meaningful uprising against the KOH, the senatorial leeches would certainly grab hold.

"You've done good work for us," Felix continued. "I know our bond was formed on tumultuous terms, but the favors you've done for me and the Heirs will be returned."

Elysande rolled her eyes. "I'm not a dog to be pet when she does a trick."

"Do you always respond to compliments with belligerence?" Felix laughed.

"Only the condescending kind," she clarified. Her eyes turned to Bryson Byrne, whose face and armor appeared unscathed despite the days of fighting. In the lowering sunlight, the knight's disguised youth radiated in contradiction to his stern demeanor. His sweaty stench, too, smelled of hard-earned victory. "I had no confidence in your knight, but he's proved me wrong. Ser Byrne has been a joy to watch this tournament."

"Most of my competitors do not understand war like I do." Ser Byrne said, the statement directed toward Ser Dance.

"And now he is in the finals!" Felix celebrated.

"And against a maimed competitor no less." Elysande added, directing her attention to the knight. "You must've seen Magnus' limp from the arena, didn't you? He tried to hide it too, which must mean it's worse than he lets on."

Ser Byrne nodded. "I saw it clear as the sun, my queen. It is a weakness worth targeting, but not one to take for granted. Sometimes mere sprains can feel worse than they are while fresh. But still, I know it wasn't a sprain."

Felix of Rezza slapped his knee in excitement. The sudden burst of energy from the lackadaisical Carcian startled Elysande and her protector alike. "Your final opponent should be the easiest to overcome. We must be in Rhomigius' favor!"

"It's best not to dwell on how the Immortals look down on us, as you may not like the answer," she warned. "And yes, one more battle lies before you, ser knight, on the turn of the new year, no less. Then you may make your request before the king... then what comes after that?"

Bryson Byrne's eyes darted to those of the senator. Receiving the cry for help, Felix interrupted: "As I've said before, Ser Bryson's position on the Praetorian Elite will be nothing more than an insurance policy. Our revolution will be peaceful, or else we're no better than the worst villains of our history."

Felix chomped into the apple one last time before chucking it into the yard. The four of them watched it bounce and tumble down the slight, green mound.

"What villains are you referring to?" Elysande asked.

"Your husband, for one," he answered. "How many failed rebels against the Gasardi dynasty are remembered fondly in the history books." He waited for Elysande to respond, but she remained quiet. "The answer is easy: none. Many a self-righteous revolutionary promises change and prosperity for the common person but brings nothing more than bloodshed and destruction. True, risk is the key ingredient in effective change, but success can be just as damaging as failure. Too many times have freedom fighters digressed into the same rulers whose atrocities motivated them to rebel in the first place."

"And yet, you threatened the lives of my children for the sake of your Republic. Have you looked in a mirror lately? The reflection may be unflattering."

Felix shook his head as if she was not understanding an apparently obvious point. "We want to reduce bloodshed, but we're not braindead idealists. I'll risk the lives of a few to save thousands, or perhaps millions more. Putting your children at stake has helped us prevent a civil war thus far. Sorry to say, but I have no regrets."

She was tempted to march out onto the green stiff grass, pick up the apple core, and shove it through the senator's sparkling eyes. He was not dangerous by himself, but the Heirs were still a threat to her so long as their numbers remained a secret. For now, he would need to live. "You're awfully ruminative, maybe to a grievous fault. Is it so boring in northern Carcia that all you people do is sit around and philosophize?"

Felix smiled his despicable smile. He patted his gut as he reflected. "Life is tranquil in my region. You may not know this, but Rezza is about half a day's ride away from Crownhold, the old city of the Gasardi dynasty. What do you know of this sacred place?"

Elysande's eyes narrowed. She hated playing games, especially with a young twerp far less clever than he pretended to be. "Legend has it the city was made of gold. Crownhold was the most advanced and intricate city humanity had ever constructed, an accomplishment even the Hallyans were envious of."

"Heh!" Felix chuckled softly. "Your inclination to say 'legend has it' fascinates me. The Gasardi dynasty ended but a few generations ago, and yet their line spanning hundreds of years has been reduced to that of myth in a fraction of the time. Anyway, I would drive to the remnants of Crownhold quite often, usually several times a month. The gold no longer glistens, and the mystique has evaporated in one sense. All that's left is an overly nourished forest obscuring the greatest accomplishment in human history."

"It must be quite the sight."

"It's as tragic as it is engrossing, that something so magnificent can be so quickly disregarded."

"So you're having a crisis of legacy?" Elysande observed. "The passing of time must be terrifying. I hate to break it to you, but one day the Roman Republic will be forgotten too."

"It's the opposite, actually," Felix corrected her. "Most revolutionaries care too much about their chapter in history before it's ever written." He looked to the dimming light over the olive garden, covering the whole backyard in bronze rays. Dark clouds rolled in from the coast, carrying with them the oncoming night. "I embrace the fleeting nature of time. In my opinion, it's what makes me the exception. It's what makes me a winner."

Ser Bryson Byrne escorted the queen and her royal protector out of the estate and to her car. Ser Dance was her driver for the night, so he circled around the vehicle and to the driver's seat, leaving her alone with her champion.

"My queen, if I may have a word." Ser Bryson started. He removed his helmet so she could get a better look at his dumb, if not handsome face in the glow of a streetlight. "I wanted to thank you for advocating for me."

Elysande sighed. "Sorry to tell you, ser, but it was not my choice."

The knight opened his arms. The silver bear sigil on his breastplate glistened in the nighttime stars. "I know, but I'm humbled by your actions, nonetheless. You may not remember it, but we've met before in Erron. I was a young boy at the time, brought to your court by my mother and father. I still recall it as if it were yesterday."

She nodded slowly. "The sight of Erron can be quite breathtaking for visitors. Or, was it the Bodewin hospitality that made the day so memorable?"

"Neither, my queen," Ser Bryson paused. "It was you..."

"Uh-huh." The knight's open posture took on an entirely different meaning.

"You were the most beautiful woman I had ever seen... and nothing has changed since." Ser Bryson's eyes slightly averted from hers. His square face flushed red. Elysande smiled slightly but warmly.

"Are you feeling brave, ser knight?" she asked, lightly touching his forearm.

In return, Bryson quivered. He gathered himself, took her by the hand, and chastely kissed her gloved fingers. With all her might, she managed to stifle a large cry from her throat as her fingers wailed in agony between his touch. "When the Republic returns, you will have no need to be married to King Caesar. After that, maybe, I was thinking-"

"Oh no," Elysande interrupted, putting her index finger to his lips. "Say no more, or else I won't sleep a night until my dreaded husband has been displaced. But until then..." Her hands shifting to the contours of his square jaw, she extended her spine and kissed Ser Bryson Byrne. The knight's mouth and tongue were paralyzed, his lips as dry as sand, but she tasted his lust, his years of quieted fantasies. Without another word, she stepped into her car and commanded Richard Dance to drive off.

"Back to the estate, ma'am?" Dance inquired.

"Don't tempt me," she sighed, rubbing her temples. Bryson Byrne's apparent infatuation had lifted her spirits, but not her energy. With heavy eyelids, she watched the passing villas soaked in starlight, tempted to join the rest of Rome in sleep. "I owe Senator Lucio a visit before the night is through. Gods, I believe all this socializing is going to kill me."

She rested her head on the window and closed her eyes. The pane was cold on her cheek, as if she were touching the nightly air itself. Everything filling her mind drifted away. The pain in her hands subsided. Slowly, sleep embraced her.

Her phone rang.

"Ah, fuck!" the queen groaned.

"Shall I let it ring?" her knight offered.

Elysande's eyes had not yet opened. Fortunately, they were not needed for talking over the phone. "Depends, who is it?"

"The legate, Drusilla."

She rubbed a hand through her thick mane of golden red hair. "I'll make an exception. Go on, put her through." A crackling sound emerged from the speakers of the car. "Miss Drusilla, how can I help you?"

"Sorry to disturb you, ma'am," the staticky voice came through. "I have some news. Nothing bad yet, but I need you to know. Commander Longinus questioned me today. Not like an interrogation or anything, but he's showed more interest in my social life today than ever before."

"And I trust you did not give him an inch?"

"No, naturally I planned for this." Drusilla assured her. Elysande fancied the confidence in her tone. "But I think he's aware of Shade's disappearance. Apologies, but I must ask: what are we going to do with Shade? If we let him out, he'll report to Longinus."

"Did you feed Shade before leaving the factory?"

"Of course I did. Also gave him a bucket for his, well, wastes."

"Then Shade is looking good on all ends." Elysande said, returning her head to its place of cool rest on the windowpane. "No need to make an impetuous decision on him now. Not at least until we know what Longinus is up to."

"Okay, ma'am. Whatever you say."

A small pause assumed between the two women. After a few seconds, Elysande said: "How are you doing? It's been a rough twenty-four hours."

"I'm tired, ma'am, but nothing I can't handle." The queen let out a slight laugh. Liscinia was concrete. It would take more than an insurrection to crack her.

"Stay strong… but what did I tell you about calling me 'ma'am?'"

"Sorry… Elysande," the legate returned, her voice shaky. "Thank you for asking."

"Don't mention it, now get some sleep while you can. No need to worry about me until I contact for you." When the phone call ended, she returned to her conversation with Ser Dance. "You realize I need you to kill Mister Shade, correct?"

Dance nodded, refusing to remove his eyes from the road. "I know."

Exhaustion blurred everything outside the car, her world reduced to splotches of color, abstract and somewhat peaceful. "And you have no moral hesitations about killing a defenseless man?"

"I've seen Shade's record. The man's a murderer, rapist, drug dealer. It would be my pleasure to end him."

*Gods, I have quite the weapon at my disposal,* Elysande thought, leaning back in her chair.

Senator Lucio Privetera made to effort to hide his disdainful skepticism when his foggy gaze met Elysande's at the door. He was in his pajamas and his thin, black hair was a mess from tossing his head about a pillow. The queen acted like she was unaware of the disturbance and invited herself into his rented villa. *It's not like he could refuse royalty.*

"Why are you here?" Lucio asked in a gruff voice. "Is Felix coming to?"

"No, no, my friend," she said, stepping around the old man and into his estate. "I came to talk to you alone. To strategize, if you will."

Lucio shook his head in complete rejection of her proposal. "I will do no such thing without the other Heirs around. We have nothing to speak about."

"Oh, Senator, we have so much to discuss." Elysande said, reaching into her pocket. Lucio was incredulous when he saw the recorder in her hand. "Now, why don't you be a gentleman and offer the lady a seat."

Lucio brought her into the living room. His shuffled footsteps echoed throughout the quiet corridors and halls as he guided her along. Elysande sat on a couch while the senator plopped himself down on a leather chair much too big for his size. The tiled floor appeared to be carved from gray rocks and stone. The white walls absorbed the overhead lights, brightening the room and giving off the illusion that it was somehow midday. Tapestries hung from the walls, the largest of the bunch depicted the Aquila of Rome over a field of red. *May Rhomigius be with me.*

"Now, what is this about?" Lucio rudely asked, nearly swallowed by the chair.

"Are we alone?"

"What?!" The elderly had a special way of testing one's patience.

"Are we the only two in the villa? No servants in the halls? No concubines in your bed?"

"Of course not!" Lucio blurted. The impudence in his tone was insulting in the presence of royalty. "State your business, then leave me in peace."

"I'll let this recording do the talking." She pressed play on her device. Witnessing Lucio's face transition from unrestrained contempt to utter fear for his own well-being was a sight to behold. He may not have known Mercurio Shade well, but hearing him reveal the conspiracy to kill Ser Galla was enough to make him squirm. The old, scornful bastard searched the room desperately for a friend, but no one would come to his aid.

When the recording stopped, Elysande let the quiet revelation seep into the room. Lucio made no notion to defend himself, instead opting to grumble deeply under his breath and noisily scratch the armrests of his chair. Finally, she broke the silence by clicking her tongue to the roof of her mouth and asking the senator: "So, what do you think about that?"

"The speaker, whoever he may be, must have been coerced into saying these lies." Lucio declared as he scratched the leather armrest vigorously. "I have no idea who this man is, or anyone he has named in that recording."

"True enough, but you know of Galla's murder. There's a trail, no matter how well you covered your tracks. Felix is a busy man, certainly he spoke to at least one of the people my confessor implicates. If the king's detectives can link Felix to the crime, your thread won't be hard to follow from there."

"This is outrageous!" Lucio waved his hand in the air as if invoking the Immortals to defend him. The queen bit her tongue to resist laughter. "I won't be threatened like this based on one recording. I don't know who this man is or why he lies so shamelessly, but I won't kneel to these absurdities!"

"Perhaps not, but you will kneel to me," Elysande said. She put the recording back into her pocket. "Or else, I can deliver this to Caesar myself."

"You would not dare!" Lucio predicted, screaming to disguise his doubt. "If I'm arrested, I'll make sure you go down with me."

"Why would I suffer the same fate as you?"

Lucio's eyes bulged. "Uh-uh! You… you advocated for Ser Byrne. Felix saw it, Rachele saw it, I saw it, and the knight saw it too. That's four names to convict you. No, bitch, you're stuck on our ship. If it sinks, you drown with us."

Finally, Elysande bore her claws. This insubordination could not be excused any longer. She stood from her seat and let loose all her furies. "You know what really bothers me, Senator? The fact that you and your conspirators think us all equals. Felix threatened me to my face, you tried to make me do tricks like a dog, and Ser Byrne just professed his love to me as if I'd swoon for him like some worthless whore in a brothel. You may have auctoritas, but I'm the fucking Queen, and you will treat me with respect!"

"Royalty falls like us all," Lucio countered. "Pride is the fatal flaw of your kind across all species in the galaxy. If Caesar learns of your part in the Heirs of the Republic, you will be brought down the same as us."

"You're a damn fool. But that seems to be a consistent theme among your lot." Elysande observed. "Even if you and every single senator in Rome implicated me, what do you think would happen? Arresting me will end the Caesar-Bodewin alliance. The king will lose Mercia and the colossal army at my father's disposal. Do you think he would jeopardize that to punish me for a miniscule role in some limp-dick uprising? No! Not on your life. I'm fucking untouchable and you will address me as 'my queen!'"

Lucio went to object, but the queen overwhelmed him. Her ears could not suffer another second of his vile insubordination. "You're an ant!" she stomped on the ground with all her might. "An ant!" another stomp, "A fucking ant! A fucking ant!"

She had reduced Lucio into a bumbling mess, spazzing in his seat like a turtle stuck on its back. *Careful now, you don't want to kill him.* She, too, took a deep breath to calm herself, fixing her hair which had flown over her face. "Look, I didn't come here to intimidate you, but to extend an olive branch."

Lucio returned to some semblance of rational thought. "What are you scheming?"

"Not what I'm scheming, what Felix is scheming. He tells me Bryson Byrne's ascendancy to the Praetorian Elite is meant ease your takeover of the KOH. He assures me that Byrne is an 'insurance policy,' but I don't believe him. So, speak."

Lucio waved his wrinkly hands in the air. "I-I-uh, that's exactly what Felix told me. He's a republican! His word is true."

Elysande leaned over and rubbed her eyes. *So tired of late; am I just getting old?* Despite her mercy, Lucio decided to pluck her last nerves. "Here's the deal: if you don't tell me what I want to hear, then I walk to one of the other names implicated in the recording. A certain Quintus Longinus, commander of the Black Dogs, seems like a good backup plan. I saw the way you recoiled when he was named. He's a common man, a hard worker too by all accounts. He'll turn his back on a nobleman such as yourself in a heartbeat. One way or another, the Heirs will implode, but I'm giving you the chance to escape before the bomb goes off."

Lucio scowled, but he relented. "Byrne is under specific directions if he is allowed into the Elite. Being that close to the king at all times, his goal is to... kill Caesar."

*Good boy.* "Kill him? That's not a risk, it's suicide. If he tries to pull a stunt like that in Rome, he must know to save a bullet for himself."

Lucio licked his yellowed teeth. His sad eyes pleaded for her to stop inquiring. "Ser Byrne is a loyal knight, and I will never speak ill of him. We will never put one of our own in such overt danger."

"Enough stalling!" she demanded, slamming her fist down on the glass table. Pain marched vigilantly up her arm, but she did her best to mask it. "Spill it all on the floor, now."

"The Synths!" Lucio cried. "We know Caesar will be on the frontlines against the Synths."

"You're betting the whole conspiracy on war with a fairytale?"

"No, no, no." he said, collapsing from his chair. "We have- we have mercs on our payroll. They'd cut his fleet off on route to Grayspace. It would be a freak battle, and in that suddenness, Caesar would be a casualty."

Elysande, too, fell back onto the sofa, her bones relaxing as they sunk into the cushions. *Have Ser Bryson by the king's side during an unexpected battle. For all anyone knows, he fell victim to stray gunfire. Clever plan, indeed.*

# KENT (VIII)

"We missed you on the practice field yesterday." Tali said, her face unable to mask her contempt. Kent had expected this. It took him all the willpower he could muster to knock on the door of her suite in the basement of Unity College. Her room was small and practical, befitting the style of a Paladin. On top the desk next to her bed was a mountain of books, some written in the strange symbols of Godspeak. He considered asking her about the books to change the course of conversation, but why waste time delaying the inevitable?

"Lady Vikander called for me to attend her war council. You do recall the Vikanders? The family protecting us." He felt it necessary to remind her of the secrets she tried to keep from him. *She's as guilty as I am. I will not slouch for penance.*

"You sound like Atticus," Tali sighed. "Aethelwulf was going to let us grow independently from his own ambitions, but his petulant niece wants us entangled in another war with the Triumvirate. History tends to repeat itself, but only a fool will allow the course to happen again so quickly."

"But we have history on our side," Kent wagered. "The Triumvirate was a shock to the galaxy when it first emerged, but now we see the chinks in the war machine."

Tali raised her eyes in mock interest. "And what are those chinks, Ser Kent?"

He went to speak, but the words could not take form. Lady Rachel was a leader and orator, a strategist and inspirer. When she spoke, every promise felt inevitable. Kent may not have understood her plans of attack against the Triumvirate, but he would contribute all he could to see them carried out. *For the sake of the Paladin Order, the Triumvirate must be eradicated.*

Seeing the Paladin struggle, Tali decided to put his embarrassment to an end. "Anyway, I guess you didn't come here to discuss politics. What is it that you want?"

"I spoke to a Denvari named Saryn Malor at the war council. He's invited us for dinner on his ship tonight. His intentions are to meet the Zoltors…"

A sickness engulfed Tali's expression. "I'm familiar with the man. Saryn's made a living by selling his 'Syndicate' to whichever warlord bids the highest."

*Well, this is rough start.* Tali's people, the Insharai, were the sister race of the Denvari. They, along with the Enfari, had lived under Denvari supervision for as long as history had been recorded.

"He's expecting us tonight. I don't see what we gain by offending him."

"What do you care?" she countered, showing newfound bitterness.

"He possesses a formidable amount of power, as you say yourself. He has an interest in our people, and with that interest could come support. The potential rewards of indulging his curiosity heavily outweigh the risks." Kent said, astutely choosing not to mention that Rachel Vikander strongly recommended they attend. She trusted Saryn about as much as Tali did, but she recognized his influence over the Bloodlands. Rachel said she would be at the dinner too, which gave him some comfort.

"Is your plan to prop up Ariel and Marion like museum exhibits?"

"You want them to be figureheads for the new Order. They need experience in diplomacy, and what better practice than tonight with us by their side?"

Tali shrugged. "All right, fine, we'll go." She had a difficult time meeting Kent's eyes.

"Thank you. I'm sorry I haven't been around as often as I should. But once we've beaten this frigate, I promise to dedicate all my time to training them. I'm still a Paladin, through and through," he stated sincerely.

Tali, however, was unconvinced. "I'll hold you to it, Ser Kent. Just remember who your people are, and don't let animosity toward the past dictate your decisions in the present."

Night came around earlier than anticipated. He was unsure how to dress for the night, so Matiyala picked his clothes for him. In the end, he left the room wearing a black doublet lined with bright orange thread. The collar scratched at his throat incessantly. A long time ago, this was his frequent attire, whether it be at formal Paladin ceremonies or diplomatic meetings, but now he felt as unnatural as a wild animal in a cage. Matiyala insisted he looked "dapper," but Kent detected more than a hint of flippancy in her compliment.

Still, there was no time to concern himself over appearances. He exited the Republic Manor and headed for Unity College, where Tali was undoubtedly waiting for him. The night air was cool and breezy, but Kent was burning on the inside with nerves. He worried about how she would treat Lady Vikander. Tali was a Paladin, meaning it was against her code to create unwanted conflict, but tensions were boiling, and the slightest word misinterpreted could send her off.

The other mages stood outside one of the thin, column-shaped buildings of the college. Tali wore a white kimono with embroidered green leaves wrapped around the sleeves, while Marion and Ariel were given new clothes likely for the sole purpose of the dinner. Marion was dressed in a grass green doublet with small, eye-shaped buttons as white as snow. Over that he wore a light gray jacket with a pointed collar. Ariel wore a long, teal blouse and a black tie knotted like a ribbon hanging loosely around her neck. Her once wild hair was brushed to control some of the chaos.

"Are we ready to head out?" Kent asked, unsure of what else to say. Asking Ariel and Marion as to how their training was going seemed tactless.

"Did you arrange a ride?" Tali asked.

"Yes..." he said. "With Lady Rachel."

Tali smiled like a doll. "Grand. I wish you had told me earlier."

Aiming to change the subject, Kent tried to ask Ariel and Marion about how they were liking Old Ulthrawn, but he was mostly met with head nods or one-word answers. He expected this trepidation too. In his preparations to save the city, he had failed them as a mentor.

*They will see in time. I can't win them over with a single conversation.*

Rachel Vikander mercifully arrived moments later in her limousine. In the backseat with her was Captain Throd, as unpleasant as always. All four mages crowded in and off they went into the outskirts of Old Ulthrawn. The conversation inside was benign enough to suit the short drive, and Kent prayed that no one mentioned the word "Rome" for the rest of the night.

Outside the city, the nighttime sky dominated the long expanse of sand and dirt. The limousine hummed along a dusty road, unperturbed by anything that may have existed in the desolate reach of the Bloodlands. Kent thought they were traveling through some post-apocalyptic land, then realized they may be in the wake of some gigantic bomb that erupted who knows how many ages ago. After all, Laktannon's surface was infinitely scarred by the toys of warfare. He looked back to the city in the rearview mirror and wondered if Old Ulthrawn stood now where a crater would soon be.

. . .

Saryn Malor's ship appeared from nowhere on the road going down an endless void of blackness. Sharp red lights glowed through the windows like fireflies in the night sky. They gave off small allusions to the greater exterior of the ship, but other than that, Malor's home hauntingly disguised most of its form in the surrounding darkness.

The driver pulled over to the side of the road, parking the vehicle right next to Malor's ship. Captain Throd emerged first, surveyed the area, then allowed everyone else to get out. As soon as the limousine was empty, the hatch of the ship dropped and out came three guards suited in moonlit armor and helmets with sky-blue visors designed in a slant across the eyes. On each of their chests was the sigil of the Eclipse Syndicate. Behind them came Saryn Malor, wearing an opulent cape of violet satin clipped to his right shoulder and a blazer so bedazzled it appeared to be made of pure silver. He smiled slickly as his guests arrived, no doubt proud of his own ability to court them into coming.

"I knew you would not let me down, Ser Kent." Saryn said with open arms. "Are these the children of the Archmage?"

"They are Ariel and Marion Zoltor." Tali interrupted, allowing the twins to walk ahead. "I'm not entirely sure of the nature of your plans, Lord Saryn, but they will not be a part of tonight's entertainment."

The Denvari laughed off the comment. "Nonsense! What kind of host would I be if I made my guests do all the work?" He addressed Marion first, grabbing him by the forearm and shaking. It was the traditional greeting of human soldiers who shared the same rank, and the sight of it made Kent sick to his stomach. "Strong lad, very much fits the appearance of a prodigal son. You seem somewhat spooked by me."

Marion cringed slightly. "I've never met a Denvari. I lived on a Roman academy for all my life up until recently… Old Ulthrawn has led me to many first-time experiences."

"Ahh, I see." Saryn said, rubbing his fingers. "The ignorant eye tends to be the most easily enchanted."

Marion shook his head. "I never said anything was enchanting."

"Well, wait until you see what's inside my ship." Saryn turned his focus to Ariel. He grabbed her right hand, raised it to his lips, lightly kissed her fingers, and said: "I'm infinitely charmed, Lady Ariel."

Her large, ember eyes expressed neither charm nor disgust, just pure, unbiased bemusement. "What was that?" she asked aloud.

"A compliment." Saryn said, a smirk cutting across his face like a dagger. He invited everyone into the ship. "Before we go to the dining hall, I would like to show you my exhibits."

"And what are these exhibits?" Rachel asked dismissively. "Something incredibly lewd, I'd bet."

"Then you don't know me at all." Saryn said, walking backward. The main entrance of the ship was absurdly spacious, making Kent further question the actual dimensions of the Denvari's home. "I'm an adventurer of sorts, and with the passion of traveling comes the subsequent hobby of collecting. It's a measure of bragging, so to speak. I do hope you will indulge me."

"I'll come," Ariel said, rather quickly. Her insistence impelled Kent to join as well. Saryn escorted them down the main hall and through a door which had to be opened by a fingerprint scan. From there, they were welcomed into a dark room with hanging orbs lit with red and orange lava. The room was a maze of sorts, with glass displays of a variety of sizes mounted from the floor to serve as barriers. The first, which was on Kent's right, was a small display on an ornate gold podium. Within the glass confines, was a skeleton's head.

Its dimensions were freakishly large, with a long snout and gaping eye sockets on the sides of its head. The mouth was ginormous too, equipped with fittingly ferocious teeth. These features were suitable for some kind of wild beast. Of course, Kent was curious. "What kind of animal is this?" he asked.

"It's not an animal… it's a Khav warrior." Marion corrected.

"Good eye, sir." Saryn complimented. "For someone so naïve to the outside worlds, you sure spotted my Khav companion quickly."

"I read a book on them recently," he said, inspecting the case further. "An old friend suggested it to me."

"My compliments to the friend. I visited the Khav home-world many moons ago, dined with their Chieftain too. A fascinating race of people, really. I've never witnessed a culture so obsessed with blood and battle, yet so clever and intuitive with their mechanical engineering. Primal in one regard, yet advanced beyond my capacity of thought in another. A real tragedy their evolution had to end so… abruptly."

"The Hallyans needed them to end the second Planter outbreak," Marion continued. "They thought they could reduce the Khav to a single biologically engineered tool, but that tool was not easily stored away with after its purpose was served."

Saryn observed the glass furtively. "The Khav desired more than what their creators designed, and thus were punished heavily for their ambition."

"What are those bugs for?" Ariel asked, diligently studying the display. Kent too noticed the oval-shaped, eight legged bugs crawling around the skull and tickling its structure with their antennae. *Ugly creatures*, he declared, their red and black striped backs were grossly exotic.

"They eat the flesh from the carcass. If not for them, this ship would possess the incredibly miasmic aroma of a dead Khav."

Saryn took them further into the exhibit of curiosities. Kent, unaware of how far they traveled, looked back and could not find the door they entered though. Surrounding him on all sides were glass cases, each indistinguishable from the last. The low lights made it difficult to see what they held inside. Saryn was taking them through a glass labyrinth, but for what purpose?

"This here is one of my most prized possessions," he said, stopping at one of the larger cases. Kent peered inside and saw a hunk of metal that at first seemed mundane, but the glowing glyphs engraved on its surface stabbed him with unease. The metal piece, which was about the size of a child, was nebulous in shape, but its sharpened and disjointed ends suggested it was torn from a larger entity. Kent turned to Tali, and they shared a moment of eerie anticipation.

"Where is this from? Ariel asked."

"Halo, from one of my more recent travels to the edge of the known galaxy. The Commandant of Halo was generous enough to allow me to cut a piece from his brig, and so I have it on display."

"You've been to Halo? So you've seen the Tear?"

Saryn's eyes flashed "How could I not? Halo surrounds the Tear, locked in perpetual orbit of the one glimpse we have into another dimension. I have a picture of it too, if you want to see."

"What concerns do you have with Halo?" Kent inquired.

Saryn looked confused. "What do you mean? It's one of the greatest landmarks of the galaxy. It's perhaps the last gift we have left from the Immortals. I have no sinister motive, I assure you, just an adventurer's lust for the mysterious."

A giant framed picture hung from the wall beside the displayed piece of divine metal. Within the gold frame was the Tear, a dimensional portal from which the Immortals made their passage over a thousand generations ago. Crossing around the Tear like a turning ring was a massive structure of black iron known to the galaxy as Halo, a construction crafted by the Immortals themselves. On its surface was perhaps a billion intricate designs etched into every centimeter of the ring, its craftsmanship beyond the capability of mortal ambition. It was not just the defensive barrier between their dimension and whatever existed beyond the Tear, but art in its most otherworldly form.

"It's amazing." Ariel said, somewhat bewitched. "I've always wanted to go to Halo. Does it live up to its reputation?"

Saryn winked. "That, and then some. Through my experiences, I find that a beautiful thing, whether it be an artifact, a landscape, or even… a person, is always at its most mystical when admiring it with the naked eye. This picture means everything to me, but it's still not enough. My memories of Halo are perhaps my most prized possessions, but they will fade over time regardless of their value. This picture is the only concrete proof I have of my journey, of the life-changing experience that slowly grows fictional. It mocks me, like it knows my dependence."

"The experience was worth it though." Ariel stated, although the lightness in her tone suggested it was more of a question. "Even if you can't channel the memory exactly as it was, at least the moment still exists."

"It does," Saryn agreed. "This picture may remind me of what Halo looked like, but it does not capture the way my heart fluttered as I saw half the ring cross slowly over the Tear, or how I gasped for air as I caught a small glimpse into another reality. Never have I felt so small, like a speck of dust drifting through space. And yet, as I recall it, those feelings have become artificial. No matter how profound the experience, time will always numb it. But in the end, it's better to have the moment in a perpetually fleeting state than to never have it at all."

"Yes, well it is certainly framed well." Rachel interrupted. "If you would not mind hurrying things along, Lord Saryn, I have much to do apart from admiring memorabilia."

The Denvari nodded in consent. They were taken further into the museum and through a dark passageway bringing them to the dining hall. It was an opulent room with a pointed ceiling and portraits of landscapes all over the walls but not a window to be had. Kent was astounded by the magnetically white tablecloth and the oddly designed chairs looking like dark oak branches reaching toward the ceiling. In the center of the long rectangular table was a silver candelabra holding gray wax candles with blue flames alight at their wicks. Saryn had seemingly planned out the seating in advance, with himself at the head of the table, Tali to his left and Marion to his right, Kent next to Tali and Ariel next to Marion, and finally with Rachel on the other end.

Kent's eyes met Ariel's as they sat, but hers darted away upon contact. *A shame, after all the progress I made with her. Marion is a student of warfare; he must understand my struggle.*

"I have some very special wine from my homeland," Saryn said as his servants approached. "They say my people have the best orchards known to man. Although I value the virtue of humility, I must say even expectations that high are still an understatement."

With a voluptuous bottle in hand, a servant emerging from some secretive corridor first poured the grape-colored wine into the glass of the host. She then moved to Tali, Kent, and Rachel. When Ariel presented her cup, the servant turned to Tali as if seeking approval.

"She's not my mother!" Ariel objected, her cheeks flushed with embarrassment. When it was Marion's turn, he was not satisfied with the amount he was given.

"I want more," he demanded, and the servant obeyed, tipping the bottle over the rim of his sparkling glass. "Pour it to the top." Much to the servant's credit, she poured the wine right to the rim of the glass without a single drop landing on the tablecloth.

"I did not know I had a connoisseur of wine in my company. Perhaps I should have prepared one of my more precious bottles." Saryn said, smiling.

"I'm familiar with the vintage." Marion said before taking a rather large gulp of it. No one made to comment, so the son of Archmage drank peacefully and plentifully. *Neither of them is making a case for expert diplomacy thus far.*

"I do have one more artifact to show to you before dinner," Saryn said, snapping his fingers. A servant retreated into the backroom and stayed in secrecy for some time. The Denvari, tapping a finger to his lips, was reveling in how easily he could captivate his audience.

The servant returned holding a thin platter. She placed it in the center of the table and, after a dramatic pause, removed the lid. Kent suspected food, but he was not so lucky. An oddity of an object sat before him, not much larger than his own hand but blacker than the night sky. He had no idea what to make of it, but its presence alone made him shudder.

"Does anyone know what this is?" Saryn asked, tilting his head. His eyes analyzed the room, like a showman daring for a participant.

After some time, Tali spoke up. "It's a voidstar, a sacred relic for Enfari religious ceremonies. The most sacred piece, I believe." She grew tense, digging her fingernail into the tablecloth. "There's no need to present one of these cursed things tonight."

Saryn shook his head. "Oh, but there is. The voidstar is not just an object of worship for the Enfari, it's a passageway into the spiritual world. I've watched them speak through it... and I've heard a voice from the other side."

"How does it work?" Marion asked, finishing his glass of wine. Kent detected a sudden but subtle ringing in his ear. It resonated from the dark object, but since no one else said a word about it, he kept his complaints to himself.

"It's presence alone allows transportation into the unseen. That's why I keep it locked up, because now that it's out in the open, its aura possesses the entire room. The Enfari do the same, only uncovering the voidstar for times of worship."

"So whatever is on the other side can hear us." Marion said, in a slightly mocking tone. "I do hope the Immortals can hear me, as I have much to say to them."

"Can I touch it?" Ariel asked. Tali abruptly coughed, or was it meant to stifle something she was about to say? Regardless, Saryn granted her permission, and Ariel leaned in over the table. Kent's eyes could not keep away from the inconceivably dark object, his mind lost in its lack of dimension. As Ariel's bony finger went to poke it, he was convinced her whole hand would slip right into the void.

Her finger did not get sucked into an interdimensional hole. Instead, she graced a pointed edge with her forefinger and quickly took her hand away. "Chilling," she said, grinning. "Like a diamond deep in a cave."

"How do you find time to collect these curiosities?" Rachel asked, with a taste malevolence. She was growing sick of Saryn's evening of theatricalities. Kent did not want to keep the Zoltors in his company for longer than they had to be.

"War can be a lucrative line of work if you know how the game is played," Saryn stated. "The Eclipse Syndicate has made me a wealthy man, so much so that it's become a burden. You see, wealth, among many things, won't accompany me on my journey to the other side. And I don't plan on having a cent of it to my name the day my ticket is called. I have been given the rare means to do what I want when I want to. So, when the opportunity for adventure presents itself, I take it."

"You must have immense trust in your syndicate to let them run operations while you're away." Rachel noted.

"Why wouldn't I? Again, my wealth has granted me many advantages, one of those being the loyalty of my outfit."

The Tigress smirked. Whatever point she was going for, the Denvari was falling right into it. "Well, Lord Saryn, you've taught your soldiers that prosperity comes through treachery."

"And are you worried about the loyalty of your own subjects?" Saryn asked, his voice sincere and almost sympathetic. In the other room, muted sounds of kitchen activity made their way into the dining hall. The wicks of the candelabra continued to burn, their blue flames reflecting on everything but the voidstar.

"Should I be worried?" Rachel returned.

Malor leaned back into his chair. "You make the mistake of assuming it is money alone that keeps my soldiers loyal, but you have not asked yourself what the source of this wealth is." The Denvari raised a first in the air. "Victory. We have followers because we win. True loyalty is only tested when the company tastes defeat, and not a singular roadblock, but a series of misfortunes. When the followers start to become disillusioned with their leader, then betrayal is at its most enticing. I accepted a long time ago the Eclipse is as strong as it is based on the fickle nature of success, can you say the same?"

"My people are united on the principles of retribution," Rachel countered. "That is why war with the Triumvirate is necessary; it's why we will win."

Saryn's eyes widened with delight. "And what happens if the victories are not as plentiful as you proposed?"

"You and Lord Vikander have made major strides in uniting the Bloodlands," Tali said before Rachel could retort. The dinner was doomed to get worse from here. "Why risk jeopardizing the peace you have created for an impossible war?"

Rachel shook her head. "Because peace cannot be obtained while the Triumvirate still dominates the galaxy. Ask Ser Kent, he knows mages will never be safe so long as Rome's registration act is implemented."

*Serios save me*, Kent begged.

"Is this true?" Tali asked. "Tell me, what is to be gained by more deaths?" The Zoltors were staring lasers through him too. He recalled the Archmage knighting him before hundreds of other mages in the Elemental Hall, and how the day had once been the best of his life. Caella was right by her brother's side. *The Wildflower, blooming over everything and everyone else.*

"It's not as simple as you make it sound." Kent started, speaking slowly to keep his temper down. "We won't be safe if the Inquisition maintains its alliance with Rome. Do you think Zakareth will allow for a new Paladin Order? The answer is an obvious 'no.' Of course I hate the Inquisition for dividing the Order and destroying it, but don't pretend like we can live peacefully together."

"You would prefer to have war. You want to continue the cycle of violence between mages?"

"No, that's not what I want, but it is the necessary option so long as some mages pay servitude to the Triumvirate."

"And what of Ariel and Marion?" Tali asked again.

Kent groaned. "What of them? They are the children of the Archmage, and I will gladly give my life for them, but let's not conflate fantasy with reality. As of now, they won't be inspiring anyone to join the Order. Rachel Vikander is the leader we need. Once we defeat the Triumvirate, then maybe they will be old enough to more seriously assume the mantle of their father."

Tali frowned. "I'm disappointed by your lack of conviction. Do you remember nothing of your studies? How can you so easily disregard the virtue of diplomacy?"

"And I'm disappointed by your naivety," he retorted. "But now that our grievances are out in the open, I must say-"

An ear-piercing sound of broken glass cut through the dining hall, causing everyone to leap from their seats. Kent searched around the perimeter to discover the source of the noise, his hand gripping the hilt of his Immortech sword. Feverish, he looked and looked and looked, only to find the answer to be right in front of him.

Ariel, hunched over, gripped a sharpened piece of the shattered remains of her plate. Her ember eyes, larger than ever before, flickered with the flames of the candelabra. Her head twisted to her left side in a ghastly way, her white teeth were bare like that of a starving animal.

"Ariel..." Kent started. Her unnerving presence caused him to choke on his words. "What's wrong?"

The daughter of the Archmage leaned back in her chair, a marionette smile strung along her face. "Oh nothing, Ser Kent. Don't worry about me." Methodically, she put her finger to her neck. "I can feel my blood pumping, my heart thumping. I'm so terribly nervous, I hope it does not show. Are you not the same?"

Kent's own heart skipped a beat. Her words sounded vaguely familiar, but his memory dodged the source. "Why?" he asked no one, caught in a stationary retreat.

Her stare on him was unblinkingly, her eyes starving for approval. "You say it's natural to be frightened before your first battle, but this is not fright, Ser Kent, oh no. I'm purely excited, no, enthralled to deal the final blow to the wannabe King in Rome."

She looked to the ceiling and her expression brightened with wonderment. That face was undeniable, like a mask disguising a demon. The memory was returning, like a dormant poison. He had merely covered an infected wound with a rag. "I gaze up into the sky and I see the moon is as red as a rose, surely a promising sign from the Immortals. This is thrilling, Ser Kent! You've taught me so well, and I promise I won't let you down. Do you think poets will write songs of this glorious day?"

*Darby*, Kent confessed, *how does she know?*

Ariel grinned fully but falsely, staring deep into his sickly soul. Her voice was higher pitched, mockingly so. When Kent looked into her eyes, he could sense she reveled in his hungering anguish, as if his rage fed her. Suddenly, her smile shifted into utter fear. She began to hyperventilate, each breath straining her lungs. Marion grabbed her hand, but it did nothing to calm her.

"What's that in the sky?" she exclaimed, eyes rolling. "Flying ships like drops of blood. Serios save us! They're raining death from above. There's no cover, no protection. We've been tricked! Duped! Look at the bodies, I see my friends turning into ash in the breeze. This wasn't supposed to happen! Gods, Ser Kent! What are we going to do?"

The Paladin was speechless, his heart served bloody red on the plate before him. *She's digging it out of me!*

Ariel turned her attention to her own feet. "I seemed to have cut my knee on something, silly me." She slouched in her chair, her eyes, wet and sorrowful, begging Kent for help. "It was green before, now it's brown and spewing all over my leg. Why are we hiding, Ser Kent? Other Paladins may still be out there, and we're cowering in a cave. Please, while I still have the strength to fight. Don't ignore me just because I'm at my end."

"Silence!" Kent swore, instinctually grabbing a dinner knife. "You will speak no further lies."

His threat went unnoticed.

"My legs are limp..." Ariel whispered, vacantly. "My arms are slowly decaying to death's grip." She coughed harshly, snapping her neck at the unexpected shift in momentum. "My heart no longer thumps, my blood no longer pumps... like it once did. I wanted a hero's death, and you deprived me of it. Why?" A sorrowful sigh floated from her lips. "I never thought you could be so afraid."

Her body relaxed, neck craned upward, and her shoulders slouched. With her last breath, she whispered, "What will be our song, Ser Kent?"

"And who will listen?" he replied, so delicately that no one else could hear. He wiped the tears away from his eyes. *I'm sorry Darby, I failed you. I failed everyone on the Blood Moon. My soul should be in ashes with yours.*

A morbid silence assumed the table. The whole room darkened, or was it merely his imagination? Regardless, Kent could not remove his stare from Ariel, and yet he sensed the condemning eyes of all those around him. *Let them ridicule me!*

"Is this one of your sorcerer's tricks." Saryn asked, insulted. Ariel's eyes closed and she fell asleep in her chair.

"I don't know what's wrong with her," Tali said. "Marion, get the plate out of her hand."

"How the fuck does she know!" Kent roared. He directed his rage toward Tali. "What did you tell her? Why are you turning them against me?"

"Calm down, Kent." Tali commanded. "She's talking nonsense, isn't she?"

"So this is how it ends!" he declared, wildly. "You're a deceptive one, you know that. And yet, you still expect me to trust a viper even after she's struck me once before."

"NO!" Ariel boomed, awake again. She grabbed a handful of her gold and silver hair, tears pouring from her eyes. "Is this what you want from her? A wildflower she is not, but you refuse to see it for the better. Oh, you lustful monster you, creating honest intentions for lascivious rewards. Why do you hate Zaki so much?"

Ariel put a finger to her chin in dramatic contemplation, her eyes raw and red and welling with tears. "Because he killed your flower? No! Too noble. It's jealousy, I think. The Enfari plucked her before you ever could, forcing you to sit alone and imagine your way to the second-best thing. And then she wilted, and then the whole galaxy lost their favorite flower, and then you never got to *fuck* her."

Something ripped into his palm. He looked down at Rachel Vikander prying his cold fingers off the sharpened edge of the dinner knife. "Kent! You're bleeding!" she exclaimed. It made no matter to him. He let his blood spill over the tablecloth.

A handful of Saryn's servants rushed through the door, grabbed Ariel by the arms and legs, and hoisted her from the room, all while she screamed her head off. Tali was at their heels, and Marion remained standing at the table, utterly incredulous.

Just as Ariel's voice was almost completely gone, Kent managed to catch one last declaration. "You're a monster! You have no right to live!"

# ELYSANDE (X)

The Temple of Rhomigius was the largest and most intricate of all the sacred palaces of the KOH. The glistening marble pillars outside the temple supported the sprawling top balcony over the iron doored entrance. The temple consisted of three, brick-shaped buildings conjoining around a central structure with a domed roof that peeked slightly above the rest. Atop every building were crenellations in which the great Immortals of legend stood mightily and watched vigilantly over the city of Rome.

Elysande was inside the temple, standing at the altar with her husband and craning her neck upward at the dome-shaped roof. Staring back at her was Rhomigius himself, spear in hand and bronze cloak flapping in the painted breeze. He was depicted in action, with his spear merely inches away from penetrating the heart of Extormitus, the betrayer who created the Planter virus and used it to nearly wipe out all known life. After defeating the Planters, Rhomigius created Last Bastion with his own Immortech, so all peoples of the galaxy could stay united even after the Immortals departed. At least, that was the story told in human fables for the past thousands of years.

She considered the tales of the Creation Wars engaging in a purely fantastical way, recognizing them as fiction and, probably, devoid of fact. *Every race thinks their favorite Immortal united the galaxy and conquered the Planters. But we're all wrong, aren't we?*

From the altar, Caesar studied the three naves and flanking aisles furtively. In just days, the temple would be filled with thousands of people in celebration of the New Year. But before that were the finals of the Gladiator Games. Depending on the outcome, Ser Bryson Byrne may be standing on the altar beside the king, wearing the brilliant golden armor of the Praetorian Elite.

As the king and queen awed at the artistry that richly decorated every inch of the temple in the forms of its slick architecture, painted walls depicting the sacred stories of humanity, and hanging tapestries tributed to the patrician families of Rome, a rumbling occurred in the sacristy, disturbing their respective trances. From behind the altar stumbled a gray-haired man dressed in brilliantly white robes. Swaying back and forth on his neck was an ornamented spearhead so heavy that it could have been responsible for the arch in the old man's spine.

His bushy eyebrows raised and long brow wrinkled as he saw them waiting for his audience. He was Dareo Cossus, an unremarkable name unbefitting of the rather remarkable title of Pontifex Maximus, the absolute head of the Church of the KOH. "Uh, apologies, my king and queen. I was not expecting visitors. Not that you are unwelcomed guests. It's my pleasure, truly."

"We did not mean to burst in on you, Your Holiness, but I was awarded a small respite from my work, so I thought it best to check in personally and ask if there was anything you needed before the New Year's mass tomorrow." Caesar said, ever so caring.

*Tomorrow?!* The revelation startled her as if a ghost had risen from the temple's hallowed grounds. *Tomorrow is my day of judgement, but how will I be judged?*

"Everything is in line for a perfect ceremony," Cossus said. "I don't dare to predict the will of the Immortals, but I suspect Rhomigius shall look down upon our tribute fondly."

"I do hope so," Caesar said, gazing around. Tending to the statues built into the walls around the aisles were the flamines, the order of priests under direct supervision of the Pontifex Maximus. "Your priests do an excellent job every year making the Temple look its most divine. I wish I could attend these masses regularly."

"Rhomigius made you king for a reason. Whatever expectations he has set for you, I'm sure you've met them," the Pontifex Maximus spoke, ever the kiss up. He paid the queen no such flattery.

Elysande brushed her wavy red hair with her pale hand. The scarring had mostly subsided, but black and blue marks covered her fingers and knuckles. If she had worn gloves all the time, Caesar would have caught on to something strange. So, naturally, she confessed. *It was a slip with the bench press bar. A freak accident. It shan't happen again.*

Gaius Caesar grabbed a chalice sitting atop the marble altar. He tipped it upside down to reveal there was nothing left inside. The act was befitting of a bored child, but utterly abnormal for the King of the KOH. It was as if he was daring Cossus to speak up. "Tell me, what do the scriptures say about the Synths?"

"Not much, other than they are unholy abominations," Cossus grumbled. "Grayspace is a kind of Hell in itself, and anything making a home out there a demon."

"So our conflict with the Synths is a holy war?" Elysande asked, sticking her tongue out slightly and smiling. She enjoyed poking at the tunneled logic of holy men. The current Pontifex Maximus was mostly a stranger to her, as he had managed thus far to be the first in a while to avoid any serious political or financial scandals.

"Well, in a way, yes." Cossus stated, ardent in his beliefs.

Caesar interrupted before she could speak again. "What she's alluding to is a request I have for Your Holiness. With our war against the unknown imminent, I would ask you to bless our legions in the Forum as they embark into Grayspace. My hunch is it would bring them courage, and at this point I would prefer to leave no advantage untaken."

"Yes, Your Majesty. It would be my honor!" Cossus bit his lip and pondered something in his mind. He walked out from the altar table and descended the huge row of steps down to the nave. Gaius and Elysande received his unspoken invitation to follow.

"If I may state a recommendation, Your Majesty," he started, pacing quickly for an old man. The flamines around the pews stopped their cleaning to watch the king and Pontifex Maximus, two nearly deified persons in themselves, interact with one another. "Perhaps clerical representation in your inner council will facilitate the word of the Immortals reaching your governance." Cossus shot a glare at his priests, who promptly returned to work.

"Ah-huh. And I don't suppose you see yourself as that perfect representation?"

"I do!" Some cheeriness returning to his voice. *Little does he know he's a rabbit playing with serpents.* "The Pontifex Maximus was a chief political advisor to every Gasardi king and queen. And in the Republic, those who possessed my title before me were relied upon by the consuls for their spiritual wisdom. This is not a request based in ambition, as I would be nothing more than a messenger for Rhomigius."

"Am I not the King of Rome?" Caesar asked.

Cossus' furry brow narrowed: "Why yes, obviously you are."

"Then who would be more capable in understanding and interpreting the word of Rhomigius than myself?" Caesar's gaze sharpened. His footsteps echoed louder throughout the temple, while the priest's shuffling seemed to have quieted.

"I would never dare question Your Majesty's connection with the Immortals." Cossus stumbled. "I was only suggesting-"

The king patted the priest on his nimble shoulder, placating the conflict immediately. "I value the word of the Immortals more than any man or woman on my council. Sometimes, admittedly, I do struggle with interpreting their messages. Fortunately, if I ever need a translator, I will know exactly where to find one. Here, in the Temple of Rhomigius."

The Pontifex Maximus bowed his head in defeat. Church bells rang throughout the spacious halls in apparent declaration of Caesar's victory. They approached the threshold of the great iron doors, where Sutorian in his golden armor stood sentry. Beside him were two other Praetorian guardsmen. Given the information Drusilla told her, not one of them could be trusted. The old guard's face expressed a morbid hesitation similar to when he reported Galla's death.

"You seem to have something on your mind, Sutorian." Caesar observed. "Out with it, then. My hour of holiness is over for the day."

"Yes, Your Majesty. I have some, well, odd news." His gray eyes flashed at the priest.

"Whatever it is, you can say it before the Pontifex Maximus." Caesar assured him.

"It involves the three frigates sent to neutralize Fyrossia. Two of the three have continued their journey into Grayspace, but one has gone missing."

"How does a bloody frigate go missing?" Elysande asked. Her brother was on one of those ships. Maybe he had something to do with it.

"I only just received word from Censor Nakamura, who himself got the message secondhand from an officer. He has the officer in the council room. If you will follow me, we can speak to her in person," Sutorian advised.

King Caesar sighed, unusually, then turned to Cossus to say, "This is where we depart for now. Do say a prayer for me, or several if you think they'll help."

A female officer stood before the King and Queen of the KOH, arms behind her back, shoulders up, and gaze straight ahead. She reminded Elysande vaguely of Liscinia, *just less... alluring*. Shota Nakamura, Kassa Savon, and Tullius Caesar were in their company too. Her father, Reynard, was fortunately elsewhere. *For the best, no doubt. He'd be a nervous wreck worrying about his prodigal son.*

The woman cleared her throat to begin. "Forgive me for the disturbance, my king and queen. I work in the Astro-communications sector, and we just received a transmission from a General Antonius Marko. He's captaining one of the frigates which took part in the assault on Fyrossia. Based on an urgent report, his ship has broken off from the path to Grayspace."

"Tell us the report." Caesar commanded. The skin under his eyes appeared heavier today. Although maintaining his kingly aura, her husband appeared uncharacteristically worn down. *Almost makes him seem normal.*

"Mages, Your Majesty." The officer was embarrassed by this answer. "An informant leaked to the army that mages were hiding on a nearby military academy. I believe it's called Romulus. Instead of having all three frigates investigate, Antonius was chosen to go alone."

"But still," Admiral Savon interrupted. She was dressed in her dark blue naval tunic. On her face shined a bluish bruise from her duel with Magnus Caesar. "A whole frigate to search for a few mages? Half the crew would overflow an off-world academy."

"They aren't just any mages," the officer began. "In his report, Marko states they are believed to be Zoltors. And they aren't alone."

A screeching silence assumed the room. Elysande dug her nails into her palms. Flashes of Fredrick and Boltof danced in her head. By the end of the siege of Erron, their once strong, youthful bodies had been depleted to charred bones. *Every Zoltor died on Spyre. Not a single one of those abominations should be left alive. And if they are, then the Inquisition failed at its primary objective.*

"First Synths, now Zoltors." Tullius chortled. "What's this galaxy come to?"

*It's come to shit,* Elysande thought. *These past few weeks have ascended all restraints of normalcy. When one nightmare comes to an end, many more appear on the horizon.* She dreaded to think what surprises waited for her in the new year.

Caesar rubbed his chin. "Fyrossia is too far out for direct communication. He must've sent you a message via relay station."

"Yes, my king. The message was sent by one of his scouts. There are very few functioning relay stations in Fyrossian space, so it could have taken the scout days to reach one."

"And potentially several more for the message to make it to Rome," Caesar pondered. "And there have been no other reports of this frigate?"

"Not one, sir. We tracked the distance between Fyrossia and Romulus, and it would require a few days' travel for a frigate to cover that kind of space. We should receive another message from Marko shortly."

"This is assuming that the operation went as planned?" Elysande asked. Depending on the powers they possessed, even two mages were a danger to them all. *And if they truly are Zoltors, it's safe to assume the worst.*

"Yes, my queen," the officer admitted. "Depending on the success of the operation."

"I can also send an alert to all our people in Fyrossian space to be on lookout," Kassa suggested. "This is peculiar though. One would think a rogue frigate would garner some attention."

Caesar tapped the desk methodically. "Regarding these mages, does Marko have any evidence they could be Zoltors?" Even hearing the horrible name spoken aloud made Elysande shiver.

"The informant Marko spoke to claims to have seen one in person. A group of mages apparently found a girl on Prisilla. The boy, as I'm told, has been hiding on the military academy for his whole life."

This perked up the Commandant. "And who in the Hell is this informant?" Tullius asked. "Sounds like a trap to me."

"Regretfully, the message does not say," the officer answered. "From what I gather, whoever the informant is, he or she is going by a codename."

"So one of my generals derailed a whole frigate under the word of an unidentified informant?" Caesar asked, brushing a hand through his cool, brown hair.

"The informant could have pictures of the Zoltors?" Kassa offered, but even she sounded doubtful.

A possibility occurred to Elysande. "Inquisitors assisted in the invasion of Fyrossia. Perhaps this is one of their schemes. Who knows what powers they possess? For all we know, General Marko is under some spell. Bring Cira into the Palazzo now! She'll need to answer for this."

"That won't be necessary." Caesar assured the council, but Elysande hardly felt any better by it. In fact, she truly felt like a child again, sensing the skin-crawling presence of the Archmage outside her home. *Immortals! Don't I have enough on my plate?!*

"Admiral Savon," the king began. He required time to gather his thoughts. A cold wind passed through the council during the perplexing silence. "Put every ship on high alert for this frigate. In fact, send a squadron of your best star-splitters out into the zone too. And if by some exceptional turn of events even one Zoltor is found alive, they must all be brought back to Rome unharmed."

*What do you mean 'unharmed?' Obliterate them in space!*

Kassa saluted: "Hail, Caesar!"

Gaius appeared frozen as he considered the rest of the council. *He's sluggish, but why?* "If we may conclude this session for today, I have a million other things I need to get done before nightfall."

the king said, removing himself from the table and stalking off to his own secluded section of the Palazzo Reale.

. . .

The queen sat on the edge of her bed, wearing a white towel. Her skin was moist and hot from her shower. She came from her gym, hoping in vain that the meditative ways of exercise would somehow guide her to the right answer. But no matter how hard she thought, she seemingly slipped further away from the truth.

The New Year was but hours away, and there was no way she could avoid it.

*If I do nothing, Bryson Byrne will win the Gladiator Games. I saw Tullius' face. His son is damaged. Byrne is too deft a fighter to lose, especially with his loyalty to the Heirs. If the roles were reversed, Magnus' ego could have been his downfall, but Byrne won't make that mistake.*

*If I do nothing, Bryson Byrne WILL be in the Praetorian Elite. He's built up too much auctoritas from his matches to be denied. Then what? He'll kill Caesar in a fluke naval attack. A good, clean kill. Natalia will resist the Heirs of the Republic, but it won't matter. Father will eventually see the Caesar cause as lost and gladly switch over, or else take his Crimson Armada to Laktannon and carve out his own empire. A war, certainly, but a comparably smaller one. But then, I'm at the mercy of the Heirs. They've promised my family freedom from the dangers of our status, but how can I expect them to fulfill their end of the bargain once they've gained what they want?*

Elysande grabbed a bottle of pills by her bedside and shook the container in her hand. The rattle of it gave her some weird sense of pleasure. If she fed these to Ser Byrne tonight, his insides would be a mess tomorrow. Even Magnus with his limp could conquer him in such a sickly state. Then, things would remain somewhat the same, but she would always feel the shiver of impending retribution from the Heirs. If their numbers were truly at the scale that Felix wanted her to believe, she would be endangering her family even further.

*It's all the king's fault!* Elysande concluded. *If Caesar had named his heir, we would not be in this position. Natalia may be his first daughter, but my children are the products of the most formidable alliance in the KOH. The Bodewin-Caesar relationship must stand. Natalia isn't a bad girl, but I hate her because of him! If only he could have committed to his position as king, and not clung to his fetish as conqueror.*

She remembered eating breakfast with Julia in the backyard a few weeks ago. Lance kept to himself, but she cherished their small interactions around the house. Both of her children had been sidelined since then. Fighting for their lives had allowed her to forget about being a mother. Did they hate her for this neglect? Did her actions to protect only put them more at risk?

A rock grew in her throat as she swallowed. Her eyes welled with warm water, but she promptly stifled the oncoming rush of self-pity.

She grasped the life of her husband in her hands. She wanted to constrict her fingers, to strangle the soul from his body, but something stopped her. *Remorse? No. Never.* Caesar could die, and she would prosper from it. The Heirs would wear themselves thin trying to contain the people of the KOH. They loved their king, for whatever reason, so convincing them to overthrow his decades of labor for a new Republic could result in their own destruction. Then, Elysande could sweep in when her enemies were all but corpses, using the Crimson Armada to take Rome and establish her own Queendom.

*What a sight that would be...*

She dressed slowly, as if in meditation. Her commitment to one path or the other changed with every article of clothing she put on. The bottle of pills was on her bed. She sighed, reached for them, pulled her hand away as if she touched something scalding hot, but eventually forced herself to pick it up and store it in her back pocket.

She left her bedroom on nervous feet and paced methodically down the hallway. Passing Lance's bedroom, muffled sounds of whatever he was watching on television broke through the white walls. She leaned against the wall and considered knocking on the door to check on him, but it served no purpose but to further delay her decision. *Make up your mind and own it. Until then, you do not deserve peace.*

Outside, a storm brewed. Sounds of thunder echoed distantly. The light patter of raindrops danced on the roof of her estate. The natural music of it drifted her consciousness into the wild outdoors. While walking through the dark kitchen, she felt alone with the tempest. An unexpected crack of lightning exposed that, truly, she was not alone.

The fierce shadow of a perched eagle casted against the flash of white tempestuous light. Startled, Elysande nearly screamed. But who would answer? Ser Dance was elsewhere, taking care of the nasty business that was Mercurio Shade. It may have been an assassin sent by the Heirs, paid to eliminate her with her purpose now served. But guessing would get her nowhere.

Desiring to dissipate any fear of the unknown with the weapon of clarity, Elysande rushed to the light switch by the threshold, unleashing scintillating brightness over the whole room. The abrupt change burned her eyes, but when they adjusted, she saw not a fierce eagle, but a broken man.

King Gaius Julius Caesar considered her coldly. Hunched over in his tall chair, Caesar aged ten years in one day. Placed in front of him was a wine glass filled to the top and a larger bottle that was half empty.

"I was not expecting you home, my king." she said, slowly approaching the table but unsure if she should sit. It was a peculiar sight to see the eagle in his nest.

Caesar traced his finger along the rim of the glass. There was something vacuous in his normally sharpened brown eyes. "Ha! 'My king.' Many a man and woman say it through gritted teeth, but none in such a patronizing fashion."

"Shouldn't you be out in the Forum enjoying the final hours of the year?" Elysande asked, taking a seat. "It's been a stressful month, you deserve it."

"I'm tired. I don't have it in me anymore to work all day and party throughout the night. You used to come with me to the city center on the eve of the new year. Julia and Lawrence used to love the fireworks over the Colosseum. Do you remember? Now, they're strangers to me, as is Natalia. As are you, come to think of it."

Elysande smiled nostalgically. Julia used to sit on her shoulders and squeal whenever a new round of fireworks launched over the city. "Work gets the better of us. They're good kids, although I'm a biased observer."

Caesar took a sip of wine. The conversation stimulated his mind back to full capacity. "You've always been honest with me?"

Her gaze shifted away. "Right…"

"Inform me then: what do you think of a war against the Synths?"

Elysande shrugged. "I'm honestly speechless."

"My feelings exactly," Gaius laughed. "It's a farce, a mockery even. A decade and a half ago, we won the most expansive war the galaxy has ever known, and now we're fighting myths. And all based on what? Some pictures and the recounts of a few soldiers. You know what? General Tarquinius has not reported one other sighting of Synths. We could search that sector for months, probably years, and not find anything. Then, I return to Orbis with nothing but embarrassment."

"So why the spectacle? What's wrong with peace under the Triumvirate?"

"Our people want war. It's what unifies us better than anything else. We're creatures of conflict. If we can't find it externally, rest assured we'll find it internally. How do you think the Civil War started? I refused to accept a demotion from the Republic, and my efforts to stand my ground launched the largest conflict since the Creation Wars."

"It's more complicated than that," she proposed. "Ambition was punished beneath the Roman Republic, while you've rewarded it."

"True, and how long until someone comes for my crown?" Caesar asked. "Too much safety makes people search for risks. If there is nothing but peace and prosperity in the KOH, someone will make it their mission to disrupt it. Ademar Vikander was my greatest friend before the war, but we mutually abandoned our years of bonding to raise our stakes in separate systems of government. I still think of him often, and how things may have been different had I been complacent."

Elysande was ready to slap him across the face. "It sounds to me like you want to blame your personal problems on everyone but yourself. Is that why you came to the villa tonight? To vent to me?"

"It is a personal problem; I'll agree with you there." Another bolt of lightning struck outside, illuminating the tops of the cityscape like metallic fingers pointing to the sky. "I miss the thrill of battle. Tullius misses it too, as does your father. I've never felt more alive living day to day on the run. I loved Ademar and many of the officers on the side of the Republic, but I loved besting them in wit and warfare even more."

"And your hope is that war with the Synths will resurrect those days?"

"It's a hope, but a pathetic one," Gaius admitted. "The war theater in Grayspace will be a parody of the one that made me king. I fought hard for this position, and yet the job itself is terribly dull. I'm a soldier dressed like a politician. You've experienced the same."

"We're destined for permanent discontent," she said. "No one makes it to the positions we have without being grotesquely ambitious. It's a drug, really, and only death will cure us." *Even with the king and the Heirs of the Republic exterminated, I won't find peace. There will always be another hill to climb and another adversary aiming to stop me along the way.*

They sat in silence for a while, the years they lived with one another stacked between them like piles of books. Elysande felt the bottle of pills in her pocket. She grinded her teeth. Again, another layer of mud atop the right answer.

Without warning, Caesar reached into his jacket and pulled something from his breast pocket. "Going off to war again has reminded me of my mortality." He handed Elysande what appeared to be a document. On the line at the bottom was the signature of one Natalia Caesar.

"I would hate to die in Grayspace without an heir to the kingdom."

"Gaius!" Elysande gasped. "How did this happen?"

"Natalia has had this in her mind for a while now. She has no interest in ruling as queen. She wants to play a role in the kingdom, but not on that grand of a scale," Caesar said. "Lawrence is my heir, indisputably."

Elysande's head fluttered, her heart stopped, her blue eyes gaped so far open that they risked popping out. She flexed her shoulders and mountains came crumbling down. She could have kissed her husband, but the idea of doing it in private was so foreign that the desire quickly subsided. And yet, she looked at her king in a different light. He did have a conscience after all.

The queen's feet slid from her chair. She turned away from her king and marched from the dining room, grabbing her coat and heading for the exit.

"Where are you going?" Gaius' voice echoed.

*You've never cared before, so don't ask now.*

# ARIEL (VII)

The Cliffs of Norin jutted from the mainland like the teeth of the largest beast myth and fable could conjure, long dead but immortalized in the grounds it once roamed. The cliffside was bumpy with hundreds of uneven rocks beaten relentlessly for centuries by ocean waves and winds. Hollowed, darkened caverns were abundant, while windswept boulders laid out on the sandy shore expressed the formidable girth the ridge once possessed. From the bottom, its curve slowly angled inward to the peak; perfect for climbing.

Ariel started her ascent from the shore of an abandoned bay. Kent Kentoshi, the Tigress of Old Ulthrawn, and a handful of her guards in their vizard masks were right beside her. They left their off-road jeep in the sand and never turned back. Rachel waved Ariel on, letting her lead up the path. Unabated, the daughter of the Archmage set a quick pace for the rest of the company to follow.

As the climb transpired, Kent fell several yards back and was forced to play catch-up, his feet clearly untrusting of the narrow and steep passageway. Ariel enjoyed the challenge of navigating the routes nature herself carved within the cliff, it forced her to stay alert in case a deceptive pebble slid from her feet. She had read about "hiking" years ago in one of her travel books. Prisilla, being a space station, lacked any natural landscapes, making something so tremendous as a cliff just as mysterious to her as magic. When Rachel offered to take her to Norin, she jumped at the opportunity, although a veiled part of her was intimidated.

Her confidence rose as she climbed. She looked out into the crystalline blue sea, but it was something on the sandy coastline that caught her attention. A dozen rusted spaceships lay moored on the beach. They did not appear to be damaged by battle, merely left to rot for no discernable reason.

"What's wrong with those ships?" she asked Rachel. "Can't they fly?"

"No, they only sink." the Tigress answered, right on her tail. "Old Ulthrawn was once a simple fishing village. Fishermen would attach nets to the backs of their ships and dive into the ocean to catch fish. Old Ulthrawn only became what it is because other bigger cities were too preoccupied with annihilating one another."

Rachel had warmed up to them a great deal since their first encounter, especially with Kent. She had confided with him the whole way to the Cliffs of Norin, whether it be talking strategies about the battle to come or bickering about her uncle's unwillingness to take action against the Triumvirate. It was good that Rachel had so much to say, for she and Kent had hardly spoken since her "outburst."

Ariel barely recalled a thing from the night with Malor after he had introduced the voidstar to the table. From what Marion told her, she had given Kent a verbal thrashing, that she recalled memories of the Druin's past she could not possibly have known. Tali concluded she may have been under someone else's control, that the cut on her neck from Slorne may have allowed him to take over her mind, somehow. Ariel was skeptical, but she kept her opinions to herself, not wanting anyone to know of her conversations with the Inquisitor.

*At least he was honest with me, while those "looking out for me" have been anything but.*

Kent had forgiven her, at least verbally, but they were detached. Ariel was sorry in a way, but Kent was being overly dramatic. And yet, her memories of the night may have been nonexistent, but the feelings, the foreign despair, lingered. As if she saw him with eyes that were not her own, the Paladin's presence filled her with untraceable mistrust.

He somehow turned up to her training sessions less than before, in fact she was certain he never would have come on the hike if not for Rachel.

This adventure was a needed break from everything in Old Ulthrawn. The city could be oppressively congestive and gray. It reminded her of the Underbelly in its staleness. The fresh and salty smell of the ocean was a welcomed sensation to her skin. The bright sun dancing vibrant white light on the waves treated her eyes so long as she did not stare for too long. Even the sight of old boats moored to a dockside was oddly exciting. The wild outdoors was her true home, and she hated the idea of having to return to that cramped prison everyone else called the Republic Manor.

She and her brother were not allowed to stray away from the Manor, and the time they got to spend outside was for sparring or meditating in the fields of Unity College. Ariel cherished that time, as she loved the deeply green lawn and the exotic aromas of the garden. She coveted the chance to improve in her swordplay and grew to appreciate the stillness of mediation. Tali insisted meditation would be her guide to discovering her powers, which was Ariel's only motivation to try it. But as time went on, meditating became a frequent part of her day, training or not. The silence was intoxicating; her demons slowly befriending her through listening and understanding.

As she hiked up the cliff, the repetition of her breathing, along with the pleasant sound of wet rocks crunching beneath her feet, carried her into a trance. She thought of her father, most of his stories coming from Tali. If she was to be believed, the Archmage himself was trained by her from childhood. Across the stars, he was known as *Stormcaster*, conjuring clouds of thunder and bolts of lightning at a whim to defeat any evil that may have emerged to challenge him. She and Marion barked with questions as their minds boiled over with imaginings of their late father. In response, Tali sternly insisted that a Paladin's priority in any conflict was to find a peaceful resolution. Despite the Archmage's unfathomable capabilities, Tali swore he never used his powers to their fullest potential.

Ariel doubted she would have such restraint. In the deepest lair of her mind, she dreamt of returning to Prisilla with her new powers. Would the pearls try to arrest her? Would Kagen and his cronies offer peace? Would all her wrongdoers kneel and beg for forgiveness? It made no difference, for they were all as good as dead. Especially Silver Wulf. He must have been dead, but it nagged her that she never made certain of it.

They were about halfway up the cliffside when the winds turned from gentle and loving to unabashedly fierce. Ariel led the ascent, tracing a path with her eyes and following it without hesitation. The rocks were wet and slippery, and the breeze bullied her away from stable ground. She loved it, nonetheless, feeling like a hero of her own adventure story and writing the pages in her head as she went along. She had taken her gloves off, allowing her fingers to touch the sand-speckled roughness of the rocks as she hoisted herself upward. The air was thick with ocean fragrance, winds pounding in her ears with a natural drum, overwhelming her senses with such force that she might have cried.

"We should start turning back now!" Kent shouted from way behind, with shaky legs and a shakier pride. "I would hate to see my hard work done away with by a slip."

Lady Vikander, who had adopted her own trail up the cliff, called out from afar: "She's a brave one, Ser Kent. Destiny has greater use for her than to be lost at sea."

Ariel laughed at Kent's grumbling consent, but the word "destiny" stung her brain like a syringe. Destiny was in her favor, so she had been told at nauseum. Born into the right family, with prestige flowing through her veins, but what of the Inquisitor? What of Slorne? He was destined too, but not for triumph, nor for anything close to eminence. By his own master's words, he was to die for her benefit, a steppingstone on her path toward something even she could not comprehend.

She felt Slorne's bitterness, his contempt for those who believed themselves to be all-knowing and superior. Underlings were nothing, but mages were something of great importance, especially the daughter of the last Archmage. *But what is that importance?* It was a haunting question. The Grand Inquisitor was willing to discard the life of Slorne, his dedicated pupil, for her: a girl who had no powers, a girl who was... confused. She had lived on Laktannon for weeks, surrounded by those who knew more of her upbringing than she ever could, but her purpose was still unclear, the portrait of her life they had painted for her deliberately vague and deceptive.

Escaping Prisilla had granted her new faith in life, but the boundless opportunities ahead morphed into demons questioning her every action. She was trapped again. She had merely traded one master for another.

Despite being in the same exact situation, Marion was not one to confide in. He had been distant too. Not that she was particularly warm in return, but his friendliness seemed contrived, scripted even. She had told him of the Tigress' plans to go to the Cliffs of Norin, but he respectfully refused.

*What better things does he have to do? Does he really prefer staying in his room over having fun? His stupid girlfriend left him, and he won't help himself get better.*

She grabbed a jutting piece of rock with her right hand, but the ledge crumbled, and gravity's hand yanked her down. Gasping, Ariel willed her body forward, and she landed rather directly into the cliffside. Hugging the rocky wall, her body trembled. *Octavia,* she thought, as if she had tapped her on the shoulder. *Where did you go?*

She was back in the frigate. Smoke and fire encircling her. Sirens blaring. Romans shooting as she retreated. She remembered stealing a rifle from a fallen soldier, Kent rushing into the fray with his Immortech sword, like a halo in his hand, and Marion standing stupidly in the middle of it all.

*He was alone, right?* Slorne had risen from the darkness, his silver jawline unmistakable. *He had his ugly Enfari steel sword and... and he threw it.* Ariel buried her face into the cliffside. *Immortals, who did he hit? Not Octavia, no, she must have been taken prisoner. Or she was working for the Romans all along...*

She remembered sitting with Marion outside the dining hall of Unity College. They were drinking, and he mentioned Octavia, something stupid about liking her dresses. *He looked so sad, looked to me for answers. Why didn't I say anything? I should have told him she was-*

*No! There's nothing to say. You don't know him, and he doesn't know you, not truly. Whatever happened between him and Octavia stays that way.* Ariel looked up, seeing she was nearing the peak of Norin. Her body shuttered with embarrassment. *Leave it alone, it's none of your business anyway.*

She let out a tremendous sigh while the winds blew loud enough to disguise it.

When she reached the top of the cliff, the Tigress was there to greet her. "How was it?" she asked, smiling.

"Fantastic!" Ariel exclaimed, her excitement dominating her reserved inclinations.

"That was fast for your first climb." Rachel complimented, extending her hand and hoisting her over the sharp ledge. To Ariel's surprise, she showed no strain in lifting her.

"I could have gone faster if I wanted, but this nature is so… enchanting." A landscape of brown rocks and fields of wild green and yellow grass intermingled like earthly lovers waited for her atop the cliff. Rows and rows of waist-high bushes separated trails of sand and gravel. Gazing farther out along the coastline, dark trees growing on the slant of the cliffs grew in the shape of rising ramps from decades of being beaten by the ocean breeze.

Rachel found a seat on an elevated slab of stone sticking up a few feet away from the ledge. She patted the space next to her as an invitation for Ariel to sit.

Once she accepted, Lady Vikander continued, "If you can believe it, hundreds of people usually walk the Cliffs of Norin every day. Sometimes thousands if the weather is right. They come from Old Ulthrawn and a few other local towns. Some hike or go to the beach, and others just sit by the ledge and look out. There's no arguing, no fighting. The ocean breeze calms everyone."

"It sounds nice." Ariel said, picturing people around the Cliffs. The idea of hundreds of people outside socializing and being friendly pleased her. It was not something she would ever find in the Underbelly.

"People outside Laktannon like to call us the 'Bloodlands' because they think we're savages. They don't know it's possible for us to get along, and, to be honest, most of us don't know it either. But it is possible, I've seen our people live peacefully. I see it every time I come to Norin."

"I'm from the lower levels of Prisilla, where the people are very poor. We're constantly attacked by the government. They have the guns, they have the soldiers, and they have all the wealth to fund their oppression, but we outnumber them ten-to-one. If my people could overcome their differences, all the money in the world couldn't save those rich dogs." Ariel said, making fists with her hands. "But we can't. We continue to fight each other; all the while still being harassed by the elites. It's sad and it's sick, but still I feel like I should be back fighting with them, no matter how hopeless it is."

"And what about the Paladin Order?" Rachel asked.

"I feel... detached," she admitted.

"It must be difficult, assuming the responsibility of your father. I, at least, had the luxury of witnessing the greatness of mine, however brief it may have been. I know what I'm fighting for. In short, you have my sympathies."

Ariel was both annoyed and amused by her diction. Opulent, as if her fancy words added credibility to whatever she was saying. "But don't you ever question it? The responsibility and duty? Do we owe our parents our lives just because they gave them to us?"

"Our responsibility does not solely belong to our parents. We have lineages to protect, or legacies to uphold. I come from one of the most prestigious families of Mercia and heroes of the human Republic. Your ancestors represented a pillar from which the Paladin Order was founded on. Would you want their generations of work go to waste?"

"I don't know." Ariel confessed, as she kicked a stone and watched it tumble away and drop into oblivion. She took to her feet and made way to the cliffside again. The ocean churned tremendously, sending forceful lashes of waves in quick strikes against the rocky ridge. The air carried droplets of water over the cliff, creating foggy apparitions that ascended into the sky. Ariel stretched out her arms, let her clothes billow in the breeze, felt the winds send spectral fingers through her hair. She opened her senses and smelled a storm.

Dark clouds gathered over the horizon like a giant hand slowly reaching for the land. The daughter of the Archmage was not afraid, feeling more at peace now than ever before.

Rachel's eyes touched her back, studying her every move. "The waiting is killing me," Ariel finally said. "So much practicing, reading, lecturing, and sparring. Everyone expects a great deal from me, and over time I've come to expect it of myself too."

"Frustrating, true enough, but vital." Rachel said, uncomfortably playing the practical role of an adult. "Even a mage must suffer the tedious exercise of practice if she wants to master her craft. I'm jealous of you, really."

This piqued Ariel's curiosity. "Jealous of what, exactly?"

"I'm but a human, and you're so much more," the Tigress started. "There's a gift in you yet to be unwrapped, while I'm out of surprises. Any day now you'll captivate us with some fantastical power, and I look forward to it dearly. Maybe someday I'll be able to control the ocean tides with my mind, but I don't expect it to ever come."

Ariel turned to the Tigress and looked deep into her black eyes. She respected Lady Rachel to a certain extent. Her fearsomeness in the face of her uncle was inspiring. "I've had this fantasy lately in my head. It's of a house on a cliff a lot like this one. I could build it myself and live there free of expectations and inevitable disappointment."

Rachel's face lightened up. "Ah, you're a lady of the sea."

"I suppose so," she laughed.

"Doesn't surprise me. The ocean is enchanting, unpredictable, mysterious… foreboding even."

"And am I foreboding?" Ariel asked, smiling. "You're overthinking me. It's the isolation I find the most enticing, an escape from the rush of this world and life."

The Tigress smirked. "Sounds nice, but wouldn't it get boring after a while?"

Ariel mused for a moment, then the revelation of infinite dissatisfaction made her chuckle. "Yes, I think it would."

Atticus was not particularly understanding of their rendezvous outside the city. "Do you understand the danger you put yourself in?" he scolded, his worn face boiling red. "Besides falling to your death, you made an easy target for a Roman star-splitter who may have flown by. War is on our doorstep, and all you want to do is make it easier for the enemy!"

Kent Kentoshi raised his head from its previously bowed state, saying: "I take full responsibility, First Scholar. The idea was brought to me by Lady Vikander. I... I should have objected."

"Don't be sorry!" Ariel demanded. They had been rounded up by Aethelwulf's soldiers as soon as they returned to Old Ulthrawn. Sergeant Parkton had taken the Tigress back to her uncle, while she and Kent were sentenced to the library to meet the reprimands of the First Scholar.

Atticus opened his mouth in preparation for another fiery rant, but Ariel darted from the room before he could begin to speak. *Why would I stay to listen to him?* she asked herself. *If he wanted to be my father, he should have saved from Prisilla a long time ago.*

The wrathful words of the First Scholar followed her throughout the halls and to the staircase outside the Republic Manor. She headed to the fields beside Unity College where she hoped to find some isolation. She was sick of how Atticus treated her, which was even more abhorrent after her incident on Malor's ship. *He thinks I'm cursed, that I'm under the spell of the Inquisition. Whatever happened that night, it was not me...*

The terrace outside the Manor was dead quiet as battle loomed ever closer. Ariel could hear her own footsteps as she paced along. Inside, her head was a tempest of faces: Slorne's sickly pale face, which watched her with an interest that no one had shown before; Marion's sad and bereft one, staring like a lost animal; Octavia's face, so horrified in the end.

*No, I saw nothing. Attachment only leads to tragedy, just look at my brother.* She sighed, disgusted with the slime inside of her. *All Marion needed was someone to talk to...*

There was a rifle under her bed, primed and ready to fire. Ariel rubbed her head, unsure of which path to take. At this point, the garden was closer. She needed to meditate, to rid those faces from her head. *What's wrong with me? What the fuck is wrong with me?* No one answered. *So, it's nothing, or everything?*

The sight of the garden granted some relief, but it was short-lived as soon as she saw who was waiting.

Ariel approached Tali, whose back was turned to her as she admired a wide array of flowers pleasantly absorbing the low afternoon sun. She looked tranquil perched on a large rock, as happy to be stationary as every plant in the garden. Even so, Ariel prepared for the worst.

"I'm not here to be scolded at," she stated. "Atticus has no right to torment me for doing as I please, and neither do you."

"Atticus cares about you," Tali whispered. "If you could have seen his face when he got word Kent had rescued you and Marion. He loves you two more than you could know, he just has a difficult time expressing it."

"Well!" she started, then thought better to subdue the defiance in her tone. Her body felt sluggish, as if poisoned. "He can't decide to be my father now. I'm too old for that."

Tali turned her violet eyes from the garden to Ariel. They were glossy and sparkling, like two small ponds reflecting sunlight. "He owes you an apology, and so do I."

Ariel was taken aback. "For what?"

"It's two apologies, in truth. I was responsible for you after your father's sacrifice; I'm the reason why you ended up on Prisilla. My incompetence resulted in the life you were given."

Ariel's first instinct was to scream. This mage must have believed her to be damaged goods. *The poor Underling girl! She doesn't know any better than to act savagely!* But then she saw the remorse in Tali's face. She was not being treated like a lesser being, but as an equal.

She caught the anger in her chest and changed it to empathy. "What's done is done. This could be a new start for both of us."

Tali breathed a sigh of relief, as if she had been granted penance. "I've screwed up your past, and now I fear I may endanger your future as well. Once the galaxy becomes aware of your presence, there will be no hiding. I'm giving you the chance to walk away, although it may be too late. I just think you should know, I reached out to you purely because it's in the best interest of our people. There are no safe places for mages anymore, but I want to believe the son and daughter of the greatest Paladin to ever live could change that."

Ariel considered her proposal carefully. "*Most well, let thy fate be mine own.*"

Tali was struck with bemusement. "*Doth the knoweth Godspeak?*"

"*Knoweth and speaketh, proficiently,*" she added. "*Tis a weapon of mine own people against the dreaded pearls.*" She had heard Tali speaking the language of the Immortals before, but never had cause or reason to show she could do the same.

"*Thou art full of surprise, mine lady.*" Tali complimented. She gazed down at Ariel's hands and asked. "*What misfortune occureth to thyne hands?*"

"Rocks," Ariel laughed. She presented her scarred, calloused hands as if they were artifacts. Tali grasped them, her hands as cool as soil. She sensed a peculiar tingling as an indescribably energy emanated between her fingers and Tali's. When the Paladin teacher removed her hands, Ariel found that her own had healed. She clenched her fists and rubbed her palms together.

"I can't remember the last time they were this smooth," she said ecstatically. A breeze picked up, capturing some colored pedals from the flowerbed and sending them into the sky. She watched them spin in the air and gracefully fall back to the earth.

"I did not mean to be so cold to you," Tali said. "I wanted you to be more innocent. It was a selfish need on my part; it was an attempt at damage control for the chaos I already let happen. I believe in you Ariel, and some day many other mages will do the same."

Ariel began to speak, but choked on the words. She feverishly scratched her palm and looked anywhere but in her teacher's direction. Her eyes became glossy. She tried to turn away, but her emotions overwhelmed her. "My last bounty was a bust. My master warned me not to screw up, but I still did. He died and I was stuck on top of a skyscraper with his stupid blood all over me."

Her jaw clamped, trapping her tongue between her upper and lower teeth and prepared to close all the way. Her heart raced like never before, nearly exploding from her chest. Breathing, she relaxed her jaw. Her confessions, once locked away, finally came spilling out. "I stood on the ledge and I... I almost kept walking. It wasn't the first time I had that urge but it was, you know, it was the most convincing time. I'm glad someone saved me from that place."

Tali reached down into the garden and plucked a bell-shaped, orange flower halfway down its stem. Near death, the pedals were wilted and brown. As she held it in her hand, the pedals pulsed back to life, until it was just as vibrant as any other flower in an early spring's bloom. She turned to Ariel, brushed her long mane of platinum blonde hair behind her ear, and placed the flower there.

"Please tell me more, if you are ready."

. . .

She returned to her room inside the Republic Manor at nightfall. Waiting for her, as always, was her Pup, who whistled joyfully as she entered. "Hey, buddy," she said, putting a hand on each of its spherical sides and resting her head on its lens. "Sorry I was gone all day. Won't happen again, I promise."

She stood in her room with her eyes closed for a while, holding her BOT.

Her confession felt like the breaking of a chain that constrained her somewhere deep in her mind. Finally, someone else could help carry this burden. She was free, whimsical in a way. The reality of her self-loathing had finally come to life, making it understandable, conquerable, human. Ariel flexed her liberated shoulders.

But a new burden emerged in its place. She willingly revealed her vulnerability to Tali, and now she was free to spread it to whoever she liked. Ariel sighed, feeling naked. Time would tell what the costs of her honesty would be. She could only hope Tali would keep her secret.

A screeching sound from outside broke her trance. Unable to locate the source of the noise, Ariel was convinced she was losing her mind, but the sound turned robotic, assuming a repetitious form. *An alarm, but for what?*

She rushed toward the window to see soldiers charging in and out of buildings, taking formation under screaming commanders, and receiving their firearms. Turrets and anti-aircraft guns sprouted from the wide square outside the Manor and on flat rooftops in the city afar. The KOH was here. She went to her drawer and tied her new belt to her waist. On the table sat her rifle taken from a soldier during her escape from the frigate. She was smart to hold on to it.

For the thrill of it, she put her gloves on and activated the gravitational pull at her fingertips. If her pistols were near, they would fly to her hands. But of course, they weren't near, they were with Slorne a thousand miles into space.

Footsteps approached her doorstep, slowly and in a prowling manner. Ariel glanced over and saw the person she last expected to see.

"The hour of judgement is here." Marion said, in a whisper. "Time to see whose side you're truly on." There was something peculiar in his eyes, something like absolute focus.

"What are you talking about?" she asked.

"I don't care if you run away with the Inquisition. At this point, we'd be better off far away from each other, but I need one more thing before you go," Marion said. She realized that her new firearm was still on top of the drawer… several feet away. Her eyes deceived her intentions.

"You won't make it," he promised. The sword in his hand casted a thin line down the right side of his face. "Go for the gun, and we both lose. You die, and I don't get the truth I need." There was no hint of doubt in his voice. He was a machine, incapable of sympathy.

Pup, sensing danger, inserted itself between them. She could have ordered it to stop Marion, but she could not bring herself to speak the command. *Haven't I tortured him enough?*

"I'll cut through your BOT if I have to."

Ariel sighed, "What do you want to know?" *Stupid question.*

Marion knelt to one knee, raised his Immortech sword to his face and contemplated the smooth design and glyphs wrought into the blade that had yet to glow. He put his thumb atop the tip, plucked his skin, and watched a fat drop of blood slide down the blade and fill one of the glyphs with crimson.

"You are going to tell me how Octavia died."

Ariel felt a pit in her stomach. "I thought she left you on the frigate." The shallowness of her tone gave her away. She convinced herself that Octavia abandoned him, that their love was hollow. Her mind flashed back to their escape, the silver cloaks billowing through ash and fiery winds, and the Enfari blade piercing through the little redhead's chest.

*And what did I do? Nothing...*

"Liar!" Marion cursed. His pain seeped through the scowl on his face, but his determination returned as quickly as it went away. "Did you think I forgot? Well, unlike you I have... had people who loved me. People I'd gladly give my life for if it meant they could return from the dead. The Inquisitor was the one who did it, lunging his sword right between her breasts. The memory is vague other than that, so I want you to go into painstaking detail over the nature of her demise. I want the image crystal clear in my head for when I slay the damned Enfari myself."

"What's this going to solve?" Ariel asked. "It was selfish of me to not ask about her. I can't imagine how hurt you are, and I was stupid not to care." A reproving nausea overwhelmed her. *I've ruined him*, she realized, watching her brother admire his Immortech sword.

"You've had more than enough time to reach out to me." Marion said, grinding his teeth. "So now, you will tell me what I want to know. And if I catch any suspicion that you're lying again, this blade is going into your stomach, slowly."

# KENT (IX)

Kent paced to the balcony outside his bedroom, absorbing Old Ulthrawn from a bird's-eye view. The city was a shadow, each building shaped like a headstone in a graveyard. An evening wind crept beneath his cloak, cooling his skin. Inside, his blood was a special, frantic kind of hot.

The sounding alarm would not let him forget of the impending conflict. War was no longer a vague threat of doom, but an undeniable inevitability of carnage. His Immortech sword would soon be painted in the souls of his enemies, and perhaps his own soul would belong to another once the last shot of battle rang over a desolate land. Whether it excited or terrified him, Kent was unsure.

"I haven't heard a noise like this in over a decade," he said, sensing Matiyala's presence behind him. "It never bothered me then, but now I'm shaking."

"I feel it too," she agreed. "It's not just the alarm of battle, it's a declaration of change. Whatever hope the galaxy has against the Triumvirate will either breathe new life tonight, or it will die in the cradle."

Kent turned to Matiyala, who was holding his breastplate, its Immortech coating reflecting off the starry night above. He let her place it on him, felt her tightening the straps around his arms, neck, and waist. Like his sword, Immortech armor could endure the most powerful types of hostile energy. It was the key to allowing mages to compete with enemy armies in ground warfare, a parting gift of protection from Serios himself. *They say guns and missiles are the future, but Immortech is eternal.*

On top of having nearly indestructible armor, Paladins were trained to fight in units. Mage knights made up the majority of a combat force, but healers, conjurers, and builders accompanied them by necessity to cover the weak points of their warrior brethren. They had to connect with each other like parts of one body, as any lesser chemistry would ensure the demise of the entire unit. In the days of Marius Zoltor, Kent Kentoshi had witnessed small groups of Paladins rout entire legions of Triumvirate forces.

But Kent was alone now. Any and all of his brothers and sisters in arms who refused the deceptive embrace of the Inquisition were dead. He knew all too well that the Tigress' forces would not have his back, but he still had to fight twice as hard if they ever had a chance of winning.

"Will you be piloting the Seshora Araman?" he asked Matiyala. In their final hour of tranquility, Kent's concerns for his clandestine lover were unrelentingly raw. Admiring her as she walked around in her nightgown, the Paladin wondered if he would ever have such a simple pleasure again by tomorrow.

"Only if I wished for certain death," she replied. Her posture was casual, somehow undaunted by the surrounding sounds of preparation for bloodshed. *She's a soldier after all*, Kent reminded himself, *she's likely been in more battles than I have.*

Matiyala continued, "Lady Vikander has gifted me with a star-splitter, so the Romans won't see me coming."

"When will you embark?" Kent asked. "The first wave of fighters is always the most vulnerable, especially in the air."

She smirked. "As an officer, there's no place I'd rather be than in the first wave. What's it to you?"

"I only want to know where you'll be." Kent said defensively. Matiyala considered poking further to really turn his green skin red. Thankfully, she expressed restraint instead.

"Don't worry about me. You're fighting alongside the Tigress. She's the one you should be concerned with. Laktannon will survive without me, but I can't say the same for her."

He changed the subject, realizing Matiyala had survived sufficiently thus far and that any of his inputs could only serve to jeopardize that streak. "I must admit, I'm feeling the pressure of keeping Lady Rachel safe. She insists on defending the city's gate. Her soldiers support her at least, and most of them would take a bullet for her if necessary."

"I wish Lord Vikander shared their faith," Matiyala sneered. "Instead, he'll be hiding in a bunker while his niece battles the brunt of the KOH invasion. It hardly seems fair."

Kent witnessed a young Aethelwulf Vikander during the early months of the Galactic War. He had a full head of black hair at the time, and a neat beard to add years to his life he had not yet earned. He would stand by his older brother, the father of the Tigress, but he was always in his shadow. The years of newfound and maybe unwanted leadership had taken their toll on the ruler of Old Ulthrawn. *Perhaps some live more comfortably in the glorious shadow of others.*

Kent watched from the balcony as Matiyala opened the drawer from underneath the bed and pulled out an orange and black jumpsuit. She removed her nightgown and put it on. She asked Kent zip it up from the back and he obeyed. When she turned around, she gasped at the unexpected sensation of Kent's arms wrapping around her.

"I was miserable after my Order fell apart," he whispered into her ear. "You allowed me connect with someone again, and I, uh, thought you should know that if something bad happens tonight."

Matiyala responded with a light kiss on his lips. When Kent went to kiss her in return, she lovingly pushed him off. "Save it for later, Ser Paladin. The most beautiful love stories are the ones that end prematurely, before both parties lose the vigor of their union. That being said, I've grown fond of you despite my best efforts. So, please do your best to make it to tomorrow."

The war room beneath the atrium of the Republic Manor was ablaze with chatter and frantic footsteps.

The compacted, steel-reinforced walls were fit to burst with soldiers, officers, and technicians, all awaiting orders from the generals who were, in turn, awaiting orders from the Vikanders.

They were herded around the tight vicinity like livestock, clucking away to one another about concerns for their own safety. Kent's eyes darted upward to study the vaulted ceiling. Strong and sturdy, but the firepower of the KOH frigate could smash the bunker into pebbles if Old Ulthrawn's shields gave way.

In between the commotion stood the statuesque Aethelwulf Vikander, analyzing a monitor laid out on the desk before him. To his left was the Tigress, with a face indecisive between boredom and anticipation, and to his right was Captain Throd. Sergeant Samuel Parkton, who served as Aethelwulf's chief military advisor, stood by his lord's shoulder, the pink scar on his face twisting as he watched Kent approach.

Behind the lot of them were the generals of Laktannon, each one dressed in their most sumptuous attire befitting of a military commander. The dress, however, did nothing to obscure their glossy, panic-stricken faces. Except for the Drakonid who had spoken out during the council meeting a few days prior. He was a seasoned veteran judging by his posture.

"Here comes our Paladin," the Tigress greeted. "My guardian is protecting me before the first missile fires."

As Kent drew closer, he could see what the Vikanders observed on the monitor. It was a ship the size of a moon with hundreds, no thousands, of tinier ships swarming around its iron mass like hornets to a nest. The frigate was equipped with cannons around its sides and turrets atop its smoothed, frontal surface. From a distant view of the drone's camera, the deck of the massive ship, with its varying proportions, possessed the same intricacies of a city flying through space. *Has there ever been a machine as perfectly bred for destruction?*

"Rachel tells me that she has picked you as one of her personal guardsmen on the battlefield," Aethelwulf said with mitigated skepticism. "Despite my warnings, she still chooses to face the enemy in the open, but I have limited her to stay inside the confines of the city. Out of respect for you as a living being, I must inform she will be fighting where the battle is at its heaviest."

"I will stand wherever she needs me." Kent replied, patting the hilt of his sword.

"If only your other mages shared the same enthusiasm," Lord Vikander said absently.

"It's time for us to part ways, Uncle." Rachel was eager lead her troops out of the bunker. In contrast to Lord Vikander, the Tigress possessed the energy of the sun.

"May the Immortals protect you." Aethelwulf prayed, a crack of concern making its way through his cold gaze.

"Father will be smiling down upon me," Rachel remarked. "Can you say the same?"

With those words, the Tigress of Old Ulthrawn turned on her heel and marched toward the armory. Kent and Throd followed along.

They were intercepted by the humanoid, Troyton Vorenus, mere seconds later. His height alone made him a formidable figure, but there was an undeniable essence of weakness around him. Kent guessed the giveaway was his fidgeting hands, which could not decide whether they wanted to be in his pockets or out. Additionally, his dark brown skin was a glossy mess of nervous sweat. Still, he appeared intimidating enough dressed in an officer's heavy armor.

"You look anxious," Rachel noted. She was downplaying the overwhelming stress painted on the humanoid's face. "Where's your mind at?"

"Exactly where it needs to be, Commander." Troyton lied, clapping his giant hands together. "Don't worry about me."

*No one is...* Kent thought. The humanoid was an unnecessary variable. He gave them the information they needed on the frigate, and any other contribution he could provide seemed superfluous at this point. On top of the mountain of responsibilities Kent already had, he would need to add watching Troyton to that insurmountable list.

Rachel patted the humanoid on the shoulder. Despite the tremendous height difference, she was by far the more intimidating of the two. "Relax. You'll be inside the city with the rest of my reserves. If our walls crumble and the battle rushes through the streets, can I count on you to fight until your last breath?"

Troyton spoke with added confidence. "Yes, ma'am. I'm with you, one hundred percent."

They entered the armory between a funnel of saluting soldiers. Lady Vikander thanked them all generously as each soldier professed their unyielding loyalty to her. Kent had never seen one person receive so much affection from such a variety of species since Marius Zoltor. The walls of the armory were coated with weapons and explosives. Kent was not an expert on the subject, but the guns he saw were thin and tiny with small cartridges. He was hard-pressed to find more than a handful of weapons equipped with auto-lock mechanisms or even scopes. A Roman armory would never have this number of outdated firearms.

*Her soldiers have passion. They know what they're fighting for, and that's more dangerous than any elite weaponry.*

And just as he deemed the Vikander arsenal primitive, the Tigress unveiled her secret. Exoskeleton armor, painted with colors as black as night and orange as fire wrapped around its formidable being. She grew three feet taller and stretched two feet wider once she stepped inside the hatch. When she moved, the suit responded as naturally as any limb would. She flexed, flaunting her wrist-rockets and the gears and wires that were the muscles of her metal arms.

"You like it?" she asked, cocking an eyebrow.

"No one could wear it better," Captain Throd admired. "Romans will shit themselves at the sight of you."

"That's an expectation I won't disappoint," she promised. "And you, Kent? Do I look as legendary as a Paladin?"

Kent rubbed his chin in exaggerated observation. "I'd offer you my sword if I could."

"I don't know the first thing of swordsmanship, but there will be plenty of time to teach me after today's victory."

Kent Kentoshi nodded humbly, "I look forward to it, Commander."

The blast doors on the opposite end of the bunker screeched open, their slow movement sounding like giant chains being dragged across the floor. On the other side of the doors was a ramp ascending to the surface of the city. Soldiers marched into formation, lining up in rows of fifty men. They moved without grace. When an officer running outside their ranks shouted an order, he may as well have been speaking nonsensical words. Mixed races, mixed dialects, and mixed uniforms; they were, indeed, a rainbow of disorder.

"Should we take the lead?" Captain Throd proposed. The barrel of his rifle hissed as he charged it.

"No better time than the present," the Tigress declared in return, unflinching confidence ringing in her speech. She gestured her army onward with a pump of her fist. Kent would have followed if his attention had not been caught by something else out of the corner of his eye. There, in a small niche of the war room all to themselves, stood Tali and the Zoltors.

"Excuse me, ma'am, I believe Tali and the First Scholar need a word with me," he said, guilt getting the better of him.

Rachel Vikander twisted her lip. "We will wait for you, Paladin, but the KOH may not."

Kent bowed and hurried over to the other mages. He was dreading their impending conversation more than the actual battle. Tali and Atticus confronted him first, separating him from the Archmage's children. Ariel and Marion had their Immortech swords placed in scabbards at their hips. Marion looked like a young Paladin destined for greatness. Ariel looked like Caella.

"Wishing the Tigress good fortune before she departs?" Atticus remarked, slyly. To think, a few days ago the First Scholar had complimented him as the last great Paladin of the Saighdiúir.

*He wants me to say it, as if it's some sort of confession.* "I have been chosen as one of Lady Vikanders personal protectors on the battlefield. At this moment, my sword belongs to her."

"And what of the Order?" Atticus asked. "Are the lives of the Archmage's children worth less than hers?"

"That's not fair to say," Tali warned. "The Vikanders were gracious enough to accept us into their home, and for that we owe them a life's debt. But that debt should not come at the expense of our own existence."

"And what happens if Lady Vikander falls and Old Ulthrawn is taken?" Kent asked rudely. He hated to have to spell out the dire situation they were in, but the naivety of his fellow mages left him with no choice. "If they lose today, we are back in the grips of the Triumvirate. Then what comes next? A certain and quick execution."

Tali considered his word carefully. "Be careful of tricks. You're possibly the last of the Saighdiúir to not be tempted by the silver serpents of the Inquisition. One by one they all have fallen, but you remained vigilant. Don't be seduced by another serpent simply because her scales are orange and black."

Kent spat defiantly. "We are about to oppose the same army that stormed Spyre and killed the Archmage. You talk about loyalties? Well, every human I kill out there is revenge for a Paladin unfairly murdered by their hands."

"Bloodlust? Is that the price of a Paladin nowadays? How cheap we have become." Atticus said.

"It's not bloodlust, it's justice," Kent specified. His mind flashed to Darby, his body slowly decaying from the leg up. *He knew he was dying. He begged me to take one last stand against the KOH, and I couldn't give him that. He must have been so ashamed, Serios save me.* "I won't let an evil like the KOH go unchecked again. Not for my sake, but for the memories of our fallen."

"Call it what you will," Atticus sneered. "But it's time to make your decision: stay with us or go out and fight with them."

Tali smiled sadly. "Kent Kentoshi has already made his decision."

Kent formed aggressive fists with his hands. There was no sense in arguing, but he could treat the wound for the time being. He cut through Tali and Atticus and took a knee beside Marion and Ariel. It was the best he could do to combat the venomous words of those he thought were his friends. "Stay in the bunker until the fighting is over. I will make sure you are safe. Despite what it may seem, everything I do is for you two and your father."

Marion nodded, his eyes distant. "I understand, Ser Kentoshi."

Ariel said nothing. When Kent considered her face, he saw not the Underling he had saved on Prisilla, but the demon who had attacked him the night on Saryn Malor's ship. *She knows more than she lets on. I never spoke to a soul about Darby... and my ugliest sin.*

"Despite everything that's happened, we can overcome this."

"I think so too," she answered, smiling plastically. Kent stood, a hollowness in his gut.

He addressed Tali and Atticus one last time: "Do not think ill of me. We will talk again once this frigate is destroyed. My life still belongs to the Order, now and forever."

...

At first glance, Kent believed there to be a dragon in the sky. Shrouded in ash and smoke and beyond epic in size, the Spear of Rhomigius, named in honor of the Immortal who slayed Extormitus to end the Creation Wars, stood solitary along the horizon. Bloodthirsty bats in hundreds of legions soared around its massive sides, eager to be let loose by their master. They loomed amid the dark clouds, slowly broken down by a royal, red sun that creeped over the horizon. *They're waiting for the sun to rise and let its rays blind us*, Kent thought, rubbing his eyes.

The war council had predicted that the young General Antonius Marko would act impetuously and attack the city as soon as possible, but the enemy leader was wise beyond his years. Instead, they made the defending army sweat in anticipation throughout the night. And now, the forces of Old Ulthrawn had daybreak working against them. The hours of waiting had given Kent time to contemplate... too much time to contemplate.

He stood on the ramparts of the eastern wall, letting the dawning sun warm his face. Beside him was Captain Throd and the Tigress. In front of them was the barren expanse of war-torn earth outside the city. The drop from atop the wall was nauseating. On the opposite side of the wall waited the bulk of the Tigress' army. Thousands and thousands of soldiers set up barricades throughout every possible street connected to the eastern gate. If the KOH soldiers were able to breakthrough, they would be met by a hail of gunfire as they entered the city.

Lady Vikander watched from the eastern wall as the frigate showed its first sign of engagement. From its underbelly sprung thousands of tiny black pods. They zipped through the air with impossible speed, landing a few miles away from the outskirts of the city, right where they could be concealed by the dip in the sandy terrain.

"There are foot soldiers in those pods," Rachel concluded. "They'll try to take the city while their air force bombards us from the sky. A pity they landed so far away; I anticipated watching our guns blow their pods into dust before touchdown."

"I'm picking their gravestones as we speak," Captain Throd announced.

"Do they deserve such a luxury? Their bodies can be tended to by crows and bugs for all they're worth." She checked her watch, then turned back to her captain. "Release the star-splitters. Let them pickoff as many on the ground as they can before their aircrafts gain the nerve to face us."

In seconds, a row twenty razor-thin ships zoomed over their heads. Another twenty came, then another. The rows grew in number with every batch until they became impossible to count. Kent prayed to Serios that Matiyala was not part of the first wave, but he had a sinking feeling she was.

The attack ships surrounding the frigate grew antsy at the sounds of bombs and lasers falling on their soldiers. They were still too far over the horizon for Kent to witness the battle unfold, but he could hear the screams, nonetheless. In complete synchronization, the enemy ships descended, sinking below the slope. Instantaneously, ships of all shapes and sizes filled the sky, fighting an aerial battle so chaotic that it was impossible to predict who had the advantage.

A few ships steered by hotheaded humans charged recklessly for Old Ulthrawn, meeting immediate and rightful vaporization from the barrel of a mounted cannon.

Some soldiers from inside the city's walls cheered at the spectacle above. It served as a reassurance that the enemy frigate could not simply approach their city without extraordinary risk. If it were to get close, the Tigress could hit it with an EMP bomb and order the entire might of thousands of turrets, cannons, and missiles to slay the hulking steel beast.

During the spectacle in the sky, the bug sized soldiers of the KOH army peeked over the horizon. In such great numbers, their legions looked like giant black bricks from afar. Rachel ordered her turrets to strike. Lasers fired from atop the parapets, but when they reached the Roman army, the staticky rays of their arching shields pulsed in protection. Kent could not figure out where the shield generators came from. The possibility crossed his mind that the shields could be magical, but it was unlikely. They had no reason to rely on magic in a field where human intellect had already surpassed.

Armored buggies drove along the flanks of each legion.

He cursed under his breath. Those buggies carried the generators casting the electromagnetic shields over their legions. If Rachel wanted to damage the foot soldiers, she would need to eliminate the buggies first.

Grunts of discomfort sparked among their ranks. *The enemy has yet to fire a single shot at them, and still they quiver.*

The shields screeched as they deflected lasers, metal, and cannon fire alike. The Romans, dressed in their bulky, gold-and-red armor, inched toward the city almost entirely unfazed. The gate they aimed for was small and compact, but decades of withstanding sieges left its material weak and brittle. A few well-placed bombings would destroy it for sure, and likely a large chunk of the wall with it. Then Rome could run wild over Old Ulthrawn with little to stop them.

"Aim all cannons at the damned buggies!" Rachel commanded. By this point, the KOH soldiers below were close enough to fire shots of their own, and they barraged the worn-down walls with brutal efficiency. Some of the soldiers on the wall, dumb enough to think themselves invincible, returned fire with no regard for their own heads. Those few who kept their heads learned their lessons quickly.

Kent felt the heat of the city's war machines on his back as they charged. The buggies sensed this too, so they sped away from their legions to move around more freely in the barren fields to break the auto-aim of the cannons. Kent counted ten buggies in total. If they could takedown half, the shield generators would be too weak to cover the entirety of the Roman ground forces.

"Our weapons are fully charged, ma'am." Captain Throd reported.

"Then fire!" the Tigress declared without hesitation.

For a split second, the barrels of the mighty cannons took one large breath that sucked up all surrounding noise. Kent was thrown off by how extended the singular moment felt, allowing himself to briefly forget the troubles he carried to the battlefield. For that moment, his mind was hypnotized by the unnerving sense of hundreds of massively charged weapons taking life in unison.

The exhale was something divine. Beams shot down to the gravelly earth like rays of heaven dissipating any nightly clouds lingering in the dawning sky and rendering all spectators momentarily blind. Briefly, the world was devoured in celestial light. When Kent regained his sight, as limited as it was, he could at least tell the Romans on the ground were still reeling in its afterglow.

The soldiers on the wall were in an uproar. They celebrated as if they had routed the enemy into a decisive victory. Such a scene was certainly worth appreciating, but only in war stories after the battle was won. Kent kept a cool head and counted the buggies. *One... two... Damn! Six still remain.* A couple hundred Romans on the outskirts of their respective legions had disintegrated into piles of ash, but they hardly represented the bulk of their force. Kent watched as the soldiers of Laktannon atop the wall continued their attacks on the legions, but as he unfortunately suspected, their shields withstood.

The Romans efficiently organized themselves and realigned in their ranks. They returned fire, covering every inch of the fortified defensive wall with gunfire. Soldiers along the ramparts fought valiantly, if not recklessly, but they were outgunned and outnumbered by the invaders. Kent ominously took note that cover along the wall was beginning to crumble.

"Order the cannons for another round of Hellfire." Rachel Vikander commanded to her captain. She was a Goddess of War in her exoskeletal suit, but her eyes betrayed the doubt in her soul.

"Um, that's not possible yet, ma'am." Throd reported hesitantly.

"What do you mean?" she demanded with equal amounts of annoyance and urgency.

"Our guns need to cool down before they can fire again... or else they'll fry on us."

"So, do we wait while the KOH steals Old Ulthrawn from under our feet?"

Kent peered out westward to the rolling hills. His ears caught the sounds of hovering amid the surrounding metal madness. "Waiting may not be an option."

A squadron of helicopters soared along the western horizon on the outside of the main city where the battle had yet to infect. Their propellors were long and strong, spinning rapidly to hold the weight of the steel birds. The helicopters were a terrifying sight, as Kent was all too familiar with their speed, freakish agility, and firepower. Shouts, cheers, and jeers were lunged from the soldiers below. The helicopters possessed the arsenal to tear down their defenses if given the right shot, and the Romans voiced their anticipation and bloodlust like ravaging animals as the city was mere moments away from breaking.

The sounds of blades slicing through the air grew ever louder, accelerating in time with Kent's racing heart. To make matters worse, the helicopters had open air so long as Rachel's mounted cannons remained out of use. Some Laktonnian soldiers shot at the choppers, but they may as well have been throwing pebbles.

"How are those cannons coming along?" Rachel asked.

Captain Throd frowned. "We still require a few minutes. Might I suggest retreating to the bunker..."

"There's no time for that!" the Tigress declared. She looked desperately at the oncoming helicopters that were starting to line side by side to attack the weakened wall with one mighty wave of a rocket barrage. They all knew it was coming, and Kent wished dearly they could find safer ground.

"Could the humanoid give us some advice?" Kent offered.

Rachel said: "No, I need Troyton protected until our ground soldiers clash with theirs." Her head flinched as if an epiphany struck her like a bullet. "Throd, order Gressna and his team of snipers to the ramparts. No one is to fire on the helicopters. We need them to feel comfortable."

Captain Throd agreed skeptically. He barked some orders to a nearby officer, and the man in turn muttered something into the comms on his wrist. "General Gressna is two towers away, ma'am. He'll be here momentarily."

"Good," she said, gazing into the city, where the bulk of her soldiers waited for battle. "Order a rocket battalion up here too. Don't tell them why, or else they may not come at all."

A rocket battalion of thirty soldiers rushed up the stairs to the top of the wall. They kept their heads down along the ramparts as they moved. Gressna and his squadron of snipers followed, riding hoverbikes and weaving seamlessly between soldiers, turrets, and debris along the wall. The rocket battalion appeared frightened as they began to realize they would be used against the helicopter. General Gressna and his men seemed unperturbed.

"Reporting for duty," the Drakonid hissed. His violet sniper rifle was the slickest weapon Kent had ever seen.

"How good of a shot are you?" Rachel asked, smugly.

"Thisss sseemsss like an inappropriate time to asssk quesstionsss you already know the anssswer to, Commander." Gressna said.

"You said during the war council that you could hit a pilot in his cockpit." Rachel reminded him. "Let's put that statement to the test."

Gressna was unamused. His thin tongued protruded from his pointed teeth. "One of thesssse pilots? I could have hit them from my tower."

Too preoccupied with taking cruel shots at helpless soldiers lined up on the wall, the helicopter pilots did not notice the Laktonnian rocket battalion as they took form along the parapet. At the word of the Tigress, the rocketeers hastily fired their weapons. The sounds of thirty high-pitched whistles screeched through the air as rockets zipped from their chambers with unrelenting speed.

Despite the prideful ignorance of the pilots, their helicopters' automatic defensive systems launched flares upon immediate detection of the oncoming danger. One hundred red comets ascended into the sky, embracing the rockets fully. The fiery projectiles exploded on impact, violently whipping hot air into the faces of Kent and everyone else along the wall. The helicopters were unscathed. However, Rachel expected this. "Now, Gressna!"

The rocket battalion dropped down and the sniper team popped up. All at once, the snipers fired. The piercing sound made

Kent jump. Smartly, at least two snipers were assigned to each helicopter, so no pilot stood a chance of avoiding a fatal bullet. Several of the steel birds tilted, then stumbled into complete drunken disarray. Before any of the surviving pilots could react, they were all devoured into an aerial collision.

They fell like dominoes, their fates decided with no chance for objection. The sounds of metal and fire slamming into morbid embrace excited Kent, and he made sure not to blink, to get all the enjoyment possible out of the small victory. The KOH foot soldiers were in awe too, much to their own demise. When those closest to the wall finally realized they were in harm's way, colossal projectiles of scorched steel were already burying them into the dried earth.

The cries of sheer agony filled the battlefield. The noises were so sick that Kent almost had sympathy for the Roman bastards. *If only they showed us any mercy on the Blood Moon. No! Don't spare them a sliver of remorse. They're trained to capitalize on weakness.*

"Phenomenal shooting, Gressna!" Rachel emphatically congratulated the Drakonid general.

Gressna was indifferent. He bowed, saying "I live to ssserve."

Captain Throd was reluctant to praise Gressna, but he ultimately stuck to his old-fashioned code of honor. "You've saved Old Ulthrawn for the time being, and we are in your debt for that. What still confuses me is how did the KOH know where the weakest part of the city would be?"

Gressna stuck out his slithering tongue. "Perhapss they sssaw a human dresssssed like a commander of the army and thought 'she mussst be protecting sssomething important.'"

A profound silence assumed over the group, as embarrassment seeped through the skin of the Tigress and her captain.

Rachel was the first to break the mood. "I am human, after all, which means I'm as good at learning from my mistakes as I am at making them. Now, Captain, have the cannons cooled sufficiently?"

"They have. Ready to use at your command."

"Let's see Hell on earth!"

The cannons heated up and fired again. This time, the ranks below were too disoriented in the fallout of the previous blunder to properly form a shield wall. The buggies, upon hearing the weapons roar, raced to form order. It was, ultimately, a futile effort. The cannons shot in unison, the souls of those on the ground practically leaping from their bodies before the deathblow embraced them. The light that emerged from the cannon fire was equally as divine as the previous, but Kent noticed something strange.

The luminescent rays were frozen in air.

A sphere of solar energy hovered between those on the wall and those on the ground outside. The lightning-colored brightness of the miniature sun was blinding, yet too magnificent to turn away from. Everyone watched with such awe as if an Immortal had come down to earth to observe their battle. Fear, admiration, and humility filled the Paladin's soul in overwhelming injections. All color, light, and sound seeped into this one incomprehensible orb, which hummed ferociously as it hovered in place.

The ball of enraged energy groaned and lashed out wildly to be released from its unnatural state. Kent, comprehending the situation before anyone else, felt his soul drop to his feet. No human technology could cause lasers and missiles to halt in midair.

"We must get down from the wall, now!" he said, but the slack-jawed, wide-eyed, Tigress was too bemused by the holy occurrence to listen.

"Rachel!" Kent yelled, bringing her back to the real world. There were three Inquisitors on the frigate, silver cloaks swaying in the smoke, granting them a ghostly appearance. "That's the work of a mage, and a powerful one at that. We need to get off the wall before it explodes!"

Rachel nodded, "Of course. Captain, order everyone on the ramparts to regroup at the-"

Kent tugged her by the black-iron arm of her exoskeletal suit, but it was not his strength that pulled her forward. The orb of energy reversed in direction, crashing into the eastern wall and sending soldiers and scrap metal reeling into the sky. The momentum of the collision pushed Kent forward into a headlong and uncontrollable stumble. He spun in terrifying, unpredictable weightlessness, until his back hit the ground. He was rendered deaf and blind. He touched is forehead and felt blood. His palms too were stabbed all over by pebbles and small pieces of torn metal.

When his eyesight returned, he thanked Serios that the blast did not push him off the wall. He felt even luckier when he peered down to the scores of broken bodies that made the several story tumble to the unyielding ground below. Upon confirming he was, indeed, still alive, he searched frantically for the Tigress. Vain optimism brought his eyes first to what was left of the ramparts, but she was nowhere to be found. With great reluctance, he again looked over the wall. He spotted the Tigress' armored suit behind the first line of defense, about one hundred paces from a massive maw that had broken through the wall.

"Commander!" Throd cried. The captain rushed to his feet, stumbled, tripped, then forcefully threw himself down a damaged flight of steps. Kent followed, although with greater trepidation; a pulsing pain spiking up his legs with every step.

A large group of soldiers swarmed the Tigress. Kent hit the floor and used his remaining strength to cut through the mob. Matiyala made him promise to keep the Tigress alive, and he would never forgive himself for failing.

"Will she recover?" Captain Throd asked aloud, his voice abnormally frantic. Kent wrestled his way through the crowd, pushed his way into the inner circle, and found Throd interrogating a medic who knelt by the head of Lady Rachel Vikander.

The medic, behaving as if the brutish captain was blaming him for Rachel's current state, gingerly removed her helmet.

The Tigress' eyes were closed, her brow flushed from the early stages of bruising. Her long black hair spilled out in sweat-soaked tangles. Even in comatose, her face expressed incredible self-assuredness. Kent saw her chest rise and fall. It granted him some relief, but not enough to convince him that she was okay.

The medic opened her left eye, then her right. He checked her face for bruising and the back of her head for bleeding. When he removed his hands from the outlines of her skull, they were clean of any blood. The whole squadron of soldiers waited in absolute silence for the medic to finish his inspection. Kent's heartbeat shook his ribcage.

*She's dying, all because I wasn't quick enough.*

The medic turned to Throd and, with some relief, declared: "Commander Vikander has suffered a concussion from her fall, but it's nothing serious. She will need to be evacuated from the battlefield immediately, Captain."

Throd sighed, ecstatic that the Tigress was not dead, but furious with himself that she was injured at all. He snapped out of his depression and directed four of his soldiers to remove Rachel from her suit and take her back to the vaults beneath the Republic Manor. Kent, too, felt relief from his own failings.

When she was gone, Captain Throd found all eyes were on him. Within seconds of the Tigress' departure, morale took a tangible dip. Most of the soldiers had yet to fight in the battle thus far, but fear had already consumed their minds having seen their comrades on the wall take their fatal falls.

"Lady Vikander risked her life so Old Ulthrawn might survive another day. Now she needs us to fight with that same courage to save our city!" Captain Throd declared with resolute authority. "The rest of us will stand and fight, understand?"

"Yes, sir!" the soldiers chanted as one. The faint rumblings of a hundred thousand soldiers and their war machines were heard approaching the breach in the wall. With their commander incapacitated, a sense of responsibility assumed the soldiers inside Old Ulthrawn.

"Glad to hear it!" Throd shouted. "Now form up along the barriers. Shoot as soon as you see the bastards in red and gold. Don't give'm an inch of ground!"

Kent crouched behind a chunk of wall reinforcement along the innermost circle of the fortification. He grabbed a rifle from a dead body beside him and charged it. Heaps of buildings blown to bits surrounded him on all sides, good for cover in case he had to reposition. To his right was the exulted Captain, more than ready to redeem himself.

The first wave of Romans was unorganized, and they succumbed to a rain of gunfire as a result of it. Throd was smart to keep his soldiers hidden and let pride lead them into a sense of safety.

Human ego would be the best weapon against them. Expecting the ragtag army to have scampered away, the invaders strutted in as if the city was already theirs. Kent was sure the next wave would not be so arrogant, nor the next, nor the one after that.

The following wave was introduced by a screeching whistle. Through the massive maw came a line of KOH soldiers, twenty in all and lined shoulder to shoulder. They were each protected by a steel, rectangular shield that unfolded from the left forearm of their suits. Embedded onto these shields, tauntingly, was the Aquila. There was a small cove on the right side of each shield for a soldier to shoot their rifle while minimizing the risk of exposure. This may have limited their aim in theory, but the way they exterminated the Laktonnian defenders provided evidence to the contrary.

The siren screeched again. The first line of soldiers paused, stepped to the side, and allowed the second line to take the forefront. Although the transition could not have been easy, the firing rate hardly ceased for a second. Kent glanced out; the legions of the KOH surpassed as far as his eyes could see.

The Laktonnian defenders fought bravely, and at least they could rely on their knowledge of the city to delay the Romans slightly. Fighters stationed on the rooftops provided quite the hinderance for those soldiers stuck in the middle of the legions. They were paralyzed within their ranks, making easy kills for the Laktonnians. However, the discipline of the legions and how they deftly switched out fresh soldiers into the frontlines allowed them to tear through Captain Throd's forces on the street. Every time that bloody whistle screeched, Kent braced for another onslaught.

The battle transformed into a desperate act of survival. Although no one retreated, Kent could sense the terror in his soldiers. The KOH demolished what negligible cover was available, and the narrow streets of Old Ulthrawn meant they would have very little space to set up another defensive fortification. Kent shot at the enemy lines with his rifle, but most of his shots either missed or deflected off Roman shields.

And then the tanks came.

At first, he believed it to be an earthquake, but then he saw the rumbling machines pave their way across the broken, concrete grounds. Upon arrival, the tanks knew what to destroy. Taller buildings from which the more useful soldiers had their way with the enemy were demolished by a single rocket each. More buildings fell like glass sculptures as the tanks continued their path of annihilation. The Immortals only knew how many Laktonnians perished in the rubble.

Finally, the first Laktonnian soldier came to his senses and made a run for safety, but the moment he entered the barren street he was promptly cut down. This may have hindered other soldiers from doing the same, but not for long.

*This is it*, Kent thought, *this is your last stand. Find redemption here, Paladin. You owe Darby that much.*

He gathered the nerve to draw his sword. It was like flashing back in time. The bravery of youth impelled him forward, and soon his feet rushed against the enemy line.

The KOH legions were astounded by the sight of him. A Paladin, dressed in Immortech armor, wielding a mythical sword, and charging their way. For a moment, the Paladin Order returned to a time of reverence, of dreamlike awe. Kent screamed wildly against thousands of opponents, feeling as divine and indestructible as Serios himself. Whether it be fear or nostalgia, whatever had captivated the legions soon wore off, and Kent heard the command "Shoot!" directed by a human officer.

And shoot they did, with the intention of blowing the mystical hero back into his storybook, but they were never given the chance. A tank, once considered to be friendly, ran over the frontline of humans with its massive wheels. Utterly confused, the rest of the legion did not know how to react. The tank aimed the barrel of its cannon against its own people and obliterated them.

The humans lost their ranks and ran for their lives. The tank continued to crush some under its wheels while annihilating others with its missiles. Finally, another tank came to rescue and destroyed the rogue, but the chaos it caused was beyond fixing.

There were no limits to his powers. He assumed the tank driver's mind instantaneously and without resistance. All boundaries were broken. He had never experienced such a strong connection to his gift. When he drove his sword into the heart of an enemy soldier, no sound was ever so sweet.

He had no intention of rallying his men forward, but the soldiers of Old Ulthrawn had joined him, nonetheless. And they fought side by side, for the first time as a unit. Kent slashed and cut and hacked, took over the minds of KOH soldiers and forced them into betrayal. All his movements were as natural as running water; the heat of battle was dictated by his will alone.

"You've got balls, Paladin!" Throd called as he charged into the thick of battle. Kent laughed deliriously. They were running through the Roman legions, breaking their lines and marching over those who refused to run. No matter how large the Roman, or how heavy his armor, Kent's Immortech sword ran through them all.

And yet, despite this newfound spirit, the superior numbers of the red-and-golds outmatched them, surrounded them, and crushed them. Kent had been too preoccupied moving forward that he had not considered his flanks. This realization crossed him when he felt the ranks tighten, but it came too late.

Laktonnian soldiers fell left and right, and those who continued to fight were losing their confidence. Kent was no longer invincible. Allies that once surrounded him were now in the dirt, and pretty soon he would have no protection from the full might of the enemy legions.

"Spread out, men!" he heard Captain Throd yell. "Don't let them surround us!" Kent continued to fight, but his arms eventually wavered. He was not as young as he used to be, and age hit him like a truck when he saw how much of the Roman forces remained. *Hordes of them. We'll have to fight for hours if we want to win.*

And when victory seemed unreachable, the Tigress returned to the field.

The orange-on-black exoskeletal suit hit the frontline of the KOH army like a meteor. Scorched bodies flew through the air, and those surrounding the Tigress stood shell-shocked in crippling panic. A short silver sword popped out of the wrist of her suit, which she used to slice through her enemies like raw meat.

The humanoid was by her side, fighting with an unreal capacity for viciousness. His aim was impossibly fast and true, his speed incalculable, and his ability to deal death to the KOH nearly divine.

The lumbering, awkward Troyton Vorenus had never looked so comfortable as he did now. He was, indeed, bred for warfare.

Captain Throd called for his soldiers to fight with the Tigress, and they obeyed with newfound enthusiasm. The enemy legions were unable to quell this rage, and soon enough they were running for their lives.

"Regroup on me!" the Tigress shouted, her voice triumphant over the screams of the routed Roman soldiers. Kent read her face, knowing exactly what she would say next. "Let's form a counterattack while we have them on the run. Am I the only one still thirsty for Roman blood?"

A resounding "No, ma'am!" followed.

"Good! Charge with me, and let them suffer the consequences of trying to take our home!"

Despite Aethelwulf's orders, not a single soul thought twice about joining the Tigress in a second helping of slaughter.

# ARIEL (VIII)

The ferocity of the bombing raids echoed throughout the bunker. Although the sounds were muted this deep into the earth, the sense that they were coming closer was undeniable. For Ariel, the distant, ground-shaking eruptions were something close to sentimental.

Prisilla's pearls generously used their arsenal against the delinquent gangs of the Underbelly. What often began as a scuffle between rival factions over a territory could easily turn into a warzone if the right people were involved. Gang leaders, especially those like Kagen, would never accept retreat from their soldiers. Suffice to say, confrontations rarely ended peacefully. If pearls caught on to these clashes, especially if high-ranking dealers or gunrunners were involved, a government-sanctioned air raid would be called to soundly neutralize all combatants, and likely a few bystanders too.

To his credit, Silver Wulf knew how the pearls operated. Like his own work ethic, they strived for maximum victory via minimal risk. Whenever she and Wulf needed a place to rest while out on a contract, he made sure to find a building with a basement deep enough to withstand a bombing. Ariel got used to sleeping through air raids, so much so that they eased her into sleep faster than anything else.

So, while the politicians and nobles of Laktannon trembled, she was as calm as ever.

She found it difficult to make eye contact with Marion. His glacial, menacing aura was birthed by the loss of Octavia and, much to her own contempt, she submitted to it. Octavia had died right in front of her, arms entwined with his. She tried to distort her memories, not wanting to deal with her brother's mourning, but her own negligence made things worse for them both.

He was a wounded animal left out in the cold, and she refused to open her door for him. His face was a frozen field as he held the point of his sword to her belly and made her recount Octavia's murder. His stare was unblinking and bold, belittling her, a reflection of measured callousness.

She also worried for Pup, who was waiting for her outside the city. She had no idea what to do with him as they were rushed inside the bunker, so she made the quick decision that Pup was better off far away from the chaos. If by some miracle the battle was won, she would have to go searching for him.

After some time, Tali approached Lord Vikander with a thought: if, Immortals forbid, the bunker was to collapse, it would not make sense for all of them to go down with it. She suggested that Ariel and Marion be transferred to the vault beneath Unity College. Although not quite as fortified, it was less of a target than the Republic Manor.

Aethelwulf Vikander's eyes reflected skepticism, but he agreed through reluctant lips. "But," he added. "You and the First Scholar must remain in the war room."

"Ah, yes." Tali answered, bowing, although she had not planned on the condition. She came to the Zoltors and relayed the message, trying her best to sound reassuring, "Lord Vikander has agreed to have you two taken to Unity College. Some of his soldiers will join you, along with Brutus Cirileo and Sara."

"And where will you be?" Ariel asked. She had expected the air between them to have twisted since confessing her secret, but Tali treated her much the same. It was almost comforting.

"I will stay with Lord Vikander. He must need me for my deft military knowledge," she remarked dryly. "Stay safe and don't leave the soldiers. I will find you as soon as I can."

They were escorted out of the war room through an underground tunnel leading directly to another bunker beneath the college. As they walked, Ariel counted over a dozen passageways connected to the main one, likely leading to other parts of the city. The intent must have been birthed from the mind of a paranoid leader, afraid of nearby armies, or air raids, or even his or her own allies. The dank tunnels were so intricate that they must have taken decades to complete. *Whoever oversaw their construction most definitely did not live long enough to reap the benefits.*

Vikander's personal officer, Sergeant Parkton, led the group onward, scowling and muttering complaints under his breath the entire time. He was a steadfast and seasoned soldier judging by the way he conducted his squadron. Brutus and Sara followed along, as Tali proposed, but Ariel questioned why they were needed. Brutus was a merc employed by Vikander. He was as loyal to the mages as any other Laktonnian, which was to say not at all. Sara had all but disappeared since they came to Old Ulthrawn. Although she did not seem especially fond of either Vikander, she was still as much on their payroll as Brutus and Matiyala. *She certainly cannot be trusted either.*

"It doesn't matter if we have one guard or one hundred," Marion whispered in the dark. "Your Inquisitor will face judgement, and my verdict will be swift and brutal. You can't protect him now."

Ariel's reflexes betrayed her, and she looked at her brother's face. He smirked as their eyes met, and she quickly returned to looking at the ground. The journey felt three times as long walking by his side. Eventually though, the bunker did reveal itself, taking form as a literal light at the end of the tunnel.

"A lot bloody quieter in here, at least." Cirileo muttered when the vault between the underground passageway and the basement of Unity College was closed. "The squeals of those noble cravens were making my head hurt."

"Watch your tongue, merc." Sergeant Parkton demanded. The human was not intimidated by Brutus, despite common sense concluding that he should be.

"And what if I don't? Who do you expect will discipline me?" Cirileo smiled sickly. He cherished confrontation, whether he engaged in it willingly or not. Sergeant Parkton recognized this and decided to step down, not from fear, but out of honor for his lord's orders. Cirileo, perhaps disappointed, stalked away. Ariel followed the merc into an adjoining room, leaving Marion to himself, swinging his Immortech sword in a sparring match against an apparition.

Brutus was smoking on a stairwell in the other room as she entered. The light at the end of his cig casted a smoky, blue gloom. A scowl welcomed her as she went to sit beside him. He wanted to be alone, but he also needed a distraction to pass time during the boredom of battle. He handed Ariel his cig, and she smoked it gratefully.

"Your brother is ready to die, are you?" he asked.

"I'm always ready," Ariel lied. The smoke of the cigarette filled her lungs. It reminded her vaguely of Blast-off, which she had not used since being locked up on the frigate.

Brutus chortled, making her feel like a dumb child. "You see the way he 'practices.' There's no sense of self-preservation. He doesn't fight to live, but to kill."

"What's your point?"

He grabbed the cig back and took a long draw of it. *He's enjoying this.* "I fought in the same way, completely uncaring of my own safety. I worked for crime lords in Prisilla, petty kings in the Bloodlands. When you see as much death as I have, detachment from the carnage becomes inevitable. Most mercs don't live this long, and it's because they think their lives are worth a damn."

Ariel was silent. Marion may not have cared for his life anymore, but to say he was detached was simply untrue. She saw the way he loved Octavia, how his eyes expressed an innate certainty they would always be together. It shook her when she first saw it, but no matter how much contempt it brought, she could not deny that they had something she never could.

*Love blinds the fact that only one thing is eternal. Marion was stripped of his happily ever after, so he will settle for tragedy in its place.*

"You were not always a merc though," Ariel cut in, longing desperately to speak of anything other than her brother. Her statement was nothing more than a guess, although her tone was solid enough to make it sound factual.

Brutus' heavy brow twitched. "And how would you bloody know?"

She shrugged casually, sensing the balance of power sway. "Your name betrays you. Brutus Cirileo. A name as grandiose as that can only come from a patrician family." She could feel the merc tense up. "So, what is it? Displaced son? Family of traitors banished from the KOH? Or are you running away from responsibilities?"

"I've got a history with the KOH, most humans do. But you're out of your element here, Underling." Brutus warned. "Go around digging up dirt on me, you'll regret it, I promise."

Ariel rolled her eyes, sensing the emptiness of his threat.

"Poor Tali's dynasty is crumbling at the foundation," Cirileo continued. "Marion's all but done with the worlds, Kent's found a new idol to worship, and you're just a rat of the Underbelly. Some rallying point you all turned out to be."

She chuckled. Brutus, whose intention was to insult her, was bemused by her response. "That's where you're wrong. I'm not a rat of the Underbelly, but a rat of the whole galaxy."

Now the merc was laughing too, his amused face moving in neglected ways. The sudden intensity of his voice was alarming. He hollered and slapped his knee, but a smile never crossed his face. "If the rest of your lot had that kind of self-awareness, then they would've recognized Kent for the killer he is."

*What will be our song, Ser Kent?* Ariel asked. The foreign memory flashed through her mind and caused her to shiver. Kent was a puzzle that vexed her endlessly. She went to indulge Brutus further on his impressions of the Paladin, but they were interrupted by one of Vikander's masked guards. The man reported that a small squadrons of KOH forces had snuck into the city, and a handful of their own men were preparing to search the upper floors of the College. Cirileo shot up and demanded he too join the hunting party. The soldier relented, his mask unable to suppress his fright.

Cirileo stomped off without a word to Ariel. She was not surprised by this sudden abandonment. They were similar creatures, and attachment was against their nature.

She was left with Marion, Sara, and a few guards under the command of Sergeant Parkton. Part of her wanted to engage in the war above, to experience the severe gamble of life and death that she had not played since leaving the Underbelly in bedlam. She had taken the risk for granted. Perhaps she too wanted Slorne to find them, so she could participate in the deadly game once again.

They were in a small room with a flat ceiling and walls of dark oak. No doubt that behind those walls were layers of compacted concrete, but the bunker itself was designed to look like the snobbish study of some college professor.

She covertly watched Marion as he continued to spar with himself in a corner. As if sensing her gaze, he looked up. She choked as their eyes met for half a second, but all was disturbed by the shockwaves of a dropped bomb that shook the room. The lights in the bunker flickered then promptly died, leaving everyone in unbridled blackness. She reached for the Immortech sword on her hip. The touch of a mage would enlighten the blade. Her touch, on the contrary, was a cruel reminder of what she was not.

One of the soldiers spoke into his comms, calling for the squadron who went upstairs to return to the basement immediately. In return, he received only a blizzard of static.

"Flashlights on," Parkton ordered. His soldiers obeyed, the ends of their rifles promptly projecting scalding rays of white light. "We're blocked off from the war room, meaning this is still the safest place we could be. Williams, relay a message to Lord Vikander. See if he can do something about the bloody power outage. Until then we-"

The earth shattered, sending everyone in the bunker into a falling frenzy. The explosion was so loud that Ariel was sure the KOH had dropped a massive bomb right over their heads. Cracks ripped through the ceiling, and the once flat floor now dipped and sunk like concrete waves. She rubbed her knees and thighs, which had taken the brunt of her fall. She then realized she was in the full embrace of Sara, who had endured most of the phantom quake for her.

"Are you good?" she asked, guiltily.

Sara nodded. She shot up, stalling for half a second to wince in pain, then checked on Marion.

"Immortals help us!" he sang, thankful that he had not accidentally impaled himself with his own sword. His legs quivered as he ascended to his feet.

"Sergeant Parkton, the basement could collapse at any moment," one of the guards reported, his voice tremulous and boyish.

The sergeant, weary of his mind, took a moment to regain his command. "We stay here. Each entrance must be guarded until the squadron upstairs reports back. Even if the college falls, our shelter will hold."

The soldiers grumbled in compliance. They were six in total, each wearing the vizard masks of Laktannon. Sergeant Parkton made them turn off their flashlights, so they may hide in the darkness. Two men were directed to each exit for "precautionary" purposes. *He's expecting invaders. We aren't quite as safe as he wants us to think.*

Ariel and Marion crouched beneath a sofa beside a classical fireplace in the central office. Sara was silently meditating, her ears twitching at the faintest of noises. "He's on his way," Marion said in a hushed voice, the rhythm of his speech was songlike. Ariel said nothing, but she felt it too. *Mages sense the presence of other mages*, she remembered reading. *Slorne knows where we are.*

The waiting made her uncontrollably eager. She despised the powerlessness. If something was coming for her, it best make haste.

Sara's nostrils flared and her brow furrowed. She opened her lucid, yellow eyes and whispered: "Inquisitors." The word was delivered with such delicacy that Ariel strained to hear it despite being right by her side. Before she could react, the sounds of faint footsteps echoed from the left side of the room. The sounds belonged to a soldier who was slowly inching toward the end of the threshold. His gun was at the ready, pointed at the exit and prepared to fire. His partner questioned him, but the soldier, consumed by curiosity, disappeared around the other side of the door without a word.

Ariel could feel her heartbeat in her throat. She thought of the abominable poison Slorne had injected into her neck through his fingernail. The memory nearly made her sick still. Marion, unable to cage his anticipation, peeked over the sofa.

Two rounds fired from the other side of the threshold, sending small strikes of white light pulsing throughout the cavernous bunker. Ariel spotted the flash of a metal jawline. A scream followed, which soon descended into a pleading whimper.

The other soldier by the door looked down the sights of his rifle, but he never had the chance to get a shot off. A sharp projectile sliced through his armor like paper. The soldier tried to scream, but only a shallow sigh of air emerged from his opened lungs. Parkton snapped his flashlight on, presenting the man's final moments for everyone in the bunker to see. The sword's craftwork was unmistakable. Only Enfari steel could be so hideous.

The dying man, impaled by the sword of Slorne, fell backwards. The sounds of gargling blood were all that was heard inside the bunker. Sergeant Parkton gestured for the remaining soldiers to surround the door, their flashlights illuminating the fine woodwork of the office.

The cloaked figure darted into the bunker like a shadow on the wall. Slorne was behind the squadron before they could trap him. He grabbed one soldier by the chin and slit his throat with his crooked fingernail. Choking, the soldier ripped off his mask in a vain attempt to retrieve air. One of his companions screamed in terror at the horrific sight. His face was riddled with worm-like veins, his eyes bulging freakishly from his skull as they comprehended the certainty of death. His mouth dropped and out came a sea of black, miasmic liquid that splattered to the floor. A second later, the poisoned man dropped too.

Ariel was pulled unceremoniously by her sleeve. Sara wrapped a clawed hand around the wrists of both Zoltors and yanked them out of the bunker and up the stairs. She never saw the end of the fight, but the bloody screams pursued her to the top of the college.

Sara finally released her grip when they arrived at the windowed atrium on the ground floor of Unity College. For a lean woman, the wolf-girl was deceptively strong.

Marion stomped his feet on the marble flooring and pouted. "We should be helping them! The Inquisitor would be dead if not for your cowardice."

"Don't be misguided." Sara said, passively.

Marion clenched his fists, "He's mine to kill, and you won't deprive me of it!"

"Let the boy dream while he can," Slorne swaggered up the steps. His pale Enfari skin looked sicklier in the morning sun. On his silver cloak were the bloodstains of Vikander's guards. They were butchered like animals, the amalgamation of their sacrifice granting the Archmage's children little more than a few seconds of reprieve.

Slorne slowly and methodically walked forward, his companions following him like thralls. The big one, dressed in scaley armor, held his warhammer in both hands. The smaller one loomed about, its nimble figure unidentifiable in a sea of cloaks.

Marion drew his sword, but Sara acted faster. She bore her claws, snarled like a wicked beast, and charged the Inquisitor with imperceptible speed. She pounced before Slorne could defend himself, but he was saved from her attack thanks to the leviathan.

The monstrous Inquisitor caught Sara and wrapped his armor-clad arms around her in a bearhug. She squirmed to escape, realizing his intent to snap her in half at the spine. Finally, she found the slit in the leviathan's helm and dug her claws into it. The Inquisitor howled, but in his rage managed to toss Sara away with unparalleled strength. She soared like a missile through the glass wall, shattering one giant panel into diamond dust. Marion and Ariel watched in awe.

"Come on!" Ariel yelled, pulling him to follow her out the window. She saw the garden outside, its once natural beauty now a field of ash and soot. The sight eviscerated her soul. Sara was laid out on the patio, unmoving.

"Get your damn hands off me!" Marion growled. "The Inquisitor owes me a debt."

"You can't kill him." Ariel pleaded, astounded by her brother's stupidity. She questioned why she even cared.

Slorne pretended to be appalled. "And what did I do to be treated like this?"

"You killed Octavia! On the frigate, you stabbed her, when she did nothing against you!"

Slorne faintly gestured to his companions to stand down. "Ah you Roman boys are all the same, thinking the galaxy revolves around your wants and needs just because life is such an easy thing to live. If it helps, I was aiming for you. No one forced you to escape, so her blood stains your hands as much as mine."

Marion gritted his teeth. "She had no part in this, but you still took her from me."

"And you've taken my whole life from me thus far," the Inquisitor returned. "Today I liberate myself from the strings of fate. The only choice you have is how easy you make it for me."

"Marion," Ariel begged. "We can still run. Brutus may be outside."

"Come now," Slorne said, checking his nails. "The Grand Inquisitor says you're the one who's supposed to slay me. Let's put his delusions to the test."

Marion shook his head. His cheeks were flushed and his eyes welling with tears. "It doesn't matter anymore." He raised his Immortech sword in the air and rushed for Slorne with rampant determination.

The Inquisitor wiped the long black bangs from his face and smiled lustfully. Marion's battle cry was fierce, rich with rage, but none of it broke through the icy heart of the Enfari. Ariel looked on, as if everything occurred in half its natural speed.

"Brave boy," Slorne said, as Marion came close to his jagged blade. The Inquisitor spun deftly, raised his sword over his shoulder, and cut down the son of the Archmage in full sprint.

Ariel gasped. She put a hand over her mouth and bit her fingers. Marion slowly turned back to her, utterly shocked and confused by how quickly it happened. A red line ripped across his body from shoulder to waist, his shirt turning black as it showered in blood. *Damn it, were you expecting a heroic death?*

He let his sword fall to the ground, and his body followed.

Slorne laughed greedily. He stepped away so the growing pool of red did not stain his boots. "I was wrong about the Roman. Most of his kind like to talk about bravery more than practice it. Now, Ariel, my sister of the misunderstood, will you come with me peacefully?"

In response, she drew her sword from its scabbard. She narrowed her eyebrows to express the illusion of confidence, or at least comfortability with a sword in her hand, but she suspected that neither came off convincingly. Slorne's bone pale face glowed with disappointment. "I'd be more afraid of you if you had these," he said, holding up his silver cloak and revealing her pistols on his belt.

Marion fidgeted on the ground. A lake of blood slowly expanded around his person. *He needed a friend, a companion, a sister, but I deprived him of all three.* For his sake, she had to fight. The wound across half his body was not so bad that he could not live through it, or so she told herself.

Thinking on her feet, she arched her arm back and launched her sword like a spear. She had witnessed Slorne do it moments ago, and she thought she could pull it off too. Instead, the sword completely missed. The blade screeched across the marble floor several feet away from the other mages, rendered completely ineffective.

"Shit!" she cursed. With that plan failed, she opted to take her chances out in the open.

She sprinted out the window, hopped onto the patio, and found herself by the body of Sara. Unconscious but still with shallow breath, Ariel shook her frantically, but received nothing in return.

"Empathy?" Slorne asked, right on her trail. "I expected better of you."

He was right. Sara was a lost cause, so she left her among the shards of glass. Her instincts as an Underling could only help her now.

She sprinted to the crater of ash and dust that was once her heavenly field and garden. She thought of the radiant flower Tali had placed behind her ear and wondered if she would ever see such exquisite nature again. War raged around her, but the primary threat was Slorne. The Enfari made a mockery of her retreat, finding merriment in watching her feet tangle among themselves. No matter how fast she moved, he was always right behind her.

*Why is he behaving this way?* she asked herself. On the frigate, he was kind, considerate even. They bonded, as brief as it may have been, discussing literature and prose, dreams and regrets, things Ariel never imagined herself doing with another person. Despite an innate strive toward civility, the mental scars overcame him. The abuse he suffered at the hands of the Grand Inquisitor were fresh, and he celebrated her death as the remedy to his surging anguish.

"I don't want to fight you," she conceded, taking her stand in the middle of the field. Gunfire hollered in the distance, a reminder that a larger battle waged elsewhere.

"Nor do I want to fight you." Slorne admitted, ashamed. As the heat of the moment subsided, his own mental madness fled with it.

"Let's leave this planet. You and me, together. We won't go to your home-world, nor anywhere the Inquisition or Triumvirate can find us. You have no reason to serve your master."

He shook his head, disgusted. "I'm not doing this to serve Zakareth. This is his punishment for trying to dictate my destiny. I thought you understood."

"I do!" Ariel implored. "On the ship, you asked me how it felt to defy my master. You want the truth? I don't feel any better. He still haunts me; he's the reason why I doubt myself at every turn. Leaving him on Prisilla did nothing for me. Zakareth's grip on you won't vanish when he's dead, nor will the pain he caused you."

Slorne said nothing. He stared at the ground in contemplation, the grip on his Enfari sword softening. Ariel continued, cautiously: "The best thing we can do is show our masters how little they mean to us. We run away, break the chains of obligation. Fuck everyone, that's what I say."

Slorne roared with laughter. The veins on his pale neck turned purple, his starving eyes bulged in red pools. He grinned wide enough for her to count each of his browned teeth. Even his metallic jawline strained with amusement. "Zakareth is an abomination. He needs to die, but first he must break. As long as you live, he will feel justified in his torment of me for the sake of his own conjured prophecy."

Ariel shook her head and sighed. *It wasn't meant to be. We are bound by hate, after all.*

Slorne extended his hand. "Come with me peacefully. You can at least see the Grand Inquisitor before you die. You should meet the man who damned us both."

She approached, her gloved hand reaching out for him. Slorne licked his pallid lips.

Then, she squeezed her hand, activating the magnetic pull on the fingertips of her glove. One of her pistols shook anxiously on the Inquisitor's belt. Confused, he watched the pistol slip from its holster and into Ariel's palm. It felt like a long-lost friend coming home. Without hesitation, she pulled the trigger in rapid succession.

The Inquisitor cried in despair as a series of ripping lasers met his armored torso. The agony was unrelenting, but he managed enough strength to charge and pin her to the ground. His long, crooked nails dug into her shoulders. She screamed as they tore through her flesh. His crimson eyes, spilling with molten wrath, betrayed his intention to kill. The pain that surged through her arms forced Ariel to drop her pistol. Her blind hands fumbled to retrieve it, but the gun was out of reach. Giving up, she decided to kick.

She did not see if her shots broke his armor, but she kicked frantically into his lower abdomen where she guessed the damage was done. At first, Slorne was unfazed, but the violent pain soon crippled his fury. The Inquisitor let out a whimper and fell over, allowing her the chance to escape.

She scurried over to her pistol, using her elbows and knees to push forward. She grabbed it and searched for Slorne, but he was already on his feet. Green ooze bled in gushes from around his belt, staining most of his left pantleg and some of his shirt. He used one hand to hold the wound, while the other was wrapped around the hilt of his sword. Ariel too was bleeding like a river from the punctured holes in her shoulders. But her adrenaline was pumping like never before, allowing her to ignore the wounds like she would a hangnail.

On the hill stood the other Inquisitors. They were like sentries watching over the duel, and she wondered why they would not help their companion. Maybe they were secretly hoping she would kill Slorne, fulfilling the Grand Inquisitor's prophecy, or perhaps they knew he was going to kill her and wanted no responsibility in the matter.

Regardless of their veiled intentions, Slorne's was dauntingly conspicuous. He lumbered for her, panting and wheezing, black liquid akin to his own poisonous magic frothing from his mouth.

Ariel went to raise her arm to shoot the Enfari, but her wounded shoulder pinned her down. She laid crippled on the black field that once was her flourishing garden.

Accepting the inevitability of oblivion, Ariel experienced an injection of tranquility and felt it flow throughout her body. She remembered the night of her last bounty, Graznys. Atop a towering skyscraper and looking down on the neon void, she dwelled on what would have happened had she followed her instinct and taken that one extra step into nothingness. It was months ago, and she had been on so many unbelievable adventures since, but ultimately it led her to the same end. She weighed the values of her wandering escapades and deemed them better than anything she had on Prisilla. She only wished she had more time to talk, more time to understand.

With death's grip on her neck, she was ready to surrender her memories to the cosmos.

A flush of fire burned into the sky. Ariel opened her eyes wider, convinced she was dying, but Slorne saw the same thing. The ball of fire descended from the hill of Unity College. Upon a closer examination, the figure possessed a human form. The flames along the contours of his body burned her irises, and yet he was impossible to look away from.

As the burning man charged along, one thing became abundantly clear: he was headed for Slorne.

The Inquisitor stepped back in defense. He held his sword with one hand across his chest, anticipating the flaming apparition's attack. It revealed a sword of its own, alive with crackling flames. It struck wildly at Slorne, who was able to deflect all the blows. The Enfari steel hissed as it clashed with the flaming sword, and sparks soared high into the air every time both metals kissed.

Despite displaying expert swordsmanship, the Inquisitor could not prepare for the wildfire which had gripped his silver cape. He was forced to fight two battles, and suddenly the wound from his gut sprouted a mortal leak. He began to sweat. His mind and body were thrown into complete disarray. The fiery figure saw these distractions, swung around, and dug his molten blade into the chest of the Inquisitor.

Slorne's eyes turned mercifully to Ariel before his entire being was engulfed in fire. He collapsed to the ground, groaning desperately as his soul blackened. The figure standing over him bellowed. Then, the fires cooled.

Marion fell to his knees, his naked skin red, hot, and pulsing. He wailed, digging his hands into the earth. Ariel considered both running away and comforting him, but her limp body would not let her do either.

"It hurts!" Marion cried. Smoke arose from his skin. His hair had completely burned away from his scalp. The cut across his torso was grotesquely crimson, but the fire had at least cauterized it. *He's a true mage after all!* Ariel laughed to herself. Despite his current state of agony, he truly possessed the aura of a Paladin, with his soul and body alight with red and orange flames.

"Then give me your hand," said a delicate voice. It was the smaller of the two surviving Inquisitors. They had come to the field without Ariel's knowing. The monstrous Inquisitor stood behind his smaller partner. They were stationary like monuments, until the shorter one removed her robes.

She was thin, her skin a pale purple, and her eyes somehow redder than Slorne's. She wore a tunic with incomprehensible symbols woven into the fabric with silver thread. Her bare arms were adorned in golden bracelets.

She was impeccably beautiful, her face radiating mystical innocence. Ariel had never seen anything like her. Her hair was long and white. She had four ruby-shaped eyes on each side of her face, and her teeth were sharpened like blades. Marion was on his knees, utterly captivated by the otherworldly creature.

And then the wings sprouted from her back, made of bones thin like the legs of a spider.

"Let me take your hand so I may share the pain," the Inquisitor offered, her voice soft but commanding.

Spellbound, Marion obeyed. His arms were weak and smelled of crispy flesh, but he managed the strength to do as she asked. He flinched when they touched, but his muscles relaxed as euphoria explored his body. He cried out in both pain and pleasure. In return, the veins on the winged woman's arms turned black, and she strained to hold her bone cold hand to his charred one.

Before her eyes, Marion's scorched skin regenerated. His miasmic stench vanished. When the girl Inquisitor released her grip, he had the strength to stand again.

"Cover him," she said to her larger companion, who proceeded to tear the sash from his armored shoulder. Marion crumbled as the thick fabric embraced his tender back.

Ariel, dodging in and out of consciousness, was barely present when the attention of the Inquisitors was brought to her. A waterfall of blood flowed from her shoulders, forming into an expanding pool of her own mortality.

"Daughter of Zoltor," the winged woman sang. "I feel your suffering too. Join us, and revel in your birthright the Paladins have denied you of."

"To Hell with my birthright," she said, groggy. "He's the one you want. He's the proper mage."

"Ariel," her brother pleaded, his eyes watering. "Her words are true. I've never felt such serenity as I do now." He was telling the truth, Ariel sensed. For the first time since meeting him, he seemed liberated.

"Leave me," she whispered, abstaining from his caring gaze. Cold darkness embraced her, meeting little resistance. The giant Inquisitor marched over, rejecting her will. Ariel used her last ounces of strength to force her body forward, but she was pathetically slow. His hand wrapped around her collar, but instead of being pulled up, she was abruptly and ungracefully tossed further into the ash.

"Fuck off from her, you bloody cunts!" Brutus Cirileo boomed. He charged straight into the fray, firing uncontrollably at the bewildered Inquisitors. Sergeant Samuel Parkton was right by his side, letting loose his rifle with equal efficiency. The large Inquisitor attempted a defense, but Cirileo's stun grenade struck him stupid. The two humans covered half the distance of the field in seconds, not allowing the Inquisitors a moment to breathe, let alone fight.

Seeing the scale of battle tipping out of their favor, the winged Inquisitor put one hand on Marion's shoulder and the other on her monstrous companion. Together, they vanished into mist.

"Balls!" Cirileo cursed. He stomped around in the shadows of the mages. A slight essence of glowing dust was all that remained.

"We'll find them soon enough." Parkton promised, valiantly. Even with the pink scar encompassing his face like a rash, he still possessed a less bestial appearance than Cirileo. "I've seen these teleporting types before; they can't travel farther than a kilometer or so."

"You're a mess," Brutus said to Ariel. "What the bloody fuck will I do with you?"

Parkton refused to let the merc make the orders this time. He marched right up to Cirileo's face and declared: "She's going to the Republic Manor. There is a medical bay in the bunker. But most importantly, Lord Vikander wants what's left of these bloody mages in his sight."

Cirileo nodded in agreement. "Aye-Aye, Sergeant." He raised his rifle and fired into the chest of Samuel Parkton, who was dead before his head hit the ground. The merc laughed at his own work. Once the joke was over, he returned to his familiar disposition of pure and unbiased contempt for everyone and everything. "Bloody Roman welp, so much for his convictions."

"Marion's found something to believe in. Can't say I don't envy him." Ariel whispered. Her body was icy and distant. She felt halfway into a dream.

Cirileo narrowed his gaze. "The rat of the Underbelly proved more loyal than the boy-soldier. Watching Inquisitors vanish before my eyes might be the second strangest thing I've seen today."

There was a long silence between them. Even with Ariel's blurred vision, she could see the cruel contours of the merc's face. She threw her head back, slipping away. A long sigh arose from her gray lips.

Brutus shook his head. "No, no, you're worth more alive to me than dead. Unfortunately, Miss Rat, the galaxy is hardly finished with you."

# ELYSANDE (XI)

The sleeping body of Ser Bryson Byrne sprawled across his bed. Feet extended past the bedpost, arms hanging over the sides, he was every bit the mighty brown bear that adorned his family's coat-of-arms. He snored like an animal too, surrounded by empty bottles of beer strewn about the carpeted floor and on the bed itself. Gingerly, Elysande grabbed the white sheet by his feet and placed it between his legs.

*He'll be suffering enough embarrassment today, the least I could do is relieve him of some shame.*

His small apartment was located near the western edge of Pullo's Shield. A relatively rural area of Rome, Elysande was confident the neighborly setting reduced the chance of being spotted by some curious eyes. That, and the fact most of the population of Rome had gathered around the Forum mere hours ago in drunken celebration of the New Year. *After a long night like that, the whole city must still be asleep… or nursing an especially belligerent hangover.*

The queen quietly searched for her clothes about the place and put each article on as she found it. She was in a rush, as she would not want to be around when the bear stirred and the effects of her pills hit him like a star-splitter. She made sure not to give him enough to cause any serious internal damage, but he would be firing uncontrollably on all ends for the better part of the morning. Feeding Byrne was much easier than intended. For such a large man, alcohol diluted his thinking quite quickly. He had only shown any significant resistance to her advances while sober, but a lustful curiosity for her body that entranced the young knight since childhood disarmed his external shield of "duty" and "responsibility."

"We can't, my queen." "This is wrong, my queen." "I must be at my best for the Games tomorrow." "If Felix finds out, he'll be furious at us both!" The objections lasted almost as long as he did.

Tidy and stark, she had no problem finding everything she needed in the apartment. She zipped up her knee-high boots, then searched for a mirror to fix her hair. When she was presentable enough to enter the outside world, she departed without disturbing a soul.

The red rim of the sun poked over the eastside of Rome, signifying the first dawn of the new year. The air was cool and fresh. It made Elysande shiver, but she embraced it fully. Her head pounded and her eyes dragged from the night before, but the songs of chirping morning birds set her at ease. She walked out of the front yard of the apartment complex, her boots thumping down the sleeping suburban street. Ever the diligent and loyal knight, Richard Dance waited by the sidewalk, her car door already open.

"Glad to see you got my text," Elysande said. "Did you get any sleep?"

"Not a wink, my queen." Dance answered, although his voice and posture expressed not a sliver of exhaustion.

She took one last look around. Not a soul was in sight. Her heart raced. The thrill of deception seduced her ego. The decision was made, her hand played. Now, she would reap the benefits, or suffer the consequences.

"Take me back to the villa," she commanded, stepping into the backseat. "We can both get some rest before the tournament finals. Is the Shade situation dealt with?"

"He's fish food," Dance reported.

Elysande took her preferred seat on the right. In the distance she heard the vague screeching of something laboriously heavy and metallic. Out of curiosity, she turned and saw a dullish green garbage truck huffing and puffing its way up the street; on its back flanks were two men in luridly yellow jumpsuits, hoisting up mountainous trash bags as they cut through the dim neighborhood. *To think of a world without garbage men? This machine is so massive, so powerful, but the smallest missing piece and it all comes falling apart.*

"Have I ever expressed how much I appreciate you?"

"Never, my queen."

Elysande relaxed her shoulders. Slowly, her eyelids drifted down too. "Oh well, you're smart enough to know by now."

The Colosseum was filled to the very top on the last day of the Gladiator Games. Stage lights, spotlights, and camera lights alike flashed and sparkled without end. Music sounded from the speakers, but it was muddled by the low thunder of the audience waiting in anticipation to see who their champion of the New Year would be.

The attendants were as electric as ever, despite being the fourth day of the tournament. Elysande gazed into the crowd and saw plenty of spectators sporting shirts or flags depicting the growling brown bear of Byrne. He was the underdog, the local hero for every common man and woman around Orbis. But no matter how vehemently they backed him, Ser Byrne would lose… she was nearly certain of it.

She sat with her king to her left, her son Lawrence to her right, and her daughter Julia one seat over. Next to Gaius was Natalia, and alongside her was Jacob Mauvern, wearing a sky-blue silk doublet in honor of his late father. For once, Elysande was able to speak to her husband's daughter without any strained hospitality.

Roaming the narrow walkways to her back were soldiers of the Praetorian Guard, conducted by the Elite Prefect, Sutorian. They were monuments in their gilded attire, standing sentry like the statues of the celestial warriors who fought alongside the Immortals thousands of years ago. And yet, Elysande was not overwhelmed with any sense of divine security. Liscinia's testimony implicated one of them as a conspirator for the Heirs. *If only there weren't hundreds to pick from.*

A few rows below her sat the sea of white robes that was the section of senators. Neither Felix of Rezza, Rachele of Venallia, nor Lucio Privetera were in her field of view. Because she had not yet received any angry calls, she suspected they were unaware of Bryson's current state.

*If I could just see their faces when they realize what an unmitigated disaster he's become.*

But she would have to wait a while longer for her ploy to finally take center stage. Before the Gladiator Games was a mock naval battle, which for many people was more than worth the price of admission by itself.

The lights dimmed, filling the Colosseum with near blackness. Excited screams sang from the rafters, adding to the mystique that shrouded the stadium. After a moment, a large ship zipped into sight, hovering above the arena, and accompanied by a phantom *vroom* that shook the stadium's speakers. This ship was not made of metal and circuits, nor did it weigh the millions of pounds a warship of that size should. Instead, it was weightless, consisting of infinite vivid orange particles emanating from some deftly hidden projector from the catwalk. Another ship appeared, of similar grand size, but this one was made of blue particles. They shifted away from each other, moving with the weight of their real-life counterparts to opposite sides of the arena.

The monitors around the Colosseum reactivated, depicting the number "5" on their wide screens. A siren sounded, starting the countdown.

"Four!" the crowd roared in unison. Elysande felt Lawrence grab her forearm, his hand shaking with anticipation. "Three! Two! One!"

The hulls of each warship opened, and out came a swarm of hundreds of digitized star-splitters, zipping around the Colosseum with untraceable speed. A unanimous gasp rocked the stadium as everyone marveled at the naval battle waging instantaneously before their very eyes. Orange star-splitters chased blue and vice versa, while the two larger warships were locked in a duel as their turrets and rockets fired relentlessly upon one another.

Somewhere, likely beneath the arena, people were controlling these digital projections through virtual reality helmets. Tournaments of mock naval battles were draws themselves year-round in the Colosseum. Elysande would know, as Lawrence had dragged her to several in the past year alone. Her condescending viewpoint of what a "gamer" was at the time crossed over into her opinions of these virtual games. *True skill in military strategy comes when real life consequences are on the line,* she had once believed, *this is a mockery of what admirals dedicate their lives to.* She was, eventually, seduced by the spectacle. If she had the time to learn how virtual reality worked, she would surely dominate the competition.

The sight of Lawrence's jaw-dropped face, covered in orange and blue particles of reflected light, warmed her heart. At one point, an orange star-splitter destroyed the engine of its blue enemy, sending it reeling into their section. The crash and subsequent pixilated explosion caused them to laugh. Julia shrieked, briefly convinced the oncoming ship would flatten her, and her vain effort to disguise her fear afterward made them laugh even harder.

Eventually, the blue star-splitters outnumbered the orange, and the rest of the match played out exactly as one would expect. The giant orange warship was the last of its side left and, despite its strength, crumbled against overwhelming odds. The audience clapped in appreciation as the game came to a close. Lance was the most elated of them all, intricately describing the events back to Elysande as if she had not witnessed them herself.

Then, it was time for the finals of the Gladiator Games.

Magnus Caesar, the champion of the A block, came to the arena first, riding a silver chariot driven by marvelous horses as white as snow. Arranged in three rows of two, the daunting beasts looked ready to take flight and carry the young Caesar to the heavens. Magnus rode them confidently, circling around the arena with surprising speed. He waved to the crowd as he passed them by, and they returned his affection, but Elysande detected some reservation. *They may adore the Commandant's son, but not as much as they do his opponent.*

Magnus halted his chariot and stepped off. Under his arm was his new helmet shaped in the sharp facial contours of the Aquila. He put it on while waiting for his opponent to come out. Elysande watched his pace studiously, not seeing any signs yet of his ankle injury.

As soon as the gates opened again, the chants of "Bry-son Byrne! Bry-son Byrne!" rang throughout the Colosseum. Elysande's own stomach flurried. *A normal man would be locked up in his bathroom all day, but he is far from normal.* Despite her choice to defy the Heirs, all her efforts would be rendered meaningless if her knight won today. Then, she would have no way of getting him off the Praetorian Elite before Caesar departed for Grayspace.

Ser Bryson walked through the gate and into the arena, greeted with nothing but love and affection from the stadium. His helmet was already on, perhaps because he was trying to hide a sickly complexion. He waved half-heartedly to the crowd. She watched his feet and observed a slight stagger. *It'll be a battle of the cripples!* she thought, sardonically.

Both warriors saluted the king and queen before picking up their shock batons. As he stood before her, Elysande could feel Ser Bryson's wrathful eyes burn through his helmet. *But he won't tell Felix of our night together, at least not before his fate is sealed.*

The match began with both men circling the arena. Neither wanted to be the first to strike. Magnus' right leg dragged slightly as he paced. *I don't know what the fool is doing! That leg won't get better the longer the fight goes!* Elysande sensed bile in the back of her throat as she caught herself rooting for Tullius' bratty son.

As if he could read her mind through his absurd eagle helmet, Magnus was the first to strike, opting for his usual strategy of agitating his opponent's limbs and being an overall nuisance. Previous bouts supported this method, as the young Caesar proved he had the cardio to drag duels out in his favor. And if her drugs did as they were supposed to, Byrne would not have the nutrients to carry on for very long.

Magnus' volleying of Byrne's arms took on a musical repetition. The knight hardly bothered to hit back, but rather moped around like a dullard. His defenses were slacking too, his shoulders slouching as if they could not support the weight of his arms. Again, a strike. Again, another strike to Byrne's fortified arms. Caesar struck and struck, but his confidence betrayed him.

Just as the music of the fight grew monotonous, the Mercian knight was gifted with a sudden burst of energy. He charged through another of Magnus' lazy swings and checked him to the ground. Elysande's heart skipped a beat. A chivalrous knight would have given his opponent a chance to stand, especially in competition, but not Byrne, not today. *He's come too far to lose to good manners.* The bear smelled blood. He bared his teeth and charged the wounded bird. He went to hit Magnus with an overhead swing, but the young Caesar was smart enough to roll out of the way, making the baton *zap* as it hit nothing but the arena floor.

Undeterred, Byrne turned on his heel and continued his relentless attack. Magnus, ever an athlete, rolled to his feet, prepared for Byrne's offense, and sidestepped away from certain defeat. From there, instinct caused him to pivot his right foot to slide naturally into facing his enemy, but the wounded leg finally gave way and caused him to stumble. As he snapped to the floor, the whole audience gasped.

Byrne saw his opening and sprinted. Completely caught up in the sudden spasm of pain, he was a rabbit trapped in a snare. The Colosseum started to cheer again, as although they sympathized with Caesar, they could also sense the underdog's victory was imminent. Elysande cursed quietly, echoing the less subtle screams of vulgarity ringing from Tullius.

As if blessed by Rhomigius himself, the pills obeyed Elysande's will and Ser Bryson Byrne collapsed to the ground with a graceless thud. Again, one unanimous gasp of hundreds of thousands of spectators. Byrne writhed on the floor. One hand clutched his stomach, but the other extended and dragged his body on a path toward Magnus.

*Gods, what is this man made of?*

His right arm alone was vigilant enough to force the body forward, armor and all. Magnus was on one knee. His eagle-shaped helmet had fallen off, so everyone could witness the amazement in his opulent, brown eyes. He returned Byrne's prior lack of chivalry by attacking him while down. This received a rain of boos from the audience, but it did not matter. *They have short attention spans anyway.*

Standing over the downed knight, Magnus Caesar wailed on the man's torso, the only thing preventing him from scoring the winning point was the working arm of Byrne that held his baton.

The blocks were shockingly defiant given his current state, as if Magnus was chipping at a brick wall with a stick. *He'll tire soon, no matter his God-given fortitude.*

Much to her disdain, Elysande realized she, as well as Magnus, had been duped. The hand of Ser Byrne that clutched his stomach came into action, like a hidden snake, and struck at the wounded leg of Caesar. Naturally, he crumbled, falling right into the ironclad bear's grip.

Byrne wrapped one meaty arm around the throat of Magnus, the one man unknowingly left standing against his king's assassination. The other arm held his baton, ready to stab Magnus right into his open belly. Byrne's legs constricted around his waist too, leaving him with no way to defend himself. But one thing still deterred the Mercian knight, the Heir of the Republic, the Bear of Byrne, from claiming victory, fleeting as it may be.

Magnus' hand held his enemy's shock baton back, but with Byrne's arm closing around his neck, he would not be able to resist for long without losing oxygen. *All this strategizing, investigating, and manipulating, and for what? The outcome would be the same had I done nothing at all.*

The young Caesar used his other hand to reach for his opponent's helmet. He dug for a long time under the gorget. The coordination was truly impressive. One arm fighting off the baton, the other on his opponent's helmet, all the while struggling for air. He managed to unstrap the helmet and rip it off despite bitter protest from the bigger man. Then, Magnus raised his own neck and violently smashed the back of his head down like a mallet on the snout of the Bear of Byrne.

The whole Colosseum could hear the Mercian knight's bloodcurdling cry, but his hold endured vehemently around Caesar's throat.

"Don't stop, Magnus!" Tullius ordered.

Again, his neck raised, and all Ser Byrne could do was watch as another mallet smashed onto his face. The hold broke, and Magnus crawled away like a freed animal. Byrne grabbed his nose, but it did nothing to abate the waterfalls of blood flowing from his nostrils. Magnus was on his feet first, but his limp prevented him from reaching Byrne before he could regain his own bearings.

Finally, the two warriors stood at a standstill. Bloody, battered, and bruised, the audience showered them in adoration at their co-opted showcase on tenacity and brutality. Magnus wiped the long, sweat-streaked bangs from his face. *If every girl in Rome wasn't already in love with him, they will be now.* He raised his baton in a daunting challenge to his enemy.

Byrne went to mirror him, but he stumbled. The bear remained on his feet, but his mind was spinning in circles. With his hands on his knees, he vomited all over the arena. The crowd groaned at the pool of blood and bile that spread around his boots. Elysande, however, chuckled.

As if he was given the task of putting a dying animal out of its misery, Magnus Caesar planted his electric baton into the chest of Ser Bryson Byrne. The hit was merciful, but it still made the knight fall over in sheer pain and exhaustion. And with him fell the conspiracy of the Heirs.

The crowd sighed in relief, disappointed the underdog lost, but relieved the elastic tension of the room was finally cut. Tullius hollered. Lance and Julia talked ecstatically to one another. The king too clapped in admiration of the showing from both warriors.

"At least I lost to the winner," Admiral Kassa Savon muttered from behind her.

"Next year, the tournament is yours," Elysande said in return.

Magnus fell to a knee. His companions sprinted from the back of the arena to his aid, half in concern and half in celebration. Bryson laid in a puddle of his own bodily fluids, unattended to. When Magnus could walk, he ordered someone to fetch his chariot. He mounted it on shaky legs and embarked on several victory laps around the arena to make sure he received the praise of every single spectator in the Colosseum.

Elysande could have sneered at his obnoxious gloating, but she too was celebrating a victory. *Felix has lost! He thought he could outsmart me, but my cunning is on another level. Best of all, Bryson won't say anything, or else endure the wrath and humiliation of the other conspirators.*

With the triumphant hands of victory massaging her back and shoulders, Elysande slumped into her seat and sighed. *So much for your 'insurance policy,' you filthy fucking liars.*

"Is something wrong, Mother?" Lawrence asked. "Did you want the Mercian knight to win?"

"Don't worry about me, sweetling," she smiled. She rubbed her son's head until his embarrassment showed. "I'm merely overjoyed by your cousin's victory."

...

After the Colosseum had cleared out of attendants, the royal family was escorted to the marble pillars and shimmering halls of the Temple of Rhomigius. They were taken to a garage beneath the stadium, packed into a limousine, and driven down Via Vittoria quickly with the help of a procession that cleared the way. The long line of cars both ahead and behind them were filled with the nobles of the KOH, that being lords and ladies, generals, governors, censors, and senators alike, all heading to the New Year's mass. This would be the first and likely only time any one of them would set foot into a holy temple for the remainder of the year.

A bold yellow sun greeted them into the afternoon, its rays sparkling off the canals crisscrossing through the city center. A faint smell of wine and citrus fruits kissed the air. Watching from afar on the elevated street of Via Vittoria, Elysande could see the Forum was bustling with activity. Merchants, street vendors, artists, and travelers were all making the best of a warm, sunny day. Many of them had likely come from the Colosseum. She wished to be in those crowds, but she had an appointment with the Immortals to attend first.

On both flanking sidewalks of Via Vittoria stood single rows of the military men and women of the KOH. Soldiers, Black Dogs, knights of the Praetorian Guard, and general police officers saluted the king's limousine as it passed by. The endless sight of them was humbling. Truly, an infinite amount of manpower was required to run the galaxy.

Gaius peered out the window, admiring the totality of his subjects who had come to pay him tribute. A slight smile crept across his sharp face; he had rebounded marvelously from the night before. His olive skin fresher, his face fuller, the weight of an entire planet and several moon colonies more manageable.

"Magnus won the Games, but he seemed to forget to make his request before you," Elysande said.

"He's a Caesar. There's little he could ask for," Gaius answered. "That being said, he told me his wish in advance, to be one of my commanding officers in the Grayspace campaign. He'll declare it publicly before takeoff."

"It's good to see the hardest workers in Rome are rewarded justly for their efforts," she joked. At least Magnus would be away from Orbis. *Hopefully the Synths put up a worthy fight. The longer the war lasts, the better.*

Caesar's half-smile reappeared on his face. In the front window, the towering Temple of Rhomigius came into sight. "The strength of the Caesar bloodline has fortunately passed down to the next generation. Magnus earned his victory today, but to one fault."

The queen cocked an eyebrow. "What fault is that?"

"Ser Bryson Byrne is a curiosity of sorts. He's a blessed warrior, but he came out of nowhere like a gift from the Immortals. For days, I was intrigued by what he would request from me if he had won, but now I'll never know."

"Well, there is always next year," Elysande offered dismissively, wanting to rid the name "Bryson Byrne" from her ears. The remainder of the ride was carried out in silence.

Every congregate in all three sections of the Temple of Rhomigius stood as King Gaius Julius Caesar and his family walked from the main entrance, down the gilded hall wrought in gold dust, and finally to the first row of pews closest to the altar where Dareo Cossus, the Pontifex Maximus, donned in brilliant white robes of silk, was standing in a line with the local pontifices and altar servers. In the hands of one of the servers was the silver spear that Rhomigius used to kill Extormitus and end the Creation Wars. *Its metal is remarkably shiny for something thousands of years old...*

Dareo and Caesar exchanged mutual nods as the king passed by and took his seat. Elysande searched around and spotted Praetorian guardsmen lurking around the upper floors of the temple in addition to the ones who stood quite conspicuously around the altar. She knew Ser Richard Dance was nearby too. He was always around her somewhere.

The Pontifex Maximus coughed to clear his throat, sending unholy grumbles throughout the multiple speakers built in the pillars of the temple. "My brothers and sisters, Carcians, Tisonians, and Mercians, and everyone of the Kingdom of Humanity, we come here to celebrate the end of an old year and the beginning of a new one. Glory to Rhomigius, who without his bravery and leadership so many ages ago, we would not be here today in this holy celebration of life."

"Glory to Rhomigius," the temple echoed. Elysande's eyes could not stop darting about the spacious halls. Every inch of wall was part of some glorious painting that, as a whole, depicted the epic story of the Creation Era, but she was not admiring the artwork. *Ser Bryson Byrne wasn't the insurance policy!* she told herself. *Felix is a liar; he played me for a docile woman, and now he loses for it.*

Despite the declarative statements, something in her felt hollow. *An insurance policy?! Why would Felix risk the wrath of the queen for an insurance policy? Byrne was his only card to play, he has to be.*

Cossus continued his sermon: "And glory to the King, Gaius Julius Caesar, whose untiring efforts have led humanity to new heights previously thought inconceivable." The old priest raised his pale arm and straightened it to the sky. "Hail, Caesar!"

"Hail, Caesar!" the crowd shouted in return, mirroring his right arm salute.

*A rat among the guards, but it would be impossible to tell which one!* Instinctively, her nails dug into the pew. Lawrence and Julia were by her side, naively listening to the Pontifex Maximus rattle on. *What if it's not a Praetorian guardsman, but an outsider sneaking into their ranks. Galla was found in civilian clothing, right? Armor like that can't be replicated easily. There's a rogue, no, a disease in their ranks.*

The senators of the KOH were regulated to the front pews on the left side of the temple. Elysande scrutinized them. *No Felix of Rezza, no Lucio, no Rachele.*

"Before our celebration can begin," Dareo Cossus started, "The king himself would like to say something to his people. So, with that said…" The Pontifex Maximus bowed humbly and stepped from the altar to a small seating section disguised in the back. King Caesar adjusted the laurel wreath on his head, rose from the pew, and marched to the center stage. As he turned to address the crowd, his Praetorian legions subtly arranged themselves into a V formation behind him.

"Thank you all for joining me here today on this mass of the New Year," Caesar began. Even while addressing thousands of people, he managed to keep his tone and disposition unfathomably personal. "As I stand here today, under the gaze of Rhomigius himself…" the king looked up to the ceiling where said Immortal was painted in his legendary pose. "Quite literally, really."

The congregates let out a low rumble of laughter respectable for the sacred atmosphere.

"As I stand under the protection of Rhomigius, I can't help but ask if not only myself, but if humanity as a whole has lived up to the image he has set for us." Caesar paused, pacing the room to let the question sit with the congregates. "We have been put in a position like no other to change the worlds as we know them. The last two decades alone will be remembered throughout our history as we today remember the Creations Wars, the rise of Elvezio Gasardi, and the construction of Pullo's Shield. And yet, as one chapter closes, another must be written. And that next chapter is in Grayspace… in battle against the Synths."

As Gaius spoke, Elysande scrutinized each of the guards. They were sentries. Stoic concrete. Unflinching. Never drawing attention to themselves, but their presence was undeniable. Then, an ungodly flinch. One of the golden statues rubbed his boot against the marble flooring, sending a piercing shriek throughout the temple. Elysande searched around and was shocked that no one else heard it. The guard continued to twitch. Compared to the average spectator, these movements were unnoticeable, but in the presence of disciplined statues, every spasm was a scream.

Lawrence and Julia stared off into space. Natalia gently stroked the nutbrown curls on the back of Jacob Mauvern's head. Tullius rubbed his nostrils, followed by a thunderous sneeze, *brute that he is!*

*Where's Ser Dance? Does he see this too?*

"People of the KOH!" Caesar continued. "I call on you humbly for your support as we head into uncharted territories. As we have proven before: united, humanity is unstoppable. We have made the galaxy a smaller entity, but our work is far from complete." The twitching guard reached slowly behind his cream-colored cloak. Elysande went to jump, but what if she made a fuss about nothing?

Gaius walked closer to the altar, closer to the rogue guard. "Every man and woman is present in the never-ending history book that is our developing galaxy, but only a select few are given the pen to author it." The guard revealed his hand, and in it was a pistol. "Now, my people, come and write history with me…"

The rogue statue raised his arm, gun pointed directly at the king of all of humanity. Caesar, whose back was to the altar, gazed out at his subjects completely unaware of the threat behind him.

"Gaius!" Elysande cried. This stirred the temple to life, as if Rhomigius himself had granted them the clarity to see the devil. This included a guard next to the rogue, who nobly, if not belatedly, grabbed him by the forearm and forced his aim away from Caesar. The two soldiers struggled, but the rogue managed to point his sidearm at the stomach of his antagonist and pull the trigger.

An ear-warping sound pulsed throughout the temple. The noble soldier was obliterated into bits of flesh and blood that splattered over the marble ground. Congregates shrieked in fear for their lives and disgust at the display of bodily horror. Elysande had never seen such magnitude of firepower from a weapon that small.

Sutorian was on top of the king instantaneously. The guards beside the rogue charged their rifles, but his unrelenting attack disoriented them. The guards on the opposite side of the transept charged their rifles too, but they were reluctant to shoot while their king was caught in their crosshairs.

Most of the crowd ran hysterically for the closest exit. Despite the wide doorframes, they quickly crammed shut, leaving hundreds of crazed spectators trapped in the halls and clawing at one another for escape.

The assassin fired again, obliterating more of the king's defenders. The weapon did not expel bullets or lasers, but a concentrated sonic boom of insane power. One brave soul managed to wrap an arm around him, knocking his helmet off in the process, but meeting the same sticky oblivion as the rest. With the helmet removed, Elysande scrutinized the assassin's face. Nothing struck her as remarkably familiar, until she glanced his mangled ear. *Quintus Longinus. A commanding officer of the Black Dogs.*

They made eye contact. Elysande felt nothing but ire radiating from his maddened stare. Impulsively, she reached for her children, throwing her body over them and spreading herself as wide as she possibly could. She closed her eyes, feeling their frantic heartbeats against hers. Her mind floated as she prepared for the end. Her soul prematurely ascended from her chest. Every nanosecond of life was utterly profound. She prayed, for the first time in a long time, that her body could protect them long enough for Longinus to be reprimanded.

But nothing happened.

She kept her eyes closed, kept her grip strong around her children, all while her ears listened to the masculine roars ringing from the altar. Finally, curiosity got the better of her. Without removing herself from Lawrence and Julia, she slightly craned her neck to see whatever horrors were occurring on the sacred ground. Sutorian and Longinus were in a wrestling match before the painting of Rhomigius. The old veteran concentrated his efforts on the deceptively powerful sidearm in the assassin's hand.

Tullius Caesar stood from the pew and charged up the transept. Jacob Mauvern followed, ignoring the horrified shrieks and reaching hands of Natalia. The king himself had retreated behind the lines of his guards, who all had their rifles drawn and ready to fire.

Sutorian, implementing his veteran instinct, pushed Longinus away, and without needing a command, the Praetorian Guard fired in unison, each ray of red laser ripping through the assassin's body.

He collapsed to his knees, filled with smoking holes. The soldiers relaxed their posture. The atmosphere of the temple dropped, but deceptively so. Quintus roared, shot back to his feet with resounding speed and agility, turned to Caesar with his gun in hand, and fired. Elysande winced. An explosion of flesh and blood erupted from the line of royal protectors around the king. Crimson rain splattered over everyone sitting in the front pews. When the torrent settled, the queen saw her king hunched over, protected by the morsels of metal and flesh that remained of his sworn defenders.

Sutorian jumped on top of the assassin, pinning him to the ground. And yet, the gun was still in his hand. With all the cauterized holes in his body, Elysande was beginning to think Quintus was an Immortal. She watched helplessly while the gun aimed for the captain's torso. Jacob Mauvern and Tullius Caesar berated him on all sides, but they too were oblivious to Longinus' sneaking hand. Elysande desired to interject, but her body refused to leave her children.

With the barrel firmly pointed at Sutorian's ribs, Elysande assumed the old veteran was fighting his final battle. But before Quintus could pull the trigger, his wrist was planted firmly to the ground. Standing over him and grinding a black boot into his arm was none other than Gaius Julius Caesar. A battle-seasoned commander himself, Caesar promptly kicked the gun from the assassin's hand, letting it skid across the altar and down the central hall.

"Hoist him up!" he commanded. Sutorian and Tullius grabbed Longinus and sat him up. The whole altar was drenched in blood. Somewhere behind a tapestry lurked the Pontifex Maximus, who stuck his head out from his hiding place when he heard the commotion had ceased.

"Are you all right?" Elysande asked her children.

"Yes, Mother!" they answered in unison, although their petrified and pale faces expressed the opposite.

She wrapped each of them in an arm and pulled them close. As she held them, she could feel their anxious hearts ease. "You are safe now; I'll make sure of it." She peered over Julia's head of curly brown hair and saw Natalia sitting alone at her pew, her clothes sodden in crimson. "Is everything okay, Natalia?"

Her expression was pale and blank. "I... I thought I was covered in my father's blood."

"Look," Elysande said, pointing to her husband. "Your father is fine. We're all okay, I think. Just breathe." She let go of her children and stood from the pew. "But I will go check on him to make sure. For the time being, the three of you sit here."

All three nodded in understanding. The queen shook her head, as if mothering the first daughter of her husband had caused a malfunction in the machinery inside her brain.

Caesar's face was filled with disdain as he looked down upon the failed assassin. Quintus still struggled to free himself, but the mutual strength of Sutorian and Tullius held him firmly in place. Jacob Mauvern hovered around too, strutting proudly as if he had contributed anything to saving Caesar. *Natalia needs you, and all you care about is looking good before the king.*

"Who are you?" Caesar demanded, his mouth grimacing. "And why do you dare make an attempt on my life?"

"Fucking usurper!" Longinus declared. He spasmed in his seat. His receding black hair was dripping in an ocean of sweat. If Elysande were to guess, she would say he was high on something. *It would explain his current tolerance to pain. But what kind of drug could be that strong?*

"I recognize his ear, my king." Sutorian observed. "I believe he's one of the commanders of the Black Dogs. Centurion Longinus, if I'm not mistaken."

"Traitors! All of you hell-bringers!" Longinus said in return. His breath was rapid. Whatever granted him invincibility was fading fast.

"Don't waste my time with riddles. Tell me what you want, or I'll blast more craters into your worthless vessel!" Caesar demanded, resurrecting a brutal coldness that Elysande had not seen since the Civil War.

Longinus bowed his head, defeated. They watched his mouth and jaw work as if he was practicing the words before he said them. Then, he bit down with a hard crunch. "For the Heirs!" he cried, as his mouth filled with saliva. His spasms grew uncontrollable, his mouth vomited a gratuitous flush of foam, the veins on his neck fattened and strained. After ten seconds of intense thrashing, Quintus Longinus was dead.

"Get this filth out of my sight," Caesar said, his tone harsh, but Elysande caught a glimpse of fragility that only years of familiarity could detect. She almost wanted to hug him. *Almost.*

Sutorian went to pick the body up, but another guard approached them. "Your Majesty!" the helmeted woman declared, frantically. Elysande possessed a grave suspicion the day's obstacles were not yet through. "There's an attack on the city! Armed soldiers have stormed the Forum and are heading for the Palazzo Reale. We've received reports from those trapped inside."

"Any idea which army?" Caesar asked. More than anyone else, Gaius was capable of striking a tone both coolly confident and boldly determined.

"No idea yet, sir." the woman answered. "But some of our soldiers say people in senatorial robes are conducting the assault."

Caesar thought pensively. Their attention transitioned so drastically that the assassination attempt seemed like a dream. *But this was Rome, after all. Bloody occurrences of this nature happened all the time before Caesar donned the laurel wreath.*

"Sutorian!"

"Hail, Caesar!"

"Rally what guards remain in the Temple and any soldier or police officer in the area. We will try to shut down this attack with manpower first, as I don't want my city ruined unnecessarily with anything heavier. Outside of that, make sure Rome's defenses remain as they are. We don't know where else we could be hit from, and it's best not to look any more foolish than we already do."

"Yes, King Caesar, it will be done." Sutorian marched off, waving for his squadron to follow.

Next, Caesar turned to his Commandant, placing his hand on Tullius' heavy shoulder. "Will you fight alongside me yet again, in the streets like we did in our youth?"

"Yes, brother. Anywhere you lead, I will follow."

Finally, the king addressed his queen. "I ask you to make sure our children are brought somewhere safe. If anything were to happen to them, then this attack will be a success."

Something in his stare gave her the confidence that the Heirs of the Republic would be put down. And as it would turn out, her inclinations were correct.

# TROYTON (VII)

The battle was a blur, a blood rush, a fever dream.

He recalled the anxiety that shook him as he marched out of the war room with the Tigress' personal guard and the hesitation that plagued him like a deadly disease while waiting with the Laktonnian soldiers inside the city and expecting every bomb that landed home to be the one to break the eastern wall of Old Ulthrawn. His last memories were of the massive orb of volatile energy hovering in the air, of the thick walls which crumbled like sandcastles, and of the golden Aquila standard as it emerged from the rubble and entered intrusively into the city. Never could Troyton have conceived opposing such an immaculate symbol, at least not until it glimmered before his very eyes, accompanied by the war cries of the army he once enthusiastically swore allegiance to.

Perhaps it was a blessing his brain had shut down before the real killing began. Troyton looked down, seeing the blood-soaked hands attached to his wrists that were strangers to him.

He was on the outside of the city, standing in the scorched remains of where the opposing legions once laid siege. The greenish sun hovered directly over the blackened sky, the smoke which blanketed the air being the composition of billions of particles that were once KOH soldiers, Laktonnian soldiers, and pieces of Old Ulthrawn.

The bodies of both armies laid across the scorched earth in heaps and piles, many of whom were more charred than the ground they died on. The air was stuffed with smoke and dust. Troyton drew a deep breath, undeterred, as his lungs were enhanced to withstand such toxicity. Others were not so fortunate. Those surviving soldiers without helmets coughed and hacked as their lungs begged for clean air.

Rachel Vikander thrived where her soldiers faltered. She radiated, despite being covered head to toe in ash. Her clothes were drenched in sweat and a mop of brown hair was plastered to her forehead as she exited her exoskeletal mech. And yet, she was as vigorous as ever, while her protectors appeared to be thoroughly exhausted.

The stone-faced Captain Throd locked his jaw in a scowl, but his eyes deceived the aching pains of battle that dragged his body down. The Paladin, Kentoshi, was equally winded, but at the same time there was an essence of positivity kindled in his eyes. Kent cleaned his sword affectionately, the intricate glyphs and whirls alight and burning through the Roman remains that dirtied the blade.

Troyton intended on watching the conversation from afar until he was spotted and promptly called over by the Tigress.

"Commander!" he saluted.

Rachel narrowed her gaze. "I have to say, Vorenus, I both envy and admire your valor. If half my soldiers possessed your instincts, there would not have been a battle to begin with."

Troyton blushed. "Sorry, it's all a fog to me. I promise you though, any of the valor I showed must be credited to your leadership."

Rachel laughed. She tried to get the Paladin and her captain to join in, but they continued to stare at the humanoid with the most antagonistic of faces. "My leadership?" she asked. "I did all I could to keep up with you!"

"I don't understand?"

"Don't play the obedient pet with me, my pride can handle it. You led the charge despite my best efforts. You were first into the fray. Without your bravery, our counterattack would not have routed the Romans like it did. I am truly grateful, and I will make sure your tremendous deeds today are rewarded."

Troyton sunk to a knee and bowed his head in deference. If he had stayed with the KOH, execution for treason would have been a certainty. Instead, Lady Vikander had offered him redemption, and he seized the opportunity to the best of his ability.

"Commander," Throd called. "We should return to the war room. Lord Vikander is waiting for you there."

"Today we earned a glorious victory." Lady Rachel proclaimed, although her tone expressed disappointment. "And yet my uncle will find a way to ridicule me."

"Lord Vikander is a tactical man. He will undoubtedly be pleased with our successful defense," Throd assured her.

The Tigress growled in return. "He would rather see Laktannon fall under his rule than prosper against it." Noticing Troyton was still on one knee, she ordered him to stand. "I can only hope the courage you showed today might mitigate his wrath. But don't worry, I won't mention your name until his head has cooled."

Troyton was not sure if he should laugh or express gratitude. His constant nervousness around the Tigress was infuriating.

A flock of star-splitters soared over their heads, heading toward the horizon where the dreaded KOH frigate still loomed. A small force of ships surrounded the colossal steel dragon, but they were a skeleton crew compared to what was before.

"We'll hit it with an EMP soon enough." Rachel said. "Sink it and find General Marko. I have much to say to him."

As *do I. Marko did nothing when the Inquisitors tried to kill the Fyrossian boy. If the KOH treats such injustices passively, then they don't deserve my service.*

Kent made an effort to speak next. However, he was not concerned with General Marko or the frigate. "Lady Vikander, there is a pilot in your service that I think you know. Her name is Matiyala… have you heard any reports from her?"

Rachel smiled gently. "Ah, yes. She's one of my best. Our air force suffered significant casualties, I won't lie, but my admirals say they performed better than expected. Don't worry, Kent, if any of my pilots could survive, it would be her."

Kent nodded, slightly reassured. The clouds of vaporized bodies were beginning to dissipate. The sun and sky brightened the earth. A sense of normalcy returned to Laktannon.

"How about you two head to the war room. I need to speak to Commander Vorenus alone." Rachel continued, patting Troyton on the shoulder. Throd and Kent dismissed themselves. When they were out of sight, Rachel continued. "Regardless of what happens next, the time will come when I will depend on you yet again, and it may be sooner than we both think. Can I count on you?"

Troyton was relieved he could finally answer her with certainty. "Yes, you can count on me."

The next few days proved to be as chaotic as the battle itself. Marion Zoltor and his sister had vanished, along with the other mages they partnered with. Without Marion, Troyton never would have rebounded. He imagined one day they would meet again, and he could sway the Archmage's son back to the side of the Vikanders. For now, though, he could not be occupied with pointless fantasies.

Rumors had also circulated that the body of an Enfari Inquisitor was uncovered in the demolished garden outside Unity College. Troyton suspected it belonged to the same mage who tried to kill the Fyrossian Emperor's son. Speculation overcame him, pushing him to check the spot. Nobody was to be found, likely burned away with the thousands of KOH bodies left on the battlefield. His wandering mind was not satisfied, the ghost of the Inquisitor continued to follow him for days.

Perhaps for his own good, he was isolated from the politics of the Republic Manor. There were rumblings from other soldiers in the downtown districts of Old Ulthrawn that the Tigress and Lord Vikander were preparing an assembly at the Tiger's Den, but no definitive date would be set until delegates of every city on the planet had come to the capital. Troyton could not help but take pride in his own dedication. Unlike more than half the provinces of Laktannon, he did not wait for the Vikander victory before throwing in his support.

He spent his nights shifting though the crowds that populated the southern tip of the city, closest to the oceanside docks. By far, it was the area least damaged by the KOH assault. It was here that Troyton received most of his updates on the happenings within the Republic Manor. A population drenched in alcohol was a population with loose tongues, and he had an eye for spotting important people willing to spill their news.

The cool sea breeze graced his skin. Talking and celebrating with the nightlife, although done with a calculated purpose, actually allowed him to feel welcomed. They were a community of grateful men and women, no longer taking life for granted after escaping the cold grip of death days before, experiencing every aspect of life with newfound appreciation under the multicolored lamps hanging over the congested but cheery streets.

Laktannon was a culture of individualism. Whereas a lab-born humanoid in a KOH legion stood out like a hangnail on the hand of Caesar, Troyton was now one creature of millions, as exceptional as he was mundane. During a night of cycling through his usual bars, he could sit at a table with ten or so others, all of whom belonged to separate species, and everyone would get along merrily.

These nights along the oceanfront were a needed escape from himself. He was given an apartment for the time being in the city center near the statue of Jradex the Foundation. His days were spent in his flat, waiting and anticipating a call from the Tigress. He would exercise in the lounge room to pass time, but his large body made nearly every workout awkward and tedious in the tight quarters. He tried moving the sparse furniture around to make it more spacious, but the only effective remedy would be to shrink his own body.

He wondered constantly of the Tigress' reward for his bravery on the battlefield. It was still a blur, but the way people approached him on the streets like a celebrity led him to truly believe he had saved Old Ulthrawn from the KOH. All the heroes of Rome had their one special moment of valor to catapult them from nameless soldier to military legend, and he may have just had his. He envisioned himself as a great general of Laktannon: a promising soldier on the verge of greatness who was betrayed and outcasted by his people, only to return with an army of his own and bring justice to those who had wronged him. The KOH was not inherently evil, but there were evil people controlling it from the inside. Rachel Vikander was humanity's hope of restoring the greatness it once had, and Troyton would be right there to aid her.

Exploring the city at night, talking to Laktonnians, and searching for clues served as his relief from the constant wondering of when the Tigress would call... and what exactly she would rely on him to do.

Eventually, he discovered training barracks close to home.

The other soldiers who frequented the barracks deterred him from complete uselessness. After a few days of stalling, he showed up to their dining common one morning and was welcomed warmly into their small squadron. They were awestruck by his body, quickness, and the grace with which he performed military drills. The soldiers, consisting of a mix of species who all deemed themselves "Laktonnians," were hungry to learn. Troyton, although not a teacher, naturally assumed the role of instructor.

The best of it all was the camaraderie.

No soldier in the barracks treated him like a freak or monster. Humbled by the experience, he would purposefully slow his own performance during drills to avoid potentially humiliating his comrades. When the day was over, the whole group would kindle a bonfire on the sidewalk and drink beers from a local brewery. Troyton would not drink, but he enjoyed the long hours of sitting around and chatting with his newfound friends.

The cycle of spending his days training and his nights wandering the oceanfront grew into a comfortable rotation. For the first time in a long time, the word "home" possessed a physical meaning. But as quickly as it started, a knock on his door one random afternoon broke the cycle of normalcy and pulled him back to relevancy.

He was laying on his bed and staring at the cracked ceiling when Kent Kentoshi came to his apartment. The Paladin was dressed neatly in black and white robes with an orange sash across his torso. The scabbard attached to his white leather belt was recently polished, as was the hilt of his Immortech sword.

"Vorenus," he said in a detached voice. "I have a message from Lady Vikander. May I come in?"

"Of course." Troyton said. Kent stepped inside, and following him was a Kalmar woman who introduced herself as Matiyala. She was significantly more jovial than the Paladin, and she looked exceptionally soldierly in a flight officer's tunic and cap. The three took their seats in the living room.

"What's the word from the Republic Manor?" Troyton asked. "I've seen hundreds of new visitors since settling here. At least some must be new supporters of the Vikanders."

"It's difficult to rally around a cause when said cause is so nebulous," Kent responded. "Rachel wants to continue the campaign against the KOH. She believes her successful defiance will unite the whole galaxy against the Triumvirate. Aethelwulf, well, it's unclear what he wants."

"It's incredibly obvious to me: Aethelwulf wants nothing." Matiyala chimed in. "He thinks the KOH will leave us be, but it's a fool's hope."

Troyton would follow the Tigress to any end of the galaxy, but even he was skeptical toward an all-out war with the Triumvirate. "Lord Vikander dealt King Caesar his one major defeat during the Civil War. He's not so much a fool as he is aware of the military power he's up against. Battling the KOH is one thing, but you can't have a war against humanity without getting the Denvari and Timanzee involved too."

Matiyala was unconvinced. "Our planet united can create an army comparable to any other. We've all seen the traffic flowing into Old Ulthrawn. Delegates from every province have come to give aid to the Tigress… if only Aethelwulf would do the same."

"She does not need Lord Vikander's support," Kent added. "I've been by her side since the turmoil between them first erupted. He's doing all he can to keep her quiet, but the Tigress can only be muzzled for so long."

"And that day may come sooner than we think. Aethelwulf will need to call an assembly soon, or else risk discouraging the same provinces he dedicated years to unify. Then, Rachel will have her chance to speak." Matiyala predicted.

Kent agreed. Even Troyton, dim as he was prone to be, could tell the Paladin wanted to kiss Matiyala as if they were the only two in the room. His eyes were sour and weary, but they showed love, nonetheless. Professional courtesy abated him, so he shifted his attention back to the business at hand. "This matter is exactly why I've come to speak with you. Rachel requests you support her at the Tiger's Den whenever the assembly is called."

Troyton was hopelessly confused, and Kent detected it. "Perhaps you could provide some anecdotes of her bravery on the battlefield. You were right by her side, after all."

"Being a former soldier of the KOH, maybe you could tell of the cruelties and injustices you've witnessed them commit." Matiyala offered. "Anything that could rally the delegates to Rachel's side would be most helpful, given you speak the truth."

Troyton froze, his consciousness transporting him from reality to the memory of his meeting with Caesar. Although most of the conversation was lost in a dreamy haze, he would always remember lying to his king. He did it for the promotion of a lifetime, but fate checked him for his dishonor. He looked at the hilt of Ser Kentoshi's sword and wondered briefly of the fate of the Fyrossian boy whom the Inquisitors attempted to murder.

*The boy must be dead too. My defiance, ultimately, meaningless.*

"With all due respect, why did Lady Vikander send you to relay the message?"

"She's under the impression that we're friends. Not sure where she drew that conclusion from though." Kent said, dryly.

Matiyala was appalled by his brutal honesty. "Kent!"

The Paladin shrugged with indifference.

"It's not a problem," Troyton assured her. "Hopefully, Ser Kent and I can one day call each other friends... Gods know he's sorely lacking them nowadays." The brash comment came from nowhere, but saying it felt oddly powerful. After all, he had no reason to show humility toward a mage.

In response, Kent Kentoshi arose from his seat, made his courteous goodbye through gritted teeth, and departed. Troyton wondered if his quip was too mean-spirited, but Matiyala's wink and slight smile as soon as the Paladin's back was turned told him that no irreparable damage had been done.

When the overly familiar silence of his apartment made its unwelcomed return, he had no doubt as to what needed to be done next. He grabbed a pen from his drawer, tore off a piece of paper from his notepad, and prayed to the Immortals that he could think of something to say at the assembly if the Tigress called on him. Time passed, but the pages remained blank.

Denial had gotten the better of him.

Even while sitting in the front row of the Tiger's Den and listening to Lord Vikander's attempts to placate the rowdy and raucous crowd, Troyton refused to believe that he would be called on to address the heated room. Lady Rachel was about to boil over as she listened to her uncle's pleas for peace. Their generals stood by the flanks of the podium and listened to their lord with deference, but the Tigress was a timebomb that began to tick the moment her uncle uttered his first word of capitulation.

And when her bomb finally exploded, it shook the walls, rafters, and the very foundation of the Den.

"Uncle, you speak of surrender as if the KOH will ever accept it. We are outlaws! Not just us, but everyone in this auditorium. The false King in Rome left us alone because he believed us to be docile, that our divisions would distract us from achieving our potential. Not only have we united the hundred provinces of Laktannon, a feat not accomplished since the reign of Jradex the Foundation, but we've proven we can match the KOH blow for blow on the battlefield."

"Silence!" Aethelwulf demanded. Despite the hostility in his voice, his reddened face suggested his will was faltering.

"I will do no such thing," the Tigress assured him. "Only a fool or craven would pass on the chance to destroy the oppressive regime that is the Triumvirate. And I'm sorry to say that I am neither of those things. A great deal of uncertainty comes with war, but I will take the route of uncertainty over the route of inevitable doom every time."

The packed crowd stomped their feet emphatically. Rachel could feel their support behind her, and she channeled it into her fiery rhetoric.

Despite the overwhelming odds against him, Lord Vikander showed no signs of intimidation. "You're young and bold, but impetuous all the same."

"And what of it?" Rachel demanded. "You try to portray my youth as a weakness, but what do old men yearn for more than to be young again?"

Aethelwulf grinded his teeth, his square jaw as hard as stone. "I've been fighting for humanity all my life. I served under the

Roman Republic and fought tirelessly against the KOH until the last of my military might was depleted. What can you tell me of the KOH that I don't already know?"

The Tigress smirked, conspicuously satisfied that the grizzled veteran had wandered right into her trap. "I may be ignorant of the innerworkings of the KOH, but there is someone who knows more about the cruelties of the Roman army than anyone else here." Her hungry eyes targeted Troyton. "Commander Vorenus, tell us of the army you once fought for."

He approached the podium on hollow legs. His footsteps gracelessly thundered throughout the otherwise silent auditorium. Aethelwulf shot him a malignant glare. Every face in the Tiger's Den merged into one suffocating blur.

"Don't be nervous." Rachel whispered, clutching his hand in hers. "Tell your war stories. You owe no one anything but the truth."

Troyton took a big gulp and felt a boulder slide down his throat. "Well, I suppose I should start with the basics," he said, turning away from Rachel and back to the mob.

"My name is Troyton Vorenus," he coughed. "I am a lab-born, genetically altered humanoid formerly fighting under the KOH. I cannot speak to all the battles waged by my former Kingdom, but I can speak to one. It was on Fyrossia. We had taken the planet with unexpected ease. When I made it to the frontlines, plans to take the capital city were already in effect. I saw many atrocities as I walked between the four great pyramids, but one stands out to me the most.

"I was with the Fyrossian Emperor and his family as they negotiated their surrender with General Antonius Marko. Three abhorrent Inquisitors were present too. One of them demanded the emperor's young son, a toddler, be executed for no reason at all... and my general did nothing to object to it."

Lord Vikander cut him off immediately. "I did not call this assembly to hear the sob story of a defector. This tale proves you're just as cold-blooded as the kingdom you fought for."

"I TRIED to save the child, Lord Vikander. And my treason has fortunately led me to Old Ulthrawn."

Aethelwulf puffed. "Even if this story is true, it shows what happens to planets when they defy the KOH. The destruction suffered in Fyrossia is what I mean to save us from!"

"The emperor surrendered before the attack, but the Romans decided to sack the city anyway." Troyton lied, the words flowing from his mouth more gracefully than a spring breeze passing through a meadow. The Den started to grumble as the delegates absorbed this disturbing, but utterly false, revelation.

The Tigress was surprised by this testimony too. She wanted a war, and Troyton was giving it to her. She promised him a reward for his loyalty. He could be a general, or the Tigress' own royal protector. He could conduct a ship, no, an armada! Lead an army into an epic battle. Become a legend himself, whose countless victories would change the course of galactic history. These wondrous imaginings swirled through his head. They sugared the lies to taste like honey in his mouth.

From there, the creative energy flowed as if he had invoked a celestial muse. As Troyton judged himself inwardly, not a single stutter of self-loathing interfered in his speech. "Marko wanted the capital to burn and the pyramids to crumble. He thought it would inspire obedience in the rest of the planet that way. Hundreds of thousands of Fyrossians died so the KOH could flaunt its strength. Surrender won't matter to them; it will only make our annihilation more enticing."

He could not stop himself from speaking, while Lord Vikander could not start a word from his throat. The delegates cried and yelled and swore, their declarations cracking like thunder and threatening to break the vaulted ceiling over their heads. Out of the corner of his eye, Troyton saw the Tigress smile.

She had her war.

. . .

The medals and badges, the fresh officer's tunic, and the new title of "general" were meaningless. They were more layers over his heart, but no matter how hidden it was, the thing that pumped corrupted blood through his veins was black and rotten. Millions were being shipped off to war, based on a deception of his own creation. Standing by Lord and Lady Vikander on a terrace at the top of the Republic Manor, he saw naïve faces on the soldiers as they filed into formation along the open square. They were a mixed army in every way imaginable, but survival had instilled them all with newfound discipline.

No star burned brighter than the Tigress herself, who had worked tirelessly since the declaration of war and seemed to be loving every minute of it. Troyton was allowed to follow her as a personal guard and assistant during her endless political errands. Her enthusiasm and energy kept him distracted enough from falling off the edge of self-loathing, and her gratitude for his testimony gave him reason to breathe the air of more deserved men and women.

Of course, she believed his lies to be true, and she often spoke of relieving the Fyrossians of KOH occupation before anything else could be done. It required much pleading from her war room strategists to change her mind.

He could not confess his crimes, for her sake. She had rallied the provinces of Laktannon against Rome, and a large part of it was due to his testimony. If word got out that he was a liar, her reputation would be damaged irreparably as well. For the time being, Troyton was trapped within the history he had devised.

Despite these successes, he had not slept for days. Guilt would not allow him a moment of release. It was one thing when he lived by the oceanfront and he could distract himself by walking the festive and pulsing city streets, but he had since moved to a suite within the Republic Manor, and it would seem suspicious if he was caught roaming around every night. So, for the most part, Troyton was locked in his room and forced to think of nothing else but his blatant deceptions.

Finally, he had enough.

Another sleepless night sent him outside. The moon shivered in the inky sky. The gaunt buildings that loomed overhead were dark and cold like giant stone monoliths. The barren streets were a welcomed sight, and the quiet rustling of litter as it swept across the concrete ground was an unusually sweet sound to his ears. With several deployments already sent into deep space, the city was at peace again where it was once overspilling with activity.

This night was not an aimless excursion through the portside nightlife. Although he tried to convince himself otherwise, Troyton acted with a clear goal in mind.

He entered the barracks closest to the Republic Manor, where one lone soldier was working the nightshift.

The man was sitting at a desk in the lobby, bobbing his head enthusiastically to whatever music was playing through his earphones. Troyton's unexpected appearance nearly gave him a heart attack.

"State who you are and what your business is," the masked man demanded.

"General Troyton Vorenus. I have come to inspect the prisoners."

The guard was delighted to hear the name. "General Vorenus!" He removed his helmet and under the weak ceiling lights did his Fyrossian qualities become apparent. "Firstly, I must say your speech was truly inspiring. I wasn't there, but a friend told me all about it. Immortals, I wish my superior had stationed me inside the Den that day."

Vorenus bowed his head. *I was bred for warfare, and yet my abhorrent lies have caused the most damage.* "Thank you for the kind words. Now, if you would excuse me…"

"However, sir, I was given no warning in advance of your arrival. I unfortunately can't let anyone in who doesn't have permission from the warden." There was a strong apprehension in the young soldier's voice, as if he was apologizing.

"You're a good soldier. What is your name?"

"Phlakka, sir."

"Okay, Phlakka. It is true that I'm not under any 'official' authorization, but I've been asked by the Tigress herself to facilitate the identification of General Antonius Marko, as I have been in the man's company personally. If you let me inspect the prison now, it would make her job so much easier. Chances are, you're not even holding him. I'll be in and out before anyone notices."

The Fyrossian thought long and hard. One overhanging light flickered. The outside commotion from a distant construction zone filled the lobby. An abrupt holler of maddening laughter rang from the floor above. "It's a-okay with me, sir." The soldier stepped away from his desk and started for the hallway. "Follow me, if you will, down the staircase. I'll unlock the vaulted door."

The Fyrossian soldier guided him along, opened the entryway into the cellblock via a special code on a keypad circuited into the vault, and left Troyton with mute trepidation as he dismissed himself.

The cells were packed with prisoners, each man provided with the same gray jumpsuit. By this late hour of the night, many had fallen into a great slumber despite the absence of pillows and blankets. No one stirred as Troyton crept along the aisles. Defeat had dulled their senses.

He barely acknowledged the packed cells with a glance. The man he searched for would have a private cell twice as fortified as the others.

Three rows in, he found the cell that stood out from the rest. It was smaller in width, only occupying a couple square feet in diameter, but it was much, much taller in height. Plus, it occupied one man alone, who was bound and fettered like an exotic animal on display at a carnival. Calmly, Troyton lifted the back of his black jacket to feel the grip of the pistol which had been tucked into the waistline of his pants.

Lucius acknowledged him before he intended on making himself known. "Troyton!" His voice was hoarse and dampened by defeat. "I was convinced Marko had you ejected out the airlock."

"I was one step ahead of him," Troyton said. Lucius went to speak again, but all his functions came to a halt when he spotted the badges over his friend's chest.

"I knew you to be deceptive, but an outright traitor? I don't know who I'm speaking to." Lucius said, his flippancy disguising the severity of the statement.

"Don't misconstrue me as some sort of mastermind; most of this happened by accident. The one thing I'm good at is soldiering."

Lucius laughed, although it sounded like a harsh cough. His black beard was long, the hair on his head wild and unkempt. A pink burn mark splattered across his face, and a chunk of his left ear was torn away. "So humble, but undeservedly so. You were always a lightyear ahead of the rest of us on Casca."

"How about I let you out of those chains." Troyton offered. Lucius extended his fettered wrists through the bars of his internment. Troyton broke the chains with one hand.

"I could've done it myself," Lucius declared.

"Why didn't you?"

"What would be the point? I survived the battle. No sense in risking any more for those conceited humans." His eyes glazed over as he reflected on the massacre. Troyton wanted to ask him of his war stories, but promptly thought better of it.

"We could've been mercs," Lucius continued. "Explored the galaxy together. Live like kings until one day our luck runs out and we die in a glorious hail of gunfire. Now where are we? Together again at another edge of civilization, surrounded by nothing but dust and death."

"I'm going back to Orbis, to retake the planet in the name of the Vikanders and the Human Republic." Troyton said, almost as a confession. Admittedly, he struggled to believe the words spilling from his mouth.

"How in the Hell did that happen?"

"That's why I'm here. I did- I did a bad thing. Remember Fyrossia? Well, I told the Tigress and all her people that we had sacked the capital city after the emperor surrendered."

Lucius smirked, his face pale and sickly. "Funny, wouldn't be the first time you started a war based on a lie."

"I don't understand my obsession," he confessed. "It's an uncontrollable disease. I swear that every time I lie, it's like an out-of-body experience."

"And are you seeking reconciliation from me?" Lucius asked, his spiteful eyes feigning sincerity. "You're a chronic liar. You deceived King Caesar, and now you've done the same thing to the Tigress bitch. Let me guess, she offered you a promotion too?" The humanoid, whom Troyton considered to be his closest friend, chortled at his despair. "What do you want me to say?"

"Laktonnians want war!" Troyton objected. "I just facilitated the process."

Lucius shot up to his feet and threw his whole body against the metal bars. A stomach-churning clang echoed throughout the prison block. "You're a selfish prick, my friend, no matter how you twist it. You accepted the rewards for your sins, and soon enough you will have your punishment too."

"You wanted to betray the KOH long before I did. I only left because I was forced to." Tears erupted in the whites of his eyes, sweat perspired in buckets over his whole body. *The lies, all the lies. Were they really performed selfishly?*

Lucius stuck his face into the bars so deeply that his flesh stretched and his eyeballs nearly popped out of their sockets. "I'm sorry, Troyton. It must disturb you to know you'll never be like the Roman heroes you pathetically worship. If you're truly as noble as you think, call the Vikanders down here and confess your sins. Only then will the guilt stop haunting you."

Troyton released his pistol and shot his friend in the chest. Lucius reeled backwards, tripped on his own feet, and collapsed against the opposing wall of his cell. He admired the fresh cavern in his chest, then turned back to Troyton, smiling.

"Rome's monster has turned against his creator. You must appreciate the poetry in that?" Lucius asked, blood flowing from his lips.

"I wish I could have met you on the battlefield."

"I wish I knew to look for you. Now, be a good boy and finish it."

Troyton did as he was told. Moments later, the Fyrossian soldier sprinted through the door. Once he analyzed the scene, his jaw dropped to the floor.

"I'll need to speak to whoever restrained this prisoner." Troyton commanded. "Someone needs to be disciplined for such negligence."

# ELYSANDE (XII)

The Heirs of the Republic burned out in a fiery display of shame, disgrace, and gratuitous projection.

Soldiers and citizens from Rezza, Venallia, and several other cities and towns in the northern districts of Carcia aligned with a skeleton crew of Black Dogs to form a measly army that successfully marched over the Forum, but failed bitterly in their attempt to storm and overtake the Palazzo Reale. They had managed to kill several Praetorian guardsmen in their invasion, as well as occupy the bottom floor of the Palazzo, but their efforts were rendered useless when the king himself arrived at the scene, donned in shimmering bronze and crimson armor, and routed the conspiratorial forces with next to no resistance.

Elysande had hardly made it back to her villa with her children before receiving word that the rebels had been defeated and rounded up by the local police force. The queen laughed to herself as her servant delivered the good news.

The senators were captured and imprisoned. In addition to the three she was aware of, seven more senators from northern Carcia had been arrested as well. She considered visiting the prison under the Capitoline Hill too see Felix of Rezza, to gloat in her victory, but deemed the matter below her and entirely unqueenly.

A conspiracy that must have taken months, or possibly years, to plan was tried and failed in a couple hours. To make matters even more humorous, the story of their insurrection was overshadowed by one of far more pressing, if not outright fantastical, stakes.

The trials were merciful, as many of the conspirators were allowed the choice of life imprisonment, life service on Halo, or, of course, death. Many chose life imprisonment, cowards that they were, and others chose death, but of the senators she knew, Felix, Lucio, and Rachele would all be shipped out on the next prison transport to Halo. And that, she prayed, would be the last she would ever need to deal with the Heirs of the Republic and their pathetic conspiracy.

*Felix expected the king to be dead. He planned for the chaos in the wake of his assassination to be the perfect time to take Rome and extinguish it of the royal family. Funny, Ser Byrne truly was his insurance policy.*

But King Gaius Julius Caesar was alive, and in more vigorous health than Queen Elysande had ever seen as she stood triumphantly beside him, riding a cream-colored chariot pulled gallantly by white horses through the Forum. Confetti rained from the sky, thrown by the thousands and thousands of spectators who flooded the Forum to see their king leave for his next campaign. Hanging from every edifice in sight were banners depicting the golden eagle of Rome, wings spread as if in tribute to the flight that the king was about to embark on.

Caesar whipped the horses with an appropriate amount of strength, accelerating the chariot forward with an abrupt force. Elysande laughed loudly as the sudden shift caught her off guard. This, along with the thousands of adoring fans, was more than enough to tickle her ego.

The king's face was painted red in honor of Rhomigius. He dressed for war in his bronze-colored breastplate, pointed shoulder guards, and crimson red cape billowing in the breeze. They each wore glittering laurel wreaths on their brows. To the common people, they must have appeared as Immortals riding through the humble plains of Orbis.

If she could have her way entirely, she would join her king on his crusade. Not for any newfound love for Gaius himself, but because of her unyielding desire to test herself on the battlefield. Despite this, she had gotten what she wanted most, her son as the crowned prince of the KOH. For that, she would have to be satisfied, temporarily.

They rode through the narrow streets of Rome to its most southern tip, the whole time flanked on both sides by devoted subjects of the KOH. There, on the oceanfront, sat a formidable armada of ships, lined up on a long stretch of tarmac. Like beached whales, the massive silver ships were drenched in afternoon sunlight. Without a cloud in the sky, the day was abnormally warm, and the white beach and light blue ocean especially crystalline.

Several armed legions were also in attendance, standing straight and soldierly and listening for the command from their king to board the ships. In every legion, one soldier in the front row bore the Aquila. Centurions ran along the brick-shaped columns, ensuring every man and woman was in proper order.

Waiting on an elevated platform before the impressive armada were the members of the king's council. Tullius Caesar, dressed in similar wartime attire as his brother, Sutorian, Admiral Kassa Savon, Shota Nakamura, and Cira, the dreaded witch and representative of the Inquisition. This would be both Tullius and Savon's last day in Rome for what would likely be months, or even years, if she was so lucky. It was a shame Cira did not go with them, as she was useless in her current role.

Placed before them were the daughters and son of the royal family. Gaius pulled the horses to the side and perfectly parked the chariot right at their feet. He stepped out, saluting. All three returned salutes, but Julia, his youngest, was the first to breakdown and hug her father around his legs.

Caesar chuckled, patting her on the back. "Don't cry for me, little one. I'll be home before you know it."

"But I want you to stay!" Julia insisted, as if she could legitimately decide for him.

Caesar sunk to one knee. "I'm relying on you to govern Rome while I'm gone. Do you think you can handle it?" Julia responded with a teary-eyed nod. Elysande's heart broke for her. *At least she has the benefit of wanting her father to be around.* "That's my daughter! You'll be so busy, you won't even realize I'm gone."

Next, the king moved on to Lawrence, the crowned prince. "My son, I count on you now more than ever before. Keep your eyes and ears open, and your mind ever curious."

"I will try my best, Father." Lawrence answered, his voice shaky. Father and son were not much the same, but with age Lawrence would hopefully adopt some of the king's better qualities. Caesar patted him on the shoulder and smiled.

Finally, he addressed Natalia. "Keep an eye on Proconsul Bebti for me. This is a once in a lifetime opportunity. Do your best to learn from it."

Natalia did not answer him, but instead returned his advice with a hug. Unlike Julia, she was tall enough to wrap her arms around his shoulders. "Stay safe, Father. I will think of you always until you return."

"Don't burden yourself," he insisted. "You've proven your independence. I couldn't be prouder of the woman you've become."

"Thank you," Natalia whispered, releasing him from her arms.

After a quick and final salute to his army and people, Caesar was ready to embark on his next crusade. Originally, the armada was gearing up for an invasion into Grayspace, but a recent revelation had changed the campaign's plans substantially, perhaps for the better. The story of the spotted Zoltors had progressed in a way that no one could have possibly predicted. According to further messages from General Marko, the Zoltors had been picked up by a rogue force and taken to Laktannon, the planet of exiles on a different edge of the galaxy.

This news caused Gaius Caesar to suspend his campaigns into Grayspace until the story played out. In another incredible twist of fate, Marko's scouts reported the rogue army was led by none other than Aethelwulf Vikander, brother to the king's old friend and rival, and he had fortified himself quite well in a small city on Laktannon. Still, Marko predicted that the battle would be won quite easily and the Zoltors, if they really were who they claimed to be, would be in his captivity in a matter of days. Suffice to say, the royal family and its inner circle of advisors were eager for the next chapter of this story to come through the relay station.

In the transpiring days, the queen's own brother, Drake, would return to Rome to confirm the near mythical reports of Zoltors. Elysande questioned to herself why he did not stay with General Marko to pursue them, but she could not be bothered with meeting him in private to deliver her ridicules. She prayed that

Marko's next report would be one of victory, that Aethelwulf and his army were eviscerated and his mages were being shipped to Rome in body bags. Then, news of defeat arrived.

The council room was shocked, except for Caesar, whose mathematical silence soon reached a solution for the problem at hand. The conspiracy of the Heirs added further urgency for action. And with that, the crusade into Grayspace was scrapped, meeting no objection from advisors and generals alike. *No auctoritas could be gained from a war against a fairytale. But against an old enemy of the kingdom, many a name could be elevated in that kind of campaign.*

"And this is where I leave you, my queen." Caesar said, feet mere meters away from the ramp of the frigate that would be leading the charge against Laktannon.

"Until next time," she replied. For simplicity's sake, they hugged and pecked each other on the lips. And then, Elysande turned away, never taking a moment to gaze back and watch her husband board his ship.

As soon as the warp of spatial sound and energy blipped in the sky, signifying the armada's transition into hyper speed, Elysande marched to her limousine and departed for home. She rushed Lawrence and Julia along, despite their naggings to stay for "just a little bit longer." They exited the runway down to the closest street by the beachfront. She identified her limousine, where Richard Dance was waiting in the driver's seat. With them all packed inside, the queen's royal protector drove off.

With several causes of her migraines deep into outer space, she felt like a new woman. The freedom was too good to be true. *More trials will be ahead of me, but I must embrace the peace for now.* Although some of her problems were gone, two were waiting for her in the villa, surprising her as she came through the door. These ones could not be ridden of so easily, as they were hereditary.

Drake Bodewin took the liberty to help himself to the royal liquor cabinet in the kitchen. With his undeniable skill of finding hard liquor, Elysande wondered if he was indeed a mage after all. He raised his glass as she entered the atrium. In return, she greeted him with a glance of concentrated disinterest. Lawrence and Julia were more ecstatic, but the queen abruptly dismissed them to the backyard to play. She could not risk her brother's influence rubbing off on them.

Her father, Reynard, was present as well, sprawling his arms across her couch and generally making himself at home in her living room. As he sat across the fireplace, his red beard and hair merged with the rising and falling flames of the holographic fire. "I take it the king has departed on his next campaign?" he asked.

"I'm surprised you were not there for the ceremony," she returned, taking up her own seat in the living room. Sunlight reflected through the large windowpanes and onto the white marble floor. Looking out, she spotted her children in the backyard, grabbing a soccer ball and kicking it back and forth.

"I will be soon," Reynard said, defensively. "The Crimson Armada will follow Caesar wherever he goes. But first, I have a mountain of arrangements to handle in Erron."

Elysande nodded, "True, such as who will act as Overseer of Mercia during your absence." She gestured toward Drake, who smirked lowly at her insistence to create conflict.

"Governing isn't my specialty," her brother said, his crystal blue eyes beaming.

"Then what is your specialty?" Reynard asked through grinding teeth.

Drake took another sip from his glass and flipped his golden auburn hair from his eyes. "Killing, probably. It's what I'm most accustomed to. Give Erron to an uncle, aunt, or cousin, if you must. The people of Mercia will thank you for it."

"You lie, brother." Elysande hissed. She craved to slap the glass from his hands and watch the shards scatter across the floor. "If you were so skilled at killing, there would not be two Zoltors continuing to infect the galaxy."

Reynard scoffed, "That's entirely inappropriate!" His normally white face flushed red with anger. The name which she spoke darkened the room, years of pain resurrected. In the corridor, she heard the footsteps of Fredrick and Boltof, marching off to their deaths.

"No, she's right." Drake conceded. "I should have killed them, but my hubris got in the way. I saw one of them with my very eyes.

Looks more like his mother than the Archmage, but the features are undeniable."

"So, what stopped you?" she asked further.

"I had another mage in the room with me, used him to draw out the boy. They had somehow integrated themselves into the academy." He paced across the living room, as if enacting the events as they were retold. "I recognized him from living on Spyre. I tasted blood in my mouth, got distracted, and I let them get away. It's a mistake that won't be made again, because I won't be getting anywhere near this war with Laktannon."

"I agree, best to leave it in capable hands," Elysande said. *Like mine own, if only I had the chance.* "But you won't find Rome as welcoming as you may think."

Reynard scoffed again. "Power has already rushed to your head. Allow me to provide the antidote: Rome is not yours with the king gone. You are the figurehead to maintain the status quo; don't expect anything but laughter from the Senate if you try to propose any new laws."

"Are you sure, Father?" She paused to allow his fears to run wild throughout the room. "I urge you to relax. Gaius and I are on good terms, and those terms will certainly improve now that we're lightyears away from each other."

She stood from her chair and went to the windows that separated the living room from the outside porch. The low sun warmed her skin. All at once, the tiredness of the past few weeks washed over her. "Lawrence is the crowned prince, something we've both wanted since his birth. I'm completely aware of what's at risk, and I won't jeopardize it... for his sake."

Reynard raised his hands in relief. He was nearing the door before she could turn to face him. *I've spoken the magic words, and now he'll disappear.* "I've underestimated you, daughter. Perhaps the KOH is in capable hands after all. And if not, Gaius has told me he is sending his uncle and aunt to Rome to make up for his absence."

"His what?" Elysande gasped. She looked desperately to Drake, who reveled in her surprise.

"Oh yes," her father began. "Manius and Claudia Caesar. They've been living on the Kappelli Isles for years, but they were eager to answer their nephew's call for help. Expect them soon, they'll be in need of long-term residency."

"I don't believe you."

"You don't have to, but you risk making a bad first impression to Lord and Lady Caesar for when they come to Rome and you have nothing prepared." And with those kind words, Reynard exited. It was, in actuality, one of their more diplomatic closings to a conversation. Drake followed his father, laughing to himself along the way.

"Are you sure you don't want me around?" Drake asked as he walked along the stark corridor to the front entrance. "Two Bodewins in Rome are twice as formidable as one."

Elysande stomped her foot to ground, feeling twenty years younger. "You have a fortnight to find something to do with your life. If you're not out of Rome by then, I'll have Ser Dance drag you out."

Drake spun on his heel and left, chuckling the whole way to the door. "Oh, I would love to see him try!"

Elysande returned to her chair and watched the holographic flames lick the stone outline of her mantlepiece. She hunched over, shoulders on her knees, hands riding through her mane of auburn hair. Caesar trusted her, but not as much as she naively assumed. She had hoped that Rome would be rid of his family, but it was not the case. She vaguely remembered talking to Manius and Claudia at her wedding, but their personalities were lost to her. It was, after all, a day she tried desperately to forget. Considering the family they belonged to, she could logically predict that they were obnoxiously determined, stern like a sheet of steel, and too smart for their own good.

*The obstacles never end. I rid myself of one flock of Caesars, and another appears as if by magic. And with the Heirs defeated, what will come along to take their place?*

She considered calling Liscinia Drusilla, but for what? The Heirs were defeated, making her practically useless. And yet, the desire to see her again persisted somewhere in her chest. She could invite her over for no reason at all. Drink wine, eat dry cheeses, and talk over the moonlight. A favorite pastime for Carcians, but in so many ways Legate Liscinia was an exception among the norm.

*You have enough on your plate. It's impractical to add more. That's how this life works.* She recalled Liscinia's deep brown eyes, like acorns in the low sunlight of autumn.

*Very few Carcians possess her drive. She was not born into nobility. The story of how she achieved the rank of legate at her age must be fascinating.* Despite the hours they had spent together, Elysande never bothered to ask.

But she was the queen of all of humanity, and even if Liscinia refused her request, she could not refuse her command. Searching her kitchen counter, Elysande retrieved her phone and dialed the number. Thankfully, her body acted independently of her mind's blatant objections.

"Hello?"

"Yes, Liscinia?"

"Yes, my queen, do you need something?"

*What did I tell you about calling me 'my queen?'* "Yes and no. I've uncovered a small detail on the... project we were working on. As with everything else we've handled, I think it's best we discuss in person."

"I completely agree," Liscinia said. "I can meet you at the factory, if it pleases you."

"No, it doesn't." Elysande paused for a second. "Come to my villa tonight. We'll talk then. I can have Ser Dance escort you."

"Tonight?" There was a slight apprehension in her voice. Elysande became horrified by the sense of exposure. "Yes, I'll be there. Don't bother Ser Dance, I can drive myself."

"You don't have a shift with the Black Dogs that I'll be interrupting?"

"No. I'm off for the next few days. So tonight, at your villa, you can count on me."

"Good. Don't leave me in anticipation." She hung up her phone and slammed it down on the kitchen counter. Her body was gifted with an imperceptible energy that made her feel invincible. Needing to spend it somewhere, she headed outside to check on her children.

Lawrence caught the soccer ball underneath his spiked cleat. Pushing it against the ground and kicking his leg out from behind him, the momentum caused the ball to spin clockwise and roll up the top of his foot and cradle on the arch of his ankle. The crowned prince kicked the ball up, sending it to his opposing knee. From there, juggling it from knee to knee was easy.

After he was thoroughly satisfied with showboating, he kicked the ball back to Julia, and the volley between them continued.

While she watched the hypnotic rolling of the ball across the lawn of stiff grass, the queen fell into a mental exercise. She considered why Felix of Rezza, or any of the other Heirs, did not name her as an accomplice to their conspiracy. Obviously, they had no physical proof, unless one was to consider the "word" of conspirators who had already proven themselves violently duplicitous. Felix could have snitched to Gaius that she was the sponsor who got Bryson Byrne into the Games, but Elysande would have denied it if confronted. Naturally, he would have sided with his queen, not from trust, but the influence of her family.

Maybe one of the Heirs did tell Gaius, and suspicion then motivated his decision to send his uncle and aunt to Rome. If that was the case, the return of the Vikanders could not have happened at a better time. The king needed the Crimson Armada for the oncoming war, which meant good relations between himself and her father were paramount. As long as the Crimson Armada remained the most formidable naval force in the galaxy, she had immunity.

And yet, the queen did not feel as secure as her position would suggest. As she watched her children play, she could not help but want to gather them inside and lock the doors of her villa forever. Many more conspirators were uncovered during the attack on the Palazzo Reale, but that did not mean they were all uncovered. She knew for a fact that one of the Heirs still lingered close by, hiding in plain sight, and his name was Ser Bryson Byrne.

He did not partake in the storming of the Palazzo, likely due to the effects of both the pills Elysande had fed him and the subsequent beating he had suffered at the hands of Magnus Caesar. Byrne roamed around Rome to this day, refusing to make eye contact with the queen, but always in her presence no matter where she turned. Byrne was probably hoping Caesar would remember him, that his showing alone in the Gladiator Games would be enough to get him on board the king's war party.

*But Bryson Byrne will have to learn that he is yesterday's news. No one ever remembers who came in second place.*

"Mother!" Julia called. Elysande's attention shot forward, sensing danger. "Come play with us!"

The queen sighed deeply. "Really?"

"Yes, please!" Julia insisted, kicking the ball to her feet. Watching it glide across the grass, Elysande smoothly stopped it with her foot. Sinister shadows lurked in every corner, but for now the golden sun was in bloom, so she would enjoy it while it lasted.

# KENT (X)

Kent convinced himself for days that Tali, the First Scholar, and the Archmage's children had merely gone missing. He waited endlessly, believing vainly that at any moment they would walk into the Republic Manor, unharmed and ready to make amends. They never did. Not a single one of them. He used every excuse he could conjure to combat the disappointment that slowly broke his spirits, but acceptance hit him with the grace of a crash landing.

After the battle, Kent traveled to the ruins of what once was the lawn around Unity College. He was exhausted from hours of fighting, but the fear of what could have happened to Ariel and Marion had encouraged him to continue searching. Each step sent whirlwinds of ash and soot into the air. The once beautiful grass and garden were now a hellish landscape of smoke. By the end of it, his dirtied and blackened clothes were one with the ruins.

The body of Aethelwulf's man, Sergeant Parkton, was the only one Kent could find completely intact. He had a large hole in his chest, his inners cauterized by a laser likely shot from close range. Beside him were the singed remains of a silver cloak. A dreadful sickness shivered down Kent's spine. He bent to a knee to investigate, but the miasmic stench of the crime scene kept him at a distance.

If the cloak was not enough to prove the work of an Inquisitor, the grotesque Enfari blade swaddled inside served as the irrefutable evidence. Charred bones were all that remained of the Enfari. Kent picked up the skull and analyzed the melted metal wrapped around its jaw and questioned what injury a man would have to suffer to need such a contraption.

*They killed the Inquisitor, but where did they run to? I should have been there to protect them!*

As he walked, his foot touched something eerily robust. Uncovering the ash at his feet, Kent reached down and grabbed a pistol. *Ariel's pistol.* He remembered nostalgically how she tried to shoot his head off with it when they first met in the Underbelly. A whispered curse left his lips. He kicked a heap of ash into the air and questioned morbidly if what remained of the Zoltor bloodline now drifted as indistinct specks in the breeze.

His investigation saw no further results. Exhaustion from the entire day overwhelmed him and he woke up hours later in the same field, clothes caked in dust and dirt. Temporarily giving up, Kent returned to his suite in the Republic Manor and subsequently slept like a rock.

The news broke to him over the course of several days. Tali and Atticus Zoltor were officially missing too. The Tigress had ordered a city-wide search for the mages, or at least their bodies, but nothing came of it. Kent held onto faith for as long as he could. The conjured image of them stepping into the atrium of the Republic Manor would not leave his head. Matiyala's presence brought him some relief, but his mind was too fixated on the Paladin Order, or whatever was left of it.

Eventually, acceptance of their betrayal came in anticlimactic doses. Logic guided him to the conclusion that all four, alive or dead, could not be missing for this long. None of them were ever loyal to the Vikanders, and they likely used the heat of the battle to embark on their escape. Reports of a missing ship all but confirmed Kent's theory, and he had yet to shake the disease of disappointment ever since. He tried to end their last interaction on open terms, but Tali and Atticus were unflinching. They could not align themselves with the Tigress, despite her generosity. The ears of the Archmage's children were likely poisoned by this thinking too, and so they fled. Ultimately, they chose freedom for the hefty price of vulnerability.

The Paladin Order, after all his work, was truly lost.

Kent Kentoshi patted the hilt of his Immortech sword as he entered the war room beneath the Republic Manor, wondering desperately what his future on Laktannon would hold. Inside the war room sat the generals who would be leading the resistance against the Triumvirate. At the head of the table, in front of a giant monitor, was Lord Aethelwulf Vikander, appearing more grave and tired than ever before. To his right was the Tigress, brimming with excitement in her chair. Both Vikanders had been impossibly busy of late treating with representatives of the Hundred Provinces of Laktannon. One Vikander was handling the pressure tremendously better than the other.

Also at the table were General Gressna, whose bronze scales shimmered under the glaring ceiling lights, Captain Throd, as stern as ever, and Troyton Vorenus, who, much to Kent's disdainful surprise, was wearing the badge of 'general' on his right breast. The final member of the war room was a man Kent had never seen before, which caught him off guard considering all the time he had spent in the Republic Manor. Given his large head and brow, low jowls, three squinty eyes, and, most of all, his corpulent body that required a silver hoverchair for mobility, the man unquestionably belonged to the Timanzee species.

"Ser Kent, please take a seat." Rachel introduced him. "This is General Qualaheen VolBrock. He will be our chief officer in the campaign against the Timanzee Empire."

"VolBrock?" Kent exclaimed. The Timanzee Empire made up one-third of the Triumvirate, next to the KOH and Denvari Union. The Emperor of the Timanzee himself was Nasquabar Gal'Een VolBrock, or as most people outside the Empire called him, "The Nas."

"Don't allow the name to alarm you," VolBrock insisted. He was dressed in a long, spotted robe of yellows and purples. The vibrant hues of his clothes made his grayish complexion appear all the more pallid. "I have no allegiance to my father, as my father has no allegiance to me."

"And how did that come to be?" the Paladin asked, unafraid of sounding hostile.

VolBrock continued, undeterred by the brazen interrogation. "I am the oldest of the Nas' plentiful sons and daughters. Naturally, I was the heir to my father's empire, until he set my mother aside on false accusations of adultery. He married another woman before my mother could be buried, and soon disowned me for their first child. To escape the same fate, I fled to Laktannon."

Rachel Vikander caught Kent's skeptical eye and added, "My army makes no division based in race or former allegiance. We are all Laktonnians. General VolBrock has been unfairly displaced like the rest of us and is no less deserving of retribution."

Qualaheen VolBrock rubbed his fleshy chin with a small hand. There was something contemptibly astute in his methodical tone. "I know my father's war strategies better than anyone else. There is no man more suitable to lead the campaign against him."

"Then where were you when Old Ulthrawn was under attack?" Kent inquired, further correcting any illusion of niceties.

"My city is on the opposite side of Laktannon. There was no time to gather an army and bring it to Old Ulthrawn, especially with KOH star-splitters occupying the sky."

The Paladin nodded, "Right."

VolBrock's attention turned to Vikander. "You did not tell me I would be put on trial. Are all your advisors so, how do you say, truculent?"

"We have matters to attend to, Ser Kent. The sooner you stop this pointless interrogation, the better it will be for us all." Aethelwulf interrupted, exhaustion taking the form of heavy bags beneath his eyes. "Excellent. For the first matter, costs to repair the city have reached an inconceivable number. Given we have a war to fund too, I have not the slightest clue how Old Ulthrawn will recover from her injuries."

"Don't think so narrow-mindedly, Uncle." Rachel insisted. "We have hostages to ransom. Plenty of sons and daughters of rich Carcians, Mercians, and Tisonians that will pay us millions of credits to have their precious children come home."

"Metal from the frigate and downed star-splitters could be worth something too." Captain Throd added. "Plenty of traders and factory managers on Laktannon alone are eager for quality KOH steel. If we look further to Prisilla, we should find lucrative offers."

"General Vorenus, you can assist in the deconstruction of the frigate. Understand me?" Aethelwulf ordered.

"Yes, Lord." Troyton coughed. The war room was cool, and yet the humanoid's skin was glossy with sweat. *Gods, do we need him though*, Kent reflected. The man had near single-handedly routed several legions of the KOH as they invaded the eastern gate. In the fog of war, Troyton appeared to be an Immortal, so utterly beyond everyone else's capacity for both bravery and savagery that his actions seemed not of these known worlds. *If the KOH is brewing other humanoids like him, we will have an arduous war ahead of us.*

Aethelwulf diligently continued his list of matters. "Has anyone seen or heard from Saryn Malor since the battle? He hasn't been spotted in Old Ulthrawn for days."

"He's missing too?" Kent asked. All things descended rapidly down a cliff as soon as he agreed to the Denvari's dinner invitation. Had he not been so naïve, the Zoltors may still be by his side. "Could he have perished during the invasion?"

Captain Throd chortled. "I'd wager that unlikely. Saryn kept his Eclipse Syndicate as far from the KOH as he could. They hardly suffered a scratch, while the rest of us were lucky to finish the day with our souls in our chests."

"I label him a coward on a generous day, and a deceiver when I'm feeling honest," Rachel declared. "Captain Throd, would you say the reservation Lord Saryn displayed on the battlefield could be considered treasonous?"

The captain's eyes bounced between both Vikanders. Ultimately, he kept his large jaws shut.

"No doubt he's reserving his strength for the wars to come." Aethelwulf said, dismissively. "Throd, keep your guards on the lookout for Saryn leaving the city."

"Do you expect anything malicious, Lord?" Throd inquired.

"Not that I'm aware of. But with a man as... enigmatic as he is, it's always in our benefit to know of his whereabouts."

"We should have him forfeit his syndicate." Rachel proposed.

"Showing division in our ranks at the dawn of war is not a wise strategy, Niece." Aethelwulf corrected, somewhat abrasively. "But on another note, a handful of our ships have launched into space. General VolBrock will be leading the Timanzee front, and I shall meet King Caesar's navy. Rachel, I would recommend you and General Gressna start planning a strategy against the Denvari Union. Once we contact Saryn, it should-"

"The Denvari Union is not a threat like the other two. They are the odd group out of this unholy trinity, and it's a waste of resources to go instigating an unnecessary fight... at least for the moment," Rachel said.

"So now you hesitate toward starting quarrels. And how else should we spend those resources?" Aethelwulf asked, clearly annoyed by his niece's constant objections to his rule.

"The Denvari Union must be kept at bay, and I would give that authority to you, General Gressna." Rachel offered. The Drakonid craned his long neck and hissed. "Uncle, I can win something far grander than a few victories over a union whose glory days are behind them. By your command, I can give you Rome."

"Rome?!" Troyton exclaimed.

The Tigress smirked. The news shocked the war council as soundly as she anticipated. "Although war against the Triumvirate was never a certainty, I could not help but plan for it. Lord Aethelwulf, I have allies in the KOH. You may think it far-fetched, but this has been my design for years. I promise you that Rome can be ours in the matter of a year. We can end the Triumvirate's tyranny without suffering the tremendous losses you expect."

Kent's head filled with dreams of storming the capital city of the KOH and taking it from those who had turned against the Paladin Order. He imagined how the Caesars and Bodewins would plead for mercy, and how cathartic it would be to channel their cruelties back onto them. He wished Tali and Atticus were here to see the benefits of staying loyal to the Tigress. *The Paladin Order will only be safe with the Triumvirate extinguished... and I can help make that day come sooner than any of us could ever imagine.*

"Have you seen Pullo's Shield?" Troyton asked, still incredulous. "Rome is impenetrable. Even with Caesar's army defeated, it could take years to properly cut it off from the rest of Orbis and force a surrender."

"Let her speak." Aethelwulf demanded. For the first time, he appeared legitimately enticed by one of his niece's propositions.

"That's where you're wrong, my friend." Rachel corrected. She went to the monitor and pulled up a map of Carcia. The sight of Orbis alone ignited a fury in Kent's soul. "Rome will have the orange and black banners of Vikander hanging from its walls by this time next year… and we start with Paranthon's Cross."

Rachel Vikander left the war council in a stupor. Even Aethelwulf was uncharacteristically open to her strategy. Invading Carcia would be no easy task, no matter the size of the army or experience of the leader controlling it. However, after her success in commanding Laktonnian soldiers against the Roman legions, Kent held complete confidence in the Tigress' capabilities.

As everyone filed out of the conference room, Rachel asked Kent if he could stay for a few words in private. Captain Throd was the last to leave, and he closed the door for them as he exited, no doubt remaining on guard on the opposite side. The fact that the captain could confidently allow Rachel to be alone in a room with him was oddly endearing.

Rachel started speaking as soon as they were alone. "There is no easy way to say this, so I will make this proposal in the bluntest way possible: I want you to be the new Archmage."

Kent felt the air squeeze from his lung. The room abruptly turned upside down and inverted on itself.

"I- I could never, ma'am," he refused. His eyes widened, and his mind fell into a trance. He pictured himself in the same robes as Archmage Marius, standing statuesque on the altar of Spyre with hundreds of Paladins under his authority. Despite the dazzling thoughts, years of practiced discipline successfully abated his ambitions.

"Is the title of Archmage passed down through bloodline?" she asked.

"No, ma'am."

"Is the title reserved for those of a specific species?"

Kent was offended by the question. "Of course not. Paladins renounce any loyalties to their former species upon joining the Order. I'm more mage than I am Druin."

"So it is possible for you to be the Archmage?" Rachel inquired further.

Kent's head was spinning, his green face deepening in color. He knew the path she was guiding him on, and his answers submitted him through this temptation. "It is technically possible... but I must be nominated by the living Archmage, then have it voted on by a council of other Paladins."

*There is no council, so I CANNOT be the Archmage.*

Rachel shook her head. "Forgive me, as my knowledge of the Order is limited, but there have been times in history in which a Paladin was declared Archmage without going through this process."

"You are correct, but only during periods of crisis."

"Well, Ser Kent, the Order is in dire need of resuscitation. Spyre has crumbled. The few mages who refuse to wear the silver cloak of the Inquisition are left as fugitives of the entire galaxy. Has there ever been a time of greater crisis for your people than this very moment?"

"No," was all Kent could mutter. He meant to say more, to refuse the honor he did not deserve, but any humble objection emerged from his throat in stutters and mumbles.

"If you are done denying yourself, I suggest you take the position," Rachel said.

"I-" Kent slapped himself, the sound cutting through the war room. "I cannot be the Archmage! Taking the role for myself would be an insult to the Order. Besides, I'm not ready for it. I couldn't protect my own squire, let alone the Order."

"How could you be this selfish? Don't take the title for yourself, but for your people. Be the rallying point they need! Seeing that the Order has nothing left to lose, a sagacious, driven Paladin such as yourself would be the perfect figure to shepherd them through these dark times."

Kent went to object again, but the Tigress cut him off, this time with a more endearing tone. "You showed unparalleled bravery and leadership against Rome. I have met many a man who desires command, but few who can live up to the task when actual lives are at risk. You were presented with an impossible challenge, and you beat it. The Paladin Order would be nothing but lucky to have you as its Archmage." She reached out and lightly touched his arm.

Kent sighed. She was right, he could establish a new Order. Mage-kind would no longer have to live in the shadows. A new, stronger foundation for the Order could be built in Laktannon: a safe haven for all mages.

"I don't want this position, but it seems to have been thrust upon me. For the sake of my people, I will... take on the mantle of Archmage."

He thanked the Tigress for her forethought, prayed to Serios for guidance, imagined himself in the glowing halls of Spyre performing the knighting ceremony that changed mages into Paladins. But the exultance he felt died with a flicker when he remembered the Zoltors. "And what about Marion and Ariel?"

Lady Rachel shrugged. "We both know they weren't captured by the Inquisitors. Desertion was their choice, and I won't do anything to change their minds. If they cannot see the validity of our cause, then why spare them a second thought?"

Kent agreed. Not another word of the Zoltors was spoken.

. . .

Matiyala nestled her cheek on Kent's chest. She was asleep and had been that way for hours. He stroked the long tentacles on her head, finding a sliver of peace as time passed. Unlike most others, sleeplessness and restlessness were not one in the same for him. Although his mind refused to shut down, Kent was happy to stare off into space, sensing the comfort of Matiyala's warm body against his and listening to the gentle pattering of a rare rain hit the roof. He made the unspoken decision to enjoy moments like this while he could, for it was impossible to know how many more they would have together with war on their doorstep.

He was Archmage now, whatever that meant. The only mages he could have had authority over deserted him. The honor of carrying on the legacy of the most vital role in the Order was certainly humbling and filled him with a profound sense of responsibility, but Kent could not help but accept that nothing in his life had changed since inheriting the position.

*Give it time. You cannot expect to rebuild the Order in one day,* he reminded himself. But doubt persisted. *What if no one comes? What if I'm never given the materials needed to rebuild? Will I morph the Archmage role into a farce?*

*A parody, that's what I'll be, me and the new Order too.*

An unexpected knock at the door alerted him away from his troublesome speculations. He discreetly removed his arm from Matiyala's shoulder and gently rested her head on a pillow. He dressed into a robe and exited the bedroom, closing the door and leaving her in a peaceful sleep.

A human woman in a long trench coat stood in the hallway. She was middle-aged, with short black hair and a tanned, thin face. Her expression seemed as surprised as Kent's when they made eye contact. She was nearly as tall as him, but something about her body language expressed frailty.

By her side, and only about as tall as her leg, was a human boy.

"Can I help you?" Kent asked. Despite being around the Tigress so often, he still possessed an instinct that was distrusting toward humans.

"Are you Ser Kent… the Archmage?" the woman asked.

"That would be me."

A smile of relief broke out on her face. "The name's Kathleen Ripley. This is my son: Talan."

"Hi." Talan said, shyly.

"A pleasure. Are you from Old Ulthrawn?"

"Oh, no. We're from the Kender province," she said. "I'm a close friend to Rachel. Our families were both from Mercia… and we escaped to Laktannon together when Caesar took over."

The human woman looked down to her son and smiled. The child, in return, wrapped his arms around her leg. "But I'm rambling on about nothing. Rachel recommended that I reach out to you. You see, my son, well, I think he's a mage. She told me that you were the one who could train him."

*Darby*, Kent sighed, biting his lip as if tasting something tart. "You think he's a mage? The difference is hardly subtle."

Kathleen laughed nervously. "You see, he's been messing with our electricity. I chalked it up to power outages for a while, but those don't cause lightbulbs to explode. There have been mages in our family history before, but they were from generations ago. I mean, way back during the days of the Gasardi kings."

Kent studied Talan. The wide-eyed boy resembled his mother. Mages possessed a sense, like a hunch, that could detect when they were in the presence of other mages. With Talan, Kent had that hunch.

"Would you like to learn from me, Talan?"

The boy turned to his mother for the right answer. "Tell him what you think," Kathleen urged him, rustling his hair with her hand.

"Yes," he said, staring at his feet. "I would like it."

"Then we will start tomorrow," Kent declared. He would make time to teach. *No excuses. No procrastination. Stop running away from your mistakes. You're the Archmage, now you must act accordingly.*

"Thank you," Kathleen said, relieved. "I felt bad for him. I'm no mage, neither is my father. You're the only one who can help control his powers."

"They're his gifts. I've trained young mages before. Talan will be all right, I'm sure of it." He went to one knee to speak to his new pupil personally. "Tomorrow morning, come to the Republic Manor, okay?"

Talan nodded, "Yes, sir."

"A necessary virtue for every aspiring Paladin is patience. Do you have patience?"

"Uh, I think so. I will try, sir."

"Good lad," the Archmage smiled. "I can't wait for our first lesson."

The Ripleys departed moments later, leaving Kent alone with gathering thoughts swirling in his mind like debris in a tornado. It was a small step forward, but any progress was good progress. *Word is already getting out. Soon, Serios save me, more mages will see this as their place of refuge. Then, we'll have a school, then a community, then an Order of the same heights as the old.*

Just as his flowery dreams danced before his eyes, Kent felt something wet in his hand. He looked down and saw his palm was soaking in blood. It was the same hand that gripped the knife at Saryn Malor's ship when Ariel, under a spell, brought his old demons to the table and let them feast on his soul. He grabbed the knife that night, but he hated to think of what he intended to do with it.

*Silence her... I'd rather silence her than have my sins spoken allowed.*

He watched the blood drip to the floor, making no effort to stop it. *I may be a monster, but don't monsters have the right to live?*

# EPILOGUE

*One way or another, the bitch will be on the shit-end of my retribution.*

Silver Wulf, bound, beaten, and stinking of piss, was still figuring out the intricacies of how exactly he would get even, but inevitably he would have it. He gave Canary a life, a reason to wake up in the morning, and protection from those Underlings who would do much worse to her than he ever did. A beating here and there was necessary to remind her of her place, but many a girl in the Underbelly would be lucky to reach her age, let alone have her security. And how did she repay his generosity? By leaving him for dead in the derelict embassy of the old Galactic Council, while the most brutal war between pearls and Underlings in decades waged from outside.

It was a massacre on both ends. Storms of lasers and bullets and rockets ripped through the lifeless air. Wulf had woken up at the very end of it, stumbled outside and watched as the pearls, caught right in the middle of the open square, allowed for the Underlings to surround them. They were masters at navigating the underground ventilation systems, so entire squadrons of Kagen's army could move silently like rats beneath the feet of the pearls. By the time they realized the setup, escape was no longer a possibility.

*No one will be taken prisoner. It's not their style; they forced our hand.*

Pearl war machines, like their tanks and armored trucks, were the last to fall to the Underling horde. Admiring from afar, Wulf lost count of how many hundreds of his kind died to take them over, but the number did not matter. Underlings were not individuals. *Thousands of them could die in one day and be replaced the day after.*

He admired the fireworks of warfare that lit up the sky. *So gray, so dead, so fucking desolate.* Entranced, he lost track of his surroundings. He forgot he was the most wanted man in the Underbelly. It was not long until Kagen's soldiers discovered him. Wulf did not resist their arrest, but his obedience was insignificant. He had taken much, much worse assaults from far more violent people, meaning someone high on the totem pole wanted him alive, just not completely unharmed.

He sat in the back of a cramped car, stuffed between two of Kagen's goons as a third drove them on. Snug tight to his left arm was a Druin male with dark green skin and long ivory horns sprouting from the sides of his head and one smaller horn pointing from his chin like a goatee. He watched Wulf with irises like dull flashlights. The Druin had given him two black eyes and a swollen lip for his trouble.

To his right was a Kalmar woman, whose heavy hair of writhing tentacles were bound by countless bands. She wore a sleeveless tank top which showed off her bare, but heavily inked arms. The designs and symbols possessed a digital style to them, as if they were inspired by some intricate computer code. The woman caught him staring and sneered.

"You like dah digitized?" she asked. Silver Wulf turned his head away and said nothing. The woman reached into her pocket and pulled out an inhaler. She put it to her mouth and breathed in. Her eyes dilated within seconds. "Blast-off. Want sum?"

"Get that shit away from me," Wulf said. *Ariel was always huffing it. That's why her mind was so fucked. I should've beaten her the first time I saw her use it.*

"Suit yerself," the woman said, returning her gaze to the window.

The car was broken down, as the incessant screeching of the back bumper against the asphalt road implored. Acting as if he were operating an armored tank, the driver zipped down street after street with equally little concern for those inside or outside the vehicle. Not that there was much to lookout for. On these levels between the Market District and the Underbelly, the giant metropolitan areas that were once massive centers for trade were reduced to cities for ghosts.

It was, to be blunt, the no man's land in the perpetual war between the Underbelly and New Horizon. The skyscrapers that remained were mostly desolate, existing for no other reason than to eventually collapse. Between them were mounds and mounds of scrap and junk, like the sand dunes of an urban desert. Waves of heavy white fog repopulated the barren streets. Some of the most paranoid of his kind believed the fog to be a gaseous poison dispensed by the elite of New Horizon to slowly kill them off, but Wulf did not think the same. *They kill our people in the open enough as it is.*

As they went deeper into the Underbelly, signs of communities emerged through the mist. They entered a different world, free from oppression. Businesses, mostly casinos and clubs run by top workers of the Eight, flashed their lurid, neon signs against the otherwise dark and decrepit streets and alleyways. Bells and whistles sounded from unseen speakers, adding cheap levity to a swampy foundation. Everything this deep into Prisilla ran on massive generators stolen from the Market District, as no one above the Underbelly would spare them a candle, let alone electricity.

Those individuals on the sidewalk stared into the windows as the car drove along. His captors made no effort to keep a low profile, but instead kept their windows down and waved casually to specific people as they passed. Wulf guessed they must have been in Kagen's territory, as no one in their right mind would be this relaxed on rival turf.

Traffic too increased in population. Streetlights, stop signs, and speed limits were nonexistent in the Underbelly. Here the rules of the road were determined by the most courageous, or rather, hostile drivers. More than anything else, gang warfare was caused by road rage, and it was not uncommon for Underlings to be out on the streets for the sole purpose of provoking a fight. Luckily for Wulf, no one dared challenge the recklessness of his chauffeur.

"Where are you taking me?" Wulf asked, boldly.

The Kalmar woman leaned over to address the Druin. "Should we tell'em?" He shrugged in return. "We're takin' you tah Kagen. You worth quite a bit to 'im." The woman smiled, revealing a mouthful of metallic teeth.

*I'm not the one he wants,* Wulf accepted, *but this is a step in the right direction.* Anything was an improvement to what he originally assumed his fate would be: discovered, tortured, and shot in the head. The two in the car with him were skilled trackers. He was too quick to be caught by anyone but the best. Kagen needed him alive, at least for now, and that was good enough for Wulf.

"The battle, what happened with you and the pearls?"

The Kalmar woman laughed. "We fucked dem up right good. Killed me a few pearls personally."

"They gettin' too greedy," the Druin added. "Comin' to our turf like tha'. Do they think we'll surrendah to 'em?"

"I surrendah to no one, 'specially pearls."

Wulf rolled his eyes. "But what caused the fight? Underlings never confront pearls so openly."

The Kalmar laughed again. Before she answered, she took another hit of Blast-off. She puckered her lips and made circles of smoke fly into the air. "You should know, Silvahman. Your girl waz turned in by anotha bounty huntah. Pearls rolled up minutes latah. We were tol' tah stand our ground."

"And we crushed'em!" the Druin declared, fist in the air. "Right undah duh mural of Selina Vortex. She'd be proud."

"She would," the Kalmar woman agreed. "Bu' we can take dah fight furtha. Come to their homes, kill them in their beds. Take dah anger, dah darkness, they caused us, and use it 'gainst dem. Unite dah Eight for dah firs' time since Selina Vortex. Rule New Horizon in her name. Put dah rulahs of Prisilla in dah Underbelly, into dah Hell they made for us!"

"But Canary!" Silver Wulf interrupted. "Do you still have her?" He was growing dangerously brash, but Kagen's sidetracked goons made him that way.

The Kalmar smiled and kissed him on the cheek. "Silly Silvahman. Why do you think we did not jus' shoot you where we foun' you?"

Wulf decided it best not to question his circumstances any further. Based on how they treated him, the Kalmar and Druin must have considered him a dead man walking. Little did they know, he still had one more card to play. *Canary screwed me over, but she's the only way I make it through the night alive.* But as confidence returned to his outlook, the Druin threw a bag over his head and something hit his skull hard enough to knock his lights out.

A freezing cold splash of what Wulf optimistically guessed was water awoke him from his forced slumber. His head pounded, his eyes burned, and his back ached, the scalding white light projected from the rafters only serving to infuriate these pains. He raised his bound hands to wipe the "water" from his face. He was in some sort of flat pit, like a small arena. Jeers and curses were shouted from all around, coming from spectators in the crowd who were hauntingly obscured in darkness. Wulf knew who they belonged to, and he understood they wanted to see him bleed.

"We brough' yer bounty, Mister Kagen," the Kalmar girl said. She planted a heeled foot on the back of Silver Wulf's neck and forced him to the ground, much to the approval of the shrouded audience.

A group of onlookers parted, leaving an empty spot around the ring. Then, the sound of clanging footsteps cut through the pit. They were scampering and rapid in nature, as if whatever was coming walked on a thousand legs. Disoriented, Silver Wulf had to concentrate twice as hard to locate the noise. Coming to the center of the stage was none other than Kagen himself.

"You did well, creature." Kagen admired. The crime boss was of such an obese size that he could not rise from his chair. Then again, all Timanzee were that way, hence the eight metallic picks sprouting from the base of his chair moving eerily like the sharpened legs of a giant spider. Wulf had dealt with many of his race in the markets of Prisilla, but none were quite so fleshy as Kagen. "And what of our girl?"

His voice was low like a raspy whisper. Of the crime lord's three eyes, the one in the center of his forehead was glaringly red, clearly a result of some cybernetic cosmetic. He wore elegant robes of ruby red and sapphire, contradicting the roughness of his gray, scarred skin.

"No sign of 'er still," the Kalmar woman reported. "Bu' she'll turn up. Thinkin' da Silvahman 'ere will snitch to us."

"Ah Canary," Kagen said, poking his right jowl. "So much promise in her. I knew she was something special, but even this surprises me. Wulf, why do you lie?"

Wulf shook his head dramatically. "No Mister Kagen, I could never. I don't know what you're talking about, I swear!"

"I was ready to have you both shot in an alley for letting Graznys die. Then, my scouts sent word that a Paladin was searching for her. That got me to researching, and it seems she's a mage too, but not just any mage. Wulf? Don't play dumb with me."

"She's nothing more than an Underling! At least... that's what I thought." Wulf admitted. "A Paladin did come to steal her from me, but I never expected it, you must believe me."

"Should I believe the bounty hunter?" Kagen asked his subjects. A unanimous roar of boos emerged from the crowd. The blaring spotlights dimmed, allowing Wulf to see more of his surroundings. The pit was bigger than he expected, making him feel like a prisoner ready for execution. Above them, in place of a ceiling, was instead an aquarium. Inside was a biome of vibrant orange, red, and yellow colors that danced in waves of hypnotic light over the pit. As Kagen spoke, a shark, at least ten times the size of Wulf, swam over his head.

"How did you find Ariel?" Kagen demanded. "And don't let me suspect any lies. They possess a pungent smell."

Silver Wulf struggled to remember. *Immortals, it must've been a decade and a half ago.* "I came across some asshole with a babe in the Market District. The man was tired, hungry, and desperate. I offered him help, and I tricked him, took the child for myself. Free labor, you know." At any moment, he expected Kagen to release his minions to feast on him like starving dogs rushing for a banquet.

"So you raised her from there." The crime lord shifted in his dazzling chrome chair, allowing his body to sprawl out comfortably. "And she never showed signs of any... powers?"

"No. Sir." Wulf insisted. "I wouldn't have her as an apprentice if I knew. That's a shitload of trouble I don't need. Bitch wasn't worth keeping on as it is." *I gave her everything and never got an ounce of gratitude for it.*

"And did you teach her obedience?" Kagen asked, his words lingering. The red metallic eye on the center of his forehead flashed malignantly.

"I think so?"

"Your bird flew away as soon as her cage was opened. You were not her master, but her captor. In order for a pet to learn its place, it must be kicked, left out in the cold, reminded of how shit its life is without you around. Your Canary is a wild animal, and it's all your fault."

"Yes, sir. Sorry, sir." Wulf was utterly confused as to if he was winning or losing his boss' favor.

Kagen continued, "My gang has won its greatest victory against the pearls since the days of Selina Vortex. The other leaders of the Eight have witnessed this, and we've all come to talking. The Elite of New Horizon have casted us to this gray Purgatory for too long, and it's time to rise like the demons we are and strip them of the luxuries that should be ours!"

A cheer of enthusiasm rang from the crowd, followed by the clanking of glass bottles. The aquatic biome on the ceiling pulsed vividly, as if it too was anticipating a rebellion. Wulf wanted to see the upper levels suffer as much as anyone else, but he was still clueless as to his own role in the matter.

"If we are to rise against our oppressors, we will need the best weapons money... and maybe magic can buy. And what better weapon to use against the pearls than the daughter of the Archmage?"

"Very smart thinking, Mister Kagen." Wulf replied. "I will do everything I can to help you eradicate those pricks in New Horizon. Point me in the right direction, and my skills are yours to use."

"You've screwed up for the last time, Wulf." Kagen stated. The room went silent. In the distance, a wintry breeze passed. "Tell me everything you know of Canary's captors and where you think they may have gone, and your reward will be a quick death."

The Kalmar and Druin charged their weapons. Two cold barrels were placed on the back of his skull, causing his whole body to shiver. A bullet to the head would be a kindness, but Wulf still had one vendetta that required repayment.

"You said my Canary is out of her cage, but you're wrong if you think she's lost." Wulf said, arousing the curiosity of the crime lord. "I always considered the chance that she'd run away, so I put a tracking device in her arm when she was an infant. Ariel is clueless of its existence, but the device is fully operational, no matter how far the distance."

"Then give it to me!" Kagen demanded, rocking in his chair. In the dark, it was hard to separate the corpulent Timanzee from his chrome seat.

"Not so fast. Only I can read the tracker. If you want her, I'm the one who needs to find her." Wulf feigned confidence as hard as he could. If Kagen detected he was bluffing, or simply did not appreciate his attitude, his option for a quick bullet to the head would no longer be on the table.

Kagen dug a long fingernail in the armrest of his seat. Wulf could sense the two goons behind him getting antsy, waiting for the nod to inflict pain. The crime lord grinned, displaying proudly a mouthful of platinum teeth. "I respect a man who puts all his cards on the table. It seems I have no option but to let you live."

"I'll bring her back to you. The bitch means nothing to me anymore." Wulf said. *Oh Immortals, I can't believe that worked!*

"You're damn right you will," Kagen spat. "Because I'll have an eye on you the whole time." He shifted his chair to the dark void behind him. "S3, introduce yourself to the bounty hunter."

From the shadows sprung a slim figure that leaped from the stage to the bottom of the pit. Once hitting the ground, the figure shifted its bodyweight forward and continued the momentum in a sharp roll across the ground, stopping inches away from Wulf's face. The lack of noise was unnerving. The jump would have shattered the ankles of any normal creature, no matter the race, but the thing standing before him was nothing normal.

Kagen clapped his meaty hands in amusement. "Wulf, meet S3, my top-of-the-line BOT, protector, unstoppable killing machine, and now your personal warden. He'll be joining you in the search for Ariel, and he'll be the one making sure my orders are followed."

Wulf stared starstruck at the BOT. Its tall body had a cylinder shape with a smooth, polished, onyx surface. Its limbs, which possessed a similar shape, color, and sleek design, were connected to the body via cords and thin metal bridges. The head possessed small monitor which projected a series of flashing white lights as it inspected Wulf. On its crest, almost like a hat, was a thin visor that went around the head like a plate.

He remembered Ariel's BOT, which she for some bloody reason treated like a pet. The thing was obnoxious, but it was helpful in frantic situations. Pup was not designed to kill, forcing Wulf to make his own modifications. This contraption in front of him, S3, was created to kill.

Despite his better suspicions, Wulf had to ask: "How do I know this thing isn't ordered to kill me as soon as we find her?"

Kagen laughed deeply. The audience, as if they were waiting for permission, laughed along. The BOT continued to stare with its untraceable face. "You don't know, and you never will. But remind me: what other choice do you have?"

Wulf scowled: *none, really.* "When do we head out?"

"Soon. But first, we celebrate a new age of the Underbelly. For freedom, for the beginning of a new unholy alliance between the Eight!" A series of hidden stereos turned on in unison, blasting a kind of techno music with a biting cybernetic beat, and an earthshaking base. Strobe lights flashed from the ceiling, turning the dank trial room into a raucous club. The audience adjusted, grinding on one another within seconds of the music starting.

*Junk DJ. Utter trash.*

The Kalmar girl bent down and cut the restraints around his wrists. The sense of freedom on his raw skin was elating. "Enjoy yahself tonight, Silvahman. It may be ye las night tah ge' righteously fucked up!"

"Good advice," Wulf replied. A drink would be good, but several would be euphoric. Before he could escape the glare of S3 and join the debauchery, Kagen grabbed his attention. From the top of the stage, the crime lord launched something from his hand, and it landed by Wulf's feet.

He picked it up and scrutinized it curiously. "Evolve from your mistakes Silver Wulf and put that collar on her." Kagen declared from his spider-like throne. "The bitch needs to learn obedience, the bitch needs to know her place, and the bitch needs

MATTHEW MARTELLA

to transform from wild animal into weapon. You will make her my pet, or you'll die trying."

# About the Author

Matthew Martella is a writer from Massachusetts. In addition to writing, he is an avid reader and traveler. He has studied literature across several countries, including England and Ireland, and is perpetually fantasizing about his next adventure in Europe.

# AFTERWORD

I never thought this novel would leave its Microsoft Word page. And yet, after six years of a love-hate relationship, Hollow Stars has finally made it to print! To my readers, I offer my most sincere gratitude, not only for putting money down on my book, but for participating (and hopefully enjoying) this crazy story. It wasn't easy to create this fantasy world and its countless characters, locations, and rules, but the end result was more than worth it.

   A sequel is currently in the works (in addition to a myriad of other projects), and I encourage you to check out my twitter: @martella_writer and my website: www.matthewmartella.com for updates.

Printed in Great Britain
by Amazon